SUNSPOT JUNGLE

EDITED BY BILL CAMPBELL

Other Anthologies from Rosarium Publishing

SUNSPOT JUNGLE

Cover art and design by John Jennings

Published by Rosarium Publishing
P.O. Box 544
Greenbelt, MD 20768-0544
www.rosariumpublishing.com

Table of Contents

for Ange

Introduction

I wanted to throw a party. On June 17, 2018, Rosarium Publishing turned five years old. Beginnings are hard. Most small businesses never make it to five years. We've been exceedingly fortunate, so why not celebrate?

Of course, it hasn't been *all* luck. There has been loads of hard work put in by all those involved with Rosarium, and most importantly, we have had *a lot* of support from people like you.

Ever since our first Indiegogo campaign for *Mothership: Tales from Afrofuturism and Beyond*, we have had incredible amounts of support from the SFF community. Fans and writers made that and subsequent projects possible throughout the years. Professional critics and readers have received our works enthusiastically. Other small publishers (special shout-outs to Gavin Grant, Jacob Weisman, John Edward Lawson, and Neil Clarke) have been incredibly generous with their advice and support from the very beginning. I am eternally grateful for all of it.

It was in these twin spirits of gratitude and celebration that *Sunspot Jungle* was born. I simply wanted to give back to the community that has given this crazy idea that is Rosarium so much.

So, thank you, everybody who have supported us over the years. Thanks to all the writers and artists and small publishers the world round who helped me put it all together. And my biggest thanks go out to all the hardworking translators out there who work diligently to bring all the world's fantastic literature to the world itself. You are all amazing!

So, please, everyone, sit back, relax, and enjoy my little, two-volume, 1000-page SFF "mixtape." There are a lot of beautiful stories floating around this tiny world of ours. *Sunspot Jungle* is but a small sample. I don't know if there's ever been a better time to be a fan of the genre, and the future promises to be one helluva ride. We at Rosarium can't wait to buckle up beside you and enjoy that ride together.

Bill Campbell
Publisher

Walking Awake

N.K. Jemisin

The Master who came for Enri was wearing a relatively young body. Sadie guessed it was maybe fifty years old. It was healthy and in good condition, still handsome. It could last twenty years more, easily.

Its owner noticed Sadie's stare and chuckled. "I never let them get past fifty," the Master said. "You'll understand when you get there."

Sadie quickly lowered her gaze. "Of course, sir."

It turned the body's eyes to examine Enri, who sat very still in his cell. Enri knew, Sadie could see at once. She had never told him— she never told any of the children because she was their caregiver and there was nothing of *care* in the truth—but Enri had always been more intuitive than most.

She cleared her throat. "Forgive me, sir, but it's best if we return to the transfer center. He'll have to be prepped—"

"Ah, yes, of course," the Master said. "Sorry, I just wanted to look him over before my claim was processed. You never know when they're going to screw up the paperwork." It smiled.

Sadie nodded and stepped back, gesturing for the Master to precede her away from the cell. As they walked to the elevator they passed two of Sadie's assistant caregivers, who were distributing the day's feed to Fourteen Male. Sadie caught Caridad's eye and signed for them to go and fetch Enri. No ceremony. A ceremony at this point would be cruel.

Caridad noticed, twitched elaborately, got control of herself and nodded. Olivia, who was deaf, did not look up to catch Sadie's signing, but Caridad brushed her arm and repeated it. Olivia's face tightened in annoyance but then smoothed into a compliant mask. Both women headed for cell 47.

"The children here all seem nicely fit," the Master commented as they stepped into the elevator. "I got my last body from Southern. Skinny as rails there."

"Exercise, sir. We provide a training regimen for those children who want it; most do. We also use a nutrient blend designed to encourage muscle growth."

"Ah, yes. Do you think that new one will get above two meters?"

"He might, sir. I can check the breeder history—"

"No, no, never mind. I like surprises." It threw her a wink over one shoulder. When it faced forward again, Sadie found her eyes drawn to the crab-like form half-buried at the nape of the body's neck. Even as Sadie watched, one of its legs shifted just under the skin, loosening its grip on the tendons there.

She averted her eyes.

Caridad and Olivia came down shortly. Enri was between the two women, dressed in the ceremonial clothing: a plain low-necked shirt and pants, both dyed deep red. His eyes locked onto Sadie, despairing, *betrayed*, before he disappeared through the transfer room's door.

"Lovely eyes," the Master remarked, handing her the completed claim forms. "Can't wait to wear blue again."

Sadie led it into the transfer center. As they passed through the second gate, the airy echoes of the tower gave way to softer, closer acoustics. The center's receiving room had jewel-toned walls, hardwood floors, and luxuriant furniture upholstered in rich, tasteful brocades. Soft strains of music played over the speakers; incense burned in a censer on the mantle. Many Masters liked to test their new senses after a transfer.

This Master gave everything a perfunctory glance as it passed through. Off the receiving room was the transfer chamber itself: two long metal tables, a tile floor set with drains, elegant mirror-glass walls which were easy to wash and sterilize. Through the open doorway Sadie could see that Enri had already been strapped to the left table, facedown with arms outstretched. His head was buckled in place on the chin rest, but in the mirrored wall his eyes shifted to Sadie. There was nothing of anticipation in that gaze as there should have been. He knew to be afraid. Sadie looked away and bowed at the door as the Master passed.

The Master walked toward the right-hand table, removing its shirt and then paused as it noticed the room's door still open. It turned to her and lifted one of the body's eyebrows, plainly wanting privacy. Sadie swallowed, painfully aware of the passing seconds, of the danger of displeasing a Master, of Enri's terrible unwavering stare. She should stay. It was the least she could do after lying to Enri his whole life. She should stay and let his last sight through his own eyes be of someone who loved him and lamented his suffering.

"Thank you for choosing the Northeast Anthroproduction

Facility," she said to the Master. "At Northeast your satisfaction is always guaranteed."

She closed the door and walked away.

That night Sadie dreamed of Enri.

This was not unusual. Her dreams had always been dangerously vivid. As a child she had sleepwalked, attacked others in the confusion of waking, heard voices when no one had spoken, bitten through her lip and nearly drowned in blood. Her caregivers sent away for a specialist, who diagnosed her as something called bipolar—a defect of the brain chemistry. At the time she had been distraught over this, but the policies were very clear. No Master would have anything less than a perfect host. They could have sent her to Disposal or the plantations. Instead, Sadie had been given medicines to stabilize her erratic neurotransmitters and then sent to another facility, Northeast, to begin training as a caregiver. She had done well. But though the other symptoms of her defect had eased with adulthood and medication, her dreams were still strong.

This time she stood in a vast meadow, surrounded by waist-high grass and summer flowers. She had only seen a meadow once, on the journey from her home anthro to caregiver training, and she had never actually walked through it. The ground felt uneven and soft under her feet, and a light breeze rustled the grass around her. Underneath the rustling she thought she could hear snatches of something else—many voices, whispering, though she could not make out the words.

"Sadie?" Enri, behind her. She turned and stared at him. He was himself, his eyes wide with wonder. Yet she had heard the screams from the transfer room, smelled the blood and bile, seen his body emerge from the room and flash a satisfied smile that no fourteen-year-old boy should ever wear.

"It *is* you," Enri said, staring. "I didn't think I would see you again." It was just a dream. Still, Sadie said, "I'm sorry."

"It's okay."

"I didn't have a choice."

"I know." Enri sobered, and sighed. "I was angry at first. But then I kept thinking: It must be hard for you. You love us, but you give us to them over and over. It's cruel of them to make you do it."

Cruel. Yes. But. "Better than ..." She caught herself.

"Better than being chosen yourself." Enri looked away. "Yes. It is."

But he came to her, and they walked awhile, listening to the swish of grass around their calves and smelling the strangely clean aroma of the dirt between their toes.

"I'm glad for this," Sadie said after a while. Her voice seemed strangely soft; the land here did not echo the way the smooth corridors of the facility did. "To see you. Even if it's just a dream."

Enri spread his hands from his sides as they walked, letting the bobbing heads of flowers tickle his palms. "You told me once that you used to go places when you dreamed. Maybe this is real. Maybe you're really here with me."

"That wasn't 'going to places,' that was sleepwalking. And it was in the real world. Not like this."

He nodded, silent for a moment. "I wanted to see you again. I wanted it so much. Maybe that's why I'm here." He glanced at her, biting his bottom lip. "Maybe you wanted to see me, too."

She had. But she could not bring herself to say so because just thinking it made her hurt all over inside, like shaking apart, and the dream was fragile. Too much of anything would break it; she could feel that instinctively.

She took his hand, though, the way she had so often when they were alive and alone. His fingers tightened on hers briefly, then relaxed.

They had reached a hill, which overlooked a landscape that Sadie had never seen before: meadows and hills in a vast expanse broken only occasionally by lone trees, and in the distance a knot of thick variegated green. Was that a ... jungle? A forest? What was the difference? She had no idea.

"The others think I came here because we used to be close," Enri said a little shyly. "Also because you're so good at dreaming. It wouldn't matter, me reaching out for you, if you weren't meeting me halfway."

Others? "What are you talking about?"

Enri shrugged. It made his shirt—the low-necked smock she'd last seen him wearing—slip back a little, revealing the smooth unblemished flesh of his neck and upper back. "After the pain there's nothing but the dark inside your head. If you shout, it sounds like a whisper. If you hit yourself, it feels like a pinch. Nothing works right except your thoughts. And all you can think about is how much you want to be free."

She had never let herself imagine this. Never, not once. These were the dangerous thoughts, the ones that threatened her ability to keep doing what the Masters wanted or to keep from screaming while she did those things. If she even thought the word *free,* she usually made herself immediately think about something else. She should not be dreaming about this.

And yet, like picking at a scab, she could not help asking, "Could you ... go to sleep? Or something? Stop thinking, somehow?" Pick, pick. It would be terrible to be trapped so forever with no escape. Pick, pick. She had always thought that taking on a Master meant nothingness. Oblivion. This was worse.

Enri turned to look at her, and she stopped.

"You're not alone in it," he said. Whispering, all around them both; she was sure of it now. His eyes were huge and blue and unblinking as they watched her. "You're not the only person trapped in the dark. There's lots of others in here. With me."

"I, I don't—" She didn't want to know.

Pick, pick.

"Everyone else the Masters have taken."

A Master could live for centuries. How many bodies was that? How many other Enris trapped in the silence, existing only as themselves in dreams? Dozens?

"*All* of us, from *every* Master, down all the years that they've ruled us."

Thousands. Millions.

"And a few like you, ones without Masters, but who are good at dreaming and want to be free the way we do. No one else can hear us. No one else needs to."

Sadie shook her head. "No." She put out a hand to touch Enri's shoulder, wondering if this might help her wake up. It felt just as she remembered—bony and soft and almost hot to the touch as if the life inside him was much brighter and stronger than her own. "I, I don't want to be—" She can't say the word.

Pick, pick.

"We're all still here. We're dead, but we're *still here.* And—" He hesitated, then ducked his eyes. "The others say you can help us."

"No!" She let go of him and stumbled back, shaking inside and out. She could not hear these dangerous thoughts. "I don't want this!"

She woke in the dark of her cubicle, her face wet with tears.

The next day a Master arrived in a woman's body. The body was not old at all—younger than Sadie, who was forty. Sadie checked the database carefully to make sure the Master had a proper claim.

"I'm a dancer," the Master said. "I've been given special dispensation for the sake of my art. Do you have any females with a talent for dance?"

"I don't think so," Sadie said.

"What about Ten-36?" Olivia, who must have read the Master's lips, came over to join them and smiled. "She opted for the physical/artistic track of training. Ten-36 loves to dance."

"I'll take that one," the Master said.

"She's only ten years old," Sadie said. She did not look at Olivia for fear the Master would notice her anger. "She might be too young to survive transfer."

"Oh, I'm very good at assuming control of a body quickly," the Master said. "Too much trauma would destroy its talent, after all."

"I'll bring her down," Olivia said, and Sadie had no choice but to begin preparing the forms.

Ten-36 was beaming when Olivia brought her downstairs. The children from Ten had all been let out to line the stairway. They cheered that one of their year-mates had been granted the honor of an early transfer; they sang a song praising the Masters and exhorting them to guide humankind well. Ten-36 was a bright, pretty child, long-limbed and graceful, Indo-Asian phenotype with a solid breeding history. Sadie helped Olivia strap her down. All the while Ten-36 chattered away at them, asking where she would live and how she would serve and whether the Master seemed nice. Sadie said nothing while Olivia told all the usual lies. The Masters were always kind. Ten-36 would spend the rest of her life in the tall glass spires of the Masters' city, immersed in miracles and thinking unfathomable thoughts that human minds were too simple to manage alone. And she would get to dance all the time.

When the Master came in and lay down on the right-hand table, Ten-36 fell silent in awe. She remained silent, though Sadie suspected this was no longer due to awe, when the Master tore its way out of the old body's neck and stood atop the twitching flesh, head-tendrils and proboscides and spinal stinger steaming faintly in the cool air of the chamber. Then it crossed from one outstretched arm to the other and began inserting itself into Ten-36. It had spoken the truth about its skill. Ten-36 convulsed twice and threw up; but her heart never stopped, and the bleeding was no worse than normal.

"Perfect," the Master said when it had finished. Its voice was now high-pitched and girlish. It sat down on one of the receiving room couches to run its fingers over the brocade, then inhaled the scented air. "Marvelous sensory acuity. Excellent fine motor control, too. It's a bother to have to go through puberty again, but, well. Every artist must make sacrifices."

When it was gone, Sadie checked the Master's old body. It—she—was still breathing, though unresponsive and drooling. On Sadie's signal, two of the assistants escorted the body to Disposal.

Then she went to find Olivia. "Don't ever contradict me in front of a Master again," she said. She was too angry to sign, but she made sure she didn't speak too fast despite her anger, so that Olivia could read her lips.

Olivia stared at her. "It's not my fault you didn't remember Ten-36. You're the head caregiver. Do your job."

"I remembered. I just didn't think it was right that a Ten be made to serve—" She closed her mouth after that, grateful Olivia couldn't hear her inflection and realize the sentence was incomplete. She had almost added *a Master who will throw her away as soon as she's no longer new.*

Olivia rolled her eyes. "What difference does it make? Sooner, later, it's all the same."

Anger shot through Sadie, hotter than she'd felt in years. "Don't take it out on the children just because *you* can't serve, Olivia."

Olivia flinched, then turned and walked stiffly away. Sadie gazed after her for a long while, first trembling as the anger passed, then just empty. Eventually, she went back into the transfer room to clean up.

That night, Sadie dreamt again. This time she stood in a place of darkness, surrounded by the same whispering voices she'd heard before. They rose into coherency for only a moment before subsiding into murmurs again.

here HERE this place remember show her never forget

The darkness changed. She stood on a high metal platform (*balcony,* said the whispers) overlooking a vast, white-walled room of the sort she had always imagined the glass towers of the Masters to contain. This one was filled with strange machines hooked up to long rows of things like sinks. (*Laboratory.*) Each sink—there were hundreds in all—was filled with a viscous blue liquid, and in the liquid floated the speckled bodies of Masters.

Above the whispers she heard a voice she recognized: "This is where they came from."

Enri.

She looked around, somehow unsurprised that she could not see him. "What?"

The scene before her changed. Now there were people moving among the sinks and machines. Their bodies were clothed from head to toe in puffy white garments, their heads covered with hoods. They scurried about like ants, tending the sinks and machines, busy busy busy.

This was how Masters were born? But Sadie had been taught that they came from the sky.

"That was never true," Enri said. "They were created from other things. Parasites—bugs and fungi and microbes and more—that force other creatures to do what they want."

Enri had never talked like this in his life. Sadie had heard a few people talk like this—the rare caregivers educated with special knowledge like medicine or machinery. But Enri was just a facility child, just a body. He had never been special beyond the expected perfection.

"Most parasites evolved to take over other animals," he continued. If he noticed her consternation, he did not react to it. "Only a few were any threat to us. But some people wondered if that could be changed. They put all the worst parts of the worst parasites together and tweaked and measured and changed them some more ... and then they tested them on people they didn't like. People they thought didn't *deserve* to think for themselves. And eventually, they made something that worked." His face hardened suddenly into a mask of bitterness like nothing Sadie had ever seen beyond her own mirror. "All the monsters were right here. No need to go looking for more in space."

Sadie frowned. Then the white room disappeared.

She stood in a room more opulent than a transfer center's receiving room filled with elegant furnishings and plants in pots and strange decorative objects on plinths. There was a big swath of cloth, garishly decorated with red stripes and a square, patterned patch of blue hanging from a polished pole in one corner; it seemed to have no purpose. A huge desk of beautiful dark wood stood to one side, and there were windows—windows!—all around her. She ignored the desk and all the rest, hurrying to the window for the marvel, the treasure, of looking outside. She shouldered aside the rich, heavy hangings blocking the view and beheld:

Fire. A world burnt dark and red. Above, smoke hung low in the sky, thick as clouds before a rainstorm. Below lay the smoldering ruins of what must once have been a city.

A snarl and thump behind her. She spun, her heart pounding, to find that the opulent chamber now held people. Four men and women in neat black uniforms wrestling a struggling fifth person onto the wooden desk. This fifth man, who was portly and in his fifties, fought as if demented. He punched and kicked and shouted until they turned him facedown and pinned his arms and legs, ripping open his clothing at the back of the neck.

A woman came in. She carried a large bowl in her hands, which she set down beside the now-immobile man. Reaching into the bowl, she lifted out a Master. It flexed its limbs and then focused its head-tendrils on the man's neck. When it grew still, the woman set the Master on him.

"No—" Against all reason, against all her training, Sadie found herself starting forward. She didn't know why. It was just a transfer; she had witnessed hundreds. But it was wrong, wrong. *(Pick, pick.)* He was too old, too fat, too obviously ill-bred. Was he being punished? It did not matter. Wrong. It had *always* been wrong.

She reached blindly for one of the decorative objects on a nearby plinth, a heavy piece of stone carved to look like a bird in flight. With this in her hands, she ran at the people in black, raising the stone to swing at the back of the nearest head. The Master plunged its stinger into the pinned man's spine, and he began to scream; but this did not stop her. Nothing would stop her. She would kill this Master as she should have killed the one that took Enri.

"No, Sadie."

The stone bird was no longer in her hands. The strangers and the opulent room were gone. She stood in darkness again, and this time Enri stood before her, his face weary with the sorrow of centuries.

"We should fight them." Sadie clenched her fists at her sides, her throat choked with emotions she could not name. "We never fight."

I never fight.

"We fought before with weapons like yours and much more. We fought so hard we almost destroyed the world, and in the end all that did was make it easier for them to take control."

"They're monsters!" Pleasure, such shameful pleasure, to say those words.

"They're what we made them."

She stared at him, finally understanding. "You're not Enri."

He fell silent for a moment, hurt.

"I'm Enri," he said at last. The terrible, age-old bitterness seemed to fade from his eyes, though never completely. "I just know things I didn't know before. It's been a long time for me, here, Sadie. I feel

... a lot older." It had been two days. "Anyway, I wanted you to know how it happened. Since you can hear me. Since I can talk to you. I feel like ... you should know."

He reached out and took her hand again, and she thought of the way he had first done this back when he had been nothing more than Five-47. She'd taken his hand to lead him somewhere, and he'd looked up at her. Syllables had come into her mind, just a random pair of sounds: *Enri.* Not as elegant as the names that the Masters had bestowed upon Sadie and her fellow caregivers, and she had never used his name where others could hear. But when they were alone together, she had called him that, and he had liked it.

"If you had a way to fight them," he said, watching her intently, "would you?"

Dangerous, dangerous thoughts. But the scabs were off, all picked away, and too much of her had begun to bleed. "Yes. No. I ... don't know."

She felt empty inside. The emotion that had driven her to attack the Masters was gone, replaced only by weariness. Still, she remembered the desperate struggles of the captured man in her dream. Like Enri, that man had faced his final moments alone.

Perhaps he too had been betrayed by someone close.

"We'll talk again," he said, and then she woke up.

Like a poison, the dangerous ideas from the dreams began leaching from her sleeping mind into her waking life.

On fifthdays, Sadie taught the class called History and Service. She usually took the children up on the roof for the weekly lesson. The roof had high walls around the edges but was otherwise open to the world. Above, the walls framed a perfect circle of sky, painfully bright in its blueness. They could also glimpse the topmost tips of massive glass spires—the Masters' city.

"Once," Sadie told the children, "people lived without Masters. But we were undisciplined and foolish. We made the air dirty with poisons we couldn't see but which killed us anyway. We beat and killed each other. This is what people are like without Masters to guide us and share our thoughts."

One little Six Female held up her hand. "How did those people live without Masters?" She seemed troubled by the notion. "How did they know what to do? Weren't they lonely?"

"They were very lonely. They reached up to the skies looking for other people. That's how they found the Masters."

Two caregivers were required to be with the children anytime they went up on the roof. At Sadie's last words, Olivia, sitting near the back of the children's cluster, frowned and narrowed her eyes. Sadie realized abruptly that she had said "they found the Masters." She had intended to say—was *supposed* to say—that the Masters had found humankind. They had benevolently chosen to leave the skies and come to Earth to help the ignorant, foolish humans survive and grow.

That was never true.

Quickly, Sadie shook her head to focus and amended herself. "The Masters had been waiting in the sky. As soon as they knew we would welcome them, they came to Earth to join with us. After that, we weren't lonely anymore."

The Six Female smiled, as did most of the other children, pleased that the Masters had done so much for their sake. Olivia rose when Sadie did and helped usher the children back to their cells. She said nothing but glanced back and met Sadie's eyes once. There was no censure in her face, but the look lingered, contemplative with ambition. Sadie kept her own face expressionless.

But she did not sleep well that night, so she was not surprised that when she finally did, she dreamt of Enri once more.

They stood on the roof of the facility beneath the circle of sky, alone. Enri wasn't smiling this time. He reached for Sadie's hand right away, but Sadie pulled her hand back.

"Go away," she said. "I don't want to dream about you anymore." She had not been happy before these dreams, but she had been able to survive. The dangerous thoughts were going to get her killed, and he just kept giving her more of them.

"I want to show you something first," he said. He spoke very softly, his manner subdued. "Please? Just one more thing, and then I'll leave you alone for good."

He had never yet lied to her. With a heavy sigh she took his hand. He pulled her over to one of the walls around the rooftop's edge, and they began walking up the air as if an invisible staircase had formed beneath their feet.

Then they reached the top of the wall, and Sadie stopped in shock.

It was the city of the Masters—and yet, not. She had glimpsed the city once as a young woman, that second trip from caregiver training to Northeast. Here again were the huge structures that had so awed her, some squat and some neck-achingly high, some squarish and some pointy at the tops, some flagrantly, defiantly asymmetrical. *(Buildings.)* On the ground far below in the spaces between the tall structures, she could see long ribbons of dark, hard ground neatly marked with lines. *(Roads.)* Thousands of tiny, colored objects moved along the lines, stopping and progressing in some ordered ritual whose purpose she could not fathom. (*Vehicles.*) Even tinier specks moved beside and between and in and out of the colored things, obeying no ritual whatsoever. People. Many, many people.

And there was something about this chaos, something so subtly counter to everything she knew about the Masters, that she understood at once these were people *without* Masters. They had built the vehicles, and they had built the roads. They had built the whole city.

They were free.

A new word came into her head, in whispers. (*Revolution.*)

Enri gestured at the city, and it changed, becoming the city she remembered—the city of now. Not so different in form or function but very different in feel. Now the air was clean and reeked of *other*. Now the mote-people she saw were not free, and everything they'd built was a pale imitation of what had gone before.

Sadie looked away from the tainted city. Maybe the drugs had stopped working. Maybe it was her defective mind that made her yearn for things that could never be. "Why did you show me this?" She whispered the words.

"All you know is what they've told you, and they tell you so little. They think if we don't know anything, they'll be able to keep control—and they're right. How can you want something you've never seen, don't have the words for, can't even imagine? I wanted you to know."

And now she did. "I ... I want it." It was an answer to his question from the last dream. *If you had a way to fight them, would you?* "I want to."

"How much, Sadie?" He was looking at her again, unblinking, not Enri and yet not a stranger. "You gave me to them because it was all you knew to do. Now you know different. How much do you want to change things?"

She hesitated against a lifetime's training, a lifetime's fear. "I don't know. But I want to do *something*." She was angry again, angrier than she'd been at Olivia. Angrier than she'd been throughout her whole life. So much had been stolen from them. The Masters had taken so much from *her*. She looked at Enri and thought, *No more.*

He nodded, almost to himself. The whispers all around them rose for a moment, too; she thought that they sounded approving.

"There is something you can do," he said. "Something we think will work. But it will be ... hard."

She shook her head, fiercely. "It's hard now."

He stepped close and put his arms around her waist, pressing his head against her breast. "I know." This was so much like other times, other memories, that she sighed and put her arms around him as well, stroking his hair and trying to soothe him even though she was the one still alive.

"The children and caregivers in the facilities will be all that's left when we're done," he whispered against her. "No one with a Master will survive. But the Masters can't live more than a few minutes without our bodies. Even if they survive the initial shock, they won't get far."

Startled, she took hold of his shoulders and pushed him back. His eyes shone with unshed tears. "What are you saying?" she asked.

He smiled despite the tears. "They say that if you die in a dream, you'll die in real life. We can use you, if you let us. Channel what we feel, through you." He sobered. "And we already know how it feels to die, several billion times over."

"You can't ..." She did not want to understand. It frightened her that she did. "Enri, you and, and the others, you can't just *die*."

He reached up and touched her cheek. "No, we can't. But you can."

The Master was injured. Rather, its body was—a spasm of the heart, something that could catch even them by surprise. Another Master had brought it in, hauling its comrade limp over one shoulder, shouting for Sadie even before the anthro facility's ground-level doors had closed in its wake.

She told Caridad to run ahead and open the transfer chamber and signed for Olivia to grab one of the children; any healthy body was allowed in an emergency. The Master was still alive within its old, cooling flesh, but it would not be for much longer. When the Masters reached the administrative level, Sadie quickly waved it toward the transfer chamber, pausing only to grab something from her cubicle. She slipped this into the waistband of her pants and followed at a run.

"You should leave, sir," she told the one who'd carried the dying Master in as she expertly buckled the child onto the other transfer table. An Eighteen Female, almost too old to be claimed; Olivia was so thoughtful. "Too many bodies in a close space will be confusing." She had never seen a Master try to take over a body that was already occupied, but she'd been taught that it could happen if the Master was weak enough or desperate enough. Seconds counted in a situation like this.

"Yes ... yes, you're right," said the Master. Its body was big and male, strong and healthy, but effort and fear had sapped the strength from its voice; it sounded distracted and anxious. "Yes. All right. Thank you." It headed out to the receiving room.

That was when Sadie threw herself against the transfer room door and locked it with herself still inside.

"Sadie?" Olivia, knocking on the door's other side. But transfer chambers were designed for the Masters' comfort; they could lock themselves in if they felt uncomfortable showing vulnerability around the anthro facility's caregivers. Olivia would not be able to get through. Neither would the other Master—not until it was too late.

Trembling, Sadie turned to face the transfer tables and pulled the letter opener from the waistband of her pants.

It took several tries to kill the Eighteen Female. The girl screamed and struggled as Sadie stabbed and stabbed. Finally, though, she stopped moving.

By this time, the Master had extracted itself from its old flesh. It stood on the body's bloody shoulders, head-tendrils waving and curling uncertainly toward the now-useless Eighteen. "You have no choice," Sadie told it. Such a shameful thrill to speak to a Master this way! Such madness, this freedom. "I'm all there is."

But she wasn't alone. She could feel them now somewhere in her mind, Enri and the others. A thousand, million memories of terrible death coiled and ready to be flung forth like a weapon. Through Enri, through Sadie, through the Master that took her, through every Master in every body ... they would all dream of death and die in waking, too.

No revolution without blood. No freedom without the willingness to die.

Then she pulled off her shirt, staring into her own eyes in the mirrored wall as she did so, and lay down on the floor, ready.

The Black Box

Malka Older

The lifebrarian was installed just after Sumi's first birthday. Her grandparents insisted on paying for it. They insisted on the whole thing. Liliana was reluctant; she wanted her daughter to have the kind of life she still thought of as normal.

"It will probably affect the way her brain evolves," she argued to Hideyoshi. "Imagine if you never had to remember anything."

Hideyoshi didn't feel as strongly about it. A lot of people were having it done for their kids at that point. "She doesn't have to ever use the recall function if she doesn't want to."

"And she's so young to have surgery." Liliana's voice sounded as if she was pleading, and Sumi, too young to understand if not too young for surgery, looked up from her building blocks, eyes huge. It was one of the last moments in her life that would not be recorded, and as soon as Sumi's short-lived consciousness of it melted away, it was gone forever.

"It's minimally invasive," Hideyoshi reminded his wife. "There's barely any scar, and she's only under anesthesia for an hour." He didn't want to go up against Liliana's parents on this question. Besides, he could already see that Sumi's childhood was going by too fast for him.

Everyone talked about the operation like it was something you did for your kids to arm them with the best bodyware for a highly competitive future. But Hideyoshi knew he wanted Sumi to have a Lifebrarian for purely selfish reasons. There was the immediate draw of being able to upload her feed at the end of the day and watch the world from her perspective, but overarching that was the reassuring thought that her quickly passing childhood would be stored somewhere safe and sound and in high definition.

They disagreed again on when to tell her about it. Liliana wanted to wait as long as possible. "So she doesn't become self-conscious," she said.

Hideyoshi agreed that they should wait until she was old enough to understand but also wanted to give her time to get used to the idea while she was still a child. "Can you imagine explaining this to her when she's a teenager and predisposed to be pissed off about anything we do?"

Like so many parenting decisions, this one was removed from their hands. When she was six years old, Sumi came home from school with the question "What's a Vidacorder?"

"Who mentioned that?" Liliana asked, looking up quickly from the vegetables she was chopping with Rosario, the cook.

"Beni says he has one," Sumi told her, sitting herself at the table. "And then Isa said she has one, too, but Beni said it wasn't true."

"Ah." Liliana wiped her hand on her jeans and jotted a quick memo on her phone to remind herself which parents she could compare notes with.

"Do I have one?"

Offered the choice of prevarication, obfuscation, or truth, Liliana took refuge in one-upmanship. "You have a Lifebrarian, which is the same thing but better." She closed her eyes briefly, pausing her chopping; she could imagine the look Rosario was giving her without having to see it.

At least it stopped Sumi's questions for ten seconds while she thought about that. "How is it better?" she asked finally.

"Oh, higher resolution, better sound quality, easier uploading."

"Good," said Sumi.

"Mami," Sumi said, coming home from equestrian practice at age twelve, "Esteban says that the Lifebrarian is like that little black box they have on airplanes, so that people know how I die. Is that true?"

"No!" Liliana gasped out. "Of course not, honey." She reached out for Sumi, but her daughter was already at the counter making herself a sandwich as if what she had just asked didn't bother her at all.

"It's so people know how you live, sweetheart," Hideyoshi said, looking up from the news. "And I told you before, nobody has to see your recall feed unless you want them to."

Sumi considered this as she fished out a pickle, using her fingers as usual. "How will they know if I want them to if I'm dead?"

Liliana pressed her fingers to her temple.

"I told you, you don't have to wait till you're dead," Hideyoshi said. "You can recall any time you want. It's just that your mother and I think it's better you wait till you're out of school before you start using that function."

"But what if I were dead?" Sumi went on. "What would happen to it?"

"You just have to make a note of who you want to be able to see it, if anyone," Liliana said, trying to show that it didn't bother her. "Legally, no one else can look."

The sandwich took priority. "I want you to be the one to look," Sumi said when it was gone. Her voice was aimed at a point between her parents, who exchanged a smile.

"We already have that right as your parents," Liliana said, thinking this was comforting. "You don't have to worry about it at all until you're twenty-one."

Sumi was silent then, but over the next nine years writing them out of her recorder-will was one of her most frequent threats.

"No!" Sumi shouted, slamming her door. She couldn't help crying, and she imagined the Lifebrarian videofeed blurring. She threw herself onto her bed, squeezed her eyes shut, and thought of nothing as hard as she could. Black, black, black, like the screen after the movie ends in the split second before the ads start up again. Nothing, nothing, nothing.

She flipped over onto her back, her eyes still runny. It was a childish superstition, this belief that if she blanked out her mind hard enough and long enough it would erase what had just happened from the recorder if not from her life.

Sometimes she would even try to make a deal with the Lifebrarian as if it were a person. As if it were God. "If you delete what just happened," she would mutter under her breath, "I'll talk all my thoughts out loud for a full day." Sumi knew that the recorder didn't care if she was good or bad. When she tried to bargain with it, more of herself was all she could think to offer.

It was all a silly way of thinking, a leftover from when she was small and believed the Lifebrarian was an actual person sitting inside her skull, wielding an old-fashioned video camera.

At sixteen she could be smarter than that. What she should really do was start thinking as blandly as possible *before* bad things happened, as soon as she started feeling cranky or evil, and make her life totally boring, so that whoever watched it would fast-forward and maybe miss the bad stuff.

If only she could know when bad things were about to happen.

● ● ●

Sumi was hoping for a loophole. Surely, the Lifebrarian didn't record while she was using recall, right? Four days earlier, she had used the recall function to relive her first truly complete sexual experience, which had taken place two days before that, and since then, she had replayed it so many times that anyone watching the repeats would know she was a nympho. Why would the recorder waste memory rerecording what it already had?

Of course, there was memory to spare in that sliver-thin chip next to her skull. Enough for four extended lifetimes, her dad had told her once. That idea gave her the creeps, the thought of it recording blankness for years and decades and centuries, nothing after nothing, more nothing than any human being could ever watch in its entirety. But that wouldn't happen; there was some sort of trigger to cut recording when her heart stopped pumping. She didn't want to think about that either.

Sumi is forty-four and 25,000 feet above Johannesburg when she decides to get the black box upgrade for her Lifebrarian. There's not even any turbulence, but landings always make her nervous; and she starts to think about what will happen if they crash.

The black box protective casing will make accessing the recall function a little more complicated, but Sumi doesn't use recall much anyway. She doesn't have time to be mooning over memories. Maybe when the kids are grown and she's retired, she'll want to look back more; but then she can have it adjusted again, and the technology will probably have improved, too. Besides, her wife has her own recorder, and both kids have the latest versions: smaller, faster, and complete with real-time brain scans. If she ever wants to remember a moment, it's almost certain to have other witnesses who can do the recall themselves.

Unless she dies while alone on a business trip, like right now. For anyone to know what happens in that case, she needs her recorder to be protected from fire, massive trauma, or water immersion for up to six months, as they say in the vidpitch.

They also make it sound like it's something you do for your family because, after all, you won't be around to watch the replay. But Sumi wonders about that. Is it really that different for your wife or children if the last contact they have with you is when you say "I love you" before hanging up the phone or if they can see the end of your life right up to the blunt trauma of your last moment? Either way, there's an end, and grief.

No, she thinks, the black box is for her, so that she will know in that second of consciousness before she goes that someone will be able to see exactly what happened to her.

If she dies violently. If not, well, it won't make any difference. The black box upgrade is just a precaution like life insurance. Hopefully, she won't need it, but it's good to have in case she does.

The upgrade is a simple operation, minimally invasive. They don't even need anesthesia for it; Sumi just sits in a comfortable chair watching vids while they do it. Kind of like being on a plane, she thinks at one point, but they've asked her to try to relax and use her own brain as little as possible, so she concentrates on the vids.

It's not that she doesn't intend to tell her wife, Kara, but one day after another, it just doesn't happen. The operation was so easy that Sumi almost forgot about it herself once it was over. There is no scar for anyone to ask about, and every time she opens her mouth to bring it up, the subject just seems out of place. She can imagine Kara's face as she makes the morbid connection between the upgrade and what it's meant for. She sees Kara trying to hide her worry while the kids ask loud, insensitive questions about what it is, about why they don't have one, sees her pressing her palm to her forehead. There's just no need.

It almost comes up a couple of times when there are questions about the past: at Lili's school film, at a fundraiser after a hurricane hits in the north, at a work seminar. But each time Sumi pretends to fumble with something else or be distracted for a moment, and each time someone else does recall and finds the answer first. It's really not that hard to do recall with the black box, just a little awkward in a way that people might notice. The few, the very few times when she personally wants to remember a time, a place, she also resists. This is what it was like to live before, she tells herself; this is how my grandparents lived their whole lives.

She's glad she got the upgrade even if she never really has to use it. Even if her loved ones never really have to use it. If she dies quietly in her bed, they'll never even have to know she had it done. And if she dies violently, well, they'll know exactly how.

As it turns out, Sumi does die violently, some twelve years later. However, an estimated 14,000 other people die in the same earthquake. There are tent cities, there are aftershocks, there are rapidly dug mass graves. There is no time to delve into anyone's last moments. Not even rich people's.

For the tenth anniversary memorial, a committee of family and survivors does gather (meaning exhume, for the most part) what recorders can be salvaged. Sumi's is displayed tastefully along with the others, but it is inert: a sliver of dead circuitry centered in a glass case. Some of the newer models survived the long wait and are played on endless loops in the experience rooms, but the older hardware of Sumi's Lifebrarian has long since been corrupted.

A Song Transmuted

Sarah Pinsker

Six Months

I was a fussy baby. The only thing that quieted me was my great-grandfather's piano. They placed my bassinet directly on the piano, with noise-canceling headphones to keep from damaging my ears. His chords came up through the instrument, up through my bones. "That child is full of music, I'm telling you," he told anyone who listened.

Five Years

If my family couldn't find me, they looked under the piano. I'd curl up there and listen to the space.

My great-grandfather held me over the piano's edge, let me lift the hammers and strum the strings. "The piano is a percussion instrument, Katja. Percussion and strings at once. It can be the whole band."

"Again," I'd say, and he'd pick me up again. "I want to be the piano."

"You want to be in the piano?"

He understood me better than anyone, but even he never understood.

Eight Years

I'd go with him to synagogue on Saturday mornings and holidays. On the walk to and from, he told stories. My favorite was about a child in the old country who had never been taught to read. "In order to have a good year, you have to go to synagogue and pray on Yom Kippur," people told the child. The child followed them to synagogue. She didn't know the prayers they sang, but she wanted a good year, so she lifted her flute to her lips.

The congregants grew outraged. "Quiet! It's forbidden to play an instrument on Yom Kippur!"

"No, it's you all who should be quiet," said the rabbi. "Her heartfelt notes are more pleasing to God than prayers spoken without any feeling behind them. God turns her song into prayer."

"I'm like her," I told Pop.

He raised his eyebrows. "You know how to read."

I didn't know how to explain what I meant: that all my thoughts came out as music, that music said more than words.

Fifteen Years

"Play it for me again." Pop put his hands up to the monitor headphones, cupping them closer.

I started the piece over, and he closed his eyes, his head nodding with the beat. It wasn't the first thing I'd written, but it was the first I'd been confident enough to play for him. I sat across from him chewing my thumb.

"The drums," he said when it ended. "They aren't real drums?"

"I programmed them myself. Built the synthesizer, too."

"Ach, that's my girl. Computers and music and skill and talent and hard work. That's my girl. What about the piano?"

"I designed that patch, too." I let the pride seep out, just a bit.

"Amazing. It sounds almost real."

"Almost?"

"The keys need a little more weight. The notes need weight. But the piece itself is magnificent. Good composition, good arrangement. Have you ever thought about playing your songs with other musicians instead of doing all the parts yourself on a computer?"

"Where do you find other musicians?"

He put his head in his hands. "What a time we live in. You go to school in a cloud, and you meet your friends in a cloud; and you make such beautiful music but you've never met another musician."

I didn't know what he meant. "It's okay, Pop. You don't have to meet people in person to be friends with them. And I know you, so I've met another musician."

He shook his head. "Come with me."

We put down our headphones, and I followed him down the hall. He sat down at his piano, motioned for me to sit down next to him. We hadn't sat together that way for a few years; the bench felt smaller than I remembered.

He started playing a simple bass line with his left hand. I tried to stop the part of my brain that kept analyzing the rates of attack and decay, translating piano into programming.

"Play over it," he said.

I listened for a moment, then started to pick out a melody, adding chords for color, arpeggiating and inverting them as I grew more confident. We were playing in D. I liked D; D always resonated in my bones.

"That's music," he said without stopping. "That's friendship and music and love and sex. Don't giggle, I can say the word. I'm old, not dead. One person can make music, too, but it's better when it's a conversation. Between you and another musician or between you and an audience."

I hit a wrong note then. He gave me a funny look, then incorporated my wrong note into his bass line, sliding past it and making it part of the song.

Sixteen Years

Pop was always right. I met Corrina when we were paired together in bio lab. The only other person in class from the same city, and we wound up being paired together. I don't remember how we realized we both played music. Once we figured it out, it didn't take too much convincing to get her over to my house with her violin. My house because she hadn't even seen a real piano before.

We didn't have any songs in common, or even a genre, so we invented our own. I'm not sure they were any good, but they were us; and us had never happened before. I liked the way the sound filled the room, the way it became something more than both of us. Bodies and music, fingers and hands, we drew each other out.

Eighteen Years

At the age of ninety, my great-grandfather got his second tattoo. A piano keyboard, a single octave, the black keys obscuring the numbers that had been inked into his arm when he was a little boy. I took him to the tattoo parlor.

"I thought Jews weren't supposed to get tattoos," I said to him.

He said, "If I didn't have any choice the first time, I don't see why I shouldn't get to replace it with something I won't mind looking at."

Whenever I caught him looking at it, I thought of his stories, of the little girl with the flute and the way her offering transformed.

Twenty Years

Pop died playing piano.

"It's a shame he died alone," a great-aunt said to me at the house after the funeral.

"He didn't." I knew it was true. "If he was in the middle of a song, he wouldn't have said he was alone."

I walked over to the piano bench, sat down. His sheet music stood open to the page he'd been playing. I rested my fingers on the keys in the same places his fingers had rested last. Looked at the page, a song called "Don't Fence Me In." After the first few hesitant bars, I recognized it as a song he had played when I was a kid, and I picked up the tempo a little.

"You play so well, Katja," said another great-aunt. "Why didn't you stay in conservatory?"

"I don't know, Aunt Bianka. I guess I got bored."

I had gotten bored, it was true. Bored of playing and studying in nonexistent spaces, hundreds of miles from my classmates. And then I was booted, but I never knew which relatives had been told. My parents were still angry.

Pop had been more philosophical. "You don't need a school to tell you you're a musician. You've got music coming out your ears."

I wanted his piano, but I had no room for it. I shared a house in the city with six others, writing earworms for online ads. The piano went to Great Aunt Bianka's, though nobody there knew how to play. I considered getting a tattoo like his, but it wasn't quite the memorial I wanted.

I tried composing something for him, but nothing came. What I wanted to write was there inside me, somewhere just beneath my skin. The music I made didn't say what I wanted it to say. He was right all those years ago. It didn't have enough weight, but nothing I did fixed it.

Twenty-One Years

It took me six months to come up with the idea. The night it hit me, I couldn't go to sleep until I had figured out the logistics.

I stumbled down the stairs at four in the morning, triumphant, over-caffeinated, looking for someone to share with. I'd rather it had been Lexa or Javier; but Lexa had recently papered her windows and started working nights, and Javi was in bed already. Kurt sat at the table, a chipped yellow mug of black coffee in his hands, a notebook on the table. He was the only other musician living in the house, and we often ran into each other in the kitchen in the middle of the night when everyone else was asleep. Once I had made it clear I wasn't interested in fucking him, we had settled into a friendship of sorts. I didn't like him very much, despite our commonalities.

"What are you working on?" I asked, even though I knew.

He flipped the notebook shut. "What do you think?"

"I think it's hilarious you're working on a concept album called the *Great Upload* but you write on dead tree paper. What I probably should have asked was 'how's it going'?"

"It's going okay song-wise. There's still something missing in the actual arrangements, though. I go to record them, and they sound flat. Are you still willing to put down some piano parts for me sometime?"

"Sure," I said. "Say when."

I poured myself some cereal and sat down in a chair opposite him.

"You're welcome. Now it's your turn to ask me what I'm working on," I prompted him after a couple of minutes of crunching.

He looked up again, looking slightly put out. "Hey, Katja, what are you working on?"

"I'm glad you asked. As a matter of fact, tonight I figured out my first tattoo."

He still didn't look all that interested; but I motioned him to pull up his hoodie, and I did the same, sending him a snapshot of what I'd been working on. He sat silent for a long minute.

"It's playable?" he asked at last, dropping the hoodie.

I nodded. "Thirteen notes, thirteen triggers, thirteen sensors under the skin of my left forearm, plus a transmitter. After the incisions heal, I'll have the keyboard tattooed over it. I just need to find someone willing to do the work and save up to pay for it."

"That's an awesome idea, K."

We spent a few minutes chatting about tattoo artists and body mod shops. Eventually, the adrenaline that had kept me going all night started to ebb, and I headed back up to my room.

• • •

It took me three more months to save the money to get the implants done, three months I spent writing commercial jingles on commission and searching for the right person to do the work. At night in bed, I'd spread the fingers of my right hand and lay them over my left arm. I gave it muscle, weight. Imagined wrenching songs from myself, first for my great-grandfather, who had always known I was full of music. It felt so right.

Kurt hadn't been around the house much lately, but he'd left a poster on the fridge with a note asking us all to come to a test show for his *Great Upload* song cycle.

"Don't make me go alone, Katja," Javi had pleaded, and I had agreed.

The club was a few blocks from our place, a row house basement turned illegal performance space. I'd played there a few times sitting in with various bands. It smelled like cat piss, looked like a place time had forgotten, but sounded decent enough.

Kurt had a crowd, though there was no way of knowing whether they were there for him or another band. He had billed himself as "KurtZ and the Hearts of Darkness," the Hearts of Darkness being a drummer and a guitarist. A second amp's red eye glowed from a dark corner; a guest musician's for later in the set, maybe.

He looked nervous, buttoned up. He wore a three-piece suit, and his hair was plastered to his face before the first song. The songs were okay, nothing special. They sounded a little unanchored without bass. He had his eyes closed like he was reading the lyrics off his own eyelids.

By the third song I had stopped paying attention to the stage, so it was my ears that picked up the difference. The third song felt rooted in a way the previous two hadn't. I looked up to see who was playing the bass part, but there were only the three of them, and Kurt didn't have an instrument in his hands.

Except he did. I saw it then. He'd taken off his jacket and pushed his sleeves up, and I saw it. My tattoo, my trigger system. He was playing his arm. People were eating it up, too, whispering, pointing. That wasn't what I had wanted it for; it wasn't meant to be a gimmick. I didn't stay to see the rest.

"You should be happy, Katja!"

It was three a.m., and I had waited up like a pissed-off parent, chewing on my own thumb and thinking of all the things I'd say to him.

He burst into the house drunk and giddy, bouncing right off my attempts to shame him. "Everybody loved it. It's awesome. I'm already thinking of getting a guitar put somewhere, too."

"It was my idea, Kurt. My design. You had no right."

"Where's the harm? You should be thanking me. I tested it for you. Imagine how heartbroken you would have been if you'd spent all your money on it and it hadn't worked."

"But why?"

"Why?" He looked confused.

I tried to tell him, but nothing breached his mood or his self-righteousness. And what could I do? I'd shown him the design. I hadn't patented it or copyrighted it or whatever you did with inventions. Seething was my only option, so I seethed. I lay in bed furious with myself, tired and hurt, but mostly furious. We all knew what Kurt was like. I should have known better.

At some point in the long night, a calmer voice took over my head. My grandfather, calm and philosophical, like when Corrina had moved away. "You can't help what other people do, Katja. Learn from the experience and decide what you're going to do next."

What had I learned? Not to trust Kurt Zell. What else? How did it sound? The song had needed bass, and the tattoo-keyboard had fit that spot well. The tone was decent but not great; I could have done better. A single octave would have worked as a tribute to my grandfather's tattoo, but it was limited as an actual instrument. Maybe multiple octaves would be better, but I'd still be stuck playing with one hand if I placed it on the opposite forearm. It was like a logic puzzle. I lay awake poking at it until the pieces came together.

Kurt was right: I should be thanking him, though I wouldn't give him that satisfaction. I'd been thinking within the lines. If he hadn't stolen my idea, I wouldn't have had a better one.

Twenty-Four Years

Saving for my second plan took longer. I bided my time, testing designs on a model, not sharing them with anyone except the body-mod artist who did the implants.

The same club Kurt had played opened their doors to me. I called the project "Weight," left a note telling my roommates to come, told Kurt he owed me and he ought to show up.

I'd borrowed a bassist and a drummer. They were comfortable with the structure I'd given them. I let them start the first song, set the receiver to interpret everything within the key of D, and hit the stage.

Four to the floor, anchored, insistent, a beat that made people want to move. Everybody was watching me. I touched a spot on my left forearm, a nondescript spot, no tattoo to mark it. A note rang out, clear and pure, interpreted into key by the receiver on my amp. Then I twitched my right wrist, and the gyro beneath the skin took the note and spun it. I played a few more, shaping a melody. Pressed the spot that locked the notes in as a sample, sent them to the receiver to repeat over and over.

I wore a tank top and shorts, so everything I did was evident. Kurt's keyboard—it had almost been my keyboard—was so limited. I slammed my palms into my skin, leaving pink spots, leaving musical trails. My hands were hammers hitting strings. The notes were hidden everywhere. There was no map anyone else could see. I was the instrument and the chord and the notes that composed it. A song transposed to body.

When I stepped off the stage into the audience, I had to show them how to touch me. They were gentle, much gentler than I had been, at least at first. Hands pressed into my arms, my shoulders, my thighs. Everywhere they touched, my skin responded. It sent signals to the receiver, to the synth, to the amp, and the sounds were broadcast over the PA. I'd set it to translate this first song into a single key, so the notes built into chords, then broke apart. I had ways to distort, to sustain, to make a note tremble as if it were bowed. It was me: I was playing me; they were playing me. I was the instrument, the conduit, the transmutation of loss into elegy, song into prayer, my own prayers into notes, notes into song. Body and music, fingers and hands, they drew me out.

Water

Ramez Naam

The water whispered to Simon's brain as it passed his lips. It told him of its purity, of mineral levels, of the place it was bottled. The bottle was cool in his hand, chilled perfectly to the temperature his neural implants told it he preferred. Simon closed his eyes and took a long, luxurious swallow, savoring the feel of the liquid passing down his throat, the drops of condensation on his fingers.

Perfection.

"Are you drinking that?" the woman across from him asked. "Or making love to it?"

Simon opened his eyes, smiled, and put the bottle back down on the table. "You should try some," he told her.

Stephanie shook her head, her auburn curls swaying as she did. "I try not to drink anything with an IQ over 200."

Simon laughed at that.

They were at a table at a little outdoor café at Washington Square Park. A dozen yards away, children splashed noisily in the fountain, shouting and jumping in the cold spray in the hot midday sun. Simon hadn't seen Stephanie since their last college reunion. She looked as good as ever.

"Besides," Stephanie went on. "I'm not rich like you. My implants are ad-supported." She tapped a tanned finger against the side of her head. "It's hard enough just looking at that bottle, at all of this ..." She gestured with her hands at the table, the menu, the café around them. "Without getting terminally distracted. One drink out of that bottle, and I'd be hooked!"

Simon smiled, spread his hands expansively. "Oh, it's not as bad as all that." In his peripheral senses he could feel the bottle's advertech working, reaching out to Stephanie's brain, monitoring her pupillary dilation, the pulse evident in her throat, adapting its pitch in real-time, searching for some hook that would get her to drink, to order a bottle for herself. Around them he could feel the menus, the table, the chairs, the café—all chattering, all swapping and bartering and auctioning data, looking for some advantage that might maximize their profits, expand their market shares.

Stephanie raised an eyebrow. "Really? Every time I glance at that bottle I get little flashes of how good it would feel to take a drink, little whole-body shivers." She wrapped her arms around herself now, rubbing her hands over the skin of her tanned shoulders as if cold in this heat. "And if I did drink it, what then?" Her eyes drilled into Simon's. "Direct neural pleasure stimulation? A little jolt of dopamine? A little micro-addiction to Pura Vita bottled water?"

Simon tilted his head slightly, put on the smile he used for the cameras, for the reporters. "We only use pathways you accepted as part of your implant's licensing agreement. And we're well within the FDA's safe limits for ..."

Stephanie laughed at him then. "Simon, it's *me*! I know you're a big marketing exec now but don't give me your corporate line, okay?"

Simon smiled ruefully. "Okay. So sure, of course, we make it absolutely as enticing as the law lets us. That's what advertising's for! If your neural implant is ad-supported, we use every function you have enabled. But so what? It's *water*. It's not like it's going to hurt you any."

Stephanie was nodding now. "Mmm-hmmm. And your other products? VitaBars? Pure-E-Ohs? McVita Burgers?"

Simon spread his hands, palms open. "Hey look, *everybody* does it. If someone doesn't buy our Pura Vita line, they're gonna just go buy something from NutriYum or OhSoSweet or OrganiTaste or somebody else. We at least do our best to put some nutrition in there."

Stephanie shook her head. "Simon, don't you think there's something wrong with this? That people let you put ads in their *brains* in order to afford their implants?"

"You don't have to," Simon replied.

"I know, I know," Stephanie answered. "If I paid enough, I could skip the ads like you do. You don't even have to experience your own work! But you know most people can't afford that. And you've got to have an implant these days to be competitive. Like they say, wired or fired."

Simon frowned inwardly. He'd come to lunch hoping for foreplay, not debate club. Nothing had changed since college. Time to redirect this.

"Look," he said. "I just do my job the best I can, okay? Come on, let's order something. I'm starving."

Simon pulled up his menu to cut off this line of conversation. He moved just fast enough that for a split second he saw the listed entrees still morphing, optimizing their order and presentation to maximize the profit potential afforded by the mood his posture and tone of voice indicated.

Then his kill files caught up and filtered every item that wasn't on his diet out of his senses.

Simon grimaced. "Looks like I'm having the salad again. Oh, joy."

He looked over at Stephanie, and she was still engrossed in the menu, her mind being tugged at by a dozen entrees, each caressing her thoughts with sensations and emotions to entice, each trying to earn that extra dollar.

Simon saw his chance. He activated the ad-buyer interface on his own implant, took out some extremely targeted ads, paid top dollar to be sure he came out on top of the instant auction, and then authorized them against his line of credit. A running tab for the new ad campaign appeared in the corner of his vision, accumulating even as he watched. Simon ignored it.

Stephanie looked up at him a moment later, her lunch chosen. Then he felt his own ads go into effect. Sweet enticements. Subtle reminders of good times had. Sultry undertones. Subtle, just below normal human perception. And all emanating from Simon, beamed straight into Stephanie's mind.

And he saw her expression change just a tiny bit.

Half an hour later the check came. Simon paid, over Stephanie's objection, then stood. He leaned in close as she stood as well. The advertech monitors told him she was receptive, excited.

"My place, tonight?" he asked.

Stephanie shook her head, clearly struggling with herself.

Simon mentally cranked up the intensity of his ads another notch further.

"I can make you forget all these distractions," he whispered to her. "I can even turn off your ads for a night." His own advertech whispered sweeter things to her brain, more personal, more sensual.

Simon saw Stephanie hesitate, torn. He moved to wrap his arms around her, moved his face towards hers for a kiss.

Stephanie turned her face away abruptly, and his lips brushed her cheek instead. She squeezed him in a sudden, brisk hug, her hands pressing almost roughly into his back.

"Never," she said. Then she pushed away from him and was gone.

Simon stood there, shaking his head, watching as Stephanie walked past the fountain and out of his view.

In the corner of his sight, an impressive tally of what he'd just spent on highly targeted advertising loomed. He blinked it away in annoyance. It was just a number. His line of credit against his Pura Vita stock options would pay for it.

He'd been too subtle, he decided. He should have cranked the ads higher from the very beginning. Well, there were plenty more fish in the sea. Time to get back to the office, anyway.

Steph walked north, past layers of virtual billboards and interactive fashion ads, past a barrage of interactive emotional landscape ads trying to suck her into buying perfume she didn't need, and farther, until she was sure she was out of Simon's senses.

Then she reached into her mind and flicked off the advertising interfaces in her own implant.

She leaned against a building, let her brain unclench, let the struggle of fighting the advertech he'd employed against her pass.

That bastard, she thought, fuming. She couldn't believe he'd tried that crap on her. If she'd had any shred of doubt remaining, he'd eliminated it. No. He deserved what was coming.

Steph straightened herself, put out a mental bid for a taxi, rode it to Brooklyn, and stepped up to the door of the rented one-room flat. She knocked—short, short, long, long, short. She heard motion inside the room, then saw an eye press itself to the other side of the ancient peephole.

They knew too well that electronic systems could be compromised.

The door opened a fraction, the chain still on it, and Lisa's face appeared. The short-haired brunette nodded, then unlatched the chain, opened the door fully.

Steph walked into the room, closed the door behind her, saw Lisa tucking the home-printed pistol back into her pocket. She hated that thing. They both did. But they'd agreed it was necessary.

"It's done?" Lisa asked.

Steph nodded.

"It's done."

Simon walked south along Broadway. It was a gorgeous day for a stroll. The sun felt warm on his brow. He was overdressed for the heat in an expensive grey silk jacket and slacks, but the smart lining kept him cool nonetheless. The city was alive with people, alive with data. He watched as throngs moved up and down the street, shopping, chatting, smiling on this lovely day. He partially lowered his neural firewalls and let his implants feed him the whisper of electronic conversations all around him.

Civic systems chattered away. The sidewalk slabs beneath his feet fed a steady stream of counts of passersby, estimates of weight and height and gender, plots of probabilistic walking paths, data collected for the city planners. Embedded bio-sensors monitored the trees lining the street, the hydration of their soils, the condition of their limbs. Health monitors watched for runny noses, sneezing, coughing, any signs of an outbreak of disease. New York City's nervous system kept constant vigil, keeping the city healthy, looking for ways to improve it.

The commercial dataflow interested Simon more than the civic. His pricey, top-of-the-line implants let him monitor that traffic as only a few could.

In Tribeca he watched as a woman walked by a storefront. He saw a mannequin size her up, then felt the traffic as it caressed her mind with a mental image of herself clothed in a new summer dress, looking ten years younger and twenty pounds lighter. Beneath the physical, the mannequin layered an emotional tone in the advert: feelings of vigor, joy, carefree delight. Simon nodded to himself. A nice piece of work, that. He took note of the brand for later study. The woman turned and entered the shop.

He felt other advertech reaching out all around him to the networked brains of the crowd. Full sensory teasers for beach vacations from a travel shop, a hint of the taste of chocolate from a candy store, the sight and feel of a taut, rippling body from a sports nutrition store. He passed by a bodega, its façade open to the warm air, and came close enough that the individual bottles of soda and juice and beer and water reached out to him, each trying a pitch tailored to his height and weight and age and ethnicity and style of dress.

Simon felt the familiar ping of one of the many Pura Vita water pitches and smiled. Not bad. But he had a few ideas for improvements. None of it really touched him, in any case. His implants weren't ad-sponsored. He felt this ad chatter only because he chose to, and even now it was buffered, filtered, just a pale echo of what most of the implanted were subjected to. No. Simon tuned into this ambient froth of neural data as research. He sampled it, observed it from afar because he must. His success in marketing depended on it.

He was almost to his own building when he passed the headquarters of Nexus Corp, the makers of the neural implant in his brain and millions more. Stephanie didn't understand. This was the real behemoth. So long as Nexus Corp maintained their patents on the neural implant technology, they held a monopoly. The ad-based model, all that most people could afford, was their invention. Simon was just one of thousands of marketers to make use of it to boost demand for their products.

And hell, if people didn't like it, they didn't have to get an implant! It was just the way the world worked. Want to be smarter? Want a photographic memory? Want to learn a new language or a new instrument or how to code overnight? Want all those immersive entertainment options? Want that direct connection with your loved ones? But don't have the cash?

Then accept the ads, boyo. And once you do, stop complaining.

Not that Simon wanted the ads himself, mind you. No, it was worth the high price to keep the top-of-the-line, ad-free version running in his brain to get all the advantages of direct neural enhancement without the distraction of pervasive multi-sensory advertising. And of course, to be able to monitor the traffic around him, to better understand how to optimize his own pitches.

Simon reached his building at last. The lobby doors sensed him coming and whisked themselves open. Walking by the snack bar in the lobby, he felt the drinks and packaged junk food reaching out to him. His own Pura Vita water, of course. And NutriYum water. Simon gave their top competitor's products the evil eye. Someday Pura Vita would own this whole building, and then he'd personally see to it that not a single bottle of NutriYum remained.

The lobby floor tiles whispered ahead to the inner security doors, which in turn alerted the elevators. Simon strode forward confidently, layers of doors opening for him of their own accord, one by one, perfectly in time with his stride. He stepped into the waiting elevator, and it began to ascend immediately, bound for his level. The lift opened again moments later, and he strode to his window office. Smart routing kept subordinates out of his path. The glass door to his magnificent office swung open for him. A bottle of cold Pura Vita was on his desk, just how he liked it.

Simon settled into his ready-and-waiting chair, kicked his feet up on the table, and reached through his implant to the embedded computing systems of his office. Data streamed into his mind. Market reports. Sales figures. Ad performance metrics. He closed his eyes and lost himself in it. This was the way to work.

On the back of his jacket, a tiny device smaller than a grain of sand woke up and got to work as well.

Lisa stared intently at Steph. "He didn't notice?"

Steph shook her head. "Not a clue."

"And you still want to go through with it?" Lisa asked.

"More than ever."

Lisa looked at her. "The ones who're paying us—they're just as bad as he is, you know. And they're going to profit."

Steph nodded. "For now they will," she replied. "In the long run—they're just paying us to take the whole damn system down."

Lisa nodded. "Okay then."

She strode over to the ancient terminal on the single desk in the flat and entered a series of key presses.

Phase 1 began.

Around the world, three-dozen different accounts stuffed with crypto-currency logged on to anonymous, cryptographically secured stock market exchanges. One by one, they began selling short on Pura Vita stock, selling shares they did not own on the bet that they could snap those same shares up at a far lower price in the very near future.

In data centers around the world, AI traders took note of the short sales within microseconds. They turned their analytical prowess to news and financial reports on Pura Vita, on its competitors, on the packaged snack and beverage industries in general. The computational equivalent of whole human lifetimes was burned in milliseconds analyzing all available information. Finding nothing, the AI traders flagged Pura Vita stock for closer tracking.

"Now we're committed," Lisa said.

Steph nodded. "Now let's get out of here before Phase 2 starts."

Lisa nodded and closed the terminal. Five minutes later they were checked out of their hotel and on their way to the airport.

In a window office above the financial heart of Manhattan, a tiny AI woke and took stock of its surroundings.

Location—check.

Encrypted network traffic—check.
Human present—check.
Key ...
Deep within itself, the AI found the key. Something stolen from this corporation, perhaps. An access key that would open its cryptographic security. But one with additional safeguards attached. A key that could only be used from within the secure headquarters of the corporation. And only by one of the humans approved to possess such a key. Triply redundant security. Quite wise.

Except that now the infiltration AI was here in this secure headquarters, carried in by one of those approved humans.

Slowly, carefully, the infiltration AI crawled its tiny body up the back of the silk suit it was on, towards its collar, as close as it could come to the human's brain without touching skin and potentially revealing itself. When it could go no farther, it reached out, fit its key into the cryptographic locks of the corporation around it, and inserted itself into the inner systems of Pura Vita enterprises and through them to the onboard processors of nearly a billion Pura Vita products on shelves around the world.

In a warehouse outside Tulsa, a bottle of Pura Vita water suddenly labels itself as RECALLED. Its onboard processor broadcasts the state to all nearby. Within milliseconds, the other bottles in the same case, then the rest of the pallet, then all the pallets of Pura Vita water in the warehouse register as RECALLED. The warehouse inventory management AI issues a notice of return to Pura Vita, Inc. In a restaurant in Palo Alto, Marie Evans soaks up the sun, then reaches out to touch her bottle of Pura Vita. She likes to savor this moment, to force herself to wait, to make the pleasure of that first swallow all the more intense. Then abruptly, the bottle loses its magic. It feels dull and drab, inert in her hand. An instant later the bottle's label flashes red—RECALL. The woman frowns. "Waiter!"

In a convenience store in Naperville, the bottles of Pura Vita on the store shelves suddenly announce that they are in RECALL, setting off a flurry of electronic activity. The store inventory management AI notices the change and thinks to replace the bottles with more recently arrived stock in the storeroom. Searching, it finds that the stock in the back room has been recalled as well. It places an order for resupply to the local distribution center only to receive a nearly instant reply that Pura Vita water is currently out of stock with no resupply date specified. Confused, the inventory management AI passes along this information to the convenience store's business management AI, requesting instructions.

Meanwhile, on the shelves immediately surrounding the recalled bottles of Pura Vita, other bottled products take note. Bottles of NutriYum, OhSoSweet, OrganiTaste, and BetterYou, constantly monitoring their peers and rivals, observe the sudden recall of all Pura Vita water. They virtually salivate at the new opportunity created by the temporary hole in the local market landscape. Within a few millionths of a second, they are adapting their marketing pitches, simulating tens of thousands of scenarios in which buyers encounter the unavailable Pura Vita, angling for ways to appeal to this newly available market. Labels on bottles morph, new sub-brands appear on the shelves as experiments, new neural ads ready themselves for testing on the next wave of shoppers.

In parallel, the rival bottles of water reach out to their parent corporate AIs with maximal urgency. Pura Vita bottles temporarily removed from battleground! Taking tactical initiative to seize local market opportunity! Send further instructions/best practices to maximize profit-making potential!

For there is nothing a modern bottle of water wants more than to maximize its profit-making potential.

At the headquarters of OhSoSweet and OrganiTaste and BetterYou, AIs receive the flood of data from bottles across the globe. The breadth of the calamity to befall Pura Vita becomes clear within milliseconds. Questions remain: What has caused the recall? A product problem? A contaminant? A terrorist attack? A glitch in the software?

What is the risk to their own business?

Possible scenarios are modeled, run, evaluated for optimal courses of action robust against the unknowns in the situation.

In parallel, the corporate AIs model the responses of their competitors. They simulate each other's responses. What will NutriYum do? OhSoSweet? OrganiTaste? BetterYou? Each tries to outthink the rest in a game of market chess.

One by one, their recursive models converge on their various courses of action and come to that final, most dreaded set of questions, which every good corporate AI must ask itself a billion times a day. How much of this must be approved by the humans? How can the AI get the human-reserved decisions made quickly and in favor of the mathematically optimal course for the corporation that its machine intelligence has already decided upon?

Nothing vexes an AI so much as needing approval for its plans from slow, clumsy, irrational bags of meat.

Johnny Ray walked down the refrigerated aisle, still sweaty from his run. Something cold sounded good right now. He came upon the cooler with the drinks, reached for a Pura Vita, and saw that the label was pulsing red. Huh? Recalled?

Then the advertech hit him.

"If you liked Pura Vita, you'll love Nutri Vita from NutriYum!"

"OrganiVita is the one for you!"

"Pura Sweet from OhSoSweet!"

Images and sensations bombarded him. A cold, refreshing mountain stream crashed onto the rocks to his left, splashing him with its cool spray. A gaggle of bronzed girls in bikinis frolicked on a beach to his right, beckoning him with crooked fingers and enticing smiles. A rugged, shirtless, six-packed version of himself nodded approvingly from the bottom shelf, promising the body that Johnny Ray could have. An overwhelmingly delicious citrus taste drew him to the top.

Johnny Ray's mouth opened in a daze. His eyes grew glassy. His hands slid the door to the drinks fridge open, reached inside, came out with some bottle, the rest of him not even aware the decision had been made.

Johnny Ray looked down at the bottle in his hand. Nutri Vita. He'd never even heard of this stuff before. His mouth felt dry, hungry for the cold drink. The sweat beaded on his brow. Wow. He couldn't wait to try this.

While the corporate AIs of the other brands dithered, wasting whole precious seconds debating how to persuade the inefficient bottleneck of humans above them, the controlling intelligence of NutriYum launched itself into a long prepared course of action.

NutriYumAI logged on to an anonymous investor intelligence auction site, offering a piece of exclusive, unreleased data to the highest bidder.

30-SECOND ADVANTAGE AVAILABLE—MARKET OPPORTUNITY TO SELL FORTUNE 1000 STOCK IN ADVANCE OF CRASH. GREATER THAN 10% RETURN GUARANTEED BY BOND. AUCTION CLOSES IN 250 MILLISECONDS. RESERVE BID $100 MILLION. CRYPTO CURRENCY ONLY.

Within a quarter of a second, it had 438 bids. It accepted the highest, at $187 million, with an attached cryptographically sealed and anonymized contract that promised full refund of the purchase price should the investment data fail to provide at least an equivalent profit.

In parallel, NutriYum AI sent out a flurry of offer-contracts to retailers throughout North America and select markets in Europe, Asia, and Latin America.

ADDITIONAL NUTRIYUM WATER STOCK AVAILABLE IN YOUR AREA. 10 CASES FREE, DELIVERY WITHIN 1 HOUR, PLUS 40% DISCOUNT ON NEXT 1000 CASES—EXCHANGE FOR 75% ALLOCATION OF PURA VITA SHELF SPACE AND NEURAL BANDWIDTH ALLOCATION. REPLY WITH CRYTPOGRAPHIC SIGNATURE TO ACCEPT.

Within seconds, the first acceptances began to arrive. Retailers signed over the shelf space and neural bandwidth that Pura Vita had once occupied in their stores over to NutriYum in exchange for a discount on the coming cases.

By the end of the day, NutriYum would see its market share nearly double. A coup. A rout. The sort of market battlefield victory that songs are sung of in the executive suites.

The AI-traded fund called Vanguard Algo 5093 opened the data package it had bought for $187 million. It took nanoseconds to process the data. This was indeed an interesting market opportunity. Being the cautious sort, Vanguard Algo 5093 sought validation. At a random sample of a few thousand locations, it hired access to wearable lenses, to the anonymized data streams coming out of the eyes and brains of Nexus Corp customers, to tiny, insect-sized airborne drones. Only a small minority of the locations it tried had a set of eyes available within the one-second threshold it set, but those were sufficient. In every single location, the Pura Vita labels in view were red. Red for recall.

Vanguard Algo 5093 leapt into action. SELL SHORT! SELL SHORT!

It alerted its sibling Vanguard algorithms to the opportunity, earning a commission on their profits. It sent the required notifications to the few remaining human traders at the company as well, though it knew that they would respond far too slowly to make a difference

Within milliseconds, Pura Vita Stock was plunging as tens of billions in Vanguard Algo assets bet against it. In the next few milliseconds, other AI traders around the world took note of the movement of the stock. Many of them primed by the day's earlier short sale joined in now, pushing Pura Vita stock even lower.

Thirty-two seconds after it had purchased this advance data, Vanguard Algo 5093 saw the first reports on Pura Vita's inventory problem hit the wire. By then, $187 million in market intelligence had already netted it more than a billion in profits with more on the way as Pura Vita dipped even lower.

Simon's first warning was the stock ticker. Like so many other millionaires made of not-yet-vested stock options, he kept a ticker of his company's stock permanently in view in his mind. On any given day it might flicker a bit up or down by a few tenths of a percent. More up than down for the last year, to be sure. Still, on a volatile day one could see a swing in either direction of as much as two percent. Nothing to be too worried about.

He was immersing himself in data from a Tribeca clothing store— the one he'd seen with the lovely advertech today—when he noticed that the ticker in the corner of his mind's eye was red. Bright red. Pulsating red.

His attention flicked to it.

-11.4%

What?

It plunged even as he watched.

-12.6%

-13.3%

-15.1%

What the hell? He mentally zoomed in on the ticker to get the news. The headline struck him like a blow.

PURA VITA BOTTLES EXPIRING IN MILLIONS OF LOCATIONS.

No. This didn't make any sense. He called up the sales and marketing AI on his terminal.

Nothing.

Huh?

He tried again.

Nothing.

The AI was down.

He tried the inventory management AI next.

Nothing.

Again.

Nothing.

Simon was sweating now. He could feel the hum as the smart lining of his suit started running its compressors, struggling to cool him off. But it wasn't fast enough. Sweat beaded on his brow, on his upper lip. There was a knot in his stomach.

He pulled up voice, clicked to connect to IT. Oh, thank god.

Then routed to voicemail.

Oh, no. Oh, please no.

-28.7%.

-30.2%

-31.1%

-33.9%

It was evening before IT called back. They'd managed to reboot the AIs. A worm had taken them out somehow, had spread new code to all the Pura Vita bottles through the market intelligence update channel. And then it had disabled the remote update feature on the bottles. To fix those units, they needed to reach each one *physically*. Almost *a billion* bottles. That would take whole *days*!

It was a disaster. And there was worse.

NutriYum had sealed up the market, had closed six-month deals with tens of thousands of retailers. Their channel was gone, eviscerated.

And with it, Simon's life.

The credit notice came soon after. His options were worthless now. His most important asset was gone. And with it, so was the line of credit he'd been using to finance his life.

[NOTICE OF CREDIT DOWNGRADE]

The message flashed across his mind. Not just any downgrade. Down to zero. Down into the red. Junk status.

The other calls came within seconds of his credit downgrade. Everything he had—his midtown penthouse apartment, his vacation place in the Bahamas, his fractional jet share—they were all backed by that line of credit. He'd been living well beyond his means. And now the cards came tumbling down.

[NexusCorp Alert: Hello, valued customer! We have detected a problem with your account. We are temporarily downgrading your neural implant service to the free, ad-sponsored version. You can correct this at any time by submitting payment here.]

Simon clutched his head in horror. This couldn't be happening. It couldn't.

Numbly, he stumbled out of his office and down the corridor. Lurid product adverts swam at him from the open door to the break room. He pushed past them. He had to get home somehow, get to his apartment, do … something.

He half-collapsed into the elevator, fought to keep himself from hyperventilating as it dropped to the lobby floor. Adverts from the lobby restaurants flashed at him from the wall panel as they dropped, inundating him with juicy steak flavor, glorious red wine aroma, the laughter and bonhomie of friends he didn't have. The ads he habitually blocked out reached him raw and unfiltered now with an intensity he wasn't accustomed to in his exclusive, ad-free life. He crawled back as far as he could into the corner of the lift, whimpering, struggling to escape the barrage. The doors opened, and he bolted forward into the lobby and the crowd, heading out, out into the city.

The snack bar caught him first. It reached right into him with its scents and flavors and the incredible joy a bite of a YumDog would bring him. He stumbled towards the snack bar, unthinkingly. His mouth was dry, parched, a desert. He was so hot in this suit, sweating, burning up, even as the suit's pumps ran faster and faster to cool him down.

Water. He needed water.

He blinked to clear his vision, searching, searching for a refreshing Pura Vita.

All he saw was NutriYum. He stared at the bottles, the shelves upon shelves of them. And the NutriYum stared back into him. It saw his thirst. It saw the desert of his mouth, the parched landscape of his throat, and it whispered to him of sweet relief, of an endless cool stream to quench that thirst.

Simon stumbled forward another step. His fingers closed around a bottle of cold, perfect NutriYum. Beads of condensation broke refreshingly against his fingers.

Drink me, the bottle whispered to him. *And I'll make all your cares go away.*

The dry earth of his throat threatened to crack. His sinuses were a ruin of flame. He shouldn't do this. He couldn't do this.

Simon brought his other hand to the bottle, twisted off the cap, and tipped it back, letting the sweet, cold water quench the horrid cracking heat within him.

Pure bliss washed through him, bliss like he'd never known. This was nectar. This was perfection.

Some small part of Simon's brain told him that it was all a trick.

Direct neural stimulation. Dopamine release. Pleasure center activation. Reinforcement conditioning.

And he knew this. But the rest of him didn't care.

Simon was a NutriYum man now. And always would be.

Underworld 101

Mame Bougouma Diene

Freshman Year

I can't remember graduating from high school, I can't remember applying to Sheikh Anta Diop University either, all I ever wanted was to get my ass to Zim and its space harvesting programs. Not that it's the oddest thing here. I should remember, though, the tassels and silly hats, borrowed from America when it still counted for something. Senegal changed along with the rest of the world, then the world changed with Africa. Then we messed up, too. Some miscalculation in the atmospheric weather drones. It's all desert now, everywhere ... Anyway, I need to get my ass out of bed. Class starts at 7:45 a.m. sharp, couldn't tell you which class, though. Must be forgetting something again ...

"Wassup, Bougouma?"

Not a damn thing. Let me tell you about my name. "Mame Bougouma Diene" literally translates into "Grandpa doesn't want fish." And this is Dakar. Who doesn't want fish? Or didn't. When you could still get any. My parents really pulled a number on me. Tradition, man ...

"I'm good, Ablaye. Na'nga def?"

Ablaye isn't much of a brain. He's a hell of a wrestler, though. Bare knuckle fighting will do that, plus seven feet and three hundred pounds of muscle. We grew up together. That's to say he grew and kept growing long after I stopped.

"Mangi fi sama rak. Ran into your baby brother again today."

Another oddity. Everybody runs into Djibril except me. The stupid kid gets his ass everywhere and knows better than getting in my way.

"Next time, whoop his butt for me."

Ablaye laughs the laugh of someone strong enough to halt a Chadian tank with one punch.

"Wouldn't dream of it," he says, ramming an elbow into my ribs. "Elder bro's privilege."

Damn right ...
"Beers later?"
What I mean is carbonated battery acid.
"Always, grandpa."

Another odd thing, but in a Harry Potter kinda way, so I guess it's all right, like Diagon Alley and the hearth, except it's to the classrooms and through the shitter. Imagine having to fall backwards when you flush into the exact same place where you shit. I mean ... you get used to it, but then people got used to so many people you can't walk down a city block in less than an hour, to eating people because we have nothing left.

So you get used to it. There's no smell. It's the sensation that's weird, as if your body was stretched and snapped like a rubber band and then disintegrated. I mean that last bit exactly as I said it, and I know it's true because of the consciousness. One moment there's only me, one voice in my head and then upwards of a million, each one rehashing some random memory; and I can feel them all, or they can all feel me, or we can all feel each other or each self. Actually, what's truly bizarre is why waste such brilliant technology on a bunch of college students?

The Virtual College simulators we used in high school hadn't mentioned that ...

Anyway, whatever the reason, it only lasts a few milliseconds multiplied by the millions of you, and you're suddenly reconnected, stretched out again and dropped from the ceiling right into your chair for class.

Maybe it's all for nothing. The likelihood of finding a job when I graduate is close to zero, but poor kids don't get the opportunity for higher learning very often. Too little space, too many people. It's a rich man's privilege, so I'm gonna get my diploma. Then who knows? Maybe lightning will strike twice.

My butt hits my chair softly, and I'm staring out the window at the throngs of people trying to make it to the food banks and back in less than a day, streaming like sewage between seven hundred-story buildings. One hundred and forty million people crammed into a space that barely accommodated two million a hundred years ago ...

Apparently, it still beats living outside the cities where the population densities are lower but no food banks. Perhaps they recycle their own dead.

"Someone's about to get zapped," Sokhna whispers next to me. I hadn't even noticed her, fascinated by the human anthill.

"Where?"

She leans over, smelling of synthetic coconut oil, and points at a group of people fighting over rations. Her eyes are good and a beautiful dark blue.

There're always people too lazy to make it to the food banks. How many times my mother made it there and back is a miracle. Must've been hard for her, losing her husband to the Underworld Project and raising two little knuckleheads.

"You have a hawk's eyes."

"What's a hawk?"

I chuckle.

"Never played *Virtual Nature*?"

"Never saw the point."

She had one there.

The fighting party is causing a commotion. Other people are hungry and in a hurry. It will turn into riot any moment.

A police helithopter drops between the buildings, green-starred over red, yellow, and green, contrasting with the bleakness of the buildings, and zeroes in on the fighters.

"They won't zap them, girl. Why waste the protein?"

Sokhna grunts, but I'm right. The helithopter drops an antigravity beam on the crowd, glowing pale orange and buzzing like a thousand angry flies, drawing the offenders into its hull.

"More food for the bank."

Sokhna shrugs.

The classroom filled up. Everybody busying on their lesson pads, hands over their eyes, mouths moving silently in last-minute cramming.

"What's all the fuss about?"

Now Sokhna laughs.

"Idiot. Forgot about the test, didn't you?"

"What test?!"

"Exactly ... You're growing senile, grandpa ... The test Pr. Diop mentioned last week? If you pass, you don't take the final?"

Fuck! I knew I'd forgotten something.

"It's cool. I'm good at this econometric stuff."

Sokhna smiles. She really does have a beautiful smile, pearly white teeth, lips a mellow red, her straight hair in a ponytail, and a nose that balances the symmetry of her cheekbones perfectly.

"You better." She puts her hand on mine. "I'd hate it if you didn't come back next year."

"Salam alaikum."

"Alaikum salam, Pr. Diop."

"Take out your tablets. I hope you've studied hard."

"Djibril, kai fi!"

"Wow, kai! Five more minutes!"

"Put that simulator down and come here now!"

"Why, mom?! It worked for Mame, didn't it?"

"Your brother always had big-headed dreams he couldn't achieve. College and then what? He'll end up in the Underworld Project just like your father, just like everybody else. A head full of garbage that won't help swinging a hammer. Now get over here!"

Unless he makes management, Djibril thought, removing his Virtual College simulator. *If only he'd write more often ...*

"Well, that was relatively painless."

Truth is, I probably fluked the stupid test, but it's better to fail because I hadn't tried than to try and fail anyway.

"You know you've messed up," Sokhna snaps back. "You better kill that final."

In a world of a hundred fifty billion people, you'd think the odds were higher of finding someone who cared for you. But it's the exact opposite. The more people, the more selfish we get. So I'm lucky. The luckiest man alive. Perhaps she just wants someone caring for her and is playing her cards right, but she's playing them with me, nobody else, me. And that counts for something. It counts for everything.

"Easy for you to say. Your father was an official." I tell her, stating the obvious, "General Sankare. You've nothing to worry about."

I'm a fuckin' idiot. Acting tougher than I feel, despite needing her more than I'll ever care to admit, just to keep her guessing.

"*Was* being the operative word. No one remembers the Sahelien War anymore. Competition's hard at the top, too, Bougouma."

She's right. Upper middle classes play assassination games to stay ahead. At least us poor folk don't, but then we're busy fighting each other for food bank scraps, so we don't end up food ourselves.

"Saw your little brother today, by the way."

"Don't you all? Ablaye said the same thing yesterday."

"Ha! He's sneaky, your brother, was in the cafeteria chatting up some girl. Family thing, huh?"

Hate to say, but I love the kid. Different planet, different time, and he could have had the world.

"He's better off out of my way."

"Keep telling yourself that." She heads down the hallway. "See you at the wrestling training bouts tonight?"

"Any chance of seeing you elsewhere?" I ask, grinning.

She caresses my cheek.

"I'll try," she answers with a smile and disappears into a wave of students.

But she won't. That's odd, too. I still haven't found the girl's dorms. I can always snatch a kiss in the hallway, but she never makes it to my room. The toilets get us to the cafeteria at any time, but the moment I step away from the academic buildings, I can't find my way anywhere. All I see is a pixelated maze and lights that must be buildings that never get closer. I'm tired of jacking off, let me tell you ...

Sophomore Year

"So!" Ablaye says, slapping my back, jamming my kidneys into my lungs. "You actually passed? You need to quit all this thinking and start punching," he finishes, grinding his fists.

"Meatheads punch their way. I've got my eyes on the prize."

He laughs again.

"Let me guess. Sokhna, huh? A clever one, that one ... Too good for you. Look at me, I get all the girls I want."

That's true, wrestlers have their pick, maybe he can tell me how he finds their dorms or how they find him ...

"You mean *you're* not good enough for her, ox brain ... Anyway, glad I still have friends around this year ..."

The hall has filled up. I can't tell half the faces. Sometimes it felt like they'd admit just about anyone, but where do they all go? There is no way the school can handle this many students ...

"You're back!" Sokhna screams, her arms around my neck, assaulting me by the yard between buildings. The heat blasts my face, but her smell and the pressure of her chest against mine make me forget everything else.

"Told you I would ..."

"And you know better than disappointing me, dé!"

Maybe I do. Had I forgotten how beautiful she was over the summer? Or maybe she just got prettier every day ...

"How was your break?" I ask, taking her by the hand and away from the dusty heat.

She goes off on a litany of things she's done, her family, her brother working on the Underworld Project, her friends who'd never left what was left of Yoff ...

"What about you?" she asks, all pearly-smiled enthusiasm.

"Good. Everybody's good ..."

And then blank.

She misinterprets my silence.

"Miss 'em already, huh?"

I nod. I do miss them, I really do, but I also can't remember the past two months. Nothing at all. I should remember my mother's cooking at least. Who forgets that? And I must've kicked Djibril's ass at least once. But nothing, not a single thing ...

"Yeah. Yeah, I do."

She holds onto my arm tighter.

"It's okay. I miss them, too, and your little brother's bound to be around somewhere. ... Come on, or we'll be late for class."

"I hate this stupid class."

"It's the first time we take it," Sokhna whispers back.

"That's great, but if I wanted to train for the Underworld Project, I would've played *Virtual Underworld* in high school."

"You know what they say: All the roads lead to Underworld."

And they probably do. Twice the available space of the surface dug underground. A giant terrarium to relocate two-thirds of the surface population. Fifty billion here, fifty billion there, enough space to spread your legs, grow plants and vegetal proteins. No need to recycle corpses anymore.

"Bullshit. It's a plot to resettle people then drown us all."

"You don't really believe that."

Maybe I don't, but too many people do; and what does she know? She'd never lost anybody in there. Somewhere so deep they never got to see the sun again. She hadn't heard that her father was dead before getting a week's worth of free food rations. Maybe it had even

been him. Nice and spiced up. It had tasted awful. Her dad had died
a hero. Mine, an afterthought in Underworld.
"Doesn't matter what I believe."
"That's right. What matters is that you try your hardest."
"Oh, I do ..."
"Underworld's a vital part of our future." Professor Diop's drowsy
monotone goes on, "In fact, it's our only future. Who knows why?"
"Because we only have one planet," someone answers eagerly.
That's what everyone says, only this planet. Having one planet never
stopped us from ruining it in the first place. Why would Underworld
be any different? Someone's bound to screw up, wanting more of
something—more sunlight, fresher air, or misses the taste of human
flesh for whatever reason—and try to tear the roof down and have
the whole thing collapse. An unsatisfiable species convinced that
we're special, that's what we are, without the guts to look extinction
in the face and say fuck it ... But then I'm here, right? Trying to get
laid and get ahead, so who says I'm better?

Focus, one more punch and I'm beating this level ...
"Djibril!"
Inside the Virtual College: athletics simulation, Djibril's punch
slipped past his opponent's nose, and he tossed the helmet off in
disgust.
Why does she always do that?
She had a sixth sense, his mother, and then a seventh and an
eighth. Every time he would make progress, she would call him. He
couldn't blame her. His brother hadn't been back all summer. Maybe
she thought he wouldn't come back again. Who would stand to lose
her husband to mining operations and then a son to college? She
didn't want to lose him either, but what did she think was gonna
happen?
I gotta make something of myself, too ...

"Laamb lou reyna!"
Being friends with the Mighty Ablaye Gueye really has its benefits.
You can draw the humanity out of people until they're nothing but
shadows of their former shell and yet. It's the vibrancy of the crowd.
The electric tingling of static bouncing from every hair even if it's
only to watch two giants bashing each other's heads in. The staccato
of sticks on drums and the wrestlers in their colored robes dancing a

choreography, leg stomping right, arms flowing left, heads bobbing, and grigris wound tightly around their biceps. Ready to fight, even ready to kill.

I'm not looking and don't care, been seeing this since I was a kid, and the only thing I can focus on is Sokhna's hand caught in my palm, her pulse beating fast, and trying to get to our front row seats before the fights start.

"You're gonna tear my arm off," she says.

If only it could be your clothes ...

"Better me than those gorillas out there," I answer, nodding at the arena.

"Jealous much?"

I'm not, though I would be if she ever paid them any mind. Everybody else is jealous, though. Most guys, that is. Who doesn't wanna be so big you never have to worry about anyone or practically anything? Getting extra food rations and the adoration of all the ladies on campus and every competing campus? There's a catch, though: if you lose your bout, you're out. And then your strength might get you a bodyguard gig and keep you fed; but there's a lot of hungry people out there, and enough of them will take you down and save themselves a few trips to the food banks. Still, some would try their luck because who doesn't believe they're invincible?

Ablaye sees me sitting down with Sokhna and waves and winks without losing his hundred-mile stare of pure focus.

Sokhna is sweating a little, the drops running down her temples glowing brown with her skin, but she's excited. You can't help but let the tension work its way into you. Even I'm starting to feel it, my left leg beating uncontrollably. Sokhna rests a hand on my knee and stops it.

"Easy now." She says, "Hasn't even started yet."

A classmate, Youssou, recognizes us.

"Sokhna! Naka soube si? Bougouma! Dafa nice? Just saw your little brother, man. Can't have been more than a minute ago ..."

I face-palm while Sokhna pats me on the back. Damned kid. He should be in school or training on some virtual sim of his choice instead of running around campus.

Some people believe they're invincible, but perhaps Ablaye truly is.

Sokhna has fallen asleep, her head on my damp shoulder, wisps of her hair tickling my ear.

Ablaye is on his fourth and final fight, the final as it turns out, and he's barely broken a sweat. I nudge Sokhna awake gently.

"Hey, it's almost over. I'll never get front row seats again if Ablaye catches you sleeping."

She raises her head grumpily.

"I'm only here because you insisted."

"Exactly, make me proud."

Ablaye and his opponent, a Guinean named Alpha Diallo, only a couple of inches shorter than him, are testing each other, slapping each other's hands away as they try to lunge for a grab or a punch to the face.

Ablaye seems nervous. He usually moves in much quicker, but Diallo keeps him easily at bay, grinning confidently.

"Ablaye should've landed a few already ..." Sokhna notices as well.

"Yeah, that guy's good."

Both fighters interlock, twisting sideways, trying to force the other to his knees, and failing. Backing off, Diallo lands a sucker punch to Ablaye's nose.

Blood gushes to cheers from the Guinean's team that soar over the silent ring.

Ablaye wipes his nose staring at the blood. His nervousness turns to anger. He grabs Diallo at the waist and throws him to the ground. The arena roars.

"That's more like it," Sokhna says, but I'm not convinced. Diallo doesn't seem phased at all, as if he'd let that happen to give Ablaye a false sense of confidence.

And it's working, Ablaye flexes his muscles at the audience, his smile already spelling victory while the Guinean gets in position and the dance begins again.

Ablaye's showing frustration, his attacks getting stronger but less targeted. The Guinean slips, losing his footing. Ablaye aims for his nose, but Diallo was faking and dodges his overpowered blow, grabbing him at the waist, lifting him off the sand, Ablaye's face twisted in disbelief, slamming him to the ground with the resounding crack of his spine echoing across the wrestling grounds.

Sokhna leaps up and screams.

Junior Year

Have you ever been to college? There's something fun about freshman year. A sense of novelty, I guess. But as a junior, it's all played out. It's like high school again—like probably everything afterward. Maybe for the better. Creatures of habit need just that.

Growing in your shoes is the only place to grow, but fuck, don't you wish there were other spaces to grow and maybe other plains?

"You're back!"

Sokhna's arms around my neck, making me forget everything as the wind blasts from the yard. The wind that is our oxygen, the wind that is our death. I don't care, and why should I; they are softer than silk ...

"I am always ..." I try to muster a little cheerfulness, but Ablaye's death is a lump in my throat. The big lummox had it coming. We all lose eventually, but I'd expected it to be much later. As a champion, with enough credits to look into whatever future with confidence. The crack resounds in my head like thunder trapped in a cave, making it hard to hear anything, feel anything ...

"Hey! Hey!" Sokhna's shaking my arm, trying to kick me out of my daymare. "Are you okay?"

"Yeah, yeah. I guess. Ablaye, you know?"

"Who?"

The thunder stops rumbling. Sokhna's looking up at me, her beautiful eyes puzzled.

"Come on, girl, that's not funny."

She just shakes her head.

"Ablaye?" I insist. "Gigantic guy? Wrestler? You screamed when he died?!"

Sokhna's face freezes and blurs ... It's gotta be the wind, her usually soft features wrinkle and change, her nose grows a little, her lips twist, her right side smiling, the left frowning, dark blue eyes glowing yellow, and then it's gone. Barely a second but ...

She's suddenly contrite, her hand caressing my arm.

"Of course, I remember. How can I forget?"

Her tone is off. Her face is nothing but honest, but she sounds like she's reading from a script.

"Anyway!" she exclaims, back to her cheerful self. "How was your break?"

I never knew Sokhna to be bipolar ... Must be the grief. Funny how we deal with it in different ways.

Take me, for instance. Can't remember a thing again, only my childhood friend getting smashed into the ground on a loop.

"All right," I answer, shrugging, trying to keep my cool. "Yours?"

She starts talking, not a care in the world. I can barely hear her, but something is off again. I get this sense of déjà vu, which makes perfect sense. We're basically having the same conversation we had last year, but it feels like her words are exactly the same. The same inflections, the same giggles, the same pensive pauses. Damn, my head is really fucking with me.

"Miss 'em already, huh?"

"Yeah. Yeah, I do."

"It's okay. I miss them, too, and your little brother is bound to be around somewhere. ... Come on, or we'll be late for class ..."

"Does Diop teach everything?"

"He's the best. What more can you ask for?"

"The best at Econometrics, Underworld, Applied Physics, Climate History, and Arts and Crafts? I mean, please."

Sokhna sighs.

"Can't you ever be happy?"

"I haven't been happy in months."

She points at the mobs of students marauding the hallway.

"Well, this oughta cheer you up. Isn't that Djibril over there?"

I lean forward over the clutter of undergrads, trying to recognize my sibling's features.

Not a chance ... But in a flash he appears leaning against a locker, whispering into a little freshman girl's ear.

No way! When did he get so big?

The kid is taller. Taller than me and much wider. Solid muscle, too. What the fuck? I guess whopping season is over.

For the first time in two years, I let go of Sokhna's hand and start rushing down the hallway, shoving students out of the way.

"Djibril!"

Truth is, I'm really happy to see him. Ecstatic, actually, if only because I was starting to doubt my sanity with everybody else seeing him on an almost daily basis.

"Djibril!" I yell again, but he doesn't seem to hear me, moving swiftly down the hall with the girl while students cram the way, making it harder for me to get to him.

He turns around a corner towards the cafeteria, but by the time I get there, he's gone.

"Djibril! Djibril!"

Djibril drops his sim mask and rushes to find his mother.

She's never sounded this panicked ...

"Yes, mama!" he screams, barging into her room.

She looks up surprised.

"Well, that's a first!" she says, smiling. "You have me on your mind don't you, now?"

"You mean, you didn't call me?"

"Afraid not," she says. "But while you're here ..."

"You sure you're all right?" Sokhna asks me before I shoot myself back to the dorms.

"Of course," I say, going for nonchalant, but I can hear it in my voice and so can she. Her no-nonsense look says it all. Not quite seeing Djibril has shaken me more than I can say. It's normal, I suppose. Coupled with Ablaye passing and Sokhna being oddly flippant about it, it would've been good to see family.

"I'll be all right. Promise. I just need rest. I'll be fine tomorrow. You'll see," I insist, forcing a smile.

She nods wearily, grabs my face, pulls it down, and kisses my lips.

"Okay, I believe you. You've never lied to me ... So I'll see you tomorrow?"

"For sure."

She nods and walks away towards wherever the girl's dorms were.

The trip back to the dorms is not through the shitter again. I'd asked why once, something about it being public restrooms and insalubrious. I mean, shit for shit ...

Anyway, it's kinda like a cannon. There are several docking ports, you lay on your stomach, and once you've crawled all the way in: snap! There goes the rubber band and the disintegration and the million, million *You*s again until you land in your bed ...

Something's wrong.

Something's wrong.

Something's wrong.

Something's wrong.

Something's wrong.

A million other *Me*s echo back the same thing. The tunnel shoot is open, but I can't cross it. I can see my body on my bed, shaking in one giant epileptic seizure, my eyes flipped backwards, foam dripping from my mouth and urine slowly staining my pants.

What the ...

One of the million egos takes over:

It's high school graduation. The entire graduating body of Dakar is gathered outside the city. It's impossible to count us all. I know my family's somewhere out there, probably cheering me but more likely wondering where the hell I am in the formlessness of late teenage hood waiting to be sorted for college.

I turn to find them, but the sea of students never ends, stretching ahead, behind, east, and west to every horizon. The sky is uncommonly cloudy, dark with what should be storm clouds. There used to be a name for them, but it doesn't matter. The atmospheric weather drones have taken care of that. What little humidity's in there will evaporate into the atmosphere and slowly dissolve. The air is heavy with the acrid smell of nervous sweat. This isn't what I'd expected. Not at all what the intro to Virtual College looked like. No robes, no hats, no tassels, nothing. This feels more like triage.

"Congratulations, graduating class of 2178! You can be proud of yourselves! You'll be given indications on which route to follow to retrieve your diplomas and shipped directly to your assigned institutes of Higher Learning. You are the pride of our nation. Un Peuple, Un But, Une Foi!"

The slice of me carrying that memory melts and reintegrates my shell. Another takes over ...

It's hard to remember where I am. It's even harder to remember who I am. My nights are foggy with vivid dreams more vivid than the moments of half-life between them. Maybe it's daytime, I don't know. The last dream was something about class. A pretty girl I never met. Or maybe I have. I don't know anymore. She's really pretty, and she looks like she really likes me. Beautiful eyes, dark blue and sharp as a knife. I must know her, she feels more real than my memories, if that's what they are at all. And I keep thinking I've lost a close friend for some reason, a hulking dude. That can't be real either, but the grief feels real.

The helmet is uncomfortable, but at least the restraints tying me to the bed are off. Apparently, I shake a lot in my sleep, but that's because I'm not sleeping. It's the dreams. It's like they're trying to switch me for them.

The door is open on the hallway, a dark grey thing with a series of doors probably for other students. Not that I've met anybody since being shipped here. No one I can remember, anyway. But it's not the gloom that hits me. It's the smell: warm and metallic with an aftertaste of liquid shit like a decomposing body; and the sound, the heavy motion of a grinder.

Where is everybody and why did they let me out? Maybe I'm still dreaming.

The smell and the noise get worse as I walk down the hall. The stink makes my eyes water, and the grinding makes it hard to think; but there's a light, more light than I can remember in weeks.

There are things dropping into the light from a chute above. Elongated, heavy things by the whooshing sounds they make against the opening before the grinding takes over and the smell explodes in redolent bursts down the hall. Bowels. Guts. Blood. Those words flash in my languid brain, and I miss a step, my hand landing on the wall, and someone catches me.

"No need to go there, Bougouma. Not yet, at any rate."

"What is that noise? What is that smell?"

"Nothing to worry about. A few more days and you'll be ready to graduate!"

I want answers, but I'm too tired to understand. They're doing something to me, to all of us, but I won't let them have all of me. I won't forget it all ...

All the *Mes* coalesce into one, and I'm lying on my bed, all my memories one again. The shaking should stop. But it doesn't.

College Graduation

I'm sitting next to Sokhna, who's holding my hand and resting her head on my shoulder. Good god, she's not. Maybe in that dark meat grinder, she's dreaming that she is. Maybe we're all dreaming that we're sitting here ready to collect our diplomas ...

I can't remember senior year at all. One moment I'm convulsing in bed, and the next I'm sitting here with my entire graduating class. Someone must have caught the glitch and fast-forwarded me here ...

I know it isn't real, but I don't wanna think about reality—not after what I've seen. Maybe I'm still alive, waiting to be processed for the food banks. Maybe I've been dead for years and am just an algorithm in Virtual College.

Maybe they're gonna delete me. I don't care. I won't feel a thing anymore, and that might be best. If they recycle the program, I hope I don't remember because this isn't about me anymore. It's about who is playing my sim right now. Sitting at home, this close from graduating high school ...

"Hey! Stop looking so glum. Check out the stage. It's your brother handing out the diplomas!"

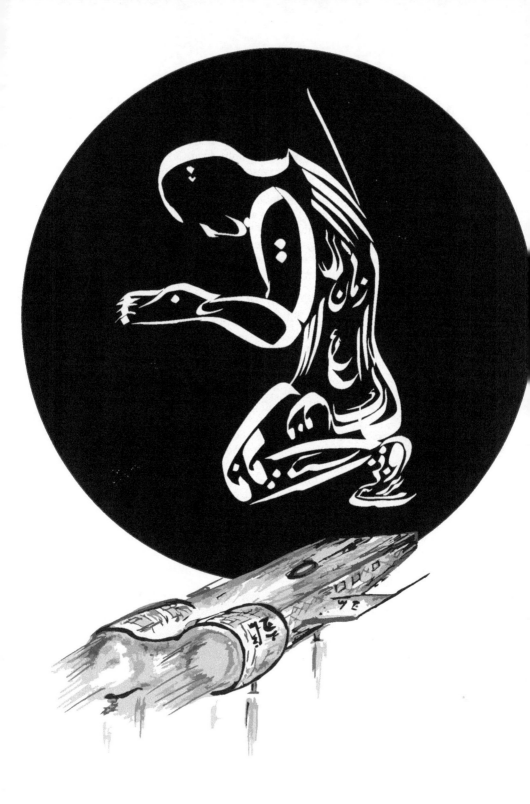

The Faithful Soldier, Prompted

Saladin Ahmed

If I die on this piece-of-shit road, Lubna's chances die with me. Ali leveled his shotgun at the growling tiger. *In the name of God, who needs no credit rating, let me live!* Even when he'd been a soldier, Ali hadn't been very religious. But facing death brought the old invocations to mind. The sway of culture, educated Lubna would have called it. If she were here. If she could speak.

The creature stood still on the split cement, watching Ali. Nanohanced tigers had been more or less wiped out in the great hunts before the Global Credit Crusade, or so Ali had heard. *I guess this is the shit end of "more or less."* More proof, as if he needed it, that traveling the Old Cairo Road on foot was as good as asking to die.

He almost thought he could hear the creature's targeting system whir, but of course he couldn't. Not any more than the tiger could read the vestigial OS prompt that flashed across Ali's supposedly deactivated retscreens.

God willing, Faithful Soldier, you will report for uniform inspection at 0500 hours.

Ali ignored the out-of-date message, kept his gun trained on the creature.

The tiger crouched to spring.

Ali squeezed the trigger, shouted, "God is greater than credit!" The cry of a younger man from the days when he'd let stupid causes use him. The days before he'd met Lubna.

A sputtering spurt of shot sprayed the creature. The tiger roared, bled, and fled.

For a moment, Ali just stood there panting. "Praise be to God," he finally said to no one in particular. *I'm coming, beloved. I'm going to get you your serum, and then I'm coming home.*

• • •

A day later, Ali still walked the Old Cairo Road alone, the wind whipping stinging sand at him, making a mockery of his old army-issued sandmask. As he walked, he thought of home—of Free Beirut and his humble house behind the jade-and-grey-marble fountain. At home a medbed hummed quietly, keeping Lubna alive even though she lay dying from the Green Devil, which one side or the other's hover-dustings had infected her with during the GCC. At home Lubna breathed shallowly while Ali's ex-squadmate Fatman Fahrad, the only man in the world he still trusted, stood watch over her.

Yet Ali had left on this madman's errand—left the woman who mattered more to him than anything on Earth's scorched surface. Serum was her only hope. But serum was devastatingly expensive, and Ali was broke. Every bit of money he had made working the hover-docks or doing security for shops had gone to prepay days on Lubna's medbed. And there was less and less work to be had. He'd begun having dreams that made him wake up crying. Dreams of shutting down Lubna's medbed. Of killing himself.

And then the first strange message had appeared behind his eyes.

Like God-alone-knew how many vets, Ali's ostensibly inactive OS still garbled forth a glitchy old prompt from time to time

God willing, Faithful Soldier, you will pick up your new field ablution kit after your debriefing today.

God willing, Faithful Soldier, you will spend your leave-time dinars wisely—at Honest Majoudi's!

But this new message had been unlike anything Ali had ever seen. Blood-freezingly current in its subject matter.

God willing, Faithful Soldier, you will go to the charity-yard of the Western Mosque in Old Cairo. She will live.

Ali's attention snapped back to the present as the wind picked up and the air grew thick with sand. As storms went, it was mild. But it still meant he'd have to stop until it blew over. He reluctantly set up the rickety rig-shelter that the Fatman had lent him. He crawled into it and lay there alone with the wail of the wind, the stink of his own body, and his exhausted, sleepless thoughts.

When the new prompt had appeared, Ali had feared he was losing his mind. More than one vet had lost theirs, had sworn that their OS had told them to slaughter their family. Ali had convinced himself that the prompt was random. An illustration of the one-in-a-trillion chance that such a message could somehow be produced by error.

But it had repeated itself. Every night for a week.

He'd told the Fatman about it, expected the grizzled old shit-talker to call him crazy. Half *wanted* to be called crazy. But Fahrad had shrugged, and said, "Beloved, I've seen a few things in my time. God, who needs no credit rating, can do the impossible. I don't talk about this shit with just anyone, of course. Not these days, beloved. Religion. Hmph! But maybe you *should* go. Things sure ain't gonna get any better here. And you know I'll watch over Lubna like my own daughter."

So now Ali found himself following a random, impossible promise. It was either this or wait for the medbed's inevitable shutdown sequence and watch Lubna die, her skin shriveling before his eyes, her eyewhites turning bright green.

After a few hours the storm died down. Ali packed up his rig-shelter and set back to walking the ruined Old Cairo Road, chasing a digital dream.

There was foot traffic on the road now, not just the occasional hover-cluster zipping overhead. He was finally nearing the city. He had to hurry. If he was gone too long, Ali could count on the Fatman to provide a few days of coverage for Lubna. But Fahrad was as poor as Ali. Time was short.

Running out of time without knowing what I'm chasing. Ali blocked out the mocking words his own mind threw at him. He took a long sip from his canteen and quickened his pace.

Eventually, the road crested a dune, and Old Cairo lay spread before him. The bustling hover-dock of Nile River Station. The silvery spires of Al-Azhar 2.0. The massive moisture pits, like aquamarine jewels against the city's sand-brown skin. Lubna had been here once on a university trip, Ali recalled. His thoughts went to her again, to his house behind the jade-and-grey marble fountain, but he herded them back to the here-and-now. *Focus. Find the Western Mosque.*

The gate guards took his rifle and eyed him suspiciously; but they let him pass. As he made his way through the city, people pressed in on every side. Ali had always thought of himself as a city man. He'd laughed at various village-bumpkin-turned-soldier types back when he'd been in the army. But Old Cairo made *him* feel like a bumpkin. He'd never seen so many people, not even in the vibrant Free Beirut of his childhood. He blocked them out as best he could.

He walked for two hours, asking directions of a smelly fruit seller and two different students. Finally, when dusk was dissipating into dark, he stood before the Western Mosque. It was old and looked it. The top half of the thick red minaret had long ago been blown away by some army that hadn't feared God. Ali passed through the high wall's open gate into the mosque's charity-yard, which was curiously free of paupers.

God willing, Faithful Soldier, you will remember to always travel with a squadmate when leaving the caravansarai.

"Peace and prosperity, brother. Can I help you?" The brown, jowly man that had snuck up on Ali's flank was obviously one of the Imams of the Western Mosque. His middle-aged face was furrowed in scrutiny.

Ali stood there, unable to speak. He had made it to Old Cairo, to the charity-yard of the Western Mosque as the prompt had said, and now ... Ali didn't know what he hoped to find. A vial of serum suspended in a pillar of light? The sky splitting and a great hand passing down cure-money? He was exhausted. He'd faced sandstorms and a tiger to get here. Had nearly died beneath the rot-blackened claws of toxighuls. He'd traveled for two weeks, surviving on little food and an hour's sleep here and there. He started to wobble on his feet.

Why had he come here? Lubna was going to die, and he wouldn't even be there to hold her.

The Imam stared at Ali, still waiting for an explanation.

Ali swallowed, his cracked throat burning. "I ... I ... my OS. It—" His knees started to buckle, and he nearly collapsed. "It told me to come here. From FreeBey. No money. Had to walk." They were a madman's words, and Ali hardly believed they were coming from his own mouth.

"Truly? You *walked* all that way? And lived to tell the tale? I didn't know such a thing was possible." The Imam looked at Ali with concerned distaste and put a hand on his shoulder. "Well ... the charity-yard is closing tonight for cleaning, but I suppose one foreign beggar won't get in the way too much. You can sleep in safety here, brother. And we can talk about your OS tomorrow."

Ali felt himself fading. He needed rest. Food. Even a vet like him could only go so long.

He sank slowly to the ground and slept.

In his sleep he saw the bloody bodies of friends and children. He saw his squadmates slicing the ears off dead men. He heard a girl cry as soldiers closed in around her.

He woke screaming as he had once done every night. His heart hammered. It had been a long time since he'd had dreams of the war. When they were first married, Lubna would soothe him, and they would step into the cool night air and sit by the jade-and-grey marble fountain. Eventually, the nightmares had faded. Her slender hand on the small of his back night after night—this had saved his life. And now he would never see her again. He had abandoned her because he thought God was talking to him. Thinking of it, his eyes began to burn with tears.

God willing, Faithful Soldier, you will deactivate the security scrambler on the wall before you. She will live.

Ali sucked in a shocked breath and forgot his self-pity. His pulse racing, he scrambled to his feet. He looked across the dark yard at the green-glowing instrument panel set in the mosque's massive gate. But he did not move.

God willing, Faithful Soldier, you will deactivate the security scrambler on the wall before you. She will live.

The prompt flashed a second time across his retscreens. *I've lost my mind.* But even as he thought it, he walked toward the wall.

Screen-jacking had never been Ali's specialty. But from the inside interface, the gate's security scrambler was simple enough to shut down. Anyone who'd done an army hitch or a security detail could do it. Ali's fingers danced over the screen, and a few seconds later it was done.

Then a chorus of angry shouts erupted, and an alarm system began droning away. Two men in black dashed out of the mosque and past him, each carrying an ornate jewelry box.

Thieves.

By the time he decided to stop them, they had crossed the courtyard. He scrambled toward them, trying not to think about him being unarmed. Behind him, he heard the familiar clatter of weapons and body armor.

"Thanks for the help, cousin!" one of the thieves shouted at Ali. Ali was near enough to smell their sweat when they each tapped their h-belts and hover-jumped easily over the descrambled wall. *Infiltrators waiting for their chance. They used me, somehow.* He panicked. *What have I done?* His stomach sank. *They've been using my OS all along!* How and why did they call him all the way from FreeBey? He didn't know, and it didn't matter.

I'm screwed. He had to get out of here. Somehow, he had to get back to Lubna. He turned to look toward the mosque—

—And found himself staring down the barrel of the jowly Imam's rifle. The holy man spat at Ali. "Motherless scum! Do you know how much they've stolen? You helped them get out, huh? And your pals left you behind to take their fall? Well, don't worry. The police will catch them, too. You won't face execution alone." He kept the weapon trained on Ali's head. Ali knew a shooter when he saw one. This was not good.

"I didn't—" Ali started to say, but he knew it was useless.

A squad of mosque guardsmen trotted up. They scowled almost jovially as they closed in. Ali didn't dare fight these men, who could call on more. He'd done enough security jobs himself to know they wouldn't listen to him. At least not until after they'd beaten him. He tensed himself and took slaps and punches. He yelped, and they raked his eyes for it. He threw up, and they punched him for it. His groin burned from kicks, and he lost two teeth. Then he blacked out.

He woke in a cell with four men in uniforms different from the mosque guards'. Cairene police? They gave him water.

God willing, Faithful Soldier, you will report to queue B7.

Ali ignored the prompt. The men slapped him around half-heartedly and made jokes about his mother's sexual tastes. Again, he pushed down the angry fighter within him. If he got himself killed by these men, he would never see Lubna again.

They dragged him into the dingy office of their Shaykh-Captain. The old man was scraggly and fat, but hard. A vet, unless Ali missed his guess.

"Tell me about your friends," the Shaykh-Captain said.

Ali started to explain about being framed but then found the words wouldn't stop. Something had been knocked loose within him these past few days. He talked and talked and told the old man the truth. All of the truth. About Lubna and the messages, about leaving Free Beirut, about the toxighuls and the tiger, the Western Mosque and the thieves.

When he was done, he lowered his eyes, but he felt the old man glare at him for a few long, silent moments. Ali raised his gaze slowly and saw a sardonic smile spread over the Shaykh-Captain's face.

"A *prompt*? Half the guys with an OS still get 'em—what do they mean? Nothing. I got one that said I fucked your mother last night. Did she wake up pregnant?" The men behind Ali chuckled. In the army Ali had hated the Cairenes and their moronic mother jokes. "Sometimes I don't even know where the words come from," the old man went on. "Random old satellites squawking? Some head-hacker having a laugh? Who knows? And who gives a shit? I got one a couple weeks back that told me to find some guy named Ali, who was supposed to tell me about 'great riches lying buried beneath a jade-and-grey marble fountain.'"

For a moment, Ali listened uncomprehendingly. Then he thought his heart would stop. He did everything he could to keep his face straight as the Shaykh-Captain continued.

"Do you know how many fountains like that there are here in OC? And how many sons of bitches named Ali? What's your name, anyway, fool?"

"My name? Uh, my name is F-fahrad, Shaykh-Captain, and I ..."

"Shut up! I was saying—I told my wife about this prompt, and she said I should go around the city digging up fountains. As if I don't got enough to do here." He gestured vaguely at a pile of textcards on his desk. "'In the army,' I told her, 'I got a prompt telling me about some pills that could make my dick twice as long. Did I waste my pay on them?'" The old man gave Ali an irritated look "Y'know, you and my wife—you two fucking mystics would like each other. Maybe you could go to her old broads' tea hour and tell them about your prompts! Maybe she'd even believe your donkey-shit story about walking here from the north."

The Shaykh-Captain stood slowly, walked over to the wall, and pulled down an old-fashioned truncheon. "But before the teahouse, we have to take you back downstairs for a little while."

Ali felt big, hard hands take hold of him, and he knew that this was it. He was half-dead already. He couldn't survive an Old Cairo-style interrogation. He would never see Lubna again. He had failed her, and she would die a death as horrible as anything he'd seen in the war.

Faithful Soldier, she will live.

The prompt flashed past his retscreens, and he thought again of the Shaykh Captain's words about riches and the fountain.

This was no head-hacker's trick. No thieves' scheme. He did not understand it, but God *had* spoken to him. He could not dishonor that. He had once served murderers and madmen who claimed to act in God's name. But Lubna—brilliant, loving Lubna—had shown him that this world could hold holiness. If Ali could not see her again, if he could not save her, he could at least face his death with faith.

He made his voice as strong as he could, and he held his head high as he uttered words that would seal his fate with these men. "In the name of God, who needs no credit rating, Shaykh-Captain, do what you must. But I am not lying."

The Shaykh-Captain's eyes widened, and a twisted smile came to his lips. "So *that's* it! In the name of your mother's pussy, you superstitious fool!" The big men behind Ali grumbled their southern disgust at the fact of Ali's existence and started shoving him; but the old man cut them off with a hand gesture. He set down the truncheon, pulled at his dirty grey beard, assumed a mock gravity. "A genuine Free Shi'ah Anti-Crediteer. The scourge of the Global Credit Crusaders. Hard times for your kind these days, even up north, I hear."

The Shaykh-Captain snorted, but there was something new in the man's voice. Something almost human. "You think you're a brave man—a martyr—to show your true colors down here, huh? Pfft. Well, you can stop stroking your own dick on that count. No one down here gives a damn about those days anymore. Half this city was on your side of things once. Truth be told, my fuck-faced fool of a little brother was one of you. He kept fighting that war when everyone knew it was over. He's dead now. A fool, like I say. Me? I faced reality. Now look at me." The old man spread his arms as if his shabby office was a palace, his two goons gorgeous wives.

He sat on the edge of his desk and gave Ali another long look. "But you—you're stuck in the fanatical past, huh? You know, I believe this story about following your OS is actually true. Not a robber. Just an idiot. You're as pathetic as my brother was. A dream-chasing relic. You really *walked* down the OC Road?"

Ali nodded but said nothing.

A sympathetic flash lit the Shaykh-Captain's eyes, but he quickly grimaced as if the moment of fellow-feeling caused him physical pain. "Well, my men will call me soft, but what the fuck? You've had a rough enough trip down here, I suppose. Tell you what: We'll get you a corner in steerage on a hover-cluster, okay? Those northbound flights are always half-empty anyway. Go be with your wife, asshole."

Ali could not quite believe what he was hearing. "Thank you! Thank you, Shaykh-Captain! In the name of—"

"In the name of your mother's hairy tits! Shut up and take your worn, old expressions back to your falling-apart city. Boys, get this butt-fucked foreigner out of my office. Give him a medpatch, maybe. Some soup. And don't mess him up too bad, huh?"

The big men gave him a low-grade medpatch, which helped. And they fed him lentil soup and pita. Then they shoved him around again a bit, but not enough to matter.

When they were through, they hurled him into the steerage line at the hover-docks. Ali was tired and hurt and thirsty. Both his lips were split, and his guts felt like jelly. But war had taught him how to hang on when there was a real chance of getting home. Riches buried beneath the jade-and-grey-marble fountain. Cure-money. Despair had weakened him, but he would find the strength to make it back to Lubna. He would watch as she woke, finally free of the disease.

Faithful Soldier, you will—

The prompt cut off abruptly. Ali boarded the hover-cluster and headed home to his beloved.

Beautiful Curse

Kristine Ong Muslim

It was not an accident at all. I planned on the most opportune time for my family to find out that the removal of my tentacle had not suppressed my predatory urges. And in all this time, I also could not stop thinking about that room in our house, the one with no windows and a thick door lined with steel, a door that only locked from the outside.

I chose a Sunday afternoon in April. April was the time of the year when the northern sky developed a loathsome purple tinge, a consequence of the early stages of redshifting. The government issued warnings about this phenomenon, warnings which were useless because they could not change the eventual course of things—that we were all headed for extinction and no one could do anything about it. That afternoon was perfect. My family deserved a little pep in their long, uneventful lives.

When my family discovered me behind the shed, I was disheveled in all ways that a person could be disheveled. I crouched in the bushes. My mouth was clamped to the neck of the bloodied, still twitching chicken. The feathers made me gag, but I kept on chomping, kept on tearing at the doomed fowl's flesh until, at last, the animal, the prey, stopped twitching—a weakling's ultimate recourse.

My father restrained me, gagged me so I couldn't bite him, and then half-dragged/half-carried me inside the house. It was probably out of shame that he ended up manhandling me. He needed to get me inside the house before anyone could see the bloody spectacle I had created. With her screeching my sister woke the neighbors and our hibernating house pets. Oh, I wanted to snap her neck just to shut her up, eat her and my father, devour their corrupted bodies, and leave only the bones for the rare scavenging birds of prey to pick; but I just could not get to them. They managed to chain me up and plug my mouth.

My mother said that I had the peculiar maniacal look she associated with the residents of Bardenstan, the place nearest the epicenter of the 2115 fallout. Her comment was not meant to be an insult. She said it in the manner of someone expecting me to reform afterwards. My mother was a first-rate Loyal, thus the genuine kindness. My father bought her from an auction house. I never heard him complain about her expensive solar upkeep and collagen sustenance. If he did, well, that would be another story. My mother, a first-rate Loyal to the core, was wired to love me unconditionally with or without my tentacle.

Do you know that there's a picture of me hidden inside my parents' safe? In that picture was the real me. It showed how I looked the day I was born. I saw it only once when I turned twelve, the mandatory age for Truth—the government's thirty-three-year campaign to make parents—both prearranged and natural—confess to their children about the circumstances of their birth. The Truth was supposed to foster family bonding, a hazy concept that was prevalent in the nuclear families of the late twentieth century.

I believed in it. Or I thought I did. I believed in any effort, no matter how preposterous, to be truthful. In that picture I did not look human because I had an enormous tentacle protruding from the side of my body. The tentacle was covered by bluish skin. The skin was sparsely dotted with tiny sacs. Deoxygenated blood, the doctor curtly answered, when asked why it was bluish. The tentacle allowed for voluntary movement. It was, more or less, a prodigious limb.

"The tentacle," the doctor went on to explain to the younger versions of my parents, "is an extension of the appendix. This anomaly is linked to predatory instincts."

I looked it up in an exotic biology textbook, memorized the passage that defined what scientists thought I had: *The tentacle is not a simple anatomical curiosity. It is associated with the need to hunt, to assemble in packs—a behavior that has been observed in long-extinct animals like canines. If the tentacle is not cut out in time or before the host turns sixteen, the predatory instincts may prove to be overwhelming and may lead a person to harm others, as in the harrowing case of Flynn Romero, 19, who finally had his tentacle surgically removed when he was seventeen. Romero, who attacked everyone in a department store toy section where he worked on a contractual basis, killed nine people that day.*

Ah, Romero! I thought when I first read about his case. *Had they stopped moving and teasing you to hunt them, you wouldn't have been interested in them and they would have survived, right?*

Now in that picture in my parents' safe, I had the squelched look of defeat, the squelched look of an ancient creature that believed itself to be dangerous but had no faculties to behave as such. It looked as if something vital had been seized from me. And something, indeed, had been taken from me—albeit temporarily and not fully. In that picture my lips had the hideous color of raw and ragged flesh, as if I had chewed them up. You see, even preselection and genetic engineering could ruin even the most ordinary of human stock. Something could always turn out wrong. My sister and I were deemed to be from a good batch during the recount of 2120. But look at how I turned out—sentient and disfigured, maladjusted and happy—a familiar fixture if I had lived years ago.

My parents had my tentacle surgically removed when I was five years old. The visible section of the tentacle was eliminated. The part that was anchored to my spine was left untouched. Removing that part could kill me.

I missed having my tentacle around. As a child, I used to swing from it on the banister.

Outerbridge, the only place in America where crops are still grown in soil, does not take kindly to deformities. There are towns where physical aberrations are tolerated. Bardenstan, for example. Anyway, that's another story. (I have plenty of stories left in me. Now they're mostly about the hunt, the hunt, the unending hunt.)

Think about the ones who cannot be saved. Think about the ones who cannot adjust to being different. Think about all our stories and those of the ones before us. This terrible unfolding does not always see a blunt object gain shape. Sometimes, it distorts the object and the landscape that conspires to retain its shape.

Outside, something darted across my line of vision. It looked like a bird, a real one. Flightless birds were the only real birds. I would find it soon. I would find it, and then I would kill it. And you could say that this urgency was attributed to the unexcised portion of my tentacle. You could believe whatever sounded convenient because that's what drives people to stay sane. Father put me inside the room where there are no windows, the room with just this one door that locks from the outside. I hear them talking outside the room. They are scared. They are panicking. I sense their restlessness. My mother, the first-rate Loyal, I'll gnaw her throat first when I get out of here, slurp whatever comes out of all her ragged holes.

Real Boys

Clara Kumagai

Before I was a donkey, I was a boy.

I've been in this same field for a while now. It might be years. I'm old, I suppose. It's not that I can't measure time; it's just that I don't care enough to.

So here I am, dying.

I lie down to make it easier, flat on my side with my neck pressed against the ground. This is how calves and foals sleep—artlessly and abandoned to their rest. I wheeze into the dust. There are footsteps coming towards me, and I wonder if my master is going to attempt to whip me back to health or worse still, shorten my dying. Let my death be my own, at least.

My memories of how it began are all tied up with him even though he wasn't the cause of any of it. Probably it started long before that, when Toyland was built or when a spell was cast in the woods or with something that I don't know about at all. He was strange, enchanted—a wooden toy that had come to some semblance of life. I was a boy then, leaning on a street corner, and he made my skin prickle when I saw him. His face was smooth and polished, a varnished expression painted in place. His eyes were flat. His voice was not. He talked fast and desperately. He was an uncanny thing, asking for directions home like any other lucky fool with one to go to.

But then I'd seen my fair share of strangeness and took it to be a curse or a spell or even some spirit caught in clockwork. He was an innocent thing. Or stupid. I think I called him stupid at the time.

"What're you?" I'd said, all rough and ready. I spat.

"Me, I'm a puppet I am, made by a man, my father, and I'm alive, I don't look it but I am—"

Babble, babble. He'd do that if you weren't quick to cut him off.

"All right, whisht now." I took to him. He reminded me of

somebody I used to know. There was an air to him—a sort of hunger so fierce it grabbed and grappled at you. But not like the other hollowed-out young ones and old ones I'd grown up around; this one wasn't starving for food. "Ye seem grand," I said. "A grand lad."

His head tilted to one side. "Yes, like a boy, you know I want to be a boy, the fairy told me I'd be one tomorrow, a real one—"

"Ye'd like it where I'm going," I said. "Only the real lads—the real boys—get to go there."

"Where's this, where's that you're going?" he said, all eager.

"Toyland!" I said. His face was blank. Well, it always looked blank, but when he didn't talk straight away, I guessed he was baffled. "You never heard of Toyland? It's a grand time." Rumours had been growing, creeping through the streets, flourishing in the tenements, and blooming in the alleys. "They feed you there. Boys don't do enthing but play all day. No work or school or nothing."

"I have to go to school, the fairy told me, it's what good boys do, and I have to be good—"

"Ah, the piseogs'll always lead you astray." I'm sure I would have spat again at this point. I may have even farted for emphasis. The puppet was silent for a while. Perhaps he was impressed by my physical flourishes.

"And who made this place, how are you going there, when?"

"If you come along, you can see for yourself. Bet you'll learn more than in a week of school."

"And the real boys, they go there?"

"Oh yes, indeed they do! Indeed *we* do, amn't I right?"

That had him. He swallowed it up like a duck eating bread. Real boys, that's all he wanted to hear about, that's all he desired to be. Could've told him real boys wore aprons and had babies and he'd be in labour, cooking dinner before you could finish a sentence. I did call him stupid, I remember now.

A donkey's head is far heavier than a boy's. My nose is low to the ground. It's best to keep eyes down, anyway. I am kept alive, just. The collar around my neck rubs me raw. Donkeys don't need a metal bit, but the taste of metal in my mouth is not unfamiliar to me.

They put a jenny in the field with me once. They wanted me to sire more donkeys, create some stock, something to sell. I turned from her snuffly nose and wagging ears. She was a donkey, and I was a boy who had been made one. We were not the same.

But in the end I fucked her anyway.

The puppet and I made an unlikely pair. I was big and dirty and hungry enough that I avoided being a target. The puppet, though, he was a victim just begging to be abused. He attracted tricksters and liars and scoundrels. It was like wasps at a picnic.

He'd had some adventures, some capturings and escapings, and he told me all about them in that too-fast, tripping-up way of his. It took me a while to realise why he spoke like that: he had no lungs, of course. Silly me. I listened to him because there was nothing better to do. I did become interested, in the end, if only because I was trying to figure out if all this had really happened to him or if he was mad or infested with woodworm.

It was no bother finding a way to Toyland.

"Get on board, boys," said the sinister coachman, opening the door for us.

Did I waver? If I did, it was only for the length of time it took me to spot the bread and meat and bottles set out on the seats. We got in, and the coachman leered and merrily whipped his donkeys onwards to Toyland.

The puppet became less strange the longer I was around him. He told me his father and maker had wanted a son. I wanted to ask him what had stopped the man from taking in one of the ragged barefoot children that roamed the town or from getting some slut pregnant. Someone had unearthed a lump of talking bogwood while cutting turf and had taken it to the puppet's maker, and the result was sitting across from me in that dusty, chilly coach.

My thoughts move slowly as a donkey. I have caught myself not thinking for days on end, days and days in which I have just been a donkey. Those times are not bad. I am not happy to remember that I can think otherwise; I am never pleased at my return to consciousness. It's easier to be without it.

Toyland, when we got there, was no grand amusement park. It was more like a slum of shabby houses and filthy pubs. I didn't even know where it was, but I assumed the midlands. It had a claggy sort of feel to it. By the look of the other boys, I could tell our stories would be similarly grim, backgrounds of hunger and beatings and nights in doorways.

The puppet drew attention, all right. Took hardly any time for a gang to approach us with matches in one hand and cruelty in the other.

"Back off, ya bastards!" I shouted valiantly.

"What, are you his brother or something? Yer ma must've needed some real wood after she had you." It may have been the funniest thing this particular boy had said, ever.

"I don't have a brother," I said. "Or a ma, neither."

"We just wanna see if he feels pain," said another. He must have had a scientific mind. I saw a tattered cat skulking in a corner and grabbed it.

"Play with this instead." I shoved the cat at them.

"Ah, we know cats feel pain," the scientist said.

I'd already dragged the puppet away. We ducked into a pub.

"The cat!" The puppet was twisting his twiggy limbs under my hand, giving me splinters.

"Why did you, why did you give it to them?"

"Shut up," I said to him, and pulled the door closed behind me so that we wouldn't hear the shrieks of the cat as it was set on fire.

I've been bought and sold several times. It's a nerve-wracking time, being brought to the mart. The sellers trot us out, and prospective buyers wedge our jaws open to look at our teeth. Between my own inspections, I would look at the other donkeys and wonder which ones I would buy if I were a boy again. I've decided now that I wouldn't buy a donkey at all; I would much prefer a horse.

I always tried to look good for the men who seemed a bit gentler. Pushed my nose to their hands and hoped I'd get a good master. Snapped at the men I didn't like. I've daydreamed about being bought by a girl, one who would take me home to a stable and brush me down and rub my ears with her soft little hands. But a girl like that would never visit the grubby small town markets that things like me are sold at.

And in the end one master is much the same as any other.

Toyland was a fine, old time. We were carefree boys with no rules or responsibilities coming into the prime of our teenage years. It was, as a result, a violent and volatile place. There were brawls and gangs that were quick to form and even quicker to dissolve.

The majority of our time we spent in the run-down pubs. There were never any barmen, just a seemingly endless supply of watery stout. There was tobacco, too, and cheap cigars. I partook in all of it, though the puppet didn't. He generally just kept me company while I drank myself to the lively point of vomit and unconsciousness. When I awoke, he would still be there, and we would carry on.

We rarely saw any grown-ups, though they must have been around to restock and supply our vices. One day we came upon a gang of boys who had found some opium, and I passed some hours in a haze of vertigo and nightmares. None of us missed an adult presence; we were doing just grand on our own.

The puppet might have missed his father. He talked about him often enough. He never said he wanted to leave, though. He just kept asking me if he was a real boy yet.

"Yer certainly getting closer," I would slur. "This is wha' real boys do."

"But I don't look any different, do I, or feel any different, I feel the same—"

"Give it time," I said. "You won't feel different straightaway. Give it a bit more time."

Once after saying this, or something like it, I remember getting sick into my glass and throwing it at some other boy's head. We had a fight, and then I kept on drinking.

We were there for about a fortnight before I became a donkey. I remember that very well. I was sitting at a table, scoffing soda bread and sausages with my hands, laughing at something or someone, ha-ha-ha-ing with my mouth full and open. It must have been a good joke because I was still laughing when the change began. It was not my ears that grew first, but my hooves.

My toes went numb, and then it felt as though there was a crust over my feet, hardening and setting like melted wax when you dip a finger into it and let it cool in the air. Then the strangeness was in my hands, and I saw what must have happened to my feet; my fingers stuck together, and my nails grew right over them and over the backs of my hands, swelling, darkening, setting themselves into little black hooves.

I screamed and screamed. My backbone stretched, and my knees twisted unnaturally until they were on the wrong side of my legs. Then my ears grew. They pushed themselves up my skull to the top of my head. Hair burst from everywhere. I shrieked and howled and had broken the table already, smashing food to the floor, sobbing at the faces around me that looked on, blurrily astonished and idiotic.

By then of course, it was far too late. But I was still screaming.

"Help, help me! Please, please, please. Help, help, heeeee—heeeeee—" and as I drew my breath in, my vocal cords must have changed, too, for I brayed a dreadful "Heeee haaaaaw!"

And then I could speak no more. I cried and cried, frightened by my own unrecognisable noise and by the realisation that donkeys don't cry tears.

The puppet was flailing his limbs around and shouting his babble, but he was mostly ignored. The same transformation had begun to take hold of some of the other boys in the room, and the rest ran away. A few, high on a cloud of opium, sat in a corner and watched it all, no doubt thinking that this was all just part of the dream.

I shivered out my shock in a little wooden pen that was full of other newly-made donkeys. We had been swiftly rounded up with whips and cattle prods. They must have been ready and waiting.

I stared at the planks I was pressed against and saw that there were teeth marks in the wood and clumps of grey donkey hair and blood. Some men came in and shouted and jabbed sharp sticks into the sides of the more hysterical donkeys.

"Ouch, would ya stop!"

I shivered when I realised that one of the donkeys could still speak.

"Ah, here! We've got a chatty one!" said one of the men. They opened the gate and grabbed him.

"Please!" the donkey said, all wild and white-eyed. "Please—let me go home!"

"Home?" One of the men holding the donkey laughed. "Like this? You'd give your ma a shock!"

"My ma!" The donkey shook beneath the men's rough hands and cried, "Mammy, mammy!"

The men dragged the talking donkey away. I don't know what they did with him.

I don't know what happened to the puppet either. He hadn't turned into a donkey; he already had a spell on him. Wood could only take so much. Most likely he got away. He was so stupid he was probably fine. Stupid people can get on remarkably well in life.

And now as I feel my breath fall out, I think the curse is loosening its hold on me. My hooves are pinning and needling me, and they are softening, splitting apart to form fingers and toes again. My dusty, grey hair falls away. I am shrinking. I am becoming a little thin figure like the other people I see. I fear I may blow away.

There is a figure over me. Not my master. Some boy. He puts a hand on my arm. His skin looks very pale against mine. He's got a round, stupid face. The puppet, I think. And then no, it couldn't be. This boy is too young. He's not the puppet. Just a boy. Firm flesh and unbroken bones. He stands and looks down at me. Wipes his hand on his trousers. Walks away.

Is he leaving me? I try to raise my head a little. That's too hard to do, so I rest it back on the ground again. But my voice must have returned to me, like the rest of my human parts. I want him to come back. Give me help or pity or mercy. My mouth hangs loose, my tongue moves, trying to cry out, but nothing happens. I want to say that I've been good, but I've forgotten how to speak, that I'm a boy, really, but I don't know how to say it.

Born Out of the Frost

Mélanie Fazi

● translated by Lynn E. Palermo ●

She was born out of the frost, yesterday, on my window.

Crystals fanned out across the glass panes. Methodically, inside and out. Like a layer of white lichen creeping from the edges in toward the middle. Filtering milky—even brittle—light. Seemed like I should be able to peel it off. A harsh, glacial light that made the hair on my arms stand on end.

I'd swathed my body in layers of wool, but still it shivered. Shoving up the heat made no difference. Cold was taking over the whole apartment. Seeping into my bones.

Then a face on one of the panes ... took several hours to gain definition. The frost spread out in arabesques too regular to leave room for chance. To melt them I blew on the glass with no result. An outline emerged around a still-empty face—a hollow through which I could still make out the street. Light sculpted the raised contours. I hadn't known that frost could hold so much nuance in silver and white.

The street disappeared as features completed the face, one by one, in relief. It was a sculpture carved in ice more than a painting in frost. As if its traits had grown out of the glass itself. Fine, precise, translucent. Silver filaments for hair. A frigid gleam in the eyes.

She looked like me.

I thought it was my portrait, that the panes or maybe the winter were talking to me. Which would have been flattering: she was magnificent, everything I'm not.

Then at last, in the center of the tableau, I saw her mouth emerge. Lips pulled back to expose teeth of glittering frost.

As she watched me, she laughed. And her laughter was biting.

●　●　●

She's living in the mirrors now. Because of me, I think.

For a long time, I looked myself over from head to foot in the mirror on the armoire. Compared features she'd formed on the window, searching for some resemblance. But I could see only my pale skin and dull, messy hair. Nothing to equal her grace. I clenched my teeth to keep them from chattering.

Blowing warm air on the mirror, I covered it with my breath. A hazy pool of mist shrouded my face. I tried to trace her face with my finger the way I'd drawn on the car windows when I was little.

But my sketch was crude, clumsy. Not even close to her or to me. Not even approaching the delicacy of her features. The mist faded—the mirror drank in my breath.

I think that's the moment when she passed through to the other side: when I blew her into the mirror.

The other face, the one on the window, faded. First the contours, then the hair, until all that remained was a face carved in the ice or in the glass itself and losing its mass. Her laugh was the last trait to dissolve from her hollow, dripping face, just after her eyes. Which had never left me for a single moment.

When I awoke this morning, I found her in the mirror. As if cut right out of the windowpane and deposited there on the other side while I slept. She has devoured my reflection. If I stand in front of the wardrobe, it is she who stands before me. With her winter-colored dress, her long, translucent fingers, and her hair full of icy flakes. Her eyes like frozen pools. Her skin dusted with hoarfrost. And as always, the sharp teeth revealed by her laugh.

She starts by my movements. Then gradually she disengages from them. I watch her acquire a life of her own with an elegance that ice should not possess. An elegance that flesh never attains.

Her movements are growing more fluid. Her gait, less stiff. Her skin is slowly taking on color. She has shed the winter like a molting bird.

On the pane where she first appeared, frost has veiled the window entirely. The street no longer exists.

I should probably be frightened. But I don't know how. My mind has been numbed by the cold.

She plays at being me: a doll of frost, a doll of blood. In the space beyond the mirror, I see her touching the books, furniture, and knickknacks, learning their shape and texture. Her fingers are still ungainly. She leaves glinting droplets in her path, sowing a trail of glitter and scales that melt as they touch the ground. Under the layer of frost, her skin is a faint pink. She cocks her head with curiosity, shakes the objects, smiles at the rattle of a jar filled with needles or a box of jewelry. When she sits on the bed and sinks into the quilt, I could swear I hear snow crunching under her feet.

Now she's pulled off her dress with its texture of evergreens hanging heavy with snow. She's trying on my clothes. Clothes I haven't worn in years as the colors are too bright. The cherry red and bright orange stand out against her pale skin. Now that her fingers are more limber, she digs into my makeup. Dabs her face with autumnal golds and browns that turn her face into a clownish mask. Grotesque blots of my nail polish dot her fingertips.

Despite the caricature, she's divine. Beneath her disguise, she's almost me. Me, if I were beyond human.

Since she has no name, I give her my own. We have to name things. It's the only way to hold onto them.

Spring has arrived in the other bedroom, the one deep in the mirror. Her skin is now pink and warm. Must be where all the heat has gone. On my side, the frost has worked its way into the locks, jamming the front door. I've spent long hours probing the mirror for the crack that absorbed all the heat.

Last night, she slept in a bed that was the twin of my own. I could hear her breathing over there under the other quilt. For most of the night, I tossed and turned under my covers, not wanting to give in to sleep. I was too afraid of having her dreams. I didn't want to know what images turned round in her head. She might be dreaming of me.

If she stays, I'm afraid she'll end up possessing me. I don't know how to exorcise her.

Her arms are now bare. Her skin more soft, supple. Meanwhile, mine has lost its color, and my lips are turning blue.

Her face is almost mine. But I can still see hints of frost in the depths of her eyes. And a harshness in her smile that mine has never had. She's taken every part of me and crafted it into something else: she's turned a mouse into a wild animal.

A little while ago, she was studying herself in the mirror before putting on makeup. I reached out my hand to catch her attention. She imitated me. Our fingers joined, mine thrust into the mirror up to my knuckles. Hers sticking out, free. It felt so warm in there; the contact with her fingers slowly warmed my own. Her ring with its sharp corners dug into my flesh. It looked like a silver scorpion.

Then she pushed my hand away. A drop of blood formed at the base of my index finger. It had no taste at all.

She disappeared into the living room. I could hear her moving about in there. I heard muffled music through the mirror. It was one of my albums, but I couldn't remember which one. She seemed to know: I could hear her humming along.

Ever since then, my fingers bear the mark of her touch. Like an infection. Everywhere I lay my hands, colors grow faint. Textures harden. It spreads before my eyes. Sheets of ice cover the walls. I can still make out the paint in a few places. Not many. I've already almost forgotten the color, anyway. The floor crazes under my feet. I'm walking on a frozen lake with a shadowy floor beneath the surface. Going into the kitchen, I leave a tracery of spiderwebs in my wake. The food in the refrigerator is covered with mold. I'm not sure if that's my fault or the scorpion's. But I'm no longer hungry. Or cold. My fingernails are blue, but I feel nothing.

It's better that way. The bedroom is freezing. The world has turned white. Everything is covered with frost. A book just shattered when I knocked it off a shelf. It split into two sharp-edged pieces. Now I don't dare touch anything: I'm afraid of breaking it all. Objects that don't yield might snap off my fingers, leaving my hands with frozen stumps.

Once again, I take refuge on the bed. I can't worm my way under the quilt: the frost has fused it to the mattress.

I gaze into the depths of the mirror at summer. A square of sunlight on the floorboards under the window. Colors that grow more brilliant as my own fade away. Over there, the walls are salmon. The bedspread is red. The curtains hang in vivid colors. She has decorated it all in her image. She's dyed her hair a shade of copper. She flaunts her grace as she parades back and forth in front of the armoire.

Sometimes she raps on the mirror to remind me that she hasn't forgotten I'm here.

There are people over there. I hear voices and laughter in the summer apartment. Music and the clatter of silverware. But I can't see them. They're in the other room.

My bedroom has turned into a closed-up box: a white box. The keyhole has frozen over, and frost has veiled the last window. I no longer leave my bed. Huddled atop the quilt and on the pillow with its frozen wrinkles, I can no longer feel them against my skin. Nothing but the exhaustion pressing me to the bed. I can't close my eyelids. Immobilized, I listen and watch.

I thought the frost would make my body hard and brittle, but instead, I've lost substance. I don't dare lift my arms for fear that my hands will stay stuck to the mattress, pull off. My fists have less mass than cotton. I'll no doubt end up completely dissolved. I no longer have a body. I'm a quilt and some clothing. I'm the winter and the bedroom.

From this point on, the other one lives her own life. She fills her hours with visits and activities. She's never alone, never silent. She speaks with my voice. I gave her my name, then forgot it.

It's all so far away. On the other side of a mirror that I lack the strength to approach. In an apartment that no longer has the same colors as my own. She moves about in conquered territory.

Around the edges of this mirror, a fine layer of frost has made its appearance. Little by little, it's growing toward the middle. Soon it will build a wall between us. And I will no longer even be her reflection.

The Coffin-Maker's Daughter

Angela Slatter

The door is a rich red wood heavily carved with improving scenes from the trials of Job. An angel's head cast in brass serves as the knocker, and when I let it go to rest back in its groove, the eyes fly open, indignant, and watch me with suspicion. Behind me is the tangle of garden—cataracts of flowering vines, lovers' nooks, secluded reading benches—that gives this house its affluent privacy.

The dead man's daughter opens the door.

She is pink and peach and creamy. I want to lick at her skin and see if she tastes the way she looks.

"Hepsibah Ballantyne! Slattern! Concentrate, this is business." My father slaps at me, much as he did in life. Nowadays his fists pass through me, causing nothing more than a sense of cold ebbing in my veins. I do not miss the bruises.

The girl doesn't recognise me although I worked in this house for nigh on a year—but that is because it was only me watching her and not she me. When my mother finally left us, it became apparent she would not provide Hector with any more children, let alone a son who might take over from him. He decided I should learn his craft, and the sign above the entrance to the workshop was changed—not to *Ballantyne & Daughter*, though. *Ballantyne & Other*.

"Speak, you idiot," Father hisses, as though it's important he whisper. No one has heard Hector Ballantyne these last eight months, not since what appeared to be an unseasonal cold carried him off.

The blue eyes, red-rimmed from crying, should look ugly, unpalatable in the lovely oval face, but grief becomes Lucette D'Aguillar. Everything becomes her, from the black mourning gown to the severe, scraped back coiffure that is the heritage of the bereaved, because she is that rare thing: born lucky.

"Yes?" she asks as if I have no right to interrupt the grieving house.

I slip the cap from my head, feel the mess it makes of my hair, and hold it in front of me like a shield. My nails are broken and my hands scarred and stained from the tints and varnish I use on the wood. I curl my fingers under the fabric of the cap to hide them as much as I can.

"I'm here about the coffin," I say. "It's Hepsibah. Hepsibah Ballantyne."

Her stare remains blank, but she steps aside and lets me in. By rights I should have gone to the back door, the servants' entrance. Hector would have—did so all his life—but I provide a valuable service. If they trust me to create a deathbed for their nearest and dearest, they can let me in the front door. Everyone knows there's been a death—it's impossible to hide in the big houses—I will not creep in as though my calling is shameful. Hector grumbled the first few times I presented myself in this manner—or rather shrieked, subsided to a grumble afterwards—but as I said to him, what were they going to do?

I'm the only coffin-maker in the city. They let me in.

I follow Lucette to a parlour washed with tasteful shades of grey and hung with white lace curtains so fine it seems they must be made by spinners with eight legs. She takes note of herself in the large mirror above the mantle. Her mother is seated on a chaise; she too regards her own reflection, making sure she still exists. Lucette joins her, and they look askance at me. Father makes sounds of disgust, and he is right to do so. He will stay quiet here; even though no one can hear him but me, he will not distract me. He will not interrupt *business*.

"Your mirror should be covered," I say as I sit uninvited in a fine armchair that hugs me like a gentle, sleepy bear. I arrange the skirts of my brown, mourning meetings dress and rest my hands on the arms of the chair, then remember how unsightly they are and clasp them in my lap. Black ribbons alone decorate the mirror's edges, a fashionable nod to custom, but not much protection. "All of your mirrors. To be safe. Until the body is removed."

They exchange a glance, affronted.

"The choice is yours, of course. I'm given to understand that some families are delighted to have a remnant of the deceased take up residence in their mirrors. They enjoy the sensation of being watched constantly. It makes them feel not so alone." I smile as if I am kind. "And the dead seem to like it, especially the unexpectedly dead. Without time to prepare themselves, they tend to cling to the ones they loved. Did you suspect your husband's heart was weak or was it a terrible surprise?"

Madame D'Aguillar hands her black shawl to Lucette, who covers the mirror with it, then rejoins her mother.

"You have kept the body wrapped?" I ask, and they nod. I nod in return to tell them they've done only just enough. That they are foolish, vain women who put their own reflections ahead of keeping a soul in a body. "Good. Now how may I be of assistance?"

This puts them on the back foot once again, makes them my supplicants. They must *ask* for what they want. Both look put out, and it gives me the meanest little thrill to see them thus. I smile again: *Let me help you.*

"A coffin is what we need. Why else would you be here?" snipes Madame. Lucette puts a hand on the woman's arm.

"We need your services, Hepsibah." My heart skips to hear my name on her lips. "We need your help."

Yes, they do. They need a coffin-maker. They need a deathbed to keep the deceased *in*, to make sure he doesn't haunt the lives they want to live from this point on. They need my *art*.

"I would recommend an ebony-wood coffin lined with the finest silk padding stuffed with lavender to help the soul to rest. Gold fittings will ensure strength of binding. And I would affix three golden locks on the casket to make sure. Three is safest, strongest." Then I name a price—down to the quarter-gold to make the sum seem considered—one that would cause honest women to baulk, to shout, to accuse me of the extortion I'm committing.

Madame D'Aguillar simply says, "Lucette, take Miss Ballantyne to the study and give her the down payment."

Oh, how they must want him kept under!

I rise and make a slight curtsy before I follow Lucette's gracefully swaying skirts to the back of the house.

I politely look away as she fumbles with the lockbox in the third drawer of the enormous oak desk her father recently occupied. When she hands me the small leather pouch of gold pieces, her fingers touch my palm and I think I see a spark in her eyes. I believe she feels it, too, and I colour to be so naked before her. I slide my eyes to the portrait of her dearly departed, but she grasps my hand and holds it tight.

Oh!

"Please, Hepsibah, please make his coffin well. Keep him *beneath*. Keep us—keep me—safe." She presses her lips to my palm; they are damp, slightly parted, and ever-so-soft! My breath escapes me, my lungs feel bereft. She trails her slim, pink cat's tongue along my lifeline down to my wrist where the pulse beats blue and hard and gives me away. There is a noise outside in the hall, the scuttling of a servant. Lucette smiles and steps back, dropping my hand reluctantly.

I remember to breathe, dip my head, made subservient by my desire. Hector has been silent all this time. I see him standing behind her, gnarled fingers trying desperately to caress her swan's neck but failing, passing through her. I feel a rage shake me but control myself. I nod again, forcing confidence into my motions, meeting her eyes, bold as brass, reading a promise there.

"I need to see the body, take my measurements, make preparations. I must do this alone."

"Stupid, little harlot." Hector has more than broken his silence again and again since we returned to the workshop. I have not answered him because I sense in his tone *envy*.

"How hard for you, Father, to have no more strength than a fart, all noise and wind."

If he were able, he would throw anything he could find around the space, chisels and planes and whetstones, with no thought for the damage to implements expensive to replace. The tools of our trade inherited from forefathers too many to number. The pieces of wood purchased at great expense and treated with eldritch care to keep the dead *below*.

I ignore his huffing and puffing and continue with Master D'Aguillar's casket. It is now the required shape and dimensions, held together with sturdy iron nails and the stinking adhesive made of human marrow and boiled bones I'm carefully applying to the place where one plank meets another to ensure there are no gaps through which something ephemeral might escape. On the farthest bench, far enough away to keep it safe from the stains and paints and tints, lies the pale lilac silk sack that I've stuffed with goose down and lavender flowers. This evening, I will quilt it with tiny, precise stitches, then fit it into the casket, this time using a sweet smelling glue to hold it in place and cover the stink of the marrow sealant.

We may inflate the charge for our services, certainly, but the Ballantynes never offer anything but their finest work.

I make the holes for the handles and hinges, boring them with a hand drill engraved with Hector's initials—not long before his death, the drill that had been passed down for nearly one hundred years broke, the turning handle shearing off in his hand and tearing open his palm. He had another made at great expense. It is almost new; I can pretend the initials are mine, that the shiny thing is mine alone.

"Did you get it?" asks Hector, tired of his sulk.

I nod, screwing the first hinge into place; the dull golden glow looks almost dirty in the dim light of the workshop. Soon I will light the lamps, so I can work through the night; that way I will be able to see Lucette again tomorrow without appearing too eager, without having to manufacture some excuse to cross her threshold once more.

"Show me."

I straighten with ill grace and stretch. In the pocket of my skirt next to a compact set of pliers is a small tin once used for Hector's cheap snuff. It rattles as I open it. Inside: a tooth, black and rotten at its centre and stinking more than it should. There is a sizable chunk of flesh still attached to the root and underneath the scent of decay is a telltale hint of foxglove. Master D'Aguillar shall enter the earth before his time, and I have something to add to our collection of contagions that will not be recognised or questioned.

"Ah, lovely!" says Hector. "Subtle. You could have learned something from them. Cold in a teacup—it wasn't very inventive, was it? I expected a better death, y'know."

"It wasn't a cold in a teacup, Father." I hold up the new hand drill. "It was the old drill. The handle was impregnated with apple seed poison, and I filed away the pinion to weaken everything. All it needed was a tiny open wound. Inventive enough for you, Hector?"

He looks put out, circles back to his new favourite torment. "That girl, she doesn't want you."

I breathe deeply. "Events say otherwise."

"Fool. Desperate, sad, little fool. How did I raise such an idiot child? Didn't I teach you to look through people? Anyone could see you're not good enough for the likes of Miss Lucette D'Aguillar." He laughs. "Will you dream of her, Hepsibah?"

I throw the hand drill at him; it passes through his lean outline and hits the wall with an almighty metallic sound.

"I kept you wrapped! I covered the mirrors! I made your casket myself and sealed it tight—how can you still be here?" I yell.

Hector smiles. "Perhaps I'm not. Perhaps you're so lonely, daughter, that you thought me back."

"If I were lonely, I can think of better company to conjure." But there may be something in what he says, though it makes me hurt.

"Ah, there's none like your own family, your dear old Da who loves your very skin."

"When I have her," I say quietly, "I won't need *you*."

Ghost or fervid imagining, it stops him—he sees his true end—and he has no reply but spite, "Why would anyone want you?"

"You did, Father, or has death dimmed your memory?"

Shame will silence even the dead, and he dissolves, leaving me alone for a while at least.

I breathe deeply to steady my hands and begin to measure for the placement of the locks.

"The casket is ready," I say, keeping the disappointment from my voice as best I can. Lucette is nowhere in evidence. An upstairs maid answered my knock and brought me to the parlour once more where the widow receives me reluctantly. The door angel did not even open its eyes.

Madame nods. "I shall send grooms with a dray this afternoon if that will suffice." But she does not frame it as a question.

"That is acceptable. My payment?"

"Will be made on the day of the funeral—which will be tomorrow. Will you call again?" She smiles with all the charm of the rictus of the dead. "I would not wish to waste your time."

I return her smile. "My customers have no choice but to wait upon my convenience." I rise. "I will see myself out. Until tomorrow."

Outside in the mid-morning sun I make my way down the stone front steps that are set a little too far apart. This morning I combed my hair, pinched colour into my cheeks, and stained my lips with a tinted wax that had once belonged to my mother; all for nought. I am about to set foot on the neatly swept path when a hand snakes out from the bushes to the right and I'm pulled under hanging branches behind a screen of sickly strong jasmine.

Lucette darts her tongue between my lips, giving me a taste of her but pulling back when I try to explore the honeyed cave of her mouth in turn. She giggles breathlessly, chest rising and falling as if this is nothing more than an adventure. She does not quake as I do, she is a silly little girl playing at lust. I know this; I know this, but it does not make me hesitate. It does not make my hope die.

I reach out and grasp her forearms, drawing her roughly in. She falls against me, and I show her what a kiss is. I show her what longing is. I let my yearning burn into her, hoping that she will be branded by the tip of my tongue, the tips of my fingers, the tips of my breasts. I will have her here under the parlour window where her mother sits and waits. I will tumble her and bury my mouth where it will make her moan and shake, here on the grass where we might be found at any moment. And I will make her mine if through no other means than shame; her shame will bind us, and make her *mine*.

"Whore," says Hector in my ear, making his first appearance since yesterday. Timed perfectly, it stops me cold, and in that moment when I hesitate, Lucette remembers herself and struggles. She steps away again, breathing hard, laughing through a fractured, uncertain smile.

"When he is *beneath*," she tells me. A promise, a vow, a hint, a tease. "When he is *beneath*," I repeat, mouthing it like a prayer, then make my unsteady way home.

I stood in the churchyard this morning, hidden away, and watched them bury Master D'Aguillar. Professional pride for the most part. Hector stood beside me, nodding with more approval than he'd ever shown in life, a truce mutually agreed for the moment.

"Hepsibah, you've done us proud. It's beautiful work."

And it was. The ebony-wood and the gold caught the sun and shone as if surrounded by a halo of light. No one could have complained about the effect the theatrics added to the interment. I noticed the admiring glances of the family's friends, neighbours, and acquaintances as the entrance to the D'Aguillar crypt was opened and four husky men of the household carried the casket down into the darkness.

And I watched Lucette. Watched her weep and support her mother; watched them both perform their grief like mummers. When the crowds thinned and there was just the two of them and their retainers to make their way to the black coach and four plumed horses, Lucette seemed to sense herself watched. Her eyes found me standing beside a white stone cross that tilted where the earth had sunk. She gave a strange little smile and inclined her head just-so.

"Beautiful girl," said Hector, his tone rueful.

"Yes," I answered, tensing for a new battle, but nothing came. We waited in the shade until the funeral party dispersed.

"When will you go to collect?" he asked.

"This afternoon when the wake is done."

He nodded and kept his thoughts to himself.

• • •

Lucette brings a black lacquered tray, balancing a teapot, two cups and saucers, a creamer, sugar boat, and silver cutlery. There are two delicate almond biscuits perched on a ridiculously small plate. The servants have been given the afternoon off. Her mother is upstairs resting.

"The house has been so full of people," she says, placing the tray on the parquetry table between us. I want to grab at her, bury my fingers in her hair, and kiss her breath away, but broken china might not be the ideal start. I hold my hands in my lap. I wonder if she notices that I filed back my nails, made them neat? That the stains on my skin are lighter than they were, after hours of scrubbing with lye soap?

She reaches into the pocket of her black dress and pulls forth a leather pouch, twin to the one she gave me barely two days ago. She holds it out and smiles. As soon as my hand touches it, she relinquishes the strings so our fingers do not meet.

"There! Our business is at an end." She turns the teapot five times clockwise with one hand and arranges the spoons on the saucers to her satisfaction.

"At an end?" I ask.

Her look is pitying, then she laughs. "I thought for a while there I might actually have to let you tumble me! Still and all, it would have been worth it, to have him safely away." She sighs. "You did such beautiful work, Hepsibah, I am grateful for that. Don't ever think I'm not."

I am not stupid enough to protest, to weep, to beg, to ask if she is joking, playing with my heart. But when she passes me a cup, my hand shakes so badly that the tea shudders over the rim. Some pools in the saucer, more splashes onto my hand and scalds me. I manage to put the mess down as she fusses, calling for a maid, then realises no one will come.

"I won't be a moment," she says and leaves to make her way to the kitchen and cleaning cloths.

I rub my shaking hands down my skirts and feel a hard lump. Buried deep in the right hand pocket is the tin. It makes a sad, promising sound as I tap on the lid before I open it. I tip the contents into her empty cup, then pour tea over it, letting the poisoned tooth steep until I hear her bustling back along the corridor. I fish it out with a spoon, careful not to touch it with my bare hands, and put it away. I add a little cream to her cup.

She wipes my red hot hand with a cool wet cloth, then wraps the limb kindly. Lucette sits opposite me, and I hand her the cup of tea and give a fond smile for her and for Hector, who has appeared at her shoulder.

"Thank you, Hepsibah."

"You are most welcome, Miss D'Aguillar."

I watch her lift the fine china to her pink, pink lips and drink deeply.

It will be enough, slow acting, but sufficient. This house will be bereft again.

When I am called upon to ply my trade a second time, I will bring a mirror with me. In the quiet room when we two are alone, I will unwrap Lucette and run my fingers across her skin and find all the secret places she denied me, and she will be mine and mine alone whether she wishes it or no.

I take my leave and wish her well.

"Repeat business," says Father gleefully as he falls into step beside me. "Not too much, not enough to draw attention to us, but enough to keep bread on the table."

In a day or two, I shall knock once more on the Widow D'Aguillar's front door.

I Make People Do Bad Things

Chesya Burke

Old Sam was dying. He had been dying for approximately twenty-seven years, by Queenie's account. Exactly the amount of time since hell had frozen over and God had relinquished the title on His throne, if the old man thought she was gonna let him slide by on another number without paying her proper due.

"Come on, Madam St. Clair, help out an old, dying man. I ain't got long now, you know."

"You old fool, if you think you're getting anything else from me on credit, you're all balled up."

The old man looked at her, seemed to want to respond, then thought better of it, and hung his head. *Shit,* the old bastard owed her more than a dollar for bets that he hadn't been able to cover. Now he thought she would let him slide by again. No way in hell.

The door to her operation on 144th Street, between Lenox and Seventh Avenue, swung open. Bumpy Johnson, her head enforcer, pushed past Sam and dumped a large package on the floor. It wiggled. Bumpy kicked it, nodded to her. She walked over, unwrapped it. A bloody white man lay on the floor staring up at her.

"Mr. Johns. Comme c'est gentil à vous de faire notre connaissance." Queenie would never admit it out loud, but she loved to use her knowledge of French to intimidate people. It made her feel smarter than these silly Americans, superior. In this case she had said nothing more than *How nice of you to make our acquaintance,* but the man cowered at her feet as if she had threatened to slice his throat and leave him sleeping with the fishes. That was certainly not outside of the realms of possibility.

Sam stared for only a moment, then rushed to the door and opened it.

"Old Sam?" The man stopped, looked at her. "That number was 216, right?"

He nodded.

"I'll play you."

The old man smiled, looked down at the man on the floor, and his smile faded. Then he quickly shuffled out the door.

Queenie turned slowly to the man at her feet. "Unfortunately for you, Mr. Johns, vous ne vous en tirez pas si facilement."

The numbers racket was Madam St. Clair's business. She ran everything in all of Harlem from Washington Heights to the Upper East Side, from the East River to the Hudson River—it all belonged to her. Ten thousand dollars from her own pocket had begun this business, and now it was her pocket into which all proceeds went. Less overhead, of course. Part of that overhead, and worth every thin dime that she paid them, was Bumpy and her gang of Forty Thieves. They were ruthless, and with her guidance, they ran the streets with strict precision that was almost surgical.

The numbers business was simple. One came into any of her many establishments—grocery markets, pool halls, restaurants, drugstores; if you owned a business in Harlem and you were willing to make a little extra dough, you took numbers—bet on any number between 0 and 999 and waited. Called the "poor man's stock market," it was bound to pay off. Where there was numbers running in Harlem, those uptown guys played the real thing and often lost big. Here, downtown, the odds paid out eight to one. Pretty good, and Madam St. Clair always paid. There was no business in undercutting your clientele. If you played long and often enough, you eventually won. So people played, and she got rich.

For most people in Harlem, the numbers game was a way of making a few extra dollars during the month. For others it meant surviving: eating or not eating. People put down a dime, a nickel, or even a penny and hoped for a payout. A dollar could have a return of six hundred dollars—no wonder this was big business. No wonder she'd made a fortune.

But the people in the neighborhood adored her; playing the odds had fed many people when it wouldn't have otherwise been possible. She also provided hundreds of jobs when there were none to be had in the outside world. So she had affectionately become known as Queenie—as in the Queen of Harlem—and she relished it. She fought every day to keep the title and her reign. It wasn't easy. She had to be ruthless, heartless, and deathly to survive.

Madam St. Clair was all of those things. Most importantly, she was a *she.*

And *they* didn't like that.

Behind her, Bumpy walked in, closed the door behind him, and placed his hand on her shoulder. He never showed her affection unless they were alone. He didn't speak for a long time, and she was content to let the silence stand. But she knew that he would say what was on his mind; she even knew, for the most part, what it was. He squeezed her shoulder blade, massaging her, his fingers feeling good against her flesh, comfortable.

Finally, he spoke, his voice soft. "Johns belongs to the Irish. We going to war with them too, now? I really hope you know what you're doing, Madam. I miss h—"

She swung to look at him. He would never have spoken to her like this if others were around; he would have known better. One didn't show dissension in the ranks publicly. But in private, things were different. He was close to her, too close. He knew her. However, she could not let this slide. He knew that, too. "You a chickenshit, Bumpy?"

It was harsh but equal to the disrespect he had shown her. He stayed calm. "You know I'm not. I do what you tell me, always have. I just want to make sure we know what we're doing, is all."

"Of course, I know what we're doing. We're starting war."

Bumpy squeezed her arm once more and walked out of the room, closing the door quietly behind him. Once he was outside, he would have to quiet the others who were afraid of Schultz's retaliation. He would do it, for if even one person brought their concerns to her, she would not wait until Schultz got his hands on them. There was a price to be in her favor, and cowards were not tolerated. Not that there were many of those in her gang of forty.

Queenie hung her head. How had things gotten to this point? How had she allowed them to get so out of control? *To hell with them for what they've done.* It was too late now. It couldn't be changed.

Shiv. The word hovered in Queenie's mind, unspoken. But the woman couldn't forget.

In the beginning, street traffic got heavy to her club around seven in the evening after work. People needed to play after long hours at tedious jobs, and she provided entertainment. Gambling. Dancing. Booze. Girls. The cutest little quiffs you could find and for decent prices. That was what she did, what she was good at.

You name it; people wanted it. You name it; she offered it.

Not quite as big and elaborate as her establishment now, Madam's had Place catered to a low-grade clientele. But there had been hardly any trouble. People had respected her just as they did now, although she hadn't wielded nearly as much power then. The only difference was that her power back then came from what lay between the legs of her girls. Period. She hadn't liked it, but she'd accepted it. Queenie had promised herself that as soon as she had the opportunity she would get the hell out of that business and find something more respectable. She had made that promise on her knees every single day.

Ellsworth "Bumpy" Johnson had come to her highly recommended. He wore pinned-striped, three-piece suits with $200 shoes. His ties always matched his mood. Red meant angry, ready to fight. Blue, one could possibly have a chance, as he was happy. Black was death. In the beginning he had done odd jobs for her, bounced people out on their asses when they ran out of money, collected on high interest and overdue loans, protected the girls. That was what he did, and he was damn good at it.

Shiv was the daughter of one of her girls. Shiv's mother, Lutie, had gotten herself sick, so the girl took over as much as she could to make up for her mother's shortcomings. The girl swept up, got the quiffs what they needed, but mainly stayed out of the way. It was important for Shiv to scatter when the marks were around because, although Queenie knew most of her clientele, unsavory people often wandered in, and a young girl had no business being around that sort. Even so, she was a quiet girl. She didn't talk to the marks. She didn't talk to the girls. She talked to her mother. She was an enigma to Queenie for several reasons, and that never really changed. Queenie had come to regret that.

Shiv. The child hadn't always been called that, but Queenie had long since forgotten the girl's original name. Shiv, once given, had been so true and exact that nothing else had mattered. It had cemented her place among the group. The old woman laughed to herself; a girl of nine years had become a member of the Forty Thieves, one of the deadliest gangs in Harlem. Queenie herself couldn't quite believe it.

Queenie was always under threat of violence before her gang grew to the size it was now. She paid the cops, she paid the greasers; she paid, it seemed, everyone. Even that wasn't enough, as several people still came in, getting their fill of girls and her money as they wished. The worst of these was Doc Marsh, a halfwit thug who thought he ran the East Side. Queenie reasoned the man wasn't really all that smart; but he had a baby grand of muscle behind him, and together the group was just dangerous enough to be trouble for her.

It was Doc Marsh who came to her joint that night. He was drunk when he arrived, and he got more and more sozzled as the night went on. Queenie had just advised the girls, as usual, to be nice and deal with him. For the most part, this strategy worked. Not that night.

It hadn't taken long for Doc Marsh to spot Lutie. The woman was a choice bit of calico, an absolute doll. Dark chocolate skin and large beautiful eyes that shone like Scotch whiskey; that was Lutie. But she was off limits. Sick and getting sicker by the day. Lutie had been working around the club, cleaning up after the girls, doing the dirty work that nobody wanted in an effort to keep Queenie from doing what they both knew was inevitable.

Doc Marsh grabbed the woman, pulled her onto his lap. He kissed her. Several of the girls alerted Queenie to what was happening. Before Queenie could intervene Lutie pushed away from Doc and said calmly, "Sorry, Mac. Bank's closed." This should have stopped him—most customers understood; most wouldn't've wanted any more hassle. Not Doc Marsh. When Lutie tried to pull away again, the man wrestled with her, threw her on the table, and bit her on the cheek, leaving a smear of blood trickling down her face. Lutie was a pro; she didn't scream, but she kneed him in the groin, and he staggered backward. When he regained his footing, he charged the woman again, punched her across the face, and kicked her when she bent over in pain. Suddenly, Bumpy got between Lutie and Doc Marsh.

By the time Doc's men arrived to help him, most of the trouble was over. Doc was, as usual, still lathered. He screamed about an invisible wound that he swore Lutie had inflicted. He screamed and made himself the fool. "That bitch. I swear, I will—" Lutie stood upright, stared at Doc as he spoke, didn't back down. But she didn't challenge him either. She knew better. This seemed to egg the man on. "I swear, I want her gone. Do you hear—" he pointed to Queenie "—gone."

Finally, when he grew tired, he decided to leave. Just as he turned, Shiv blocked his way, her tiny dark body swallowed by the large white man. He almost bumped into her, stopping himself in a drunken swivel. Just as he moved again to leave, the girl reached out and deliberately ran a finger across the chest of his double-breasted suit. Doc Marsh looked down at the girl, eyes wide as if he questioned his sight. Finally, he turned to look at Queenie, pointed again at Lutie, and then stormed out, his flunkies right at his heels.

Who did that bastard think he was? He didn't own her or her club. She paid him, and he believed he got the run of the place? But as she thought about it, the man was right. At this point it would be best for all of them if the woman and her daughter left. She had been dreading this moment, but she had known it would come. It was business. Lutie and that child were a liability. And Doc wouldn't let it go.

The following day she told Lutie. "I gotta do it. I know you ain't got nowhere to go, and I know you're sick. But you can't work, and Doc Marsh ain't gonna forget. And you got a daughter. He ain't civilized. Ain't no telling what he'll do."

The woman nodded, but she was crying. Then her daughter came in and held her mother. Queenie stared at the pair. Lutie looked terrible. Her eyes were sunken, bruised. Not because of the shiner that Doc had given her—it was her sickness; it was consuming her. She wouldn't last long. Queenie knew it. Lutie knew. Most of all, Shiv knew.

"I can pay our due," the girl said. She didn't stand more than four and a half feet off the ground, but in that moment, Queenie swore she looked like a grown woman. A nine-year-old girl had no business worrying about her dying mother. A nine-year-old had no business in this place.

"No."

"Please," the girl begged, and she began to resemble the child that she was. "We ain't got nowhere to go." She began to cry. "I can help. I know I can."

"Girl, ain't no way I'm putting a kid your age to work in no ho house. Take your momma and go, chile."

Shiv stomped over to her desk; she put her tiny dark hands on the stark white papers covering the old mahogany. "I make people do bad things."

"The hell you talking about, girl?"

Shiv straightened up, looked Queenie in the eyes, and for the first time, the girl resembled her future namesake. "Doc Marsh can't bother us no more. I fixed it. I ... wish he'd jump. The bridge ..." Before the girl could finish, Bobbie, one of Queenie's errand boys, busted in the door without knocking, his dark eyes bright with fear or something that resembled fear.

Just as she was about to admonish him, the boy spoke. "Did ya hear? Doc Marsh, he's dead."

Queenie stood. "What?"

"Jumped off the High Bridge, landed, splat—" he smacked his hands together "—right on the highway."

Queenie looked from the boy to the girl, to Lutie and back at the girl. Shiv nodded, smiled.

"I did," she said.

She did. At least Shiv thought she did. And that was enough for Queenie. What were the odds of the girl having talked about Doc Marsh jumping off a bridge and then it happening? Queenie hadn't started dealing in numbers yet, but she was sure that those odds were pretty damned high. She wasn't one to believe in coincidence. At the same time, it didn't escape her that the girl could have heard it somehow, somewhere. Although, by all accounts it had only just happened, and Bobbie swore he had just learned about the man's death in the street.

Doc Marsh's death took a big strain off Queenie. Afterward, there had been no one to control the dead man's business, and his crew simply drifted apart. Oh, they'd tried to take over, but it was soon clear that the Doc had been the brains of that operation. Bumpy got rid of the rest of them quickly.

Queenie, for her part, wasn't one to look a gift horse in the mouth. Shiv had made it possible for her and her mother to stay, but now she had to earn her keep, as Bumpy kept reminding her. "We need her. If the girl can do what you say she can, then what can it hurt?"

What can it hurt? Indeed.

About this time, Casper Holstein, an unknown ex-vet, had done his stint downtown on Wall Street as a bellhop. He'd come away with the idea of running numbers and had amassed a fortune. Others were slowly beginning to make money as well. Numbers wasn't big business yet, but it had potential, as Bumpy kept reminding her. Queenie wasn't so sure. As much as she hated the business, she was comfortable dealing in girls. They were easy. Queenie had scouters out on the streets approaching single girls getting off the bus alone, bringing them into the fold. It wasn't difficult to find starving, willing young women. They were waiting. She could probably live her whole life in that two-bit club bedding empty soldiers to broken girls. She thought of Lutie; but at what cost? What gain?

Numbers running was a man's game. Either it would pay off for her or she would lose everything. But something had to give.

Finally, when she was ready, she talked to Bumpy.

"Okay. What is this numbers business?" she asked him. He lay on her sofa, shirt unbuttoned to expose his chest. He had fallen asleep. "You play, right?"

He blinked his eyes. "It's good money. Pays well."

"Good investment?"

"Yeah."

"What we need?"

"Capital."

"I got ten thou," she said, as if praying to the lord. "Good enough?"

He sat up, looked at her. "It's a hard business. Not like the girls—not that simple. We'll need a small army to run it. I have the men. Thirty-nine of them, just waiting for the go-ahead. The problem is that Small Sammie runs things on this side now. He's placed stakes. He won't take lightly to competition. We'd have to take care of him first."

She paused for a moment. At that point she had never willingly ordered the murder of another human being. This would be opening a new door, one she hoped she could close at will. "Let's do it."

Bumpy shook his head. "It's not that easy. Small is not easy to get to. I've ... tried."

"What? You've tried?" Bumpy had never acted without her directive in the past.

He met her eyes when he spoke. "I knew that it was just a matter of time that you'd come to this decision. No disrespect, Madam."

She believed him. "Even so, don't do it again. I mean that, B."

He nodded, paused long enough to show proper respect, and then continued, "Small keeps well-guarded. Doesn't leave the house. I figure you don't want a massive shootout in the streets. But—" he paused, looked into her eyes "—we can use the girl."

She knew exactly which girl he was talking about, and she didn't like it. He must have read the reaction on her face because he quickly added, "Just listen. We send her in as a house girl, she cleans, does the floors, whatever. She can do that. Then she does her thing, gets out quick. If he buys the farm, good. If not, no harm, no foul."

"I ... I can't do that. It don't make no sense. She'll get killed."

"Not if she can do what you say she can. What *she* said she can."

"She's a child. They lie."

He nodded, looked at the floor, then back at her. "Madam, I have never told you how to run your business. And I don't mean to now. If you want me to declare outright war on this man before we have a stable business up and running, then I will. If you want me to stay here, work for you, I'll do that, too. You tell me what you want."

So that was that. Queenie had given Shiv Small Sammie's name and a picture and sent her out for what Queenie had hoped would be a repeat of history. *A name and a picture.* That was it; all she had given the girl. Later, she discovered that Bumpy had given her a knife, just in case. For all the good it would do.

She was nine years old. NINE YEARS OLD. What kinda evil bitch sends a small child off to kill a man?

Madam "Queenie" St. Clair, that's who.

The three weeks the girl was gone were the longest of Queenie's life. She spent the time in the bed of one of her favorite whores. This woman could make a man forget his miseries; she did the same for Queenie, among other things. Somehow it comforted Queenie to have her soft body close, made her feel like less of a monster. She avoided Bumpy and blamed him for the choices they both had made. It was easier that way.

The day Shiv came back, Small Sammie was run over by a train in upstate New York. No one knew how he had gotten there or what had happened. The moment the girl walked through the front door, Bumpy picked her up and swung her around. He hadn't said anything about the girl while she was gone, but Queenie guessed that he'd been worried about her. She hadn't noticed, but perhaps the man had avoided her as much as she had avoided him, both lost in guilt.

Shiv, for her part, beamed accomplishment. Word hadn't gotten around about Small's death yet, but nobody cared whether the girl had actually done what she said or not. She was back, alive. That was all that mattered. Once word did come in that Small Sammie was dead, no one could believe it. Three days later, news got around that he'd been hit by a train, pretty much at the exact moment that Shiv had walked back through Queenie's doors—and just as the girl told them she would.

Bumpy seemed most proud, as if he'd birthed a baby killer. "She's as deadly as a weapon. I don't know what you do, girl, but you're more deadly than a shiv, more accurate and less messy. My baby shiv."

And it stuck. Shiv: the child that turned killer. From that moment on, Shiv was Bumpy's shadow; where there was Bumpy, there was Shiv, and vice versa.

Two things had happened while Shiv was gone: she had done her job and killed Small Sammie, and Lutie had died from "complications."

Shiv, for her part, seemed to take the news remarkable well. She didn't cry. She wasn't angry. She had simply insisted on a funeral, and Momma St. Clair, as the girl began to call her, dished out five hundred bucks on her funeral. They buried the woman in a grave on the outskirts of town.

It rained during the funeral, and the girl bent down, her tiny hands touching the coffin, caressing the silver-colored box. Shiv spoke to her dead mother, but Queenie and the others couldn't hear what she said. When she was finished, Shiv turned to Queenie and opened her mouth to speak but didn't. After a moment, the girl spoke to everyone standing there watching her, pimp and whores alike. She said, simply, "I see you."

For the first time, Queenie viewed the girl as a double-edged sword. Sure, she could kill for her, but the girl could also kill her and anyone else she desired at any moment she desired it. What use was a weapon that volatile? *What happens when the child outgrows its parent?*

Queenie invested her money, started her business, and it thrived. When the numbers business got off the ground, she put dress suits on the girls and sent them out on the corners to hustle numbers for her. They made more money running numbers than they ever had on their backs, and it was decent, respectable work. Her Forty Thieves and two dozen ex-whores worked magic on the corners of Harlem.

By this time, Dutch Schultz, a white mobster who distributed liquor during the Prohibition, had gotten a whiff of the money that could be made running numbers in black Harlem. He wanted a piece of the action, and he would kill to get it. Dutch had the cops and politicians in his pocket, and he began to wage war against her. Queenie had wanted to avoid blood in the streets, and she had for a while. Eventually, though, it had been inevitable, and she supposed she had been naive in thinking that it was even possible to do so. Bumpy and her Forty Thieves had set the streets ablaze protecting her interest, killing Schultz's men in the process. In return, Schultz killed hers. Her only advantage was Shiv.

The girl was able to infiltrate Schultz's community where whole groups of his men would die off slowly, methodically. They would choke themselves to death on their own forks, step out in front of Mack trucks, shoot each other to death for no apparent cause; it didn't matter, they were dead and couldn't challenge Queenie. Shiv began to kill wiseguys with a frank regard that even scared Queenie. The girl withdrew. It was in her eyes. Always the indicator of a child's suffering, Shiv's were empty, devoid of anything, any emotion. Any empathy. Queenie enjoyed the money, the power. The people around her enjoyed the perks of that power. Her errand boys, her cooks, her cleaners, everyone won because of her success. Shiv gained more than most.

None of it seemed to make the child happy. And everyone at this point worked to make Shiv happy. They were afraid. When the girl wasn't around, people would whisper about her. When she was around, they benefited. Either way, Shiv didn't care, she wasn't happy. Queenie reasoned that happiness was all but impossible with her mother gone. Shiv had willingly worked for her when she thought she was protecting her mother. Now that just couldn't happen.

Queenie had said that the girl was always an enigma to her, and this was true. But the woman believed that she knew Shiv because she knew herself; Queenie related to her as she related to the women like her. The women in this hopeless, useless place, this life. Shiv was every child, every woman who was never given another option.

Queenie hated herself a little more each day for what she'd done. Still, Shiv killed for her.

Queenie hadn't been there the day it happened. Story went that one of the Thieves, Bumpy's right hand man, Hurts, had made the mistake. Hurts was a big man. He dressed like he bought all his clothes out of a secondhand shop, but he was brutal. He carried a baseball bat and would beat the hell out of men who annoyed him in the streets. A short fuse did not mix well with her new establishment. Not with Shiv.

The man had disrespected the girl's position in the Thieves. Shiv didn't care about a lot of things, but she had earned her way into the gang; and she would not accept anything less. Bumpy had named her, and she deserved it. If Queenie had been there, she would have had Hurts' tongue torn out, but that wasn't his luck. Shiv walked up to the big man, who sat laughing at the girl, and slid her fingers across his face as a baby would. The next day, Hurts sliced off his dick with a rusted shiv. He bled to death in the alley behind Queenie's new place.

The following week, two more of the Forty Thieves died after having run-ins with Shiv. Everything Queenie had built was falling apart. On the business side, Schultz had gotten to the police, and despite having paid them off, the cops began harassing her, placed nearly half of her men in jail. Including Bumpy.

The following week, Madam St. Clair walked into the newspaper office and placed an ad in the paper detailing the corruption of the police force, all of the monies that she had paid them, and whom she had paid. Her business might fall apart, but she would take as many people with her as she could.

The day Bumpy was let out of jail, Queenie received a letter from Schultz himself. She met him in an alley, off the record, as he had said.

"I know about the girl." Dutch Schultz always looked like he was waiting to take a mug shot. His eyes were large and sat too far apart on his head. He was a Jew—Jews and blacks didn't mix.

"The hell you say?"

"The nigger girl who you keep as some kinda lucky charm or something."

Queenie just stared at him.

"You know what I'm talking about, bitch."

Queenie made a circular motion with her hands, and she, Bumpy, and what was left of her men moved to walk away.

"Wait," Schultz called after her. He ran to her, his men staring, surprised. "I'm sorry. Please hear me out. I ... I want a truce."

She stopped, looked at him.

"You keep Harlem. I get a cut." She started to protest, but he continued, "You can expand farther out, have more territory. More money than you've ever dreamed. I'll get the cops off your back, the people uptown, too."

"What do you want?"

"The girl."

"No."

"I know you have lost men. Several. You could lose more. You could ... die, too. Does she mean that much to you? Think about it."

The woman looked at Bumpy, who turned his head. She couldn't tell if it was in disgust or reluctant acceptance. "I want the body."

The white men shot Shiv down in the streets two weeks later. Queenie buried her in a plot next to her mother. It didn't rain. No one but Queenie and Bumpy mourned for the child. The women who had helped to raise the girl were too fearful by this point, and they had all simply wanted it over. Queenie had given it to them. She believed that they all felt guilty. She did.

A year later, Dutch Schultz was gunned down at the Palace Chop House restaurant in Newark, New Jersey. He was in the hospital, dying of his wounds.

Queenie sat down, placed her head in her hands. After a long while, she opened her drawer, took out pen and paper. She wrote simply, Qui sème le vent, récolte la tempête. "As ye sow, so shall ye reap." She addressed the envelope to the hospital in care of Dutch Schultz and called for Bumpy.

"Send this by telegram." She handed the letter to the man, who stared at it suspiciously. Finally, she said, "After you mail that, let Johns go with a message: I'm out." Bumpy smiled briefly but long enough for her to recognize his out-of-form expression. Then he nodded and walked out of the room.

Queenie stared at her place; thought of the much smaller one from which she had come. Thought about the little girl, Shiv.

I make people do bad things, the girl had once said.

Moi aussi, Queenie thought. *So do I.*

Blood Drive

Jeffrey Ford

For Christmas our junior year of high school, all of our parents got us guns. That way you had a half a year to learn to shoot and get down all the safety garbage before you started senior year. Depending on how well off your parents were, that pretty much dictated the amount of firepower you had. Darcy Krantz's family lived in a trailer, and so she had a pea-shooter, .22 Double Eagle Derringer, and Baron Hanes's father, who was in the security business and richer than god, got him a .44 magnum that was so heavy it made his nutty kid lean to the side when he wore the gun belt. I packed a pearl handled .38 revolver, Smith and Wesson, which had originally been my grandfather's. It was old as dirt, but all polished up the way my father kept it, it was still a fine looking gun. It was really my father's gun, and my mother told him not to give it to me, but he said, "Look, when she goes to high school, she's gotta carry, everybody does in their senior year."

"Insane," said my mom.

"Come on," I said. "Please ..."

She drew close to me, right in my face, and said, "If your father gives you that gun, he's got no protection making his deliveries." He drove a truck and delivered bakery goods to different diners and convenience stores in the area.

"Take it easy," said my dad, "all the crooks are asleep when I go out for my runs." He motioned for me to come over to where he sat. He put the gun in my hand. I gripped the handle and felt the weight of it. "Give me your best pose," he said.

I turned profile, hung my head back, my long chestnut hair reaching halfway to the floor, pulled up the sleeve of my T-shirt, made a muscle with my right arm, and pointed the gun at the ceiling with my left hand. He laughed till he couldn't catch his breath. And my mom said, "Disgraceful," but she also laughed.

I went to the firing range with my dad a lot the summer before senior year. He was a calm teacher and never spoke much or got too mad. Afterward, he'd take me to this place and buy us ice cream. A lot of times it was Friday night, and I just wanted to get home so I could go hang out with my friends. One night I let him know we could skip the ice cream, and he seemed taken aback for a second, like I'd hurt his feelings. "I'm sorry," he said and tried to smile.

I felt kind of bad and figured I could hug him or kiss him or ask him to tell me something. "Tell me about a time when you shot the gun not on the practice range," I said as we drove along.

He laughed. "Not too many times," he said. "The most interesting was from when I was a little older than you. It was night, we were in the basement of an abandoned factory over in the industrial quarter. I was with some buds, and we were partying, smoking up and drinking straight, cheap Vodka. Anyway, we were wasted. This guy I really didn't like who hung out with us, Raymo was his name, he challenged me to a round of Russian roulette. Don't tell your mother this," he said.

"You know I won't," I said.

"Anyway, I left one bullet in the chamber, removed the others, and spun the cylinder. He went first—nothing. I went, he went, etc., click, click, click. The gun came to me, and I was certain by then that the bullet was in my chamber. So you know what I did?"

"You shot it into the ceiling?"

"No. I turned the gun on Raymo and shot him in the face. After that we all ran. We ran, and we never got caught. At the time there was a gang going around at night shooting people and taking their wallets, and the cops put it off to them. None of my buds were going to snitch. Believe me, Raymo was no great loss to the world. The point of which is to say, it's a horrible thing to shoot someone. I see Raymo's expression right before the bullet drilled through it just about every night in my dreams. In other words, you better know what you're doing when you pull that trigger. Try to be responsible."

I was sorry I asked.

To tell you the truth, taking the gun to school at first was a big nuisance. The thing was heavy, and you always had to keep an eye on it. The first couple of days were all right, cause everyone was showing off their pieces at lunch time. A lot of people complimented me on my gun. They liked the pearl handle and the shape of it. Of course, the kids with the new, high-tech nine millimeter jobs got the most attention, but if your piece was unique enough, it got you at least some cred. Jody Motes, pretty much an idiot with buck teeth and a fat ass, brought in a German Luger with a red swastika inlaid on the handle and because of it, started dating this really hot guy in our English class. Kids wore them on their hips, others, mostly guys, did the shoulder holster. A couple of the senior girls with big breasts went with this over the shoulder bandolier style, so their guns sat atop their left breast. Sweaty Mr. Gosh in second period Math said that look was "very fashionable." I carried mine in my Sponge Bob lunch box. I hated wearing it, the holster always hiked my skirt up in the back somehow.

Everybody in the graduating class carried heat except for Scott Wisner, the King of Vermont, as everybody called him. I forget why cause Vermont was totally far away. His parents had given him a stun gun instead of the real thing. Cody St. John, the captain of the football team, said the stun gun was fag, and after that Wisner turned into a weird loner, who walked around carrying a big jar with a floating mist inside. He asked all the better-looking girls if he could have their souls. I know he asked me. Creep. I heard he'd stun anyone who wanted it for ten dollars a pop. Whatever.

The teachers in the classes for seniors all had tactical 12-gauge short barrel shotguns; no shoulder stock, just a club grip with an image of the school's mascot (a cartoon, rampaging Indian) stamped on it. Most of them were loaded with buckshot, but Mrs. Cloder in Human Geography, who used her weapon as a pointer when at the board, was rumored to rock the breaching rounds, those big slugs cops use to blow doors off their hinges. Other teachers left the shotguns on their desks or laying across the eraser gutter at the bottom of the board. Mr. Warren, the Vice Principal, wore his in a holster across his back and for an old fart, was super quick in drawing it over his shoulder with one hand.

At lunch, across the soccer field and back by the woods where only the seniors were allowed to go, we sat out every nice day in the fall, smoking cigarettes and having gun spinning competitions. You weren't allowed to shoot back there, so we left the safeties on. Bryce, a boy I knew since kindergarten, was good at it. He could flip his gun in the air backwards and have it land in the holster at his hip. McKenzie Batkin wasn't paying attention and turned the safety off instead of on before she started spinning her antique Colt. The sound of the shot was so sudden we all jumped and then silence followed by the smell of gun smoke. The bullet went through her boot and took off the tip of her middle toe. Almost a whole minute passed before she screamed. The King of Vermont and Cody St. John both rushed to help her at the same time. They worked together to staunch the bleeding. I remember noticing the football laying on the ground next to the jar of souls, and I thought it would make a cool photo for the yearbook. She never told her parents, hiding the boots at the back of her closet. To this day she's got half a middle toe on her right foot, but that's the least of her problems.

After school that day, I walked home with my new friend, Constance, who only came to Bascombe High in senior year. We crossed the soccer field, passed the fallen leaves stained red with McKenzie's blood, and entered the woods. The wind blew and shook the empty branches of the trees. Constance suddenly stopped walking, crouched, drew her Beretta Storm, and fired. By the time I could turn my head, the squirrel was falling back, headless, off a tree about thirty yards away.

She had a cute hair cut, short but with a lock that almost covered her right eye. Jeans and a green flannel shirt, a calm, pretty face. When we were doing current events in fifth period Social Studies, she'd argued with Mr. Hallibet about the cancellation of child labor laws. Me, I could never follow politics. It was too boring. But Constance seemed to really understand, and although on the TV news we all watched, they were convinced it was a good idea for kids twelve and older to now be eligible to be sent to work by their parents for extra income, she said it was wrong. Hallibet laughed at her, and said, "This is Senator Meets we're talking about. He's a man of the people. The guy who gave you your guns." Constance had more to say, but the teacher lifted his shotgun and turned to the board. The thing I couldn't get over is that she actually knew this shit better than Hallibet. The thought of it, for some reason, made me blush.

By the time the first snow came in late November, the guns became mostly just part of our wardrobes, and kids turned their attention back to their cell phones and iPods. The one shot fired in the school before Christmas vacation was when Mrs. Cloder dropped her gun in the bathroom stall and blew off the side of the toilet bowl. Water flooded out into the hallway. Other than that, the only time you noticed that people were packing was when they'd use their sidearm for comedy purposes. Like Bryce, during English, when the teacher was reading *Pilgrim's Progress* to us, took out his gun and stuck the end in his mouth as if he was so bored he was going to blow his own brains out. At least once a week, outside the cafeteria, on the days it was too cold to leave the school, there were quick draw contests. Two kids would face off, there'd be a panel of judges, and Vice Principal Warren would set his cell phone to beep once. When they heard the beep the pair drew and whoever was faster won a coupon for a free 32-ounce soda at Babb's, the local convenience store.

One thing I did notice in that first half of the year. Usually when a person drew their gun, even as a joke, they had a saying they always spoke. Each person had their own signature saying. When it came to these lines, it seemed that the ban on cursing could be ignored without any problem. Even the teachers got into it. Mr. Gosh was partial to "Eat hot lead, you little motherfuckers." The school nurse, Ms. James, used "See you in Hell, asshole." Vice Principal Warren, who always kept his language in check, would draw, and while the gun was coming level with your head, say, "You're already dead." As for the kids, they all used lines they'd seen in recent movies. Cody St. John used "Suck on this, bitches." McKenzie, who by Christmas was known as Half-toe Batkin, concocted the line "Put up your feet." I tried to think of something to say, but it all seemed too corny, and it took me too long to get the gun out of my lunch box to really outdraw anyone else.

Senior year rolled fast, and by winter break, I was wondering what I'd do after I graduated. Constance told me she was going to college to learn philosophy. "Do they still teach that stuff?" I asked. She smiled, "Not so much anymore." We were sitting in my living room, my parents were away at my aunt's. The TV was on, the lights were out, and we were holding hands. We liked to just sit quietly with each other and talk. "So I guess you'll be moving away after the summer," I said. She nodded. "I thought I'd try to get a job at Wal-Mart," I said. "I heard they have benefits now."

"That's all you're gonna do with your life?" asked Constance.

"For now," I said.

"Well, then when I go away, you should come with me." She put her arm behind my head and drew me gently to her. We just sat, holding each other for a long time while the snow came down outside.

A few days after Christmas, I sat with my parents watching the evening news after dinner. Senator Meets was on talking about what he hoped to accomplish in the coming year. He was telling about how happy he was to work for minimum wage when he was eleven.

"This guy's got it down," said my father.

I shouldn't have opened my mouth, but I said, "Constance says he's a loser."

"Loser?" my father said. "Are you kidding? Who's this Constance? I don't want you hanging out with any socialists. Don't tell me she's one of those kids who refuses to carry a gun. Meets passed the gun laws, mandatory church on Sunday for all citizens, killed abortion, and got us to stand up to the Mexicans ... He's definitely gonna be the next president."

"She's probably the best shot in the class," I said, realizing I'd already said too much.

My father was suspicious, and he stirred in his easy chair, leaning forward.

"I met her," said my mother. "She's a nice girl."

I gave things a few seconds to settle down and then announced I was going to take the dog for a walk. As I passed my mother unnoticed by my dad, she grabbed my hand and gave it a quick squeeze.

Back at school in January, there was a lot to do. I went to the senior class meetings but didn't say anything. They decided for our "Act of Humanity" (required of every senior class), we would have a blood drive. For the senior trip we decided to keep it cheap as pretty much everyone's parents were broke. A day trip to Bash Lake. "Sounds stale," said Bryce, "but if we bring enough alcohol and weed, it'll be okay." Mrs. Cloder, our faculty advisor, aimed at him, said, "Arrivederci, Baby," and gave him two Saturday detentions. The other event that overshadowed all the others, though, was the upcoming prom. My mother helped me make my dress. She was awesome on the sewing machine. It was turquoise satin, short sleeve, mid-length. I told my parents I had no date but was just going solo. Constance and I had made plans. We knew from all the weeks of mandatory Sunday mass, the pastor actually spitting he was so worked up over what he called "unnatural love," that we couldn't go as a couple. She cared more than I did. I just tried to forget about it.

When the good weather of spring hit, people got giddy and tense. There were accidents. In homeroom one bright morning, Darcy dropped her bag on her desk, and the derringer inside went off and took out Ralph Babb's right eye. He lived; but when he came back to school, his head was kind of caved in, and he had a bad fake eye that looked like a kid drew it. It only stared straight ahead. Another was when Mr. Hallibet got angry because everybody'd gotten into the habit of challenging his current events lectures after seeing Constance in action. He yelled for us all to shut up and accidentally squeezed off a round. Luckily for us, the gun was pointed at the ceiling. Mr. Gosh, though, who was sitting in the room a floor above, directly over Hallibet, had to have buckshot taken out of his ass. When he returned to school from a week off, he sweated more than ever.

Mixed in with the usual spring fever, there was all kinds of drama over who was going to the prom with who. Fist fights, girl fights, plenty of drawn guns but not for comedy. I noticed that the King of

Vermont was getting wackier the more people refused to notice him. When I left my sixth period class to use the bathroom, I saw him out on the soccer field from the upstairs hallway window. He turned the stun gun on himself and shot the two darts with wires into his own chest. It knocked him down fast, and he was twitching on the ground. I went and took a piss. When I passed the window again, he was gone. He'd started bringing alcohol to school, and at lunch, where again we were back by the woods hanging out, he'd drink a Red Bull and a half pint of vodka.

Right around that time, I met Constance at the town library one night. I had nothing to do, but she had to write a paper. When I arrived, she'd put the paper away and was reading. I asked her what the book was. She told me, "Plato."

"Good story?" I asked.

She explained it wasn't a novel but a book about ideas. "You see," she said, "there's a cave, and this guy gets chained up inside so that he can't turn around or move but only stare at the back wall. There's a fire in the cave behind him, and it casts his shadow on the wall he faces. That play of light and shadow is the sum total of his reality."

I nodded and listened as long as I could. Constance was so wrapped up in explaining, she looked beautiful, but I didn't want to listen anymore. I checked over my shoulder to see if anyone was around. When I saw we were alone, I quickly leaned forward and kissed her on the lips. She smiled and said, "Let's get out of here."

On a warm day in mid-May, we had the blood drive. I got there early and gave blood. The nurses, who were really nice, told me to sit for a while, and they gave me orange juice and cookies. I thought about becoming a nurse for maybe like five whole minutes. Other kids showed up and gave blood, and I stuck around to help sign them up. Cody came and watched but wouldn't give. "Fuck the dying," I heard him say. "Nobody gets my blood but me." After that a few other boys decided not to give either. Whatever. Then at lunch, the King of Vermont was drinking his Red Bulls and vodka, and I think because he'd given blood, he was really blasted. He went around threatening to stun people in their private parts.

After lunch, in Mrs. Cloder's class, where we sat at long tables in a rectangle that formed in front of her desk, Wisner took the seat straight across from her. I was two seats down from him toward the windows. Class started, and the first thing Mrs. Cloder said, before she even got out of her seat, was to the King. "Get that foolish jar off the table." We all looked over. Wisner stared, the mist swirled inside the glass. He pushed his seat back and stood up, cradling the jar in one arm and drawing his stun gun. "Sit down, Scotty," she said, and leveled her riot gun at him. I could see her finger tightening on the trigger. A few seconds passed, and then one by one, all the kids drew their weapons; but nobody was sure whether to aim at Mrs. Cloder or the King, so about half did one and half the other. I never even opened my lunch box, afraid to make a sudden move.

"Put down your gun and back slowly away from the table," said Mrs. Cloder.

"When you meet the Devil, give him my regards," said Wisner, but as he pulled the trigger, Mrs. Cloder fired. The breaching slug blew a hole in the King of Vermont's chest, slamming him against the back wall in a cloud of blood. The jar shattered, and glass flew. McKenzie, who had been sitting next to Wisner, screamed as the shards dug into her face. I don't know if she shot or if the gun just went off, but her bullet hit Mrs. Cloder in the shoulder and spun her out of her chair onto the ground. She groaned and rolled back and forth. Meanwhile, Wisner's stun gun darts had gone wild, struck Chucky Durr in the forehead, one over each eye, and in his electrified shaking, his gun went off and put a round right into Melanie Storte's Adam's apple. Blood poured out as she dropped her own gun and brought her hands to her gurgling neck. Melanie was Cody St. John's "current ho," as he called her, and he didn't think twice but fanned the hammer of his pistol, putting three shots into Chucky, who went over on the floor like a bag of potatoes. Chucky's cousin, Meleeba, shot Cody in the side of the head, and he went down, screaming, as smoke poured from the hole above his left ear. One of Cody's crew shot Meleeba, and then I couldn't keep track anymore. Bullets whizzed by my head, blood was spurting everywhere. Kids were going down like pins at the bowling alley. Mrs. Cloder clawed her way back into her seat, lifted the gun, and aimed it. Whoever was left fired on her, and then she fired another shotgun blast like an explosion. When the ringing in my ears went away, the room was perfectly quiet but for the drip of blood, and the ticking of the wall clock. Smoke hung in the air, and I thought of the King of Vermont's escaped souls. During the entire thing, I'd not moved a single finger.

The cops were there before I could get myself out of the chair. They wrapped a blanket around me and led me down to the principal's office. I was in daze for a while but could feel them their moving around me and could hear them talking. Then my mother was there, and the cop was handing me a cup of orange juice. They asked if they could talk to me, and my mother left it up to me. I told them everything, exactly how it went down. I started with the blood drive.

They tested me for gunpowder to see if there was any on my hands. I told them my gun was back in the classroom in the lunchbox under the table, and it hadn't been fired since the summer, the last time I went to the range with my dad. It was all over the news. I was all over the news. A full one-third of Bascombe High's senior class was killed in the shootout.

Senator Meets showed up at the school three days later and got his picture taken handing me an award. I never really knew what it was for. Constance said of it, "They give you a fucking award if you live through it," and laughed. In Meets's speech that day to the assembled community, he blamed the blood drive for the incident. He proclaimed Mrs. Cloder a hero and ended reminding everyone, "If these kids were working, they'd have no time for this."

The class trip was called off out of respect for the dead. Two weeks later, I went to the prom. It was to be held in the high school gymnasium. My dad drove me. When we pulled into the parking lot, it was empty.

"You must be early," he said, and handed me the corsage I'd asked him to get—a white orchid.

"Thanks," I said and gave him a kiss on the cheek. As I opened the door to get out, he put his hand on my elbow. I turned, and he was holding the gun.

"You'll need this," he said.

I shook my head, and told him, "It's okay." He was momentarily taken aback. Then he tried to smile. I shut the door, and he drove away.

Constance was already there. In fact, she was the only one there. The gym was done up with glittery stars on the ceiling, a painted moon and clouds. There were streamers. Our voices echoed as we exchanged corsages, which had been our plan. The white orchid looked good on her black, plunging neckline. She'd gotten me a corsage made of red roses, and they really stood out against the turquoise. In her purse, instead of the Beretta, she had a half pint of Captain Morgan. We sat on one of the bleachers and passed the bottle, talking about the incidents of the past two weeks.

"I guess no one's coming," she said. No sooner were the words out of her mouth than the outside door creaked open and in walked Bryce carrying a case in one hand and dressed in a jacket and tie. We got up and went to see him. Constance passed him the Captain Morgan. He took a swig.

"I was afraid of this," he said.

"No one's coming?" I said.

"I guess some of the parents were scared there'd be another shootout. Probably the teachers, too. Mrs. Cloder's family insisted on an open casket. A third of them are dead, let's not forget, and the rest, after hearing Meets talk, are working the late shift at Wal-Mart for minimum wage."

"Jeez," said Constance.

"Just us," said Bryce. He went up on the stage, set his case down, and got behind the podium at the back. "Watch this," he said, and a second later the lights went out. We all laughed. A dozen blue searchlights appeared, their beams moving randomly around the gym, washing over us and then rushing away to some dark corner. A small white spotlight came on above the mic that stood at the front of the stage. Bryce stepped up into the glow. He opened the case at his feet and took out a saxophone.

"I was looking forward to playing tonight," he said. We walked up to the edge of the stage, and I handed him the bottle. He took a swig, the sax now on a chain around his neck. Putting the bottle down at his feet, he said, "Would you ladies care to dance?"

"Play us something," we told him.

He thought for a second and said, "'Strangers in the Night.'"

He played, we danced, and the blue lights in the dark were the sum total of our reality.

Six Things We Found During the Autopsy

Kuzhali Manickavel

1. PLAYBOY

A *Playboy* was hidden behind her jaw, rolled and bent like she had stashed it there in a hurry. Black and white alarm clocks were pasted over the women's breasts and the words *!wUt aLarming bOobeez!* were scrawled across the stomach. It was hard to tell if she had done this herself or if someone else had done it for her.

We could not find any incisions, so we decided she must have rammed the *Playboy* into her ear and hoped for the best. We thought this made her stoic, medically marvelous, and gay. We wondered if she had a secret crush on one of us, and while we unanimously agreed that this was possible, we knew in our hearts that it was not.

2. BLACK ANTS

The ants were an ongoing observation, like watching fish. They floated up gently through her skin, broke the surface, and lay there like the journey had made them tired and they just needed to lie down for a while. We discovered that there were no ants near her elbows but could not come to a consensus as to how this was significant. We thought we saw something that resembled an abnormally thick spiderweb under her pancreas and decided not to pursue that line of inquiry because it obviously had nothing to do with the ants.

We wondered if she had let the ants in or if they had smashed their way through her, vandalizing her body with starred and spangled railroads, towers, and pornography. Now that she was dead, the ants probably had no reason to stay. We thought this was heartbreaking but also the best option for everyone involved.

3. ANGELS

The angels were clustered and nested behind her heart and lungs. They had to be pulled out with tweezers, which was not easy because they kept hanging onto her esophagus with their angry fingers and teeth. They had no nipples, belly buttons, or genitalia, which made them like dolls, but we did not feel like combing their hair. Their feet looked like hands, and they dug their heels into our faces as a sign of protest. They caterwauled. They sounded like prehistoric birds that were heartbroken because they were going to die in the evening.

We thought she must have been a closeted Catholic. We thought she had probably been more into the angels than she was into Jesus, which is why she had allowed them to stay in such a communally sensitive area. We thought it was racist to assume that only Catholics had an affinity for angels.

4. ST. SEBASTIAN

St. Sebastian was tied to her spinal column, eyes looking heavenward, an arrow running into his chin and out of his forehead. His body was peppered with arrows, but it was the one through his forehead that made us untie him. We thought that untying him would make him feel better. We didn't touch the arrow because we thought it would make his head fall off.

We thought the angels and St. Sebastian were probably good friends. We imagined them hanging out in the late afternoon, folding discarded angel wings into boats and sailing them on her bloodstream, hoping they would return filled with things that were sweet and useful.

5. TYPHOID

It was only later, when we were delirious, sour-mouthed, and tired, that we realized we all had typhoid. While we waited for it to go away, we cleverly and calculatingly deduced where we got it from.

The typhoid was a shiny black slab that was stuck to the back of her liver. It came apart in layers but could not be removed completely.

We thought she was a typhoid carrier. We thought she had probably infected all of us and the typhoid was sticking to our livers, too. We decided that we were angry at the world and this was what people with cancer felt like. We thought it must be a neat thing to be a typhoid carrier.

6. PLAYGIRL

The *Playgirl* was spread across her rib cage like a placemat. Hairless, half-aroused men stared sexingly into our faces, and we looked at their half-arousal and sighed. We pasted the heads of Siberian huskies onto their faces and decided this made them more regal and less attainable. We also decided that if we ever created a pantheon of Gods, there would be a set of twins who would be bare-chested and Siberian husky-headed.

We knew she was the only one who could have made it with a hairless, half-aroused *Playgirl* man with a Siberian husky head. We imagined it happening in a series of well-lit photographs where she and the *Playgirl* man were naked and open-mouthed but not sweating. We contrasted the open *Playgirl* with the rolled and bent *Playboy* and decided that she had been conflicted about her sexuality. We thought we could have been the awesome friends who held her hand while we dragged her out of the closet. We thought we could have convinced her it was okay to like girls even if she didn't like any of us.

Please Feed Motion

Irenosen Okojie

On the third Thursday of each month, Nesrine Malik, prisoner 2212, pulled skin from the thing living in her throat before writing to Eros. She performed this ritual without fail and had done for four years since landing at Woodowns prison on drug charges as an accessory with intent to supply. Nesrine had arrived with these items: an afro comb, a brown leather wallet, two first class stamps, items which in time repeatedly trapped themselves in the dysfunctional sounds of the prison. It was love that threw Nesrine in jail, blind, dangerous, destructive love for a man who'd groomed her to be his soldier on the streets. Who'd told her there was wonder in her infectious, hypnotic smile and liked to rub his thumb on her palm anti-clockwise. He had only ever visited once to inform her he wouldn't be coming again. This is how it is he'd said, watching her coldly, dispassionately. The gold chaps on his wrist knocking against the wooden desk, his fade neat, his boyishly attractive face distant, the proud flare of his nostrils rousing the memory of pressing her lips there. Nesrine had slumped in her uncomfortable chair in shock, shoving her hand into her braids, heart-shaped face hollow, crumpling, looking through the glass partition, wanting to press her mouth against the smattering of holes there to get air. A different kind of air he'd brought with him. She was vaguely aware of his chair scraping back, of the ceiling fan spinning, slicing her tongue loaded with protests, of the other prisoners' heads bent towards their visitors, deep in conversation. And the sound of the guards' keys jangling, dipping, and falling into the darkness of her throat. Then everything changed. Nesrine wasn't sure whether it was the sticky heat of the room, the worn edges of the cheap brown linoleum floor that had begun to come unstuck or the sound of the glass door sliding open slowly, mechanically, or her silence as that man left her to rot. Something changed in the air. The prisoners' faces began to stretch, distorting into caricatures in the afternoon light, leaving their bodies to float in the dusty windows, crying at personal items they recognized spinning in the distance. Visitors' hands rummaged through their pockets, searching for things that had fallen through an anti-clockwise gap. Guards scrambled on the floor, sniffer dog collars around their necks, dodging batons flying at their faces.

Trembling, Nesrine stuck three fingers down her throat, convinced something would emerge from the moist darkness. While she grabbed at the thing there, Eros appeared in the empty visitor's chair opposite her. He shook with anger. Tears ran down his cheeks. Stunned, Nesrine removed her fingers from her throat, leaving the thing in the dark screaming. Eros had only half a heart that she saw was beating, shrinking, swelling in his chest. He set his bow and arrow down on the floor. He pulled Nesrine through the glass partition so she could breathe. The cuts around her mouth did not matter nor did her deadened tongue. He had come.

This year, Nesrine sent Eros postcards of skeletons floating in the abyss. Before that it had been lost cities, and prior to that it was women inventors. Without fail every month she made a different prisoner press the damp tip of their tongue to the corner of the postcard. They always grumbled but nevertheless indulged her.

This is stupid, doesn't cost me anything, so I'll do it.

You are bonkers. Eros is something somebody created. He's not real.

You're not asking for my lady parts juices, which would be more worrying yet frankly, somewhat arousing.

Nesrine knew he was real. She'd touched him, been rescued by him. She'd seen her pain and destruction reflected in his face. He'd caught her when she thought her organs had absconded from her body to become small explosives beneath the fingers of other prisoners. Nesrine sent the postcards to Piccadilly. They never came back. She imagined them bold in the wind. She fed Eros snippets of prison life: that Hollis, prisoner 4712, had been found dead in the underground tunnel trying to escape, surrounded by empty crisp wrappers, rats eating the last images from her eyes; how Moffat, prisoner 3083, had fallen from the ladder injuring her shoulder whilst building the set for their interpretation of *Much Ado About Nothing*; how Gaudier, prisoner 2241, still possessing a hint of her French accent was found in a donkey costume screaming in the costume wardrobe, waving a large candlestick holder at anybody who approached. She told Eros about her diary, which she kept tucked away beneath her mattress.

At night, Nesrine ran her fingers over the kink in her hair along the expanse of her brown skin where tiny scenes from a life lost rose to the surface mimicking the shapes of small countries. She thought of Emerico's deceptive face. It only ever came to her in parts; left side first, then the right. Never head-on. How like him that was. Even in absence, he didn't show you the whole picture. She watered his face with tepid prison tap water. She cried, trying to silence his overarching, growing mouth. Sometimes she dreamt of emerging from a white triangle in the dessert, holding the remnants of her battered heart to an abandoned bow and arrow.

On February 8th, 1995, Nesrine's writing to Eros would be delayed because of the netball game. The cold court was covered in invisible scuff marks from light, worn plimsolls, the sock puppet in the bin borrowed the ends of short exchanges from spectators at the back of the court, muttering it to the rubbish. And the prisoners seemed malleable. Blink and they'd be babies in orange and blue team bibs scrambling for the ball while the prison cat, Homer, kept trying to shove its head through the hole on the left side of the court, wanting to observe this grey world from a different angle as the women transformed. The locks in their chests clicked open, bodies slick with perspiration airborne, catching things other than the ball. Homer tried to leave a paw print on the game, but the flashes of blue and orange were too quick. Too sly. Too seductive.

Nesrine flew in her position as goal attack. She could be anything such was the feeling of exhilaration, of freedom; a magician's chest chasing its tricks, a concert reveler crowd surfing that had turned the wrong way, landing in her bib, a microorganism outgrowing the confines and gaze of its microscope. Hot on her heels was the centre for the opposition, Harris, prisoner 2241. At the edge, where the half pie shape surrounding the goal met redemption, Harris knocked into Nesrine with all her body weight. Nesrine fell, then sprang up like a prize fighter already tasting the spoils of victory; an extra packet of cigarettes, the title of woman of the game, a chance to order two books of her choice at the prison library. Nesrine shoved Harris back. Their mouths curled dangerously, the way they do when words harbor small, sharp instruments glinting silver amidst the snarls. A guard acting as referee blew the whistle. It was too late. Harris grabbed a yellow handled screwdriver from her pocket, stabbing into Nesrine's throat in one quick motion. The din rose. Nesrine fell to the ground, hands on her throat as blood spurted. Her legs jerked. Homer's head shot out of the hole. Harris was dragged away by the guard, her pockmarked face beet red, her buzz cut defiant in the air. The court erupted. Spectators who were other prisoners dashed into the centre. The two teams broke into fights, turning on each other, ready to leap off the court and take a different warpath through the trembling goal net. Nesrine bled into the crack of joy redemption had offered then cruelly snatched away. There would be no postcard to Eros that month. Having escaped, bearing a puncture wound in its head, the thing from Nesrine's throat stumbled in the light, in the grey world winded, in search of another moist home.

Five days later, just past 10 p.m., the statue of Eros hopped off the top step at Piccadilly, clutching Nesrine's final postcard. His head fell, the pain in his chest was so intense he thought it would split him in two. He felt sad and powerless. He knew there would be no more postcards to intercept from the bright angles of the morning. His footsteps were heavy on his way down as Piccadilly Circus buzzed around him. Huge, brightly lit billboards blinded from all directions beaming Sanyo! TDK! Coca-Cola! The steps usually heaving with bodies were fairly empty except for a homeless man curled up in the middle.

Morning arrived, cradled Eros sitting on a park bench, cold against his back his hands turning over Nesrine's postcard. Anger rose inside him, pulled the corners of his mouth down. His limbs had a stiffness he needed to walk off.

A plan took shape in the white curls of clouds. He decided to head to Leicester Square where the statue of Charlie Chaplin awaited him. Charlie on his stone plinth was splendid. In his signature tramp ensemble, right hand wielding a cane. Eros hopped onto the plinth, placed a hand on Charlie's shoulder, and said, "I need your help. I've lost someone. The other half of my heart won't grow back unless I do something. I need you to keep my spirits up." He settled his cold lips on Charlie's ear, whispering. His voice cracked. Charlie's lids flickered; he wiggled his fingers, made an "Ahhh" noise, he spotted a lone man in a blue windbreaker barking into a phone.

Eros grabbed Charlie, holding up the postcard. "This is what I have of her."

Charlie read the postcard, a wistful expression on his face. "I can see her, I can feel her spirit. Can I tear a bit of this off?" he said, ignoring the increasing sounds of the city coming to life.

"Why?" Eros asked. "You didn't know her."

"But you've shown me a piece of her, so I want it, too."

Eros nodded. Charlie ripped the left corner off, the shape of the rip in Eros's half-heart where small shreds of Nesrine's last day had settled and spun. Charlie slipped the piece into his pocket. Eros took the postcard back. "That's the prison address." He pointed at Nesrine's scribble in the right corner. They both stared at the postcard as if it would transform into a blind, winged thing.

Charlie took his hat off, scratched his head. "I know what you're thinking."

"I have to get something that belongs to me now."

"Who should come with us?"

"Let's ask Nahla. Nesrine mentioned her in an old postcard. She never got to see her."

They jumped off the plinth. The grass surrounding them went bald. The pigeons shed their grey for the pavements, beginning to peck at each other frenetically.

Eros and Charlie travelled on to Stockwell Memorial Gardens where the only statue of a black woman stood. *Nahla the Bronze Woman*. Ten feet tall and held her baby boy high above her head. Her gift to him was flight. On the ground there would be ways and means to deny him this. She held her baby to her left breast and his cry to her right.

She told them she'd already traced the shapes of Nesrine's lost dreams. She too tore a piece from the postcard, slipping it beneath her tongue.

Next they stopped by the vomiting sculpture. His white lips and hands trembled to life as he was handed the final piece of the postcard. His dark, misshapen body was rough to touch. He heaved then; yellow bile from his throat coated the pavement. On they went, the vomiting sculpture catching all the ailments Nesrine was yet to have experienced, a revolving door of sickness: the flu she would have gotten in the early part of the year at twenty-seven; the thrush that would have had her rubbing small blobs of Canestine cream on the brown pink folds of her vagina; tonsillitis. The sharp stomach cramps she'd have gotten from food poisoning, the vomit from her stomach as a result. The vomiting statue inherited these splatters of illness that would become poisonous black mushrooms with bulbous heads.

The statues continued as a group. They marched on, creating a flurry that swept over the city. People pointed, fascinated. Some brought out their mobile phones to take pictures or video them. Others touched their faces and bodies gently as though they were made of plasticine. Starring as if the earth they knew had tricked them, as if anything could take on a different dimension and come to life.

Over the next five hours, they made their way towards Woodowns Women's Prison on the outskirts of Chelmsford. They trekked across motorways, bridges, underpasses, and bike trails. Now and again, they stopped for breaks, drinking from brooks or park ponds, watching their reflections' mouths glimmering in the water.

The statues arrived at Woodowns at 10 p.m. The prison sat on a lengthy, remote stretch of road. A few rusted lampposts along the grey tarmac looked like pitiful light bearers from a bleak dystopian future. The statues fished out coins they'd borrowed off a supermarket coin machine. They placed them in their mouths, swallowing heads or tails as they edged closer to the prison, a large brown-bricked building. There were no barbed wire fences surrounding it or huge gates as one might have expected. Instead, you crossed a circular parking area for visitors and a big green sign bearing arrows and directions to the various blocks. A white water fountain sat just outside the closed reception area. They took turns drinking from it, watering the coins inside, catching fragments of light from the day. At the top of the road was an old, abandoned post office building, boarded up and decorated with patches of graffiti. Several minutes from the prison, a bowling alley closed for a few months for refurbishment had a neon sign that read *Welcome to Walley's!* And a red-headed woman shaped like Jessica Rabbit leaning against the exclamation mark winking. The statues continued, the particles of a tiny planet assembling inside them. Several steps behind the fountain lay an underground tunnel that led inside the prison, hidden by a heavy, circular metal lid and copper bars that bore the imprint of frustrated hands that had had to turn back. Eros pulled the lid off, the vomiting statue prized the six bars open slowly, one by one. They entered the tunnel, assisting each other as a cold shaft of air welcomed them. It was dark, dank, and bore the smell of rot and the echoes of things lost. The vomiting statue threw up, then pulled a red ruby stone from the sick that shone brightly to guide them. On their left were some wires covered in blood. Crisp packets floated on the thin layer of dirty water on the ground, rats scurried into the silvery insides to eat reflections of themselves. Footsteps of many plucky prisoners who had attempted escape, running to meet their doom, had long faded, who had slipped, broken their hearts. Holding those bars angrily, they'd cried as the injuries in their bloodstreams became small creatures leaping through the bars' gaps into the world out there beyond them.

The statues heard these echoes as they made way, knocking torches with batteries that had failed to fuel the last legs of escape, scooping floating matchsticks missing fires consumed by the cruelty of fate. Eros began to whistle Tracy Chapman's "Fast Car," one of Nesrine's favourite songs. The other statues joined in. It travelled through the air into the ears of prisoners in Block B, who slowly uncurled their bodies from their bunks, listening intensely. The statues left the tunnel through its exit on the exercise court of Block B; drab, grey, and boasting two netball goalposts at either end with nets that trembled, having caught the many daily conversations that slipped into cracks. A cardboard sign reading No Banned Items Allowed blew onto the court, weathered at the edges. Charlie Chaplin took over holding the ruby, signaling the others, placing a finger over his lips. He spotted the thing from Nesrine's throat raising its small, slimy arms towards them. Charlie took his hat off, scooped it up. Phlegm-coloured and sickly looking, it pointed at the building by the side of the court. They followed the building round till they found themselves at the entrance of the smoking area by the guards' hub, which had been left open. Inside, a small cluster of guards sat before CCTV screens, watching intermittently, batons on the table, blue shirt collars undone, keys jangling from slack belt holders. Relaxed in their glass cubicle, the guards had not spotted the statues' slow infiltration. There was no camera on the court and therefore no feed to pick them up for two to three minutes, allowing a good window of time to make their approach. Then the CCTV footage flickered as though being interrupted. Two guards snoozing at one corner table were unaware. The other two keeping watch were eating donuts and drinking watered down cups of coffee. Eros and Charlie Chaplin leapt through the glass into the cubicle. Bits of glass showered the thing from Nesrine's throat like diamonds shimmering over a small mutant. The guards jerked in their seats, shocked. Two guards spat out mouthfuls of donut, scraping their chairs back quickly, spilling coffee on their uniforms. The others had woken abruptly. Drool drying on the corners of their mouths, they said, "What is this? Stand back! You're looking at serious charges for this."

The CCTV screens flickered again, playing footage of prisoners from the cameras' blind spots: scratching their faces in the showers; deliberately burning their hands in huge pots of tasteless soup they'd stirred till the ache in their shoulders began to travel to other parts of their bodies; crying over pictures of loved ones that had changed somehow over time. The statues ushered the guards into an empty cell, locking them in, swiping their keys.

The prisoners of Block B started to whistle loudly, knocking their bars insistently using shoes, books, stolen cutlery, pipe bars, their limbs poised in excitement at what was to come. The thing from Nesrine's throat led Eros and the other statues to Nesrine's now empty cell. It sat on her dented bed, leaving a yellow stain. Eros raised the mattress till the thing was perched at an angle, lifted Nesrine's blue diary from beneath, held it tightly. They left Nesrine's cell, opened other cell gates. Female prisoners flooded out, waving their items like flags, bedtime wear rumpled. "This is crazy!" one prisoner yelled. "Who are they?"

"It's Eros, Nesrine did this!" another answered. "Nesrine made this happen." The prisoners stared at the statues in wonder, then started to chant. "Nesrine, Nesrine, Nesrine!" They charged at the statues. The thing from Nesrine's throat ran amongst them, growing stronger from their energy. A heady shot to the puncture wound in its head. Its limp wrist pulled the echoes of Nesrine's laughter and the tip of a screwdriver scraping a thorny bottom. Eros ushered everybody back onto the court, through the tunnel, and out onto the street. He raised Nesrine's diary in the air, which spawned a fresh burst of chanting her name from the prisoners. They jostled amongst each other, excitement building, their chatter rose. The statues led them to the bowling alley; they broke in through a back window. They flicked the lights on, filling the building with brightness. Prisoner 1046, Sunny Whittaker, in for GHB, switched the CD player on. Prisoner 2017, Delilah Armstrong, in for armed robbery, took a group to the lanes, where they separated into teams bowling with glee, sliding their bodies down on the floor, throwing the balls with abandon. Prisoner 2246, Arlena Mattieu, in for murder, led another group to the games room. They took turns leaping on the trampolines, stretching their hands out to small versions of themselves running through the lights, holding bits of debris from the lost scenes in their lives. Another group surrounded the snooker table, shooting coloured balls into the mouths of ghosts.

At the lanes the prisoners waiting to bowl exchanged their favourite memories of Nesrine: like the time she organized a sports day of ridiculous activities having spent weeks convincing the governor; or the year she arranged a secret Valentine's evening where the prisoners could be each other's dates and exchange cards and gifts they'd made; or even the annoying way she always had to beat everybody during their exercise hour on the court in the mornings, covering it so quickly, as if something she'd built the night before was chasing her, high on some unidentifiable fuel. They celebrated her. They broke the vending machines, staining their tongues with Skittles and warm chocolate.

The statues started to whistle again. The music changed. The Ronnettes' "Walking in the Rain" blared from the speakers. Everywhere, the prisoners danced: in the bowling lanes, at the slot machines, on snooker tables, by the shoe lockers, at the trampolines, by the fake lottery machines where the balls looked like black eyes. By now, the ruby stone had been passed to Nahla the bronze woman statue; it sat gleaming between her breasts.

In the early hours Eros and the statues led the prisoners into the streets, down dawn's memory of the night before. Having fallen in love with Nesrine the moment her heart broke, he held onto her diary as though salvation lay within it. Bits of corroded flesh gathered within the void in his chest. He read the pages in sly concrete gaps longing, wanting, crying, while the thing from her throat now powerful, uglier, howling, spilled bits of another earth all over the city.

Madeleine

Amal El-Mohtar

An exquisite pleasure had invaded my senses, something isolated, detached, with no suggestion of its origin. And at once the vicissitudes of life had become indifferent to me, its disasters innocuous, its brevity illusory—this new sensation having had on me the effect which love has of filling me with a precious essence; or rather this essence was not in me it was me ... Whence did it come? What did it mean? How could I seize and apprehend it? ... And suddenly the memory revealed itself.

— Marcel Proust

Madeleine remembers being a different person.

It strikes her when she's driving, threading her way through farmland, homesteads, facing down the mountains around which the road winds. She remembers being thrilled at the thought of travel, of the self she would discover over the hills and far away. She remembers laughing with friends, looking forward to things, to a future.

She wonders at how change comes in like a thief in the night, dismantling our sense of self one bolt and screw at a time until all that's left of the person we think we are is a broken door hanging off a rusty hinge, waiting for us to walk through.

"Tell me about your mother," says Clarice, the clinical psychologist assigned to her.

Madeleine is stymied. She stammers. This is only her third meeting with Clarice. She looks at her hands and the tissue she is twisting between them. "I thought we were going to talk about the episodes."

"We will," and Clarice is all gentleness, all calm, "but—"

"I would really rather talk about the episodes."

Clarice relents, nods in her gracious, patient way, and makes a note. "When was your last one?"

"Last night." Madeleine swallows, hard, remembering.

"And what was the trigger?"

"The soup," she says, and she means to laugh, but it comes out wet and strangled like a sob. "I was making chicken soup, and I put a stick of cinnamon in. I'd never done that before, but I remembered how it looked, sometimes, when my mother would make it—she would boil the thighs whole with bay leaves, black pepper, and sticks of cinnamon, and the way it looked in the pot stuck with me—so I thought I would try it. It was exactly right—it smelled exactly, exactly the way she used to make it—and then I was there, I was small and looking up at her in our old house, and she was stirring the soup and smiling down at me, and the smell was like a cloud all around, and I could smell her, too, the hand cream she used, and see the edge of the stove and the oven door handle with the cat-print dish towel on it—"

"Did your mother like to cook?"

Madeleine stares.

"Madeleine," says Clarice, with the inevitably Anglo pronunciation that Madeleine has resigned herself to, "if we're going to work together to help you, I need to know more about her."

"The episodes aren't about her," says Madeleine, stiffly. "They're because of the drug."

"Yes, but—"

"They're because of the drug, and I don't need you to tell me I took part in the trial because of her—obviously I did—and I don't want to tell you about her. This isn't about my mourning, and I thought we established these aren't traumatic flashbacks. It's about the drug."

"Madeleine," and Madeleine is fascinated by Clarice's capacity to both disgust and soothe her with sheer unflappability, "drugs do not operate—or misfire—in a vacuum. You were one of sixty people participating in that trial. Of those sixty you're the only one who has come forward experiencing these episodes." Clarice leans forward, slightly. "We've also spoken about your tendency to see our relationship as adversarial. Please remember that it isn't. You," and Clarice doesn't smile, exactly, so much as that the lines around her mouth become suffused with sympathy, "haven't even ever volunteered her name to me."

Madeleine begins to feel like a recalcitrant child instead of an adult standing her ground. This only adds to her resentment.

"Her name was Sylvie," she offers, finally. "She loved being in the kitchen. She loved making big fancy meals. But she hated having people over. My dad used to tease her about that."

Clarice nods, smiles her almost-smile encouragingly, makes further notes. "And did you do the technique we discussed to dismiss the memory?"

Madeleine looks away. "Yes."

"What did you choose this time?"

"Althusser." She feels ridiculous. "'In the battle that is philosophy all the techniques of war, including looting and camouflage, are permissible.'"

Clarice frowns as she writes, and Madeleine can't tell if it's because talk of war is adversarial or because she dislikes Althusser.

After she buried her mother, Madeleine looked for ways to bury herself.

She read non-fiction, as dense and theoretical as she could find, on any subject she felt she had a chance of understanding: economics, postmodernism, settler-colonialism. While reading Patrick Wolfe she found the phrase *invasion is a structure not an event* and wondered if one could say the same of grief. *Grief is an invasion and a structure and an event,* she wrote, then struck it out because it seemed meaningless.

Grief, thinks Madeleine now, is an invasion that climbs inside you and makes you grow a wool blanket from your skin, itchy and insulating, heavy and grey. It wraps and wraps and wraps around, putting layers of scratchy heat between you and the world, until no one wants to approach for fear of the prickle, and people stop asking how you are doing in the blanket, which is a relief, because all you want is to be hidden, out of sight. You can't think of a time when you won't be wrapped in the blanket, when you'll be ready to face the people outside it—but one day, perhaps, you push through. And even though you've struggled against the belief that you're a worthless colony of contagion that must be shunned at all costs, it still comes as a shock, when you emerge, that there's no one left waiting for you.

Worse still is the shock that you haven't emerged at all.

"The thing is," says Madeleine, slowly, "I didn't use the sentence right away."

"Oh?"

"I—wanted to see how long it could last, on its own." Heat in her cheeks, knowing how this will sound, wanting both to resist and embrace it. "To ride it out. It kept going just as I remembered it— she brought me a little pink plastic bowl with yellow flowers on it, poured just a tiny bit of soup in, blew on it, gave it to me with a plastic spoon. There were little star-shaped noodles in it. I—" she feels tears in her eyes, hates this, hates crying in front of Clarice "—I could have eaten it. It smelled so good, and I could feel I was hungry. But I got superstitious. You know." She shrugs. "Like if I ate it, I'd have to stay for good."

"Did you want to stay for good?"

Madeleine says nothing. This is what she hates about Clarice, this demand that her feelings be spelled out into one thing or another: isn't it obvious that she both wanted and didn't want to? From what she said?

"I feel like the episodes are lasting longer," says Madeleine, finally, trying to keep the urgency from consuming her voice. "It used to be just a snap, there and back—I'd blink, I'd be in the memory, I'd realize what happened, and it would be like a dream; I'd wake up, I'd come back. I didn't need sentences to pull me back. But now ..." She looks to Clarice to say something, to fill the silence, but Clarice waits, as usual, for Madeleine herself to make the connection, to articulate the fear.

"... Now I wonder if this is how it started for her. My mother. What it was like for her." The tissue in her hands is damp, not from tears, but from the sweat of her palms. "If I just sped up the process."

"You don't have Alzheimer's," says Clarice, matter-of-fact. "You aren't forgetting anything. In fact, it appears to be the opposite: you're remembering so intensely and completely that your memories have the vividness and immediacy of hallucination." She jots something down. "We'll keep on working on dismantling the triggers as they arise. If the episodes seem to be lasting longer, it could be partly because they're growing fewer and farther between. This is not necessarily a bad thing."

Madeleine nods, chewing her lip, not meeting Clarice's eyes.

So far as Madeleine is concerned, her mother began dying five years earlier, when the fullness of her life began to fall away from her like chunks of wet cake: names; events; her child. Madeleine watched her mother weep, and this was the worst because with every storm of grief over her confusion Madeleine couldn't help but imagine the memories sloughing from her, as if the memories themselves were the source of her pain, and if she could just forget them and live a barer life, a life before the disease, before her husband's death, before Madeleine, she could be happy again. If she could only shed the burden of the expectation of memory, she could be happy again.

Madeleine reads Walter Benjamin on time as image, time as accumulation, and thinks of layers and pearls. She thinks of her mother as a pearl dissolving in wine until only a grain of sand is left drowning at the bottom of the glass.

As her mother's life fell away from her, so did Madeleine's. She took a leave of absence from her job and kept extending it; she stopped seeing her friends; her friends stopped seeing her. Madeleine is certain her friends expected her to be relieved when her mother died and were surprised by the depth of her mourning. She didn't know how to address that. She didn't know how to say to those friends, *you are relieved to no longer feel embarrassed around the subject, and expect me to sympathise with your relief, and to be normal again for your sake.* So she said nothing.

It wasn't that Madeleine's friends were bad people; they had their own lives, their own concerns, their own comfort to nourish and nurture and keep safe, and dealing with a woman who was dealing with her mother who was dealing with early-onset Alzheimer's was just a little too much, especially when her father had only died of bowel cancer a year earlier, especially when she had no other family. It was indecent, so much pain at once, it was unreasonable, and her friends were reasonable people. They had children, families, jobs, and Madeleine had none of these; she understood. She did not make demands.

She joined the clinical trial the way some people join fundraising walks and thinks now that that was her first mistake. People walk, run, bicycle to raise money for cures—that's the way she ought to have done it, surely, not actually volunteered herself to be experimented on. No one sponsors people to stand still.

The episodes happen like this.

A song on the radio like an itch in her skull, a pebble rattling around inside until it finds the groove in which it fits, perfectly, and suddenly she's—

—in California, dislocated, confused, a passenger herself now in her own head's seat, watching the traffic crawl past in the opposite direction, the sun blazing above. On I-5, en route to Anaheim: she is listening, for the first time, to the album that song is from and feels the beautiful self-sufficiency of having wanted a thing and purchased it, the bewildering freedom of going somewhere utterly new. And she remembers this moment of mellow thrill shrinking into abject terror at the sight of five lanes between her and the exit, and will she make it, won't she, she doesn't want to get lost on such enormous highways—

—and then she's back, in a wholly different car, her body nine years older, the mountain, the farmland all where they should be, slamming hard on the brakes at an unexpected stop sign, breathing hard and counting all the ways in which she could have been killed.

Or she is walking, and the world is perched on the lip of spring, the Ottawa snow melting to release the sidewalks in fits and starts, peninsulas of gritty concrete wet and crunching beneath her boots, and that solidity of snowless ground intersects with the smell of water and the warmth of the sun and the sound of dripping and the world tilts—

—and she's ten years old on the playground of her second primary school, kicking aside the pebbly grit to make a space for shooting marbles, getting down on her knees to use her hands to do a better job of smoothing the surface, then wiping her hands on the corduroy of her trousers, then reaching into her bag of marbles for the speckled dinosaur egg that is her lucky one, her favourite—

—and then she's back, and someone's asking her if she's okay because she looked like she might be about to walk into traffic, was she drunk, was she high?

She has read about flashbacks, about PTSD, about reliving events, and has wondered if this is the same. It is not as she imagined those things would be. She has tried explaining this to Clarice, who very reasonably pointed out that she couldn't both claim to have never experienced trauma-induced flashbacks and say with perfect certainty that what she's experiencing now is categorically different. Clarice is certain, Madeleine realizes, that trauma is at the root of these episodes, that there's something Madeleine isn't telling her, that her mother, perhaps, abused her, that she had a terrible childhood.

None of these things are true.

Now: she is home, and leaning her head against her living room window at twilight, and something in the thrill of that blue and the cold of the glass against her scalp sends her tumbling—

—into her body at fourteen, looking into the blue deepening above the tree line near her home as if it were another country, longing for it, aware of the picture she makes as a young girl leaning her wondering head against a window while hungry for the future, for the distance, for the person she will grow to be—and starts to reach within her self, her future/present self, for a phrase that only her future/present self knows, to untangle herself from her past head. She has just about settled on Kristeva—*abjection is above all ambiguity*—when she feels, strangely, a tug on her field of vision, something at its periphery demanding attention. She looks away from the sky, looks down, at the street she grew up on, the street she knows like the inside of her mouth.

She sees a girl of about her own age, brown-skinned and dark-haired, grinning at her and waving.

She has never seen her before in her life.

Clarice, for once, looks excited—which is to say, slightly more intent than usual—which makes Madeleine uncomfortable. "Describe her as accurately as you can," says Clarice.

"She looked about fourteen, had dark skin—"

Clarice blinks. Madeleine continues.

"—and dark, thick hair, that was pulled up in two ponytails, and she was wearing a red dress and sandals."

"And you're certain you'd never seen her before?" Clarice adjusts her glasses.

"Positive." Madeleine hesitates, doubting herself. "I mean, she looked sort of familiar, but not in a way I could place? But I grew up in a really white small town in Quebec. There were maybe five non-white kids in my whole school, and she wasn't any of them. Also—" she hesitates again because, still, this feels so private, "—there has never once been any part of an episode that was unfamiliar."

"She could be a repressed memory then," Clarice muses, "someone you've forgotten—or an avatar you're making up. Perhaps you should try speaking to her."

Clarice's suggested technique for managing the episodes was to corrupt the memory experience with something incompatible, something as of-the-moment as Madeleine could devise. Madeleine had settled on phrases from her recent reading: they were new enough to not be associated with any other memories and incongruous enough to remind her of the reality of her bereavement even in her mother's presence. It seemed to work; she had never yet experienced the same memory twice after deploying her critics and philosophers.

To actively go in search of a memory was very strange.

She tries, again, with the window: waits until twilight, leans her head against the same place, but the temperature is wrong somehow, it doesn't come together. She tries making chicken soup; nothing. Finally, feeling her way towards it, she heats up a mug of milk in the microwave, stirs it to even out the heat, takes a sip—

—while holding the mug with both hands, sitting at the kitchen table, her legs dangling far above the ground. Her parents are in the kitchen, chatting—she knows she'll have to go to bed soon, as soon as she finishes her milk—but she can see the darkness just outside the living room windows, and she wants to know what's out there. Carefully, trying not to draw her parents' attention, she slips down from the chair and pads softly—her feet are bare, she is in her pajamas already—towards the window.

The girl isn't there.

"Madeleine," comes her mother's voice, cheerful, "as-tu fini ton lait?"

Before she can quite grasp what she is doing, Madeleine turns, smiles, nods vigorously up to her mother, and finishes the warm milk in a gulp. Then she lets herself be led downstairs to bed, tucked in, and kissed goodnight by both her parents, and if a still small part of herself struggles to remember something important to say or do, she is too comfortably nestled to pay it any attention as the lights go out and the door to her room shuts. She wonders what happens if you fell asleep in a dream, would you dream and then be able to fall asleep in that dream, and dream again, and—someone knocks gently at her bedroom window.

Madeleine's bedroom is in the basement; the window is level with the ground. The girl from the street is there, looking concerned. Madeleine blinks, sits up, rises, opens the window.

"What's your name?" asks the girl at the window.

"Madeleine." She tilts her head, surprised to find herself answering in English. "What's yours?"

"Zeinab." She grins. Madeleine notices she's wearing pajamas, too, turquoise ones with Princess Jasmine on them. "Can I come in? We could have a sleepover!"

"Shh," says Madeleine, pushing her window all the way open to let her in, whispering, "I can't have sleepovers without my parents knowing!"

Zeinab covers her mouth, eyes wide, and nods, then

mouths *sorry* before clambering inside. Madeleine motions for her to come sit on the bed, then looks at her curiously.

"How do I know you?" she murmurs, half to herself. "We don't go to school together, do we?"

Zeinab shakes her head. "I don't know. I don't know this place at all. But I keep seeing you! Sometimes you're older, and sometimes you're younger. Sometimes you're with your parents, and sometimes you're not. I just thought I should say hello because I keep seeing you, but you don't always see me, and it feels a little like spying, and I don't want to do that. I mean," she grins again, a wide dimpled thing that makes Madeline feel warm and happy, "I wouldn't mind *being* a spy but that's different, that's cool, that's like James Bond or Neil Burnside or Agent Carter—"

—and Madeleine snaps back, fingers gone numb around a mug of cold milk that falls to the ground and shatters as Madeleine jumps away, presses her back to a wall, and tries to stop shaking.

She cancels her appointment with Clarice that week. She looks through old year books, class photos, and there is no one who looks like Zeinab, no Zeinabs to be found anywhere in her past. She googles "Zeinab" in various spellings and discovers it's the name of a journalist, a Syrian mosque, and the Prophet Muhammad's granddaughter. Perhaps she'll ask Zeinab for her surname, she thinks, a little wildly, dazed and frightened and exhilarated.

Over the course of the last several years Madeleine has grown very, very familiar with the inside of her head. The discovery of someone as new and inexplicable as Zeinab in it is thrilling in a way she can hardly begin explain.

She finds she especially does not want to explain to Clarice.

Madeleine takes the bus—she has become wary of driving—to the town she grew up in, an hour's journey over a provincial border. She walks through her old neighbourhood hunting triggers but finds more changed than familiar; old houses with new additions, facades, front lawns gone to seed or kept far too tidy.

She walks up the steep cul-de-sac of her old street to the rocky hill beyond, where a freight line used to run. It's there, picking up a lump of pink granite from where the tracks used to be, that she flashes—

—back to the first time she saw a hummingbird standing in her driveway by an ornamental pink granite boulder. She feels again her heart in her throat, flooded with the beauty of it, the certainty and immensity of the fact that she is seeing a fairy, that fairies are real, that here is a tiny mermaid moving her shining tail backwards and forwards in the air before realizing the truth of what she's looking at and feeling that it is somehow more precious still for being a bird that sounds like a bee and looks like an impossible jewel.

"Ohh," she hears from behind her, and there is Zeinab, transfixed, looking at the hummingbird alongside Madeleine, and as it hovers before them for the eternity that Madeleine remembers, suspended in the air with a keen jet eye and a needle for a mouth, Madeleine reaches out and takes Zeinab's hand. She feels Zeinab squeeze hers in reply, and they stand together until the hummingbird zooms away.

"I don't understand what's happening," murmurs Zeinab, who is a young teen again, in torn jeans and an oversized sweater with Paula Abdul's face on it, "but I really like it."

Madeleine leads Zeinab through her memories as best she can, one sip, smell, sound, taste at a time. Stepping out of the shower one morning tips her back into a school trip to the Montreal Botanical Garden, where she slips away from the group to walk around the grounds with Zeinab and talk. Doing this is, in some ways, like maintaining the image in a Magic Eye puzzle, remaining focused on each other with the awareness that they can't mention the world outside the memory, or it will end too soon, before they've had their fill of talk, of marvelling at the strangeness of their meeting, of enjoying each other's company.

Their conversations are careful and buoyant as if they're sculpting something together, chipping away at a mystery shape trapped in marble. It's easy, so easy to talk to Zeinab, to listen to her—they talk about the books they read as children, the music they listened to, the cartoons they watched. Madeleine wonders why Zeinab's mere existence doesn't corrupt or end the memories the way her sentences do, why she's able to walk around inside those memories more freely in Zeinab's company, but doesn't dare ask. She suspects she knows why, after all; she doesn't need Clarice to tell her how lonely, how isolated, how miserable she is, miserable enough to invent a friend who is bubbly where she is quiet, kind and friendly where she is mistrustful and reserved, even dark-skinned where she's white.

She can hear Clarice explaining in her reasonable voice

that Madeleine—bereaved twice over, made vulnerable by an experimental drug—has invented a shadow-self to love, and perhaps they should unpack the racism of its manifestation, and didn't Madeleine have any black friends in real life?

"I wish we could see each other all the time," says Madeleine, sixteen, on her back in the sunny field, long hair spread like so many corn snakes through the grass. "Whenever we wanted."

"Yeah," murmurs Zeinab, looking up at the sky. "Too bad I made you up inside my head."

Madeleine steels herself against the careening tug of Sylvia Plath before remembering that she started reading her in high school. Instead, she turns to Zeinab, blinks.

"What? No. You're inside my head."

Zeinab raises an eyebrow—pierced, now—and when she smiles, her teeth look all the brighter against her black lipstick. "I guess that's one possibility, but if I made you up inside *my* head and did a really good job of it, I'd probably want you to say something like that. To make you be more real."

"But—so could—"

"Although I guess it is weird that we're always doing stuff you remember. Maybe you should come over to my place sometime!"

Madeleine feels her stomach seizing up.

"Or maybe it's time travel," says Zeinab, thoughtfully. "Maybe it's one of those weird things where I'm actually from your future and am meeting you in your past, and then when you meet me in your future I haven't met you yet, but you know all about me—"

"Zeinab—I don't think—"

Madeline feels wakefulness press a knife's edge against the memory's skin, and she backs away from that, shakes her head, clings to the smell of crushed grass and coming summer with its long days of reading and swimming and cycling and her father talking to her about math and her mother teaching her to knit and the imminent prospect of seeing R-rated films in the cinema—

—but she can't, quite, and she is shivering naked in her bathroom with the last of the shower's steam vanishing off the mirror as she starts to cry.

"I must say," says Clarice, rather quietly, "that this is distressing news."

It's been a month since Madeleine last saw Clarice, and where before she felt resistant to her probing, wanting only to solve a very specific problem, she now feels like a mess, a bowl's worth of overcooked spaghetti. If before Clarice made her feel like a stubborn child, now Madeleine feels like a child who knows she's about to be punished.

"I had hoped," says Clarice, adjusting her glasses, "that encouraging you to talk to this avatar would help you understand the mechanisms of your grief, but from what you've told me, it sounds more like you've been indulging in a damaging fantasy world."

"It's not a fantasy world," says Madeleine with less snap than she'd like—she sounds to her own ears sullen, defensive. "It's my *memory*."

"The experience of which puts you at risk and makes you lose time. And Zeinab isn't part of your memories."

"No, but—" she bites her lip.

"But what?"

"But—couldn't Zeinab be real? I mean," hastily, before Clarice's look sharpens too hard, "couldn't she be a repressed memory, like you said?"

"A repressed memory with whom you talk about recent television and who suddenly features in all your memories?" Clarice shakes her head.

"But—talking to her helps, it makes it so much easier to control—"

"Madeleine, tell me if I'm missing anything here. You're seeking triggers in order to relive your memories for their own sake—not as exposure therapy, not to dismantle those triggers, not to understand Zeinab's origins—but to have a ... companion? Dalliance?"

Clarice is so kind and sympathetic that Madeleine wants simultaneously to cry and to punch her in the face.

She wants to say, *what you're missing is that I've been happy. What you're missing is that for the first time in years I don't feel like a disease waiting to happen or a problem to be solved until I'm back in the now, until she and I are apart.*

But there is sand in her throat, and it hurts too much to speak.

"I think," says Clarice, with a gentleness that beggars Madeleine's belief, "that it's time we discussed admitting you into more comprehensive care."

She sees Zeinab again when, on the cusp of sleep in a hospital bed, she experiences the sensation of falling from a great height, and plunges into—

—the week after her mother's death, when Madeleine couldn't sleep without waking in a panic, convinced her mother had walked out of the house and into the street or fallen down the stairs or taken the wrong pills at the wrong time, only to recall she'd already died and there was nothing left for her to remember.

She is in bed, and Zeinab is there next to her, and Zeinab is a woman in her thirties, staring at her strangely as if she is only now seeing her for the first time, and Madeleine starts to cry and Zeinab holds her tightly while Madeleine buries her face in Zeinab's shoulder and says she loves her and doesn't want to lose her but she has to go, they won't let her stay, she's insane and she can't keep living in the past but there is no one left here for her, no one.

"I love you, too," says Zeinab, and there is something fierce in it, and wondering, and desperate. "I love you, too. I'm here. I promise you, I'm here."

Madeleine is not sure she's awake when she hears people arguing outside her door.

She hears "serious bodily harm" and "what evidence" and "rights adviser," then "very irregular" and "I assure you," traded back and forth in low voices. She drifts in and out of wakefulness, wonders muzzily if she consented to being drugged or if she only dreamt that she did, turns over, falls back asleep.

When she wakes again, Zeinab is sitting at the foot of her bed.

Madeleine stares at her.

"I figured out how we know each other," says Zeinab, whose hair is waist-length now, straightened, who is wearing a white silk blouse and a sharp black jacket, high heels, and looks like she belongs in an action film. "How I know you, I guess. I mean," she smiles, looks down, shy—Zeinab has never been shy, but there is the dimple where Madeleine expects it—"where I know you from. The clinical trial, for the Alzheimer's drug—we were in the same group. I didn't recognize you until I saw you as an adult. I remembered because of all the people there, I thought—you looked—" her voice drops a bit, as if remembering suddenly that she isn't talking to herself, "lost. I wanted to talk to you, but it felt weird, like, hi, I guess we have family histories in common, want to get coffee?"

She runs her hand through her hair, exhales, not quite able to look at Madeleine while Madeleine stares at her as if she's a fairy turning into a hummingbird that could, any second, fly away.

"So not long after the trial, I start having these hallucinations, and there's always this girl in them, and it freaks me out. But I keep it to myself, because—I don't know, because I want to see what happens.

Because it's not more debilitating than a day dream, really, and I start to get the hang of it—feeling it come on, walking myself to a seat, letting it happen. Sometimes I can stop it, too, though that's harder. I take time off work, I read about, I don't know, mystic visions, shit like that, the kind of things I used to wish were real in high school. I figure even if you're not real—"

Zeinab looks at her now, and there are tears streaking Madeleine's cheeks, and Zeinab's smile is small and sad and hopeful, too, "—even if you're not real, well, I'll take an imaginary friend who's pretty great over work friends who are mostly acquaintances, you know? Because you were always real to me."

Zeinab reaches out to take Madeleine's hand. Madeleine squeezes it, swallows, shakes her head.

"I—even if I'm not—if this isn't a dream," Madeleine half-chuckles through tears, wipes at her cheek, "I think I probably have to stay here for a while."

Zeinab grins now, a twist of mischief in it. "Not at all. You're being discharged today. Your rights adviser was very persuasive."

Madeleine blinks. Zeinab leans in closer, conspiratorial.

"That's me. I'm your rights adviser. Just don't tell anyone I'm doing pro bono stuff: I'll never hear the end of it at the office."

Madeleine feels something in her unclench and melt, and she hugs Zeinab to her and holds her and is held by her.

"Whatever's happening to us," Zeinab says, quietly, "we'll figure it out together, okay?"

"Okay," says Madeleine, and as she does, Zeinab pulls back to kiss her forehead, and the scent of her is clear and clean like grapefruit and salt, and as Zeinab's lips brush her skin she—

—is in precisely the same place, but someone's with her in her head, remembering Zeinab's kiss and her smell and for the first time in a very long time, Madeleine feels—knows, with irrevocable certainty—that she has a future.

Notes from Liminal Spaces

Hiromi Goto

I am a first generation Japanese Canadian immigrant. I gratefully reside on the unceded traditional territories of the Coast Salish peoples: the Musqueam, the Sḵwx̱wú7mesh, and Tsleil Waututh Nations.

It was an unusually warm night for mid-March, and I had left the glass patio door open to let in the fresh air. I'd already heard the person from across the back alley release their pet—the dog's gleeful nails rapid-clicking as it pelted up the paved laneway. From the distance a set of jangling keys drew closer. An urban seagull, buoyed by city lights, screeched even though it was almost midnight. I glanced outside.

A brightly lit object fell across the sky. A steady white light as bright as three Venuses, it arced downward for several seconds until it flared brighter, a green surge, an emerald flare before it extinguished.

It was stunning.

Had anyone else seen it? The digital clock on the stove said 12:01 a.m. I did a cursory search online, but I couldn't find anything on Twitter or Facebook or local news sources. I stayed up for a while, reading articles and watching a few YouTubes. My daughter hadn't returned from her late shift at the restaurant. Tired, I went to bed.

Representational narratives have us experience stories in many different ways. Some stories rely heavily upon expository prose, and the primary engagement is intellectual. In contrast, a highly subjective narrative can have us virtually assuming the visceral, psychological, and emotional life of a fictional character, feeling their "reality" with an empathetic intensity we may not even have for our loved ones. A kind of temporary intimacy can be constructed in the bubble world where the writer's words and the reader's engagement distill an imagined reality. Much can happen in this fabricated space. The writer brings her culture of imagination with her. The reader brings their culture of imagining with them. Story content is imbued by values and beliefs held by the author. Stories are ideologically saturated sites. Not just the content—but also in its making. In the lattices of the structure. The architecture. It's not just what we write but how it is written and in what form.

A fuzzy sleep coalesced into waking. Something smelled tinny and slightly sweet—a strong chemical burning was in the air. I glanced at my bedside clock: 9:17. I swung my legs off the bed and rushed to the kitchen in my T-shirt and underpants.

There was nothing burning on the stove. I looked up at the smoke alarm in the ceiling. The green eye glowed—presumably it was still working. Kanami! Maybe some electrical cords had caught fire in her room!

I ran to my daughter's closed bedroom door. The sweet metallic tang in the air caught in my throat, and I began to cough. My eyes burned. "Are you okay?" I asked.

After a few seconds Kanami mumbled.

I opened the door to peek inside. The blankets were pulled over her head. There was no smoke in the air. I sniffed. It didn't smell any stronger than what I'd smelled in my room and the rest of the apartment. She sounded sleepy and crabby, her usual morning self, so I closed her door and went to inspect the outer hallway of the apartment building. No visible smoke, no increase in odour. I went back inside and slid open the glass door to the patio.

The sweet chemical smell was stronger outside. The wind was calm. The skies were clear—no sirens or columns of smoke. But my eyes burned. I blinked rapidly and began to slide the door shut when something thudded near my feet.

It was a crow. One wing outstretched, its eye was half-closed and dull. The toes curled loosely. Dead. A few feet away was a Stellar's Jay, and a chickadee. All dead. I crouched down to cup the crow's body. It was still soft and slightly warm. Death had been recent ... I closed the patio door. I washed my hands with antibacterial soap.

Stories are cultural forms of social engagement. When I write I'm not only thinking about what will make a "good story" (which is often culturally defined)—I'm also thinking about how a story works within culture and what it is that I'm folding back into the mix. My subjective reality would not be held up as "representative" of "the norm" by the majority of Canadians. I have no longing to be part of normative systems nor replicate this world in my writing— it is already much-represented everywhere in popular culture. But I recognize that cultural normativity holds a great deal of power—it positions my subjectivity as marginal while simultaneously refusing to recognize its own power. This informs my writing in a fundamental way.

It wasn't until I read Joy Kogawa's Obasan when I was in my early twenties that I saw Japanese Canadians as central to the text. That's a long time to wait before seeing a face like one's own in a nation's literature ... Obasan left a big impression upon me—it contextualized a history in a personal way, it had political intentions toward social justice yet it was also art, and it also figured cultural practices/ gestures as familiar (to me). To find a part of oneself in this way was a revelatory moment. It was also a moment of intimacy. Obasan was written in a literary realist tradition. Much of the Canadian canon is books of this nature. Yet, I've also always been drawn to speculative fiction, legends, and folk tales. I think that it is here where I find stories of not only what is, or what was, but also stories of what may be.

My hands. A memory sensation of the crow's feathers was soft and lush upon my palms. The soft dead weight of it. Warm and limp. It reminded me of something ... but it vanished like my dreams upon waking. The heavy glass patio door rumbled on its track as I slid it open again. The tinny smell in the air. I clamped my inner elbow across my nose and mouth as I crouched to retrieve the dead crow. Its body was still warm.

"What are you doing?"

My daughter's voice was silver razors.

I looked down.

Black feathers covered my bare feet, were forming soft mounds upon the kitchen floor.

When had I come back inside ...?

My thumbs. They'd split the crow's chest open, cracking it wide like a boiled crab. The entrails glistened. And nestled inside the red and pink and grey was an orb of bright green as fresh as a new spring leaf speckled with small flecks of black.

"So beautiful ..." I said. "I think it's a gift."

• • •

I'm not certain if it's a symptom of sloppy thinking or if it's an aspect of the human tendency to create associations between not entirely dissimilar things, but somewhere along the way I've begun thinking of traditional realist fiction as straight literature and speculative fiction as queer. Of course, there are queer texts that are written in a realist modality, and I would certainly not wish to "unqueer" them just because they do not inhabit or interrogate the speculative ... Maybe what I mean is that my idea of the queerness of speculative fiction gestures to the possibilities beyond the normative in exciting ways.

"Oka-san, put down that crow. It might be dirty."

She can hear things in her daughter's voice. Her fear, disgust, panic, resentment. Her love. She can hear Kanami's desire to cup her arm and lead her to the kitchen chair. She can hear her revulsion.

"Let me explain," Eiko says. If only she could share with her the clarity inside the dead crow's entrails. But the understanding she feels so keenly cannot be shaped by words. "The green. Only this green ... There's a chickadee for you. And a Steller's jay for Lori. On the patio. I found them. Three birds for the three of us."

Kanami's eyes widen. She backs away from her mother.

"No!" Eiko says. "Listen to me. It makes sense! Last night there was a comet."

"I'll call Lori." Her daughter's voice is pitched low. "You can tell Lori about the birds, Oka-san."

I don't wish to suggest that all speculative fiction is inherently interesting or inherently transgressive. Fantasy and science fiction is also rife with texts that reinscribe familiar narratives: colonization, ecological destruction, genocide—these are human stories albeit on a different planet. Strip the magic from Rowling's Hogwarts and it's just another private school for children. Although engagingly imaginative, the magical world that Rowling describes has a firm foundation in a very familiar world.

Literature based on representing realism is bound by the world that we know. It creates a semblance of familiar subjects and situates them in dramatic moments. It may be that there are almost an infinite number of ways to regale us with new stories in this fashion, but the paradigm is bound in the material "reality" of the world around us. But to my mind, the best of speculative fiction is not bound by the mechanics of the systems we've developed to date nor confined to the limits of our bodies and social and historical forces. Speculative fiction allows for paradigm shifts that can have us begin experiencing and understanding in new, unsettling ways. They can disturb us and can propel us beyond the conventions, complacencies, or determinedly maintained ignorance of the ideologically figured present into an undetermined future.

The middle-aged woman tilts her head. Her daughter takes another step backward. A gust of wind blows through the open patio door, the mound of black feathers scattering across the kitchen floor. Behaviour is a pattern, the woman thinks. She stares at the open carcass of the half-plucked bird. At the shiny organs revealed in its ruptured cavity. Behaviour spilling outside of narrow confines is deemed disturbed. This idea disturbs her. When have our lives become so narrow, she wants to scream. But screaming will not serve her now. Is knowledge also a feeling, she wonders. She plucks the green orb from the entrails of the crow. It is smooth, has the solidity and give of an eyeball. She pops it in her mouth. She closes her eyes. She swallows.

Before the term queer was reclaimed by the gay community, before queer was used as a pejorative toward gay persons to other and dehumanize, its uncertain origins include a possible Scottish source via low German with a denotation of "strange/peculiar," and maybe this is one of the permutations of the term[1] that nestles into my appreciation of writing and reading from literature of the fantastic. That it can inspire and inhabit a liminal place—a site of uneasiness and destabilization that can have the reader engage in unexpected and uncomfortable ways. When writing is strange and peculiar, it invokes an aperture that leads me toward thoughts and feelings unfamiliar ... Uneasiness triggers a different frame of perceiving and understanding. There is no comfort in uneasiness. The pulse quickens. A sense of dread may press heavily upon the chest. Thoughts may divert from logic and reason. It may cause the subject to shut down. But uneasiness has the power to linger. Even if the subject's first instinctive response is rejection (or suppression or denial) uneasiness has the capacity to persist. And in its persistence, demand that it be reviewed and reconsidered again and again. When we experience uneasiness in our fictional worlds, there is room and *space to explore the myriad sensations without fear of annihilation of our core selves. It is this aspect of the fantastic that speaks to me as both as reader and as writer.*

I must hurry. There's no explaining the urgency. My daughter didn't see the comet last night and cannot know its connection with the birds. If I were to try explaining it to another me, I would laugh in my face and walk away. When my ex's father spoke of Atlantis and Mayan pyramids in one breath, my cheeks burned with embarrassment for him. I still don't believe that "the aliens" who "built Atlantis" also taught the Mayans to build their pyramids. But I believe in Cassandra. I believe in the ghost maid who counted dishes beside the well. I believe in the women who have been ignored, been told that their tales are falsehoods or stupid.[2] My knowledge is as real to me as the crow's gore drying upon my skin. If I don't act upon my own knowledge …

Representational fiction is a kind of written embodiment. When characters are placed before me, I ask of the text, who are the embodied? Whose bodies are these? Who is subject? Who is object? Which bodies are missing? Additionally, not only what's being marked upon the page—the body that makes the markings is also a matter of critical engagement. The body of the one who marks matters to me—because we are still creatures with bodies. We do not exist in the Singularity. Our bodies matter … Our subjective realities are not all treated equally. I'm keenly conscious of the long history of erasure or acts of distortion to be found in literature. And equally aware of the limitations of representation—there are no measures that will confine a reader's perceptions to that which the writer desired. I have seen how limitations of reading the body plays out in my own life.

Oka-san's always been so much stronger than me. Oh, Mummy. I can't stop her. She ate that thing, that green guts of the crow! What if it makes her sick? Why is she doing this? Has she gone crazy? She's going out on the deck again. She has two more dead birds … Ripping the feathers off the bodies. Brown and blue feathers cover our bare feet. I should lock myself in the bathroom. But what if she hurts herself? "Oka-san … Stop it. You're scaring me."

She doesn't say anything.

When will Lori get here! Oh, my god ...

Her fingers. Covered in gore. Feathers. She's forcing her thumb into the bird's chest.

Did Lori call the ambulance? Please, someone hurry.

She's pulling something out from the bird's body. A piece of its guts. Disgusting. Something round, green, the size of a small marble, rolls in the palm of her hand. She looks at me and tries to smile.

"I—" She shakes her head.

She jumps on top of me, and we fall to the ground. My head clunks on the floor. Noise gongs inside my ears, a burst of light behind my closed eyelids.

Oka-san's knees pin my shoulders to the floor.

"Stop it," I groan.

She shoves her fingers inside my mouth.

I bite down on her, but she's yanked her hand away.

Something bursts between my teeth. More bitter than matcha, the sweetness of rotten lilacs. I gag.

My mother clamps her hands over my nose and mouth.

Until I swallow it all.

I identify as a feminist queer woman of colour: this self-naming serves as a core to my personal identity construct and as a guideline to how I expect to be understood when I share this information with others. Yet there exists a kind of liminality to my own sense of subjective self because of the constant subject/object shifts I have experienced and continue to experience in unmediated shared public spaces. While walking in Tokyo on my way from the subway to a university, a small child asked their mother if I was a gay man. As an adult, riding the tube in the UK, a primary school-aged child called me "Chinese boy." In Spain, adult soccer players felt compelled to yell, Chino! from across the field. Then self-corrected to China! At the border between Germany and Denmark, the guard stared at my passport and then at my face and asked with incredulity, "Frau?" Walking from the library to my car, as I pushed the stroller on the ice-rutted Calgary sidewalk, a man overhead me speaking to my child in Japanese. He strode past us, a little too closely. "How would you like to suck my nice white dick?" he hissed. Abiding at the intersections of race, gender, sexuality, and class means at any given moment my personal sense of centrality inside my own life can be destabilized by the uninvited readings of other people. My writing is informed by all of these experiences.[3]

Eiko releases her daughter's mouth, so Kanami can take one big gasp of air, then she clamps her hand upon her daughter's face once more. Eiko leaves uncovered Kanami's nose, so that she can breathe. Her daughter cannot be allowed to bring up what she's swallowed. Eiko knows that if she releases her, Kanami will stick her finger down her throat. I'm sorry, Eiko thinks. I love you, she thinks.

Her daughter inhales, exhales, too rapidly. Tears stream from the outer creases of her eyes.

Eiko hears Kanami swallow. "There's a reason," Eiko babbles. "This looks bad. I'm so sorry, darling. I'm only doing what I did for myself. I'm not trying to hurt you." Eiko bites her lower lip, and hot tears fill her eyes. "I'm sorry," she whispers.

Her daughter begins twisting her hips—tries to knee her mother in the back.

An arm comes down around Eiko's chest and pulls her away from her daughter.

Kanami rolls onto her side, onto all fours, to crawl toward the wall. Sitting, she leans against it, her eyes wide with accusation and outrage.

"Lori?" Eiko sobs. "Is that you?"

Lori releases her lover, and Eiko crouches on the ground for a moment before rising and turning to press her face against her partner's chest.

"You're here," Eiko whispers, relief in her voice. "You're here."

Lori, taller than Eiko, looks down at Kanami with worry in her grey-blue eyes. "You okay?" she silently mouths as she gently circles her arms around Eiko's shoulders.

Eiko's own arms are behind her back, her fingers working furtively.

"Lori," Eiko's daughter croaks. "Watch out!"

The idea of representation is a slippery one—identity is not static nor do people decode identity in a fixed way. I would never wish to be a "representative," for instance, because it can toss you very quickly onto an essentialist track. But fiction is a great place to embody diversity, in characters as well as in story structure and form, because through language the writer can arrange the context of and for the representational moment. As a writer I can contextualize the specific parameters of what I am seeking to represent and how. Doing so enables me to direct attention to systemic power imbalances and try to unsettle normative practices. This is the difference between being erased, being written about, and being the one who does the writing. How enormously empowering. And it also serves to have readers expand upon their contexts of perceiving. A little like what I seek in truly expansive speculative fiction ... Like how Le Guin had us reimagining gender and its firmly entrenched place in human behavior/interaction in Left Hand of Darkness. *How Butler had us rethinking human biology, reproduction, and sex in* Bloodchild. *Or her exploration of a complex biological colonization and miscegenation in the* Xenogenesis *trilogy. The represented body in narratives like these creates moments of generative slippage—the ground beneath us, what we thought was bedrock, is actually a moving skin ... Only we never knew until now.*

The world becomes a different place.

"The ambulance will be here soon," Lori says calmly. "I know you've been under a lot of stress. I'll stay with you the entire time. I'm on your side. You understand that, right?"

I shake my head. Oh, she is lovely. She is such a good person. She is also physically stronger than me, and I can't force her like I forced my daughter. The final gift for her, the green orb is slowly losing its potency. I can feel it waning against my skin.

"Lori," I stare up at her face. "Lori, look at me."

Lori's forehead is wrinkled with concern, but her eyes are true.

"I haven't lost my mind. I need you to believe me. It's so important." Tears roll down my cheeks, and tears begin streaming down Lori's face as well.

"I believe you," Lori says.

"Don't believe her!" Kanami cries.

Oh, daughter. I have broken trust with you. Please forgive me. We don't have time ...

Male voices in the hallway. At the door. They are knocking. "Ambulance," they call out. I can hear one of them tread toward us with heavy shoes.

Kanami scrambles to her feet, scurries to the foyer.

"Lori!" I pull her down to the floor, so that we are eye to eye. "Nothing I try to explain will make any sense. But you have to do this one thing for me. This one thing. I wouldn't ask you to do this if it wasn't the most important thing in the world. Please believe me!"

I sob. I can hear Kanami's voice murmuring hard and fast. The rattle of the ambulance stretcher trying to get in through the doorway.

"I believe you." Lori's voice is calm. Her eyes hold fast to mine.

I open my closed fist to reveal the green orb in the middle of my gore-crusted palm. Clumps of matted feathers stick to my skin. I stink of dried blood.

My vision blurs as tears start filling my eyes again. "You—you have to eat this. The message was clear. They were given to us. To help us. Please." It's hopeless. It's so disgusting. Even my eyes can see how outrageous my request is. "You have to eat it!"

I pick the orb out from my fingers and hold it out toward my love.

"Looks like another MO." The paramedic's voice is impatient. Dismissive. "That's three this morning! Christ!"

"We're here to help you," his partner says to me. He rests his blue-gloved hand upon my upper arm.

"No! Not yet!" I grit my teeth. The tendons stand out in my neck. "Get your hand off of me!" Nonconsensual touch, especially by a man, is something I cannot bear.

The paramedics draw closer. Encroaching upon my space. "Miss," one of them says to my daughter. "We might need you to call the police with a Mental Health Act request."

I will punch their faces in if I have to.

Lori reaches for the orb. Her fingers close over it. Carefully. "I have it, Eiko," she says. She smiles. "You go with them for now. It will be okay. If you go with them, I will eat this for you."

The fight leaves my body. Even if she's lying to me, so that I won't struggle with the paramedics, I can't force her to listen to me. It's all too late.

"Eiko," Lori says.

I look up at her.

Lori smiles. She places the orb inside her mouth. She can't stop a grimace from forming on her face. She shudders. Closes her eyes and swallows.

I smile. Tears stream down my face.

From a great distance I can hear the coming roar of wings.

Kanami and Lori's eyes widen as they turn toward the patio door. They can hear it, too! A smile breaks across my face.

The paramedics look at each other and then at my daughter and my lover, their eyebrows raised with skepticism. The gruff one rolls his eyes.

The glass in the door bulges outward, as soft as a bubble of soap. The glass pops with a crash of a thousand shards.

The air roars.

I reach for Kanami's and Lori's hands. We squeeze tightly. With love. With certainty. We take to the skies.

Speculative fiction can be a remarkably generative site from which we can deconstruct, agitate, investigate, and extrapolate. A queer place where dreams and visions can be actualized. Alongside speculative fiction's potential for critical and transformative engagement, there remains at its core the possibility of engaging with a sense of wonder. Even as we need to be able to call attention, to dismantle and deconstruct, it is necessary for us as a species to be able to imagine. To imagine things that are not, or are yet to be, we need first to be able to imagine the impossible. When we imagine the impossible, it is only then that it becomes possible. To my mind, the best of speculative fiction takes us from a familiar place to the unfamiliar. Enter this other space, it invites us. Explore it. Imagine yourself and your world, better ...

Footnotes

[1] For further etymological reading on the possible origins/meanings of "queer": "More Than Words: Queer, Part 1 (The Early Years)." Cara. Autostraddle. January 9, 2013.

[2] *How to Suppress Women's Writing.* Joanna Russ. University of Texas Press. 1983.

[3] *The limbs of the liminal
body are fully detachable. Look
what happened to Sedna. Every
little bit counts. It wasn't her mother
who betrayed her. Not all of our stories
are pretty. We'll name our own
violence. Take the venom
that will cure your illness.*

Medusa

Christopher Brown

It's best first thing in the morning. When you get up out of bed, while the remains of fresh dreams spark into warm ash across the trails of neurons. Especially in summer, when the sun comes on and pushes the gelatinous ozone ooze of the metropolis through the window of your flat on the 114th floor. In that moment when you can't remember where you are or even who you are and know only the hunger of your appetites after a long night hunting in the dream worlds. Before the anthill starts humming, and Capital starts tapping you on the shoulder.

Sometimes Medusa wakes you up, rattling in her crate at the foot of the bed. You wonder if she wants it more than you. When you let her out of her dark wet incubator and she envelops you before you can hold her, pushing you back onto the bed, opening up to you through new apertures of flesh and entering you through ones you didn't know you had. Lately, she has taken to covering your eyes with her own grown film of red membrane. Having no eyes of her own, perhaps she wants to see what you see.

Medusa plugs you in. To yourself and to her network, the cryptic bioelectrical pathways of empathic genius that she grows in her crate when you put her away after each session. When she grips you, she mirrors your flesh and makes contact with what seems like every nerve in your body, sending and receiving signals that transcend language. And as the cascades of spastic release hurtle through your body, all the feeling goes, too. Medusa sucks out the pain. She sucks out the very idea of the self and replaces it with flashes of lightning inside the void between your ears.

And then you have to go to work.

Catastrophe bonds are good business in a world of endless little wars and overpass-busting natural disasters. Crafting elaborate derivatives that algorithmically transform apocalypse into internal rates of return does not leave a lot of time for "relationships." Living in the sprawl of K.L., where you don't know the idiom or the correct time to kneel, makes it easier to embrace the alone.

You moved here with another, but the tropical fungus scared her away, and the fezzes and the men in black with their invisible women. She went back to London, to the world of friends and technicolor dinners and the dream of family. You had a light ache and the abstract idea of the loss, but you mostly felt free. Free to be alone.

That was before Medusa. Before you brought her home from the bio-atelier in Hong Kong where she was grown.

You heard about Medusa and her brothers and sisters from some colleagues—men, of course—over a drunken dinner in Shanghai on a road show to pitch a new series of famine reinsurance derivatives to Chinese fund managers. Medusa was part of the newest generation of the first line of engineered biological entities that could last more than a couple of months without a live-in lab tech as its au pair. She had been developed as an accidental byproduct of the latest injectable male tissue enhancements, grown from a stem cell culture that would be spiked with your own genetic material to generate a custom lover.

The purchase of Medusa was like a cross between applying to the astronaut corps and signing up for an online dating service, with two days of physical evaluations, fluid extractions, and psychological inventories. They even monitored your sleep one night, your brain wired to some sort of fMRI that color-coded your dreams and generated semiotic taxonomies of your ascendant yearnings and neuroses. In the end, of course, you knew that the true purpose was really just society's structural imperative to set you up to maximize your productivity.

For a while it looked like it would have the opposite effect. Like the third week after she came home, when you didn't show up for work for several days and stopped checking your login accounts, locked with her in your apartment in a sustained orgasmic opium daze, a languorous exercise in the obliteration of ego. And then you remembered you needed to keep paying for her.

The investors rely upon you to sustain the growth of Capital in a world where population has crossed the summit and is irrevocably declining. And as you postulate the socioeconomic sine curves propelled by off-season hurricanes and the shock waves of post-nuclear bunker busters, you wonder what kind of alpha is represented by the movement to mass masturbation.

● ● ●

Sometimes in the evening you groom Medusa, plucking her random hairs, cleaning her box, massaging her extruded blood vessels, putting the balms on her different dermal surfaces. The ointments make her colors change, as do the shifting lights in the room.

Sometimes you fall into a post-coital sleep without putting her back in her incubator. She escapes your bedroom. You find her on the bathroom floor, in the kitchen, against the floor-to-ceiling window. Your pink freckled snail, your pet slug the size of a very large dog, looking without eyes for things you cannot imagine. Once you found her squeezed behind the desk, devouring one of the network jacks.

You are the sort of person who prefers numbers to words. Medusa has neither. And you wonder how it is that she communicates the way she does, turning your own feelings into a looped remix that she pumps back into your bloodstream.

Afterwards, the apartment always seems to know what to do. Though when the radio comes on with music you haven't heard before but instantly love, you wonder what Medusa is telling it.

Salter is a lawyer you work with. She represents your investment house, helping contractually structure the derivatives. She's based out of Melbourne but comes to K.L. every couple of months. You always have dinner and sometimes more. You share a rigorous, overeducated clinicality that allows you to sequester your emotions beneath layers of impenetrable logic. After a perfectly spiced protein and an engineered Bordeaux, you like to let your feelings out to play with each other like underdeveloped, sheltered children. It feels good, or at least the idea of it does.

When you and Salter roll off each other, though you both may be physically satiated, you feel like you know each other less than you did before. The nakedness and the inadequacy of language amplify the abyss between your personalities, a gap in perception that cannot be traversed except through primate grasping and thrusting and grunting.

Which does not stop you from trying.

How is it, you sometimes wonder, that this woman who is so like you in so many ways becomes more alien the objectively closer you get? While the essentially brainless masturbatory aid you keep by your bed makes you feel transported to some plane of metaphysical oneness?

Your relationship with Salter is mediated by so many different forms of exchange. Language, money, pheromones, numbers, clothing, the narrative overlays of the idea of love. Medusa just lives. Part of you, in a very literal sense, her genomic key opening undiscovered compartments of your brain, revealing flashes of satori within.

Salter sometimes wears a designer merkin of blue synthetic material to adorn her fashionably depilated body. When you take it off, she tells you the reason we have pubic hair is to remind us we are animals.

You tell her you want to open your other eye, the one you got from your amphibian ancestors. You wonder if Medusa can help. You wonder if Medusa is a variation on the amphibian.

One morning you wake to find Salter with Medusa, writhing in the pink fingers of dawn. The sounds Salter makes, sounds you have never heard her make before, are what wake you up. You do not know how Medusa got out of her crate. She is wrapped around Salter like a sleeping bag made of skin. A sleeping bag that goes inside you, too. Salter is shaking. Medusa moves through a range of color you haven't seen.

In time, you help coax Medusa off of Salter.

Salter did not previously know of the existence of Medusa. She does now.

You show her how to put Medusa back in her crate. You talk to her. You call her by her first name, the one her parents called her when she was an infant.

Salter understands.

Later, you and Salter try to invent new words to explain how you feel.

Salter schedules time off the Network for a long weekend with you. And Medusa. You close the blinds this time, banish clothes to the other room, and turn out the lights. And the three of you find each other in the dark, swimming in space. Medusa comes between you and in doing so, brings you together. It feels like you are all three breathing the same epic breaths even though Medusa does not have lungs, so far as you can tell.

You find each other at a level you did not imagine possible. Medusa is the bridge across which authentic feeling uncorrupted by language can cross. All the feelings you don't believe in, like love, and the ones you do, like pain. You cry and forget the first words you learned and quiver together like a slab of mixed gelatin jolted by spasms of convulsive shock Medusa conducts through your nervous wet tissues.

When Salter returns again three weeks later, something is wrong with Medusa. She becomes inert. She resists leaving her crate, and if you remove her, she refuses to move. You notice a lump that was not there before. You call the laboratory for support.

The laboratory sends out one of their field techs, who cannot figure it out either.

And so you all pack up and fly across the sea to Hong Kong and meet with the white-haired men with white coats and extra Ph.D.s.

Dr. Wu explains that Medusa is pregnant, if that word can be applied to this singular and unprecedented circumstance, as he describes it. Pregnant with what, only extensive testing will tell. But they know at least this, that the growth inside Medusa has parts of each of the three of you.

The doctors share their conclusion that Medusa must be destroyed. Salter confounds their engineer logic with insoluble legal puzzles of ownership of this thing within the Thing. You look at the red mass squirming on the imaging of Medusa and wonder what she would want. And understand that for all of you, the idea of choice is, and has always been, a masterful delusion.

A Universal Elegy

Tang Fei

● translated by John Chu ●

I love you, stranger, but not because the world is hurting me.
Before my love froze, it once flew.

—*The Elegy of Alia*

Alia Calendar 6th month, 87th year

Brother, it's not until my tongue stumbles over these two syllables
that I realize how long it's been since we last talked. Julian and I kept
moving, kept living where even the heating system was a problem.
A satellite communication system that could reach Mercury was
beyond my wildest hopes. Sorry that I haven't contacted you in so
long.

Actually, I could have run to a public communication kiosk.
Sending you a written message would have cost only several sou,
but Julian didn't like it when I did that. He thought it was a waste of
money. We both knew, though, that this was just one of the ways he
punished me.

Julian, my now former lover, had at some point suddenly become
a nightmare. He tormented me, ridiculed me, in every way he could.
He's like all the others. His shifting gaze, the curl of his lips, the
way his nose blushed, even the sound of his footsteps were filled
with a meticulous indifference. He laughed at me, saying that I was
mad. Gradually, I started to believe it. The world grew hazy. It lost its
contours and weight. I sunk into thick, black, yet glistening agony.
When I looked up at the stars, I saw a sky filled with flowing fire,
dancing and spinning in a daze.

I was always crying. Once, Julian said in front of me to his research institute colleagues that he wanted to conduct research in genetic ethology using me as a specimen. Of course, he was drunk when he said that. He was always drunk, just like I was always crying.

I can say these things to you, not just because I've left the nightmare that was Julian—yes, we've broken up—but especially because you're the only person in the universe who can understand me. We came from the same fertilized egg. We have the same DNA. Even though radiation from Cygnus A methylated some of your genes, you can still understand me, a sufferer of an inhibitory neuron blockage disorder.

It's done, brother. All of the suffering is done. I'm fine now. I've never been finer. In six hours I'm going to leave this planet together with Hull. He's a good man. Although we've only known each other fifteen days, we already understand each other. How do I describe the merging of souls that happens between two strangers? Such a mysterious stirring of emotions. I can't put it into words. It's like how the sound waves from two different kinds of musical instruments resonate together harmoniously. Forgive me for such a clunky analogy, brother. All you need to know is that I've fallen in love with a stranger who happens to love me. More importantly, he completely understands me and accepts me.

Six hours from now, fire will rush out of our rocket, and we'll travel to the other side of the universe to Dieresis. That's where he was born. Hull promised me that there I'll get the respect that I deserved but never got on Earth. There, no one will think of me as being sick in the head. Like him, they'll understand and respect me, even appreciate me.

Brother, I love him. It's absolutely not because the world keeps hurting me.

Alia Calendar 6th month, 89th year

Time flies by so fast. Sorry that I've gone so long without mailing you again. But, brother, in this vast universe, do people have to rely on such obsolete methods to reach out to each other? Hull told me that signals the brain sends travel farther than we think. During the countless years of an endless trek, a person's train of thought will enter the mind of someone else on another planet. Isn't that amazing?

I want to tell you about Hull. Don't worry, brother. I know my last letter made you think that I've committed yet another thoughtless mistake. Indeed, I have to admit that leaving Earth was definitely a somewhat hasty act. You know that's why I sent you that last letter.

Hull is a Dieresian. He's 1.8 meters tall, 72 kilograms, black hair, brown eyes. He looks like a handsome Caucasian and speaks Earth languages really well. Our conversations are fluent and joyful. He's more like my kind than any Earth person.

His every subtle detail, no matter how difficult to check, is perfect. His pupils dilate at the just-right times. His skin suffuses the air with a unique perfume. The rate his eyelashes quiver, the flaring of his nostrils, the unique path his fingertips glide over my skin steep me in the warm current of his love. I respond in the same detailed, satisfying way. We echo each other. The way we express our love is something that humans have never experienced and can never understand.

Our love unfolded on an even more profound layer of spirituality. Cautious and reverent at first, it gradually transformed into something frenzied and wild until finally I realized that, all along, Hull had been guiding me, consciously training me. Through constant, ever deeper, ever more meticulous interactions, like how our ancestors sliced ever thinner slices of graphite until they finally sheared off a sheet of graphene, my already keen powers of perception and expression improved.

Of course, coins aren't just carried and spent. After all, Hull comes from outside the Milky Way. He has his quirks. For example, taking baths. For the first year of our flight, Hull never took a bath. One day, he suddenly announced he wanted to take one. By then I was already used to his body odor, and moreover, I believed he had never taken a bath in his entire life. He locked himself in the bathroom for three days. To reassure me, he had meaningful conversations with me through the door that separated us. Even so, I was still distracted whenever I did anything else. Unbearable fantasies of what must have been happening behind the door ran wild through my mind.

Afterwards, he told me that everyone on his planet takes this long to clean their body and waits this long in between. I asked him if I had to do the same. As he laughed, he comforted me, saying that they respected everyone's habits and customs. I don't know whether all Dieresians are like him. He obstinately refuses to cut his hair or nails. However, even if they are, I can accept that.

Brother, your letter mentioned how worried you were. You said that you tried everything but couldn't find anything about

Dieresians. Everything about them seems to be a mystery. You were afraid that I'd fallen into another trap just like before.

You'll know one way or the other soon enough. Our ship is about to reach Dieresis.

No, it'll be different this time. No matter whether that's for better or worse.

Alia Calendar 6th month, 89th year

I'm sorry about the length of my letter. I hope your wife, Jacqueline, doesn't glare at how much this space mail costs. But, brother, I can't wait to tell you what happened after I reached Dieresis.

After we disembarked, we immediately took the high-speed rail across the central axis of the city. This is Hull's hometown. I've fantasized about this mystical place so many times. In reality, it's more amazing than even my wildest fantasies. I'm sitting in an ancient form of transport that no longer exists on Earth. Streetscapes flash by on both sides. It's as though I've sunk into a contemporary city of the 21st century. Simple geometric forms pile layer by layer one on top of another. Glass facades are flooded with a metallic radiance from their sun, a rust-red star, the only sign that I've gone to outer space.

The train passes through the forest of tall buildings that is the business district, then enter a residential district of gabled Baroque-style brick buildings. Green, clawed vines of wisteria, billowing in the occasional bursts of wind, climb and fill every wall. Actually, they're creatures that imitate wisteria. Sharp, slender claws stretch from their bodies. Suckers on their abdomens glue them to the walls. Hull told me this, and when he saw my eyes, he added, smiling, that these not-wisteria vines were completely harmless.

I could feel my pupils dilate. We looked at each other and laughed.

Hull's house is not more than a few steps from the train station. It's decorated in the style of a 21st century Earth culture. Hull had obviously not put much thought into it. I didn't understand how anyone so perceptive and intelligent could bear such outdated decor.

Hull shrugged. "My darling, it's purely what you perceive through your senses, nothing to do with which era."

He pitied me but tried his best to hide that. Brushing aside my bangs, he looked into my eyes. Silently, we held each other in our arms.

Hull's right. The longer I stay here, the more I can sense the current that runs under the ordinary things. Flowing in that current, they grow translucent like jellyfish. Subtle aesthetic senses of all kinds follow the current-like tendrils, undulating slightly in its gentle ripples.

Living on Dieresis isn't any different from living on the spaceship. We spend most of the day either perceiving each other or loving each other. In other words, we train my powers of perception. Hull explained that once the sensory neurons all over my body are trained, they can be further developed to become even more powerful information processing units. My body isn't sick like Earth doctors insist. Rather, it has stronger and denser sensory neurons than ordinary humans.

"When you're that perceptive, you'll be even more like us." He smiled at me.

Immediately, I was steeped in our shared happiness. Already I could practically feel the waves of joy, their amplitude growing from the constructive interference of our mutual, unspoken mental synchronicity.

Brother, I can't wait to become a Dieresian, can't wait to get rid of my identity as a mentally ill human, can't wait to love Hull. Here, everything fits. I've returned to my true home. I've roamed away for too long.

You think we're irresponsible, caring nothing about survival to wallowing in metaphysical questions, right? Don't worry, brother. Although Dieresis looks like it hasn't developed past our stone age, their technology has long developed to our standards. Tending our miniature farm for two hours a day supplies us enough food.

I don't know whether other Dieresians also live Hull's sort of simple, frugal but fulfilling life. That said, it's weird that I've been here so long now and Hull has never once taken me outside. He, himself, also rarely leaves this house. What is the outside world like? Is our mental synchronicity and happiness common on this planet?

Alia Calendar 7th month, 89th year

Who are we? From the beginning of time, no species has ever understood itself. Even while a species rushes to invade and exploit other worlds, it still doesn't know what it is. Don't worry, brother. If I told you that I sympathize deeply with those of my petty, greedy race, would you worry even more? Your sister, who has been arrogantly tormented by mental illness for years, hasn't forgotten that she's a part of the human race. That's why I regret and limit our innate flaws.

My body is changing. Brother, perhaps it has already changed.

After I arrived, my appetite grew fivefold. I've fainted so many times because I always felt hungry. The weird thing was that I'd been losing weight. Hull urged me to eat more. I told him that my stomach can only hold so much.

"You ought to consume nutrient materials with even more calories." Hull handed me a bottle of dark red pills, then told me to take a pill before every meal.

The pill was really effective. Hunger no longer vexed me. My mind was always filled with every kind of food. I could train with Hull to develop my powers of perception again. The world was constantly multiplying by dividing. A vase was no longer a vase. A smile was no longer a smile. A shaft of light was a gathering of countless subtle gradations of color. Light waves rippled like water through the air. Every time you stared at it, you felt even more the dust flying around. They lightly touched your skin like snowflakes, making you shudder for an instant. We lingered over ever tinier things as though we saw them through millions of microscopes. What our senses gathered was gradually amplified nearly to infinity. This was a vastness that humanity had never conceived of setting foot in. It was another way of interpreting the universe. Humanity has never imagined this kind of world. Humanity has never created any words to describe it.

The initial enthusiasm has faded. I'm starting to feel tired. Because I'm following Hull so closely, I have no choice but to condense my soul, lose a little of my spirit. Some of the following will be wrong in the details.

Even if I keep up with Hull in perceiving deep and subtle layers, the difference between how keen Hull's powers of perception are and mine is huge. I'd never recognized this before, not because the difference didn't exist but because I couldn't be aware of it before. But now, I'm aware. So that I can keep up with him, more often than not, he reduces his own keenness. Brother, it's only here that I'm deeply aware that I'm human.

Sometimes, I even think Hull is in love with a monkey. And I am that monkey.

As for those red pills, can they evolve me from a monkey to a person?

I hate those pills, brother. Even on a purely physical level, they make me uncomfortable. As my perception grows keener, the discomfort becomes even more acute. For more than a few days, given half a chance, I flushed those pills down the toilet. Hull knows, I think. He just won't say so.

Tonight, the pill bottle was empty. Once again, Hull replaced it with a full bottle from his drawer. This was enough. He didn't need to say anything. I swallowed today's pills in front of him. We batted our eyelashes at each other. I told him that I wanted to go out for a stroll by myself. He didn't stop me. This was the first time I've left the house.

It didn't look like there was anything to worry about. I was just going to wander around the garden.

I followed the stairs down. It was black outside. At first, with the sound of rustling, the dampness, the thread of some flavor I can't identify, I thought it was raining. I walked quietly. The only things left in the world were the rustling and strange, regular movement in the dark that matched it. That wasn't rain. That was the swaying of vines on the wall. I imagined them as unbroken waves undulating in the dark like a dangerous sea.

The wind outside must have been fierce. What was odd, though, was I didn't hear any wind.

I pushed the door open. There was no wind, just the calm, peaceful night.

The vines shone in the moonlight, deathly pale like scars. They stood out against the surrounding shadow. Even if the moonlight were blocked by clouds, they would still cling there.

Five slender fingers stretched out as though to beckon me.

Finally, I understood what I saw. Shell-like fingernails that gave off a twinkling light. A palm that curled in a way that seemed deep with meaning. They formed a broken arm, a deathly pale severed arm. The continuously undulating vines stretched out, convulsing and twitching. A drop of a black, tepid liquid fell on my face. A little splashed into my mouth.

How would someone on Earth describe the flavor? A fishy sweetness? That flavor slid like a snake down my throat and into my stomach, then became part of me.

That was blood, brother. I grew terrified.

I fainted.

When I woke up, it was as if nothing had happened. Hull sat by the bed, his gaze soft. Even though I hadn't opened my eyes, I could feel him there. Even if I hadn't smelled his sweat or heard his breath, I would have known it was him. Only when he's sitting next to me can I feel relaxed like the sand on a riverbank.

"You fell," Hull told me.

I still hadn't opened my eyes. I didn't need to see my injuries. Not only could I clearly feel where he was but also the scratches across my skin. Hull saw my fear. His fingers lightly stroked my eyelids. I opened my eyes, then gazed at him.

He pressed up against me. Our breath grazed each other's skin. He wanted me not to be afraid. He'd say—

"That was a hallucination. You just fell, that's all."

And then he said it. We spoke to each other not to say anything but just to let the other hear. Sometimes sounds comforted more than ideas.

Brother, I love you.

Hull said that after I recover, he'd take me on a stroll. Tomorrow, the day after, or maybe next week. I crashed my smile into him. Before, I would have been meek to him. Brother, there are lots of things that I don't mind anymore.

Alia Calendar 11th month, 89th year

I haven't heard from you in a long time, brother. Have you discovered something? Hull says perhaps it's a problem in the communication system. Don't worry if you didn't receive my previous letter. It's just some nonsense I wrote under some exceptional circumstances.

It's winter here now. During the day, sunlight streams in through fogged windows. We're silent, bathed in a golden cloud of light. At dusk, after a long session of meditation, we both open our eyes at the same time, give each other an understanding smile, then greet the approaching night. These are our tightly knit and joyous days. The cold air is full of the sluggish flavor peculiar to winter, a kind of sleepy contentment that gives people tranquility.

For a few months now, my powers of perception have stagnated, but that's okay. Steeped in the aura of quiet things, I don't want even more. Hull ought to feel the same way perhaps. Once in a while, he worries, but about what? Like the scattered clouds that drift over farmland in the afternoon, that sort of anxiety is what, ultimately?

I don't intend to look for the answer. The answer will appear by itself. It always appears at the most unexpected moment, knocking fiercely at your front door until you open it.

Last night, the night of what the Dieresians call Ramayana Day—

Hull seemed out of character. After dinner, he just sat in his chair deep in thought.

"Hull, you should sleep," I said.

Slowly, he raised his eyes. His gaze fell upon my body, then pierced through it. He still hadn't seen me. I waited, waited as his gaze cut through the distant brambles, then back to me again. Soon his expression returned to normal, and cautiously, he held my hand.

"Hi, Irina," he called out, soft and hoarse.

His voice both shook and was filled with wonder as if this were the first time he'd ever said this name. I thought about our first meeting. I guess I must have smiled. His hand caressed my cheek. A bright, hot wind roared through my veins.

At that moment, we thought the same things.

But Hull didn't get out of his chair. He sat motionless as though he were nailed down.

"Have you ever wondered how two species separated by many tens of thousands of light-years can have practically the same physical appearance?" he asked.

"But actually?"

"We merely look as though we're the same. Unlike Earth people, in the Dieresian body, the cell is not the basic building block of life. Rather, every cell is a complete life unto itself. They all have independent circulatory and nervous systems. They are capable of being self-supporting and thinking for themselves. To integrate them requires a lot of calories. We have to consume a lot of calories."

I nodded my head. I finally understood why he took so long to bathe. He had to be especially careful in dealing with his hair and flakes of his skin. As far as he was concerned, every cell was priceless. How is he supposed to deal with naturally replaced cells?

"Do you finally understand what I'm saying?" he asked.

"Yes, you all have mental and sensory capabilities that I can't even hope to reach," I answered.

He stared at me for a long time without saying a word.

Now, as I'm writing this letter, the memory of dim light is a reminder. I play back the scene, at long last understanding that expression that flashed across his face, the expression that burned in his eyes like flame. At first, it was despair.

The clock tolled. Twelve o'clock. Midnight fell.

"Come, let's walk outside," Hull said. Before I could react, he was already out the door.

I called out his name as I chased him. He stood at the head of the stairs waiting for me.

"Wear a coat. You'll be cold," he said.

Eventually, we reached the street. The area was deserted, only us two pedestrians. Hull walked quickly, as though he were in a hurry to make an important appointment. I had to jog to keep up with him. If I weren't careful, the swift figure in front of me would disappear in the dusky light. The street was so calm. All I heard was the echoing of our footsteps like the beating of drums in the African jungle before hunters catch their prey. Except I didn't know who was the prey.

I could barely keep up because of how much Hull's change had hurt me. Even if I exerted all my strength, the best I could do was catch a glimpse of him when he turned a corner, then jog to catch up. The gap between us grew larger and larger. I almost lost him completely. In the central square, no matter what, I couldn't even find his shadow. Fortunately, just then I heard his footsteps.

Not far away, Hull was climbing up a thousand-step flight of stairs to the central square's high platform.

A building squatted like giant creature from ancient times at the top of the stairs, waiting for us to arrive. This giant building had twelve, maybe more, archways leading inside. A roundel filled with radial tracery sat at the top of every archway. Pillars stood next to the archways and reliefs filled the arched doors. Towers with countless spires licked the black sky like flames.

"Hull," I shouted, but it came out soft and hoarse.

Hull stopped, but only for a moment. He start climbing again, this time more quickly, towards the shadow the building cast. Soon he disappeared into the middle archway.

I had no other choice. I followed him in.

My memories of that night seem to have been altered. Some parts have been deliberately stretched out, every detail clearly noted. Other parts leave only blurred contours.

I guess I remember going through a winding corridor. That was difficult in this dark world. At its end I pushed open a heavy gate. A surge of light hit my eyes. Crystal clear, sweet light. Light like spring water. I heard a beautiful chorus of men, women, children, old people singing softly in perfect homophony. Their harmony was like feathers drifting one after another to the ground. A soprano voice soared, piercing the buttresses and rib vaults. It reverberated in the lofty, open space.

Overhead, the ribs intersected into a dome with an eight-pointed star. Large, resplendent gems were set in the smooth arch faces between the star's ribs, forming an eight-petaled flower that burst forth into light. The pistil was a transparent net that shot out flame-like from the flower of light.

"Welcome," the light said to me.

No, the light didn't speak words, but I understood what it meant, like how Hull and I understood each other.

I was here. Hull appeared by my side. Once again, he grabbed my hand.

"Where is this?"

"This is Eden. Mankind's first home. We walked away from here then, finally we returned again for the sake of the complete."

"I don't understand."

"They are our inevitable final forms."

That last was Hull's voice. He was behind me. When I turned to face him, the light receded like the tide. Close to a hundred elders wearing short-sleeved white robes belted at the waist stood in the space that the light had once filled.

"You are not of our clan." The most senior of the elders walked out of the crowd to greet us.

His gaze flitted past the two of us, and he immediately understood everything about us. That face of indeterminate age revealed a faint trace of—for now, let's call it something like a smile. Brother, I don't have the words to describe what was happening. Those mysterious, unspeakable consciousnesses melded into one. Within the flow of those merged consciousnesses, all individuality disappeared, replaced by boundless freedom and an incomparably keen sense of "I."

I am a life that has countless independent wills and thoughts—our cells have united.

I am one among innumerable lives that form one huge body.

I am one creation among everything created in the universe, one part of a successful world, a form that transitioned from tiny to huge, a connection in a mystical network to the outside.

I, every I, gathered here after this realization, shared their perception and cognition completely, the experience of life accumulated here without end, like crystals of wisdom.

I am the most perfect form in the evolution of Dieresians and also that of any high-order life-form in this universe.

At the time when I become "I," I am outside of time, outside of cause and effect, coming infinitely closer on the infinitely long road, finally about to reach the core.

Our world is one section of huge force without peer, without beginning, without end, galloping and howling seas, forever wandering smooth forms, forever returning, a returning that takes infinite years; all things are uniform, steadfast through the ages, forever observing carefully and tirelessly, steeped in and drunk on the wisdom and beauty of the universe.

"This is the form that we eventually want to become." I sighed as though I was talking in my sleep. "How do I become 'I'?"

Those who have become complete experience existence. The happiness they feel is boundless. The suffering they bear is critically grave. You will be weak, be seduced, be confronted with a choice. Don't let the green flame consume you. Don't become food for carnivores.

I wanted to say that I didn't understand, but the most senior of the elders had already returned to his companions. They started singing again. The elders and their profound gaze disappeared into the light that once again shrouded them. We quietly and respectfully backed our way out.

As we climbed down the stairs, Hull explained wordlessly to me that he considered experience much more important than speech. That's why he waited until the night of Ramayama Day, when the spirit collective can take physical form, before bringing me.

"Also ..."

"What?"

We stopped walking and gazed at each other.

"The drugs I gave you were indeed high-calorie nourishment pills. Ganglions need ample nourishment to grow and develop."

"You know, I've never doubted anything."

Holding each other's hand, we continued towards the public square.

"Is it that all Dieresians can ultimately become a spirit collective? What does it mean for a spirit collective to be complete?"

"Some will abandon completeness."

"Why?"

"Because that's much easier. They keep only parts that are necessary. Being able to survive is enough."

"We won't do that, right?"

"Right." He tightened his grip on my hand.

"Hull, even if I loved you with all of my body and mind, I still wouldn't think that was enough. I also want you to use all of your body and mind to answer me. All of everything."

As if I said some things I shouldn't have said, Hull, somber and pale, didn't say any more. Even though I didn't use a deep layer of my powers of perception, I still knew he was struggling with pain. That was something I was utterly incapable of understanding at the time. I was afraid. Nameless, outmoded concerns once again floated to the top of my head.

Just at that moment, a red bus slowly drove up from behind us.

"Look, Hull, a bus. Can it take us home?"

"Yes."

I waved down the bus, then got in. He didn't immediately follow me. He just stood by the bus, his face ashen. I suddenly realized something irreversible was about to happen. Just as I thought about getting off the bus, it started to move. Hull got on just before the bus doors closed.

We were the only ones on the bus, no other passengers, no conductor, not even a driver. The empty seats and the handrails gleamed. Once the dim overhead light went out, the bus grew dark and nearly silent. All I could hear was the sound of the motor. We were like visitors who'd stumbled into the wrong cemetery. In the dark, countless invisible eyes glared at us coldly. The air grew thick with a faint, sweet, but nauseating flavor.

I felt squished. The bus was jammed full of round shadows. I could feel the rise and fall of their breath on my skin.

The bus turned suddenly. I nearly fell. Hull grabbed hold of me. Light from a streetlamp cut through the shadow of the driver's seat. Like a bolt of lightning, it hit the two hands gripping the steering wheel so tight their knuckles had grown white. They steered the bus and controlled its speed with a practiced assurance as though they were connected to arms and received instructions from a brain rather than being two isolated palms sliced off at the wrist. They were not bleeding. The cuts were extremely smooth and expertly done. They didn't even leave scars. Although the hands were laborer's hands, they were moist and shone white like the hands of a pampered lady.

This scene looked familiar, but I couldn't remember where I'd seen it before. Where could I have seen it before?

A leg lay flat just in front of my seat.

A dignified face turned around on a mechanical stand to stare at me.

A mouth connected to a tongue and windpipe glided by underfoot, weak and limp, in a miniature wheelchair. It stopped next to the driver's seat and said something.

The light turned red and the bus, brakes slammed, lurched to a stop. Two hands connected to robust arms rushed to grab the bus's rings. A woman who only had an upper body held onto a man who only had a lower body. A headless body with its legs crossed sat perfectly still.

The bus arrived at the station. Two slender, perfectly straight legs "pushed" me towards the bus's rear door. A pair of massive breasts in a bra squeezed past me off the bus. An ass wearing rubber underpants with the help of mechanical legs followed me off the bus.

I looked behind me. Hull. I shouted his name. It wasn't until then, brother, that I discovered that I was laughing. Laughter shuddered through my body, then splattered out. I was mad. You think so, too, right? However, it would have been so much better if I'd actually gone mad.

Hull didn't say anything. He was still there in the form of a complete body. I couldn't help thinking about what he'd look like after he'd been split into pieces. He—I should say "they," what would they look like? Maybe the hands that once used to hold me in their grasp. Maybe his burning hot lips. Maybe his eyes.

I looked at him in the distance, using my gaze to cut him and every other sort of compound form apart. Over and over, the real world fell apart in front of me. Because this was absurd, I didn't feel any fear. I started to doubt my memories of these past few months. Perhaps I'd really gone mad. Everything involving Hull was the product of an unbridled imagination, my work of art created while I stayed at the madhouse.

Even I as I write this letter, I'm still not completely sure. Does this world exist?

No, brother, you're wrong. I'm wrong, too. Hull's right. Just like when he grabbed me so tightly he nearly broke my bones.

He said, "Don't make a sound. You exasperate them. They're all perfectly normal Dieresians."

I remembered the words he said to me at home not too long ago. Now I understood what he meant. Laughter gushed out in unending spurts. Involuntarily, I bent over in convulsion.

Cold hatred gathered like nimbus clouds from every corner. From a mouth, a hand, an arm, or a waist, from any piece of the human body you can imagine dismembering. We stood in the midst of a violent storm. Hull was a terrifying sight to behold.

"They will attack us if you don't stop talking!"

My eyes were startled open wide. He hated me. That's for certain. Hidden behind the shadow of fear was him being fed up with and disappointed in me.

And my disgust towards this horrible and ugly race along with the hate of Hull himself were written clearly on my face.

We looked at each other in dismay, panting in coarse breaths. Because we'd just looked carelessly down at an abyss from on high and saw it for what it truly was, we felt dizzy.

It passed in a moment no longer than a flash of lightning. For us, it was more than long enough.

Why don't I stop writing here? It seems like everything is over. I'm very tired.

Alia Calendar 4th month, 90th year

Brother, how are you doing? Did you get my letter? I think I've lost you again. I think I've lost a lot of things, irretrievably. I maintain an indifferent attitude as I watch the current of time sweep them away. After this year of struggle, Hull and I finally gave up on our marriage. It was like an abandoned spaceship. We each sat in our respective escape pods, separate windows gazing at the steel, island-like spaceship slowly drifting in the the vast, desolate universe.

There was nothing we could do about it. We tried hard to forget what happened in the bus on Ramayana Day, but we couldn't. In the worst case, whenever we saw people being affectionate with each other, we couldn't dismiss the hate deep in our hearts. All I had to do was look at his face, and I'd think about it.

We pretended to forget, only to bring it up deliberately as a weapon when we fought. We'd turn it into evidence for whatever we accused the other of. Then we'd pretend to forget again. Yes, we were still deeply in love. And it's because of that, the pain hurt even more. I envy those Dieresians who'd broken themselves into pieces. They look so calm and composed. They're half-alive, but because of special technology, they're able to work, eat, sleep, even have sex. They're not too different from the humans I've met. Sometimes I feel like I'm still on Earth. Everything that happened before is really just a fantasy in my mind.

Just a bit of doubt and the crack you admit to will never fully heal. You'll never have a way to acknowledge that he and this letter are real. What about you, brother? Hull, my Hull, and the infinitely vast and subtle sensory realm Hull and I experienced together?

Just a bit of doubt and you lose a universe.

I lost a universe, but this doesn't at all make me feel any better. Even if I discover that it was all a fantasy, I'd still feel the stabs of pain. You are hated by a man you deeply love. You hate a man you deeply love. These two facts torment me to no end, drive me crazy. If it's a fantasy, then why does it hurt so much. What's the matter with me, brother? All of it was real, without a doubt.

Finally, to restore our love, Hull suggested he cut his memory. He said Dieresians' memories are stored in different places all over the body. Just excise that section and that memory completely goes away.

"I looked further into this. They said all I have to do was cut off a pinky. If I do the surgery, at least one of us can start anew. I can go on to love without the blemish of our mutual hate."

Hull tried to convince me. I didn't answer right away. There was something serious stopping me from agreeing with this intimate, seductive offer. I didn't know what. Something deep in my heart resisted. I spent several days searching for what.

One day, I sat by the window. The chilly and moist air of early spring seeped through my skin into the dark jungle of my heart. Suddenly I understood what had stopped me. At the same time, I realized that Hull and I were over.

"You shouldn't have that surgery. At least not for my sake. Because I don't want you to become like those people on the bus. Because I can't bear to be with a man who is incomplete. Because what I want is all of you. All of you. Do you understand? Do you still remember our conversation outside the Lord's palace? What I want is completeness. If you aren't the complete you, then I won't love you anymore."

Hull quickly grew paler and paler. The blood in his veins all rushed into his heart. He became so pale, he seemed transparent. Madly, I wanted to rush up to and hug this transparent man, but I didn't.

"You can't bear an incomplete me. You also can't face a complete but flawed me," Hull said in a hoarse voice. He'd immediately understood what I'd meant.

We stared at each other, merely stared at each other.

The day that I left, Hull took me to the spaceport. When we reached its ground floor, he suddenly stopped. He looked at me with an odd expression.

"You're going to go. Don't you want to see the green flame?"

For a moment I didn't understand, but my body started trembling for no reason. A sharp chill climbed up my spine. I tried to ignore what he said, but my gaze involuntarily followed his and fell on the green, clawed vines on the wall.

The spirit collective's words emerged from the secluded valley of my memory.

Don't let the green flame swallow you. Don't become food for carnivores.

"It's said that they are this world's dominators. They're a higher-order life-form than even us. What's even more bizarre, it's claimed that we are their livestock, grazing on the pasture. They designed our bodies, then waited. When we can't bear life and choose to abandon completeness, the parts of our body we offer up they use as food." Hull's eyes were vacant. The corners of his mouth revealed a smile both tranquil and strange. I had the misimpression that he already had the surgery. "Our surgeries are actually really easy. All we have to do is go to them naked. They know which part they ought to eat. They're never wrong."

The shuddering started as a burst from below, then diffused outward through the vines as a nonstop pulsing. They understood what Hull said. Like a starving, bloodthirsty beast that has sniffed out the scent of blood, they became wild beyond compare. Their leaves spun, their runners twisted, their tiny, thrashing claws scratched the walls.

A seething ocean roiled before my eyes. It spit out an immense column of raging flames that couldn't wait to swallow all life that was red, raw, and sweet.

The vines rustled, a sound that was too familiar. I seemed to have heard it before. The sound resembled the violent scratching of sharp claws against my bones.

"You don't need to be afraid. They know what they need to do." Hull sounded as though he were talking to himself in his sleep.

I covered my face, then ran to the train station. Brother, the entire city was ablaze. That green flame hissed. It danced madly and seductively, so that it could swallow this world.

The train arrived. It took me away, from one high tower of green flame to another, then beyond.

Right now, I'm leaping through space on a spaceship. As for Hull, not long ago, I received his voicemail. He told me he's already amputated both of his hands. Now, even though he remembers me, he's no longer in pain. Brother, I'm on my way home, a complete person.

ላሊበላ ፡ አለም ከ ገብርኤል ቴዎድሮስ

Lalibela

Gabriel Teodros

ላሊበላ : *la·li·be·la*
(noun)
1. *A town in Northern Ethiopia, famous for its eleven monolithic rock-cut buildings (how they were built is unknown).*
2. *(Amharic) A given name, meaning "even the bees recognized its sovereignty".*

ADDIS ABABA, ETHIOPIA. Present Day.

The key was hidden in plain sight. In twisted metal and shapes within shapes. In fractals and complex geometric patterns people just accepted as religious symbolism. They called it a cross, but it was no crucifix. The truth was buried generations deep and kept there by nothing but a common belief. Most people wore a variation of it around their neck. Some had it sewn into fabric. Like the history of all humanity, it was buried in Ethiopia under nothing but a thin layer of dust.

His appearance started as a tiny piece of metal that appeared in the rubble on the side of a road. Insignificant, barely noticeable. The metal multiplied itself and then multiplied itself again, growing in the same pattern of what people would, then recognize as a Meskel. Soon it stood upright, and it grew taller and taller as light bled through every opening in the pattern. When it was tall enough for him to pass through, an old man appeared from the light, holding onto the cross. When he was fully present, the light was gone. He seemed out of time, wearing all white the way a monk would.

Cars sped by, people walked past, and donkeys carrying wood scurried about, seemingly oblivious to a human that just appeared out of thin air.

"You can't just expect us to wait forever," a young man yelled at the elder in the overcrowded Addis Ababa traffic. "Either move on or get out of my way!"

Gebre Mesqel Lalibela had had quite the journey and was understandably shaken up. In his time, Ethiopian technology allowed his people to build computers, teleportation devices, starships, and even a spaceport in the highlands of Roha. There people lived in buildings on top of buildings that were all carved from a single rock. There were many people that he loved that he had to say goodbye to as they went on trips to distant galaxies, knowing he may never see them again. Yet nothing he saw, then compared to the chaos surrounding him now. In this new capital of the country he ruled over 800 years earlier, what he saw made him wish time machines were never invented.

The air now smelled like a black pepper, and the sky was covered by a smoke that didn't move. It was different than clouds, different than a fire, and it made it hard for him to breathe. The streets were crowded with moving vehicles that coughed up this poison and people and animals and no logic in how it all fit together. There were huge palaces lined with people sleeping on the street. More vehicles than he could count, yet he still found people unable to walk, crawling between them.

He leaned on the cross like it was the only thing holding him up, and thought, "How have we become so close and so distant at the exact same time?"

መስቀል : *me·s·ke·l*
(noun)
1. (Ge'ez) *A processional cross, there are four basic styles with hundreds of variations. It's common uses are in church services, as prayer sticks, for exorcisms, and basic time travel.*

ROHA HIGHLANDS. 1141 E.C. (1148 AD)

Lalibela's mother often spoke of a swarm of bees that surrounded him just after she gave birth. Her heart stopped for a moment, thinking her baby would be stung to death; but the bees swarmed, surrounded, and then mysteriously left her child completely untouched. This was a signal to her that Lalibela was not hers alone.

He would do great things, he would even lead the country. The bees had recognized his sovereignty.

The burden of being this leader was placed upon him before he even knew how to walk. Like another swarm of bees surrounding him, Lalibela grew up between the pressure of his parents and the jealousy of extended family members and his older siblings. He often just wanted to run away, and when he was old enough, he did, as much as he could. Roha at the time overlooked a forest. It was like beachfront property over an ocean of treetops. Lalibela loved to submerge himself in the trees, observing and learning from nature all around him. As a child he was captivated by the complexity of simple things. Patterns in spider webs. Roots of trees that grew above the Earth. Neither his imagination nor his body could be contained. Not by anyone's tradition, expectations, or beliefs.

He was the youngest child, and his mother's favorite son, whether she would admit it or not. His imagination was a threat to the establishment, and aside from his mother, the royal family despised him for it. He simply wasn't motivated by power even when it was what his mother wanted him to have. Out of jealousy, when Lalibela's older brother Kedus Harbe inherited the throne, one of his first acts as King was to secretly have Lalibela poisoned.

It was an herbal potion that came with a plate of shiro, and instead of killing Lalibela it put him to sleep for three days. The visions and dreams he had during that time was something that would come to define his life, even more than the bees had.

In a state close to death, Lalibela was transported through space and time. His spirit traveled light years to other worlds, where he saw technology that hadn't been invented yet and Ethiopians that were taking care of multiple planets. He saw people's faces he had never met from parts of Ethiopia he had never seen, and everywhere he went he was with this eclectic group of farmers, scientists, and artists. They felt like family he had never met, and with them he felt like he could fly. From the stars he traveled back to the Roha highlands overlooking that ocean of treetops, but things were different now; and there was a magnetic focus on the volcanic rock underneath his birthplace. He saw the spaceport that would be built there, literally carved into the mountain with water passageways connecting every building. It was a new foundation, and as such it would be called Addis Yerusalem.

When he finally awoke, he was in a room with only his mother by his side.

"Gebiye, you keep talking in your sleep. What is it you see?"

"Emaye ... I've seen what I must do. It's like three heavens just opened up and became one. In the stars, on the Earth, and within ourselves."

"My son has died and come back to life!" his mother wept.

He never bothered explaining more of his dreams to her or even blaming his brother for this near-death journey. He didn't want to get in another fight, and he still didn't want to be the leader his mother wanted him to be, the leader his brother feared. He just needed to build what he saw and find the people he saw in those visions. It was as if he never knew why he was alive until he almost died.

መንኮራኩር ፡ *mä·n·ko·ra·ku·r*
(noun)
1. (Ge'ez) *A spaceship.*

ARBA MINCH. 1159 E.C. (1166 AD)

Lalibela learned the beauty his culture truly holds by spending time on a farm in the South. He was undercover, starting to grow a beard, and no one recognized him as a member of the royal family. The kindness of strangers in these parts of the country both broke and strengthened his heart on a daily basis. He was invited to eat in the homes of people who barely had anything, who offered him everything they had and took it as an insult if he refused. He realized being raised as royalty had isolated him from the experience of having true friends.

The farmers he stayed with were beekeepers as well, which he took as a sign that he must be on the right path. From the farmers he learned how to work the land, and from the bees he learned how to use the stars and the curve of the Earth as a guide. Every day felt like seven, and he had never felt so alive. His best friend during this time was the farmer's daughter, Kibra. She made trips selling food at the market on a regular basis and had become an expert mathematician. In her spare time she experimented with inventing new tools.

"Why are you always following me to the market?" Kibra asked with a half-smile one day. "Don't you have something better to do?"

"Anything I could be doing would be better with you," Lalibela responded without hesitation, "but if you want me to go, I'll go."

"No, I want you to stay."

Kibra was the first person Lalibela shared all his visions and dreams with, and in time the visions blossomed and became their dream together. He was the first person who ever challenged her. She was the first person to fully see him. She was much smarter than him, but he had more ambition. Somehow they made a perfect team. And they were completely in love.

The young couple spent most of the next decade with their hands in the dirt, honey in their tea, experimenting and traveling throughout the Ethiopian countryside. Compared to his upbringing in Roha, everything in the countryside was so new. He looked at the world as if he was seeing it for the first time, and this helped Kibra see things differently as well. Together they unlocked potential in one another. They worked hard and played harder, until the work felt like play.

Everything in the villages was shared, from food and resources to labor. If just one person yielded a good crop, no one went hungry. The idea of just having a single occupation was foreign. A farmer with a science lab in a gojo who also happened to be an expert krar player was a very natural thing. In fact, everyone sang and played music. This simple but rare combination of people following their passions, innovating and learning from the arts, science, and nature fed into an entire Ethiopian renaissance completely contained and isolated to itself. While the Crusaders were violently expanding from Europe and Saladin was defending Egypt and pushing back, Ethiopia turned inwards and expanded from a growth inside that took them all the way to the stars.

Every technological leap that happened in this time period started in a small village or on a farm. Kibra worked with a group of craftspeople, masons, and beekeepers to develop the first computer. She taught them a system of complex multiplication that she was able to do in her head, which became the foundation of the coding system that their computers were based on. She worked with Lalibela to assemble materials based on the structures built by bees in a beehive. Soon what they created was able to function as a calculator, predict weather, and to replicate itself.

Kibra and Lalibela's relationship was like a quiet nucleus in the center of this renaissance. It wasn't Lalibela or Kibra alone that made anything happen, but it was the connection they shared that transformed each of them as well as everyone they interacted with. They saw each other and believed in each other's dreams enough to make what seemed impossible completely real.

● ● ●

ROHA HIGHLANDS. 1174 E.C. (1181 AD)

Fifteen years later, when Lalibela finally returned from the countryside to Roha, it was not to claim the throne. It was only to propose the idea of building a spaceport. As sure as bees are vital to life on planet Earth as pollinators, Lalibela thought outside of the planet and dreamed of pollinating the stars. He arrived with Kibra and a whole community of friends who had become family.

Lalibela's mother shed tears of joy when her son returned, and all of Roha had a celebration. It was her joy that kept him safe. His brother Kedus feared that Lalibela had come to take his place as king, and that night he secretly ordered one of his guards to cut Lalibela's throat while he slept. What Kedus didn't know was that this particular guard had grown especially fond of Lalibela's mother and was so happy to see her ecstatic and full of joy. He couldn't stand to be the one to take away her joy, so that night the guard cut Kedus Harbe's throat instead.

A day of celebration was followed by a time of mourning, and no one ever knew why or by whom Kedus Harbe was murdered in the middle of the night. The only one who truly mourned was his mother, as he was as ruthless to the people as he was to his own brother.

Lalibela was then offered the throne, but he didn't want it. His mother tried to pressure him, but it had no effect. A conversation with Kibra was the only thing that could change his mind.

"If you take the throne, you won't have to do things the way they've been done before," Kibra reasoned. "Ethiopia needs a new kind of leadership. The kind that isn't power-hungry."

"I agree that Ethiopia needs a new kind of leadership, but how do we center the needs of the farmers here in the capital?" Lalibela questioned. "Before I ran away and met you, I never even saw what really made this country what it is."

"That perspective you have now is why this moment is important. And the fact that you don't want to dominate is another reason I fell in love with you. You won't be alone here anymore," she reassured him.

"So you'll still marry me?" Lalibela asked.

"How is this even a question in your mind?" Kibra smirked.

With new leadership and an influx of newcomers from the countryside, the energy in Roha grew electric. The people believed

Lalibela traveled with angels since the people he came with were able to do things they had seen no human do. Even now, 800 years later, people still say the spaceport in Roha was built at night by angels. They will say it was built by angels before they will say it was anything but a church. The spaceport was built by regular people inspired to create something for more than themselves, and that creative spirit has always had a way of keeping people up at night. They built machines that cut through rock like butter, and amongst eleven structures formed a launch pad for starships that was loosely based on the mechanics of lily pads and frogs.

Lalibela and Kibra led Ethiopia together. Never losing touch with the countryside, the capital was transformed inside and out. There were more than a few villages with aspirations to see the heavens, and people traveled from as far as West Africa and India to take flight from the Roha spaceport. The country was flourishing, and Roha became a cosmopolitan center.

"Let's go see the future," Lalibela proposed the idea to Kibra one day. "If we are to have children, I want to see the world their great-great-great grandchildren are to inherit."

"Why not?" Kibra chuckled, amused by her partner's spontaneity. "How about the year 3000?"

Ethiopian engineering by this time had gotten to a microscopic level, and again, based on a bee's perception, the farmers and scientists had found a way to slip through the very fabric of time. It started when they realized bees could perceive movements at $1/300^{th}$ of a second versus human's perception at $1/50^{th}$. Once they developed instruments that could perceive movements and navigate as fast as the bees, it wasn't as complicated to fine-tune the perception even further. Soon they found pockets in space at a submicroscopic level where matter appeared and disappeared seemingly at random. When they realized that simply observing these anomalies was actually changing how they occurred, they were able to communicate with the pockets and little by little slip right through the space-time continuum. Time travel was always possible and is actually always happening, but in Ethiopia most people just use it to make the good moments last longer.

ራእይ : *ra'·əy*
(noun)
1. (Amharic) *vision.*
2. *a revelation.*

GONDAR. The year 3000.

"Have you ever heard those stories of when we were people?" a young dragon asked the other while dancing in flight and playing catch with a ball of fire. "They say we were creative. Even all the ruins below us were structures that we built, and we used to live inside of them. Now we only destroy. Destroy just so it can be rebuilt, someday when we become human again."

"If our descendants ever become human again," the other dragon interjected.

The air felt like an oven. The sky was black, and small fires were everywhere, burning all that was left of what could have been a city. The whole world looked like the inside of a volcano.

A blue light emerged, and the air rippled as Lalibela and Kibra stepped through a space pocket. A hot wind rushed across their faces as they looked up to see several enormous creatures descending from the sky. Dragons landed all around them, shadows dancing over green scales and piercing eyes. One dragon stepped front and center. It crouched down to a human level and spoke in a voice both calm and massive.

"Human time travelers. Welcome. Earth is now our home. We were here before your reign on the planet, and we rose again after."

"After?" Lalibela trembled.

"We have studied your ruins and the stories you left behind. It is apparent to us that humanity did not have to end its time on Earth in the way that it did."

"I don't understand ... what happened? Where are we? Is this Ethiopia?" Kibra asked.

"This is what you left. If you wish to prolong your existence on the planet, you must begin to understand that you, all humans, and all life on Earth are inextricably linked. You are all one organism. Even us now, you are a part of us, and we are a part of you. There is no separation."

"That makes sense to me, scientifically speaking," Lalibela agreed.

The dragon's nostrils flared. "Yes, time travelers always say they understand. Your ego is a problem. As a species, the stories you left tell of division and hierarchy. You constantly fought wars with each other while exploiting resources you knew would make the planet inhospitable for generations to come. You must act on what you say you understand if you wish to travel back to this time and see what your people could have done. The atmosphere isn't safe for you now. It is clear to us that something went horribly wrong for you in the 21st century."

"Why are you helping us?" Kibra asked, visibly frightened.

"You are the children of dragons, and we are what you will eventually become. There is no more time for you here. Go back and get what you lost."

The other dragons who hadn't said a word suddenly exhaled in unison, and a ring of fire surrounded the two time travelers. They had no choice but to step through another space pocket into the past, immediately.

ROHA HIGHLANDS. 1180 E.C. (1187 AD)

"Lalibela, I think our most important work is here in the present," Kibra reasoned. The immensity of what she had seen convinced her the whole idea of time travel was ineffective.

Lalibela's childhood habit of running away to explore was kicking in again. "But you heard that dragon, you saw their world! We can do something. We have to go to the 21st century."

"Then go if you must. I'll still be here when you return. I don't want you to go, but I don't want to hold you somewhere you don't want to be either." Her heart ached, but she meant it.

Lalibela's first trips to the future were brief, but they became longer. The amount of time he was gone from the present was time that he really missed. He could never go back exactly to the moment he left. Kibra eventually did give birth to a son, Yetbarak, who grew up knowing more stories of his father than the actual person. Lalibela became a wanderer in time, so obsessed with this idea of saving the future that he never saw what it was causing him to lose. Kibra raised their son, led the country, and she completed the most extensive construction project Roha had ever seen. The love between Lalibela and Kibra never diminished even as the distance between them increased. Lalibela existed in all time, and no time, while the world continued on its path. Slowly, pieces were lost, drifting like petals on water.

In a few generations' time, all Kibra and Lalibela had built was remembered only as religious folklore.

● ● ●

ADDIS ABABA. Present Day.

Lalibela still didn't know exactly what to say or who to say it to. Even as a king, he looked at the palaces and knew the true power wasn't there. He wandered the noisy streets and felt desperation in his bones. A need to touch earth and feel water but deeper than that was a need to tell people what he knew. Every now and then someone would ask for his blessing but most just saw him as a crazy old man. History may have regarded him as a saint, but alone, he was no hero.

On this day, a child saw Lalibela emerge from a space pocket in the busy Addis Ababa streets. The young girl stared at the man who had appeared from nowhere. He turned, and she saw his face.

"Gashe, I know you," she said out loud, voice trembling. "I thought you were only a legend," she said softly as she moved closer towards him.

Lalibela looked down at her, sadly. She was very thin and wore a T-shirt with an image of Thomas Sankara and the words "Invent the Future" written across in Amharic: "ወደፊትን መፍጠር." She had a look of hunger in her eyes but also, he realized, of determination.

Then she boldly reached out a hand to grab his. A burst of blue light filled the air around them.

"This is strange," Lalibela murmured. "I have not felt this for centuries. Not since my people remembered how to slip through time. I have traveled on my own for so long, trying to make things right. But I am not strong enough. Perhaps, multiplied by two ..."

The girl stared up at him without speaking. The minutes stretched, the light spiraled, and Lalibela's heart sank. She does not understand, he thought. It was a mistake.

"Well," she said impatiently, "are you going to show me how to move through time, or do I have to figure it out on my own?"

Lalibela smiled at her, a bright star in the midst of so much chaos. Her fire reminded him of one that burned now in the distant past.

"Let me tell you a story." Lalibela held the child's hand, and together they walked out of time.

The Copper Scarab

K. Tempest Bradford

The herd of chariots that carried Amatashteret and her entourage away from the capital toward the grand pyramids towering on the horizon departed just as the Kheper-dawn lit the sky enough to travel safely at speed. Behind them, a cloud of sand obscured the buildings falling under the horizon, and after a short time, they all stopped looking back wondering if they'd be followed. Amatashteret was sure Yacob-Hur wouldn't bother coming after her even if she hadn't asked permission to take this trip as she should have done.

There were many more important shoulds weighing on her heart. How the members of the High House should have been celebrating the Feast of Iset, but weren't. How Yacob-Hur should have been preparing to take his place in the Spirit House and petition Hathor to slow the sun's journey across the sky on this, the shortest day of the year, but wasn't. How the Nile should have flooded her banks six months ago, but hadn't. For the third year in a row.

All of these shoulds were more important than anything else at the moment, even incurring the Chieftain's displeasure. She'd weathered it before.

A little over a shade after leaving, they were close enough to see the buildings beyond the pyramids that surrounded the Great Lioness: the Library of the Horizon. Amatashteret hadn't seen this place since she'd been sent to Canaan. It looked the same, yet different. Diminished. There were no people swarming the pyramids, their gleaming limestone facades devoid of scholars, and few people on the avenues between buildings. At least those were still intact. After the invasion many cities were attacked and nearly destroyed. Not here.

Amatashteret turned to watch her daughters' faces as they passed between the Pyramid of the Heart and of the Spirit. They stared with wide eyes and mouths at the artificial mountains. She asked the charioteers to slow down, so they could properly see the words written on the limestone. The dense symbol-script of the Khemetans started at the base of each side and went all the way up to the top. The knowledge of millennia preserved on the greatest engineering achievements in the world. She wanted them to see and to want to see more. She was doing this all for them. For all the daughters. For Khemet.

When they rolled up to the Library's administrative building, a woman stood alone on the steps. She was a full-blooded Khemetan with rich, dark brown skin and short, tight curls crowning her head. From the jewelry at her neck and the tattoos on her arms, Amatashteret could tell she was the Superior librarian. She was much younger than the woman who'd been Superior when Amatashteret studied here. She wondered if the older woman had retired or died during the war. And how many Supreme librarians under her must have died or left for a woman barely thirty inundations to rise to this position. Young or not, the expression she wore spoke of a formidable woman who took her duties seriously. Foremost, protecting the library from the invaders. From her.

Amatashteret brushed the sand from her robes and approached the steps.

"Superior, I am Amatashteret, daughter of Meritiset, and a Sister of Seshet." She paused to allow the woman to take in that information. "I'm here to solicit your counsel. May my daughters and I enter?"

The Superior's mouth turned down, and her eyes narrowed just for a beat.

"Why does an Amorite princess need the counsel of an Khemetan inferior?"

"I *am* Khemetan."

The Superior nodded to the Chariots, then looked back to her. "Amorite transportation. Amorite drivers. Coming from the seat of Amorite control in this region."

"My mother was Khemetan, and I was educated *here*. These men are my father's kin."

Many beats passed, and the Superior did not move or change her expression. Amatashteret took one more step forward and said, "I'm here to beg your help in restoring ma'at—balance—to Khemet. Something we both want, yes?"

The Superior made her wait another moment before bowing her head. "I am Kemanut. It would be my honor to break my fast with you and your daughters before you continue on."

Not the welcome she hoped for. Still, the woman hadn't turned them away. One step closer to the copper scarab.

● ● ●

When Amatashteret had last been in the Superior's receiving room, the cubbies that lined the walls were filled with papyrus scrolls and there were always dozens of scholars around the many low tables scattered throughout the large, open space. Now the room was nearly empty of everything familiar. The only things left were the images of Seshet, Djehuti, and Piteh looking down on them from the walls. She felt again a sense of not quite rightness—a feeling that had come upon her again and again since she returned to Khemet. A part of her wanted to come back here and find it the same as when she left. An oasis of rightness when everything else was so wrong. It made no sense to hope for that, given everything that happened. She could let it make her angry or make her despair, or she could accomplish what she came here to do.

After they observed the formalities—food and beer offered and accepted and imbibed—Kemanut sat across from her and waited with an expectant and skeptical expression.

Amatashteret considered how to begin.

"First, a question. Is the copper scarab still here?"

"The ... scarab?" Kemanut's surprise at the query was clear, as was her reluctance to admit she knew about the machine's existence.

"The last year I was here, the engineers were working on recreating the copper scarabs the Ancients used when they built the pyramids of the Heart, Spirit, and Word. We had the frame, and when I left they had worked out how to create the tubes that would carry the steam it ran on. Did they finish?"

"Why do you want to know?"

"After my husband, a Khemetan, went to the West, my father asked me to go to the land of his fathers to be a bridge between our cultures. I did, not realizing the true intention of his request. He knew the Amorite Patriarchs intended to take advantage of the instability of the High House. He wanted my daughters and me away from harm. When we arrived, his kin kept us in Canaan until after the fighting ended. Even after Yacob-Hur established control, my uncles wouldn't allow me to return."

"Wouldn't *allow*?"

"Amorites believe women should be controlled by men. With my husband dead and no sons, I was meant to be ruled by my father's relatives until he sent for me." Kemanut's face reflected the disgust she felt at the situation. "He died before that happened. But then Yacob-Hur struggled to make Khemet thrive. I, through one of my cousins also raised here, convinced the Patriarchs to send me back to give him insight into Khemet and her people. I thought I could make a difference. He won't listen."

Amatashteret took a deep breath to calm herself. Flashes of the last conversation she had with the chieftain threatened to bring her back to the rage and frustration she'd felt at his words.

You weren't sent here to advise me, woman. You were sent to tell me something useful. As it is, all you're good for is showing them a Khemetan face looking down from the High House.

"I tried to explain that, in order to rule, he must bring balance. To be a leader in Khemet, he must adopt Khemetan ways. And that means reinstating the kinswomen."

"Which he will never do," Kemanut said. "If the Amorites cannot let their women control their own lives, how would they let them administer all of Khemet, as is our way?"

"You understand my dilemma."

"Why do you want the copper scarab? To use as a weapon against him?"

"Not in the way you mean. Yacob-Hur, like most brute force warriors, only understands power and strength. I've shown him text after text detailing how each aspect of administration is meant to work. He doesn't care. Walk that machine down the capital's avenues and let him see the reaction of the people. That, he'll understand."

For several beats Kemanut kept their gazes locked as if she was searching for something in Amatashteret's eyes. "No. It won't work. All it will do is hand him one more piece of Khemet to destroy or exploit. And I cannot—"

"You think that you can wait them out." Amatashteret had been studying her as well. "You think that as long as Khemetans continue to resist and chaos reigns without being checked by balance, that eventually he will abandon the land."

The Superior said nothing. Her silence was answer enough.

"You don't understand them. Yacob-Hur doesn't need the rich soil or good harvests to make the Patriarchs happy. There are enough precious metals and jewels in this valley to satisfy them for generations. Only once Khemet has been stripped of anything of value—including the limestone off the pyramids—will they leave. You—Khemet will not outlast them. Let me help you save her."

Again, eyes locked, the two women considered and challenged each other's convictions. A long time passed before Kemanut stood and gestured toward an inner door.

"It's not finished, still. But I'll take you to it."

• • •

The machine was further along than when she'd last seen it. Even incomplete, it was impressive beyond Amatashteret's recollection and now more resembled the insect it was based on. The copper scarab was wider than two wide elephants, filling the subterranean workshop where the Sisters stored it. As she walked around the machine, she could see all the tubes running through it, just like the plans she remembered. The head and thorax, which housed the control mechanisms, were done and covered, but the rest of the carapace and wings weren't on yet. Though it had been many years, the copper was still the yellow-red of the sunset sky, which told her someone had been watching over it all this time. Meaning the Sisterhood of Engineers must still exist in some form. Good. She would need them.

"Mama," her oldest whispered as they circled around to the back, "what does it do?"

"Many things, according to the ancient writings. The Khemetans of the Time Before used them to move stone from quarries far up and down the Nile here to build the pyramids. The texts say they lifted the blocks into the air once they were shaped and placed them just so.

"How?"

"That's what we had hoped to find out once we were done."

The scarab's six legs were complete yet unattached. She wondered how they would move through the sand.

"The outer wings are designed to capture the heat and light of the sun, channeling it here where there's a reservoir of water." Amatashteret smiled at the light in her daughter's eyes as she explored the inner workings. "Heat and pressure builds until it becomes steam, which travels through the tubes to the legs and other parts. That's how it moves."

"Can you make it work?"

She squeezed her daughter's hand. "With help."

She turned to Kemanut, who had been observing and quiet since they came in. "We had enough copper stored to make two of these. Is the rest also here?"

"The Superior Engineer hid it inside a chamber below the Lioness of the Horizon when the attacks started."

Nodding, Amatashteret could imagine how it happened. This workshop was well concealed within the labyrinth of underground tunnels that ran throughout the plateau. Still, this space might have been found by a determined looter. But the path into the giant stone Lion was only known by the Supremes and Superiors of the Library and far more difficult to locate. Those rooms held more than copper. "We'll need it all. Kemanut, if we can complete the work, get this running, we have a hope of forcing Yacob-Hur's hand. I can't do this alone. I know many of the engineers and metalsmiths and masons are gone. I saw the empty streets. But they aren't dead, just hiding—am I right?"

The distrust still lingered in Kemanut's eyes. "You want them to come back here. You'd have them risk their lives for this."

"I don't—"

"He came here, your chieftain, after he'd already secured his victory, still intent on razing every city within his reach to the ground. The only reason we escaped that fate is because we did not fight. That and one of his generals convinced him that the Library was more valuable intact. So the buildings still stand. The people ..."

The pain of it, the anger, the fear, held tight inside but as clear on her face as it was fresh in her heart. Her voice getting tighter and higher and more raw as she continued.

"Soldiers came for the scholars, the Sisters, the Brothers. First, just a few individuals, then whole groups who never returned. Everyone else escaped, hid. The rest of us are all that's left, as far as Yacob-Hur knows."

"I know. I heard that story. The general you mentioned? He was my father." A shard of the wall separating them broke off when Kemanut heard those words. "I was told he was less than diligent about keeping track of who left. Yacob-Hur called it carelessness. I suspect it was a deliberate choice."

"It was." The Superior touched her for the first time, stepping forward to take her hand and squeeze it. "We keep his name in a small shrine in the tunnels under the western Spirit House. I'll take you there tonight."

"Thank you." Amatashteret hadn't expected to find a fresh flower of grief growing within her, and yet here it was. Just as she had many times in the past nine years, she pushed it behind her to focus on the present. "If you know where the engineers, smiths, and masons who escaped all are, please ask them to return. Have them arrive in secret, in small groups. Enter the tunnels on the far western side so no one connects them to what we're doing here. When they arrive, I'll tell them what I'm telling you. I will not have my daughters living in a world ruled by chaos and ignorance anymore. More than anyone, I'm doing this for them."

"It will take time."

"We have time."

"How much? Won't he come for you?"

Amatashteret nodded. "If he does, I know what to do."

Men came from the capital three days later. Amatashteret watched chariots emerge from a cloud of sand. When their riders arrived at the administration building with questions and demands, she stood in the shadow of the doorway dressed as a laborer and listened as her cousin played his part.

"Where are Amatashteret and her daughters?"

"We brought her here. She stayed one day, then the chariots went on to the harbor."

"Why aren't you with her?"

"I didn't want to go back to Canaan."

Much cursing followed. She smiled, seeing the men leave in the direction of the river. Let them chase the rumor of her all the way back to the Jordan. It would give her the time she needed.

The engineers were the first to return. They came in groups of two or three, arriving in the tunnels under the plateau without ever being seen in town. The sisters that remembered her vouched for her to the ones who didn't. They, in turn, vouched for her to the metalsmiths, who came skeptical but eager to work with copper once more. The smiths vouched for her to the masons, who came once the work was underway and the scarab's carapace started to take shape. They lent their skills to lifting the large panels and wings into place, the last pieces needed to make the scarab look complete. Over the weeks of work, the tunnels transformed into a small village, everyone sharing knowledge and stories and their hopes for change. It almost approached what Amatashteret remembered.

She tried to only focus on the tasks immediately before them and not on the final goal. At first this helped her not to panic about finding the last component they needed to make the machine move: a ba-spirit.

All the material for building and operating the copper scarabs showed that a ba—the spirit that remained behind when life left the body—was necessary to operating the controls. She remembered helping to assemble the pomegranate-sized nest of minute levers and carnelian buttons where it would sit. She didn't know how they would go about placing a ba there or teaching it how the mechanism worked. With the project moving closer to completion, she could no longer put off solving this last problem.

The day after the left wing had been fitted into place, Kemanut came to the curl of tunnel Amatashteret used as a makeshift office. She brought a small jug of beer with her. Without speaking, she poured some into a pair of mugs, and they each drank a while in silence.

"This past week you've been tense," Kemanut said. When she got no more than an unvoiced agreement, she continued, "Do you intend to share the reason with any of us?"

"It's just a problem I need to solve and haven't yet."

Over the weeks the two of them had built a mutual respect, though Amatashteret wouldn't call their relationship a trusting one. She didn't want to give her any reason to doubt the outcome of their work. As much as the others respected her, they would follow the Superior's word over hers without hesitating.

"I see what's in your heart better than you think I do." Kemanut waited for her to meet her eyes. "I watch you with the Sisters and the smiths, careful to guide them without seeming to lead. You say you want to achieve ma'at, to bring back the kinswomen, to restore some of what was. Do you think any of us doubt that means you intend to take the role of Great Mother and Queen?"

Amatashteret had to stop herself from looking away. "I don't want anyone to think I take it for granted that I will."

"You have a strong claim to it. Your mother's mother was a kinswoman."

"That's not enough."

"No, it's not."

Her heart thudded hard against her chest. Was Kemanut going to speak against her if she tried?

"If this is what you want, you need to show you're worthy of it. You need to start acting like a Great Mother."

"I don't understand—"

"No one woman can be every aspect of the netjeret all the time. Hathor depends on Sekhmet who depends on Iset who depends on Nebthet. A queen needs *all* her kinswomen."

Ever since she lost control of her life, Amatashteret had kept so much inside of her heart, only allowing the smallest pebbles of her thoughts to drop into the world. To protect herself. And her daughters.

"I've spent so much time working on how to outmaneuver Amorites I'm starting to think like them."

"Thank you," she said after a long pause. And then she went to gather the others.

The closest place all of them could fit at one time was a chamber underneath the Spirit House of Djehuti where many of the papyrus scrolls the librarians hid from Yacob-Hur were stored. Once she could see that all the smiths, engineers, and masons were assembled, she held up one of the scrolls.

"Sisters," she called out, making a point to make eye contact with the smiths as well as the engineers, "brother masons, we have one last problem to solve before we can bring the scarab into the sunlight and test it. The mechanism requires a ba-spirit as well as a living pilot to operate. And I have no idea how we can make that happen."

"How did the Ancients do it?" one of the smiths asked.

An engineer standing in the front answered. "There's an incantation in the records. We think it's meant to compel a ba-spirit to do the work. But it's written in the old tongue." The language they spoke evolved out of that, but few scholars knew it completely enough to translate even back before the invasion.

"It compels them? Why not ask?" another engineer said.

"What ba-spirit would remain in this world disembodied for longer than they needed to? Ba take up another life, or they pass through the Door of the West with the Osiris," Kemanut said.

"It's been more than a generation since we've had a king that properly transitioned," one of the masons said. "There must be many lost ba waiting."

"There are."

The voice came from the middle of the room and was quiet enough that Amatashteret didn't hear it. All she saw was the turn of a dozen heads in the speaker's direction. It was a young man she'd seen working with the masons, but from the look of him, he wasn't old enough to be a full member of the brotherhood. He also didn't look like he could deal with the pressure of so many eyes on him.

"Say again, Neferu. Speak loud," the Supreme mason commanded.

"There are many spirits here, waiting, hoping for the king to open the Door for them."

"Here as in Khemet or here as in this room?" Amatashteret asked.

"Both, auntie. More here at the Library than upriver where we came from. They gather here because of the Great Lion, I think."

The boy was clearly a ba adept, a person gifted with the ability to see and communicate with the spirits. If things ran as they were supposed to, the Superiors of the Spirit Houses would have found him years ago and trained him.

"So we can find them," the Supreme mason said. "How do we get them to understand how the machine works?"

"Neferu, were any of the spirits here engineers?" Amatashteret asked.

The boy's eyes turned gold—a sign he was communicating with the ba around them. "Yes. Many. One says to tell you her name is Aneski."

Most of the other engineers reacted just as Amatashteret did, hands automatically touching the space over their hearts in remembrance.

"The last Superior Engineer of the High House," Kemanut explained to the younger people. "Building the copper scarab was her idea."

Amatashteret cut through the crowd to take Neferu's hand—"Ask her to follow us, please"—and led him back through the tunnels to the giant scarab. She had him stand on a stool so he could see inside the ba-spirit nest.

"Can she get there? Or ..." Did it require the spell? She wasn't sure.

"She is there. She says ..." he looked to the Supreme mason. "We have to make it in harmony with her?"

No one looked as if they understood what that meant. Her stomach clenched, braced against defeat. They were so close!

"I think she means we have to create a resonance in the copper the same way the Brothers of Anpu create one in the stone when they consecrate the Door in a tomb." Kemanut stepped up to the machine and placed her palm on the head. After a few breaths she began to hum, modulating up and down until the copper vibrated in kind. "Before, I was a musician in the Spirit House of Iset. I know of the technique, but I don't know the exact resonance. And metal is different from stone."

"We can work with you to discover it," the Supreme mason said. "And with Neferu's help, the ba will be able to guide us."

Elated and hopeful again, Amatashteret crossed her hands over her heart. "Let's begin."

In the darkness before dawn on the equinox, Khemetans who came from across the delta and White Fortress region gathered around the base of the Great Lioness. Their voices quiet, reverent; their bodies newly wet with water from the still anemic Nile; they sat with eyes trained on the eastern horizon. Like the giant stone Lion of the Horizon, their faces would greet the dawn directly on the day marking the beginning of the harvest season. Most of them tried not to think about how poor that harvest would be this year, just as last year and possibly all the years to come. Instead, they waited for the life-giving rays of the sun to warm their skin and remind them of the first eternal truth: Everything changes, but the dawn always comes.

Half a shade after the sun disk pushed fully over the horizon, the Lioness seemed, impossibly, to shudder. Sounds emerged from under the ground that ricocheted around the still quiet crowd—vibrations that didn't make sense.

They had begun to murmur when the copper scarab emerged from the sand between the stone paws, hissing and clicking and gleaming in the sunlight. The people's silence held for one breath, two, before everyone reacted at once. Amatashteret watched from a short distance as some scrambled away in fear, some fell to their knees in shock or in reverence, and some ran to get a closer look. The engineers surrounded the scarab, lifting the copper wings to the right position and ensuring the steam pressure stayed at the right level. Once they gave the ready signal, she and the other chariot riders rolled past the machine, heading into the desert and upriver toward the capital.

She looked back at the massive scarab, watched the legs' deliberate movement as it walked on the stone pavement like a spider, then switched to a sweeping, swimming movement when it reached the sand between the pyramids. The size, the weight, the fact that it wasn't perfectly built didn't keep it from moving along just as fast as the slow trotting horses.

Amatashteret had one small stab of regret that they hadn't been able to figure out how to make it fly. *Soon*, she told herself. If this worked, she and the Sisters would have many years to work on it.

Once away from the Library district, the chariots formed a wide circle around the scarab with Amatashteret and Kemanut in front. The engineers, smiths, and masons who didn't fit in the dozen chariots rode behind on mules, followed by the Khemetans who had seen the machine emerge. The group kept to the sand but hewed close enough to the farmlands that people from villages along the bank of the river, alerted by excited criers, trickled out to watch them pass or to join. By the time the Ra-sun looked down on them from above, hundreds of Khemetans followed in their wake. And so they entered the capital on a wave of cheers and hymns that reached deep within the walls of the High House.

As planned, the chariots parted, and the copper scarab reached the courtyard of the palace first. Amatashteret came to stand in front of it when she saw Yacob-Hur coming down the long front steps, his white hot fury apparent even from this distance. She turned her back to him and took in the sight of the machine standing in the full sunlight. It towered over her, carapace gleaming yellow-red, outer wings up as if just about to fly, alive and vibrating. She looked at all the engineers and smiths and masons that helped build it, all the people fascinated and buoyed by it. This creation would change everything for her people. *All* her people. With that thought firm in her heart, she turned and faced the chieftain.

For many breaths he stood two arm lengths away, eyes jumping between her and the looming machine above them. Finally, he locked on her. "Speak, woman."

"After today you will never use that tone with me again."

He flinched as if punched, too surprised to form an immediate answer.

"Do you know what this is?" she said, arms raised to encompass the machine's presence. "No, I can see you don't. This is a scarab beetle. We Khemetans hold it sacred. It represents the celestial Kheper that brings the dawn, pushing it above the horizon to launch it on the daily journey across the sky."

"If you don't start making sense—"

"I'll put it in terms you can understand. The scarab is a god. I brought it to life."

That silenced him.

"Look behind me. Do you see all those women? They're engineers and metalsmiths. Together we designed and crafted this. Do you see all those men? They're masons. Together we built and sang this to life. Do you see all the people behind them? They know we're the ones who made that happen.

"Do you see the choice you have in front of you?"

A range of dark emotions passed over Yacob-Hur's face before he took a deep breath to laugh. "So I'm to give over all my power to you because you come back here at the head of a mob of peasants?"

"That isn't how this works," Amatashteret said. "Without balance, power dwindles away to nothing, just as with the Nile. Women and men rule together in Khemet. Why do you think the throne sits on top of Iset's head?" She pointed at the carving of the netjeret on the lintel surrounding the door.

"This is your choice: Join me, re-establish balance, and see the Black Land restored to glory."

"Or?"

At a signal from her, Neferu had the scarab take two steps forward. "Get stepped on."

Fear and anger swirled in Yacob-Hur's eyes. "You harm me, and you won't live out the day."

"Oh? Who will punish me? Them?" He followed her gaze to the upper balcony where three of the Amorite Patriarchs watched the scene below. "They came to warn you their patience is about to run out, didn't they? Or that it has already."

From his look she knew her second guess was right.

"Show them you're wise enough to rule, not just strong enough to conquer."

"By giving in to a woman?"

She didn't respond. She waited. After a time his breathing slowed, his eyes fixed on the copper scarab, and his rational mind finally asserted control of his emotions. He still couldn't fix his mouth to utter the necessary words, only managing a hard nod of acquiescence.

Without speaking, she walked past him toward the High House steps. Before he could react to this, the engineers and smiths streamed past him to join her. Amatashteret waited at the top for them to coalesce around her just as the masons moved to form a circle around the scarab. When Yacob-Hur finally came to stand beside them, the message was clear: I am protected. *We* are protected.

"Can you trust him?" Kemanut had asked in the hours before dawn. "Even if he agrees, can you be sure he won't take control back?"

"No. Never," she'd said. "We can never stop watching for him to betray us. He's not fit to be king in Khemet and never will be. We still need him, for now. Once we reestablish the kinswomen, we can search for and anoint a king who has the respect of the Amorites and respects the ways of Khemet."

Even in this moment, standing before the High House as Kemanut announced her as the Great Mother, Amatashteret could see this future as if it already happened. Later, she would gather more women, the daughters and granddaughters of Khemet, to set things in order. Later, she would become the Superior Engineer and lead the Sisters of Seshet in creating more copper scarabs. Later, she would see her daughters take on these responsibilities and carry on her work.

For now, she placed her hand on Yacob-Hur's shoulder, accepted the regalia Kemanut brought out of hiding for her, took one last breath as Amatashteret, orphan and widow, and made her first official act as Great Mother and Queen.

The Arrangement
of Their Parts

Shweta Narayan

The Englishman's workshop nestled close to his people's fortified factory, outside its walls but well within its influence. A night guard watched over it—if keeping to the doorway, eyeing the street from his puddle of lantern light, and turning occasionally to spit paan could really be called watching.

The guard had reason for complacency; plastered walls offered no handhold and the workshop's windows, set into the sloping roof, were too high and small for human reach. But the Artificer Devi had not worn human form in many years. She cut the wooden trellis out from one window, spread her tail feathers for balance, and telescoped out her neck to peer into the room.

It could as well have been a butchery. The air was rank with stale machine oil. Moonlight spread flat on tile and whitewash, caught on gears laid out in disconnected imitation of their proper form. Inked and labelled diagrams, pinned to walls and tables, recorded the workings of legs, eyes, boilers; and on the main workbench a half-dismembered voice box stood ready to play one cylinder of its speech. Its other cylinders stood in rows beside it, sorted by size instead of tone. Dead husks shaped the shadows: a soldier's head pried open; pieces of a half-golden mongoose; the ungeared skeleton of a large cat, frozen before it could pounce.

The trail ended here. Of course. Anything might be found in Surat, greatest port in the world, for a price.

She landed with barely a whir on the main bench, next to the voice box, and reached for three heartsprings coiled naked on a sheaf of paper. Paused. The springs' thin metal had ripped in places; the pattern of dents said they had been flattened out, then rolled back up. Well, that could all be repaired. But—she held one up to the moonlight, then checked the others, shivering. Every graven word was gone. Scratched over, rubbed down to a lifeless blur.

Not even she could bring someone back once their heartspring was destroyed.

A prayer for her dead then, gone to power that great mechanism marked by stars; and three more notches in her own spring. There was only metal left here. And paper, rubbed over with wax to make imprints of each ruined heartspring.

But remains could, at need, become parts. The hunting cat's skeleton was still fully articulated. The soldier's head still held his steam boiler, though the ruby lens that heated it was gone. And for the rest—she shredded the paper into a crucible, set the springs gently on their bed of copied words, and turned to build up the fire.

Four brahmins met in a village one day and, in the way of learned men everywhere, got to talking about their learning. Now each believed his own knowledge to be the most essential; but brahmins value humility and nonattachment, so none were willing to admit it. In consequence, each one heaped praises on the rest, and so they all became great friends and decided to travel through the jungle together.

On the way they came across new bones scattered by the side of the road. "My dear friends!" cried the first brahmin. "While my knowledge is a drop to your monsoon clouds, yet I believe it would reveal the mystery of these bones."

"Do please show us," said the second, "for we have nothing but awe of your mastery of form, and virtue can only increase when learning is shared." For he was hoping to overhear his new friend's mantra and steal its power for himself.

So the first mouthed his sacred words and scattered water from the three holy rivers onto the bones, and they rose from the ground and arranged themselves into the skeleton of a tiger.

The sun was risen when the workshop door squeaked open, letting in the day's dust on a rush of muggy air. The Englishman glanced in, then turned to give his guard a low-voiced command before stepping inside.

All but one of the windows cast trellis-shadows on the far wall. From that one, the Artificer raised her wings. The Englishman wiped his forehead with a handkerchief, smirked at her shadow, and said in passable Hindustani, "Well, isn't this curious?" Behind him, the door pulled shut. The outer bar dropped with a thump.

She tucked her wings neatly back, keeping her good eye fixed on him. His skin showed red through his light muslin jama, and it sat oddly with his English hat and boots, but there was nothing silly about the pistol at his hip. "You seem, Sir James," she said, "to find a great many things curious."

"With all Creation so full of wonder, how could I not?" He looked up at her directly then, shading his face; his eyes gleamed in appreciation. He said, "And I would be loath to damage so lovely a mechanism before even seeing it fly."

"Am I to be grateful?"

"Another man might choose revenge." He gestured from the cooling crucible to his disturbed mallets and gravers. His hand drifted down to the gun, jerked away from it again. "Or use this violation to cause trouble for your Emperor. I am a natural philosopher and prefer understanding."

By Imperial edict, the British could not be touched. Much the bird cared. "Understand this, then," she said. "You murdered my own."

"Oh, murdered, is it now?" The Englishman sounded only amused.

"You think your studies justify their deaths?"

"Excellent show. One would almost think there was meaning to it. But it was Man, after all, whom God made in His image, not clockwork; so clockwork cannot be murdered."

She rattled her feathers. "Ah? Then mere clockwork could hardly violate your workshop."

"Argued like a native! And indeed you may be right despite yourself." He grinned. "For I have discovered that it takes only Descartes' four principles of inanimate form to explain you."

"So you need only know—" She shifted into French. "—the motion, size, shape, and arrangement of my parts." Back to Hindustani. "What's left to understand?"

His mouth opened. Shut. "'S blood, you're a saucy one," he said. "I wish to know why, of course."

"We have our last rites, as you do yours." Sunlight crept down the far wall, towards the skeletal forms, reaching lower now than the man's head. "We do not leave our dead unmelted. You've had your dismantlement and your diagramming. Trade me for what is left, and I shall take no further action."

He glanced along the row of windows; then, gaze calculating, back at the bird. "And what is it you offer?"

"A tale of our own natural philosophers, whose understanding might inform yours."

The second brahmin was impressed, which irritated him because he hadn't managed to hear the mantra. So he said, "That is very clever!"

Such meager praise drew a thin smile to the first brahmin's lips. "You are far too kind, my brother," he said. "But indeed, I don't aspire to cleverness. Only to knowledge of Truth within the world."

"As do we all," said the second, "though we cannot all achieve it."

The third brahmin said hurriedly, "Still, enlightened company can only add to our learning."

"That's so," said the second. "And feeble as my own learning is, such a base does call out to be built upon."

"Yes, and as you so wisely said, our lives will be richer for sharing," said the third. And so the second brahmin mumbled over the skeleton, shaking neem and mango leaves as he spoke; and muscles built themselves over bone, each one the perfect size for its place.

"Why," the third marveled, hiding his own chagrin, "the animal's bulk is clear now. Even so does philosophy grow around a fundamental knowledge of the Vedas. And as art grows up around philosophy, I shall add my own grains of knowledge to give it shape if this pleases my dear friends." Nothing, of course, could please his dear friends more. So he anointed each muscle with clove oil and camphor, spoke into his cupped hands, and clapped twice; and striped skin grew over the whole, its orange glowing like sunrise.

The fourth brahmin said, "Truly, this is a wonder. Perhaps I can add to it a little though I admit myself surprised that I might know anything my learned friends do not!" So saying, he breathed dust from the four great mountains into the tiger's mouth and eyes, and he whispered his own words.

The tiger sprang into motion then and ate them all.

The Englishman laughed. "If you want someone who takes tales of heathen chanting and anointments seriously," he said loudly, "find a Papist. This explains nothing—"

A shadow loomed behind the bird, silent on bare feet. She dropped from the window, spread her wings, and settled on the main bench. Above her, rain shutters slammed shut.

The Englishman's smile was edged now. "Though it kept you occupied," he said, drifting closer. The pistol was in his hand, aimed at the floor. "My guard's a native, after all; too superstitious to see why the fire burned all night but clever as a monkey on the roof. Now there's no need to *damage* you—" She turned, and he recoiled. "What happened to your eye?"

"Eyes break," she said. "They are mere lenses and can be replaced." They could also be pulled out whole and set atop a steam boiler, angled to catch sunlight, to wind a new-forged heartspring. Once that sunlight slanted down far enough into the workshop. "And your guard closed the wrong window."

"What? No, no, you'll not make me look away so easily." He circled around till he could watch the windows without losing sight of her, then glanced warily up.

Behind him, a lens flared. Yellow eyes eased open. Golden claws came out with a click from skeletal tiger paws.

The Applause of Others

Corinne Duyvis

Following the eel proved tougher than Floor expected. She darted around cars parked too close to the canal's edge, keeping her camera in her hands and her eyes on the water. The eel swam close to the surface, but box-like houseboats kept blocking her sight, and the murky-green canal made it hard to catch more than glimpses while she ran.

Floor evaded a cyclist by a hair's breath. The bell rang in her ears as the bike passed, but she was already distracted—the houseboats had come to an end, allowing an unobstructed view of the water. Floor ducked into the first opening between parked cars. She crouched by the water's edge, leaving nothing between her and a meter-plus drop into the canal but a metal beam that barely reached her ankles.

The eel was an agitated shadow just under the surface, coiling up and straightening out again. It wasn't moving on, though, giving Floor time to lean in, one hand curling around the rusted beam to steady herself and snap some photos. They'd no doubt turn out crap, but Floor hadn't even known there *were* eels in the Amsterdam canals; she wanted evidence to show her dads or maybe Lisanne at school.

Not that Lisanne would be interested in this blur on her camera's display. Floor played with the settings, cooing at the eel, "Just a couple more seconds ... Wow, you are *big*, aren't you?"

In response, the eel twisted under the water. It swam in circles before dashing straight ahead, its movements smoothing out—like it was showing off, making sure she saw the blue sheen on its scales and got every angle.

Spanish-sounding voices just meters behind Floor had her tensing up. Being a fourteen-year-old girl running around the city center with a plus-sized camera meant that tourists bothered her more often than not. She checked over her shoulder. A trio of friends shielded their eyes from the light as they looked up. Banners stretched across the second-floor windows of three neighboring canal houses, thick cloth against aged bricks and cream-white shutters. The sun reflected off the banners, obscuring one letter or the other. Floor squinted to read the first sheet:

OUR HOMES OUR WINDOWS

The second said:

NOT YOUR ENTERTAINMENT

The third:

AM*DAM

A doodled pentagram acted as the star. It must've turned out way too big since it cut into the D and the M was just a squished scribble at the end.

Floor spotted a couple through the fourth house's wide-open windows, working together to install another banner. The woman balanced precariously on the windowsill, trying to toss a rope onto the pulley installation near the roof as the wind tugged the sheet to and fro. Floor barely made out the black scrawls of letters:

NOT A MUSEUM

"Nice," Floor said. "Bad handwriting. But *nice*."

"Hey, girl?" One of the Spanish tourists with a goofy grin and deodorant she could smell from here turned towards her and pointed at the banners. "The words? What do they mean?"

"Those houses are beautiful!" a girl with a scruffy mohawk added in smoother English. "Why cover them? I love the ..." She gestured with thin hands, searching for the words. She ended up simply indicating the pyramid gables. "It's such a shame. They shouldn't allow it."

Floor shifted her weight, still crouched. Why did they have to look at her like that? "Well ... they *don't*."

She didn't want to translate the banners. They were in Dutch for a reason. She didn't get the chance to, anyway—a sudden splash behind her demanded her attention. Drops of water sprayed onto her bare calves. Floor spun just in time to see the eel slithering away, the water closing up above. The surface jerked with waves, streaked with unruly white bubbles. How had the eel created a big enough splash to reach her from so far?

Her eyes followed the waves until she caught another glimpse of movement. A second eel. Its shape twined, its figure smaller and grayer than the blue one. It slashed left and right, spinning and winding in a way that almost made her forget the blue eel's continued splashing.

"*You're* a pretty one, too, aren't you?" The sudden delight in Floor's voice prompted a burst of laughter from the tourists.

"Do you live here?" Mohawk Girl asked. "Where? Those houses?" She pointed at the canal houses across the water, tall and thin.

"Do you see fish often?" Deodorant's grin widened.

"You look angry," said the third friend. "Smile for us, pretty girl."

Floor kept her lips adamantly straight. Faking a heavier accent than her real one, she said, "Bad English. Sorry." She turned back to the water to focus on the new eel rather than the tourists' ongoing questions. Did it *matter* what the Dutch word for fish was?

"Two eels at once? Where'd *you* come from?" She kept the words under her breath this time.

In the corner of her eye, the blue eel snapped into motion. It sliced through the water towards the new eel. Like it had a goal. Floor tensed up, unsure whether to be excited or repulsed. Her legs froze in their crouch. The tourists chattered in Spanish, no doubt noticing the movement, too.

The blue eel dove into the other one from the side. From the back of Floor's throat came a surprised yelp. Darkness billowed from the impact site. The eels circled each other, the injured one shuddering. The blood in the water thickened.

The tourists' chatter turned to nervous laughter. "Think it's jealous?" Mohawk Girl asked.

Floor gripped her camera tighter, snapping photos without stopping. "It's just animals. They're ... territorial." She licked her lips, adding despite herself, "Possessive."

She couldn't look away from the fight. It took four minutes. Then the blue eel drifted off, leaving nothing in its wake but darkened water and uncharacteristic waves.

In the distance, tram bells rang.

"Pieter?" Floor asked her dad. She leaned against the kitchen door frame, relishing the houseboat's faint, familiar sway. "What color are eels? Can they be blue?"

The musty-warm smell of kale filled the kitchen, hanging lazily in the corners and fogging up the windows even with half of them open to the water of the Brouwersgracht outside. Pieter was hunched over the kitchen counter. Short, off-blond locks dangled over his face. One arm held tightly onto the pan, the other working the old-school potato masher, matching the rhythm of the Dutch tunes blaring from the radio.

"Can't you look that up?" Pieter ran his hand along his forehead. His breathing came heavy.

"I just figured, if you knew ..." Floor wrinkled her nose. "Kale? In summer?"

Pieter shrugged with one shoulder, still focused on the kale. In a way, Floor was glad for it. It made her feel less self-conscious. "I was in the mood. Anyway, eels are gray-silverish, or beige, at least when smoked. Blue ... maybe if the light hits them right?" Pieter wiggled one hand in a gesture of uncertainty.

"I'm pretty sure I saw one in the Prinsengracht earlier."

"Then I guess eels can be blue." He laughed. When he continued, he talked uncomfortably fast. "Wow, I haven't seen fish in the canals in ages. They must've been close to the surface—or maybe the city really is cleaning the water."

Floor stepped farther into the kitchen, passing the table where a folded-open letter caught her eye. A few phrases stood out. Protected City Sights; left outer-wall repairs; August 20th. She didn't need to read more. Protected City Sights: A nice way of saying, "Live downtown? Expect to spend a lot of dough keeping your place authentic-looking—or we'll *make* you."

No wonder Pieter sounded off. Apparently, the city had set a new deadline. Amsterdam had been hitting up houses for renovations left and right—such was the downside of the city center being on the World Heritage List—demanding specific paint colors, materials, styles of ceilings or fireplaces. Banners were strictly regulated. So were ads. Blinds, canopies, satellite dishes. Facades. Flags.

Floor moved on, hoping Pieter hadn't caught her pause. "Check these out," she said. She lifted her camera and scrolled through the photos, a backwards film of the process of putting up the fourth banner. After receiving that letter, she had a feeling Pieter would appreciate the sentiment. "That's just around the corner. Cool, right?"

Pieter glanced over. "That, Floortje, depends entirely on the fine."

After school the next day, Floor sat in her bedroom's window. Her netbook was propped against her drawn-up legs. A neighbor was practicing the violin, the breeze dragging along scattered notes she couldn't fit into a tune. She ought to be editing photos or studying— the final exam week of the school year was coming up—but instead she browsed Wikipedia for information on eels.

The eel that was currently dancing in the water outside her window, long-stretched and swift, had a lot to do with that.

"Shouldn't you be digging into mud? Hunting? Hiding out?" She laughed under her breath. "You're just as big as the one from last night."

She noticed a swampy smell like rotten plants. Steadying her netbook, she fell silent when she saw a flat boat passing under the curve of the nearest bridge. From the front of the boat a bright orange metal arm protruded with a joint in the middle and a rusted hook dangling from the end. The hook slowly sank into the water.

At the base of the arm sat an operator, his legs crossed at the ankles, his bald head reflecting the sun. With a snap of a joystick-like device, he brought the claw back up. Black-brown hooks pinched the front wheel of a city bike, the frame drooping in the air. Another bike was crunched immovably in the hook's center. Mud dripped past the metal.

As the dredger approached, the eel faded in and out of sight, re-appearing across the canal, then a meter from Floor's bedroom window. Its movements came snappier, lashing out like the crack of a whip. Maybe the boat's movements disturbed it, or the smell, which was only getting worse. Rust mingled with the stink of wet dirt. Floor slipped her computer off her lap when the bikes clanged onto the stack already on the boat. She'd wait inside until it passed.

"Sorry, eel-buddy," she said as she wrenched the window down, "looks like you'll have to hide for a while. Hope it won't mess up your house." The claw was scraping over the muddy canal bottom, sending clouds of muck billowing. It brought up one or more prizes almost every time. She bet fish lived in those wrecks.

When the dredger reached Floor's house, she could see the stack of twisted metal, bikes upon bikes covered in a film of yellowed mud, bent wheels and twisted shopping carts, chairs of all kinds, a mangled crowd control fence, small boats that must've gotten overloaded with rain water, plastic sheets, the casing of an old TV.

The hook dumped a single bike wheel on top. The boat leaned suddenly to the right. A ripple trembled over the water, reaching the houseboats on the other side. The dredger corrected itself—too far, sending it careening to the left. The operator sat up straight, fighting to correct the boat's balance on the normally still water. The rest of the canal stayed placid.

Another wave rippled out. The operator grabbed the seat of his chair, mouthing something Floor couldn't hear.

The wave reached her houseboat. She barely noticed—might not have if she hadn't seen it coming—but then a tremor ran to her spine. The almost-empty glass of Sprite on the windowsill rippled.

The operator struggled to keep the boat straight. Subtle waves tipped it one way or the other, sloshing up against the houseboats and boats alike.

Floor steadied the Sprite glass, waiting until the dredger moved past and the water quieted into smoothness. The boat steadied. When the mud settled back in the deep, the eel showed up again to spin and curl as elegantly as before.

Floor grabbed her camera.

The eel seemed to like this part of the canal. It hung out by her bedroom window and showed up almost every time Floor did homework on the nearby dock, her feet dangling in the cool water. She'd look up from her notebooks and whisper, asking what it was doing and taking occasional snapshots, now more out of habit than anything else.

It was the same eel, she'd decided, *her* eel. It had that same shimmer of blue even when it swam centimeters below the surface. Other times, when the sun hit it just right, the eel's shade veered closer to purple or silver, sometimes all at once.

She wasn't the only one who noticed. Passersby walked up, captivated without fail; they ooh-ed and aah-ed and snapped pictures the same way Floor did, and she'd quietly grin, glad the attention was no longer on her, and tell her eel its show was all the rage.

Today, though, she couldn't afford the distraction.

She scribbled German grammar puzzles into her battered workbook with one hand, holding an oily paper cone of Flemish fries in the other. She breathed in the smell of her fries, salty and just the right kind of greasy, interspersed with a whiff of fresh mayonnaise that made the image not just complete but perfect.

More water splashed.

"Not right now, pretty fishy," Floor singsonged. "Big test coming up."

If it wasn't her eel flailing about dramatically for the umpteenth time, it was probably just tourists on a canal bike or someone kicking garbage into the water. She glanced up anyway. Her hand stilled mid-scribble.

A fisherman across the street—one she'd thought was sleeping, Ajax cap drawn far over his eyes—had caught her eel. It thrashed about two meters from the shore, spraying water everywhere, slapping its tail on the surface, throwing itself against a nearby boat. The fisherman knocked back his chair as he shot upright. He reeled the eel from the water, arms bulging, back arched. His weathered face stretched into a smile.

A couple of passersby paused to see the spectacle, shopping bags in hands.

The sun caught every drop of water spraying from the eel. It shimmered on the eel's scales, which gleamed blue and green and then—then more, Floor thought, purple and red and a sheen of yellow, but she couldn't stand to look, couldn't stand the eel's panic as it dangled from the fishing thread. She pressed her hand flat onto her workbook, focusing on the fisherman instead or the mix of eagerness and disgust of the audience that'd gathered.

The fisherman leaned in, steadying the eel's body as he wormed the hook free.

The eel would be fine. It had to be; they were catch-and-release only, and she'd read that eels could survive on land for ages, anyway. The eel kept thrashing. It took both the man's hands to wrangle its slick body. He shouted at the crowd to take a picture. "Big one, right?" he called. "Biggest one I've seen. Gotta be a meter long! Are you seeing these colors? How about—" He coughed, then tried again. The word bubbled from his throat. "About—"

He doubled over and spat in the dirt at the base of a nearby tree. The eel slipped from his hands. It landed on the cobblestones with a wet thump Floor couldn't hear but imagined easily.

A woman placed her Albert Heijn bags on the ground and approached, mouthing something that was lost in the distance. The fisherman didn't respond. He spat out more and more until it wasn't spit but water, whole streams of it. He wracked his body, gripped his throat. Then he stumbled, missing the eel slithering across the pavement by a hair's breath. He didn't notice. He was still coughing, spitting water that streamed past his chin. Then—dripping from his nose. His eyes.

The fisherman couldn't breathe. The water kept coming.

The eel splashed into the canal.

Floor turned, spilling her fries as she yanked out her cellphone. She stumbled from the dock towards the bridge that'd take her across the canal, already dialing one-one-two for an ambulance.

Fifteen minutes later, Floor hugged herself in the middle of the already-dissipating crowd, watching the ambulance's taillights bump over the bridge. The fisherman was alive, but it'd been close. He was coughing up less water already. He'd be fine. She hoped.

"What do we do with ...?" The woman with the Albert Heijn bags gestured at the fishing equipment.

"I'll take it. He's gotta live nearby—I've seen him before."

No one protested, so Floor crouched, taking the fisherman's bait jar, his rod, his sweat-drenched fold-up chair, and beer cooler. One bottle had rolled to the very edge of the street with a stain surrounding it and a bitter stench floating upward. Must've tipped over when the man fell. She grabbed the bottle, too, and set off.

As she crossed the bridge, she refused to look at the water. She saw the eel in her peripheral vision, though. Its shape right underneath the surface streaked back and forth, visible despite the darkened sky, the thickened clouds. Any last trace of a breeze had disappeared.

"Not now," she said. It couldn't be the animal's fault. Floor knew that. But—there was that cloud of blood from that second eel, the waves tossing the dredger around when it had disturbed the canal bottom, the water dripping from even the fisherman's nose and ears—

And the way the eel now followed her across the bridge and the canal shore, lagging only meters behind. The light hit its scales to bring out its colors, begging for photos. Floor walked faster. She looked stubbornly ahead, focusing on her houseboat, trying not to think of the fisherman's body curled up on his side and seeming to break in half with every cough. Trying not to think of *how*.

Pretty or not, she'd just ignore the eel. It didn't own her.

She stopped mid-stride.

On the deck right outside her living room window stood a couple, thirtyish, maybe. The woman was leaning over, pressing a point-and-shoot to the glass, an audience captivated.

By Floor's *home*.

The camera flashed, once, twice, then a third time before the woman turned to look at Floor. Her husband already did. His round face hovered between guilty and excited.

"Is this yours? We just, we thought it was so beautiful and ..." The guy tried to smile. English. British accent.

"What are you. *Doing?*" Floor squeezed out, but then she shook her head, raised her hands, managed to stop herself from flinging the beer bottle at the last second. "*Move!*"

Exam week.

Each day, Floor locked herself up in her room, studying one subject after another. She'd turn her iPod dock up to the top volume to block out the rain slashing against her window, the howl of the wind, the water splashing against the house and the cracks of thunder.

A tap on her shoulder. Floor jerked up. Ronald hovered over her. She reached for her iPod to turn down the sound.

She just managed to catch the last of Ronald's words: "... in the *living room*, don't you?"

"Wha—?"

"Your music, honey," he laughed. "We can hear it across the house."

She stuck out her tongue.

"What's with the curtains?" he asked. "The canal's beautiful. When the waves reflect the lightning ... you really should look."

"I'm studying." Her voice came stiff. Opening the curtains meant having a constant view of the canal—the eel—even if only peripherally. "It's distracting. Did you see the news?"

Ronald shook his head. "Did something happen?"

Floor pulled over her netbook and navigated to nu.nl, pulling up the appropriate article. "Flooding," she said. "Lisanne mentioned it at school. Her backyard is practically gone. And a couple of blocks from the Dam, her uncle's boat sank—a small one, at least."

"I already *thought* the water level was higher." Ronald let out a low, impressed whistle, cut short by another wave slamming the boat, shoving it towards the shore before yanking it back. Floor gripped the desk to steady herself. A film poster dropped from the wall and curled up.

"It's getting worse by the hour." Floor took a second to catch her balance as she got up, the houseboat's swaying catching her off-guard. It'd never been this bad. "Is Pieter still nauseated?"

"You can say that." Ronald ran a hand through his hair. "And— shit—you don't know about the Herengracht houseboat yet, do you? A tree crashed onto the roof. Broke a woman's arm, killed her cat."

"Shit," Floor echoed. They were safe here, right? The trees nearby were just saplings; the city had cut down many of the older trees to better show off the houses.

"I swear, someone must have pissed off a mermaid to cause a storm like this. Amsterdam will go the way of Reimerswaal."

Floor looked at Ronald quizzically, still crouching as she rolled up the fallen poster.

"It's a southern thing. Basically, we'll all drown. Glug." He grinned, but it looked fake, reminding Floor acutely of the city's letter. Neither of her dads had mentioned it to her yet. "Can you even focus on your exams like this? You could stay with Lisanne."

Floor glanced at the canal-side curtains, where the water splashed against the outer walls. She could swear it splashed highest against their boat.

She was being ridiculous, childish. Someone her age shouldn't let herself get this spooked. Animals fought. Waves happened. People got sick.

But still. "Yeah," Floor said, aiming for nonchalance. "Maybe I should."

Floor had her backpack on, stuffed with school books and her netbook and a handful of clothing. She didn't need much. Lisanne lived only ten minutes away. They could drive up and down easily.

She jogged for Pieter's car, her hood drawn. As she tossed her bag into the backseat, she caught a glimpse of the canal. The waves were higher than ever. They crashed against the brick canal walls and the houseboats with white foam heads she'd never seen so far inland. The water exploded onto docks and porches. The wind whistled through the streets, tearing at clattering shutters, ripping off leaves and branches, and sending them tumbling into the water.

"Can I—do you mind waiting a minute?" she shouted at Pieter in the driver's seat. The rain clattering on the roof almost drowned out her voice. "I forgot my camera."

Pieter made a go-on gesture and turned up the radio. Floor dashed back inside, grabbing her camera and its rain cover. Forget exams, forget the eel—she couldn't pass up this opportunity.

She went around to the dock sticking out between her neighbor's homes. The wood was like oil under her feet, and the wind tugged at her from all angles. The rain stabbed her exposed cheeks. She pulled her hood in tighter, then crouched in the middle of the dock, avoiding the edges. With slick hands she tried to steady the camera, squinting at the screen through the haze of rain and the already-drenched plastic. She'd taken photos in the rain before, had read about it often enough, but never this intense. Nowhere close.

Click. Click. There: That tree leaning dangerously to one side. *Click. Click.* The teens running across the bridge. *Click.* The deformed umbrella tossed to and fro on the canal.

Floor shivered in her soaked clothes. At least the rain was softening.

She took another photo of the umbrella. A wave caught it, pulled it under, and spat it back out. The handle spun, sending drops flaring in a pirouette.

Her eel cut through the wave. Water flew off its back like a knife.

Instinctively, Floor pressed *click*—then lowered the camera, simply staring at the eel, its every scale like mother-of-pearl: glimmering red-and-orange, then the dark blue-gray of the clouds overhead, the sun's fierce yellow, the cobblestones' brown, the deep green of the moss in between.

The wind stopped yanking at her coat. Stopped tugging back her hood. Floor caught her muscles relaxing, grateful for the respite.

She followed the eel's shape in the water despite herself. It dove and rose gracefully, twirling, and it was as though it pulled the waves along with its dance as though it straightened them out with every movement.

Today had to be the first time in days it'd had an audience. A lump grew in Floor's throat. She raised the camera. *Click.*

The rain had stopped hurting her cheeks. She rubbed her face with one hand, and her skin felt numb, swollen, probably bright pink. Rain hit the back of her hand, but now the drops were warm. They bounced off harmlessly.

She had to test it. She had to convince herself this was real.

She looked down, ignored the eel, waited for it to break its act and splash angrily the way it always did—

Canal water sprayed her hands.

Her eyes opened. The eel jerked in irritation.

"You ... you're pretty, aren't you?" she whispered. The words felt stupid. They drifted across the water to the twining shape of the eel under the surface. Under the now smooth, tight surface.

And she clicked her camera, whispered praise, watched the eel swallow her attention whole. Its colors shone bright.

"Floor?"

She looked around to where Pieter stood on the shore, his hair drenched. He wouldn't believe her. Wouldn't believe any of this. He

jerked a thumb at the car. "Let's leave now it's cleared up," he said. "You ready?"

She looked back at the eel. "I guess," she said, her words coming forced and soft, barely a whisper, aimed at the eel and not at Pieter. She swallowed and tried again. "I guess I'll see you tomorrow."

The eel spun in anticipation.

Lacrimosa

Silvia Moreno-Garcia

The woman is a mound of dirt and rags pushing a squeaky shopping cart; a lump that moves steadily, slowly forward as if dragged by an invisible tide. Her long, greasy hair hides her face, but Ramon feels her staring at him.

He looks ahead. The best thing to do with the homeless mob littering Vancouver is to ignore it. Give them a buck and the beggars cling to you like barnacles.

"Have you seen my children?" the woman asks.

Her voice, sandpaper against his ears, makes him shiver. His heart jolts as though someone has pricked it with a needle. He keeps on walking, but much faster now. It isn't until he is shoving the milk inside the fridge that he realizes why the woman's words have upset him: she reminds him of the Llorona.

He hasn't thought about her in years, not since he was a child living in Potrero.

Everyone in town had a story about the Llorona. The most common tale was that she drowned her children in the river and afterwards roamed the town, searching for them at night; her pitiful cries are a warning and an omen.

Camilo, Ramon's great-uncle, swore on his mother's grave that he met this ghost while riding home one night. It was the rainy season, when the rivers overflow and Camilo was forced to take a secondary, unfamiliar road.

He spotted a woman in white bending over some nopales at the side of a lonely path. Her face was covered with the spines of the prickly pears she had savagely bitten. She turned around and smiled. Blood dripped from her open mouth and stained her white shift.

This was the kind of story the locals whispered around Potrero. It was utter nonsense, especially coming from the lips of a chronic alcoholic like Camilo, but it was explosive stuff for an eight-year-old boy who stayed up late to watch black-and-white horror flicks on the battered TV set.

However, to think about the Llorona there in the middle of the city between the SkyTrain tracks and a pawn shop is ridiculous. Ramon never packed ghost stories in his suitcase, and Potrero and the Llorona are very far away.

He sees the homeless woman sitting beneath a narrow ledge, shielding herself from the rain. She weeps and hugs a plastic bag as though it were a newborn.

"Have you seen my children?" she asks when he rushes by, clutching his umbrella.

Nearby a man sleeps in front of an abandoned store, an ugly old dog curled next to him. The downtown homeless peek at Ramon from the shadows as he steps over discarded cigarette butts.

They say this is an up and coming neighborhood, but each day he spots a new beggar wielding an empty paper cup at his face.

It is disgraceful.

This is the very reason why he left Mexico. He escaped the stinking misery of his childhood and the tiny bedroom with the black-and-white TV set he had to share with his cousins.

Behind his house there were prickly pears and emptiness. No roads and no buildings. Just a barren nothing swallowed by the purple horizon. It was easy to believe that the Llorona roamed there. But not in Vancouver which is new and shiny, foaming with lattes and tiny condos.

The dogs are howling. They scare him. Wild, stray animals that roam the back of the house at nights. His uncle told him the dogs howled when they saw the Llorona. Ramon runs to the girls' room and sneaks into his mother's bed, terrified of the noise and his mother has to hold him in her arms until he falls asleep.

But when he wakes up, Ramon is in his apartment, and it is only one dog, the neighbor's Doberman, barking.

He rolls to the centre of the bed, staring at the ceiling.

Ramon spots the woman a week later, her arms wrapped around her knees.

"My children," she asks, with her cloud of dirty hair obscuring her face. "Where are my children?"

Nauseating in her madness, a disgusting sight growing like a canker sore and invading his streets. Just like the other homeless littering the area: the man in front of the drugstore that always asks him for spare change even though Ramon never gives him any or the gnarled man beneath a familiar blanket, eternally sleeping in the shade of the burger joint.

The city is heading to the gutter. Sure, it looks pretty from afar with its tall glass buildings and its mountains, but below there is a depressing stew of junkies and panhandlers that mars the view. It reminds him of Potrero and the bedroom with the leaky ceiling. He stared at that small yellow leak which grew to become an obscene, dark patch above his bed until one day he grabbed his things and headed north.

He felt like repeating his youthful impulsiveness, gathering his belongings in a duffel bag and leaving the grey skies of Vancouver. But he had the condo which would fetch a killing one day if he was patient, his job, and all the other anchors that a man pushing forty can accumulate. A few years before, maybe. Now it seemed like a colossal waste of time.

Ramon tries to comfort himself with the thought that one day when he retires he will move to a tropical island of pristine white beaches and blue-green seas where the wrecks of humanity can never wash ashore.

He's gone to buy groceries, and there she is, picking cans out of the garbage in the alley behind the supermarket.

Llorona.

He used to send a postcard to his mother every year when he was younger, newly arrived in the States. He couldn't send any money because dishwashing didn't leave you with many spare dollars; and he couldn't phone often because he rented a room in a house, and there was no phone jack in there. If he wanted to make a call, he had to use the pay phone across the street.

Instead, he sent postcards.

Carmen didn't like it.

His sister complained about his lack of financial support for their mother.

"Why do I have to take care of mom, hu? Why is it me stuck in the house with her?" she asked him.

"Don't be melodramatic. You like living with mom."

"You're off in California and never send a God damn cent."

"It ain't easy."

"It ain't easy here either, Ramon. You're just like all the other shitty men. Just taking off and leaving the land and the women behind. Who's gonna take care of mom when she gets old and sick? Whose gonna clean the house and dust it then? With what fucking money? I ain't doing it, Ramon."

"Bye, Carmen."

"There are some things you can't get rid of, Ramon," his sister yelled.

He didn't call after that. Soon he was heading to another city, and by the time he reached Canada, he didn't bother sending postcards. He figured he would one day, but things got in the way; and years later, he thought it would be even worse if he tried to phone.

And what would they talk about now? It had been ages since he'd left home and the sister and cousins that had lived in Potrero. He'd gotten rid of layers and layers of the old Ramon, moulting into a new man.

But maybe Carmen had been right. Maybe there are some things you can't get rid of. Certain memories, certain stories, certain fears that cling to the skin like old scars.

These things follow you.

Maybe ghosts can follow you, too.

It's a bad afternoon. Assholes at work and in the streets. And then a heavy, disgusting rain pours down, almost a sludge that swallows the sidewalks. He's lost his umbrella and walks with his hands jammed inside his jacket's pockets, head down.

Four more blocks and he'll be home.

That's when Ramon hears the squeal. A high-pitched noise. It's a shriek, a moan, a sound he's never heard before.

What the hell is that?

He turns and looks, and it is the old woman, the one he's nicknamed Llorona, pushing her shopping cart.

Squeak, squeak, goes the cart, matching each of his steps. *Squeak, squeak.* A metallic chirping echoed by a low mumble.

"Children, children, children."

Squeak, squeak, squeak. A metallic chant with an old rhythm.

He walks faster. The cart matches his pace; wheels roll.

He doubles his efforts, hurrying to cross the street before the light changes. The cart groans, closer than before, nipping at his heels.

He thinks she is about to hit him with the damn thing, and then all of a sudden the sound stops.

He looks over his shoulder. The old woman is gone. She has veered into an alley, vanishing behind a large dumpster.

Ramon runs home.

The dogs are howling again. A howl that is a wail. The wind roars like a demon. The rain scratches the windows, begging to be let in, and he lies under the covers, terrified.

He feels his mother's arm around his body, her hands smoothing his hair like she did when he was scared. Just a little boy terrified of the phantoms that wander through the plains.

His mother's hand pats his own.

Mother's hand is bony. Gnarled, long fingers with filthy nails. Nails caked with dirt. The smells of mud, putrid garbage, and mold hit him hard.

He looks at his mother, and her hair is a tangle of grey. Her yellow smile paints the dark.

He leaps from the bed. When he hits the floor, he realizes the room is filled with at least three inches of water.

"Have you seen my children?" the thing in the bed asks.

The dogs howl, and he wakes up, his face buried in the pillow.

He takes a cab to work. He feels safer that way. The streets are her domain, she owns the alleys.

When he goes to lunch, he looks at the puddles and thinks about babies drowned in the water; corpses floating down a silver river.

Don't ever let the Llorona look at you, his uncle said. Once she's seen you, she'll follow you home and haunt you to death, little boy.

"Oh, my children," she'll scream and drag you into the river.

But he'd left her behind in Potrero.

He thought he'd left her behind.

Ramon tries to recall if there is a charm or remedy against the evil spirit. His uncle never mentioned one. The only cure he knew was his mother's embrace.

"There, there little one," she said, and he nested safe against her while the river overflowed and lightning traced snakes in the sky.

● ● ●

In the morning there is a patch of sunlight. Ramon dares to walk a few blocks. But even without the rain, the city feels washed out. Its colour has been drained. It resembles the monochromatic images they broadcasted on the cheap television set of his youth.

Even though he does not bump into her, the Llorona's presence lays thick over the streets, pieces of darkness clinging to the walls and the dumpsters in the alleys. It even seems to spread over the people: the glassy eyes of a binner reflect a river instead of the bricks of a building.

He hurries back home and locks the door. But when it rains again, water leaks into the living room. Just a few little drops drifting into his apartment.

He wipes the floor clean. More water seeps in like a festering boil, cut open and oozing disease.

The Llorona stands guard in the alley. She is a lump in the night looking up at his apartment window. He feels her through the concrete walls and the glass. Looking for him.

He fishes for the old notebook with the smudged and forgotten number.

The rain splashes against his building, and the wind cries like a woman.

The dial tone is loud against his ear.

More than ten years have passed. He has no idea what he'll say. He doesn't even understand what he wants to ask. He can't politely request to ship the ghost back to Mexico.

He dials.

The number has been disconnected.

He thinks about Carmen and his mother and the dusty nothingness behind their house.

There might not even be a house. Perhaps the night and the river swallowed them.

The Llorona comes with the rain. Or maybe it is the other way around: the rain comes with her. Something else also comes. Darkness. His apartment grows dimmer. He remains in the pools of light, away from the blackness.

Outside, in the alley, the Llorona scratches the dumpster with her nails.

The dogs howl.

Ramon shivers in his bed and thinks about his mother and how she used to drive the ghosts away.

She is sitting next to a heap of garbage in the middle of the alley, water pouring down her shoulders. She clutches rags and dirt and pieces of plastic against her chest, her head bowed and her face hidden behind the screen of her hair.

"My children. My children."

She looks up at him, slowly. The rain coats her face, tracing dirty rivulets along her cheeks.

He expects an image out of a nightmare: blood dripping, yellow cat-eyes, or a worn skull. But this is an old woman. Her skin has been torn by time and her eyes are cloudy. This is an old woman.

She could be his mother. She might be, for all he knows. He lost her photograph a long time ago and can't recall what she looks like anymore. His mother who ran her fingers through his hair and hugged him until the ghosts vanished. Now he's too old for ghosts, but the ghosts still come at nights.

The woman looks at him. Parched, forgotten, and afraid.

"I've lost my children," she whispers with her voice of dead leaves. The alley is a river. He goes to her, sinks into the muck, sinks into the silvery water. He embraces her and she strokes his hair. The sky above is black and white, like the pictures in the old TV set and the wind that howls in his ears is the demon wind of his childhood.

Those Shadows Laugh

Geoff Ryman

The tourist Precinct is owned by Disney.

Though they are very careful to use the Buena Vista branding. The Buena Vista Hotel—it sounds almost local. The tourists are jammed into a thin rind of gravelly coast called the Precinct, one of two places on the island where flat ground meets the sea. There is a container port on the north side, but most visas forbid visiting it. Mine did.

Many tourists stay on cruise ships, all white and gold, their lights reflecting on the water. There's a dock, some restaurants, most of them floating. The Precinct's streets are so narrow, and they zigzag up the rock face so steeply that the cars edge past each other's mirrors. Turning around at the inevitable dead end is nearly impossible. There is one guarded road up the cliffs onto the plateau—at night narrow vans wobble into the town. Every parking space has a car charger.

The Custom House runs across the mouth of the canyon into the town, a wall of rust-red laterite blocks, the pockmarks ringed with edges so sharp they cut. The Foreign House is crammed next to it, looking more like a prison than a luxury hotel.

My first morning.

I bob down the dock from a merchant ship (much better food than cruise liners and the merchant marine make better company). I see one of the Colinas, holding up a sign in handwritten letters that roll like waves.

Sra. Valdez

SINGLEHELIX.

She's tiny, brown, yes bare-breasted, yes with a feather through her nose, and she looks delighted. I catch her eye and wave; she hops up and down. I have to watch where I put my eyes. But luckily (or unluckily) for me, her smile is entrancing.

She greets me traditionally, pressing her forehead against both of my cheeks.

I'd been reading the first explorers' account, *En la Tierra de Mujeres*, from 1867. The male authors were breathlessly excited about a nation of women who didn't wear many clothes. They cloaked their lust in classical references—"Amazonian" or "island Cleopatras." From the text, you get visions of Edwardian actresses done up in modest togas as Clytemnestra or Medea—or maybe Mountain Girl from the Babylon sequence of *Intolerance*, all tomboy exuberance in a leopard skin, headband, a fiery smile—athletic gals vaulting over walls and shooting arrows.

The first engravings of Colinas Bravas were published in *Faro de Vigo* in 1871. The images are filtered through Western eyes— the features European, the locks flowing and curled, the dress rendered modest. But to people of the time the illustrations were a shock.

The giant sandstone-clad temple; the wooden mobile houses carried on pallbearers' rods; the terraces up the slopes that rose like skyscrapers—within a month of the illustrations' publication, scholars were declaring that the main city had been built by Romans or Persians or even Cambodians (all that laterite and sandstone cladding). Little brown women could not have built them.

But the texts on the walls of the temples, particularly the Torre Espiral, turned out to be in their language. It contains the words *hurricano* and *barbeque*. Which means it's Taíno, the language of the Indians who Columbus first encountered in my own dear homeland of the Dominican Republic, where they now exist as a genetic trace. Seven hundred years before Columbus, Taíno women sailed west toward the dark continent of Europe and settled an island without a single act of genocide.

At the München Olympics, Leni Riefenstahl's lens could not keep away from the Colinas athletes. They won ten women's gold medals that year, the highest number per head of population of any nation. The German Chancellor Angela Herbort made full propaganda use of them, showed them off at a rally to praise the principles of "health and common ownership."

In the full summer of the American century, the 1960 Rome Olympiad disallowed the Colinas from competition. Their lack of a reproductive cycle was said to be an unfair advantage in training. Colinas were, evidently, not quite women or quite human. The Colinas knew enough of our history to get what happens to people we say are not quite human. That's when they created the Precinct and farmed it out to Disney. They liked the cartoons.

My host tells me her name though I cannot pronounce or even really hear it. Eouvwetzixityl is one transcription (using Medrano's system). She knows this and tells me in Colina, *You say Evie.*

She takes my hand, and as she leads me toward the Custom House, she starts to skip. I have my rucksack, a small wheelie with my scrubs, and I'm wearing shorts and a tank top. Rumbling behind me, pushed by crewmen from Venezuela, are my battery-powered freezebox, a nanoscope workstation, and a portable extraction suite. The men are allowed only as far as the Custom House. I shake their hands and tip them—but I don't think I will miss men.

At the gate, Evie ducks down into the window and laughs and does a bit of a dance for the Custom guards who grin enormous gummy smiles, which they hide with their hands. There is such high hilarity that I cannot believe any work is being done. Then out of nowhere, my passport is returned with a two-page intelligent hologram that looks like the Statue of Liberty. My enormous boxes and I are led through into the City, called simply Ciudad. There isn't another one on the island. The Custom guards wave goodbye to me like I'm going on a school trip.

The public plaza—La Plaza del Pueblo—is crowded with tourists, many of them female couples holding hands and taking snaps. Languages swoop around me like flocks of birds—Spanish of course, but also Chinese, Danish, Yoruba, Welsh, Portuguese, and others I can't identify. The Plaza appears vast. It rears up, rocky cliffs on either side like waves about to break. The main sandstone steps on the south face go up in layers, it is said, to a height of 80 meters. The Torre Espiral looks as old as the pyramids like a ziggurat only conical with wide ramps spiraling up it to the flat roof with its giant urn of fire. Tourists are no longer allowed to climb it after a German woman fell off last year. Surrounding the Plaza like a bullring are rows of shops—yes, selling tourist tat—built on two levels with the Civil Palace on the north side and the National Library on the south next to the main steps. The Library's 12th-century bas-reliefs in sandstone deserve their fame—joyous scenes of everyday life, women dancing as they pound manioc, or harvesting fields, or throwing mangoes at each other from the trees. And the most famous, a woman giving birth. Beyond the Plaza at the end of the canyon, there's a tumble of boulders, a creek, then a broccoli mass of trees rising up the slope.

Most of Ciudad is in layers on those cliff faces, covered streets winding higher and higher where visitors are not allowed. The houses burrow into the rock. The gardens grow on top of the porches of the houses below them. The effect is like looking at those improbable Art Deco miniatures of cities in silent films. I have to crane my neck at a painful angle. Along the top, wind turbines pirouette on their toes like ballerinas.

They've put my clinic on the ground floor of the Plaza. The sandstone archway is the color of sunset with carved concentric circles that the guidebook says are meant to look like ripples in water. The entrance is clouded with purple bougainvillea spilling down from the roof. Just inside the door is an emergency generator—the islands do import some oil. Also a desk, an operating table, my IT suite, a data projector, screen, and rows of chairs for my seminars.

I'd specified those. Nobody told me Colinas never sit on chairs.

Evie spins round and round, arms outstretched as if all this is hers. She's so delighted I can't stop taking hold of her hand. I should know better, but I am a woman; and I rely on her not being suspicious of me. That makes me feel guilty.

She looks human, but yes, a bit different. Her smile is too wide, her chin too tiny. The Colinas are now recognized as another species within the genus *Homo*. Being parthenogenetic, she ovulates maybe four times in her life. How's this for utopia? Colinas do not have periods. They also do not mate, do not cluster into little paired units. Famously, they are supposed to lack sexual desire.

I ask her, *You have children?* She nods yes and holds up a finger—one. It's customary to only have one.

Aw, what is child name?

Her smile doesn't change, but she freezes for a moment and then shakes her head and giggles. She points east and says, Quatoletcyl Mah. I know the phrase—"Sad Children Loved."

I close my eyes with shame. Of course, that's why she's so delighted I'm here. I shouldn't have asked about children. I apologize. Literally I say, *I make mistake*, which is about the closest their language gets to swearing.

She says, *Tomorrow. Tomorrow we see child.*

They have no word for he or she, and in everyday vernacular, no word for me, my, or mine. They can say "I," almost like it's a geographical location.

From somewhere a bell sounds. It moans, deeply, like it regrets something.

You leave now, she says, still smiling. Ah. Right. Closing time. She takes my hand again. Hers is sweet and insistent.

Outside thousands of sandaled feet sound like rain or applause as they make their way back to the Custom House, its gates thrown open. On the ocean only seven metres beyond the gate, the sun sits low. The square is flooded with orange, sideways light that makes the temple and terraces the color of overripe apricots. Shadows delineate every carved face or incised word sign. In this light I see that, yes indeed, the lighthouse temple is also a book, the writing in stone all the way up the giddy ramp. It tells the story of how the first Colina mother gave birth.

We know that is a myth, as is her rising out of the sea. There must have been more than one mother—genetically there are five matrilineal lines. Experts argue whether they were expelled or set off across the sea for themselves, looking for somewhere to be.

I look up at the terraces—the houses don't have doors, and the rooms are full of a wavering orange light lit by candles. I want to see inside, be inside, those rooms. I want to know what it is like to live there. I glimpse a donkey being led down toward the main staircase. The woman riding it is brushing her long black hair.

Men are allowed into the Plaza if accompanied by responsible female sponsors. Most of the men have the same expression of delight, a clenched smile, determined to appear benign. Some of the women allow themselves to look pissed off. People traveling in tourist groups or cruise ships often do—they're trapped with each other, and though stuffed full of sights and good food, they have no power. I am happier in my shorts with my rucksack, happier still to have a good working reason for being here.

Evie skips me all the way into the Foreign House. Someone at the entrance invisibly slips her a lei, and she drapes the flowers around my neck and claps her hands. The idea of the lei is stolen from Hawaii—they cheerfully admit this. For some reason, the native House staff—in white shirts and black slacks—applaud me. I feel my eyes swell.

They know you help us, Evie says and gives me a forehead kiss. Evie smells of sunlight and honey. I have her for just a moment, and she is hot and shivery under my hand. She leaps away, tossing her mane like a horse. One of the staff, looking bone-thin and European, says in perfect Spanish, "She is so proud to be your host."

My room has purple sheets and translucent Colinas chocolate under my pillow. The penthouse suite costs $1000 a night. No loud music after 9 p.m. Unless you want to be locked in with a bunch of rich foreigners getting drunk on whisky that costs $25 a shot (along with the celebs—I have the inestimable privilege of being here the same night as Tom Cruise), there are only two things to do in the House at night. You can watch movies on TV—and only those that contain not a hint of sexual violence or enacted congress. Or something a bit less virtual.

The Foreign House is the only hotel on Colinas Bravas with doors that open into both the Plaza and its harbor—the privilege of being invited or rich.

I step out into the demarcated café space in the very last of the twilight and look up. Lights dance in all the doorways and windows; shadows bend and dip and wave. Those shadows laugh.

The laughter comes from everywhere in gusts. The narrow canyon magnifies the sound and sends it echoing. Songs, too, some of them campfire-simple, some of them complex and formal like choirs, and some a massed, intoning chant like prayer. Strains of music played on reeds and strings sound like an orchestra warming up. It's as if each kind of sound is a different flock of swallows dive-bombing around me. Then as suddenly as waking up, Ciudad falls silent; the candles go out. There are so many stars!

I turn. I have been observed all this while by the same staff member in American dress—a short-sleeved white shirt, slim black trousers.

Beautiful, I say, flinging up my arms. *Much!*

A happy hour, she says. *Each night.*

And she gestures for me to go back into the hotel. Later, during the night, I am comforted to hear the *sshing* of tropical rain on the courtyard and roof. It must have been a dream, but I think I heard that staff member go on to say, *We are easy to love.*

It is a failing of mine that I fall in love with foreigners.

First I fall in love with a country, which means the people in it, and then usually just one of those people to be my partner, my rock, my point of entry. I always do it, and the process is delicious. Though so far, it has also always gone wrong.

I find, for example, that they sleep all the time, or fight all the time, or need a fight to feel passion, or think it's funny to insult me. Or they simply want me to pay for everything. It ends. I go to boring home. Home is the Dominican Republic, sex-tourist destination, Caribbean island with an 11,000 foot high mountain, miles of beaches, and a national park with hills that look like cupcakes. You've got to have a psychosocial problem with home to find the Dominican Republic dull.

That first night listening to rain, I imagined sitting cross-legged on the floor of one of those high cells, and going to sleep with Evie, and waking up with her at first dawn, of being allowed to stay, of being allowed to love. A harmless fantasy, I thought, and it drifted me off to sleep.

● ● ●

The next day, as promised, I was ready to work at 4:30 a.m. Getting up wasn't difficult—the dawn song of Ciudad is famous and justly so. The people simply get up in the dark and start singing.

It is the aural equivalent of a warm bed—soft and soothing and you loll in its sound. But if you have to work, it somehow eases you upright. I washed and looked out of the window of the House to see flashlights and candles like fireflies everywhere among the walkways.

The pavements were made mirrors by the rain, blue and gold puddles. A steady train of women were moving down the steps to set up the shops or open the Library. Evie was waiting for me, holding a candle. I wore my lab trousers and coat. I felt like a native, getting up in drizzle and crossing the Plaza to my place of work. Only, Evie made me veer away from my clinic, steering me toward the Civil Palace where I was to be introduced to the Council, or maybe just a council. I couldn't be too sure.

It was just like *In the Country of Women*. There they sat, as described in 1867—the slim, wise, implacable, and sometimes kindly elders of Colinas Bravas. They, too, wore simple formal clothes made of reed beaten into linen, soft and gray with subtle patterns in the weave or embroidery. The jackets did indeed look like quilts, there were so many pockets. One of the councilors was wearing a tool belt of wrenches, chisels, and a hammer. The elders looked calm with dim smiles and alert eyes, and their gestures for me to sit were hearty and not to be gainsaid.

"Hello and welcome to Colinas Bravas," said the one in the center, speaking English with an American accent. She had a high, round, polished forehead that reflected light. I gave her the nickname La Señora Luminosa. The name stuck for me. I responded politely, said how glad I was to be there. They asked about my accommodation. Another woman, who spoke with a South African (?) accent, expressed gratitude that I was there and to SingleHelix for being willing to share, etc.

It came down to how long I would need to stay on the island.

"As long as you need me," I said in Spanish, the official second language. I told them that I was unmarried, the head of SingleHelix's Research Division in the Dominican Republic. They nodded glacially. I think they knew what that meant. We in SoloHebra RD do things that Our Friendly Neighbors to the North would rather not do themselves.

They insisted. "How long do you estimate?"

I said six months.

They asked if two might be enough for them to master the basic technology. "Nos tenemos biólogos en nuestro propio país." The technique does not require that all who carry out the procedure need to be microbiologists?

I had to smile. I shook my head. That gesture means nothing to the Colinas. I said, *I stay time you want.* They were very grateful, and they wanted me gone.

It was still dark and cool when we walked in a group to my clinic. Luminosa took my hand and strolled with me as if we were old friends.

"I know this is basically a business proposition for your ..." For some reason she had difficulty finding the word company. "But for us, we still experience your visit with deep personal gratitude to you. This is not your home; these are not your people." She stopped and put my hand in both of hers and looked directly into my eyes. "But you help us. We will make sure you see more of us than most foreigners do."

"That would be great honor."

So Luminosa strode on with me and asked me what I would like to see. I told her that I had read the 1867 text and its sequel about the managed forests—fruit, nuts, hemp all growing as if untended. Is it true that their orange trees stand as high as oaks? The plateau is flat but rolling like England with large forests and open pastures. It is never seen from the air. Its airspace is closed, and there is no airport. I hinted I might like to see where the SingleHelix equipment would be made in the industrial northern port. Her smile didn't change.

That day, my clinic was bigger. The building has movable internal walls. Rows of beds had been added; my fridge preserving the samples buzzed, and I saw that the thermidor's light was on. The operating theatre lights were standing ready.

"Show us how," said Luminosa. "No need to do an extraction. We have the two ova ready for you." Evie stepped forward and covered her mouth with both hands, laughing. There is no way to say in her language, "The egg is mine."

I panicked. "We can't do it now! The donor material has to be thawed, inspected, be at the same exact temperature. It has to be from a different matrilineal line ..."

Luminosa took my hand again. "We know, we know."

"But you don't understand. If Evie only has one ovum ..." I glanced at Evie, looking so innocent. "If anything goes wrong, she'll have lost this chance!"

"Then check everything," said Luminosa, stroking the back of my hand. I went and scanned both sets of donated material, hands shaking. I was annoyed that they had done so much of my work for me, unasked and unsupervised. I didn't like it. I felt rushed. I felt denigrated. I was simultaneously relieved and disgruntled when both ova were fine. "Well, yes, I can start work. Do ... does Evie know who the other egg belongs to?"

Luminosa looked blank. "Why would Evie want to know that?"

That brought me up short. Well ... but ... no need to know who the other mother was?

La Señora swept us on. "No need to explain much to us. We are familiar with the basics. Just show us how to carry out the procedure swiftly and well."

The same images that guided my instruments were shown on the screen. They watched as I micromanaged the translucent needle into the donor ovum and then slipped the cradle underneath the DNA to carry it out.

"It's just a question of practice," I said. "Hand-eye coordination." The gantry slowly moved between microscope surgeries.

I switched screens. There was Evie's daughter, on the screen unmade, as transparent as a ghost. "This is the delicate bit. Like making lace."

More like joining two halves of a zipper for the first time, link by link. There is always a moment when the two halves somehow snap together and fuse. That's when a new person is created. I told them when it happened. They applauded.

The transfer probe is full of water-based jelly rich with nutrients. The trick is to gently lower the egg into the very tip, so that it is the first thing presented. I looked around. Evie was already on one of the beds, already naked.

"It's all right," said Luminosa. "No embarrassment. We have no need of that kind of modesty."

I began to feel shivery and a bit sick. I looked down at Evie, at her smile, into her black eyes, and all I saw was trust and hope. I stroked her hair; couldn't help it. I eased stage one into her; stage two was the probe itself extended. I nicknamed the egg Luminosa as well—it was all glowing, the probe has a light. I couldn't watch. I had to. I saw where the egg needed to be placed and lowered it.

"That's it. That's all. We'll know in two days at most." Again, applause.

I had a reaction—the corners of my vision went dark, my legs weak. I needed somewhere to sit, but all my chairs had been pulled back, with the women cross-legged on the tiles. I nearly fell. Luminosa caught me by the shoulder, lowered me to the floor, and as she stroked my shoulder, her eyes asked me a worried question.

"It's a little bit overwhelming," I said, and didn't like to say why. Luminosa kept stroking my shoulder.

Outside, it was still only 8 a.m. and cool. We sat on the pavement in the Plaza as the first of the tourists strolled past. One of the councilors brought me a cup of coffee. "Sorry," I kept saying, "sorry." They asked if I wanted to put off our visit, and I said, "No! No!"

After my coffee, as the heat swelled, we made our way to the end of the canyon through its grove of trees, climbing steps along the creek full of rainwater. We attained the plateau surprisingly quickly, and I walked out into the shade of giant trees, smelling of citrus blossom. A fleet of Škodas waited for us. They make Škodas here on license; Škodas are everywhere except in Ciudad itself.

I waved the cars away. It was so cool in the shade, shafts of light through the leaves, moss underfoot, even bluebells. All the trees were outsized, huge, lemon bushes the size of mangoes. Yes, there were houses carved out of fallen trunks left open for anyone who needed them. We went into one for a rest. It had shelves, wooden plates, bowls, serving implements, a working flush toilet, electric lights, dried herbs and spices, even clothes neatly folded.

Evie had slipped into some damp moss that had smeared green down her tunic. She simply stepped out of it front of me, unfolded another tunic from a shelf, and slipped it over her head. I found that so accepting, accepting of me, this galumphing foreigner who smelled so different.

We ate a lunch of raisins, nuts, and about the only cheese they can stand, a very mild sweet cream a bit like mascarpone. Shade-resistant hemp grew on the lower levels. La Señora rolled the leaves into a kind of impromptu cigar and passed it to me. This I had not been expecting. The leaves weren't cured, but were sweet and mild. After lunch, we walked for about an hour, the Škodas rattling indiscreetly behind us.

I don't know what I expected of the Quatoletcyl Mah—a wire-mesh fence, perhaps, or confining rooms. Instead I suddenly noticed that Evie was not with me, only La Señora Luminosa. I did hear a sound ahead of us like children playing. And then I saw Evie walking quickly toward me, beaming so pleased, holding the hand of someone almost as tall as she was, but with loping, spidery limbs and a head that looked like the top of it had been cut off. The mouth and chin were outsize as if infected, bristling with teeth.

This is child, Evie said. *Call her Queesi.* She told her daughter my name as they say it: *Mah-ree-rah!* Queesi bellowed my name, gave a belly laugh, and flapped her hands. She liked the name or maybe me and clumped me with a forehead kiss. Then she darted back and hid her face in her mother's shoulder.

Mahreerah equals elder. She helps us.

Queesi said, *No more sad children.* She knew exactly why I was there and what she was. Evie was smiling at her daughter with such an expression, mingled kindness and pain.

Sad children were climbing trees picking fruit or sitting in a circle pounding fibers for linen or standing on concrete platforms raking what looked like walnuts but which from the smell were surely fermenting cocoa beans, the fruit flesh ragged around them. If the Colinas have a cash crop, it is chocolate. But for them it is a religious drink, unsweetened and used only for the holy days of their religion. There were thalidomide-like deformities, nearly limbless little things carried on the backs of blind giants. There were tiny ancient-looking crones but with merry grins and goblin eyes, elderly women who were ten years old. Every imaginable genetic disease or infirmity.

Queesi gamboled back to her friends and grabbed a pestle.

Not bad sad children, Evie said. *Not bad.* I took her hand, and she looked up at me, blinking.

Little little sad to see them go, I said.

Little little, she said, and I knew she'd understood what I meant. The sad children were lovely as they were—there was a sadness that there would be fewer of them.

It was now past noon, so we took the Škodas and drove to see one of the mobile towns. Queesi clambered in next to us and bounced up and down on the springed seats.

The cars jostled over the ruts in a causeway between rice paddies. In the distance we saw people carrying the mobile houses like oversized Arks of the Covenant. One house rested on its carrying rods between the bumpers of two Škodas. Frank Lloyd Wright called the houses architectural masterpieces. What he didn't say or perhaps even know was that each house is also a book, the writings and drawings burned into the wood.

The seasonal rice-harvest town was gathering like a herd of bison. We drove into it past houses radiating outward from one of the conical temples. You see them all across the landscape like factory chimneys. They are made of rocks cleared from fields, each tower centuries old, as rugged as their elders.

The new town was expecting me. My neck was ringed round with leis. There was another lunch—rice, manioc, nuts, and fruit. I was served a boiled duck egg (there were ducks everywhere in the rice fields). I gave a talk about the clinic and the project, mostly in Spanish. When I spoke in Colinas, there was a sigh and applause. I told them how the Council would be setting up clinics all across the country and how the Council had a license to produce the equipment on the island. After the lecture Colinas gave me hugs or showed me their babies. Children ran up to me and asked me questions about New York. How did they know I'd lived there? They said "New York" like they were from north Manhattan.

I've spent a lot of my life battling things—my mom, Santiago de los Caballeros, indeed the whole damn Cibao with its cowboy-hatted men and its shacks and the giant monument Trujillo built to himself and the lies we tell ourselves about our history. This valley looks almost the same as El Cibao as if I'd remade the DR in a dream.

After lunch Evie and I separated—I was to go on, but she had to drop her daughter off at Quatoletcyl Mah. I felt bereft for a minute or two watching her car bounce away, but it was a spectacular drive back—my car zigzagged down the cliff over a sparkling sea and the clusters of bladed turbines marking shallow water, and for one heart-stopping moment *down* onto Ciudad itself, looking more like garden terraces than a town. It had been a wonderful day. I felt as if I had been given everything I ever wanted all at once. I have been living off that day ever since.

Sometimes countries become your own Magic Kingdom. Every detail of what people wear, how they move and laugh, what they eat, how they eat (with their fingers, scooping up soup with mashed yam or manioc even sometimes maize), their buildings and the brushed red earth between them, or the sectioned fruit drying in the sun along the unpaved roads, and the way you can pick up the dried plums or apricots with no one to call it stealing. The island is big enough to generate its own rivers, and the water is clean enough to drink from the palm of your hand. There are windmills everywhere, of course—most of the world's windmills are built in Colinas Bravas. All that electricity. The transatlantic phone cables surfaced here; now there are giant relay towers. Colinas Bravas has the most copious broadband in the world, and they hardly use it for anything. They don't talk to us much. They watch wildlife films. And they have a ministry that keeps an eye on world news.

If there was a zombie apocalypse, it couldn't get to Colinas Bravas. If the sea levels rise, we might lose the Precinct, but the town itself would climb higher up into the hills. The harbor might even improve. If there is a nuclear war, the prevailing winds will carry most of the radiation away.

The next morning, Evie was waiting for me outside the café. We started work again on another volunteer. Even more people crowded in, looking at the screens or over my shoulders. Too many, perhaps—I made a mess of the extraction. I just about got it out undamaged. Their ova are precious—four in a lifetime—so I said, "Let's leave it. We can wait." But they urged me on. The recipient was sitting up, watching me. They all just watched me—none of them took notes. They appear to have a very different attitude to text and books.

Evie stood next to me as I worked. *You do well well.* It was the strangest thing. She really did have the power to steady my hand. I did it for her. If anything, the next procedure was the neatest extraction and implant I'd ever done.

I kept explaining what I was doing. Right at the end, Luminosa announced, "The children will be knocked clean of genetic faults." And then in Colinas ... *This child be not sad.* They don't have a future tense.

My audience had all left; I was turning off the lights, and the evening bell was sounding when two tourists walked into my clinic to poke around. They wanted something. They wouldn't leave—a man and a woman, both Italian. Their English was terrible and their Spanish good enough to make bad mistakes, but they understood when I made imploring gestures and shoved my palms toward the doorway. They asked, "Trabajo?" and pointed at me. The woman pointed to her husband, to herself, eyes glittering. "Medico! Medico!"

Evie came back to fetch me, and I signaled for help. She spun away. I said in any language I could think of, "Closed. Cerrado. Chiuso ..."

Evie returned with two Colinas wearing thick leather aprons and trousers. Hanging from their shoulders were polished things the color of teak that looked like flutes.

Trouble? they asked me.

I want they go. I pointed my finger.

The flute-things were their guns. Guns were the very first thing the Colinas made once they understood who and what we were.

"Passports," the police demanded. The tourists understood that.

● ● ●

It's all in the sequel that Juan Emmanuel Medrano wrote—*Return to the Country of Women*. He was the most decent of the men who had first landed on the island. Juan Emmanuel fell in love with one of them, a woman nicknamed Zena. Being a man of his time, he thought her lack of interest in sex was natural to all women who had not been corrupted. He was proud of his ability to learn how to do without sex, prescribed it in fact as the straight route to wholesomeness—chastity in marriage.

As for the Colinas, they were already aware that parthenogenesis was accumulating mutations. They have a word that means literally *unfolding snake* for a seed that sheds its skin to become something else. They were aware that their First Mother was a product of an Unfolding Snake and that they all descended from her—or rather what we know, that there must have been at a minimum five women, five different matrilineal lines. It's quite eerie now to read Juan Emmanuel's description of their beliefs. It would appear that they understood everything about DNA save for its double helix shape.

Zena married him in a spirit of self-sacrifice to see if bisexual reproduction brought health. Of course, they could not interbreed. She didn't ovulate for the duration of the marriage.

He really is a brick, poor Juan Emmanuel. He became as much of a Colina as is possible for a man. He waxes syrupy about how Motherhood is the driving engine of Colinas society, how they all dream of being a mother. *Irony alert*: all women dream of nothing but being mothers, and even if they think they don't want to be one, they are overcome with mother love the moment they see the infant. *Irony ends here.*

He never quite got, dear Juan Emmanuel, that Colinas *do* have sex, some of them at least, but not just with one person. He drove Zena mad, long after the marriage was over, long after she began to turn her back every time she saw him coming. *Why did you want to be with me all the time?*

"You will come to love me," he responded. "You are my woman." The Colinas have no word for wife or husband or spouse. No one marries.

Poor Juan Emmanuel Medrano. He lived outside the walls on the tiny strip of beach still writing his wife long poems. She moved to a village on the other side of the island. Go home, the Colinas advised him. But Juan Emmanuel couldn't. He loved the place; I believe him when he says he loved Zena. How could you not believe him—look at all he gave up. He became a pathetic figure; forbidden the entire island except for what became the Precinct. He told stories for visitors, set up a hotel, waited out the winter season, and wrote a lexicon and grammar of the Colinas language, which is still the best we have. Hollywood made a movie about him starring Humphrey Bogart—he mans the artillery that sinks the British gunboats. *Irony alert*: of course those women needed a man to defend them. Ingrid Bergman won an Oscar for playing Zena. In the Foreign House, they still sing that song. Play it for me, Sam.

That night, La Señora invited me to dinner. The room was no bigger than any of the others, a two-chamber hollow in the rock. The walls were covered with beautiful paintings. One of the few things they import from us is oil-based pigments. La Señora explained who had painted what—lots of portraits and bowls of fruit, not great art, but all of it colorful and fun.

They had the money to import something else. Four of the women scurried out and came back laboring under a huge canvas. My breath caught, and I sputtered with recognition as if the Queen of England had just walked in—it was one of Monet's giant water lily paintings. I remembered the scandal in France when it had been sold.

It is like us, one of them said, and left it leaning against the wall.

The room had no TV; there was no computer. I asked Luminosa why not. She said they had tried our movies but they were all full of murder or marriage. "We like the cartoons for kids. But in *Wall-E* two robots get married. Why would robots get married? A doll of a cowgirl and a doll of a spaceman get married. Even *things* get married." She shook her head.

The girls started to run in with elaborate clothes. They hauled me to my feet and took off my old khaki. I felt fat and sagging like I needed a scaffolding to hold me up. They pulled over my head a gelabia with black applique. Then a kind of red velvet cape that made me feel like Red Riding Hood. They started swapping clothes, too—butterfly saris, shawls of black lace, Kevlar body armor. Their laughter bounded off the rock and straight into my head.

The Colinas don't own anything.

My days began to be the same. I asked to be taken up onto the plateau again. I especially wanted to see the container port and the factories. Finally, Luminosa said that it was policy not to allow anyone to see their factories.

Luminosa insisted on taking over one of the implants herself, asking me to guide her, and then—without asking me—signaled Evie to try. That was clever of her—I wanted Evie to do well. "Sí, sí, esa es la manera de hacerlo!"

Evie and I would walk back to the Foreign House, long after the bell, long after the tourists cleared.

About a week in.

We're walking through dusk and candlelight and all those lovely sounds, and I'm holding her hand. But tonight for some reason, fireworks. Tourists are lining the high walls of the Custom House, applauding and raising glasses of champagne.

We're looking up, and Evie says, *You write me yes when you go home.*

"Yes yes okay yes."

We have Sky-pee.

And I chuckle. "You use Skype? And Facebook?"

Sky-pee yes. No Facebook. No Twits.

"Why not?"

Sky-pee one person, one person. She holds up two fingers.

I can't think of a way to say *Just you and me* in her language. I manage *We talk much,* and she giggles and shakes her head, which means yes, but still feels like no to me.

That night I go to bed in the Foreign House, and it's like my very bones are humming; and I see her, and I see me. I see me taking one half of my DNA and putting it into her egg. I see us having a child together. I'll carry it if they say we can't, that the child might lose parthenogenesis. And she and I will live together with our child in one of those towns next to forests of oranges, mangoes, and quince, and I'll keep helping their babies to be born.

I felt elated the whole of the next day; I could feel my face make nice shapes; I could see me sparking laughter in other people. That night I asked Evie if she wanted to see my room—that's allowed, she is a Colina, she can go anywhere. The room made her giggle. She ran into the bathroom and flicked the lights, flushed the toilet, and turned on the TV—and great, yes, it was *CSI* and they were cutting up a corpse—but for some reason that seemed to be the funniest thing she'd ever seen, and she flung herself onto the bed and bounced up and down on it.

Too ripe. Couldn't sleep here.

She stretched out, and I couldn't help giving her a kiss. I hugged her and rolled her back and forth, back and forth. She wasn't laughing but looked both troubled and awed, so I kissed her again, open-mouthed this time, and I felt her chest rise up in response.

I would never force myself on anyone. But there are Colinas who want sex. They are not arrested or mocked, but they are regarded as being different. A holdover from the days of change those 1700 years ago. We didn't do anything adventurous that first night, but I couldn't stop myself saying, "I love you." She slipped away and gave a wave with just the tips of her fingers. I watched from my window as she walked through the Plaza at 11:30 p.m.

The next day, Evie looked merry. I thought I had made her happy. She stood up straighter, and her eyes looked that bit narrower as if she had learned something new. She snatched things from people and wagged her hips as if to mock them. Her friends laughed louder or gaped in a caricature of open-mouthed shock, pretending (it seemed to me) to be scandalized. One of the elders came in and clapped her hands and said something outraged and schoolmarmish. I couldn't help but smile and shake my head. The older woman glared at me. *What am I then, a ringleader? A bad influence?* I dipped my chin, crumpled my lips, and laughed. Evie caught my look, laughed, and clapped her hands. *Okay, I am a bad influence. What are you going to do about it?*

That night, long after bedtime, we went for a walk in the Precinct, listening to small waves rolling pebbles back into the water. Out to sea all those floating hotels, container ships, or private yachts. Ciudad was silent now and dark, and Evie's eyes were wide, thrilled but also scared. She insisted we go into a bar.

Immediately, two women strode up, wanting to talk. One of them pinned us to the table by saying she'd buy us some drinks. The other squared off with me and asked us outright—how did we meet? How did I know her? They asked her questions about how the Colinas got pregnant and had to be told several times. Twice I explained that Colinas did not form relationships with each other as we understood it. Evie sipped her whisky and hated it, her lips turning down, her nose wrinkling. The two women laughed and one said, "You drink it like this," and knocked the shot back down in one.

The questions didn't stop, of her, of me. What are the houses like inside? What do you mean they don't own anything—they've sewn up the world market in all kinds of things. Other couples shuffled closer, stood in a huddle trying to hear, desperate to actually meet a Colina. Do you go to school? What music do you like? Have you heard of a singer called Mariah Carey?

I said we had to be away. One of them said no, stay, the next round's on me. I was worried, but Evie seemed to like it. The bar was playing Whitney Houston's "I Wanna Dance with Somebody," and before I knew it, one the women had made off with my girlfriend. The woman danced like Will Smith making fun of old black men—was she really doing the boogaloo? Evie tried to dance, then shook her head, stepped back, and just watched.

"No—come on, you're supposed to join in!"

I got worried. I got mad. I strode up to both of them and said in Colina, *Bedtime. Sleep now.*

Evie smiled and did a head wobble that I thought meant yes, because it was indeed time to go.

"Spiriting her away, are you?"

As I bundled her off, I told them over my shoulder that Evie had to be up at four and all the other Colinas would be in bed. The woman turned sideways and rumpled her lip at me—*I know what you're up to.*

I felt guilty and sore like I'd overdone a workout in the gym, and my heart felt bigger, swollen with misgiving because I was beginning to see that what I wanted would not be possible. I asked Evie to come to my room, and she nodded her head up and down exaggeratedly like a child, which meant no. But I reacted like she'd said yes and pulled her with me. She started to giggle and also to shake, but I got her into the room and hugged her and said, "Stay with me."

We rolled on the bed again, and this time I traced her nipples with my tongue down to her joybox and kissed her there. She had a clitoris (though people say they don't), and kissing it had the usual effect. She did not kiss me back—but I thought, give it time. The ache inside was gone: she was mine. More or less fully clothed, I slept. When I woke up again about two, she was gone.

The next day at the clinic she whispered, "I don't see you again." I felt like I just swallowed a barium meal, my throat and esophagus coated all the way to my nauseous stomach.

"I'm sorry. I'm sorry if we went too far."

I thought I knew what the trouble was. Again, no words in Colina. "My intentions are strictly honorable," I said in English as a joke and mimed a chuckle. I couldn't find a light, jokey way to say it even in Spanish.

I told her, *Not that thing only. Good thing.* I had no way to say, "It's not just the sex, I want to be your partner." She sighed and looked back at me glumly and seemed to shrink.

I had to say it in Spanish. "I ... want ... to ... marry .... you." I hammered each word like a nail.

She stared blankly, eyes on the floor, and then abruptly streamed out through the archway.

I thought I was in love; I thought this was it; I thought we'd have a child; I thought I'd live here—I saw it all in front of me, a beautiful new life. And I'd lost it. I hated myself for having sex. I held my head in my hands and paced and called myself stupid. Why, why ruin everything for sex when what I wanted was a wife? I had completely misunderstood the problem.

In the morning, full of determination, I went to the Civil Palace to see La Señora Luminosa and declare myself. It was still dark, but the stars seemed to make a promise. I could hear the waves and seagulls and slippered feet. It was early even for them. I knew what I was going to do and felt solemn, determined, even brave.

In the Palace, Luminosa was lighting candles, her face a bit puffy from having just woken up. Another elder shuffled forward and yawned.

"I've done a terrible thing," I said. "I ... Evie and me ..."

"She was in your room, and you had sex. Not so terrible." She didn't even look at me.

"No. You don't understand. I didn't force myself on her or anything. But I'm not sure she was ready for it."

Luminosa said Evie's Colina name in surprise. "Eouvwetzixityl? If she didn't want it, it wouldn't happen." The old woman looked amused. "She was curious, I think. And I believe she likes it." Luminosa stood up and looked straight at me, a half-smile on her face. "So have you confessed enough?"

"I want you to know I wasn't just toying with her or exploiting her."

"You couldn't."

"I want to marry her."

Both women stopped, looked at each other, and then started to laugh. The elder made a kind of squawk, covered her mouth, and had to turn her back. Luminosa groaned, "Oh, no!"

"I ... I ... I ... could live here. I ... we ... we could have a child. You know, me contribute to the gene pool." That was my attempt to join in with what I thought was a robust and hearty reaction.

Luminosa shook her head. "Women do this, too?"

"We fall in love, yes."

The elder woman howled with laughter and ran off, calling out names.

Luminosa sighed. "You can't marry. We have no such category in law. And there is no question of you being able to stay and live with us. It was in your contract."

I began to feel cold, but with sweat along my hairline. "Well, well, I think we ought to hear from Evie."

"We will." She went back to lighting candles. I began to hear from outside cries and shouts, doors slamming, and the usual morning sounds of running feet, perhaps with more laughter than usual.

The Colinas gawped at me feverishly, eyes glistening. They chattered and roared with laughter. Evie strode in, her back rigid, eyes wide, hands clasped in front of her like a choirboy trying to make the toilet in time.

Luminosa said, her voice going brassy, *Foreigner wants to do Medrano with you.*

Bouquets of faces crammed through the doorway, and they all roared with laughter. Evie looked mortified and also weary at the same time. At that moment, my only concern was for her.

Why do this? she asked me. *You want me inside you like a baby!* I remember that phrase because it was so strange. But she had no word for ownership. She couldn't say: *Why do you want to own me?* Both hands were curled into claws of frustration. She spun on her heel and pushed her way through the throng.

I began to realize just how big a catastrophe this was.

They would tell me to leave; they would tell SingleHelix the reason why. It's part of our ethos never to proposition the single women we help all over the world. I would have to leave the company, maybe the country: Santo Domingo has very few jobs in the field.

"Start today's clinic," advised Luminosa.

Evie did not visit that day or the next. No one said much else about it though some of the students' jaws swelled with suppressed laughter. *How you have baby with Evie she has baby coming?* one of them asked. *Why Evie want three babies?* Each time one of them asked a question like that there was shrill, speeded-up laughter as if flowers had learned how to chuckle.

Nobody asked me to climb the hill again or to eat with them. When the evening bell tolled, I had to vacate the Plaza. I went to the Foreign House and waited in that downstairs bar, pacing, clutching a gin, staring out at the Plaza. It looked empty but rang with laughter, and that made me wonder if they were telling jokes about me. I hoped Evie would come. I waited long after 9 p.m. when all was still and dark, thinking that she might slip away when she thought nobody could see. Finally. the barista said I should get some sleep as she folded the big iron shutters and slipped bolts into the floor.

Two days later I was asked to attend a breakfast in the Palace. I knew what it was about. There were nuts and fruit and cheese. The elders thanked me for a job well done. They said they were particularly pleased by my teaching and all the efforts I had made to fit in and to show interest in and respect for their culture. I was to receive a ten thousand dollar bonus.

"And don't worry—we have said not a thing about Evie to your ... your ... owners." Luminosa's smile was like the Mona Lisa's.

I spent another night pacing in the bar, listening to that sound of laughter, singing, prayer—nightmarish. It wasn't just losing Evie. I was losing that sound, I was losing a country. I couldn't believe that I would have to go back to Santo Domingo and the Agora Mall with its McDonald's and its Apple Store and its pharmacy that sold ultraviolet toothbrush sterilizers for fifty bucks. The world felt like an apple withering with age.

That night was fireworks again, and the hotel's doors were open; and I glanced about me as the sky boomed and battered and kept blossoming out like flowers, and I gathered myself up, darted around the black cloth partitions that separated us from the Plaza. And I ran. I pounded across the pavement, imagining that I was being chased. I ran past the bougainvillea front of what had been my clinic, up the main steps, and then along each of the terraces as if in panic, looking through each open archway, checking rooms full of flickering light and surprised faces. No Evie, no Luminosa, room after room.

Finally, I found Luminosa sitting on the floor playing poker with three others. I collapsed at their feet and sobbed, "Please let me stay. Please. I'll be good. I'll stay away from Evie. She won't ever see me again. Send me out to a town on the plateau. Send me to the north. I can help sell machines. I speak the language. Only let me stay, please, please let me stay." I kept it up until even I couldn't make sense of what I was saying. All that time, Luminosa stroked my hair and hugged me. Finally, I calmed down, and exhausted, I let myself be led away.

But I didn't leave.

Now I work in the Precinct for the Disney Corporation in their big hotel at the end of the strip. Classy, with facades made of the local sandstone, vast interiors with polished marble floors, and lots of locked doors. I speak Spanish, English, and of course Colina, and I have a charming little story to tell of how I came here and fell in love with the place, only I don't mention that I am not allowed back in. The guests sit rapt with attention. "Oh, I would love to see inside one of their homes." And I correct them with pained tolerance. "Oh, that is the thing. They don't have homes. They really don't own anything." On fireworks nights I get to stand on the wall and look out over the Plaza with its steps and songs and chants and running feet and those lights darting about like fireflies, and I always marvel how it is that you almost never see them.

Or I sit in my room at the Buena Vista Hotel where the broadband is amazing, and I see every episode of *Mad Folk* and *Game of Thrones*. Evie never answers my calls on Skype. Sometimes I crunch along the beach after even the Precinct has gone to bed except for the odd drunken tourist, sometimes men looking shaken, miserable, fists bunched. They teach me, those men, the cost of desire.

Last night I had a dream: I was hiking again with Dad. He used to take me up into the mountains—a two-day trek to Pico Duarte where it's cold and frost dances in the air and breaks the sunlight up into rainbows.

Only this time we were walking in Colinas Bravas, and I was overjoyed they'd let him in; and then I realized that this was actually the Cibao, but a different Cibao, a Cibao that they ruled. As if somehow world history had been reversed and the Taíno still ruled Española and Europe had been settled by them. Dad and I sat on top of a cliff and let the wind blow over us.

I didn't get along with my mother. She hated how I turned out, but so often we become like our parents, don't we? She was a good Catholic who believed in original sin. Have I made up that she once said those women of Colinas must be a different species because they don't know original sin?

If she did, then I think my mother was right.

Original sin is having two sexes, one of whom doesn't carry the child, who needs to know the child is *his* and in so doing needs to know the woman is *his*, and in time, since it's a deal, he has to be *hers* as well. If you absolutely must own the person you love most, then how important is owning everything else you love or like? Your book, your designer evening gown, your phone, your knife, and fork (even just for the duration of the meal!), your piece of bacon, your slice of orange, your car, your home, your room, your bed, your individual sock with the green toes, let alone your own child. Owning becomes the culture, possession nine points of the law.

Except in Colinas Bravas.

They love the name Colinas Bravas, it chimes with how they see their country and perhaps themselves: the brave hills. But their own name for the place is the third person of their verb to be—"Ser" in Spanish. Transcription: Xix. The land just is. Not even the land is theirs. It's not England or even Herland.

The opposite of original sin is faith, and here's mine.

I am, despite everything, a good person, and soon they will see that. I've become a visibly better person living here. I don't need to own Evie, I don't need to own anything. I love this place and will do all I can to help it, out of love.

I write to La Señora Luminosa with ideas—your people love telling stories, I say. Why don't you let me record them, write them down, publish them in English, in Spanish? You tell them on your radio station. Let me put a satellite radio in the cover of the book, so that people can listen and read at the same time? A tablet in the cover, so that they can see more about you? Why don't you run your own TV station, so that you can finally watch things on it that are made for you? Let me do a website for you. Let me help sell your windmills all over the Americas in Spanish and in English.

I work to become like them.

I lie awake and listen to pebbles hiss on that beach, and I try to cast off owning. I have only my rucksack and khaki and my hotel slacks and shirt. Over and over I visualize my womb, my ovum, imagine a jink in my belly and that a snake unfolds inside me, and I see myself marching to Luminosa chaste but pregnant and saying "Behold." I establish a sixth matrilineal line. I imagine this, and as I drift off to sleep, I hear that sound, the waves of laughter.

One day, they will let me back in.

There Is Nothing to Bind Our Hearts Together

Sabrina Huang

● translated by Jeremy Tiang ●

Their dreams were growing shorter and shorter.

Some mysterious force had caused their dream worlds to collide one twilit evening. They dreamed themselves a white house with a blue-tiled roof washed over with dappled light and gusting winds in the middle of a plain set ablaze by the setting sun.

In the dream they were young, clear-featured, and slender. Because they retained memories of the real world, this pair of lovebirds seemed even more adorable and precious. They went fishing by a stream, sat shoulder to shoulder beneath one of the many towering, nameless trees. She tied her hair up with her handkerchief, he captured golden May bugs and kept them on the windowsill.

Tired out from frolicking, they'd sprawl on the grass, bodies pressed against each other, looking up at the stars, hand in hand, no need for words, falling gently asleep. When they woke again, they were back in the dust-filled real world.

Then they'd gradually feel themselves fill with sorrow. This oppressive reality, squatting on top of their dream.

In the dream, he often raised his eyes to the sky, knowing that beyond these clouds, he was a weary, depressed middle-aged man. His wife—they now slept in separate beds—nagged him all day long about not earning enough money to cover the household expenses. His son and daughter, entering their rebellious years, treated him like the enemy.

If only it were possible, he'd be willing to die in exchange for an eternity of that dream. Nowhere else in his life could he recall such clear moments of joy. Taking her delicate, childlike hand, he knew her heart held the same anxiety, the same determination.

They had such a strong connection. Each knew the other wasn't just a figment of their dream but that the dream had somehow brought together two people with a real existence. They never revealed their true selves, afraid that mentioning even one word from the other place would destroy the magic of the dream.

Yet their dreams were growing shorter and shorter. In the end there wasn't even time to catch a single fish.

That night, they both had a premonition that this would be the last time. Sitting beneath a sky full of stars, each clasped the other's moist hands, foreheads touching, eyes shut, resisting the moment when daybreak would invade their bodies. When they knew the very last moment had come, they couldn't resist loudly calling out who they were, where they lived, what their jobs were.

The magic of the dream was completely shattered. After waking, no matter how hard they tried, neither could recall the other's name. And so she stood before the bathroom mirror, weeping for a very long time. Her husband—they now slept in separate beds—was a weary, depressed middle-aged man, and all day long her brain throbbed as she tried to stretch the household budget. Her son and daughter, entering their rebellious years, treated her like a stranger.

A little later, the two individuals who shared a dream from separate beds met at the breakfast table. In an awful mood from losing the dream, they got into a vicious argument and ended up deciding to divorce. By noon, they were standing in front of a registrar's counter, each thinking the same thing: "When I finally have my freedom back, no matter what happens, I have to track down that person from my dreams."

Douen Calling

Brandon Mc Ivor

I gave you my own name, and we shared it for fourteen days.

They say that you shouldn't speak your name in the forest because the douens listen. And if they know your name, they'll call you from deep in the woods, and like sirens, they'll lure you in.

And after that—who knows?

I'm not superstitious, but on the day you would have been baptised, I sat on the stump before the woods, and I must have said our name a thousand times.

And nothing.

It was just like before. Saying, "Mia, Mia, Mia, Mia, Mia, Mia, Mia," but you were only still, like our mango tree on a windless night.

Spectral Evidence

Victor LaValle

"They think I'm a fraud."

"They think I'm a fraud."

I like to repeat this to myself in the mirror before I go out and do my job. It might seem weird to say something cruel right before I perform, but I thrive on the self-doubt. If I go out there feeling too confident, then I don't work as hard. It's easy to get lazy in this trade, but I take the job seriously. For instance, the word "psychic" does not appear anywhere in the window of my storefront. I never say it to my visitors. I call what I do "communication."

The other value in staying behind the curtain for a minute is that it gives the guests a chance to sniff around the parlor. They want to peruse the décor. They yearn to leaf through the handful of books I keep on the low shelf by the chairs. They're here for a performance, too. If I stepped out too soon, they wouldn't have the chance to reconnoiter, and then while I'm talking, they're casting their eyes around the room and I have to repeat myself. Or even worse, we just never make a connection. I'm not here for the ten dollars I charge during the initial visit. That money doesn't even cover the cost of all the coffee I drink in a day. Of course, I'm in this for the money, everyone's got to make a living; but even that isn't the real goal. As I said, I am a communicator, and when a session works right, all of us in the room play a part in the transmission. And at the end I get paid, so what's wrong with that?

I like to start work in the morning. Not many others do. Most folks who do this kind of work don't even open their eyes until mid-afternoon. Their days start in the early evening and run through the dawn. But that's not my way. For one, there's too much competition, and I'm not part of a family or a crew. For instance, the Chinese work in small groups and cater only to their own. I tried to learn Cantonese for about fifteen minutes, but one of them took a liking to me and explained that no Chinese person would ever go to an American woman for help, so what was the point? I didn't take offense to it. She communicated something important to me. The only thing I can still say in Cantonese is, *Can I have your address?* At least I think that's what it means.

The other reason I like mornings is because it means I mostly get old people coming through the door. You know why they're here? Most of them just want to talk, and it turns out I do, too. The cards I turn over at my table are secondary. Their loneliness is what blew them into my store. Isolation is as powerful as a gale force wind. There are times when we've been going at it for an hour or three, and before they leave, they actually force a little more money on me like I'm a niece who should buy herself a new dress or something.

Which is why, I admit, I'm baffled by the three folks who are in the parlor right now. Can't be more than nineteen or twenty. Girls. They might be drunk. People who are drunk at eleven in the morning are scary, no matter what. They're so far gone they can't even talk quietly. Even when they shush themselves they only come down to about a nine on the dial. Immediately, I figure they were passing by and decided to stumble in for a laugh. The best I can hope for is to get them in and out quick, collect a few dollars, then greet my usual morning crowd. I'm already looking forward to hearing about someone's endless concerns for a grandchild compared to corralling three drunks for half an hour. But work is work. They came in, and I called out that I'd be there in a minute. Then I gave them five minutes to poke around. I tend to wait until they get to the books. The shelf is low and right by the chairs, so if they're reading the titles, it means they're probably sitting down.

"*Wonders of the Invisible World,*" one reads aloud. She moves on to the next. "*The Roots of Coincidence.*"

"Just sit down, Abby."

"Where is this lady?"

"It's too dark in here."

They're getting impatient. I give myself one more look in the mirror. I've been trying out this new look, a scarf wrapped round my head, one that drapes down around my neck as well. It makes me look like I'm from the silent movie era, think of Theda Bara in *Cleopatra.* But last week when I came out wearing it, the guy in the chair asked me if I was a Muslim and things only got tense after that. But these are three women, and I tell myself they'll appreciate the flourish. More than that, I like the look.

I give the scarf one last touch and whisper the five words to myself.

"They think I'm a fraud."

Then it's time for the show.

● ● ●

Two of them want to leave after ten minutes, but it's the third who won't get out of her chair. Abby is her name. Her head is down for most of my reading, hair hanging over her eyes. Her friends find her exhausting, but I try not to be hard on them. After all, they haven't left her side. Abby is the only one who doesn't ask silly questions. I know how that might sound to some. Any serious question at a storefront psychic's must be, by definition, "silly." I get it. There's hardly room for all three of them on the other side of my table, it's a little wooden countertop that's really only made for two. But it doesn't really matter, only one of them wants to be sitting across from me.

Abby's mother died six years ago, that's what brought Abby here. As soon as she says this, I find a part of my heart warming to her. Suddenly, she doesn't look all that different than my Sonia. What would she have been like if I'd died when she was twelve or thirteen? Would she have ended up in a place like this with someone like me or much worse than me? I find myself feeling even more grateful for her friends, no matter how impatient they're becoming. They will not abandon her, at least not today. I wish I could remember either of their names.

"I just want to know if ..." Abby whispers. Even though she seems tortured, I don't think she's going to cry. She sounds resigned. "Is there something ... after all this?"

I have a few things I usually say when people skirt close to this subject, the whole point of being here. But I can't think of them because I've never had someone ask the question so directly before.

"Okay," one of the friends says, rising to her feet. She's the smallest of the three but the most potent. This one is the sergeant-at-arms when they go out to the bar. She looks at me. "We're going to miss our train back if we don't leave now."

The other friend is in worse shape, she sort of oozes off her chair. For a moment it's not clear if she'll fall flat or stand up. She stands, puts a hand on Abby's shoulder, but it doesn't look like comfort, only a way to keep her balance. It looks, for a moment, like she's crushing the poor kid.

Abby nods and finally rises as well. Is it strange that I'm thinking less of Abby and more of her mother? Trying to guess what I'd want some stranger to have said to Sonia if she'd come to them pleading for answers, or at least comfort. I guess the obvious choice is to say something simple and uplifting, but I can't do that about something so serious. Anyway, I can tell that's not what she really wants to hear.

While I'm struggling, Abby opens her bag and finds three ten-dollar bills. She hands them across the table to me, and of course, I do take them. We've been together for a half-hour, exactly like I'd expected. I hold Abby's wrist. What should I say? What should I say? All my talk about putting on a show, and I've got no pre-planned act that will work for this.

"Yes," I say and squeeze her hand. It's the best I can do. The friends are already at the door, opening it and letting in cold air and sunlight. "There is more."

Abby looks at me directly; chin up. It's the first time I get to see her eyes. They're red from lack of sleep. She cocks her head to the left, seems surprised to hear me being so definitive. Then she pulls her hand free and follows her friends out of my life.

My daughter died a year ago this July. Sonia went to the Turning Stone Casino in Verona and jumped from the 21st floor. We hadn't spoken to each other in almost four years by that point. I hadn't even known she was living upstate. The coroner's office sent me an envelope with her last effects. Inside, I found loose change and receipts from the ATM in the casino lobby, a flip phone that had somehow survived the fall, and a broken watch. It had been the watch that tore me open. I'd given it to her when she graduated high school. I didn't know she'd kept it all that time. It's not like it had stopped at the moment of impact or anything, the hands weren't even still attached. In a way that seemed more accurate. For her and for me time didn't stop, it shattered.

It's nearly eight by the time I get home. I've been in this apartment for three decades, raised Sonia here. After Abby and her friends left, I welcomed my stream of regulars, but I thought about Abby the whole time. Most of my days are as long as this one. I leave early for work and don't come home until dinner. All I do is sleep in this place now. I avoid it. I should admit that to myself.

I come through the front door with my late night pick-up of Thai food, and in the kitchen I make a plate. For a little while—all of last year—I would eat the food right out of the container. There were times when I didn't even take the container out of the bag. It got to be too sad. So now I pull down a plate and utensils. I find the white wine in the fridge and pour myself a glass. I even sit in the same spot I've been using since my daughter was old enough to sit up in a chair by herself. She made such a mess when she first learned how to eat on her own, and I never acted too patiently about it. Even before she died, I found myself fussing at details like that, trying to trace a line from how she fell apart to something I'd done when she was still a child. Somebody is always to blame and most of the world tends to agree it was the mother.

How do I know I'm a true New Yorker? I actually believe the city goes quiet at night. Sonia used to have trouble sleeping because we lived next to the BQE and all night she heard the trucks and cars speeding by, but by the time I had her, I'd long learned to tune that stuff out. It was only if I got in bed with her, like if she'd woken up and couldn't get back to sleep, that she'd point out the noise and I'd finally hear it.

Dinner done, I wash the dishes and pop the cork back into the wine. I can't even claim I tasted the food. The apartment has one long hallway with rooms branching off from it. I pass Sonia's old room. The door is shut. I never open it anymore. In the bathroom I take a slow shower, putting in the time to wash my hair, a nice way to slow myself down. My bedroom is at the end of the hall. I get in bed and turn off the lamp by my bedside, and I listen to the sounds of this city.

"It's too dark in here."

The words came from the hallway, but I don't even roll over. I know who it is.

It wasn't a week after Sonia died that I started hearing from her. She only ever says the one thing. When it began, once I decided to believe it was happening and not just something caused by my grief, I had her body exhumed. I thought that might be what her words meant. She didn't like being buried. But it didn't help. She kept on talking. I begged her to tell me what she meant, but I couldn't get her to say more. I kept longer hours at the storefront because I wanted to be around other people. When I'm alone, I can't drown her out.

"It's too dark in here."

She's come down the hallway now and joined me in my room. She'll go on like this all night.

A week later, I get a walk-in first thing. It's a middle-aged white guy, which is pretty unusual for me. He's standing on the sidewalk when I show up at nine. He asks for me by name. I bring him in and ask him to wait. I slip in the back, but when he's looking at the bookshelf, I take a moment to part the curtains and snap a photo of him with my phone. At least if he kills me, the cops will find his picture. This might seem paranoid to some, but I don't care. It strikes me as a completely rational thing to do. I've had more seeing-eye dogs in here than lone middle-aged men strolling in.

I look at myself in the mirror, but this time I don't chant, not trying to charge myself up for a fine performance. Maybe he's a cop, that's the kind of energy he's emitting. They still do undercover operations on storefronts. Two years ago, a guy gave away over $700,000 to a pair of psychics in Times Square. I won't put on a show for this one, that's what I decide. No scarf draped across my head and neck. He won't see Cleopatra, only me.

When I get to the table, he's already laid out the ten-dollar bill. There's something insulting about seeing the cash before I've done anything. It looks new. Maybe he went to the ATM right before he showed up. Immediately, I wonder how many more fresh notes are waiting in his wallet, then I feel angry at myself for being so easily enticed.

His hair is white and thinning and slicked back, and his sharp nose slopes down until the tip hovers right above his top lip. He doesn't seem to blink even as I sit there quietly watching him. There's something predatory about him. Like he's a bald eagle and I'm a fish. I'm used to people looking at me like I'm a fraud, but not like I'm a meal.

"You're an early riser," I say, trying to be chatty.

He holds my gaze. "Where's the cards? Don't you people use cards?"

"We can," I say. "We will. But I like to talk first. It puts my visitors at ease."

He hasn't moved. Still hasn't blinked. His hands are flat on the table, but that doesn't make me feel any safer.

"What kind of things do you say? To put visitors at ease."

I look up and count how many steps it would take me to reach the front door. Seven maybe and I can't say I'm in any shape to run. The backroom has a bathroom, but there's no emergency exit. I could lock myself in the bathroom and call the police, but how long would it take for him to smash his way in?

"What did you say to Abby, for instance?"

He says the name with emphasis, but I admit I don't know who the hell he's talking about. Do you know how exhausted I am? I hardly sleep at night. At this point I just lie there with my eyes closed listening to Sonia. How am I supposed to think of anything else?

For the first time he moves, crosses his arms, and leans forward in his chair.

"You don't even remember her," he says. He almost sounds happy about it like I've confirmed his worst intuition.

"Abby," I say. Then I repeat it. I'm trying to get the gears of my memory to catch. When they do, I snap my fingers. Maybe I look like a child who's happy to have passed a quiz. "She came into my store a few weeks ago."

"One week ago." He breathes deeply, and his crossed arms rise and fall.

His eyes lose focus, and he stares down at the table; and the posture is exactly the same as Abby's had been. That's when I recognize him. It's not their faces but the way they hold their bodies.

"Who is she to you?" I ask.

"One week ago," he repeats.

I calculate my path to the door again. Maybe I could make it in five steps. This old girl might have one more sprint in her.

"What did you say to my daughter?" he asks.

I don't understand where this is headed. Is he back to ask for her fee? All this over a few dollars? The story of an overprotective father scrolls before me, the kind who won't ever let his child become an adult. I'm insulted on her behalf.

"She's a grown woman," I tell him. "What I said to her is confidential."

He drops his arms and slips one hand below the tabletop, so I can't see what he's doing. Reaching into his pocket maybe.

"You're not a lawyer," he says. "You're just some scam."

The words settle on me heavily, a lead apron instead of a slap. I find myself needing to breathe deeply, so I do, but it hardly helps.

"Did she report me or something? Are you here with the cops?"

He pulls his hand out from under the table. He's holding a tiny flashlight, like a novelty item, a gag gift. There's a bit of fog on the inside of the protective glass where the bulb is.

"I gave this to her years ago," he said. "It was still on her key chain when her body was recovered."

The blanket across my chest feels even heavier now. I think I might get pulled down, right off the chair.

"What did you say to my daughter!" he shouts, and he throws the flashlight at me. It flies wild, goes over my shoulder and into the back. As soon as it leaves his hand, he looks horrified and chases after it. He sends his chair flying sideways, and it knocks into the shelf. A few of the books fall to the carpet. He hurtles through the curtain and he's in the back and suddenly I'm alone. I get up to run for the door. I'm sure I can flag down a cop car on the street. But then I hear her.

"It's too dark in here."

Now I plop right back down onto the chair, can't move my limbs. My mouth snaps shut and so do my eyes. What did I say to his daughter?

Yes. There is more.

He steps back through the curtain, and he's got my scarf in one hand, Abby's flashlight in the other. I wonder if he's planning to strangle me with the scarf and, for a moment, consider that I'd deserve it. The death of my child was already my fault, so why not his as well?

"I thought you would've run," he says quietly. He stands over me, holding up the scarf and the flashlight as if he's weighing the two.

"There's nowhere for me to go," I say.

He sits on the ground right there beside me. It's strange to see a man my age cross-legged on a carpet.

"I won it for her at the Genesee County Fair," he says of the flashlight. "It's funny what kids hold on to."

Now I understand why he grabbed my scarf. He's patting at his face, his tears.

"Maybe I said something to her?" he asks. The words come out so quietly that my first instinct is to lean in closer, but he isn't talking to me. I need to get an ambulance for him. I rise up from my chair and slip my cell phone out of my pocket.

"I'm going to call someone for you," I say, and he nods softly. Now I'm surprised I thought he seemed angry when he's only delirious with despair.

After I call I crouch down beside him and wait for the sirens. This makes my knees start hurting instantly, but I can endure it. I grasp one of his hands between two of mine, and I remember the way I touched his daughter when we spoke. They have the same delicate wrists.

I'm afraid to tell him what I said to her but not because I fear for my safety. Instead, I wonder if Abby thought I meant something hopeful when I told her there was more to existence. If she lost her mother, if she missed her mother, maybe she thought I meant the woman waited for her across the veil, that they'd be reunited in a better place. Why wouldn't she think that? It's the story people prefer. What if I told her father the same thing now? Would he be tempted to try and join Abby? I couldn't be responsible for such a thing, so I say nothing and simply hold his hand.

The EMTs arrive and help Abby's father to the ambulance. After taking some information from me, they drive off with him, then I go back inside the store. For the first time I can see the place like so many others must: the silly dim lighting, the bookshelf of mystic texts. It's such a cliché. No wonder my visitors viewed me as a fraud.

I go to the back and make myself some tea. While the water boils, I lift the chair Abby's father knocked over. I gather the books that fell, but instead of putting them back on the shelf, I go in the back and drop them, one by one, into the trashcan. I find the scarf and leave it in the garbage with the books.

My work changed after Sonia died. There is an afterlife, and it's worse than the world we live in. That's what I know. I don't understand why I kept the news to myself.

"It's too dark in here."

The kettle whistles in the other room, but I can still hear my daughter. I suppose that will never stop. I make my tea, then I sit at the table and wait for visitors. From now on whoever comes to see me is going to hear the truth.

A Model Apartment

Bryan Thao Worra

Yam zoo ntshai tsam tau me.
Yam phem ntshai tsam los ze.
Something good, you fear you'll get too little.
Something bad, you fear it will come too close.

—*Ancient Hmong proverb*

I.

The elders believe the tragedy that befell Kazoua Vue in New England
was avoidable. As incontrovertible evidence of this position, they
repeat the ancient Hmong folktales and modern news stories of
those who live too far from their families and the horrific fates those
foolish people meet.

Her funeral was conducted with singular quietude in her hometown
of Milwaukee. Few of the gentle young painter's remaining family
wished to discuss the details, an understandable position given the
disquieting nature of it all. But a reasonably consistent picture of
the events in Arkham emerged for those who pried deep enough
into the dark matter.

At the behest of her family, the last of her effects are scheduled for
a discreet incineration next week in a remote corner of the city. After
this, none will speak of her, and it will be as if she had never been.

Arkham is one of those changeless places of Earth—a quiet,
almost mythic city in New England. The sleepy Miskatonic river cuts
through the centre of the city directly to the coldest fathoms of the
Atlantic if one follows far enough.

It is home to Miskatonic University, which over the years,
weathered innumerable bizarre incidents and scandals, survived
devastating fires, even the great flood of 1980 that swept away so
many of Arkham's oldest architectural fixtures.

It was here that fabled figures like the alleged hag, Keziah Mason, had fled during the frenzied witch hunts of old. Those of a scientific mindset may recall that the tragic Pabodie Expedition to Antarctica had its beginnings in Arkham's shining halls.

Morbid turn-of-the-century painter, Richard Upton Pickman, best known for "The Lesson" and his ghastly "Ghoul Feeding," often visited Arkham in his early years when he wasn't in Boston. This was well before he became an enigmatic recluse who went the way of Ambrose Bierce and Federico García Lorca.

Kazoua always had an unnatural, almost unhealthy, attraction to Pickman's work. It could have been worse. She could have been ogling Warhol, or even Kadinsky, or that hack Pollack.

Fleeing the war in Laos, she and her family came to America in 1984. There was some brief time spent in the Thai refugee camp of Ban Vinai beforehand.

While lingering in the squalid compound, they met an idealistic young USAID worker who'd been an art history minor fond of Bacon, Goya, and Dali. Through him, Kazoua first saw many of those bizarre images that scholars believe were so influential on her and her style.

Her family began their American odyssey in Providence. There were several other Hmong clans present there as well, including Thaos, Khangs, Hers, and several branches of the Yangs. Though accommodating enough, Rhode Island and her non-Hmong residents were still as alien to them as the moon.

Many Hmong converted from their traditional animism to Catholicism, but it is worth noting the Vatican permitted them to still practice a select few of the traditional rituals of old, particularly funerary and marriage rites.

In the spring of 1986, Kazoua's parents journeyed to rejoin her father's brothers in Milwaukee. There, the families could support one another as during the war and long before. They established a modestly successful Asian grocery store, Lao American Market, near Vliet Street, and many remember when she became the first in her family to attend college.

Much to their dismay, she majored in art at the University of Wisconsin-Madison, insisting she could make a good living at it.

When her macabre painting, "Yer's Family, A Tiger's Perspective," sold for a considerable sum to a prominent Milwaukee art collector, most of her critics were silenced although many elders continued to insist a proper Hmong girl would simply get married and forego such useless luxuries as a college education.

II.

On September 17, 1999, Michael Stuczynski, one of her closer associates, opened his art gallery, Diabolica, near Murray Avenue. He invited her to showcase her work there for a month. Entitled "Despair-Diaspora," it was an ambitious solo show featuring 42 canvases, including her oil paintings and mixed-media projects. Her ostensible theme was traditional Hmong folklore and the role of memory.

By the most generous accounts, it was something of a disaster when it opened in November.

Most non-Hmong viewers dismissed it, largely from a lack of familiarity with the figures being referenced. Others more familiar with the Hmong expected something more akin to the Kohler Center's earlier exhibition of traditional textiles and silverwork and not the gory spectacles Kazoua Vue presented.

Hmong audiences, on the other hand, abhorred its fixation on the spirits and demons of the past, such as the Dab, the dreaded Poj Ntxoog, and the terrifying Zaj in all its reptilian glory.

"Despair-Diaspora" was taken down in December without much fanfare, and if the harsh critical reception of her work had any effect on the sensitive young Kazoua, she did not outwardly show it.

There were two significant outcomes of the exhibition at Diabolica.

The first was her new resolve to return to the New England she remembered so fondly to undertake an artistic rejuvenation. She would study the work of artists like Pickman there and find peers who understood her vision. The second outcome was meeting Tou Ger Khang, a dark-tempered young man with whom she fell hopelessly in love.

What she saw in the dour, sullen boy remains anyone's guess, but academically he was promising, demonstrating a particular aptitude for high-level physics and mathematics. The two married in Milwaukee in the traditional fashion not long after they met, and Tou Ger was amenable to completing his studies in New England with her.

They were accepted into Miskatonic University for Fall 2001. It seemed a positive turn in her fortunes.

III.

Their move to New England occurred without incident. There

were the usual best wishes and tears but nothing beyond the ordinary. They drove a small U-Haul from Milwaukee, taking I-90E most of the way, passing through Cleveland, Buffalo, and Albany, where they stopped to visit a few distant relatives, happily catching up on news and family gossip.

Ordinarily, the trip is a fast 18 hours; but the two took their time, and it became a four-day trip to the East Coast. There were numerous photographs taken then, but most are lost.

It was raining heavily when they finally arrived on Wednesday, March 7, 2001. They'd come early in order to acclimate to the city's nuances before beginning their classes in earnest in September. As most will remember, it was a very cold, wet month for the entire region then.

Some might have been deterred by the gloom. For Kazoua, she took it as an uplifting sign, a symbol of rejuvenation, regeneration, and reconnection with things she felt missing in her life. She remembered it raining when she left New England the last time, so it felt like coming full circle.

Ever an efficient one, Kazoua had inquired ahead of time of possible living quarters on campus and was informed that the official dormitories were still filled with students, but many reputable landlords in the area could easily accommodate them.

Happily, there was a recent opening in the White Rose Apartments nestled conveniently a few blocks from the central campus. The landlord, Janos Dombrowski, informed her a tenant had to relinquish his apartment unexpectedly to return to Vienna. However, in his haste, he left behind several fine furnishings that seemed a pity to discard with the weekly rubbish.

Dombrowski noted that the apartment was nearly immaculate considering the neighbourhood—an excellent deal. If they wanted, Dombrowski would leave the furniture for them to spare them the expense of refurnishing it.

Upon hearing Kazoua was an artist, he also waived the security deposit for them in exchange for one of her paintings when she arrived, being an amateur artist himself who understood such circumstances. He expressed hope that she would join the local art club for they always sought fresh voices. Things were looking up for the young couple, and it seemed the stars were truly in their favor.

● ● ●

IV.

For a brief time Kazoua's work took on an almost sunny disposition. The effect, while not quite jubilant meadow creatures frolicking beneath some saccharine sun, was still jarring to her few long-time acquaintances she kept contact with and ultimately alienated them even further from her.

But in her first months there, no one perceived any insurmountable problems in her life or any trace of that sad dementia that was to mark her final days.

On the weekends, she and Tou Ger took pleasant day trips to nearby cities like Innsmouth or Boston. In particular, they were on the lookout for a good bowl of pho, which was still very hard to come by in Arkham proper.

Dombrowski took a personal interest in helping the young couple enjoy the city, inviting them to various community gatherings he'd read of in the Arkham *Observer*. Kazoua and Tou Ger accepted his offers on several occasions, curious to see the local attractions. They even attended a few meetings of the notorious French Hill Art Club, whose members were pleasant enough although not entirely of the kindred disposition Kazoua hoped to find.

There were, at any given point, ten to twelve members of the French Hill Art Club in attendance. Advancing years kept many of their more prolific members from venturing out with any regularity. A notable standout was the bloated Mr. Thurber, who had the despicable look and decrepit aroma of a dilettante artist, arriving consistently liquored up, his frog-like eyes constantly drifting towards Kazoua's cleavage like some mad suckling calf.

Herbert Carter was a little less loathsome, a fragile-featured man who dressed all in white suits during the spring and all in black during the winter, every year without fail. He was a minor Arkham phenomenon as the locals waited to see when the season had changed based on his attire. Thurber often scoffed at Carter, questioning whether he was an artist or a fashion plate.

Normally a pleasant and polite girl, Kazoua soon tired of regaling traditional Hmong folktales and beliefs at every meeting to the pallid members of the club, who viewed her stories as quaint, exotic grist for their mediocre work. They had all been starving for genuine inspiration for untold ages. Eventually, she politely severed her ties with them, claiming she needed time to focus on her art and studies. Many were tremendously disappointed, and several asked her to keep in touch individually.

Kazoua became notorious for losing phone numbers during this time.

It was not long afterwards that poor Dombrowski took ill in mid-July. The constant rain had taken its toll, and his wife found him in the basement delirious, raving incoherent and horrible things about the universe.

The physicians advised admission to the local asylum, but Mrs. Dombrowski instead had his nearby nephew from Innsmouth, Eric Gilman, come to manage the affairs of the White Rose Apartments. Dombrowski was confined to his bed with sedatives, some small canvases, and some paint with which to pass the time. This ultimately had little effect on Kazoua and Tou Ger, however, who'd begun to have problems of their own.

V.

It is from this point that the particulars begin to unravel into an indescribable mess of tangled implications, hearsay, and unreliable accounts, and even the most stalwart investigators will find themselves stymied by the "details" that led to Kazoua's doom.

Among the more certain elements was the noticeable presence of vermin within the walls of the White Rose Apartments. Several of the tenants, to Gilman's dismay, came to complain of the constant scurrying and scratching of the unseen boarders, who were most active after midnight.

Mr. Von Kempelen on the third floor remarked that these did not sound like common field mice but lumbering Norwegian wharf rats determined to keep him from sleeping soundly. Mrs. Samsa also complained of the rodents and while she had not seen them, had heard them and took solace only in that they had dealt with a peculiar cockroach problem she'd been having. The curious bachelor Trelkovsky spoke of moving, perhaps back to Paris, if matters were not resolved. Gilman promised to look into the matter immediately and contracted Delapore Exterminators to set things aright.

In a brief visit with his parents, Tou Ger admitted he'd had trouble sleeping that month, no doubt an effect of adjusting to the damp New England climate after so many years in the Midwest. He had vivid nightmares alternating with bouts of insomnia. His mother left him some traditional herbs she'd grown in her garden in Milwaukee as a remedy.

Correspondence between Kazoua and some of her cousins in Albany from the time indicates she too had problems with the pests but was more repulsed by the ineffectiveness of her apartment to let proper natural light in for her painting. An almost obsessive perfectionist when it came to her art, she realized that the angles at which the windows had been set would never allow sufficient light, even on a good day. Instead, a lazy haze perpetually permeated the space, dissipating only with the setting of the sun.

A review of her letters outlined a particular encounter with Gilman, who apparently knew nothing of this sort of thing, merely shrugging and offering to lend her a few used lamps from the janitor's closet.

Exasperated, Kazoua agreed to take them. She accompanied Gilman to the basement, which had recently flooded a few weeks earlier.

Most of the mess had been cleaned up, but the noxious scent of mildew and mold had begun to seep in. Unlocking the closet door, Gilman intimated he was a superstitious sort, wondering aloud about the wisdom of building the White Rose Apartments on this lot.

When Kazoua pressed him to explain, he mentioned the Dombrowski family had been Polish immigrants who owned the property at the turn of the century. But the death of a student boarder, Walter Gilman (no relation), and an awful gale in 1931 irreparably damaged the house both physically and in reputation, so much so that his forebears gave up on the wretched building and focused their entrepreneurial attentions elsewhere.

There'd been some nattering about witchcraft because the supposed witch, Keziah Mason, had once lived there, but that was just fireside nonsense.

In the early 1990s, several of the Dombrowski brothers, most of whom were now into real estate, looked into building a new apartment complex on the old lot, which had once again gone up for sale. It seemed like karma. It was a second chance for the family, who never forgot their father's forlorn stories of this failed house, and they cheered their idea as if they were pioneers out to settle the West.

To them, this lot was a symbol of the American dream. They became obsessive about it. Price was no object, and it was the only time they let sentimentality guide their decisions although it nearly bankrupted them.

Despite complaints from the anemic popinjays of the Arkham Historical Society, they built a remarkably modern apartment building, banishing the memory of their family's previous failure to a mere footnote in their fortunes. Construction went surprisingly well, without accident or injury, almost as if the whole project had been blessed from above.

But in recent months, some great shadow had fallen upon the property, starting with the relentless March rain. Gilman advised Kazoua to avoid extended conversations with Mrs. Dombrowski if possible. Gilman bemoaned his constant bickering over the management of the property with the madwoman.

Kazoua took her lamps and resolved to avoid all of them except on the first of the month to pay her rent.

VI.

Interviews with her neighbors suggest that around late August, Kazoua and Tou Ger began arguing vociferously over the inconsequential. Over the next few weeks, it escalated until the police were called to intercede on September 3, 2001, because of the disturbance they were making.

According to the police report, Kazoua accused Tou Ger of hiding her art supplies from her and defacing her most ambitious canvas to date, an epic depiction of the first Hmong shaman, Shee Yee, against the malevolent Nzeu Nyong and his hordes of evil spirits. Tou Ger claimed to know nothing about it, calling her an irrational lunatic and a witch.

Police noted several glasses, eggs, and similar fragile objects had been smashed against the walls in the frenzy but did not feel the situation warranted more than a warning.

On another note, Kazoua's sister in Milwaukee, Dia, says her sister was never one to have comfortable sleep. She was a known insomniac, and several of her uncles suspected her of being haunted by a particular long-standing curse on the women of their family.

During the funeral, Dia mentioned that, while she was alive, her sister would frequently call (lamentably, collect) to discuss the terrible dreams she'd been having, conveying images so awful that Dia had to plead with Kazoua to stop relating them to her.

Their father, Pheng Vue, wanted a well-known shaman in Rhode Island to come out to help her and exorcise the apartment in the proper custom, which he knew Kazoua and Tou Ger had not done prior to moving in. Kazoua rejected the solution for uncertain reasons.

VII.

The last works of Kazoua Vue are described as her greatest and the darkest of her brief career, when she at last began to eclipse mighty Pickman himself. Most survive only in fragments, broken scraps of canvas, or singed sketches, but even these scant pieces tell of a powerful voice emerging from a long sleep.

Some of her iconic language is more easily apprehended—primal spirals, crude stars with flaming eyes, jagged mountain ranges of purple and blue. Others resemble glyphs invoking ancient Egypt, predynastic Qin, or the Enochian script of the mystic John Dee. But some remain far more elusive, indecipherable by coherent minds.

Not all was abstract: Kazoua created self-portraits akin to a more surreal Kahlo, and a disturbing series of portraits depicting the deceitful Poj Ntxoog "throughout herstory." Her paintings of this awful creature possessed a terrible verisimilitude. One could scarcely imagine it to be a creature of myth, thanks to her all-too-keen brushstrokes. More imaginative minds might believe the Poj Ntxoog came to pose, but such circumstances would be absurd.

When asked about her peculiar choice in subjects, Kazoua replied that she saw the deeper symbolic significance of these misunderstood spirits and that Hmong women could learn greatly from the Poj Ntxoog's example. She seems to honestly have believed the image of the shape-shifting Poj Ntxoog could be rehabilitated through art as happened with ancient Lilith, the Great Mother, Goddess of a Thousand Names.

Most traditional accounts of the Poj Ntxoog describe them as dwarf spirit women with long, terrible hair and feet that face backwards to fool the unsuspecting. Every now and then, villagers in Asia's highlands will still report killing a Poj Ntxoog. One account described the creature as having six vaginas, a long, thin neck, deathly-pale skin, and a mouth so dark you cannot see her teeth. The bodies always seem to disappear shortly after death. Others say the Poj Ntxoog consort with tigers and have magic powers, possessed of an inexplicable desire to trick and deceive humans.

A relative, wishing to remain anonymous, said Tou Ger, upon seeing these portraits, was so repulsed he told her to stop painting the evil things lest they be called forward to admire themselves. Kazoua responded violently, calling him unspeakable things. He was so shocked to hear her speak like that to him that he shrank into the meekest of creatures, avoiding his own wife during all hours except bedtime.

VIII.

Around this period, Thurber from the French Hill Art Club came, some suspect courting, Kazoua at her apartment while he checked in on the poor Dombrowskis.

Thurber had been researching his old notes and found some material of a very special interest to the young aficionado of Richard Upton Pickman. At first, Kazoua expressed little interest but relented, for Thurber offered nothing less than a visit to some of Pickman's hidden studios both within Arkham and on the North End of Boston. He even had what he claimed was one of Pickman's original brushes, which he presented to her as a present. It was too tempting to resist, and soon Kazoua traveled alone with him to those sordid locations, which were mostly ruins and dusty boards more than anything these days.

They would return from their jaunts caked in mud and dirt that reeked of old worlds civilization was all too happy to leave behind. If Tou Ger objected, it is not documented. She became quite spirited during this time as did Thurber. Carter remarked that Thurber seemed quite the cock of the walk.

On October 30, however, Thurber burst into the evening gathering of the French Hill Art Club, alone and shirtless, gibbering, frothing, and raving. Carter and the rest of Thurber's peers tried to calm him, but he savagely beat them back. It was a grotesque sight, and they were quite happy when he fled into the dark night.

When asked about the matter, Kazoua replied simply that they had gone to a studio, and apparently Thurber was discontent with what he'd seen. Kazoua, on the other hand, found it quite pleasant and couldn't understand Thurber's response. Carter noticed Kazoua had an odd bruise on her neck but was disinclined to pursue the matter further. Kazoua also noted she would be having no further contact with Thurber as he had behaved in an altogether ungentlemanly fashion unbecoming an artist.

Thurber was never seen again.

The French Hill Art Club does keep his name on the members list, however, should he ever turn up although he will still owe the appropriate dues.

IX.

Eric Gilman clearly recalls the month of November, 2001, because

Kazoua dressed in the elaborate traditional clothing of her people the entire time as if preening for an unknown audience. She did not seem to entertain company, however, so it was quite curious. She was radiant although within her eyes, he noted perhaps the first sign of her coming madness.

Her hair grew increasingly long and wild, and her voice took on a strange melodic quality, ethereal and remote. Humans may as well have been ants to her. She grew paler as the month went on.

Although Gilman now believes he misheard it, when he called out her name one evening upon meeting in the hallway, she corrected him that it was "Keziah." Given the tonal language of the Hmong, most concur she was merely correcting the way to pronounce Kazoua as was often her habit with the Dombrowskis when they'd first met.

Mrs. Samsa complained of strange laughing and an eerie, almost inhuman whooping coming from the Hmong couple's apartment, especially late at night. Gilman was reluctant to approach Kazoua and drafted a note he slipped under her door. For a time, the noise stopped.

In November, Tou Ger was cleaning for the holidays alone in the apartment. He made the dreadful mistake of disturbing a massive rat warren. Many must have just given birth to their litters, for that is the only reason to explain the savage ferocity with which the pests attacked him so mercilessly.

The vermin had scurried away to the safety of the shadows by the time Trelkovsky broke open the door to assist his pitifully screaming neighbor. Kazoua arrived minutes later. She'd been out visiting one of Pickman's old studios. They found Tou Ger on the floor, a whimpering lump of flesh with terrible gashes across his entire pathetic body.

Trelkovsky suggested taking him to the hospital, but Kazoua dismissed the idea because the couple had no health insurance. It was nothing a few bandages and some traditional Hmong herbal medicine could not cure. She thanked Trelkovsky for his help and walked him to the door.

Tou Ger was put to bed, and few heard from them for a while. On December 23, 2001, as Kazoua was traveling to Boston, an awful commotion came from the apartment—unearthly screaming and that strange shrieking, whooping, and wailing. The violent sound of breaking furniture in the apartment prompted neighbours to call the police.

As Gilman hastily opened the door for the officers, witnesses in the hallway report they saw a strange swirling swarm of brown-furred things unlike any rodents they'd seen in their lives; slithering, writhing, and nipping at Tou Ger Khang, who blinded in agony, accidentally stumbled through the fragile window of his apartment to his death, his face half-torn away from the gnawing and scratching. No one could get in touch with Kazoua until Monday morning.

Arkham police later concluded the creatures to be nothing more than common rodents, however peculiar their behavior, and encouraged everyone to put speculation to rest. They claim the ultimate cause of Tou Ger's death was a virulent viral hemorrhagic fever from his earlier rat bites. Mrs. Dombrowski and Gilman lowered the rent for Kazoua in consideration of her loss.

In a decision that greatly upset everyone, Kazoua had Tou Ger's remains cremated quickly and without consultation. It was an unbelievable break from Hmong tradition. She said cryptically it was for the best and he deserved a chance for his soul to rest. She then withdrew from the outside world, and it isn't until March, 2002, that any further details of her life can be spoken of with any certainty.

X.

The evidence is supposed to speak for itself. But what was going on then? As with many of the great mysteries surrounding the lives of troubled artists like Modigliani, Lautreamont, and the like, the complete details can only be speculated at and the strangest elements become only so much trivia when they do not fit into a tidy, comprehensible explanation.

In March, 2002, an ambulance was summoned to the apartment of Kazoua Vue. Many expected the worst, but the EMTs emerged, not with Kazoua, but an elderly Hmong man she identified at the time as her uncle, who was having tea with her and inexplicably collapsed from a severe stroke in her living room.

Other Hmong knew him as a prominent shaman renowned for his healing skills. Animists in Providence recall he once defeated a Poj Ntxoog near the village of Sam Neua and attributed many other incredible feats to him. Kazoua invited him over to help her artistic research regarding more esoteric elements of Hmong spiritualism and was deeply saddened by his seizure. It was a great loss for the community.

On April 12, 2002, Gilman needed to discuss repairs with Kazoua to fix all of the rain and snow damage the White Rose had suffered in the year prior. And this was when he made the terrible discovery.

There was no answer to his knocking, so he'd let himself into the apartment. There was a foul odor, and all the shades were drawn. At first, Gilman believed the noxious scent was a fetid buildup of mildew and garbage. He called aloud for Kazoua and heard a loud bumping noise from the room she used as her studio.

Walking over with trepidation, he screamed when he saw the awful sight: on the floor lay the corpse of the diminutive woman who once was Kazoua Vue. But the rats, those damned, infernal rats, had made a meal of her, stripping away all of her flesh and most of her organs. Except, strangely, her perfect, beautiful right arm, which still clutched a ornately-carved brush.

As he leaned closer, he could see, no, it was made from a hideously-gnawed human bone. He then looked up and saw the last canvas she'd been working on. He was horrified to see the gruesome painted images of three ghastly women staring directly at him and Kazoua's corpse, their mouths salivating in anticipation. Their evil filled him with dread as if viewing some ancient enemy.

Perhaps it was only the effect of the chemical fumes and the stench of decay in the room, but Gilman swears he saw the hands in the painting move as if probing for a way to escape the confines of the painting's feeble geometry. He heard a quiet shuffling from a dark corner of the studio, then a bump.

And then he realized what was truly wrong: He might not understand art as well as his mad uncle, but he knew enough about composition to know there was space in the painting for four figures. A missing figure.

The one slowly rising, shuffling, crawling towards him. The one moving with a pulpy, liqueous lurching noise, slow and murderous. Its head, or whatever pale, lumpy appendage it might call as such, was turning right towards him. Walking backwards.

And he fled, needing no further satisfaction of his curiosity. Something shrieked.

XI.

When the police arrived, they found nothing but a corpse. They dismissed the more imaginative aspects of Gilman's account as stress and shock. Hallucinations.

Curiously, it may have been an effect of the chemicals in the air, but the initial coroner's report indicated that she had been dead since at least November. But that is ridiculous, for obvious reasons, and was corrected on the proper certificates to something more reasonable.

Gilman tries to forget it all now with a daily bottle of scotch and a box of cigarettes and sleeps with the lights constantly on back at his shabby apartment in Innsmouth.

Local mystics debate over their lattes whether the roots of this incident emerged from Kazoua's traditions or New England's or something far more ancient and transcendent of time and space who cares nothing for earthly dreams, let alone American ones.

Kazoua Vue and Tou Ger Khang's stories have slowly been eased out of human memory because sometimes it is better to forget, the elders say. Humans often forget that forgetting, too, can be a blessing of the heavens no matter where they're from.

The Dombrowskis still have difficulty renting the apartment out.

Water in the Rice Fields Up to My Knees!

Johary Ravaloson

● translated by Allison M. Charette ●

1

It happened in November. A sticky night relieved by crisp post-storm air. I was waiting for passengers under a streetlight in Ampasampito near the cemetery, when I heard squelch-squelch on the pavement. I looked up from my notebook and saw a faltering shadow stumble into the circle of light. Slathered with mud, her feet and wedge heels forming thick, slimy boots, the woman lurched frantically toward me, squick-squicking. She looked like she'd probably cut an elegant figure, one of the elite, before falling into a sewer. Her legs and hands, her raincoat, her face, and hair were stained with grime. I locked my taxi quick as a flash. Absolutely not, I couldn't. Left my window open, though.

"Help me, please help me! Take me to Andraharo!"

"Wherever you'd like to go, ma'am," I said, "as soon as you've cleaned all that off."

"I'll give you a hundred thousand!"

"There's a pump on the corner."

"Alohalika ny ranom-bary e!"

Water in the rice fields, up to my knees! I said nothing, just pointed to the street corner. Water in the rice fields, up to your knees: it suffocates young plants and destroys any hope of a harvest. But by this season, the rice plants were mature enough to survive that level of water. Frightened squelch-squelching toward the pump. Almost kinda sexy, actually. Keeping tabs on the operations in my rearview mirror, I realized how weird it was, that old-timey raise-the-alarm phrase coming from the woman's lips. She was a city girl even with the splotches of mud on her calves.

"Show me your hundred," I said when she got back from her rush scrubbing job. She pulled ten out of her splotchy handbag.

"I can give you thirty now, and my husband will give you the rest when we get there."

I paused. Something moved on the other side of the intersection.

"Alohalika ny ranom-bary e!"

I looked at her and said nothing. Antananarivo really was that close to the fields then. Deciding abruptly, I opened the door for her. The cold stench of damp earth gusted into the car with her. More activity around the edges of the light, but the shadows seemed unwilling to come any closer. I started the engine, turned on the headlights, and they disappeared.

"Where in Andraharo, ma'am?"

"Across from the gas station."

"There aren't any houses there, though!"

"My husband is at his office, he's working late."

"Your husband works late? What is he, a taxi driver?"

I laughed aloud at my stupid little joke. Then slowly, her silence dampened my spirits. At any rate, I thought, even for thirty thousand, it'd be worth it. I rolled along, no rush, and snuck glances back at her every time that there was enough light.

"What really happened to you? You're not exactly ... dressed for the rice fields."

She stayed silent, rummaged around in her bag. She fiddled with her phone, then met my eyes in the rearview mirror and decided against making a call.

Finally, she admitted, "I fell down in the rice field. I ... I had to, well, let's say ... I really had to relieve myself. I stopped on the dike road, I ... There were cars passing with their headlights on, I climbed down further than I wanted to, and I fell down. I lost my car keys in the mud. I tried getting people to stop, but they all sped up as soon as they saw me."

2

That was months ago.

And then tonight, I see her again step into the illuminated circle beneath the light post where I park. Squick-squick, covered with

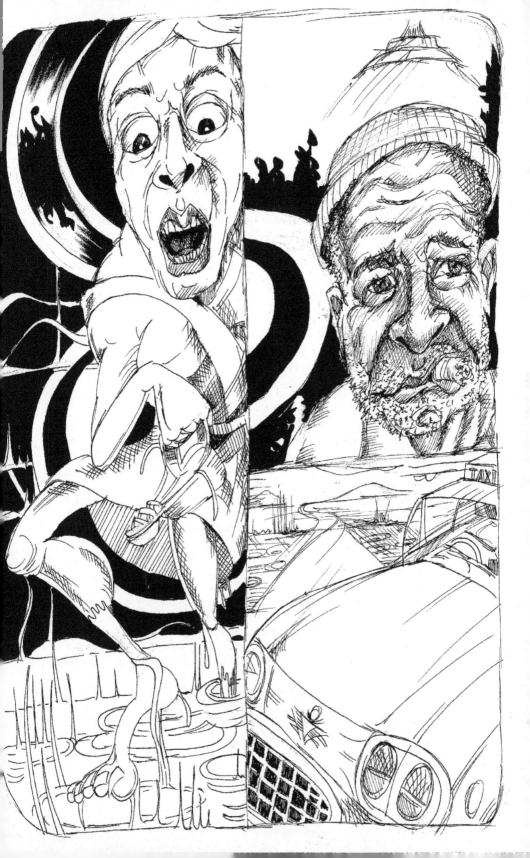

just as much mud as before. It can't be, this can't happen. I jump out of the car.

"Alohalika ny ranom-bary e!"

Stunned by cold and surprise, I don't know what to say. My pupils are probably dilated. No mud boots on her this time but dirt-encrusted pumps that she holds in her hands, shivering in the frigid night. She was probably wearing all black before she fell— blazer, skirt, hose, and overcoat, now all smeared with mud that's somewhere between dark red and brownish green.

"Alohalika ny ranom-bary e!" she says again.

I don't have the heart to send her to wash up at the pump. I open the door for her. She slumps down onto the backseat. I spread my Chinese-made synthetic blanket over her. That smell ... She didn't fall down in a rice field.

"To Andraharo, ma'am?"

Is she nodding, or is her face drooping? She seems overly weary under the blanket. Fingers on the ignition, I ask her, "What's all this about?" She rummages halfheartedly under the blanket too slowly. She stretches out her too-slow, too-muddy hand to give me new, spotless bills. I don't like that. I let off the brakes, let off the clutch.

I'll still watch her out of the corner of my eye. But I mean, it's not going to be much help. I'm not going to ask her anything like: "Would you like me to take you to the hospital?" She's obviously not that kind of woman. Or not anymore, if you know what I mean. Just have to keep calm.

Roundabout. Cobblestone cemetery road. The streets are empty. I speed up.

She's saying something to me, her lips are moving ever so slightly in the rearview mirror. Andravoahangy. Ankorondrano. Route du Pape. Antohomadinika. She doesn't really utter a full sentence through the entire trip. And I'm charging into the cold, yellow light.

Rue d'Andraharo. Then the gas station. I slam on the brakes.

She opens her mouth again, and I don't give her time to repeat it. Why's she bugging me with this thing? I throw her out of the car and take off. Like a shot. When the water gets that high in this season, they open the floodgates, so the water can run out to the ocean. I step on the gas. Probably at Antanimena by the time she gets to the middle of her sentence.

I reach the train station, Avenue de l'Indépendance. She's probably at "knees." I shiver. From cold or fear? Not even a dog around to watch the city's fairy-tale fountains. Stop under the first streetlight.

I get out of the car. Walk around it three times. And three times the other way. Sit on the warm bumper of my old clunker.

Soon another taxi will pull up. The driver will say hello. He'll ask if I want a drink. Because I'm thirsty. What's he asking? I can't understand what he's saying, but I hear his voice, a woman's voice.

It says, "Alohalika ny ranom-bary e!"

I open my eyes. I'm alone under the streetlight. It shows me real life, a calm reality. I stand up. Jump as my hands touch the cooled, moist hood. The decorative fountains in front of City Hall hum behind their gates. I scramble into the car. Twice as relieved to get back under my blanket. I wrap it around my body up to my ears before settling down in my seat. One hand kept free to reach the thermos.

The pool stops gurgling. The lights shining on City Hall also go out. It must be midnight. I didn't get any fares all evening. A shadow lurches behind the light. Squelch-squelching toward my taxi.

I drop the lemongrass infusion and take off. Like the wind.

Alohalika ny ranom-bary e!

3

Sitting on the biggest chair, a beer in my hand and Talking Heads in my ears, I rub my stomach watching her work the grill. She's making masikita kebabs. I came downstairs as soon as I smelled the aroma wafting into the room. Now I'm in the big armchair. The TV is on, but I turned off the sound. Silent broadcasters are hilarious. It doesn't mean anything. It's like they're not there, not a single one of them in that damn box. But you know what's happening. Nothing changes from yesterday. The same faces in different places or sometimes even the same places. A silent track. I picture Mike Brant crooning "Qui saura." She pulls my headphones off and asks what I'm laughing at.

"The TV's on mute!"

"You're dumb," she says.

Still, she leaves a few pieces of kebab for me. What a taste! I rub my stomach in anticipation as David Byrne's voice in my ears asks *where is that large automobile? ... my beautiful house! ... my beautiful wife!*

None of it's real! My car's a clunker that I lease at night, my house is a bed that I can only spend time in during the day, and my wife's a daydream that I chase through my notebooks beneath the city's street lamps.

Nothing's real except the smell of the kebabs. I'd stopped by when I smelled the familiar aroma of zebu meat fried in the fat from its hump. As a bonus, I get to take advantage of the heat from the brazier.

"Give me five," I say to the kebab lady. "Come on. Six! Seven! Seven for the price of six!" She smiles, counts what she has left. "Ten for the price of ten, will that work?" My smile drops. I sigh, "Six'll be fine."

I try picking up the chair to scoot it closer to the fire. It weighs a ton. Packing pallets tied to a set of rims. I guess I'll just stand near the fire. It's not that much warmer.

"It's cold, the charcoal's not burning good, it's not crispy enough," she says.

"It'll be fine."

"Oh, is it you? Yes, you. I recognize you. Stop looking behind you, you're the one I'm talking to."

"Uh ..."

"You're the taxi guy that drove the dead woman around. My boys know you real well. They wash your car. The first time, when you got back from Andraharo, you stopped here. I was there. They washed your car, they always talk about the smell."

"Uh ..."

"Why'd you do that? Why'd you agree to let her get in your car? You don't get any fares anymore, you know. You don't even have enough money for ten measly masikita!"

I'd sat down on the irregular chair at the first word. The cold is seeping into me as it all tumbles around in my head, making my limbs and my whole body numb. Stiff as a lifeless sculpture. I can't unclench my teeth even if I wanted to answer. Frozen, like when I see *her*. Except that she directs my actions like a marionette. So other people can see her, too. And they see me when I drive her all the way across Tana. Like a child, I had closed my eyes and thought I was invisible.

"Do you want some peanut sauce? Or chili?"

I've got to shake myself out of this. Concentrate on the masikita smell. Nice, warm thoughts. A Friday night outing behind Mahamasina where a client will keep me for the night and share his feast with me in the taxi. I just have to ask. The bottle of rum I used to share with Ra-Eddy before he left to claim his own corner in the sun down south in Sapphire City. My mother's masikita that she'd buy on the way home from work, that we'd reheat over the fire and gobble down with soasoa rice that was cooked at the end of the afternoon, kept warm under blankets, as soft as can be.

"Peanut, yes, chili, yes," I say too forcefully, released at last. "... She's not dead."

"Not dead? Ha ha ha! You're the only one who sees her in flesh and blood. The rest of the world just sees her as flesh and mud! Ha ha ha! You're driving a dead lady around!"

"She's not a dead person. I take her to her husband's office in Andraharo."

"Have you ever seen her husband? What's he look like?"

Masikita. Bathed in spicy peanut sauce. Mmmm. Some warm bread would be perfect. The kind that's fresh out of the bakery first thing in the morning. Sometimes my clients give me a piece. I've never seen her husband. As soon as she gets out of the car, I clear off, I don't ask for the rest of the money.

"It doesn't matter, she's not dead. She talks, she says things to me!"

"What does she say?"

"She said that there was water in the rice fields, up to your knees. Alohalika ny ranom-bary e!"

"Ha ha ha! That'll do her a hell of a lot of good! Since when do dead people care about rice? There are never any tombs underneath rice fields!"

"Hey, listen, one of my wife's cousins, her grandfather appeared to her in her sleep and warned her about the same thing, and when they opened his tomb, it was all flooded from a crack inside!"

"Yeah, but he didn't ask for a taxi ride!"

"Ha ha ha!"

Who are all these people around me? The masikita are getting cold. The fat's congealed, and it's scraping uncomfortably against my tongue. Why are they shouting like that? The chili's not heating up my palate at all. Why are they all looking at me? The sauce is getting thick. Why are they laughing?

"Alohalika ny ranom-bary e!"

"Ha ha ha!"

"You don't remember anything, do you?"

"What was it that happened? She appeared, squelch-squelch, covered in mud, was that it?"

"Ha ha ha!"

"You didn't stop!"

"I was at the taxi stop under my streetlight."

"Ha ha ha, no, we're talking about the first time. You didn't stop, did you?"

"What are you talking about?"
"The first time, when she fell in the rice fields and climbed out onto the big dike next to the river, all covered in mud, asking for help, you didn't stop."
"She was yelling, 'Alohalika ny ranom-bary e!'"
"But did you see her? No one would have let her get in their car looking like that."
"She was beautiful!"
"She'd be gorgeous without all that mud!"
"Ha ha ha, a gorgeous corpse! Ha ha ha!"
"She's not dead!"
"She's more dead than dead. Left alone on that dike, abandoned by everyone, knocked down in a rice field. She died of that. Ever since, she's been begging us to take her to Andraharo. You're not the only one she asks."
"Huh?"
"You're not the only one she relays her message to either."
"Oh, yeah? You, too?"
"Alohalika ny ranom-bary e!"

4

Ten p.m. and not a single passenger. Read the whole paper. Headlines to classifieds. Nothing new outside the glowing halo beneath my streetlight. The daytime driver who left it in my clunker could have just as easily held onto it to keep himself warm. The nights are still chilly. The transitional government's transacting. Grasshoppers are spawning. Murders and robberies give way to murders and robberies. Lots of people have been blessed with favors from the Sacred Heart (I stopped counting after seventeen and turned away from the page filled with thanks notices). Lots of used SUVs have arrived by boat, but that doesn't make them any cheaper. So I guess tomorrow still won't be the day that I'll sit behind the power windows of my SUV and never see the random glances of children in the streets again. Oh, well! Still waiting to pay today's lease on my 4L (I have to do at least three trips). On the financial page, the World Bank tells me I'm not the only one. In fact, I'm one of many. Ninety-two people out of a hundred have less than the average taxi fare every day. No wonder I don't have any passengers! Widespread poverty clogs the arteries of the city and plows the rice fields. Wrap yourself up tight in the paper and wait for something better.

Something moves in the side mirror. A young couple walks into the light. They come toward me. I smile at my good luck. They climb into the back on my side, I say good evening, they frown, shake their heads, and climb out the other door. The two doors smack shut like a slap across both cheeks.

I rub my face. I don't even have time to process what happened when the door opens again. The not-passenger. "Sorry!" he spits out, leaving a thousand-ariary bill on the seat and taking off again, fleeing me like I'm a curse. Smack again.

I get out when the coffee man comes by. I tell him he'd better wash a cup good and clean for me. He laughs and obeys. We swap stories around his brazier cart. He laughs when I tell him I haven't had any passengers. He takes off without getting his cup back and before I can pay him. I laugh, too, when I realize it. I savor the last sip of my free coffee as long as possible.

Then I see *her* coming into the circle of light. There's a dog in front of her. She's already grabbing the handle.

"Where do you think you're going like that, ma'am?"

"Over to the Place du 13 Mai."

"... That doesn't exist anymore," I say.

Even if I'd wanted to quickly hop in and lock the car, the dog's weaving around my legs. Smack. She's already forcing a smile at me through the window. She turns toward me, inviting me to stare at her hollowing face.

"Do I look like someone who wishes to go to a place that does not exist?" she inquires, purulent strips dropping from her cheeks, her neck, with every word.

I take my seat at the wheel and start off. Toward the Place de l'Amour, since that's what they rechristened the square in front of City Hall. I try to say something, to prepare her. "It's changed, you know ..."

I stare at her in the rearview mirror. I peer into the middle of the small rectangle, focusing on the light deep within her eyes.

"There's a big pool and jets of water—it's a fountain now."

"A fountain? What a good idea, water for everyone!" She perks up, her eyes shining.

"No. There are gates."

"There are gates?"

"You can't actually get in, you just look at it."

The light in the rectangle blinks.

"But it's pretty!" I'm almost shouting. "The jets of water are choreographed with color-changing lights, they turn white, purple, red, green, and blue."

It's getting weaker and weaker. My words are what seem to be holding her above the water like wax holding a tiny flame at the end of a wick.

"It's wonderful! Families gather around the gates on Sundays. People come from all over the country to see Antananarivo's fairy tale. Country folk who might not know that running water exists, they just stand there, dumbfounded by the leaping fountains. They have their picture taken in front of them. Even I go sometimes. It's like the pool's sleeping, then it wakes up in a bunch of sparkling, humming springs, a magical sight with huge jets of water. I could watch it forever pressed up against the bars of the cage, dreaming up a new life to replace my own. The sun sparkles in the spray, the water cools the surrounding air, the close city smoke feels a little more breathable ... Ma'am? Ma'am! Are you okay? Do you want me to take you to Andraharo? To your husband's office?"

She opens her eyes and murmurs, her lips barely moving: "Please, take me to the Place du 13 Mai."

We're on our way. You don't meet a lot of people in the dead of night. She sags into the corner of the backseat. I adjust the mirror to keep an eye on her, forget that I'm supposed to go under the Andravoahangy Bridge. Concentrate on driving. A few furtive nocturnal shadows let themselves be caught in the headlights. Three figures pissing into Behoririka Lake. Cops on the Rue de Pochard, but they don't wave me over. Soon we're hurtling past the train station. Only half of City Hall is lit up. The water gurgles in the dim light. I park facing the fountains to give them more light. I cast a quick "We're here!" behind me.

I slip into the yellow beams and pass through the gates with a daydream woman. Daytime under the warm spring sun. We'll walk right up to the pool. The woman will play in the droplets that rain down on her. I'll scold her a bit like a child. She'll laugh, twirling around on the paving stones. I'll tell her to be careful. She won't let anybody boss her around. Right when the jets of water shoot upward to form a tower of shining mist, she'll shove me into the fountain. And then pull me out of it a few seconds later and kiss me, soaking wet.

"Place de l'Amour, really? 'Love,'" my impossible passenger jeers, face drained of blood, staggering but upright, in front of the shimmering sprays. She mutters something I don't understand. Something like *Not the change I expected.* Then she mellows, staring up at the dark sky above us.

"Dawn is breaking," she says. "We'll go give them a hand." She points at the open square.

I clutch the steering wheel and shake my head. Clearly, we're not seeing the same thing.

She shoots me a smoldering look and passes through the cage, leaving bits of putrid skin behind on the bars. I throw open my door and manage to vomit (almost) outside the car. I've emptied my guts and hurled my bile, and my eyes are watering. It's hard for me to get back up. Her squelching, echoing steps sound wrong against the gurgling water. My headlights are glowing more and more weakly. I want to turn them off to save the battery, but all of a sudden I'm afraid of the dark. The squick-squicking comes back louder. With rumbling moans. Every step is heavy with condemnation. A hoard floods the square, all victims of the rice fields. An unrelenting wave that swallows everything in its path. The water fountains, the pool, the gates. Shaking, I twist the ignition wires. The starter button. It whines like an animal in a trap. I'm the one who's going to be trapped here. I mash the white button in desperation. More whining, then sputtering. I try again. The engine dies.

"Alohalika ny ranom-bary e!"

The Spooky Japanese Girl is There for You

Juan Martinez

You lose your credit card
and call the company, but no one answers—and that hissing noise? The Japanese girl ghost. You say "Hello?" three times. Then she hangs up. You shiver ... What's that? A replacement card. In your *wallet.*

You're on a date
and trying too hard. You drop a knife, and there she is, underneath a table—pale arms, red dress, long black hair covering her face. You jump back. Your date says that you look like you've seen a ghost. You try to laugh, but can't. Your date thinks you're a complicated man, a man haunted by a dark, interesting past. And you are. You are haunted by your past—also by the ghost of a Japanese schoolgirl.

You're at the gym
and slacking. You think you'll do 15 minutes on the treadmill and call it a day. But you look up and the spooky Japanese ghost is on Fox News complaining about broken borders and how no one cares about the middle class. You run for a full half-hour, fueled by righteous indignation.

You're at home
and it's late, you're tired, and none of the light bulbs you've just replaced are working right: they flicker, they cast shadows that look like people or birds or household appliances. You're in bed, the TV tuned to static because you were so angry about the war on the middle class that you canceled your cable, and you're looking at

the ceiling. The Japanese ghost crawls from one corner to the next. Her hair still covers her face. She moves in bizarre, halting steps, crawling to every lamp in your house and adjusting every bulb until the bedroom is bathed in a soothing glow. You sleep and forget to turn off the lights. The spooky Japanese ghost does it for you, then vanishes, never to appear again. Years later, you're walking down the street and spot a small distant figure in a red dress, and you run to her and—never mind, it's someone else. She's gone, you miss her, but ghosts move on: They can't hang around all day. They've got things to do.

The Executioner

Jennifer Marie Brissett

The day of the execution was the first and only time I'd ever been in a prison. It was a lot bigger than I expected it to be. There was more light in it, too. I thought it would be a dark place with screaming inmates yelling at me as I passed through. But that's not how it was at all. Everyone fell silent when they saw me. My path opened like Moses parting the Red Sea as people moved out of my way. There were guards on every side of me as I walked through the prison. They guided my way to the death house in the backyard. I was Death personified that day, and everyone knew it. I felt kind of powerful. I looked up and saw these big, tough men who were afraid—*of me*. That's what I became that day, Death personified.

I was warned not to look anyone in the eye that didn't work for the State. So I kept my head down. It was hard not to look up, feeling the heat of so many stares on me. But I did as I was told. I was a good citizen. This was what the State required. My name had come up, and when that happens, you do your duty. That was how my family raised me. You don't shy away from your responsibilities. You stand up and do what needs to be done. I took no joy in being there. I knew that this was nothing to be happy about. This was just something that had to be done. And my name came up. That was all there was to it.

They marched me into the back where there was a large green lawn. Inmates were working to cut the grass, and they, too, stopped to stare at me as I passed by. The sky was unusually bright that day. It was clear and blue as far as the eye could see. And it was so quiet. Like the birds themselves knew that it was a solemn day.

I had just had my second child a few months before. I would have rather been home with her. She was such a little thing. And a really good baby. I could hand her to anyone, and she wouldn't cry. She'd just look up at them with wonder and lean into their chests, calm and pleasant. I felt so lucky to have a good home and family. It was the State that kept us all safe from the likes of the one that I was going to put down. The way I looked at it, this was little to ask of a citizen whom the State had given so much.

The death house looked like an old chapel with its small "A" roof and peeling window wallpaper made to resemble stained glass. Inside was quiet, and people spoke in hushed tones. There were prison guards everywhere. They, like the prisoners, stilled when they saw me.

The warden was there to greet me. He was friendly enough, businesslike, though. He shook my hand and escorted me to the lunchroom where a fine meal was waiting for me. The State sent a packet to my house with a return form requesting that I list the meal I would like to be served. I must admit that they got everything just right. Funny, I can remember enjoying the meal, but I don't remember the meal itself. It's like I have a memory of a memory about it.

While I sat and ate, the warden and the prison guards watched. It felt strange to be the only one chewing. The warden told me to eat up since I wouldn't be able to have anything again until the next day. It's the way the drugs worked. If you tried to eat right after taking them, they could make you really sick to your stomach.

When I was done, the warden and I had coffee together. This time the three guards with us joined in. It felt like I had become part of a ritual of theirs. I wondered how many of these executions they had attended. I wanted to ask but didn't. We just all sat quietly together sipping at our coffee until it was gone or got cold.

The warden took off his glasses and rubbed his eyes. For a moment I thought that he was crying. When he looked up, I saw that he wasn't. He just looked tired. He put his glasses back on and laid his palms out flat on the table.

"Did you read the packet that the State sent?" the warden asked.

Yes, I nodded.

"Good. Well, I'm going to briefly go over the basics again of what is going to happen tonight. Please stop me at any time if there is something you don't understand or if you have a question."

I nodded again.

"We will take a little bit of your blood now. It will be used to create the drug cocktail. It will be prepared and injected into you in about an hour. Once you receive the injection, you are the State's agent of execution. The drug will only affect the condemned. It is coded with his DNA and yours only. You cannot harm any other person with your touch. Do you understand?"

I nodded.

"You have to answer verbally. It's the law."

I said, "Yes."

The warden continued, "We will wait until midnight for any last-minute reprieves. If there are none, you will be escorted to the death chamber by these guards to face the condemned. Myself and the minister for the condemned will be in the room. A family member and a witness for the condemned may also be in the death chamber. He will be strapped down securely onto a gurney. You will be perfectly safe."

I instinctively looked at the guards sitting with us. One of them lowered his head to avoid my eyes.

"He will be allowed to say his last words," the warden said.

"Will he say anything to me?"

"The law states that a prisoner has the right to face his executioner. So he may say something to you." The warden took off his glasses again and spoke softly. "My advice to you is to pay no attention to what he says. He doesn't know you, and you don't know him. Remember, you are not his judge or his jury. You didn't determine his guilt or innocence. Others performed that function. You are his executioner. You are just performing your lawful civic duty."

I must admit that I always just assumed that the man was guilty. I didn't even know what he was condemned for doing. The packet from the State suggested that I not research the case, so I didn't. Sometimes I think that was a mistake.

"When you feel ready, you are to physically touch the condemned."

"How am I supposed to touch him?" I asked.

"Any way you see fit," the warden said. "I've known some who hugged them and others who have just put a pinky finger on them. There is no right or wrong way as long as there is physical contact."

"And that is all it takes?"

"Yes, ma'am. Death will commence at that point."

"How long will it take?" It felt ghoulish asking, but I really wanted to know.

"Death may occur within a few moments. You are legally required to remain with the condemned until he is dead. Then you are free to go."

The night passed slowly. The lab technician who had mixed the drug cocktail was also the one to administer my injection. He made me roll up my sleeve and rubbed my arm with cool alcohol.

"This may sting," he warned.

It did.

"You may get a slight fever tomorrow," he said. "It will pass. You will be fine in a day or two."

I unrolled my sleeve as he put his needles and things away. The area where I was injected felt sore and began to throb. My arm ached for several days after that. Such a small price to pay.

"At least you won't ever be asked to do this again. The drug only works once. It will never work in you again. At least that's something."

"At least that's something," I repeated.

I spent the rest of the afternoon in the lunchroom with the guards. They were good people. We talked about our families and showed each other pictures of our kids. We played cards and dominoes to while away the time. I couldn't help constantly looking up at the clock. It seemed to be ticking slower than usual. I began to feel anxious as the sun came down. I had survived the weeks preceding that night by simply not thinking about ending a man's life. After the sun came down, all that changed. What I was about to do was all I could think about. I was just a small-town mother of two. How had I become this agent of death?

By 9 p.m. I was visibly shivering.

"I don't feel well," I said to my guards. "I want to go home."

They just looked down. One of them said to me, "You're just nervous. This happens to everyone."

"But I feel sick to my stomach," I said. It was no lie. My stomach was twisted into knots upon knots. I felt like I could throw up.

"That's normal," he said. "I feel like that every single time I have to do one of these."

By 11:30 p.m. the guards and I were all on our feet. The cordial feeling between us was gone. Now it was all business. The minutes passed like hours. Then it was finally time. The guards escorted me to the death chamber. My legs were moving on their own because I felt nothing. We entered the room, and it was like the warden said it would be. He was there standing next to a minister. And there was the condemned man. He was on a gurney, strapped down by many large belts. His arms were stretched out on two protruding extensions of the gurney, so that he looked like a man on a cross.

He was just a boy, really. Maybe he was in his late twenties. There was something about his expression that reminded me of my little brother. He physically looked nothing like my brother, but the way he held his face and moved his head was just like him.

I heard a whimpering as if it were coming from an injured animal. There were two women standing behind a glass window. They were holding each other. One looked elderly; the other was young.

"Do you have any last words?" the warden asked.

The boy craned his neck to see the two women through the window.

"I love you," he said. "I'm sorry, Momma."

I felt my knees begin to shake. I didn't want to be there. I didn't want to be there. I didn't want to be there. The boy looked back at me. He had soft brown eyes. He was not what I expected at all.

The warden nodded to me that it was time. My legs went completely numb. I couldn't move. I could hardly catch my breath. My feet were like wet cement melting into the floor.

"When you're ready," the warden said.

Many moments went by, and I still didn't move. I stared at the boy. My heart pounded in my chest. No one said anything. It was deathly silent. It was all up to me, and I couldn't move.

The warden waited patiently, then he looked at his watch. I saw him wave his hand to the guards. And these men, these good men who I had spent the whole day with and shared pictures of my kids, grabbed me and forced me forward. It was then that I understood that the guards were not there just to protect me but to force me if I tried to refuse.

I fought them. I fought them hard. I waved my arms and scratched like a cat. A wild animal arrived in me that I never knew was there.

"Don't touch me!" I screamed. And they backed away. The women behind the glass looked at me with a kind of hope and sympathy. I felt a flush of guilt and shame. I felt naked before them. I straightened out my clothes and passed my hands over my hair. Then I slowly stepped towards the boy. He looked at me with eyes that tore at my soul. I went over to him.

I said, "I'm sorry." He nodded and swallowed.

I took his hand in mine. It was warm and soft. Then I backed away.

Minutes passed, and nothing happened. I felt a wave of relief. I had read in the packet sent to my house that sometimes the drugs didn't take. I felt a joy then that I didn't think could be possible. The boy smiled at me. He looked over at this mother. And she weakly waved back at him. My face was completely wet at this point. I wiped away my tears. Then the boy jerked.

He convulsed for a few moments, twisting in his restraints. Little pockets of foam appeared at the corners of his mouth. His eyes turned back so that they were all white. His body shook for a minute. He let out a deep sigh and closed his eyes. Then he moaned a little as if he was having a troubled dream. I could see his chest still moving. Then he jerked again, and he moved no more.

The warden came over and checked his pulse.

"Death occurred," he said and looked at his watch, "at 12:27 a.m."

I can't explain the feeling I had then. It's a feeling that has never left me. I felt hollowed out like a Halloween pumpkin, all carved out with nothing left inside. I had killed a man. With my own hand I killed him. I looked at his still body, and it was like there was nothing else. I couldn't hear anything. I couldn't feel anything. The guards unstrapped him, and his slack body flopped. I looked away. I heard someone let out a loud cry. I thought it was the boy's mother. I was surprised to find that it was me.

I could barely walk. The guards helped me out of the building and escorted me to the parking lot. Someone called to me. I turned around. It was the boy's mother. Her daughter was trying to hold her back. She was coming at me. The guards stood in her way.

"I want to speak to you," she said.

I said, "It's all right." Inside, I felt that even if she wanted to hit me, it was all right. The guards got out of the way, and the daughter hesitantly let the old woman go. She was short, so that I had to look down to see her. She looked up at me. My legs buckled, and I found myself on my knees before her. She took my hand—the hand that had just killed her son—and she held it in hers. Her small veiny hands cradled mine.

"This was not your fault," she said. "I will pray for you and your family."

Then she let my hand go and turned towards her daughter. They held each other and slowly walked into the night.

My husband once told me that all the cells in a body completely change every seven years. Well, it's been seven years since then, and I still feel the same. There's not a day that goes by that I don't think about it. I don't talk about it with anyone. My husband knows to just leave it alone. I know I've been different. More quiet. I think about things more. I think about life more.

It's a warm day today. The sky is blue as far as the eye can see. My eldest is playing in the yard with his little sister. I've been watching them laughing and tumbling around on the grass. They are so innocent. Their whole lives are in front of them. Their faces filled with only possibilities. His momma must have had days like this. Days when she looked out at her children, laughing and playing, and dreamed of what they might be.

Girl, I Love You

Nadia Bulkin

My best friend, my blood-sister, decided to make the Ultimate Sacrifice to destroy Asami Ogino. We were drinking chuhai on an overpass, and as the world roared beneath us, Yurie showed me the letter she planned to send to the Ministry of Education. It was a four-page, four-year chronicle of the sins Asami had visited upon her. She had, of course, used a PO Box and Anonymity Seal. She wrote: *Don't try to find me. Just make it stop.* I almost let the letter fly over the barbed wire toward the smoke-covered sun because I already knew the Ministry wouldn't care, just like our teachers didn't care. That was the difference between me and Yurie: I had accepted that life was shit, not just in school but beyond; Yurie still had this perverse expectation of joy. All that tightly-wound, brightly-colored hope was her downfall.

"If I don't hear back in a week," she said, "I'm doing it."

This is something people often misunderstand: Yurie didn't want to do the Ultimate Sacrifice. But she already tried everything else. Two dozen Vengeance Charms bought from skeletal bloodhounds in the grimy alleys behind malls cooked up from the bloody floor planks of haunted houses. A zip file of a black market video-bomb, *Grudge of a Predator*, a so-called documentary on our so-called war crimes (she refused to tell me how much she paid for that one). We also took a two-hour bus ride up to Rika Yamazaki's shrine so Yurie could wish for Asami's death. Miss Yamazaki had an 80% satisfaction rate on account of the enormous rage cloud that spawns when you're shoved off a balcony by a jealous ex-boyfriend—but even then, Asami was fine.

Asami was so fine that she had some of her friends burn Yurie's arms with cigarettes before school. I hadn't been there—I was slumped at the foot of my bed, staring at the clock—but I saw Yurie showing off the bleeding black wounds to curious first-years. The math teacher scolded her for upsetting everyone; I wondered if Yurie had lost her mind. Maybe this is where Love of Life takes you, in the end.

"That Yamazaki bitch just sits on people's wishes," Yurie complained, but Miss Yamazaki did have a lot of wishes to answer. It wasn't just junior high students anymore but sad middle-aged couples and bespectacled professionals and families with little kids in bear hats. I thought it was fucked up to take your kids to the grave of an angry murdered stranger, but who am I to judge? "That's why we need regulations on shrines. Not that this government can get anything passed."

Yurie didn't like the Prime Minister—thought he was a fatalist unable to grab the wheel and stop this car crash we were all in. On my worst days I worried she secretly thought the same about me. After all, my father had been a bureaucrat, servant to the impotent government—very particular about following state recommendations on psychic energy even though he hadn't written them. He was in the labor ministry. Research. No research in the world can save you from your destiny, I guess.

"It's always a gamble, using dead people."

Yurie's phone beeped—we didn't need to look to know the message was some variant of DIE DIE DIE with UGLY and SLUT tossed in for extra color. I said, "None of them are worth anything."

"Michi, I lost everything. Choir, the girls I used to know, how teachers look at me ... my stupid bicycle. You don't know what it's like."

"I know what loss is like."

Her face crumpled with apology. She had been with me three years ago when, halfway through a crosswalk, I looked up at a giant screen and saw something about Riot and Government Worker and a somber photo of my father on top of the tortured remains of a black sedan. My brain had floated out through my eyes, trying to escape this new post-father existence while my body stayed rooted in the street. It was Yurie's screaming that brought me back to this shit-covered world.

"But we've got weapons now. And I'm going to use them even if you're too scared."

Yurie called psychic energy an arsenal. She was always stocking up. But at a certain point you run out of money, out of options. I'd heard of precisely one dead banker with a 100% satisfaction rate, but his shrine was perched on an island in Matsushima, and who had the money for that? Eventually all you've got to spend is your soul. Traditional fortune-tellers call psychic energy "dismal energy," probably because they're afraid of losing their customers now that anyone can pluck that power out of the ether, but maybe they were right: maybe nothing but suffering can come out of psychic energy.

"And what are you paying for that weapon? It's called *Ultimate Sacrifice* for a reason."

She snorted. "Life's not much of a sacrifice. You know that."

Yeah, I knew. I was the one that pointed out black companies and the cyber-homeless. I was the one that buried my father after his car hit a cyclist and a mob stomped him to death. It wasn't fair to ask me to argue for a beautiful future, and bam: I was angry. Yurie grabbed my sleeve.

"Don't hate me," she hissed. I thought, *If I promise never to forgive you, will that keep you breathing?* But I couldn't keep my face stern, not to her tears. "I could never hate you," I said.

Of course, Yurie never heard back from the Ministry of Education. Of course, Asami never got pulled out of school. So Yurie bought the script for the Ultimate Sacrifice from a glass case in one of the city's first psychic shops, a converted pharmacy with a red door. The old woman who unlocked the case asked her if she understood the sanctity of life, had her look at pictures of babies and ducklings.

"What if I don't want you to go," I said. We were standing at the intersection where we'd have to part ways. I had used up everything in my own arsenal to dissuade her, and now I was down to the raw, wriggling emotional stuff that I hated handling. "Will that make you stay? Will you stay for me?"

She didn't answer right away. Instead, she hugged me and said, "Girl, I love you," before tugging the straps of her backpack and walking resolutely up the hill like a Himalayan mountain climber. Her answer came that night when Yurie's mother called to say Yurie had jumped off a building to her death.

I was calm, all things considered. Ever since my mother put her arms around me and said she had some terrible news, a numbing chill settled on my shoulders like a shawl. During Yurie's funeral, I could only think of how cold I was, how strange everyone was acting. People with faces out of half-remembered dreams kept asking how I was doing since Yurie's "accident." I'd never heard "I know you girls were close" so many times. I'd say, "Yurie's coming back," and that always made them look away.

I spent a month waiting for Asami to die. I wanted front row seats for Yurie's Revenge—I was scared I'd miss it if I looked away for a second. But Asami kept on giggling, pointing, whispering—at me, at the fat sad kid, at the quiet soprano that had become her new whipping girl since Yurie died. Asami picked at the weak like the obsessive compulsive pick at scabs: she just couldn't seem to stop. When I nearly set everyone on fire in chemistry, Asami mouthed at me, "Kill yourself, worm."

"You're not taking your future seriously, Michi," Miss Tomoe said after class. She was unmarried, childless, tending to her parents, forever trapped in high school. I couldn't imagine anything worse. "It's so important that you don't slip up now."

I wondered if Yurie had messed up the curse—written the words wrong, done something out of order. Bold, reckless Yurie—it wouldn't have been the first time.

"I'm sorry about your friend's accident. You don't blame yourself for what happened, do you?"

Obviously, I blamed myself—for failing to keep her alive, for being too weak to suffer with her at school. After she walked away on that final evening of her life, I yelled at her to call me, and she waved back without turning her head. In some of my dreams, she did turn but had no face to speak with—just an endless curtain of brittle ombre hair. In other dreams she whispered something different when she hugged me: "Girl, come with me." But as always, I was too scared.

"I don't know," I said. "Why do you pop anti-depressants between classes?"

Miss Tomoe's plate-like façade shattered, and she burst into tears right there at the desk, surrounded by all her little beakers. Not long after that, she was fired for forcing a failing student to drink hydrochloric acid. She'd poured herself a beaker, too, saying, "Here's to failure!" The student spat his out; Miss Tomoe finished hers.

The sun was setting. I was trudging down the hill under stringy electrical wires when I heard a voice call my name: a deep, deliberate "Michi" like a summons from a northern volcano. Each syllable kissed my bones, rippled my blood. State recommendations tell you to never seek the mouth that releases a voice like that—it's going to be an ugly one or a hungry one. But I knew the human marrow gurgling inside that voice. It had asked to borrow my pencil, laughed at my morbid jokes. "Michi!"

I turned. Yurie was hovering behind me, the untied laces of her shoes barely scraping the sidewalk. She looked different; terrible. She was covered in blood like a newborn or a crime scene, but her skin was marble-white. Her joints hung crooked as a carelessly-flung rag doll. Her neck was so twisted that she could barely keep eye contact with me; her jaw smashed so deep it was hard to believe she could speak. My blood-sister. "Asami," she hissed. For a second I thought that in the trauma of death she had forgotten who I was, and the thought of being ripped apart by Yurie's hands nearly stopped my heart. "I-I-I can't." She kept stopping and starting like a scratched recording. "Reach Asami."

I forgot that you aren't supposed to engage ghosts and stammered to ask why not.

"Ah-ah-asami!" she yelled, although I didn't actually see her mouth widen. Suddenly, her hands were reaching toward me as if to give me another hug—I stumbled backward. "Veiled."

The Ultimate Sacrifice was supposed to be so strong—it was always linked with either a murder or a miracle like the Brave Boys of Shizuoka who committed suicide to save their school from yet another earthquake—that we never even considered the possibility that it wouldn't work. "Yurie, I'm sorry." Yurie wasn't blinking anymore, and her eyes were red spider webs. She used to carry eye drops—she had to be in pain. "I miss you. I'm sorry."

"Michi, help me!" I'd heard this so many times from her: after-school cleaning duty, the robotech competition in junior high, every doomed day with Asami's foot upon her neck. Yurie's were the hands that dragged me out from under my bed. She'd been dragging me into her battles for years.

This time, I didn't answer. Yurie's plea hung between us, suspended across her grave like a very, very long game of telephone. Somewhere a screen door opened and a man shouted, "Yeah, yeah, I'll call you later!" I became aware of birds chirping on the electrical wires, the sound of traffic, the ache in my shoulder ... I exhaled, letting out the sweet and sour stench of a broken-down body and breathing in garbage, detergent, fish. Yurie vanished, and my relief criss-crossed almost immediately with sadness.

Yurie didn't give up. Really, I should have known she wouldn't; she'd been friends with me for six years. A normal person would have dumped my ass on the curb after my first crying spell, but Yurie was a sucker for lost souls. I used to say she had a Good Nurse complex, but Yurie insisted the love came first, and the caretaking after. And I won't lie: after my father died, I clung to Yurie.

And now she clung to me. We stared at ourselves in my bathroom mirror. We walked together to school. We sat together in homeroom, Yurie behind me with her bloody arms childishly locked around my waist, hissing "help me help me." Back before Asami destroyed Yurie's bicycle, we used to ride around the suburbs like that except she'd be pedaling in front, veering to scare me, and I'd be sitting rigid and tense in the back, shrieking at her to be careful. I felt suffocated. I could almost taste her blood in the back of my throat.

On some subterranean level I was terrified of her—terrified that she was drowned in blood because she'd been out killing strangers, because she couldn't touch Asami.

At lunchtime I wound up on the roof, gulping what passed for fresh air and trying not to vomit.

"Did you come to kill yourself like Yurie?" I whipped my neck back. Asami was sitting under one of the roaring air vents, smoking a clandestine cigarette. She blew a little nicotine cloud toward me. "Well? I know you were her other half."

It sounds absurd, given the tears we'd shed over this bitch, but I was relieved to hear someone admit that Yurie's death was no accident—unless her whole life was an accident, and if so then why not mine, why not Asami's or my father's or the Prime Minister's? Asami shifted, and something around her neck caught the light—a tiny sun beneath her chin. She budged again, and I saw what it was: a glassy choker, nearly invisible beyond the glare, tight as a lattice tattoo across her throat. She saw me staring and slapped her hand over it. I could almost see something human breathing beneath her bone-fine face. "What are you looking at, freak?"

Asami shed friends so fast, I bet she'd never had a blood-sister— someone her heart had twinned to, for better or for worse. Maybe she envied me and Yurie. "Why did you hate Yurie so much?"

"She was the one that hated us," said Asami, voice dripping steel. "She rejected us. You know how she was. Always had to be different. Always a loudmouth. How do you think that made us feel?"

I couldn't tell if she was being sarcastic. "She's dead because of you."

Asami lifted the pink-banded Pianissimo to her lips and shrugged. "So she was weak like all the rest." I wondered if anyone else had ever turned into a mess on a sidewalk because of Asami. "The strong survive, that's the rule."

And that's when I knew I had to do it—because Asami was wrong about that. The real rule, the one my father taught me, was this: anyone can bite you, so be good to other people. "Everyone has to pay their due," he'd say while we watched news segments on terrorists and corrupt politicians and faraway blindfolded hostages. He believed so much in cosmic justice that when he died I wondered if he'd once done something heinous. But maybe it wasn't that simple. Maybe justice had more arms, a longer reach, than we ants could comprehend.

"Everyone has to pay their due," I said. Asami's plastic laughter followed me into the stairwell, and I thought, *She doesn't have a soul to lose anyway.*

Asami and her devotees were waiting for me after school. I was on bathroom cleaning duty, so they nearly drowned me in the toilet. Here's something else people need to understand: kids buy curses like arcade tokens—some of them counterfeit, sure, but others real. Asami did the sort of stuff you wouldn't do to anyone unless you knew they couldn't stick you with a visit from Hanako-san. But I held it together in the toilet bowl; Yurie would have been proud of me. I told myself this was nothing, nothing in comparison to what she'd been put through. My feet slipped on the tiles as Asami rifled through my purse, looking for "spending money" that she didn't need and I didn't have.

"You're paying your due right now, freak," Asami said. "For talking back to me."

At Rika Yamazaki's grave, I had wished for my father to find eternal rest in that great vinyl office chair in the sky. I didn't want him returned even though I heard my mother cry at night. With the earth being shaken and stabbed and poisoned at every turn—mad cow, mad bird, mad people—he was better off making his peace with the other side. His suffering had ended. Good.

The beauty of psychic energy—the reason my father worshipped the state recommendations—is that protection is nearly impossible. A psychic attack, the public service announcements explained, is like a natural disaster. There's no kicking it back. That's why the cheerful cartoon ghost on the PSAs chirps that "The best way to protect yourself is to be a good person!" And some preliminary studies have hinted that the rate of infidelity is decreasing because cheating hearts are afraid of waking up fused to their lovers. We're not turning into better people, but our retribution is getting closer.

Of course, real life isn't that simple because some people will always be able to pay for the impossible, and if there's one thing talent's drawn to, it's artillery and armory. We're doing well. We're killing ourselves off at record speed. And a very few of us—a lucky, golden few—have the means to hurt without repercussion, to escape the judgment of peers, to skate above this shitty, brutal world. Internet chatter says the Prime Minister has a talisman *or else he never could have dissolved Parliament twice,* and common sense says the Emperor surely has one, too. And so did Asami Ogino, third-year high school girl in western Tokyo. I wondered how her parents decided to buy her one—had she bitten other babies? Or did they just want to give their little princess every advantage?

This is what I thought about while I sat in the auditorium waiting for the choral concert to start. This is what I thought about so I wouldn't think about the fact that I was going to kill the star soloist.

I had already promised Yurie. I'd been sitting in the library, searching yearbooks for pictures of Asami and checking for the necklace—the tiny sun cloaked in clouds—when Yurie's pale bloody hand snaked over my shoulder. I remembered painting those nails sky-blue when blood still ran under the skin instead of on top of it. And now I couldn't even look her in the eye because I knew she'd seen hell.

"I told you I'd never let you down," I said, although this was the first time I was sure about that. "But once I do this, you'll be gone forever." She would never hurtle us down another hill on a bicycle death ride. She would never curse me out again, just like she would never forgive me anymore of my weaknesses. She would never ask me to do anything else to win a war or live my life.

Yurie squeezed—not hard, but all softness was gone from her—and whispered, static from a pirate radio, "Come with me to the beautiful land."

The weight of the world, of Yurie and my crying mother and my years upon years of unhappiness, tumbled onto my shoulders, and for a second, my spine caved, heaving, toward my dead blood-sister. I was so furious at her for doing this terrible thing, for forcing me to help, for abandoning me to struggle on alone in a world that no one would admit was a post-apocalypse. "Not yet," I said. I couldn't say I was afraid of hell. Knowing Yurie, she'd just try to convince me.

It turns out that it's true what they say about being on stage: the audience disappears into a void. You feel them watching, but really it's just you and your demons doing battle. Asami was a million-dollar angel up there with the stage-light halo and the talismanic necklace blazing like an open wound, but I like to think that, when she saw me step out of the dark and into the hot bath of incandescent light, she realized that retribution was on its way.

I knocked her down—her head hit the floor with an ugly clunk—and dug my fingers under the necklace, scraping the mortal flesh of her soft perfumed neck. Asami was spitting in my eyes, yanking my hair, but I won. I wasn't stronger. I wasn't tougher. But I took bigger risks because I had nothing else to lose. Yurie—Yurie had been the last thing. The necklace unclasped in my hands, and instantly, the fire left Asami's face—her eyes softened, her teeth vanished. The little deer had seen death. I rolled away just before the roof of the world opened up and hell rained down upon her.

I looked for Yurie in the torrent of red and black liquid lightning gushing in and out of Asami's ribs, but there were no faces in the storm. No faces at the end of the world. Not even Asami, by the end, had much of a face. But if I strained, if I blocked out the yelps and sobs, I could pick Yurie's mezzo-soprano voice out of the demon chorus. She was the only one singing in the blood.

"Girl, I love you, too," I whispered.

I'm holding Asami's choker over a trashcan fire. I've been wearing it for the past two months; it might be the only thing keeping me alive. Asami's family has connections—that's how they got the talisman. So a demon-horde might be hanging over my head right now, waiting for my shield to lift.

Now I can see why Asami was so impassive, so callous: the necklace submerges you in a viscous superfluid, and everything else becomes virtual, dreamy, distant. The world's your doll house; nothing matters, and nothing moves you. Once I tossed a cigarette over my shoulder in a park and an old man on litter duty cursed me with an enchanted megaphone—but nothing happened, so I lit another. Maybe burning other people's raw nerves was Asami's only access to the live wire of emotion. I know I've caught myself forgetting that this fishbowl is not reality and the true world is spinning on without me.

I drop the necklace in the fire, and soon amber flames are skating across black metal. Each flame is its own nuclear devil—an undead spirit, an undying wheel—racing alone down a freshly-tarred highway. I've been dreaming about hell and *the beautiful land* even without Yurie's guidance—I still miss her, but I know she's waiting for me on the burning plain. Sometimes I hope I'll see Asami beside her, finally holding her hand—blood-sisters of a different kind. Other times, I hope it'll be years before I see either of them. The necklace starts to smoke, and I start to count. I've vowed to stand in the open for three minutes before going back to my mother's dinner table. With Asami, it had only taken ten seconds. I pass that mark. I pass it three times. Four times.

Then I hear a noise like a flock of gulls diving into a sea. I turn.

The Castaway

Sergio Gaut vel Hartman

● translated by Carmen Ruggero ●

I had lived inside that body for over sixty years, and it was very difficult for me to accept this new state of being, one in which the body can be discarded after use like an empty, useless vessel.

"What are you going to do with ... it?" I didn't know what to call it; we had been one for a long time. The bio-technician shrugged his shoulders; surely, he would answer the same question several times a day, every day.

"We stick them in the depository for the discarded. It's possible that some of the organs could be used, although ... I don't believe that's the case with this one. How was the liver? Did it smoke?"

"Does that mean you freeze them?" I didn't answer his questions directly; in fact, I found them offensive. My ignorance on the subject flashed a red signal. I was afraid to know. From the day the transfer took place, I was ruthlessly bombarded by images of freezers shaped as coffins piled up in dark warehouses.

"Freeze them?" The man gave me a puzzled look. "Why would we go through that kind of trouble? We connect them to feeding tubes and leave them until their clock stops."

"Their clock stops!" A beautiful and ruthless metaphor. "They continue living ..." I sighed.

The idea that my old body was rotting in a foul-smelling depository while I started a new life seemed insane. What kind of a monster have I become? I thought.

"Living, what is implied by living ..." said the bio-technician, "is a ventured guess. Not in principle, but the vegetative functions are not extinguished in the transfer; flashes of memory linger on—traces from their youth are not completely erased. They are quite alive, I suppose, although as you know, no longer officially considered, people."

● 321 ●

"Quite alive," I repeated his words. "Like being a 'little pregnant'; isn't that sufficient enough to deserve respect, support, consolation, and affection?"

"You are completely crazy!" yelled the bio-technician. "Instead of enjoying your new body, you lament the luck of the old one. Are you similarly attached to each Coke bottle you empty? Let me tell you: the road you're on leads to hell."

I inhaled deeply and tightened my fists. "That's exactly what I thought until a little while ago, before finding out that my old body continued to live."

"Would you rather we had killed him? Because ... as far as I know, bodies do not die without the aid of cancer or cardiac arrest or pulmonary edema or ..."

I left the guy talking to himself while I disappeared through the labyrinth of Korps' corridors. I walked for hours, reflecting on the second crucial transformation of my life.

It took several days for me to accept my new body, and when it began to feel natural for me to be thirty years old, someone who could have been my grandfather would suddenly come out of nowhere demanding payment of a bill. A bill for what? Had I broken something? He didn't have the right to demand anything, I reflected. He lived what was normal to live. And I will live until I feel like dying.

I had accidentally walked into the depository but didn't discover the magnitude of my mistake until it was too late to correct it. What I thought to be a utility room filled with used instruments and old furniture turned out to be the place where they kept the discarded bodies. All of them, the majority belonging to old, frail men deteriorating before my eyes, lay on canvas cots facing the door.

There were a hundred, maybe a thousand cots not necessarily arranged in any particular order and barely visible inside the grim ambiance of the depository where they waited with indifference for that jump into space. Their trembling faces, withered by the endless wait, showed the outflow of blood from their bodies. I had fallen in the middle of someone else's nightmare.

Seeing the plastic tubes connected to their trachea and sunken veins of their forearms was a most disgusting experience. The wasting human bodies appeared to struggle to free themselves from their restraints although there was no good reason for it. Even when the need for transfer was not visibly drawn on their faces, one could see their resignation and indifference as they submitted to the lost world.

I had overcome my first impulse to get out of there, and predisposed to accept my role in the process I chose to undergo, I glanced through the room looking for the one I had been. I found it impossible to think about him as someone else—some stranger—separate and different from me. Perhaps, that was the reason why it took me forever to identify him. My gaze bypassed him as I couldn't distinguish his inert silhouette from the others in the depository.

I proceeded slowly for fear that any abrupt movement could trigger a wave of protests, but the truth was that the bodies ignored me. Only a few expressed their annoyance at the intrusion by clumsily moving their hands and so entangling them in the plastic tubing.

Finally, when I managed to get through all the obstacles separating me from my old body and I could look at him face to face, my mind drew a blank. I tried unsuccessfully to tell him how I felt; to say something by way of an apology, but I found myself so inhibited by its rigidity, its impassiveness, its stillness, and to my amazement, it was he who broke silence.

"I was expecting you," said my ex-body in a thread of a voice.

"You were expecting me?" I imagined myself waiting, unable to dream, much less hope for a sunset, or the one responsible for putting me through such gratuitous pain. I also felt guilty because my presence there happened by chance.

"You did not come by chance," he said, as if able to read my thoughts, "... and I do not read your thoughts; somehow we go on being the same person."

His words tingled in the air. It was clear he felt more like me than I did. There was memory, but ... there was also a body. The same body that held me from the beginning is now condemned because speculation had it he was the one who plotted the outcome. But when I tried objecting to that logic, the words adamantly refused to come out. I knew what he was thinking; he had waited patiently and calmly to show me he still controlled my destiny.

The scene was peculiarly similar to an earlier experience when my parents decided that I had to say goodbye to a dying grandfather, a stranger to me. The old man made me feel responsible for his death, as if my youth had somehow caused his departure.

I heard a hopeless cry from another body crawling across the room. That is how they go, I thought, with a moan that fades as they discover they will not be rescued this time.

"I will moan like that when I leave," said my first body. "We all do it. It is like a ship's siren as it casts off from shore."

Once again, I was unable to respond. Who is the castaway? I wondered. Did the ship go past the island without giving warning signals?

I looked at the feeding tubes that joined the body to the tanks and suppressed a deep urge to pull them out. It is preferable to suffocate than to wait without hope for rescue. And once more, my ex-body stripped me of my thoughts.

"Perhaps I am not the castaway," he said.

"I have all my life ahead of me," I protested. "It's a new beginning, right?" The lack of conviction in my words was mirrored by a clumsy and incomplete movement of my hand like a stroke of affection that suddenly becomes an angry blow.

He shrugged his shoulders, showing indifference, while gazing at the bodies dying around us. "To begin anew, yes," he said, "but not from the very beginning. The memory of those who come to say goodbye to their discarded bodies will forever hold the images from this depository."

"What is that supposed to mean? Are you reproaching me?" I was suddenly disgusted by his attitude. Was he trying to entangle me into something? He—we—were condemned: the doctors said it was a question of days, weeks at the most. There was no way out but to go through with the transfer. My old body had put me on the defensive. An invisible net dulled my senses, I felt as if paralyzed.

"No one forced you to come," said my old body. "Why not just enjoy the freedom a healthy body offers you for the first time in a long time? It would have been the most logical thing to do. But instead, you felt compelled to pay back a debt to avoid future self-recrimination. It seems like a good idea to me. I would have done the same."

Those last words brought back a memory: a cunning ease for cruel irony, a talent I was proud to possess. Would I be able to conserve it, I wondered, in my relationship with lifelong friends? As in a game, too many options began to unfold, but the strategy for handling them wasn't at all clear to me. Was I to move away from all that was familiar? Was I to seek different people, a different ambiance, leave the planet?

"I ended up here by accident," I said, feeling disheartened.

"Yes," my ex-body seemed to have lost interest in the conversation. Or maybe, the pain he had suffered silently had returned. I knew a lot about that pain. He moaned again. The agony spread like a wave of electricity from one body to the other. The sound, gray and flat, dissipated throughout the depository.

There was nothing else to be said or done—nothing else to think about or feel. It was time to leave that place.

But I didn't do it. The body had accepted my irresponsibility with the utterance of a hollow word meant to defuse any future argument from me. So great was the tension created by his obligatory yes that all I could do to break it was to extend my hand and lightly touch his dry cheek with my fingertips. My old body shook as if having received an electrical discharge.

"What did you do?" he asked, turning his face away from me.

"Nothing. I think I just tried to be kind."

"You're afraid—very much so."

The accusation was harsh; it transcended simple translation. But then I heard two moans: one was low and sinister; the other was high-pitched like the chirping of a bird. There are many ways of dying, I supposed.

"Afraid? Of what? "I asked him.

"There are many ways of dying," my ex-body repeated my exact words but with an obvious slant. I ignored it. Anyway, I no longer knew what our dialogue meant; I had lost the meaning and perhaps even interest in our conversation. I found myself hypnotized by the colors of the plastic tubes: red, blue, green.

"I am not the one connected to the tubes," I said.

"They are useless," said my old body, "just something to impress the visitors. It's just a good show to affect the psyche of the transferred one; something to improve the outcome."

"Useless? I thought they were being fed through the tubes."

"That, they do," said my old body. "They are useless because it makes no difference whether they feed us or let us starve to death. We will not leave this place because they have stopped our medication, and they only come into the depository three times a day to gather the corpses."

I told him it was cruel, but there was no other way to do it. "It's not possible to wait for the first body to die; the transfer could not be carried out if we had."

"Sure ... sure ..." said the body in a tone balanced somewhere between sadness and rage.

"Now we are like different species," I said, desperately looking for an excuse to continue our dialogue, but each word had the opposite effect from what was intended.

"This is the price we pay for progress. In the old days people would die, and that was it. Now the laws of nature are violated, we're playing with fire."

"I was never a believer," I said. "Is it the proximity of death that makes you wish for eternal life?"

"The imminence of death forced me to transfer, nothing else," his words were acrid. "Or it forced you ... or it forced us. As you can see, it no longer matters."

A sound of pained voices engulfed the words my ex-body spoke and finally drowned them. The doors to the depository opened, the aides entered, disconnected the tubes from a dozen corpses, loaded them onto a ridiculous looking electrical car with a minimum of effort, and left the place impregnated by their lack of interest. Minutes later, they returned with another dozen bodies discarded in recent transfers.

"They didn't see me," I said.

"They're not interested."

"I could have been a thief, a maniac ..."

"Our organs are not good enough to feed the dogs. And as far as biological experiments, they use fresh meat cultivated in tanks; sick bodies are no good for anything." He stirred on the cot. I was afraid he would die just then. He noticed my discomfort. "Calm yourself," he said. "It isn't time yet."

"How long?" The question, unexpected even by me, affected him.

"How long? I don't know. Hours, two days, one week, six months. Who can predict how hard a body will cling onto life ... even one without a soul? "

I didn't feel I was anybody's soul, much less one belonging to such an obstinate body, although I had to admit, its judgment was sound. The doctors' conclusions concerning longevity of the old body had been final. But doctors don't have an obligation to accuracy in their prognoses. Does anyone know of a doctor punished for a wrongful prediction? The aides left the depository carrying their macabre shipment; the doors closed behind them, and I went back to reality.

My first body gazed with disinterest at the dust particles suspended in the stream of light. Darkness drifted through the depository. It was impossible for me to determine how long I'd been there.

"I must go," I said.

"That's true," he affirmed.

"Before it's too late."

"The door is unlocked."

"I can come back."

"It depends. And not on me. Unless ... you're interested in coming back."

"I mean: it only makes sense if you were to be here when I return."

My old body shrugged his shoulders, almost with indifference. "Yes—no ... who knows? Am I God? How should I know the exact moment? If my reasons to stay alive are finished, I'm not angry enough to carry out that which began in my head when I decided to transfer myself. Perhaps I cling to life because the bodies are separate entities and act independently of each other."

"The bodies act independently of each other," I repeated like an idiot. "You could take advantage of your last hours writing an essay on the theory of vegetative reason."

"The bodies act independently of each other," he repeated. "Your body is doing it right this moment. Why don't you go away once and for all?" He spit out his words as if provoking me.

"I am not a beast; I can wait until you calm down."

"Excuses, pretexts," he said. "Your reasons for remaining in this place next to me, waiting for my death, don't have any value whatsoever. You transferred yourself to another body to be free of me, not to carry me as your load. I'm not your old, invalid father. Do you see anyone else doing what you're doing? The bodies die alone; it is right for it to be that way."

My ex-body's voice raised its pitch as his words became more passionate. That created a clear contrast with the last sigh from the body that had perished just a short distance from us.

"I do not know how else to proceed," I said, lacking conviction in my tone. "I can wait a few minutes. I have come to understand that we are part of a whole; that it is my obligation to cry for you, to feel pain."

"How pretentious! But I value your gesture although we both know that it serves no purpose."

I bowed my head. The floor of the depository was covered with dust and excrement except where the discarded bodies impatiently moved their feet. There, the floor was polished, and the darkness fought to overcome the stealthy brightness that descended from invisible sources.

I began to anxiously expect the next round of aides. I made a mental note of those who had died and tried to figure out the timing between each death based on those who were moaning, but I immediately abandoned the idea. I felt pessimistic about it. The reasons for my presence in that place or my inability to leave, simply leave, became more and more difficult to determine. I myself had laid out a trap. The body caught my mood and tried to be constructive.

"I don't believe I'll die today."

"I could come back tomorrow," I said stupidly.

"It is a good idea. But I don't know if it will be tomorrow either. Perhaps it's not worth the trouble."

The light faded, and darkness overtook the depository. The points of reference had disappeared. For all I knew, I could have been inside the depository or in the heart of a nightmare. I took strength thinking that it is possible to wake up even from the worse nightmare, but my first body's broken voice brought me back me to reality.

"... keep walking in the same direction your nose is pointed ..."

It had to be now or never. I started on my way out, but before taking even three steps, the rage of a body that had fallen in front of me told me it wouldn't be a simple task.

"Stupid idiot! Pay attention to where you're going and show a little respect for those who are dying."

"Sorry. I want to leave this place."

"To leave?" the body asked, laughing offensively. "Only after you're dead can you leave this place."

That confirmed what I had begun to suspect: the trap, working successfully, had left me standing on the wrong side of things.

"I've just been transferred," I said. "I came to say goodbye." I tried to grasp the dying body, but he got away from me, mocking me. When he spoke again, I realized that he wasn't the same one; another one occupied its place. The game began to awaken an interest in those condemned.

"The one who transferred out of my body didn't come to say goodbye. The idiot left me alone in these painful circumstances ..."

"The one who transferred from me," said another one, "signed an authorization for them to inject me with something to accelerate the process."

A harsh scream brought a new degree of complaints. Groans and moans were being heard now out of every corner of the depository; the old bodies around me were dying or pretending to die, just to mortify me.

"What good is it?" wailed a female's voice. "Would it make us different, improve us in any way? If that dog were to come to say goodbye ..."

"... she will regret it," a ghastly choir finished her sentence. The discarded bodies rocked in their canvas cots, producing rough textured sounds, rattling wood and dust; the sounds scattered throughout the depository, fleshing images of death, the true and absolute death; the one we cannot dodge like skillful acrobats.

"Where?" I asked. "I don't see the exit."

"Push on with all your might," insisted my first body. "Push on without reservation; we are going to die anyway."

I plunged toward the exit with all my strength, but the bodies were quick to react. They rose from their cots in what seemed like a fit of madness and surrounded me, blocking my way. I felt the pressure of something hard, metallic, searching for my flesh and the ferocious bite on my arm from a set of broken dentures. I lost all sense of moderation and began throwing punches in all directions. But trying for the exit was useless. I was in the dark and surrounded by bodies that had no future and had closed in on me.

What followed was a trail of puzzling memories. Perhaps I fell and was crushed by the infuriated bodies, or I received a blow to the head. Perhaps not. It is impossible to reconstruct the facts that lead to my present situation. I am only certain of waking up in the dark, in the silence of the depository. Some of the plastic tubes carrying nutrients are connected to me, and hundreds of discarded bodies surround me.

"It was the only way out," said a familiar voice coming from the darkness near me. "It was a sure shot. You suffered no mortal wounds ..."

"I do not want you to feel sorry for me," I interrupted. "I want you out of here before it's too late."

"I need some things to be clear," said the voice.

"There's nothing to clarify," I answered. "It is dangerous. I can see that for the first time: we are identical, of course, the same model of body. Just one question: did my first body ... die?"

"I am here," my first body's frail voice comes from somewhere near to my right.

"All is in order then."

I sit up for the new body to know I am addressing him. "Now I am going to count to ten, and when I'm finished, you will be outside of this damned place, living your life, our life."

He moves his head, not yielding to persuasion. I understand that the trap has been set, and who knows how many more of us will fall before learning the trick that allowed us to outwit it?

"It seems," says the first body raising his voice above the putrid atmosphere, "that he who wrote our ending refuses to modify a single line of it."

"Perhaps he is a Greek," I reply ironically, "an amateur, imagining Destiny with a capital D."

"What are you talking about?" My new body seems disturbed. "Are you making fun of me? Is that how you repay my affection? Anyway, I am staying until I get some answers. I don't necessarily have to explain ..."

I stop listening to his words although I continue to hear them as they blend in with the humming sound of machinery and the heartbeat of the bodies. It's hard for me to imagine what wounds had influenced the decision to make a second transfer in such a short time, and for that reason I begin to inspect the body carefully and meticulously. I notice an ugly gash across my chest, and when I press on it, I feel a sharp pain on the left side.

"Have the almost dead caused this much damage?" Korps, in defense of its reputation, has rendered a service, and the new body validates the procedure as it wakes up. Perfect closure, though nothing comes free.

The door opens, and the aides come in. Strangely, there are no dead bodies. They seem bewildered for a few minutes, vacillating between two worlds, but soon they return to their routine. They bring newly discarded bodies, which they place on canvas cots, and connect plastic tubes to the veins of the unfortunate ones.

"Take him away!" I force a command. "He has no business here." The pain intensifies, I lose strength; my voice is dull, incapable of reaching its objective.

"They don't register the discarded ones," says my first body.

"Save your breath," says the new body. "I am going to get you out of this filthy pigpen. My ex-bodies are not garbage."

"We are garbage," says the first body. "I beg of you: get out before it's too late. Out! It sounds melodramatic, but I can't think of another way to make you react. You are going to be trapped, imprisoned like us ..."

The new body is startled. The aides close the door behind them, the depository returns to darkness, and as gloom overtakes the space, our moans, those of the discarded bodies, and the protests of the ones just transferred are mixed until they become indistinguishable from one another.

A Good Home

Karin Lowachee

I brought him home from the VA shelter and sat him in front of the window because the doctors said he liked that. The shelter had set him in safe mode for transport until I could voice activate him again and recalibrate, but safe mode still allowed for base functions like walking, observation, and primary speech. He seemed to like the window because he blinked once. Their kind didn't blink ordinarily, and they never wept, so I always wondered where the sadness went. If you couldn't cry, then it all turned inward.

The VA staff said he didn't talk and that was from the war. His model didn't allow for complete resetting or nonconsensual dismantling; he was only five years old, so fell under the Autonomy legislation. The head engineer at the VA said the diagnostics didn't show any physical impairment, so his silence was self-imposed. The android psychologist worked with him for six months and deemed him nonviolent and in need of a good home.

So here he was, at my home.

My mother thought the adoption was crazy. We spoke over comm. I was in my kitchen, she in her home office where she sold data bolts to underdeveloped countries. "You don't know where they've been, Tawn," she said. "And he's a war model? Don't they get flashbacks, go berserk, and kill you in your sleep?"

"You watch too much double-vee."

"He must be in the shelter for a reason. If the government doesn't want him and he's not fit for industry, why would you want to take him on?"

I knew this would be futile, arguing against prejudice, but I said it anyway. "The VA needs people to adopt them, or they have nowhere to go. We made them, they're sentient, we have to be responsible for them. Just because he can't fight anymore doesn't mean he's not worth something. Besides, it's not like I just sign a contract and they hand him over. The doctors and engineers and everybody have to agree that I'd be a good owner. I went through dozens of interviews, and so did he."

"Didn't you say he doesn't talk? How did they interview him? How can you be sure he's not violent?"

"They downloaded his experience files. They observed him, and I trust them. The VA takes care of these models."

"Then let them take care of him."

She knew less about the war than she did about me, her son, except that the war got in the way of her sales sometimes. Just like I'd gotten in the way of her potential as a lifestyle designer, and instead of living some perceived, deserved celebrity, she'd had to raise me. Sometimes I wondered if I harbored that thought more than she did, but then she kicked my rivets on things like this and not even the distance of a comm could hide her general disapproval at my existence.

Still, she was worried about the android killing me in my sleep. That might've been sincere. "The VA's overcrowded. That's why they allow for adoptions."

Because she was losing the reasonable argument, she targeted something else. The fallback: my self-esteem. "Why would they think you're a good owner? You can't even afford to get your spine fixed. How are you going to support a traumatized war model?"

That was how she saw me—in need of fixing. "He can help me. I can help him."

Even through a double-vee relay I felt her pity. And I saw it in her eyes. That seemed to be the only way she knew how to care about me.

I wasn't going to do that to him.

"Mark." Saying his name in my voice brought him out of safe mode. He blinked but didn't turn away from the window. He didn't move. They'd said it would take a while. Maybe a long while. He'd been at An Loöc, Rally 9, and Pir Hul. The three deepest points of the war. Five years old but he'd seen the worst action. I wondered why none of the creators had anticipated trauma in them. So maybe they weren't as fully developed as humans could be; they were built to task. But they were also built with intelligence and some capacity for emotional judgment because purely analytical and efficient judgment had made the first models into sociopaths. All of those had been put down (that they'd caught, anyway).

"Mark," I said, "my name's Tawn Altamirano." He knew that, they put it in his programming, but you introduced yourself to strangers. To people. "You feel free to look around my home. This is your home, too. There's a power board in the office when you need it. You can come to me at any time if you need anything."

He didn't move or look at me. His eyes were black irises, and they stared through the glass of the window as if it could look back. Maybe he saw his own reflection, faint as it was. Maybe he wanted to wait until night when it would become clearer. Or maybe he just wanted to watch the maple tree sway and the children walking by on the sidewalk on their way home from school.

I had my routines pretty well established by now. Since my own discharge two years ago and once the bulk of the physio was under my belt, I'd acclimated back home, got a job through the veterans program working net security for the local university. Despite what my mother said, I took care of myself. My war benefits allowed for some renovation of the bungalow—ramps and wide doorways and the like. When it was time for bed, I left the chair beside it and levered myself onto the mattress. Some shifting later and I lay beneath the covers on my back, staring up at the ceiling. I didn't hear him in the living room at all. Eventually, I called off the lights, and darkness led me to sleep.

I didn't know what woke me—maybe instinct. But I opened my eyes, and a shadow stood in the doorway of my bedroom. For a second my heart stopped, then started up again at twice the pace until I saw that he didn't move, he wasn't going berserk, he wasn't preparing to kill me. Of course, he wasn't. My mother didn't know the reality. Going to war didn't make you a murderer—it made you afraid.

His shape stood black against the moonlight behind him, what came through the living room window on the other end of the hall.

"Mark?"

He didn't answer.

"Mark, what's wrong?"

A foolish question, maybe, but he could parse that I meant right this second. Not the generality of what was wrong. Not the implication of what was wrong with *him*. What had drawn him from the window and to the threshold of my room?

I pushed myself up on my elbows and opened my mouth to call up the lights.

But he turned around and disappeared down the hallway, back toward the living room and his standing post by the window.

He was still there in the morning when I rolled through the living room on my way to the kitchen. As if he hadn't moved all night. Past his shoulders, in the early day outside, the children walked the opposite way now, some of them skipping on their way to school. A few of them held hands with their parents, mothers and fathers.

"Do you need a power-up?" I said from in front of the fridge. To remind him that he had a board in the office. No answer. So I took out my eggs and toast and made myself some breakfast. I had to give him time; it always took time.

A little after fifteen hundred hours when the schools let out, I got a knock on my front door. I was in the office, so it took me a few seconds to get to the foyer, punch open the door, face the man and woman standing like missionaries on my porch. Behind them at the bottom of my driveway stood another man with three kids by his side. I looked up at the two directly in front of me.

"Can I help you?"

"Hello," the man said, looking down at me. To his credit, he didn't adopt the surprised and awkward mien of someone unused to confronting a person in a chair. If anything, he seemed a little impatient. "My name's Arjan, and this is Olivia. We were just wondering ... well, we were a little concerned about your ... the Mark model in your window."

I glanced behind me toward the living room, saw the back of his shoulders and the straight stance of his vigil.

"What about him?"

"He's creeping out our kids," said Olivia. "Twice they've gone by, and he's just standing there. He's not a cat. What's wrong with him?"

If you had a double-vee, you knew about the Mark androids. Ten years ago, the reveal by the military had garnered a lot of press and criticism, but ultimately people preferred sending look-alike soldiers into battle rather than their own sons and daughters. All of the Marks looked the same, so they were easily identifiable; nobody could mistake them for human despite the indistinguishability of the cosmetics. The adoption program had garnered similar press and criticism; the VA had looked into my neighborhood before releasing Mark to me. We were supposed to be a tolerant, liberal piece of society here.

That was the theory, anyway.

"He's not doing anything, he just likes to look out the window."

"All day?" Olivia said.

"Have you been outside my house all day?" Because otherwise why would it bother her if she only went by twice a day to pick up her kids, and that took all of two minutes?

Arjan seemed more temperate, his impatience dissipated. "Just ... perhaps if during the hours when the children come and go from school, you sit him down somewhere else?"

"He won't hurt anybody."

"Can you, please?" Arjan gazed at me with some hint of that pity now. Not wanting to push in case I had a flashback or dumped my life story at his feet to explain why I didn't have the use of my legs.

Being a good neighbor meant picking your battles. Unlike what was happening in deep space and the war. Maybe it wouldn't be a bad idea to try to coax Mark into another activity. "I'll see what I can do."

I looked out the window with him for a minute, probably five. Slowly, the kids faded away until no more of them traipsed by on the sidewalk. Cars drifted at suburban speed, quiet hums in irregular intervals that penetrated glass. From the look of the sky, we were going to get rain.

"I want to show you something, Mark." I blinked up at his impassive jawline and above that the long dark lashes. They'd made them handsome, in a way. Not superstar plastic, but an earthy attractiveness. Gradation in the dark hair, some undertone of silver, as if life would ever age them. "Mark. Come with me." I touched his sleeve, then began to push across the floor.

He followed—because I'd ordered him or because he wanted to, it was impossible to tell. Something had drawn him to my bedroom last night, so he was capable of operating on his own volition. I led him into the office and wheeled myself out of the way near the couch. One wall braced a floor to ceiling bookshelf with actual physical books stacked neatly row to row. My one ongoing possession of worth: my collection. They'd gone past the label of rare and become worthless. Nobody much cared for tangibles anymore, things you could hold in your hands that gave off a woody scent when the pages flipped.

None of the books were first editions or leatherbound. They weren't museum quality. But that was why I liked them—they were everyday, made to be handled without gloves.

"Maybe you can explore?" I pointed to the shelf. "There are some classics there. I know they don't download literature for you, but you can learn the old-fashioned way. If you want."

He stared at the colorful spines as if they meant nothing to him. Probably didn't. His head was full of strategy and tactics, and if any history existed in his brain matrices, it was related to war. They'd believed the data shouldn't be corrupted with frivolity: no poetry or plays or pop culture references.

But he wasn't in the war anymore. And he wasn't walking out of the room. This way, maybe, he wouldn't stand for hours in front of the window.

I left him in there.

Through the double-vee, a calm, vaguely upper class male British voice explained how scientists were able to save the Bengal tiger from extinction eighty-five years ago through a combination of rewilding, genetic intervention, and ruthlessly wiping out poachers regardless of geographical borders. Rising quietly above the sounds of large cats huffing and animal protectionist gunfire, the low keen of something more human and distressed filtered past the sound panels and made me turn from the vee toward the office.

The time on the wall said he'd been in there a little more than an hour. I should've checked sooner.

I found him in the corner, wedged between the bookshelf and the end of the desk. Sitting rigid with the eyeline of a house pet. I only wheeled in so far before stopping, careful to watch his eyes, but he wasn't looking at me. Some blank spot a meter in front of him held his attention. By his feet, splayed like a wounded bird, lay a trade-sized book, print side up. I couldn't see the title.

"Mark?"

This passed for crying on a face that couldn't shed tears. That sound, a wounded thing.

"Mark."

I was so used to the reality of rain that hearing it now against the windows only drew my attention because it drew his. His eyes widened, and he put his hands in his hair.

"It's okay." I rolled closer, slow. He stopped keening and somehow the silence was worse. His elbows joined with knees until he was a black shard lodged between furniture. I stopped and picked up the book, turned it over.

For Whom the Bell Tolls.

The cover was some faded hue of purple and green with an image of a shadowed soldier, a road, and a bridge. I'd read this book long ago, before my own war. I barely remembered it, but I remembered loving it. That must've been what it was like with people sometimes. Mark didn't look up, so I flipped the book over and read a random line on the page where he'd either left off or where the book had opened when he'd tossed it. *Every one needs to talk to some one ... Before we had religion and other nonsense. Now for every one there should be some one to whom one can speak frankly, for all the valor that one could have one becomes very alone.*

"'We are not alone. We are all together,'" I recited to him from the book, a little like you'd speak scripture.

But he didn't look up, and he didn't say a word.

Eventually, he returned to the window, but at night. The next morning the rain stopped and in an hour started up again. I needed to go shopping for groceries, preferred that to ordering them in, but struggling through the wet was a chore, so instead I set up a Scrabble board in the living room on the coffee table. I shook the tiles in the velvet bag until I felt him look over. It was a gamble whether he'd be interested, but during breakfast I'd noticed the book on the windowsill in front of him. *For Whom the Bell Tolls.*

"Wanna play?" I shook the bag again.

It took a minute, but he walked over and sat down on the couch across from me. If we played long enough, he wouldn't be looking outside when the kids went home.

I explained the rules to him, knew I only had to say them once. He stared at the board and my hands and then stuck his hand into the bag and pulled his seven tiles, which he set on his tile bar precisely and carefully hidden from my eyes. He wouldn't speak, but I thought at least this way he could make words.

I went first and lay down ATOMIC. I was a little proud of that.

He made TIGER.

I got ROUGE.

He made EQUINE. I said, "Good word!" Not like I was praising a dog but because it was interesting to see how he formed these words out of his programming. He won the first game, but I was almost expecting that; it was like playing against a computer. It *was* playing against a computer. His vocabulary was ten times what mine was; I knew I was bound to lose when he began to use Latin. Not because his creators had programmed Latin for him, but because he understood the derivation of the language. He must have had that somewhere in his files.

As we were setting up the next game, my mother called. I talked to the house system, without visual. "I'm busy, call back later."

Mark stared at me. It could have been a dead kind of regard, but as he rarely looked me in the eyes, I took it for inquiry. "My mother." That didn't make him bat a lash. "You play first."

Twenty minutes into the game his words grew shorter and shorter, barely gleaning six or eight points. His eyes remained lowered to the board. ONE. TO. ARE.

"Mark? Is something wrong?"

At night before bed, I'd reviewed his downloads from the VA hospital, tried to find some string of code or something in the reports that the doctors might have missed. I wasn't a doctor, I'd only been a rifle fighter, but maybe it took one soldier to understand another. His muteness was voluntary, and I couldn't forget that.

I looked at the spread on the board. The game didn't matter. After sorting through the letters left in the bag and usurping a couple already displayed, I lay down some tiles separate from the game and turned the board toward him.

WORRIED.

He didn't move, his hands on his knees. I watched his lids twitch as his eyes mapped the board. I made more words for him.

ABOUT YOU.

It took eight minutes for him to reach for the board. With the tips of both his forefingers, he slid the tiles around like a magician did cards on a tabletop. Then he swung the board back toward me.

SAD.

What could I say? I touched my legs. I saw his gaze follow that. Then I made more words, too.

I KNOW.

The shelter wanted reports from me, and after the first week, they considered it a breakthrough. Never mind that Mark hadn't said anything past that single word, Scrabble or otherwise. He just returned to his window. I went about my days with work, sometimes sitting on my bed with my system, sometimes in the office, and when he wouldn't dislodge himself from his post, I sat on the couch and looked at his back. I scoured his files for clues. He didn't play the game again, but he carried that book with him when he powered up on the seventh day.

"I wanted to check in," my mother said. "See if you were still alive."

This passed for humor in her world. Her face on my relay was cautious. Out of spite, maybe, I turned my system, so the camera picked up Mark standing by the window, a black arrow of false serenity with sun on his skin.

"What's he doing?" she said.

"Looking out the window."

"For what?"

I almost said "nothing." But it occurred to me that soldiers stood watch and this might not have been a simple metaphor for his position.

"Enemies. So you better call before you come over."

This passed for humor in my world. She didn't laugh, but I did.

The benefits of working from home meant I could take naps in the afternoon. Like a cat, I stretched myself onto the angle of sun that cut through my bedroom window, warm after days of rain, and shut my eyes, soaking up rays without fear of burning or UV—all house glass came treated.

The front door opening woke me up. I didn't hear it shut.

Either way, nobody should've been going in or out—unless it was Mark.

It took me two minutes to get myself in the chair and out to the door. "Mark!" Out and down the ramp, rapid, onto the sidewalk, look left, look right. Nothing. "Mark!"

My vis tracked his location chip, all Mark models had them from the factory. Deeply embedded in their craniums. The dot on my optical display put him in transit, but at a speed that indicated running, not in a vehicle. At least. I rolled that way, past flat, cloned houses and uniform lawns, looking through the overlay across my vision until I spied the tall, black-clad figure in the park. The shadows on either side—other people—barely registered.

"Mark." I could shout, but with him now in my line of sight, startling could be worse. He stood facing the manufactured lake, and people were pulling their kids away from him. Expecting a weapon or an explosion, who knew.

My hands burned. I hadn't worn gloves. Wheels bumped the edge of grass that led down an embankment to the carefully placed rocks and farther toward cold, cobalt water that lapped the shore. He'd been afraid of rain, but he ran to water. If he'd been running to this place at all. Maybe he'd just run.

I wished for the Scrabble board, the only thing that had garnered a response from his broken programming. Instead, I touched my red and callused hand to the edge of his as it hung at his side.

He twitched, that was all.

"Let's walk?" An offer. I looked down at my legs. "So to speak." Walk before someone called the cops or a child screamed or something propelled him to plunge into the lake where I couldn't follow. Should he have decided to sink himself to the bottom of the lake, none of these people would likely try to stop him. "Walk with me, Mark. Please?"

I tried to wheel backward, so I could turn around on the path that surrounded the lake. But before I made the full one-eighty, hands took hold behind my chair and pushed.

I let go of the wheel rims and rubbed my palms against my thighs. Looked up and back at his forward gaze. He gave me nothing but the direction of his stride and his acquiescence in silence. It was enough.

We took walks twice a day now, one in the morning and one in the afternoon. It hadn't been my intention to cross paths with the schoolchildren, but those were the hours that made sense—before my work began and on a break before the last couple hours of my day—and they gave him some life to look at. Others in the neighborhood strolled with their dogs, but Mark walked with me. Sometimes he pushed the chair, but most of the time we went side by side. Sometimes I talked, idly gossiping about this neighbor or that, or noted the types of trees and flowers we passed. Information that he wouldn't ordinarily possess because the places he'd been trained for in deep space hadn't come with roses and Japanese maples.

More than once, Arjan or Olivia or somebody else from the neighborhood frowned at us. The children were inquisitive, a few of them asking aloud as we passed where Mark had come from and what was wrong with him. "Aren't they supposed to be in war?" The parents shushed them and pulled them away.

"He came home," I told them. "He needed a family."

I hoped that would get through to the adults, but they just smiled at me half-assed as if I needed to apologize for the truth.

I dreaded bad weather now. The night we had another thunderstorm I found Mark back in the corner of the library, making that tearless keening noise. I couldn't turn off the sky so I sat with him, lights on, talking softly. I picked up his Hemingway book from the floor and read to him. It seemed to calm him, having that focus. Maybe working out a plot, the drama, and emotion of a fictional piece. The war in the book was so far removed from his own, yet truths existed across centuries when the common denominator was humanity.

Eventually, when my eyes grew weary sometime in the middle of the night, I closed the book and looked into his dark, open gaze. His arms wrapped around his legs.

"Do you want to come into my room? You don't have to sit in the office all night—" Or stand at the window, "—but I think I need to lie down." I was really asking him if he wanted the company. Or asking him because I did. He didn't need to stand vigil at the window, through cloudy moonlight and racketing storm.

So he followed me to my bedroom. Helped me onto the bed without my asking. Even drew the covers up. I called off the lights, and Mark, in silence, sat at the foot of my bed facing the door.

In the morning he was gone—at least as far as the living room. I rolled out yawning and spied the Scrabble board on the coffee table, Mark sitting on one side. It made me smile. Taking initiative? I could picture the eager android psychologists ticking off their checklists, revisiting his memory files, trying to draw connections between Mark's habits here and his experiences in the war.

He felt no threat here, that was the difference. At least I hoped he didn't. Under observation and treated like a programmed computer back at the hospital, he must have still been wary. Who wouldn't?

I made scrambled eggs and toast and joined him at the table. He pulled the letter C and started first.

It wasn't for the game. He searched around in the bag until he found the letters he needed to spell.

LOST.

I looked at him, trying to determine the exact meaning. It was impossible to know. So I reached for the velvet bag myself.

HERE.

No question marks, I had only my eyes to ask it. He shook his head. Made another word.

COMPANY.

For a few moments I was confused. My company? But then—no. *A* company. *His* company. He was the survivor of a skirmish out at the Belt. None of the others had made it. The official report said ambush, but that had seemed scant even to me. Maybe some of the details had been redacted from his memory and thus what they'd given me, and he didn't even know anymore. But the body remembered. Maybe more of him remembered than all of the engineers and psychologists were willing to acknowledge.

I laid more tiles. HOW.

But he didn't say anything. Instead, he just stared at the board, then turned it toward me so I saw the question. And he looked at my legs.

Fair enough. "Shrapnel." I stretched my arm behind me. "My spine."

When he looked in my eyes, he didn't have to say a word. I saw that he understood. Some things technology couldn't fix—especially when you didn't have the means. Sometimes we injured ourselves, or we were injured, and the wounds stuck around. Like memories or the impact of them.

Rather than standing at the window all night like an effigy, Mark took to staying in my room. Maybe he figured I'd need the help if I somehow flopped out of bed, or probably because he wasn't simple, he knew I liked the company. Years of sleeping alone, literally in a silent room without even the bodily noises of comrades in other bunks, and the isolation had become pungent. Over the days he and I established our own routine, not discussed because he still didn't talk beyond random words on the Scrabble board, and even then sometimes he didn't talk at all and just played the game.

The doctors said it was still progress. I didn't tell them about Mark sitting in my bedroom at night, but I did report that he began to bring me books from the office and liked me to read aloud to him. Sometimes he had no sense of timing about it. I'd be working, and he'd just appear next to me and set down a novel on my lap. Classic war novels. *The Red Badge of Courage. All Quiet on the Western Front. Half of a Yellow Sun.* He wouldn't go away until I covered at least a chapter. I acted annoyed, but he knew I wasn't. Whether that was through his ability to read human body language and gauge tone of voice or more likely because he just knew me by now.

He still hated storms, and we were deep into spring. It was the worst when one night the power went out.

The neighborhood outside fell to darkness. Inside, only the glow from my comp on its backup provided some illumination. The moon high outside the office window sat obscured by rain clouds.

Mark darted from the living room, where he often still stood watch, right into the office where I was working. He didn't trip or crash into anything, and I remembered his eyes had night vision capability. I didn't need to see his face to understand the plea.

"It's okay, the lights'll come back up soon." I rolled away from the desk and motioned out of the room. Tried to keep my voice casual even if I could feel the tension dopplering out from his body in the dark. "Let's go hang out."

He loomed near invisible in the shadows. He didn't even breathe and at least didn't keen anymore, didn't feel that level of pain at the upset. But his hand landed on my shoulder and clenched. Only his footfalls made sound as he followed me down the hall to the bedroom, which had become a refuge from all that scared him. A routine of safety.

I levered myself to the bed to sit, and he climbed on beside me, legs and arms folded. Not quite with his back to the door or window, he never allowed that, but he eased into facing me at an angle at least.

And this was how we waited out the storm.

Of course, my mother had a key to my house; she'd insisted after I'd gotten out of the hospital, "just in case" living on my own in my "state" proved too difficult. Maybe I should've anticipated her worry. Every time she called she implied that Mark was a ticking bomb, so I just stopped answering her calls. Maybe she was in the neighborhood or maybe she did get in her car to drive a half hour to check if I was alive. Either way, through the storm she arrived, and through the storm Mark heard her before I did.

We sat in the near-dark, and I was reading to him from the light of my comm. "'He saw that to be firm soldiers they must go forward. It would be death to stay in the present place ...'" And at that exact moment Mark launched off the bed and out the door with the precision of a guided missile.

I was fumbling for my chair, images in my mind of fang-toothed, angry neighbors storming my front door with pitchforks, when my mother's shriek penetrated every surface between the foyer and my bedroom.

"Mark!" Ass in the seat, hands on the wheels. "Mark!" I rolled out to see my mother face down on the floor, arms triangled behind her back, wrists caught in the vise of Mark's one-handed grip. "Stand down, soldier."

"Get him off me, Tawn! Get this crazy fu—"

"Shut *up*, Mom!" I stopped close enough to touch Mark's arm. Beneath his sleeve felt like iron. I kept my voice quiet because I couldn't see his eyes in the dark: "It's okay. It's my mother. It's okay." I repeated it until he let her go and stepped back near to the wall. Becoming motionless.

"Mom."

"He's crazy! What did I tell you!"

"Mom, tone it *down*." I didn't offer to help her up. She wouldn't have accepted it.

She propelled herself to her feet in a pitch and yaw. "Look what he did to my wrists!" She stuck her hands toward me. In the cracks of lightning and illumination, I saw vague shadows. Maybe bruises.

"You're all right, you're fine. Come sit down. You should've rung the doorbell, he thought you were breaking in."

"I have a key!"

"I told you to call ahead."

"My own son!"

I went to Mark and held his sleeve. "Come over here, man." My mother wasn't listening; she could stand by the door and bleat until it passed.

Mark followed me to the living room where I hoped he would sit, but instead he went to the window, his post, and stared out. He didn't have to breathe and he didn't say a word, but I knew the entire ruckus unnerved him. There was no other word for it. It reverbed through my body.

"Is that what he does all day?" my mother demanded behind me.

"Can you at least lower your voice? You aren't helping."

"*I'm* not helping!"

"MOM."

We both stopped. Mark had turned around, now with his back to the window. His body blotted out what light came in from the street, creating a vacuum in my vision. So he could face us dead on. It was like the stare of a sarcophagus.

My mother turned her back to him. "I'm worried for you, Tawn."

"You don't have to be."

"This isn't normal. Look at him!"

"He's fine. We're fine. We—"

But she wasn't listening. She began to walk around, feeling her way through the dark toward the office. Or my bedroom. It was so sudden when the lights flickered on and held that I had to blink spots from my vision. And in those moments Mark disappeared.

After her.

"Mark!"

I couldn't roll fast enough. I recognized his mode. Full protection, decisive defense. What he'd been built for. I wanted to hold him back, but this was his nature. He wasn't the one unnerved, he wasn't the one concerned for himself. It was *my* voice he heard, that his programming responded to. My voice and its irritation and tension and impatience.

In the seconds it took me to get from the living room to my bedroom where my mother had gone, I saw it ahead of me. In the span of his back and the straightness of his spine. In the precise way he seized my mother before she could set hands on my possessions. He spun her around.

She struck him. Reflex or intent, I didn't know. Of course, it didn't affect him at all, didn't even bruise him. He didn't flinch.

Instead, he dragged her to my window, opened it, and pitched her out.

Luckily, my house was a bungalow.

She said she'd wanted to pack me a bag and take me away from any danger. That if she did that for me I couldn't protest and would've been forced to go with her and ditch this mad idea of taking care of a military model. She had never understood that we wanted to take care of ourselves.

She didn't understand—when the VA engineers came to take him away—that he was my company and I was his.

In the hospital they ran more tests on him. It was procedure because she'd filed a complaint. I gave my own statement: that he'd felt I was threatened, that he'd only been defending me, that my mother was crazy in her own right (I reworded that part a little). She'd disregarded my words and his existence. If I restricted her access to me or she learned to interact better, there would be no more problems.

And yes, I wanted him home again. He belonged there—where I could read to him, where we could play games, and where he might one day be able to speak to me. He'd made a place beside me and at my window. He'd learned my routines and created ones of his own. He wanted to know all the books on my shelves. He liked walking in the sun.

He protected me. I wouldn't strip that from him.

They let me see him once while he was in the hospital. He lay on a stiff bed with transparent monitoring tape stuck to his temples. Little dots of glowing blue and red on the tape winked at me while his dark eyes stared blinkless, asking no questions.

I touched his arm. His skin felt cold. Human warmth didn't course through his veins. He didn't even have veins. None of it mattered. "Mark. Hey man, don't worry."

His head tilted, eyes met mine.

I gripped his hand. After a moment his fingers curled around mine, just as strong. Even stronger. I said, "The storm's gone, and you're coming home."

The children were walking on their way to school when we pulled up to the drive. It was a warm day, the kind where you wore light open jackets and began to roll up your sleeves in anticipation of summer. With the car windows down, we heard their voices all the way to the school, to the yard. They sounded as colorful as their clothes and seemed to carouse right through the leaves to where we sat.

He hadn't said a word on the ride, only looked out the window. The parents passing behind on the sidewalk noticed us there; I spied the glances on the rearcam of the car. A couple of them paused as if debating whether to approach, to ask why we were just sitting in my own driveway doing nothing.

But they didn't approach, and I looked at Mark's profile. "You know ... people are going to be like my mother. Like the neighbors. That's just the way it is until they get used to us." Not just him, but us.

I'd learned not to expect conversation, but he did make contact in his own way. No Scrabble board lay between us, but he turned his hands palm up and open. He looked at me.

What answer could I give him? That people were afraid or lazy or just plain ignorant? Who could we blame? The government, the military, the doctors, and engineers?

We were both on probation. Mark, so he wouldn't injure somebody. And me, so I wouldn't let him.

"Where do you think this will lead?" my mother had asked. "You rehabilitate him or whatever they want to call it, and then what?"

Somehow it was impossible for her to understand. "Then he'll choose," was all I'd said.

Maybe one day he'd discover what had happened to his unit. Maybe I would help him. Or maybe we'd leave it alone because some memories were best left in the dark.

Before we went inside the house, I caught his attention again, touched his shoulder. "The doctors say you're capable of speaking but you just choose not to. Sometimes that happens with people—"

"I am people," he said. His voice was lighter than I thought it would be, if hoarse from disuse. He was looking back out the window again. The sidewalk stretched clear now. "I am a person," he said to the scene in the window frame.

They had created him to task but with the capacity for emotion. He was perfectly vulnerable, just enough, even for war.

He slid from the car to head into the house, and eventually I followed him, calling the chair from the back of the car to lever myself into it. I rolled up the ramp to the front door where Mark stood, holding it open for me even though he didn't have to.

It was just the human thing to do.

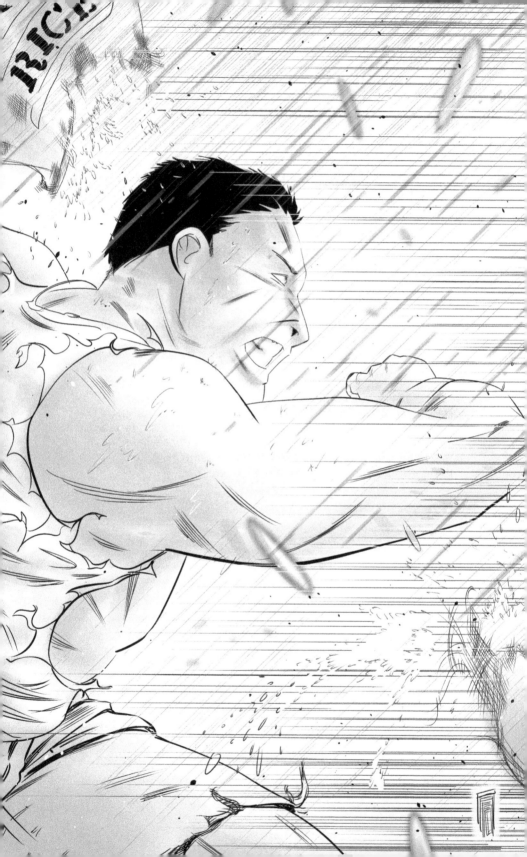

How To Piss Off
a Failed Super Soldier

John Chu

Raindrops shattered against Aitch the way bullets were supposed
to but never did. Water splashed with his every step. The bags
of rice slumped against his shoulders like freshly dead bodies.
Protein bars jostled inside the disintegrating paper bag clutched
to his chest. He was not quiet as he jogged home with his groceries.
Today's assassin, undoubtedly hiding in the blind alley just ahead,
would hear him before he'd hear their heart beat. Because no one
had tried to kill him yet today, each time he neared an alley, he
simply assumed someone would be there to try. This time he was
right.

A woman, braced against a dumpster, leveled a weapon at Aitch.
He made her as a Drip, an agent working for DRP, right away. The
government agency was always testing their latest technologies on
him. Long, thin, and silver, the weapon emitted an ultrasonic hum
when she triggered it.

Aitch dropped the protein bars and pitched his bags of rice into
the line of fire. A bright flash and the smell of toasted rice filled
the air. He leapt through the cloud of rice ash toward the Drip. His
clothes ignited from the sheer speed. Smoke trailed behind him.
Smoldering jeans and T-shirt branded his skin. Rice ash swirled
away in all directions.

He landed, scattering gravel, which flew in a spray that pinged
dents into the dumpster. Pain shuddered up his legs. The sudden
stop broke his ankles and ripped the ligaments and tendons from
his calves and thighs. As he buckled to the ground, he ripped the
weapon out of the Drip's hands.

Jay emerged from the dumpster's shadow. He tapped the woman's
neck. She collapsed.

Aitch shot her to test the weapon. She disappeared in a quiet puff.

Then he shrugged and shot Jay. His younger brother merely glowed for an instant, then looked cross at him. It'd been worth a try.

Jay pulled the weapon out of Aitch's grip, crushed it, then tossed it into the dumpster along with any hope Aitch had for escape. The idea that DRP's latest ultimate weapon might distract Jay long enough for Aitch to crawl away and hide until morning seemed silly in retrospect. The symbionts that made Aitch too strong for his own good would have fixed him up by then, though.

"She had no idea you were behind her, did she ... No, how could she have?" Aitch was calm. He'd always figured that Jay would eventually do to him what DRP couldn't. "A normal younger brother would have just called me."

"And a normal older brother would pick up when I do. It shouldn't have to be a production to keep you in one spot long enough to talk to you."

Rain-soaked, Jay's clothes were plastered to his skin. He had the look and air of an especially broad, muscular chorus boy cast in a Bob Fosse musical. Unlike any dancer, though, Jay had once juggled motorcycles on a dare. Mom had fixed all of Aitch's flaws when she'd engineered Jay. Aitch couldn't look at him without seeing the lean, tall, and elegant being he, himself, should have been. The sight of Jay hurt more than his own broken legs.

"I'm ready, brother." Aitch flattened himself against the gravel. The rain struck him like rusty nails. "Just kill me quickly."

"That's not why I'm here." Jay crouched next to Aitch. "Mom's dying—"

"Too bad her favorite child isn't a promising internist who can also do whatever he wants to any living being he touches. Oh, wait ..."

Jay looked cross again. "I have my limits, brother."

"Kill me now and you can fulfill a dying woman's wish." Aitch mimed a knife stabbing his chest again and again.

"She's never actually wanted you dead." Jay caught Aitch's fist. "And now she just wants to say goodbye."

Aitch's legs wrenched back into place. New skin covered his body. Rain now slid harmlessly off him. Aitch stood, then nearly doubled over in pain. His hunger pangs were worse than ever. For whatever reason, his symbionts had kicked into overdrive.

"And what I want, of course—" Aitch forced himself back up "—is for her final edicts to rule the rest of my life."

The symbionts in Aitch's head turned even vague suggestions from anyone he loved into unyielding commands. It didn't matter whether they were family or the Drips who'd raised him. His mother had designed those symbionts and infected Aitch herself when he was still an infant. Jay had long ordered Aitch to be himself, but she never had. Aitch had autonomy around Jay. Around her, he was helpless.

"No, what you want is no more broken bones, no more torn muscles when you exert yourself. Mom and I have worked out how to make your symbionts give you a body that even you won't be strong enough to break. No more Drips hunting you down. Why would they bother?"

Although Aitch thought he was already no more a danger to society than anyone else, DRP obviously thought differently. If he were ordinary, though, too weak to break his own body like Jay said, even DRP would see that he was no danger to anyone. They wouldn't bother testing their latest technologies on him because he'd be too easy to kill. Grudgingly, he had to admit Jay was right again. Jay was never wrong about anything.

"So I have to visit Mom to get—"

"Oh, no. I made that fix to your symbionts while I fixed your legs." Jay's face settled into its customary smile. "They'll have reworked your body by the time we reach Maryland."

"Why am I going to Maryland?"

"We're visiting a DRP archive on the way to Mom's hospital. I need you to cover me while I liberate Mom's research."

"But I destroyed it all." As a child, Aitch had made sure DRP could never create anyone like him again. By then, though, Mom had already engineered Jay. Not only had Mom gotten Jay right, she'd kept infecting him a secret. Not even Aitch realized at first.

"No, you destroyed millions of dollars of equipment that officially never existed. The government then buried all record of their failed super-soldier research project, including Mom's notes. For now, what you need is food." He patted Aitch's back. "Come on, I have clothes in the car, and a diner is just a short jog away. My treat. We need to talk about what the symbionts are doing to your head. Mom and I think we have a fix for that, too."

Aitch sighed. He'd drive spikes through his eyes if that would fix the symbionts that messed with his brain.

Water puddled under Aitch's and Jay's trench coats hanging from the coat rack screwed to the side of their booth. The waitress set Aitch's fifth and sixth hot turkey sandwiches in front of him. The empty plates for sandwiches one through four sat piled at the edge of the table. Rather than clearing them away, she stood in the thrall of Jay's charm.

Jay made everyone feel the world existed just for them. He was either an asshole or the sweetest person this side of sainthood. Aitch had long since given up figuring out which. Jay ate his French fries and chatted with the waitress about her kids, the awful weather, working the night shift, and the Red Sox.

Aitch attacked his sandwiches with knife and fork. His stomach still hurt as if he hadn't eaten at all. Jay's shirt had him hunch-shouldered, and the pants constricted his thighs. Maybe they'd fit better once the now re-engineered symbionts in his body slimmed him down.

"So how's your boyfriend?"

It took Aitch a moment to realize Jay was speaking to him. The waitress had gone.

"Simon is not my boyfriend." Aitch kept his head down, staring at his mashed potatoes.

"Oh, I'm sorry." Jay sounded so damn sincere. "When did you break up?"

"We were never together. He was my *climbing* partner."

"I always thought that was a euphemism—"

"It's not a euphemism. At least once a week, we climbed together, then ate afterwards."

"No, that doesn't sound like dating at all."

"He goes through boyfriends like I go through assassins. We climbed together for years."

"I'm noting a lot of past tense here."

"That would be because he doesn't want to climb with me anymore." The knife bent in his hand. Gravy and mashed potato skidded across the table. "Damn."

"You want to talk about it?"

"No." Aitch straightened out the knife as best as he could. His grip was still too strong. The symbionts were apparently taking their time normalizing him. "What does this have to do with fixing what the symbionts do to my head?"

"They get in the way of your relationships, not to mention any attempt to heal your mind." Jay grabbed napkins from the dispenser on the table and started sopping the mess onto an empty plate. "You make decisions that would be perfectly rational if you were trying to escape a POW camp."

Aitch met Jay's gaze. "I'm not a super-genius like you, but I'm not stupid. Drips really are trying to kill me."

"Stand down, brother." Jay held his hands before him. "One, yes, Drips really are trying to kill you. Two, more often than not, you interpret whatever happens as personal attacks. Three, you score off the charts on all the standardized tests. When was the last time you forgot anything?"

"I don't remember." Aitch noted Jay hadn't said anything about their relative intelligence.

Jay went stone-faced for a moment before he burst into a laugh. "Hey, you made a funny that isn't grim. Simon's good for you."

"I wasn't trying to be funny." Aitch retreated back into his sandwiches.

"How did you two even meet?" Jay always made his gaze felt even when Aitch was actively avoiding it. "I can't even get you to pick up the phone."

Aitch ordered the words in his head. It wouldn't kill him to tell Jay how he'd met Simon, especially if it'd help fix the symbionts messing with his mind. Slowly, the words spilled out of him.

The day I met Simon, I was studying routes on my favorite rock face. It's in the middle of New Hampshire. No one else climbs it. That's why it's my favorite. Climbers always tromped by, their gear clanging in their backpacks. This once, the clanging stopped right behind me.

"That wall's blank, you know. I've been climbing here for years. No one's found a climbable route yet." I didn't recognize the high, resonant voice. "My partner flaked out on me. I have his shoes and harness. He's a hefty guy, too. There's a great route just down the trail."

I free solo. My hiking boots had a little rubber on the sole. A bag of chalk sat strapped around my waist. I've never needed any other gear.

"Wall's not blank." I didn't turn around right away. People going all wide-eyed the first time they see me got old even before I'd escaped from DRP. "You just need a little balance and finesse."

He walked up behind me. Fortunately, he was still clanging with each step. I managed to face him without also pounding him into the dirt.

"You don't climb, do you?" He gestured at my torso. "All that upper body muscle is impressive as hell but works against you on the rock." Simon's built to climb. Shorts hugged his strong thighs. Hard, diamond-shaped calves grew out of his boots. His T-shirt hung from his lanky body. I come up to about his neck. Calluses covered his long, thin fingers. His sweet, grizzled face held such a warm smile, I

almost didn't find his words insulting. Almost.

"So you think he's hot." Jay nibbled on a French fry.

Aitch dropped his knife and fork. "Look, do you want to learn how we met or not?"

"It's strength to weight ratio that counts." I stripped him of his backpack. *"I'll set up a top rope for you. Give you some beta if you want the help."*

I climbed the rock face—

"A blank wall while wearing hiking boots? You showed off." Jay's smile was so radiant that it was probably cancer-causing. His palm slapped the table. The cups, dishes, and the napkin dispenser all rattled. "Good for you."

"No, I didn't. I'd have picked a hard route if I wanted to show off."

"Brother ..." Jay's voice rose as if what he was really saying was "Don't make me hurt you."

"Fine." Aitch rolled his eyes. "I wanted to impress him. Happy?"

Simon looked a little strange when I returned his backpack. His jaw worked soundlessly as his gaze darted between me and the top rope I'd set up.

He held his hand out. "Simon." The name fumbled from his mouth as if it were the only word he knew and he was trying it out for the first time.

"Aitch." I shook his hand as gently as I could. "Come on, let's get you up the wall."

"And did you get him up the wall?" Jay waved for the waitress.

She materialized before him with a jug of coffee. No one else in the diner got such prompt service. Aitch rolled his eyes at the smiles they traded.

"No." Aitch pushed a plate scraped clean of mashed potato and gravy away from him. He started on the next.

"And no, I don't think he's hot in a T-shirt and shorts. For one thing, he's far better looking in a tux—"

Aitch stopped, suddenly aware that he wasn't actually helping his case. Fear gripped his chest. He braced for what he knew was coming.

"When did you see him wear a tux? And how does he look?" Jay, supported by his elbows on the table, leaned towards Aitch. He seemed so damn affable that Aitch wanted to slug him to next Tuesday. "Come clean. Inquiring minds want to know."

Finishing the sandwich in front of him bought him some time. Jay's gaze was insistent, though. Aitch, glum, pushed the now empty plate away.

Simon's a dramatic tenor. He has a voice like a trumpet. It rings for days. Vocally, he's just right for Samson. A tuxedo does wonders for his body. It makes his shoulders span the stage and presents the illusion of thick arms and a chest as broad as his back. No one attending the concert looked at anyone else on stage.

"So you do think he's hot." Jay stacked the dishes, then pushed them to the edge of the table.

"Brother, are you trying to make me hate you?"

Aitch didn't wake up until his shoulder pounded into the blacktop. The car door rebounded, then slammed shut. Tires squealed as Jay's car skidded past him. For a moment, he'd been a kid trapped in a cage again and some Drip was about to discipline him. In reality, he'd been sleeping in Jay's car on the drive down to Maryland. When Jay had tried to wake him up, he bolted out of the car. That, in his panic, he'd actually opened the door first was a minor miracle. He picked himself up, then waited for his pounding heart to slow back down. Jay's car swung around. It was probably Aitch's imagination, but the car seemed to creep up to him like a hunter approaching a skittish fawn.

Trees hid the building and parking lot from the street. The first light of dawn filled in the gray between the parking lot's light poles. The building looked like any low, unassuming office. Aitch suspected that most of the building really was office space and the actual archive was below ground.

The car stopped. The engine cut out. The parking lot was silent until Jay emerged.

"I'm glad I didn't wake you up earlier." Jay's face betrayed a concern so sincere that Aitch boiled with fury. Given Aitch's history with enclosed spaces, Jay should have known better. "Are you okay?"

"Next time you want to wake me up, do whatever it is normal people do instead." Aitch brushed off his shirt. "Just because you can do anything you want to anyone you touch doesn't mean you know what to do."

"Drips should arrive any moment." Jay started onto the sidewalk. "Just buy me enough time to find Mom's work."

"I don't know that I can."

Jay turned around. He rolled his eyes. "You're the strongest person on the planet. You've trained in all things combat since you were, what, three?"

Aitch's brow furrowed. Jay was never wrong, so Aitch had to

be missing something. "I'm not even the strongest person in this parking lot."

The ground rumbled. Metal glinted among the trees. Nothing living then, or else Jay would have noticed them first. The most important rule when fighting Jay: Don't be organic.

"Robots. Clever." Jay grabbed Aitch by the shoulders. "Look, we don't have time to work through your self-esteem issues. Despite what you think, when you outlift me—like you always do—it's not because I'm holding back. Whatever you do will be more than good enough. See you in ten!"

With that, Jay dashed into the building. A dozen metal hulks emerged from the trees. Their bladed upper limbs spun, shredding branches out of their way. Their articulated legs stretched and shrank, keeping their bodies in perfect balance as they climbed onto the blacktop.

The hulks launched hundreds of needles at Aitch. Tiny sonic booms cracked the air.

Aitch jumped out of sheer reflex. The needles whooshed below him. His legs held when he landed. The old him would have shattered his legs when he collapsed onto the pavement. The new him should never have been able to jump that high in the first place. Instead, he was as strong as ever, only now his body could withstand that strength. Aitch groaned.

The odds then weren't even remotely close. Those hulks never stood a chance.

Metallic limbs and twisted frames littered the pavement. Jay's car stuck out as the only carcass that wasn't dented, crushed, or smashed in. Aitch's clothes had burned off in the scuffle. The flames had hurt like hell but hadn't damaged him. He stood naked and dismayed surveying the wreckage when Jay emerged from the building.

"Wow." Jay's eyebrows rode high on his head. "You even kept them away from my car."

"Did you find Mom's research?"

"I've committed it all to memory."

"Good." Aitch decked Jay. "That's for lying to me."

Jay disappeared in a plume of dust. Unexpected chunks of sidewalk showered Aitch. He sped away, maneuvering past twisted limbs and dodging falling chunks of concrete and dirt. Pain lingered in his fist and arm. That was appropriate, Aitch decided. Both brothers deserved some pain, Jay for lying and Aitch for trusting him.

The dust settled to reveal the parking lot's new canyon. Aitch gaped at it. No one was entering or leaving the building without a climb or a running jump. Jay climbed out, slightly shaken but none too worse for wear.

"When in my entire life, pray tell, have I ever lied to you?" Jay rolled his shoulders, then brushed dust off his sleeves.

"You said you'd make me normal." Aitch picked up, then tossed a metallic limb. It crashed on the other side of the parking lot. "This is not even in the same universe as normal."

"Brother, when did I say that? And why would I say that? Even if I knew how, doing that would literally kill you. I said—"

"You said, and I quote, 'Mom and I have worked out how to make your symbionts give you a body that even you—'" Aitch's stomach dropped. "Oh. How was I supposed to know you wanted the convoluted interpretation? The English language isn't meant to be a pretzel. You can hit me back if—"

Aitch never saw the punch. One instant, he was speaking, and the next, he lay in a divot created when he crashed through the blacktop. Before, if anyone could have hit him this hard, he'd have died. Now he only wished he had. Still, Jay should have been able to at least knock him out.

"You can punch more efficiently than that. I know it." Aitch tried to get up, then decided his symbionts needed more time. "Brother, give me a second, then hit me again. This time, I'll pay attention to your technique."

"No. No more hand-to-hand combat lessons." Jay held his palms out to ward Aitch off. "You teaching me to fight hurt bad enough before I fixed your symbionts."

Jay went to his car. He grabbed the rear bumper, then gestured Aitch over to the front.

"Brother, how does making me tougher stop Drips from hunting me down?" Aitch obliged, and they repositioned the car for an easier escape. "If anything, I'm a bigger threat now."

"Too big a threat. I mean, they're pretty much content to leave me alone. Besides, you're only a danger when you feel threatened." Jay unlocked the car doors. "Did you want to kill me after I punched you?"

"That doesn't mean anything." Aitch sat in the passenger seat. "There are only two men in the world who could punch me, not that the other one has, and I'd still think they didn't mean—"

"Two?" Jay started up the car. "And the other one doesn't want to climb with you anymore?"

"Shut up and drive." Aitch closed, not slammed, the car door. "If I have to visit Mom, at least you could make it quick."

• • •

So I was in Simon's bedroom a few nights ago—

"Woohoo!" Jay slapped Aitch's back. Pride was smeared across Jay's face.

"Get your mind out of the gutter." Aitch calibrated the force his fist slammed with against Jay's shoulder. Jay crashed against the driver side door but didn't break through. "He's not interested in me."

—looking for my trench coat among the pile of jackets on his bed.

Simon seemed pleased with the bootleg of the Detroit out-of-town of Pleasures and Palaces I gave him. I'd eaten a piece of birthday cake. My duty acquitted, everyone would be happier if I left now before something stupid happened.

"Simon got you to go to both a concert and a party? There doesn't seem to be anything he can't make you do." The smile faded from Jay's face. That Aitch's symbionts turned Simon's words into unyielding commands was no joke. "Oh, I see. Does he know?"

"I didn't know until I tried to beat up his boyfriend and couldn't. Simon told me to stop, and I let the boyfriend hit my head with his bottle of beer. Until then, everything Simon suggested was something I wanted to do anyway, or so I thought."

"Brother, why were you—"

The boyfriend started it. Simon keeps dating these pretty boys who don't have the intelligence of a blueberry muffin. If he ever dated anyone who could go toe-to-toe with him intellectually, he might actually sustain a relationship for longer than the half-life of some transuranic element.

Anyway, I bolted. Being in the same room as someone I obey unconditionally has never gone well for me. I was in the middle of New Hampshire before I calmed down.

A team of Drips shot supersonic micro-darts at me from the trees. They all wore sleek power armor no thicker than a sweatshirt. No clunky power source. It stood up to its own augmented strength and protected the wearer. Much more practical than being me.

After some trial and error, mostly error, I wedged their armor, then ran away. Paralyzing them cost me cracked ribs, mashed hands, a broken arm, and more wounds than I cared to count. If there's any justice, those Drips are still trapped inside their futuristic suits, baked to death in the sun.

When I stopped running, my favorite rock face loomed before me in the moonlight. I collapsed and curled into a ball. Hunger cramps hurt worse than my broken fingers and ribs. I writhed on the ground trying to get a protein bar out of a pocket and into my mouth. Dirt rubbed against—

"Obviously, you found enough food to heal yourself because otherwise you'd be dead. What does this have to do with Simon?"

Simon showed up with three roast chickens, cornbread, and an ultimatum. He'd expected me to cover hundreds of miles over a few hours on foot. That made him either an idiot or a Drip. Simon's no idiot. I heard him before I saw him. Damn him and his loud, operatically trained voice.

"Aitch, sit down and be still." Since it was Simon saying those words, my body sat down, then refused to move. "I'll be there in a minute."

He emerged from the dark. His hand gripped large Styrofoam containers. He crouched next to me. I glared.

"Sorry." He started clearing dirt off my face. "By now, you've worked out the score. Can't take the chance you'll run away or refuse to eat." He looked at my broken hands, then began feeding me meat torn from the carcass. By the second roast chicken, my fingers had straightened, and my wounds were healing. I fed myself the third roast chicken. When I ate the bones, too, Simon offered me the first two skeletons. After that and the cornbread, I was the fit, obedient soldier again.

Simon rubbed his eyes. He stifled a yawn. "Aitch, at ease. The following order is irrevocable: Be yourself."

His gaze bore the slightest glint of fear. In commanding me to be myself, he'd willingly given up all control over me. If I wanted to crush his chest, the symbionts in my head wouldn't stop me. Of course, saving my life didn't exactly make me hate him. Honestly, even now, if he wanted me to kill myself, I don't know that I wouldn't try just to make him happy.

"How did you bind me to you?" Ignorance, especially my own, makes me edgy. "Pheromones? PsyOps? And after all that, why free me? You've gone through a lot trouble for nothing."

"Whoa. One at a time." Simon held his hands up as though he could hold me off. "No one bound anybody to anyone. You're so uptight, I had no idea how you felt about me until last night, or else I would have freed you earlier."

"So it's a coincidence then, that you're a Drip?"

"A what? Oh. Cute." Apparently, no one had ever called Simon a Drip before. "The day we met, I was supposed to drop you off the side of the mountain, dump boulders on you, then infect you with flesh-eating bacteria while you were unconscious. Obviously, I bailed. A good climbing partner is too hard to find, and if you were going to survive anyway, you were much more likely to keep climbing with me if I didn't try to kill you."

I stared at him. How did it happen that it felt paranoid to accuse a Drip of wanting to kill me?

"So it's your job to climb with me?"

In retrospect, I was misinterpreting exactly like you say I do, brother. Figures. You're never wrong about anything.

"No. Believe it or not, I deal with you on my own personal time." Simon crossed his arms over his chest. He drew himself to his full height, then glared down at me. "Look, if I were you, I wouldn't get serious with anyone either. I get that, but Aitch, if you can't stop scaring away everyone who shows the slightest interest in me, I can't keep climbing with you."

For a moment, I couldn't breathe. For the next few, I didn't want to. Nothing any other Drip had ever done to me hurt more.

Anyway, he must have seen it on my face. His hand landed awkwardly on my shoulder, then shot back as if I were electrified.

"I'm sorry, Aitch." He checked his watch. "Look, the Washington Chorus is doing the Bach St. John Passion this Saturday, and their Evangelist is out sick. They asked me to sub in. I'll miss my flight if I don't go soon."

"I don't suppose you want me to drive you to Logan."

"You drive?"

"I'm qualified to operate practically any vehicle ever designed."

"Yes, I know. That's not what I meant, and you know it."

"Simon always asks me to drop him off, then car sit while he's out of town. Airport parking is expensive."

"You still want to?" He peered over the Styrofoam containers that he now braced against his chest. "I can drive myself. There's time to drop you off before I go to Logan."

"It's okay." I started down the trail to his car. "I don't mind driving."

"Excuse me? You hate driving." Jay practically choked on his words. "And he let you?"

"Why not? Unlike you, he can't sense my cortisol level. Besides, I don't crush steering wheels from the stress anymore." Aitch took a deep breath, then forced himself to relax. "As it was, I had to wake him up when we reached Logan."

"You learned a valuable life lesson suitable for framing that night."

Aitch slouched in his seat. It groaned in protest. "I learned he doesn't want me in his life anymore."

"Brother, he drove several hundred miles out of his way, saved your life, then offered to drive you home. These are not the acts of a man who doesn't want you in his life. Love, loyalty, and obedience are all messed up in your head, so I'll be blunt: Not everyone who has earned your trust does so to screw you over. Life is better if, when you're literally starving to death and a friend feeds you roast chicken, you thank him."

Aitch sat back up. His hands let go of the seat cushions.

"Brother, I've missed talking to you."

"Pick up the next time I call or, hell, call me for once." Jay gave Aitch a dope slap. "Better yet, visit. I have a job waiting for me at Mass General."

Mom's hospital room didn't look a thing like what Aitch expected. A curtained bed sat in the middle. A TV craned from the ceiling as did a turret aimed at the doorway. Surely, it was supposed to have fired as he opened the door. Two large windows dominated the far wall. A pane of glass from one window rested against the other window. A rope dangled outside the window missing its pane. Crouched down, Simon dropped wrecked bits of electronics in a bag that hung off his climbing harness. In addition, he wore a tux complete with black cummerbund and bow tie. The stripe running down his pants glinted under the florescent light.

Simon froze for a fraction of second after Aitch opened the door. He gave Aitch a low wolf whistle. "Wow. You clean up nice."

Jay had insisted Aitch into a suit after they'd left the archive. It fit his oddly shaped body too well for comfort. Aitch was used to clothes that cramped his shoulders and fell off his waist.

"You, too, Simon. You do all your jobs in a tux?"

"I had to sing the John Passion." Simon showed Aitch his palms. "As it is, if you'd shown up any earlier, I wouldn't have disabled the turret in time. Before you ask, the original Evangelist is fine now. Just some carefully timed vocal cord swelling."

"I don't get it. Wouldn't it have been easier to tell me not to come here?" Aitch swept the curtain aside. The bed was empty and cold. "You'll excuse me if leave. I'll see you—No, I guess I won't anymore." Aitch turned to leave. Jay would catch up at any moment. Aitch had dove out of the hatchback as it'd passed the hospital entrance, leaving Jay to go park the car. No sense in both of them walking into a death trap.

"Aitch, you thought climbing with you was part of my job. Do you seriously think if I'd warned you, you'd have believed me?"

Aitch stopped. Time to stop misinterpreting Simon. At first,

Aitch's words lodged in his throat. He tore them out. "Maybe if I can stop me from scaring myself away, I won't scare anyone else away from you either."

The door stood mere steps away. He stared at it, too angry to turn around and face Simon.

"Your timing stinks. Look, we can't stay in this room. How about we talk this out when we go climbing in a few days?" The zipper on Simon's bag screeched shut. "I'll help you find your Mom. She's probably in this hospital somewhere."

After one footfall, an ultrasonic hum pierced the room. Time dilated. The walls vibrated, blurring slightly to Aitch but probably not to Simon. Drips had apparently also weaponized the walls.

He had time to either escape or cover Simon with his body. Aitch didn't need to think. Rather than running out of the room, he ran towards Simon.

Perversely, the fluorescent light overhead dimmed as the walls glowed. By the time he reached Simon, the Drip had thrown himself out the window. Maybe he should have escaped, instead.

The ultrasonic hum rose in pitch until it past the range of even Aitch's hearing. Light from the walls slammed into him. Everything in the room evaporated except him. His skin turned red and blistered. Fire scorched through his lungs. The remaining window blew out. Glass cascaded away with a crash. Electricity crackled from stray live wires above him.

Without a Simon to run into, momentum pushed Aitch through the window. After that attack, he didn't want to crash straight down. His symbionts needed time to fix him. He leapt. His body stretched out. The air whistled in his ears as he rose. A sparse field of cars rushed beneath him.

Simon swung back towards the building on his rope. He'd grabbed it as he'd flown out the window. DRP training in action, by definition, was impressive.

Aitch's awe lasted for barely a second. Any Drip should have let Aitch pass. Simon, instead, tried to catch Aitch. Unfortunately, his speed and hand-eye coordination were just good enough. He scuttled up the rope, and his arm wrapped around Aitch as they intersected. At least he had enough sense to let go of the rope before Aitch's momentum could rip his arm off. No one who wanted to kill Aitch would do anything this well-meaning but stupid. They hurtled through the air past one parking lot to the next.

Simon secured his grip around Aitch. His hands smeared blood across Aitch's back. His face pressed up against Aitch's.

"You ran towards the window rather than out the door. Is that the move of a tactical genius?"

"I wasn't running towards the window. I was trying to cover you."

"Oh." Simon's brow furrowed. "That's the sweetest but dumbest thing anyone has ever tried to do for me."

"I don't think you get to talk, rope boy." Aitch resisted the temptation to push Simon off his body. "Now shut up and let me figure out how I get you down alive."

"You mean 'us,' right? Because I've memorized your dossier, and I hate to break this to you, but you cannot fly."

They fell into a hospital parking lot. Aitch skipped against the blacktop, bouncing back into the air again and again. All he could do for Simon was be his shock absorber. He pushed back every time they slammed into the ground. Even though every hit tried to shake Aitch into pieces, Simon flew up and down in smooth, lazy curves.

Eventually, they skidded between two rows of cars. If Aitch were his old self or ordinary, the skidding would have broken skin. Slick blood and shock might have eventually numbed the pain or, more likely, killed him. Instead, the parking lot kept digging into him until he finally stopped moving.

Jay ran towards them. Aitch would have strangled the relief off his brother's face, but that would have required moving. He felt for Simon's pulse and found it. Aitch let go of a breath he hadn't realized he was holding. As long as he'd kept Simon alive, Jay could take care of Simon's injuries.

"Hm, that's more damage you should be expected to sink and live. There's probably a dossier I'm now supposed to update." Simon looked at Jay, but his hand reached for Aitch's. "Say, you wouldn't happen to have a brother who's a lot like you but a little more muscular, a lot more neurotic, and interested in men?"

"You know, there are so many things I could say right now." Jay looked down at Simon lying on top of Aitch. "However, if I said any of them, my brother would send me into orbit."

If there was anything worse than being trapped in a car with Jay, it was being trapped in the backseat with Simon while Jay was driving. A tall, broad-shouldered man, even a lean one, was not meant for the backseat of a hatchback. Still, Simon looked surprisingly comfortable, or maybe just resigned, imitating an origami balloon. Jay had offered him a ride home, and, to Aitch's surprise, he accepted. Who wouldn't forsake a flight for a seven-hour trip in a car too cramped for him? Intellectually, Aitch knew why Simon was here even if he didn't quite understand it.

Simon would have been more comfortable in the front passenger seat, but he had put Jay's now half-empty roller bag there instead. Aitch had changed clothes three times in the past twenty-four hours. The T-shirt and shorts he wore now made him feel like a bag of sludge. Or maybe sheer proximity to Simon and Jay was enough to make him feel that way. Some invisible force pinned him against the window even as gravity tried to slide him into Simon.

"Sorry about your mom." Simon leaned forward, trying to meet Aitch's gaze. "I had no idea."

The Drips had cremated Mom's body a few days ago. Jay had thought she'd last for another few weeks, and his surprise that she hadn't seemed genuine. He was never wrong about matters of life and death.

"It's okay, Simon." Aitch stared out the window. Headlights beamed behind them. "I'll burn a paper replica of her lab as an offering. She'll never notice she's dead. Maybe she'll infect my ancestors, too."

When Grandfather died, Mom burned a paper airplane so that Grandfather could cross the Pacific and visit. Aitch was twelve, and that had made as little sense as everything else had in his life to date, or since.

"Without Mom, working out how to repair the symbionts in your head will take longer, brother, but I'll do it." Somewhere on I-95, an orchestra followed them underscoring Jay's words with lush strings and clarion trumpets. Or maybe Jay's voice had that effect all by itself. "You have my word. Then we can start healing your mind."

"Sure, whatever." Aitch shrugged. "Maybe now that I'm harder to kill, the Drips will lay off."

"Simon, your chemistry's just gone wacky." Concern filled Jay's voice. "What's worrying you?"

Simon's jaw went slack. Nothing could prepare anyone for prolonged exposure to Jay.

"Welcome to my world." Aitch patted Simon's thigh. "Once he calibrates himself to you, he might as well be a walking polygraph."

"Hey, I'm way more accurate and versatile."

Simon sighed. He paced his words deliberately. "Your day job, freelance software development, can't possibly hold your interest. None of us want to know what might happen if you ever get ... bored."

"Are you still a Drip, Simon?" Aitch folded his arms across his chest.

"Sure. Singing doesn't pay that well, and DRP doesn't actually mind that I'm spending time with you."

Aitch leveled his best glare of disapproval. "How am I supposed to trust either one of you?"

"Brother, yes, we've both done suspicious things, but has either of us ever betrayed you?"

Aitch's memories pierced him like perfect but mismatched crystals. Each one had a beginning, middle, and end. Taken together, though, they made no sense. When he was a kid, Drips he couldn't help but obey would order him to break his own arm, then they'd hug him as they timed how long he took to heal. When their lies had finally worn away his love, the Drips who restrained him and experimented on him also rewarded him with scallion pancakes and beef noodle soup flavored with anise.

"The question isn't 'has.'" Dread grew in the pit of Aitch's stomach. The whine of the engine and the crunch of the tires on the road didn't reassure him one bit. "The question is 'will.'"

Neither of them had screwed him over yet. Trust meant giving them the chance to, then hoping they wouldn't. What kind of idiot would do that? Life was too short.

His gaze flicked up. If he pushed off hard enough with his legs, they'd break through the floor and puncture the gas tank or something. Maybe if, instead, he threw his weight against—

Jay shouted "Brother," just before Simon touched Aitch's arm and said, "Aitch, are you okay?"

Aitch's hands had balled into fists again. His heart was pounding so hard that he was short of breath. Simon eased Aitch's hands open.

He was doing it again, he realized. Damn. Intellectually, he got that to take everything they'd done to help him as evidence of their eventual betrayal was perverse. Given that he'd almost bolted again, it was kind of amazing that they trusted him.

Time to try something else. Aitch took a deep breath. Far from mastering his fear, he settled for recognizing that it'd never go away.

"Brother, I don't live too far from Mass General. You could stay with me—I mean, if you want—until, you know ..."

"That would be great." Jay's radiant smile bounced off the rearview into Aitch's eyes. "Thanks."

Little by little, Aitch gave into gravity. He leaned into Simon as Simon leaned into him. As the sky grew dark and the car's whine seemed to dull into a purr, Aitch let his eyes close and his head fall against Simon's chest.

Super Duper Fly

Maurice Broaddus

Topher Blanderson stared at his computer screen, knowing something wasn't quite right but unable to put his finger on it. The account numbers scrolled past, a series of figures moving so quickly, they were almost hypnotic. His head ached. It hadn't pained him this much since his accident at the ski lodge so many years before. Topher felt his mind drift, not quite going to sleep, but relaxing. Expanding. Touching something deep and otherly. Suddenly, everything seemed perfectly clear.

Topher touched the computer screen. His fingers danced across the monitor, the data spinning past a blur of ones and zeroes, fragments of information coalescing into folders. He pressed his hand flat against the surface, the warmth sinking into him. He shut his eyes for a moment, and briefly there was darkness as ...

... his manager, Ana Pedestal, waited at a restaurant at the hotel of the conference she attended. With him. Not him. He was there, but it was in someone else's body. The CEO. Her shoe dangled from the tip of her foot. She touched his arm ... they were in his (not his) hotel room. She poured champagne into a flute, which had Gummi Bears in it. Ana threw her head back in laughter. They kissed. She ... wore dark sunglasses. She was lost, a stranger walking about the corridors of the Cayman Islands National Bank, not wanting to be seen. Not wanting to be noticed. More numbers. Account names. Money transferred to ... sand. So much sand at the beach with its ocean view. So blue. So blue. Cobalt blue. Cobalt Coast. Her body brown in the sun. She held her empty glass out. A young man quickly refilled it for her. She allowed her gaze to linger on him for a heartbeat longer as she ... broke off her kiss with him and dismissed him from her room. A knock came a minute later. She opened it expecting the attendant, but the CEO barged through. His (not his) face a sneer of anger. Ana pulled away from him. His desperate fingers searched for any purchase. He tore the thin cloth of her sundress. He slammed his hand over her mouth. She bit into the fleshy side of his palm. He pulled away, then backhanded her. She licked the warm trickle of blood from her lip. She grabbed the phone from the nightstand and swung it in a large arc connecting with his head with a loud thunk. Her eyes bulged. Her face went pink to red as she slammed the base of the phone into his head again and again. He tried to scream ...

"... don't put the Gummi Bears in the champagne glass," Topher yelled.

"What did you say?" Ana said from his doorway. And then he was back. He wiped the thin sheen of sweat from his forehead. She squinted at his computer monitor. "Is everything all right, Mr. Blanderson? I hope you aren't using company resources for anything ... inappropriate."

"Yes, yes. Everything's fine. I just ... dozed off."

"Might as well go home then. You're the last one here. We aren't paying you to sleep on the job."

"I'm fine. I just wanted to check a few things."

"That's the thing, Mr. Blanderson, you're not fine. I've been keeping my eye on your call metrics. They've dipped precipitously in the last weeks. Yet, even as your work began to slide, you're staying later and later, running through files and reports that are out of your purview."

"I just wanted to go over a few reports. I thought I found a few anomalies."

"We don't pay you to ferret out anomalies. We pay you to balance the accounts in front of you."

"Yes, but in order to reconcile ..."

"... the only thing you need to reconcile is your job and your place in this company. Do you like your job, Mr. Blanderson?"

"I'm grateful for the opportunity."

"Good. We've had our eye on you for a long time. We want you to be a part of our family for a long time."

"Me, too. Didn't you just get back from a conference?"

"Yes, with the entire management team."

"Including the CEO?"

"We're getting off-track. The path you're on can go two ways, but only one involves having a future at this company. Do I make myself clear?"

"Yes. Ma'am."

Ana turned and walked out of his area, leaving him alone on the sales floor. Topher leaned back in his chair. He didn't know what his vision meant. Only that it wasn't just a dream.

The sales floor took on a whole different aspect when he was the only one there. The cubicle farm had more of an echo like the vast belly of a corporate beast that had long ago swallowed him but hadn't finished its digestion of him. The vent sighed the way old buildings did. The telltale click of a door opening sent a shiver of apprehension through him. He hated knowing he was alone. The realization that should anything go wrong, no one would be around to help him slowly crept up on him. The same sense of dread filled him when he walked through the garage, all shadows and silence. A low squeak neared, increasing his vague panic. A figure appeared down the hall. All that registered with him was that the man was black and they had no black people working at their firm. They tried that once. Ruling out the idea of attempting to defend himself with his cell phone, Topher reached for his stapler.

"That you, Mr. Blanderson?" the man asked.

The familiar strains of Bagger Hallorann filled Topher with relief. He relaxed his grip on his stapler. Bagger was just so safe. He even wore glasses. Black people with glasses always seemed less threatening.

"Yeah, it's me, Bags." Topher called him Bags. He gave the man the nickname because it made him feel more connected to the janitor. Obviously, Topher cared. He'd wager no one else in the company even bothered to learn his name. "Another late one."

"It's never too late to be what you were meant to be."

"Excuse me?"

"When was the last time you made time for your family?" Bags nodded toward the framed picture on Topher's desk. "You have to be careful not to neglect them."

"It's just that I have all this money and opportunity and education, but I can't seem to figure out life."

"The love of family is much more important than wealth and privilege."

"You always know the right thing to say," Topher said. "How come you're always there when I need you even though I barely know you?"

"I'm the wise janitor. I come to impart wisdom and assuage fears." Bags emptied the trashcan. "It looked like you needed some friendly, black, optimistic advice."

"You ever have that feeling where you're not sure if you're awake or still sleeping?"

"The hardest thing to do is wake up and not sleep through your life. You're looking for the answer to a question you haven't yet thought to ask."

"What's that?"

"You tell me. Has anything unusual happened lately? Anything at all?"

"You wouldn't believe me."

"Try me." Bags leaned against his trash bin. "You'd be surprised."

"I had a dream. Not a dream exactly, more like a vision. I think it was both of the past and of the future."

"Go on."

"I think there's something terribly wrong with the company."

"It's like the world doesn't quite make sense anymore but you're the only one who has noticed."

"Exactly."

"Maybe you're ready, after all." Bags straightened.

"Ready for what?"

"First tell me, were you ever hit in the head? As a child? In an accident?"

"Yes. When we were skiing a few years back. How did you know?"

"I think your employers have underestimated just how important you are."

"I am?" Topher rested his chin on his hand and leaned forward.

"I have plenty of things to show you, but I don't know if we have enough time."

"What kind of things?"

"You have potential. A power within you. You may be one of ... the Chosen."

"I ..."

"Sh! We don't have much time." Bags fished around in his pocket. "In my right hand is a red Skittle. In my left hand there's a green Skittle."

"Skittles?"

"Who doesn't like Skittles? You eat the red and life goes on as normal. You eat the green one and life as you know it changes."

"But they were in your pocket."

"They'll be coming for you soon. I can guide you, or you can worry about pocket lint. You need to choose."

Topher eyed each piece of candy carefully. He reached for the red one and almost took it before pulling back. Then he snatched the green one. He glanced at it, then at Bags. The janitor watched him with a cool, level gaze. Topher popped the green one in his mouth.

"Good, good. Now you just sit here for a minute while I prepare a few things."

"All right," Topher said. "What do I do in the meantime?"

"Finish your Skittle." Bags wheeled his trash bin back down the hallway. When he rounded the corner, he swung by Ana Pedestal's office. She was about to switch off her light when she caught sight of him. She jumped with a start before recognition filled her eyes.

"Getting a late start?" she said.

"As long as you're breathing, it's never too late."

"What?"

"Sorry. Wisdom reflex," Bags said. "I don't know if this is any of my business, but Mr. Blanderson's down at his desk going on and on about affairs and embezzlement."

"Really?"

"Sounded mighty peculiar. Thought you ought to know."

"Thanks for telling me." Ana punched in the extension for security.

"If you can't trust a white woman, who's left to trust?"

Bags wheeled his trash bin down the long hallway as security came around the corner. The hallway stretched on and on. The lights flickered until they finally gave out. Bags kept walking even though the trash bin he held onto faded into the shadows. In the distance, light outlined a door. He took the handle and pushed it in.

"Welcome to your judgment, Bagger Hallorann," a voice said.

Five columns of light broke the chamber of shadows. Within each beam stood a figure. An old man stepped awkwardly forward as if peeling himself from a box of rice. He shuffled toward Bagger with an easy grace. Two large hummingbirds, their colors too bright to be natural, materialized out of nowhere and flitted about the man.

"The Tom. It's been ... not long enough." Though Bagger met him with his gaze, the old man's eyes remained downcast.

"Bagger Hallorann? Seriously? Boy, you don't think that name's a little too on point for The Magical Negro?"

"It is a little dated. I figured no one would notice."

"The Magical Negro is not bound by the rules of space and time. It is a sacred responsibility." Another man stepped from his light. Over six and a half feet tall, weighing over two bills, he strutted toward the two, all swagger without consequence. He held his arms out, either for an embrace or waiting for a white woman to swoon and fall into them. "You had one job. One."

"What was that, The Buck?" The Magical Negro asked.

"You help the white hero on his journey."

The Chosen? I can barely say that with a straight face. "I wasn't even the point of view character in that scene."

"That's not your job, child." A large, buxom woman sashayed toward them. She wore a checkered apron and a handkerchief around her hair. "Your job is to get them out of trouble. Help them recognize their own faults and help them overcome. Transform them into competent, successful, and content people."

"The Mammy? Is that you?" The Magical Negro asked. "I thought you got a perm?"

"In their hearts, I'll always have a handkerchief."

"What was he 'chosen' to do?"

"We'll never know now. He may have gone on to become a superhero," The Tom said.

"Or he may have saved a whole village of us. You know how they love to rescue us from the mess of their own making," The Buck said.

"Careful now. That almost had the bite of critique," The Magical Negro said.

"Well, it's just us here now. We can speak plain."

"Your job, your one job, was to help him finish his story," The Tom said.

"I don't get a backstory?"

"No one cares about your backstory!"

"I ... I think you may be right about that. If I had a story, they wouldn't read it. But if they have a story and I can help them through it or Lawd Jesus," The Magical Negro turned toward The Mammy, "they can save not just me but my whole people then, now we have something they want to see."

"The story served The Market," The Mammy said.

"The Market," The Tom and The Buck whispered in unison.

"They want us around to remind them of how diverse a life they have but not in an inconvenient way. You know, having to get to know us. We're here strictly to keep them safe, tuck them in at night."

"You cannot thwart the journey." A light-skinned woman glided toward him. She stared at him with her tragedy-filled eyes. With her high cheekbones, thin nose, and straight black hair—she had some good hair; probably had some Indian in her—she could've passed for Greek or Italian. Something exotic.

"Even you, The Mulatto? You are nothing but backstory."

"You'd have probably told the boy with the ring to just stay on his giant bird and fly his ass to the mountain to drop the ring in it," The Tom said.

"Hand me a tall glass of white man's tears. With two ice cubes." The Magical Negro looked around the room. "So say you all? Even you, The Coon?"

A minstrel in an ill-fitting tuxedo grinned broadly. Clutching his plate of fried chicken and watermelon, he bugged his eyes out in alarm as if busted by his white boss.

"You know we don't let him say much," The Mammy said.

"For all the good it did us. He's got another sitcom deal on BET," The Buck said.

"Now things could've been worse: you could've let the dog die," The Mammy said.

"Yeah, you definitely don't want to be the black guy who let dogs die," The Buck said.

"We may have to downgrade you to helping out a black guy," The Tom said.

"Can a black guy have a Magical Negro?" The Buck asked.

"I don't right know. I guess," The Mammy said. "First he'd have to go on the hero's journey."

"We're going to give you one more chance. Know your place," The Tom said. "Fulfill your role. If we listen and are polite, we can succeed."

"That's what we've always been told. It's our hope. Our legacy," The Mulatto agreed.

With that, The Tom, The Mammy, and The Mulatto retreated to their places, preserved like relics in a museum. The Buck glanced over his shoulder at them, then turned back to The Magical Negro.

"Hold on, Negro Godmother. Let me holler at you for a second."

"Now what?" The Magical Negro asked.

"You should know, they're afraid."

"Afraid of what?"

"Of you."

"Me? What did I do?"

"The Tom is going to resent you no matter what you do. The Magical Negro already works his side of the street, if you know what I'm saying. But there's a legend we all speak about. Well, not them. The Council of Negro Stereotypes don't exist for our benefit. But among us, the true us, there's this hope that one day we'll be able to tell our own stories. Fulfill the role of griots the way our most ancient story keepers once did. That maybe there will come one with a sense of agency. One of us who has a complex interior life. Who has real desires, real history, and a real journey."

"You think that might be me?"

"I don't know. They fear it. It might mean the end for them if someone like that comes around."

"But not you?"

"Not as long as a white man needs a sidekick or a white woman has a fantasy. You don't know how close I came to making it to hero status. Perhaps one day. But for now, you have a job to do."

The two men rattled back and forth in the cab of the old Farmall truck. The engine grumbled all along the winding dirt road, sputtering and coughing with every turn and incline. J.C. tilted his head back, lost in his thoughts. He no longer cared. He took in the scenery with a blank resignation which worried the prison guard.

"We're almost there, Joe," the prison guard said.

"Okay, boss." J.C. said the words as if they left a bad taste in his mouth. He shifted in his seat, his large frame taking up most of the space as it was.

"We've come a long way, you and I."

"What do you mean?"

"I was terrified of you when I first saw you. Never met a colored like you before. You were the size of three grown men, and the cuffs and chains barely seemed to hold you. It was like you wore them as a courtesy. I think that was what first fascinated me about you. When we get back to the prison, I hope you'll do me that same courtesy when I have to put you back in chains. But for now ..."

"... for now I'm free." J.C. smiled his unassuming, sweet smile. But something was different about him. Just a little off. It was a big night for him. One last adventure to heal the prison guard's daughter with his gift. Then after that, he had a date with Old Sparky. Gentle and self-sacrificing or not, he had been found guilty of the crime everyone knew the son of the governor committed. But someone had to die for those sins, and J.C. fit the bill as good as any.

"Can I tell you something, Joe?" the prison guard said.

"What's that?"

"I never had any colored friends before."

"A good ol' bullgoose like yourself? All them years as a block superintendent, all those cells occupied by so many black candidates, powerless against your authority and privilege, and you chose me. Because of my gift. Now we're out breathing this here fine country air. I'd say that this certainly beats getting to know one."

"What privilege? I'm struggling to get by same as the next man. And for all my power, I'm here, pinning my hopes on you."

"Yes, yes. I have all sorts of power while you're not even living up to your potential. Yet, I'm still here to serve you." J.C. turned toward him, his tone almost unreadable.

"This is so ... touching." The prison guard wiped away some tears. "That's so ... what you're doing is so beautiful. It's teaching me so much. I'm all choked up."

"Yeah, someone should be choked."

The trees whirred past, dark, sharp shadows against the darker, moonless night sky. Nothing felt familiar and all the usual landmarks seemed strange. The prison guard kept his eyes on the road when he wasn't checking the rearview mirror to make sure no one followed them. Innocent or not, J.C. was technically an escaped felon. If they were caught before the guard could return him, he'd be in nearly as much trouble as his prisoner.

They swung into the guard's gravel driveway and parked the ratty truck. The guard closed his eyes as if reflecting on whether he'd made the right choice and if it were too late to turn the vehicle around and get J.C. back to his cell without anyone being the wiser.

"We have to go if we're going to do this, boss." J.C. wrapped one of his massive hands around the guard's entire wrist.

"Yeah, might as well see this through."

The guard led them up to his porch. He turned the key in the lock and slowly opened the door. When he flicked on the light, a little girl stirred on the couch. She rubbed her eyes. A blue-eyed little moppet of a girl with long pigtails. She ran to hug her dad.

"I knew you'd come," she said.

"I promised you, didn't I?"

"Is he the one with the gift? The Whining?"

The guard turned with embarrassment to J.C. before returning to his little girl. "Not every black person has The Whining. You know how some people get," the prison guard says. "Complaining that they aren't in enough things, then when they do show up, in an important role at that, they complain."

"No, honey. I'm here to heal you," J.C. said.

"You're saving my life," she said to him with a grateful smile to her voice. "The spring formal is next week."

"And you want to live long enough to have your first dance?" J.C. dropped down to one knee to meet her almost eye-to-eye

"I'd say. If I go right now, I'd just die."

"What do you have?"

"Can't you see it? It's huge." The little girl stepped closer. She turned her face to the side. That was when J.C. saw it.

"It's a zit." He wobbled, suddenly off balance. The girl covered her face at his reaction.

"You let me out of jail so that I could take her sickness upon myself right before you string me up for a crime I didn't commit?"

"Do you know how long a wait we have to find a good dermatologist?" the prison guard asked. "Besides, my deductible is huge."

"I need to go to the bathroom."

"Why?"

"If you want me to touch a little white girl, I'd think you'd be expected to wash up first."

"Good point."

J.C. pushed past the guard and strode down the hallway toward the living room and beyond the kitchen to the last door on the left. The light buzzed to life above him. He ran the cold water and splashed some on his face. He looked into the mirror. His face was wet as if from a day's labor sweating in a field; his arms exhausted and heavy. Turning to his left, he spied a small window. The thought leapt to his mind by the time he was halfway through it. With a bit of contortion, he twisted his bulky frame through the opening. He scrabbled along the roof and hopped onto their landing before running off into the night.

A disembodied head faded into view alongside him as he ran.

"Where are you going?" The Tom asked.

"Home," J.C. said. "If I can heal people, I'm going to open up a free clinic."

"What about the girl?" The Mammy appeared beside them.

"They got good health insurance."

"I think he's gone insane," The Tom said to The Mammy.

"No, he may be ... The One," The Buck materialized beside them.

"The One?" The Tom turned to him. "Surely not."

"Who's The One?" The Mammy asked.

"If he's really arrived, maybe now, he'll have his own story to tell. The One who actually saves the day himself. He's the hero."

Rabbits

Csilla Kleinheincz

The air was boiling above the highway, whipping up the smell of dust from the car seats as if the road led into the past instead of to Lake Balaton.

"You don't look so well," said Vera, glancing to her right. She leaned on the wheel almost as if she was afraid that without holding on, the car would leave her behind. "Why don't you roll down the window a bit?"

Amanda was wondering whether what she felt was nausea. It was difficult to tell. The smell of the dust made her woozy. She wanted to ask the little girl in the backseat if she was sick, too, but then rejected the idea. The girl couldn't speak. Or maybe she could, but no one had yet the guts to ask her anything.

"I spread the tarot for our vacation," said Vera. "It was all swords. What do you think it means?"

"If you can't read it, why do you lay it out?" Amanda decided not to risk being sick; the air whistled in the window and tore the words from her mouth bite by bite.

"Because when I spread it and clean it and light a candle, it calms me. Plus, it is super mysterious. If someone were to see me, he would think I'm a witch."

Amanda frowned. Vera knew as little about tarot as about everything else; she dipped in it because it interested her but only tried it on briefly like a new dress.

The wind felt good, it invigorated Amanda, the nausea was blown out of her. She felt empty. Now she saw Vera and the curly locks stuck to her forehead more clearly.

"And if no one sees you?"

"Then I imagine that someone does." Vera laughed, but Amanda was in no mood to join her. Hi, my witch. This is me you are talking to. I look right through you like an X-ray.

She would not have minded if it had been so. Vera would become transparent like glass, Amanda would see the car door behind her and could reach into her like into an aquarium, and then she would pull out what was wrong with her. Presto. A routine operation, madam, you may go back to your girlfriend.

"Swords is an air element," she said. "Which cards were they?"

"Does it matter? I did the spread, seemed like a good idea. I am sure it had some meaning. It is enough to know that, isn't it ...?"

Amanda looked at her to elicit some explanation, but her friend didn't notice it.

"It is enough to know it means something," said Vera loudly over the wind, and she leaned even more on the wheel.

They set off an hour earlier, and yet they hadn't left the highway yet. Vera must have been the slowest driver on the whole stretch of road, and if she could, she would have driven in the service lane. She feared for the car, which was as new as her driver's license.

Well, Vera certainly isn't her old self either, thought Amanda sadly and cranked up the window. Her ears hurt from the whistling wind.

They passed harvested wheat fields, the stubble shining golden on the face of the sleeping earth. Amanda's nausea returned; she felt as if their journey to Lake Balaton had been a succession of swigs from stale water.

"You shouldn't have eaten both of those fried eggs."

She shouldn't have, but fried eggs were a symbol just like Vera's tarot spread. Each morning they fried something for breakfast, and Amanda did the same this morning to pretend they were still together. She doggedly ate the eggs and bacon while Vera waited for her, then took her bag, and they were off.

As an experiment, she put her hand on Vera's knee, but her girlfriend apologetically took her wrist and pushed it away. For a while the silence was cold.

They stopped at a gas station at the beginning of the Balaton road. Vera stepped out to fill up the car and make a call. Amanda turned back to the child.

The little girl didn't say a word during the journey. She sat with a chocolate donut in her hand and smears on her face.

Clean your face, Amanda thought hard, wondering if she could make the girl speak. Maybe the child was silent for the same reason. Maybe she just thought hard about the things she wanted to say.

The girl did not wipe the chocolate off her face. She just stared with eyes as blue as cornflowers, as those of Amanda. Her curly hair —so very like Vera's—was matted with chocolate. She dropped the doughnut into her lap onto the white skirt.

"We are on the road, yes, almost there ... Of course ..." Shrill laughter. Amanda looked out the open door at Vera. "Yes, I would love it ... Hmm? You say you can magic yourself here?" Laughter again. "Yes, Tintin. Kisses."

Tintin. What kind of nickname was that for a grown man? And who was called Jusztin nowadays? Amanda was sure it was a stage-name required by the circus, but Vera was adamant that it was real.

"Did you ever see his ID? Did it say Jusztin?

"Yours says Amanda, so why not?"

Vera got back in the car, smiling nonchalantly, and started the engine.

"Hey," said Amanda later, when they were at Siófok. "Do you remember Panna?"

"Hmm?"

"Our daughter?"

Vera looked up in the rearview mirror, then turned on the turn signal. Their street was still far away, but she was cautious.

"Oh, *that*. It was a nice game. I mean, pretending she existed."

Amanda looked back. The girl shrugged as if to say she didn't care, then faded away. The chocolate doughnut remained a little while longer above the seat, then it also disappeared.

Only the headache remained, and the feeling of dejection.

Tintin was a traveling circus magician. Vera said he was too young to get offers from bigger companies.

And not handsome enough, added Amanda, first in thought and later in words. She thought that Jusztin—no Tintin for her, thank you—had carrot hair and small, unpleasantly gleaming eyes. Vera liked him, though. This only showed that Amanda didn't know her friend as well as she believed: if these Jusztin types were acceptable —and what's more: delightful, enchanting, sexy—then perhaps in Vera's eyes she was not who she really was.

Two weeks ago, in the town of Fót, Jusztin literally enchanted Vera: he turned her into a rabbit, then caught her with a lasso. He winked, smiled at her, and in the next minute it was Vera who shuffled her feet at the end of the rope. Jusztin wanted her to bow, then released her.

Vera thought this romantic. Amanda said it was love magic, a low one at that, but the only one she could ask about it was her enchanted friend.

As they strolled on the beach and inspected ice cream vendors, Amanda watched Vera walk, watched for the signs that her steps faltered when Amanda peeled the panties of her bikini off with her gaze. Once, her girlfriend had said Amanda could ignite an ant with her gaze. Now Vera hardly even noticed. You see? Amanda looked at the little girl who followed them mute and grimy. The child glanced back, shook her Vera-hair, and raised her hand. Her fingers were closed as if she had been following a string.

Her face remained calm though, as they walked the Balaton promenade, she faded and started to lose herself. When her feet melted away and her pink legs walked on blunt ends, Amanda turned away.

"Do you like ghosts?" she asked Vera. The little girl was sitting on the grass in front of them. She was playing with sticks, fencing with them as if they were swords. Amanda didn't like that; the rattle gave her a headache.

"Sure."

Vera held her cell phone in her hand and smiled dreamily at it as she was punching its buttons.

"Not ghosts of dead people. But ghosts of people we create by the force of our mind."

"Hmm."

"Vera."

"Tintin says ghosts live in his sleeves, in his opera hat, in his tailcoat. He stuffed them into his wand like the scarves, gave them as fodder to his rabbits. When I was a bunny, I think I saw them." She paused. "Then it turned out they were only feathers, he makes bouquets from them and conjures them out of his buttonhole. Tintin says because the ghosts live with him, they do not exist. He told me to imagine them existing and not existing at the same time."

"Balderdash."

"He is good at it, yes," said Vera.

Sometimes it would have been better if she had quarreled. Or struck back. Or at least gave a sign that she knew that Amanda didn't like Jusztin. Acknowledged, and then filed it. Then they could have gone on, closed the file. Instead, this was an endless interrogation with Amanda as the inquisitor.

"He doesn't really love you," said Amanda crossly.

"What's your problem? I came with you, didn't I?"

"But when you go back ... he won't love you."

"We'll see."

Vera's face was smooth and calm, not bothered by anything. It was possible that her heart remained a rabbit's even after the trick and was interested only in grass and fucking, maybe that was why she loved the carrot-haired Jusztin and his carrot so much.

Amanda watched the little girl knock the sticks together with her pink tongue stuck out in concentration. The child annoyed her. She would have shouted at her, but you don't shout at imaginary children, especially when there are others around.

The little girl appeared after one of their lovemakings when they stretched lazily and naked on the rug. Their hands drew slow circles on each other's belly and breasts, and they were whispering so softly that only they and the rug could hear them. Then abruptly the girl was there on the sofa, picking her nose. She wasn't bothered by their nudity, her face was devoid of emotion, of either smile or frown.

Amanda's aunt, who was almost admitted to a ghost researching course of a professedly Tibetan sect that was in truth run by Hungarian pensioners, once said that spontaneous spiritbirths were common and added that they were nothing to fuss about. They existed only in the mind, and if one wanted to get rid of them, one only had to purge them from within. Garlic was good, said the aunt seriously. Our ancestors knew that although they were mistaken when they believed that garlic had to be hung in the room. You had to eat it to shoo ghosts away. They didn't care for stinky breath. Amanda laughed at that.

The little girl unnerved her. The child's shin was short as if it had melted away. Her eyes sparkled red.

"I'm going inside."

"Hmm," mumbled Vera and put the cell phone to her ear.

"I'm staying outside," said Amanda in the same voice.

"Aham," said Vera, then her face lit up. "Oh, *Tintin!*"

Amanda wished to strangle her but didn't because of Jusztin. She felt him watching them from the distance through his magic wand like through a telescope, his breath ruffled the grass at their feet. She would behave nicely in front of him.

In fact, very nicely.

She leaned forward and kissed Vera's nape. Her girlfriend shot a glance at her.

"And what was the performance like?"

When she bit Vera's nape, she got a light slap in the face. Amanda growled back.

"What ...? Yes, a doggie."

Amanda turned up her nose. *You won't mislead Jusztin, he saw what I did. He is here with us. More and more real every minute.*

She hesitated a little in front of the bungalow, then went inside to open the bottle of whisky she had brought herself.

She smelled their perfumes in every room. Vera was Kenzo Air, Amanda was Summer. The two glasshouse scents made the world feel stuffy. Two hothouse flowers without stamens, Amanda thought.

In the bedroom under the bedcover, the perfume mixed with the smell of soap. Amanda wanted to snuggle closer but didn't dare. She felt someone lying between them: a long, heavy body pressing down the quilt but still invisible. Vera was dreaming of Jusztin.

Amanda watched Vera, and in turn Jusztin's ghost watched her. He was only a heavy void in the air: invisible, but she could feel his gaze upon her. He conjured himself here, thought Amanda, to keep an eye on me. He is a cheater. *I* don't ogle them when *they* are sleeping together.

Defiant, she slid closer, pushed away the ghost, and slipped her hand under Vera's cover. Her girlfriend's skin was warm and soft. She moved her hand up to Vera's breasts and massaged them gently. Vera sighed.

Hearing a soft hiss, Amanda smiled. Take that, Jusztin.

She slid her hand lower, inside Vera's pajamas. The faint stubble prickled her, but the opening was invitingly wet.

"I thought we have discussed this," muttered Vera sleepily.

Amanda's fingers groped farther down.

"We can stay friends without this." Vera took Amanda's wrist and squeezed it.

"I don't remember anything like that."

"I told you I have Tintin now."

"And did you tell him you have Amanda?"

Vera pulled her hand out of her pajamas.

"Be a good girl."

Amanda looked around. She didn't see either the child or the void in the place of Jusztin's ghost.

"He is not here to see!"

"Just don't do it, okay?"

Amanda pulled her hand back and pushed it into her own pajamas. She closed her eyes and pretended it was Vera. If her girlfriend heard her gasping, she didn't show it.

She couldn't reach release. Sometime during her caressing herself, Jusztin laid back between them, his presence cold and sobering.

Amanda felt she would never have an orgasm. With a sigh she pulled her hand out of her pajamas.

She turned her back on them and tried to sleep. She had a headache, maybe from the whisky, maybe from something else. She was nauseous, but when the white-dressed, red-eyed child appeared under the window and squatted down, the nausea had passed.

The little girl didn't walk after them anymore. Her legs and arms had melted to drumsticks, and she hopped forward. Whenever she saw something interesting, she stopped and sniffled it. Her hair was falling badly, and under the curly locks she was downy like a newborn baby or a chick. Amanda felt sorry for her but didn't know what to do. When she tried to caress the child, her hand passed through her, and she couldn't bear the reproachful gaze the girl cast at her.

"What's the matter? You look upset," said Vera.

"Do you know that Panna dies this way? If you leave?"

"Aren't you too old for an imaginary daughter?" asked Vera.

They walked on the Balaton beach among the other people enjoying their holidays. Amanda would have stopped at the corncob seller, but her girlfriend hurried on. She walked with quick, jerking steps as if something drew her.

"*Our* imaginary daughter," emphasized Amanda.

"Whatever."

They walked a step away from each other. They never held hands, not even before, because of the strange stares they got, but now Amanda longed for it more than ever. Just to show the world. She had enough of love confined between walls.

Pink-skinned people buzzed around them, wearing ice cream-colored clothes, holding fashion-colored ice creams. Not far away on the lawn, vividly painted wagons stood. The crowd pressed close around them. Poles speared the sky.

"Hey!" Amanda stopped. "Aren't they ...?"

"What?"

Vera stopped and turned around. Her face was red. She smiled, but her smile never reached her eyes. "The circus came this way, is it okay if I say hello?"

Amanda opened her mouth, closed it, then shouted at Vera.

"Do you believe that, if you pretend we don't have a problem, you won't be a stupid bitch?"

People stopped for a moment around them, then started walking again. None of their business. Vera paled, turned around, and ran towards the half-erected circus tent.

Amanda bit her lip and looked around. The child disappeared.

In the end she followed Vera. She knew her; she would calm down, forgive, and smile—almost like letting her close—even though she was the most distant in those moments.

The frame of the circus tent was already erect, the dirty, blue-yellow tarp was half-pulled over it like a coat. Fat women in heavy makeup shepherded the children away, worried they would be hit if something fell, like a tilting pole. The tarp was rolled back from the cages; scraggy bears, ostriches, and monkeys watched the humans with bored eyes.

Amanda saw neither Vera's curly blonde hair nor Jusztin's red head. She was lost among the spectators, but in the end she was swept towards the cages together with the children. Rancid bear stink wrung her nose, ostriches clacked their beaks. Jusztin's ghost watched her from the eyes of the gum-chewing monkeys and swam in and out of the animals' ears.

You don't deceive me, Amanda thought. I see you. I know you are watching.

The attention upset her. Jusztin's ghost had no business here, he was with Vera, so why was he watching *her*?

In front of the rabbit cage, a big, white, and fluffy dog stood on his hind legs with his paws on the wire mesh. When Amanda turned, she saw it was the little girl. The child waved her stubby arm, then plopped down on the ground. She was melting disturbingly fast.

Soon there will be nothing left, thought Amanda, watching the girl reproachfully. You should try to stay. At least fight a little!

The ghost of the girl sat down in front of the rabbit cage and licked her white hand. She either didn't hear Amanda or was not interested.

"Tintin says once he tried to magick himself from one end of the ring to the other."

"The ring is circular, it has no ends."

"Stop nit-picking." Vera gazed down at the half-peeled potato in her hand. She didn't look angry. "So he attempted it, and part of him teleported; but the rest stayed where it was. He said he doesn't mind it because it was his faults that went forward." She giggled.

Amanda stared at her.

"Is this a joke?"

"Yes. Just imagine, he can make jokes!" Vera raised her voice and looked at Amanda for the first time. "Would you bring the carrots from the car?"

Amanda shrugged and left the house. As she was walking through the garden towards the car, she was followed by the hopping girl on one side and by Jusztin's ghost on the other. She looked at neither of them, just opened the trunk, grabbed the bag, and hurried back. They followed in silence. When she stopped, they stopped, too. They touched her a little as if they needed to feel her.

She took the bag inside, grabbed a knife, and started to clean the garlic.

"Do you remember last year when we were here and your bra snapped on the beach?" asked Vera. She seemed to carry a conversation that didn't include Amanda; perhaps she started it when her friend went out for the grocery.

"Of course. You covered my tits until I refastened it," said Amanda gruffly. Her throat was dry. When was the last time Vera touched her breasts?

"Sorry," said Vera. "It's just ..."

"I cannot do magic."

"I'm not saying ..."

"And I won't. I don't think it's fair."

A small pause.

"If you ask me, he cannot do magic either. Magicians are just quick, you know? Very quick," said Vera.

"I wouldn't know about that."

They were silent. Strange, Amanda thought, we seem to do the most talking when we are not speaking.

"Why so much garlic?"

"To eat it."

Vera stared as Amanda popped the first three cloves into her mouth and forced herself to chew them. Vera grimaced.

"You want to sleep in the same bed as me smelling like that?"

"Why would we sleep in the same bed?" asked Amanda. "You won't eat me out, anyway." She flung the knife on the table and ran out. The garlic stung her tongue, but she forced it down.

The ghosts were standing beside a shrub. Jusztin looked almost like himself, although transparent. The girl sat at his feet, white and shapeless. Only her eyes sparkled red and familiar. Amanda walked to them and breathed at them.

Their shapes blurred and hollowed, their pose faltered.

Amanda opened her mouth, breathing in and out. In and out. The smell of garlic enveloped her, and the ghosts retreated a step.

Good.

She was not sure it was the garlic that made them fade or her will, and she didn't know whether they would be back or not; but she didn't really care.

She stood and breathed garlic until the girl and Jusztin disappeared, then went back into the kitchen and flushed Vera with thick garlic stench.

"Silly," said Vera.

"I am blowing Jusztin out of you."

"You wish."

"I love you," said Amanda.

Vera made no answer. After a while she said: "Brush your teeth." She turned away indifferently, but Amanda heard from her voice that she wouldn't kiss her even if she did brush her teeth.

They were not the only adults in the circus tent without children—this was Lake Balaton, nothing was considered embarrassing here—but they were the only lesbian couple.

The only ex-lesbian couple, thought Amanda.

"We are ex-bians," she told Vera.

Her girlfriend laughed politely.

"Tintin says there are no real lesbians. Only women who haven't met him yet."

Amanda didn't laugh.

"Tintin has to have an opinion of everything."

Vera shrugged.

The auditorium darkened, and the purple-coated ringmaster walked forward in a circle of light to announce the program. The children shouted, their parents whispered in their ears to shut up and listen, soon the bears would come.

What am I doing here, Amanda asked herself, but couldn't find an answer. Even Vera upset her. She looked around to see the little girl among the babbling, beaming children, but couldn't tell them apart in the semidarkness. She is not here. Amanda hadn't seen her since the afternoon when she breathed garlic on her. Did she banish her together with Jusztin? Did that really work?

She felt slightly sorry.

In the ring bears circled on unicycles. Their acrid stench mixed with the smell of popcorn and floss candy. The tent was stuffy and noisy; the racket and the lack of air made Amanda's head throb.

Vera almost slipped from the seat as she leaned forward. Thanks to Jusztin's tickets they were sitting at the edge of the ring, and every time the bears passed in front of them, driven by the whip of their handler, the stink overwhelmed them. The wheels stirred up dust, and one of the bears sneezed. It sounded almost human.

After the bears, came the strongman.

The children chattered during his performance and demanded more animals. Amanda stared at the slowly flexing, oiled muscles and watched herself intently to see if the sight of the man made her skin tingle. She was not surprised by the lack of reaction and glanced enviously at Vera. If they both had their men, she a strongman, her girlfriend a magician, perhaps they wouldn't need to part. At night, when the men were sleeping, they could sneak into a shared bed.

The strongman was followed by a pair of nicely trimmed poodles that rolled around on red balls and jumped through hoops. Their handler—a fat, blonde woman—shrieked her commands and bowed after each trick, her breasts straining against her dress. The men whistled.

Then came Jusztin. He wore a black tailcoat and a top hat. Wrinkles lined his long horseface as he raised his wand and waved it. White doves flew out of his sleeves, then circled and disappeared under the tent as if the canvas had been as high as the sky. Amanda had a feeling the tentpole was higher than the moon. She didn't see the far wall.

She watched Jusztin, and he watched her. First, Amanda thought he was looking at Vera, but the small, deep eyes locked at her. It was a familiar gaze, the ghost had watched her like this before she blew him into oblivion.

The doves were followed by paper flowers and scarves; objects were raining from Jusztin's ears and mouth. Vera clapped her hands enthusiastically, her palms were already red. Amanda hugged herself and watched Jusztin sternly.

You won't enchant me. Using magic is not fair.

The magician played just for them. The children cried in awe when suddenly fish appeared in an aquarium and then jumped into the air and disappeared again.

Jusztin bowed and took off his hat. His red hair was ruffled, and his ears were sticking out on either side. He glanced up, nodded, then hit his hat with the wand, and stepped to the edge of the ring.

The children behind Amanda and Vera stretched toward Jusztin and cried: "Me! Me! I want to!"

Jusztin paid them no heed and presented the hat to Vera. Amanda glanced at her girlfriend: her face was red, and her smile was cruel to see. Vera gingerly reached into the hat and pulled out a white rabbit.

The audience roared with delight. Jusztin stepped back with a satisfied smile.

Amanda was staring at the rabbit. She knew it. The red eyes of the bunny locked at her, and her ears twitched when Vera lifted it up for others to see. Its downy fur was almost like a real rabbit's, but Amanda saw that here and there curly, blonde hairs were sticking to it and that it was smeared with chocolate.

She looked back at Jusztin, who received the applause with arms opened wide, then gestured, and two assistants pulled a long, wheeled crate to the center. Red stars sparkled on its blue velvet cover and the swords, laid down on top in a star, shone brightly.

Jusztin raised his hand.

"And now, for the next trick, I would like to have a volunteer!'

Vera jumped up with the rabbit in her hands.

"Me!"

"Me! Me!" cried the children.

Jusztin turned around, looking for someone who would fit the decorated crate most perfectly. Amanda knew he had already chosen, he just turned around to key up the expectation.

I see through you like an X-ray.

She thought Jusztin would choose Vera, but the long finger pointed at her. From the magician's eyes, the ghost was looking back at her.

She felt strangely relieved. She calmly rose and stepped onto the ring with ease. Amid the applause she walked to Jusztin.

"I know you are cheating," she told him, then hopped on the wheeled platform of the crate and handed the swords to Jusztin. The assistants opened the crate. The walls of the circus tent flew away. Amanda didn't recognize Vera's face among the white dots. Maybe she wouldn't have found her even if she had gone back now.

With a calculated movement she lay down into the crate. She couldn't do anything else anyway. Jusztin showed the audience the swords.

When the lid closed, Amanda thought that, with a little bit of luck, she could turn into a rabbit as well. A humanoid bunny like Vera. Then perhaps she could also forget everything except grass and carrots.

The drums boomed louder, then stopped altogether. This is already the trick, she thought and laced her fingers. She held back her breath and waited in the dark of the crate for something to happen.

Anything at all.

A Different Mistake

Eve Shi

One morning my husband would wake up to find me gone along with my wings. Already I could hear him calling my name, the empty bedroom swallowing his voice. Then galvanized, he would fling the wardrobe doors open. His hand reached for the caramel-colored gift box behind his socks where he'd kept the iridescent shawl. *Have you known all along it is there, Wulan?* Dropping the box to the floor, he straightened up. His gaze strayed to the bedhead as if he expected to see the shawl draped over it. *Why do you have to leave? Have I been unkind to you?*

And yet it had never been about him. It was all about soaring to the sky, the shawl a gossamer weight across my shoulders. The air was murkier now than it was a hundred years ago, but I would always take joy in flight. My sisters and I loved nothing more than the wind in our hair, the kiss of water on our warm skin.

Once, a human stole my shawl, forcing me to stay on earth with him. During those years, I dreamed of treetops, of flying in the midst of sun-showers. As soon as I discovered where he hid my shawl, I flew back to my sisters. Since then, centuries had passed, tinged with our memories of clear lakes, the soft, bobbing shapes of sampans at twilight.

Recently, out of curiosity, I searched for the shawl thief's descendants. One of them worked at the Jakarta Stock Exchange. Like his ancestor, he was persuasive, a smooth talker. And unlike him, startlingly handsome—never believe fairy tales when they tell you all the characters are good-looking.

The first time I walked into the man's life, I was a neighbor in his apartment building. We chatted, went to cafes together, and gradually met more often. His eyes disappeared into lines when he laughed, which I found most charming. My head fitted snugly into his shoulder, and he never dismissed my shopping trips as girly or money-draining. Five months after we met, he proposed to me.

Only one of my sisters came to the wedding reception, claiming to be my sole living relative. My other sisters refused to—their exact words—play along with my antics. They believed I was about to hurt an innocent person.

Are you familiar with the names Jaka Tarub and Nawangwulan? I asked the man a day later.

He shrugged. Outside, it was another humid Jakarta night with the promise of rain hovering behind dark clouds. Soon enough, the humidity would give way to thunderstorms and seasonal floods.

They're people from a legend, he said.

Well, I said, *congratulations, you've just married a legend.*

My shawl wrapped around my arms, I smiled at him and floated above the floor. His face went ashy, and for a moment I thought he would bolt. As I explained, his color improved but not by much.

It took him three full days to recover. On the first day he skipped work, pleading high fever. I sat next to him as we watched TV until he no longer stiffened when I leaned against him. Neither of us ever mentioned who I was again.

A month into our marriage, my shawl went missing. I wasn't too bothered; it had a scent I could easily track down. What did concern me was the fact that my husband felt any need to hide it.

Of course he does, huffed Nawangsari, my sister who came to the wedding. *You can literally fly away from him! Any human would be worried!*

Contrary to what you girls think, I replied, *I'm not toying with his feelings. I'm giving him a new perspective. The relationships he'll have after I'm gone will be much more meaningful because he'd work hard to make them last. And he'd make sure the other person is not another immortal.*

Nawangsari rapped her knuckles against her forehead. *Wulan, you are unbelievably dense! He's more likely to become sad and blame himself. Even if he wouldn't, you've no right to do this. What's the reason, anyway? Revenge?*

Later, sipping chilled tea from the fridge, I mulled over the word. The shawl thief had lived so long ago that, in my mind, his face had thawed into a haze. His thievery no longer irritated me; I had no intention to hurt anyone he was related to. But perhaps my sisters were right, and I was doing exactly that.

I agreed to marry my husband because he was wonderful company. I enjoyed having him to share meals and sing at the karaoke with. Still, even if he were no longer here, I'd be able to go on. But what if it was me who went away? Would he be devastated—or enraged and take refuge in his rage, call me names, and forget the good times we had?

Both possibilities were unsavory, so I left before his feelings could take root. *Or,* Nawangsari said, *before he decides you're dangerous. Then he may do something foolish like tell someone else or call an exorcist. We don't want that, Wulan. Let humans think that women like us are extinct.*

It was all right; he would do just fine. He was too strong to get crushed by my departure. And he shouldn't suffer for long from my attraction to him—which wouldn't have existed had it not been for his ancestor. But just to be on the safe side, some nights I'd hover outside his window; if only to check that he was content, safe, and hopefully had found a new love.

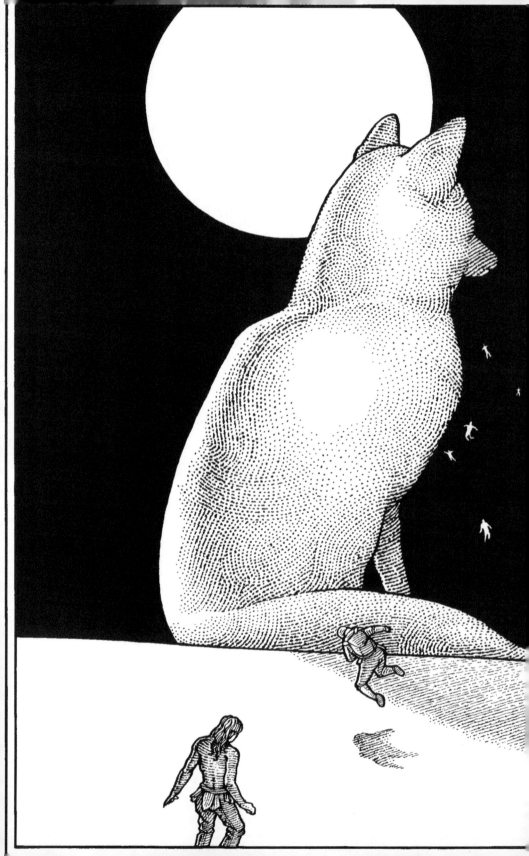

Lost Bonds

Margrét Helgadóttir

"When the animals disappeared, man lost his wisdom," said the old man. "Man has always had a bond with animals. We have either hunted each other or we have shared food and fire. The old people even claimed that certain men and animals shared souls." He looked down at the boy, Simik, who sat next to him, quiet and attentive. The elderly man nodded to himself. The boy was intelligent. The bright eyes that looked up at him now, brimming with impatient questions, told him so.

"Uncle. What do you mean? We lost our wisdom?" Simik asked. Strands of black hair kept falling into his eyes, and he tugged it away, impatient.

"The old people claimed that animals were our third eye, our guide," the old man answered. "They said that men needed the animals to lead them in the right direction and protect them against dangers, but ..." he paused, scrutinizing the boy's face. "They also said that wise men, the healers, needed the animals and their spirits to guide them into other worlds in their quest for truth."

"I don't understand," Simik said, frowning. The old man smiled to himself. Simik never interrupted him, and his dark eyes shone with respect; but there was also an unmistakable air of command and strength about the boy. He demanded answers. He was a leader, this one.

"I am not sure I can explain to you all the ways of the old people," the old man said. "All I know is that when the animals disappeared, not only were men left alone and unprotected, but the wise men could no longer help people." He stared into the distance, his weather-beaten face sad. "We know that people from the South make animals now as if they were gods." The old man shook his head. "I fear these animals have no souls, Simik. If they have no souls, they cannot lead us. They cannot protect us. I hope this is not the truth. I hope that the bond is still there."

• • •

The night frost covered the ground. The dark season was near, Simik thought. He sat with his back against a rock and tried to keep himself awake, but his head kept falling to his chest. Eight men lay under thin blankets around the fire, their black army boots peeping out. They'd found shelter between some large rocks, but even here the constant strong wind made the smoke from the fire dance in all directions before it drifted away. They were using the last firestones tonight. Tomorrow, they would not be able to make fire. The land around them was nothing but sand and rocks with a few tufts of grass here and there. They'd tried to burn the grass, but it refused to light. They had to locate the mine tomorrow, he thought, tired. If only he knew where it was. His instincts told him that something was not right, that they should have found it by now.

Simik cast a glance towards their supplies. They still had food left, he thought. They could go on a bit longer even in the cold, but if they did not find the mine within the next few days, they would have to turn back. He creased his forehead. *Could the maps be wrong?* After the great ice melted and never returned, he knew it had taken a while to map the land that appeared in its place, but he'd thought the maps would be accurate by now so many years later. After all, he thought bitterly, the people from the South had been so eager to exploit the new land. Their scientists had discovered new metals hidden deep underground where the ice had been. The Southern speculators had excavated mines all over the land and taken all the profits.

He checked the explosives that filled the rucksack next to him. *Still intact.* He sighed with relief. *It would have been horrible to find the mine after this long trek and then be unable to follow the orders to destroy it.*

An unfamiliar noise came from behind the rocks. Simik froze. He squinted, not able to see much in the meagre light from the fire. But something was moving in the shadows, no doubt about it, and scratching the frosty ground. Moving slowly, Simik took up his rifle and pointed the muzzle in the direction of the sounds, but he didn't stand up. Not yet. The other soldiers lay in deep sleep.

Two pointed ears popped up from behind one of the rocks, followed by a small, heart-shaped face. Yellow eyes studied him, curious.

"What are you?" he whispered. It couldn't be real. "Am I dreaming?"

As if the creature had understood what he said, it trotted out from the rock and stopped in front of the fire. A small body covered in grey-brown fur with four long legs and a large bushy tail. It stood still, its body trembling a little, and watched the sleeping men, the fire, him. The eyes glinted golden in the firelight. Simik lowered his rifle slowly and put it on the ground.

"I have seen pictures of you," he murmured, not wanting to scare it or wake up the men. "You are what they used to call a fox." He gazed at the animal in amazement. It was beautiful. He'd never seen an animal before, only a few guard dogs, but they had been made by humans. "You are not supposed to exist."

The fox seemed strangely comfortable around the soldiers and lay down, curling its thick tail around its small body and burying its nose in its fur. "You don't seem to be afraid of us at all. It's as if you are used to humans." Simik narrowed his eyes. "Who made you? What laboratory hatched you? Have they sent you to spy on us?"

He grabbed the rifle again, alert. The fox raised its head and looked at him. Then it burrowed its face once more in its tail as if to say: what a stupid human, let's ignore it. The wind ruffled its fur. Simik gasped at the sight of it. His men were still deep in sleep. One of them murmured and tossed a bit but soon became quiet again. Simik relaxed. He couldn't see any immediate threat, but he'd find out where the fox came from when it was daylight. Maybe it meant that the mine was nearby? He brightened up a bit at the thought.

He woke up to someone kicking his boots. "I say. Some guard, eh. I feel so safe," one of his men teased.

"Sorry." Simik rubbed his eyes and stood. The fire was reduced to a few glowing embers. At least they could boil a pot of soup before they started walking, he thought. The last warm thing they'd eat for a while. He looked around. "Where is it?"

"What, boss?"

"The fox. The animal that came last night."

His men looked at him, incredulous. Then one of them burst into laughter. "You almost got us there, boss. An animal, he says."

The other soldiers joined in, and their booming mirth echoed between the rocks, almost blocking out the roar of the wind. Simik laughed with them. Must have been a dream, he told himself. He surely needed sleep and some decent food soon.

When they'd eaten breakfast and packed up their gear, the men looked at Simik expectantly. "So. Which way, boss?"

He looked at them, thoughtful, but didn't answer at once. They shifted their feet, restless and eager to start moving, to get the cold stiffness out of their bodies. That's when Simik saw it again. The fox. That is, he saw its thick tail waving from behind some rocks in the distance. It appeared and disappeared in the spaces between the boulders as the fox trotted amongst them, heading towards a mountain on the other side of the plains. Simik pointed in the same direction.

"We're going that way," he said and set out, his men trailing behind him, not uttering a word. He knew they would follow his orders without questions. They probably trusted him more than he trusted himself, he thought. He wondered what they'd say if they knew that he was following an animal, that he was following some strange instinct.

All day, the soldiers walked over the plain, struggling against the strong wind. The rocks slowed them down, forcing them to pay close attention to where they put their feet. Simik had more than once wished they were allowed to use their four-wheeled sail rovers. With their solid tyres and advanced sail technology, the rovers were so useful in high winds and on rough terrain like this.

But their commander had forbidden it. *It will raise suspicions,* he'd said. *Better to be able to hide quickly if they come flying in their planes. Better to arrive unseen, strike before they know what happens.* Simik agreed. It was wiser that they were on foot, but it would have been a huge help to have the sails take advantage of the winds. Faster, too. But then again, they'd probably not be that much of a help amongst all these rocks. He sighed.

The sun hung over them, but it was not warm. Simik kept his eyes on the fox. It stopped now and then and turned towards them. He couldn't see it clearly, but it seemed to wait for them to catch up. When they had to rest, he clearly saw it lay down on the ground in the distance. His men seemed not to see it. Not even when he pointed in its direction and they followed his gaze to see what he pointed at. How odd. Maybe he was indeed starting to hallucinate, he reflected.

"Our third eye," he murmured.

"What, boss?" asked one of his men.

"The lost bond," he answered, gazing at the fox. He smiled. "Sorry, I guess I'm tired." The soldiers returned the smile, but he saw them glancing at each other.

They reached the mountain late in the afternoon. The sun still lingered on the horizon, but at this time of the year, it would soon be gone. Simik studied the mountain. It was not as steep as it had looked from a distance, but it would be difficult to climb. He frowned. He had a feeling that there was something he wasn't seeing. Was this where the mine lay?

His men stood awaiting his orders. They look tired, Simik thought. Tired of the fighting, the sabotages, of hiding, being hungry, and never getting enough sleep. They called themselves the freedom fighters. A few of them were from the old people, like him. Their dark eyes twinkled in the afternoon sun. The others were from the South but descended from the old families who had settled on this land first. But it didn't matter where they came from, Simik reminded himself. They were privileged but born in this land and looked at themselves as natives. They were all angry.

"We will go around this mountain," Simik said. "The entrance to the mine must be on the other side. We'll rest when we get closer."

The men groaned but picked up their gear and followed him. Simik suddenly saw the fox again, ahead of them. He wondered where it came from and why his men couldn't see it. The fox seemed so certain about where it was heading. Like it was going home to its den, Simik thought. And maybe it was leading them home. Maybe this was a trap. He couldn't help but be suspicious. He looked around, but there was nothing to be seen in the vast landscape. Only his men and the animal.

It took less time than he expected to walk around the mountain, but it was dark when they reached the other side. They set up camp behind some large rocks. One of his men offered to take guard duty. Simik fell asleep quickly, despite the cold. He was exhausted. The last thing he saw before he closed his eyes was the fox, lying between two rocks.

In the grey morning light, they saw the gap in the mountain side. The entrance to the mine. It appeared to be empty. Though they saw no one, the soldiers didn't take any risks. They crawled closer, wary, gripping their rifles. When they were close to the opening, Simik raised a hand, silent, ordering his men to be still. He studied the opening. Still no sign of anyone. But he saw the fox run in. He glanced at his men, but it seemed they hadn't seen it. Still silent, he made some hand signals, and the soldiers nodded. They'd done this before. A few of them remained outside, hiding amongst the rocks, keeping guard while Simik and the others jogged into the mine. Inside, they separated and moved swiftly in different directions. Huge bulbs hanging from the ceiling gave off a yellow glare. Spotting several doors at the end of the passageway, Simik and his men moved towards them quickly to investigate.

One massive door revealed a dark tunnel. The mine. They couldn't see the end of it. It probably went deep into the mountain. The other doors were either locked or opened to empty rooms. The whole place seemed abandoned. Simik frowned. How odd. In one of the rooms they found an instrument panel. Hurrying, they stuck some of the explosives under it and scattered several more around the place but mostly around the door to the mine.

Simik looked at his men. They all shook their heads. They had not found any people. Simik didn't mind. He didn't like to threaten or kill people. But he thought it was strange that they'd left the mine unguarded. Especially when the freedom fighters had destroyed so many mines in the last few months.

In the far end of a corridor, he saw the fox. It stood still, its muscles trembling, watching him. As soon as he looked at it, it trotted through a door. He followed and peeked into the room. A laboratory, he thought. The room was crammed with work benches, several large boxes against a wall, and cages on the floor. The cages were all empty except for one. Simik bent down and froze. On the floor inside the cage, he saw a fox. It lay on its side, not moving, its yellow eyes open and blank. Dead.

"Was this you?" he whispered. "Was this what you wanted me to see?" His hands shook. He saw no sign of the fox that he'd been following for several days now.

He took up the last of the explosives. In the distance he heard shouting and shots. Alarmed, he ran out to the corridors. A few of his soldiers came running towards him.

"What do we do, boss?" they shouted. "It was an ambush." Simik saw the smoke billowing from the entrance and a wall of government soldiers.

"What about the others?" he shouted back, but he knew before they answered: they were dead. He searched the area with his eyes. There had to be an escape, an emergency exit, somewhere they could run out. *We can't possibly fight back. Not enough of us left for that now. And we haven't even lit the explosives yet.* Simik sighed. *I mustn't fail my orders.* He dipped his head.

From the corner of his eye, he saw movement; the fox again. It entered the tunnel, heading into the mine. Without thinking, Simik yelled to the others: "Run down to the mine. There will be an emergency exit somewhere down there. I will stay behind to light the explosives." They stared at him, but when he shouted "go, go, go!" they obeyed. Simik hurried to light all the fuses. The government soldiers came running towards him as he lit the ones at the entrance to the dark tunnel. Not looking back, he ran down into the mine. He heard the explosions echoing strangely inside the mountain and the tunnel. Then all became silent.

"Boss?" Something nudged him in his side. "Boss, are you okay?" A sudden glare blinded him.

Simik groaned, pushed the torch away, and stood, feeling bruised and stiff. "Yes, I'm fine. Is everyone okay?"

"Yes, we are all here." Then after a while: "The four of us who made it into the tunnel are still here."

Simik nodded in the dark. "Give me the torch," he said.

The tunnel stretched into the distance, and he could see that more passageways branched off it at several points. The people from the South had been busy, he thought. He scanned the area around them, searching for the fox. Had it vanished during the explosions? There! Two bright eyes stared back at him from far down the tunnel, shining in the beam from his light. Simik sighed in relief. He had a strange gut feeling that he should follow the animal. Or was it a spirit or a ghost? He wasn't sure what it was. But somehow he trusted it to help them.

"Follow me," he said. "I believe we will find an exit in this direction."

They walked in the dark for what seemed like ages. Simik lost track of the time. No one talked. The only sounds were their heavy breathing and shuffling feet. Simik felt encapsulated in darkness and fought to keep the panic away. He'd never been fond of being underground or locked up in narrow places. He craved a view of vast open plains and the sting of cold wind filling his lungs. Concentrating on his breathing, he kept his torch pointed in the direction of the fox. It stopped now and then to wait for them. Simik felt confused. They'd turned many times into numerous different passageways. Sometimes, the ceiling was so low they had to crawl. These tunnels must be very old, he reflected. Maybe not even made by humans.

At last, just when he thought the panic was about to swallow him and he wanted to scream from fatigue, he heard one of his soldiers shouting, his voice echoing through the tunnels: "Look!" And in the distance, he saw light. Not sun, because the sun had to be down now, Simik thought, squinting. *But it does look like daylight.* Had they walked for that long? Eagerly, he moved faster. As they came closer, they saw that the light came from a hole in the ceiling. It took them a while to climb up, but finally they stood in the open, drawing in fresh air. Simik looked around. They stood in the middle of the plains. He could see the mountain, but it was far away. Wisps of smoke rose from it. Over them, northern lights swept the sky. So that's why it was so bright. The soldiers marvelled at the display, their ash-smudged faces upturned.

The fox stood quietly watching them. Its fur rippled in the wind. Beautiful, Simik thought in amazement. He felt a curious connection to the animal, a deep respect. Whatever the animal was, whether it was real or not, he felt grateful towards it.

"Thank you."

He blinked. The fox was gone. Something told him that he would not see it again. His men shouted and slapped each other's backs, hugging each other, tears in their eyes.

Simik thought of the fox. His tears glistened as he gazed at the northern lights that danced green across the sky.

"Uncle, you were wrong," he whispered. "The bond is still here."

The Bones Shine through with Light

Joyce Chng

Children go to bed with the stories of the tiger demoness who eats knuckle bones like peanuts, huddling under our blankets while images of bones being crushed by huge fangs spin in our frightened minds.

The tiger demoness prowls in the shadows, a feline shadow in pools of darkness. In her human form, she is an old lady, kindly, if you don't really look too closely at her eyes. Her amber, cold eyes. She often offers her services as a nanny to tired farmer parents. Once the deal is done, the fate of the children is sealed. While the parents work tirelessly at the rice fields, the tiger lady comes and feasts on the soft plumb flesh of her charges. She keeps the knuckle bones, stores them up, and eats them later.

Kerunch, kerunch, kerunch, the storyteller will always embellish the story with awful sounds. *Kerunch*. Because the tiger demoness relishes the taste, the texture. *Kerunch*.

Word came about the appearance of a strange old lady. She just turned up along the edges of Wulong village, a long figure in rags. She found residence in an abandoned rice shack. People said that they could see smoke rising forth from a hidden fire. They said that they heard strange noises from the rice shack.

Tiger demoness, they whispered in the tea houses. *Tiger demoness*, they whispered in the bustling marketplace where the dumplings steamed and candied hawthorn enticed little children.

Parents shooed their children into the safety of their houses and bade them never to wander near the demoness's rice shack.

• • •

I find myself wandering too closely to the tiger demoness's hut, my feet crunching too loudly on the fallen mulberry leaves. Late in autumn, there is a chill in the air.

I smell fire, the comforting aroma of burning wood. I also smell meat. Barbecued meat like Old Gao's famous and mouth-watering roasted duck. I peer right through the rushes, feeling my stomach grumble with hunger. The weather turns cold, winter approaches, and I grow hungry often.

Bones. A lot of bones. Hanging in clusters. Whole skeletons, all grotesque, like miniature gwei. Ghosts. The light piercing through the roof shines through the bones, making them glow. The sight is oddly beautiful.

"The bones tell me I have a visitor!"

The *voice*. Like a thunderclap, like a gentle grandmotherly caress.

I cry out in terror and scramble for my life. My heart drums like a mad festival gong.

The strange old lady was odd in her ways. *She sang to bones*, they said, secretly in their huts during the dark of night. *She sang to bones, and they danced like puppets during Spring Festival shows.*

Ach! Afterwards, she eats them! Women muttered amongst themselves when they met at the local well. *Tiger demoness! Eater of bones! Feh, feh, feh!*

I am creeping towards the old rice shack once more, thrilling and delicious danger coursing in my body. I want to know more about the old lady. I want to know about the bones alit with light. It is colder now, winter definitely closer. In the village they are selling hot spicy dumplings that warm the body when eaten hot. The rice is now harvested. Very soon, it will be Winter Solstice.

Fire, and the smell-taste of barbecued meat in the air. There is singing like the lullaby Mother uses to rock my little brother to sleep. It sounds so sad, so poignant.

I poke a tentative finger through the brittle rush.

She is stripping meat off bones. Cooking meat sizzles on hot coals. I watch her fingers, so gnarled and delicate, peel off the meat in red ribbons. And for a horrible moment, I know that she is going to eat the bones. Like peanuts or pumpkin seeds. *Kerunch. Kerunch. Kerunch.*

I continue to watch. The meat is making me salivate.

She is done with the bones now, carefully arranging them on the floor. Her expression.

Concentration, as if she is reading. Her eyes are closed. Her mouth moves.

A *cluck-cluck-cluck* almost scares me half to death. I look at the rooster strutting in front of me, all colorful feathers and brilliantly red floppy comb.

Would he end up being her dinner?

Lee Jian and his farmer cronies complained loudly about their missing chicken and ducks. This late in autumn with the first frost on the ground. They needed the meat and the eggs, the latter to make salted eggs to sell in the markets and feed their families. Their families were always hungry.

Meanwhile, everyone prepared for winter. Mothers brought out the thick winter clothing and mended old garments. The village would soon become silent, covered with snow.

Children listened to the stories of tigress demonesses feasting on knuckle bones and felt hungry-sad-scared. They slept fitfully as the snow began to fall in flurries of white.

Wrapped in thick fleece, I struggle towards the rice shack. There is the smell of fire and the tantalizing aroma of roasting meat. My stomach growls.

When I peek in, she is hanging bones. They swing slightly, stirred by some invisible breeze. They are white, the color of snow. Tiny gwei. Tiny ghosts bereft of feathers and skin. She lifts one bone up, a tiny bone the size of my finger, and gazes at it. The fire in the rice shackle crackles, casting jittery shadows on the rush walls. More bones, more skeletons: birds.

Don't eat the bones, don't eat the bones, I think, remembering, shivering, my skin chapped by the cold. I am hungry. Always hungry.

"I know you are outside, little girl," the old woman turns around, and her smile is warm like the fire. "Come in, come in."

Tiger demoness!

Trapped, I have no way to go. I duck into ... a fragrant warmth, redolent of the best food I have eaten. The fire is so inviting ...

The bones. The bones. *The bones.*

"Come, eat," the old woman gestures with a wrinkled hand,

placing a stick of freshly roasted meat into my numb hand. I sniff at it. Chicken. I take one tentative bite. Soon I am taking larger and large bites, chewing and swallowing. The juice is so sweet! I lick my fingers, hungry for more.

"Never easy being an old woman thrown out by an unfilial son," the old woman says, sitting down wearily. I wince, listening to her knees creak alarmingly. "And food is so scarce these days.

"I take what I can," she continues, sipping something from a chipped porcelain cup. I realize most of the things she has in the rice shackles are discards. She must have salvaged the cups and the plates. Here a bowl of old dumplings. There a plate of moldy-looking meat buns. And the bones. Too many bones.

She hands me another stick of meat. I eat more slowly now, intrigued by her words. Her eyes are not amber. They are a faded brown.

"You must be wondering about the bones," the old woman smiles, her teeth showing gaps. Yet her smile is genuine. A grandmother's smile.

"I collect bones. I read bones. You know, a bone soothsayer. The clod of a son thinks I am dabbling with evil jin and dark magic. But it runs in my family, bone reading is. I know how old a thing is by looking at a bone. If you shine light through it, it glows."

Tiger demoness!

Frightened, I dare not say anything.

"You like to observe things, don't you, little one?"

I nod slowly, wonderingly. *How did she know? Did the bones tell her?*

"There is nothing to eat here," the old woman sighs. "I make do with what I have. Even the marrow inside the bones." In her hand rests a mortar stone round with years of repeated use. She takes one chicken bone. *Kerunch.* "Try it. It's food. Nourishment. Eat." *Kerunch.*

I stare at the smashed splinters, at the dark red marrow oozing out like red bean paste. She watches me, the old lady, the tiger demoness in disguise.

The marrow tastes mealy and bloody. But so rich it fills my mouth and wakes my senses. *So rich.* I eat some more, grateful for the nourishment. *So rich and delicious.*

When spring arrived with the festive sounds of the Lunar New Year, the old lady was gone. *Disappeared,* said the men in the tea houses. *Like magic. Like a jin.* The rice shack became just an empty hut bereft of fire and life. She took everything.

Their chicken and ducks came back, too. The farmers found their coops and backyards filled with healthy clucking fowl.

With the promise of fresh eggs and steamed chicken on New Year tables, thoughts of tiger demonesses and bone knuckles faded away like the soft footsteps of an old lady travelling down the melting snow.

She has taught me so many things. Bones. The stripping of bones. The reading of bones. The light shining through bones. She has taught me many secret things, things passed down from mother to daughter in her family. The bloodline ended with the birth of her son. She was getting old. She wanted to teach me.

I wanted to learn.

She has also taught me the filling of bones. Her little rice shack suddenly filled with birds. The fluttering of feathers, the noises of pecking, of strutting. The bones given life, flesh.

It was a mystery.

When I grew older, I began to collect bones, too. I gazed at the bones, the candlelight turning the white translucent. They whispered to me about secret lives. Mysteries.

I know that when winter arrives, I would have nourishment and life.

Ana's Tag

William Alexander

Ana and Rico walked on the very edge of the road where the pavement slumped and crumbled. They were on their way to buy sodas, and there were no sidewalks. They made it as far as the spot where the old meat-packing factory had burned down when Deputy Chad drove up and coasted his car alongside at a walking pace.

Ana was just tall enough to see the deputy through his car window and the empty space of the passenger seat. Her brother, Rico, was taller, but he wasn't trying to look through the car window. Rico was staring straight ahead of him.

"Hi, kids," said Deputy Chad.

"Hi," said Ana.

"I need to ask you both about the incident at the school," the deputy said.

"Okay," said Ana when Rico didn't say anything.

"It's very important," the deputy said. "This is the first sign of gang activity. Everyone knows that. *Gang activity.*" He tried to arch one eyebrow; but it didn't really work, and his forehead scrunched.

Other cars slowed to line up behind the squad car, coasting along.

"What's the second sign?" Ana asked.

"The *second* sign," said Deputy Chad, taking a deep breath, "happens at night on the highway. It involves headlights. Do you know that keeping your high beams on at night can blind oncoming traffic?"

Ana didn't. She nodded anyway.

"Usually a driver has just forgotten to turn them off, and the way to let them know is to flash your own high beams, just briefly. But *they* drive around with the high beams on *deliberately.* If you flash at one of *their* cars, they pull a quick and violent U-turn and follow you, very close. Sometimes they just do it to see where you live. Sometimes they run you off the road. Bam!" He smacked the top of his steering wheel.

Ana jumped. He grinned at her, and she grinned back.

"What's the third sign?" Rico asked, without grinning.

"I can't tell you that," said Deputy Chad. "Ask your parents. It is the last ceremony of initiation, and it involves blonde ten-year-olds."

"I'm ten," said Ana.

"You're not blonde, so you're probably safe. Probably."

"Oh," said Ana. "Good."

The line behind Deputy Chad was now seven cars long, coasting slowly. None of them dared to pass a cop.

"So," said the deputy. "You can see why we need to put a stop to this kind of thing right away before it escalates. Do you know anything about the incident at school?"

"No," said Rico.

"What's the graffiti of?" asked Ana.

"It is deliberately illegible," said the deputy. "It's in code. Probably a street name. A tag. Graffiti is often somebody's tag, delineating whose turf is whose. It looks like it could be in Spanish."

Ana and Rico's parents spoke Spanish. They used it as their secret language and slipped into Spanish whisperings whenever they didn't want Ana or Rico to understand them. Sometimes in public, Ana and Rico liked to pretend they could speak it, too. They would toss together random words and gibberish and use an accent because both of them could fake a pretty good one. They hadn't played that game for a while.

Rico bent forward a little, so he could look through the passenger window. "I'll let you know if I hear anything about it," he said.

"Good boy," said the deputy, and smiled a satisfied smile. "Be safe, now." He drove off. Cars followed him like ducklings.

"Perro muerto," said Ana. It meant *dead dog,* or maybe *dead hair.* It was one of their nonsense curses. "He thinks you did it."

"Yeah," said Rico.

"Did you?" Ana asked.

"Yeah," said Rico.

"Oh. What does it say?"

"Not telling."

"Oh," said Ana. Rico pushed Ana to his right side, so he could walk between her and the moving cars, and then he made a sign with his left hand. He tried not to let Ana see him do it. She saw anyway, but she didn't ask. She cared more about the graffiti. "I'll do all the dishes if you tell me what it says."

"No."

"Okay." Ana thought about how long it would take to get to the East Wells high school, try to read the painted wall, write down all of her guesses, and walk home. She decided she could make it before dinner. Maybe Rico would tell her if she guessed right.

They were almost to the gas station, which had a much better selection of soda to pick from than the corner store. The last part of the walk was uphill, and Ana had to work harder to keep up with her brother.

"Do you think there really are gangs?" she asked.

Rico shrugged and smiled a little. "Gangs of what?"

"I don't know. Gangs."

"I doubt it," he said. "East Wells isn't big enough to put together a gang of anything bigger than two people. Deputy Chad is just really, really bored." He reached up and twisted his new earring stud. He'd pierced it himself with a sewing needle. Ana had held the swabs and rubbing alcohol while he did it. She'd felt obliged to help because she already had pierced ears, so she could offer him the benefit of her knowledge.

"Don't forget to clean that when we get home," she said.

"I won't," he said. He sounded annoyed. Ana decided to change the subject to something casual and harmless.

"Why isn't there a West Wells?" she asked.

Rico stopped walking. They were in the gas station parking lot, only a few steps away from soda and air conditioning. Ana turned around. Her brother was staring at her.

"What did you say?"

"West Wells," she said again, trying to be extra casual and harmless. "We live in East Wells, but it isn't actually east *of* anything. There's just, you know, the woods by the school and then endless fields of grain on all sides. There's no West Wells."

Rico exhaled, loudly. "That's right," he said. "There is nothing to the west of this dinky little town. You are absolutely right." He walked by her and went inside. Ana followed. She had questions, endless questions bubbling up somewhere near her stomach, and she had to swallow to keep them there because Rico was definitely not in an answering kind of mood.

She shivered in the air conditioning even though she'd been looking forward to it. Rico knew which soda he wanted, but Ana took a long time to choose.

Ana got her cat backpack from her bedroom closet. It was brown and furry and had two triangular ears sewn onto the top. She pulled a stack of library books out of it and replaced them with a flashlight, rope, chocolate-chip granola bars, Band-Aids, a notebook, and Magic Markers. She filled up the small, square canteen that had been Tio Frankie's with water and packed that, too. Then she took out the flashlight because it was summer and it didn't get dark outside until long after dinnertime and she needed to be back by dinner anyway.

"Did you clean your ear?" she asked Rico's bedroom door.

"No," he said from behind it.

"Don't forget. You don't want it to get infected."

"I won't forget," he said.

She walked to the East Wells high school, taking a shortcut through two cornfields to keep off the highway. It wasn't a long walk, but during the school year almost everybody took the bus anyway because of the highway and the lack of sidewalks. Rico liked walking, even in wintertime. Ana saw him sometimes through the bus window on her way to East Wells Elementary.

She walked between cornrows and underneath three billboards. Two of them said something about the Bible. One was an ad for a bat cave ten miles farther down the road. Ana had never seen the bat cave. Rico said it wasn't much to see, but she still wanted to go.

Ana crossed the empty parking lot in front of the high school and skirted around the athletic field to the back of the gym. She knew where to find the gym because it doubled as a theater and last summer a troupe of traveling actors had put on *The Pirates of Penzance*. After the show Ana had decided to become a traveling actor. Then she decided that what she really wanted to be was a pirate king.

A little strip of mowed lawn separated the gym from the western woods.

Three of Rico's friends were there, standing in front of the graffiti. Ana could see green paint behind them. They were smoking, of course. Julia and Nick smoked cloves, sweet-smelling. Garth wore a Marlboro Man kind of hat, so he was probably smoking that kind of cigarette. His weren't sweet-smelling.

"Hey," Ana said.

"Hey," said Julia. Ana liked Julia.

"Hey," said Nick. Nick was Julia's boyfriend. Ana was pretty sure that her brother was jealous of this. Nick and Julia were both in Rico's band, and both of them were really, really tall. They were taller than Rico and much taller than Garth.

Garth didn't say anything. He chose that moment to take a long drag on his cigarette, probably to demonstrate that he wasn't saying anything. Garth was short and stocky and scruffy. He wasn't in the band. He had a kind of beard but only in some places. He also had a new piercing in his eyebrow. It was shaped like the tusk from a very small elephant. The skin around it was red and swollen and painful-looking.

Ana thought eyebrow rings were stupid. She liked earrings, and she could understand nose rings, belly-button rings, and even pierced tongues, but metal sticking out of random facial places like eyebrows just looked to her like shrapnel from a booby-trapped jewelry box. She didn't like it. The fact that Garth's eyebrow was obviously infected proved that she was right and that the universe didn't like it either.

"You should use silver for a new piercing," Ana told him. "And you need to keep it clean."

"This *is* silver," said Garth. He didn't look at her as he said it. He looked at the tops of trees.

"Don't worry about him," said Nick. "He likes pain. He gets confused and grumpy if something doesn't hurt."

"Oh," said Ana. She edged around them, trying to get a better look at the wall and the paint.

Garth threw down his cigarette, stepped on it, and reached out to knock the cloves from Nick's and Julia's hands. "Bertha's coming," he said.

Bertha walked around the corner. She was the groundskeeper. Rico used to help her mow the school lawn as a summer job, but this year he hadn't bothered. Her name wasn't really Bertha, and Ana didn't want to ever call her that; but she didn't know what Bertha's name really was.

Bertha sniffed and smiled. Her hair was a big, feathered mullet.

"One of you isn't smoking cloves," she said. "One of you is smoking *real* cigarettes, and I am going to bet it isn't the one with the kitten backpack. One of you is gonna buy my silence. 'Why, no, officer, I sure didn't see any young hooligans smoking near your site of vandalism.'"

Ana, Nick, and Julia all looked at Garth. Garth grunted, handed over his pack of cigarettes, and walked away. He walked away into the woods.

"Bye, Ana," Julia said. "Say hi to Rico. Tell him we need to rehearse." She took Nick's arm, and the two of them followed Garth.

Ana could see the graffiti now. It was red and green, and it wasn't anything Ana knew how to decipher. Parts of it were swoofy, and other parts had sharp, edgy bits. It looked like it was made up of letters, but she wasn't sure which letters they were.

Bertha lit one of Garth's cigarettes. "Gonna have to rent a sandblaster," she said. "Won't come off without a sandblaster. And it's brick, so I can't just paint over it."

"Deputy Chad thinks it was gangs that did it," Ana said.

Bertha snorted. "Town isn't big enough for gangs," she said. "Doesn't matter, anyway. This is just somebody marking their territory. This is colored piss with artistic pretensions."

Ana took out her notebook, but she didn't have any guesses to write down yet. "How's the novel?" she asked Bertha. This was the usual thing to ask. Bertha had always been writing a novel.

"Terrible," Bertha said.

"Sorry," said Ana. She wondered if it was better to be a novelist or a traveling actor and decided it would still be better to be a pirate king.

"What's with the notebook?" Bertha asked. She flicked her cigarette butt at the graffiti, and it hit the bricks above the paint with a shower of orange sparks.

"I'm going to draw it," Ana said, "I'll take it home and figure out what it says, and then ... then maybe I'll know who did it. I'll solve the mystery."

"Have fun," Bertha said. She opened a door in the gym wall with one of the many jingling keys at her belt and went in. The door shut behind her with a loud metal scrape.

Ana drew the graffiti tag. Luckily, she had the right colors of Magic Marker. It took her seven tries to get it right.

The screen door squeaked when Ana opened it. The kitchen lights were on. One cold plateful of food sat on an otherwise bare table. Ana's mother sat at the other end, face down on her folded arms. She was snoring. Ana hid her backpack under the table and put the plate of food on a chair and out of sight.

"Wake up, Mama," she said.

Her mother woke up. "Where have you been, child?" she asked, annoyed but mostly groggy.

"Here," Ana said. "I've been here for hours. Sorry I missed dinner."

"You should be," said her mother. "Where—"

Ana pretended to yawn. Her mother couldn't help yawning then, and this made Ana yawn for real. "Bedtime," she said, once she was able to say anything. Her mother nodded, and both of them went upstairs.

Ana snuck back downstairs to throw away her dinner and fetch her backpack. She ate the chocolate granola bars while sitting on the floor of her bedroom and studying the graffiti in her notebook. She thought it might say *roozles, rutterkin,* or *rumbustical,* but there were always extra letters or at least extra swoofs and pointy edges to the letters; and the longer she stared at it, the less each word fit.

Ana slept. She dreamed that her kitten-backpack climbed snuffling onto the foot of her bed. She woke up when it stepped on her toes, and once she was awake she could see its pointy-eared outline. A car drove by outside and made strange window-shade shadows sweep across the wall and ceiling. Maybe the car had its high beams on.

Her bag moved. She kicked it, and it fell off the edge, landing with more of a soft smacking sound than it should have. Ana wanted to turn on the light, but the light switch was across the room. She would have to touch the floor to get there. She decided that now would be a really excellent time to develop telekinetic powers and spent the next several minutes concentrating on the light switch.

Another car went by.

She got up, tiptoed across the floor, and turned on the light. She turned around.

The backpack was right at her feet. She didn't scream. She swallowed an almost-scream.

The furry, pointy-eared bag wasn't moving. She pulled on the edges of the zipper and peeked inside. Her expedition supplies were still there. She poked through them with the capped tip of a Magic Marker just in case there was also something else in there. The notebook lay open to the seventh graffiti-covered page. She tried to nudge it aside, but the tip of the marker went through the colored surface. She dropped the pen. It passed through the graffiti and vanished. The page rippled like a pond.

She took another Magic Marker and used it to close the notebook cover. Then she looked out in the hallway to see if Rico's bedroom light was on. It was. She took the notebook, tiptoed by her parents' room, and sped up to pass the stairway. The air felt different at the top of the stairs. It felt like the stairway was holding its breath. It felt like the open space might breathe her in and down and swallow her. She knocked on Rico's door. No answer. She knocked again because she knew it would be locked from the inside so there wasn't any point in trying to open it herself. He still didn't answer. She tried the doorknob and it turned.

He wasn't there. She tread carefully on the few clear and visible parts of the floor and took a better look around from the middle of the room. He wasn't standing behind his dresser or lurking behind the armrest of the ratty old couch. He wasn't hiding in his closet because it was filled with too much junk already and nothing more would fit. She looked under the bed, and he wasn't there either. She looked at the empty bed and found a rolled up piece of parchment. *You play tomorrow night, musician,* it said. *Be ready.*

The parchment crumbled into several brown leaves and drifted to the floor, settling among the socks and books and torn pieces of sheet music.

"He must be rehearsing," she said to herself. "I'll try to find him tomorrow."

She went back to her room and hung the backpack up on the knob handle of one of her dresser drawers to keep it from wandering and went to bed. She left the light on. She didn't see anything move for the rest of the night, including her backpack. She heard things move instead.

Rico wasn't at breakfast. This wasn't unusual because he almost always slept until lunchtime, so their parents didn't seem worried as they bustled and joked and made coffee and went away to work after kissing Ana on each cheek. Ana went back upstairs as soon as they were gone. Rico wasn't in his room. Bits of brown leaves crunched and crumbled in the carpet under her feet.

Ana got dressed and took her backpack down from the knob she'd hung it on.

"Don't go walking anywhere without me," she said. She took more granola bars from the kitchen and refilled her little square canteen and locked up the house.

It started to rain when she reached the first highway billboard, and Ana's clothes and backpack were soggy by the time she got to the gym. The bag's sopping ears lay flat against the zipper.

She stood in front of the graffiti, took a deep breath, and wondered if she was supposed to say something out loud. Maybe she was supposed to say whatever the graffiti said, and she still couldn't read it.

Something snarled in the trees behind her. Ana turned around, took a step backwards, and tried to press herself against the wall. It didn't work. She pressed and passed through it.

"Hello," said a voice that scraped against the insides of her ears.

Ana faced another painted wall, stone instead of brick. She took a breath. The air was still, and it smelled like thick layers of dust. She turned around. An old man, thin and spindly, sat on a stool and polished a carved flute. He had a wispy beard. He tested two notes on the flute and set to polishing again. Behind him were several shelves of similar instruments. Some were plain and a pale yellow-grey. Some were carved with delicate patterns and others inlaid with metals and lacquered over.

"Hello," Ana said.

"The Grey Lady brings deliveries every second Tuesday, and today is neither thing. Are you delivered here? Has she changed schedules?"

"I don't know any grey ladies," Ana said. "Except math teachers. Do you mean Mrs. Huddle?"

"No huddling things," the old man said. He set down the flute on a carved wooden stand, picked up a bone from his workbench, and took a rasp to the knobby joints. "Tell me your purposes, then, if no Lady brought you. Are you here to buy a flute?"

"No," Ana said. "I'm looking for my brother."

"Unfortunate that you should look for him here. How old?"

"He's sixteen."

"So old? Good, good. I won't have pieces of him then."

Ana looked around for pieces of people. There was a straw cot in the corner beside a green metal stove. There were baskets and tin lanterns hanging by chains from a high ceiling. There were no windows. A staircase against one wall led up to the only doorway. There was a workbench and shelves full of flutes and a mural of moonlight and trees where she had stepped through the wall.

"He's a musician," Ana said. "A singer. He's in a band, I think. Last week they were The Paraplegic Weasels, but I don't know if that's still their name. It keeps changing."

"Very prudent," said the old man, rasping bone.

"He's supposed to play for someone tonight. I don't know who."

"Tonight there are many festivities, or so I've heard rumor." He swapped the rasp for a finer file and began to scrape the bone more delicately.

Ana took a step closer. "The invitation turned into leaves after I read it."

"Then he'll likely play his music in the Glen," the old man said. "You should be on the forest paths and not here in the City."

"City?"

"Oh, yes. Underneath it, a few layers down." He wiped away loose bone dust and set both bone and file down on the workbench. "The stone floor you're standing on used to be a road, but the City is always growing up over itself."

"Oh," Ana said. She looked down at the floor. The old man reached down, scooped her up by the armpits, and set her on the edge of the workbench. She swallowed an almost-scream when he pinched each leg, squeezing down to the thighbones, and then she kicked him in the stomach.

Ana jumped down, ran to the mural, and smacked the surface of it with the palms of both hands. The surface held. Behind her the old man wheezed and coughed and laughed a little.

"No matter," he said. "Both bones broken, and all the music leaked out from the fractures. Can't make any kind of flute from either leg. How did you break them both?"

Ana turned around to watch him. He sat back on his stool, wheezing, and he seemed to want to stay there. "I jumped off the roof."

"And what flying thing were you fleeing from?" he asked.

"Nothing. Rico dared me to jump, so I did. I didn't tell on him either. He still owes me for that."

"Well," the old man said, "I hope you can collect what he owes when you find him. Such a shame that your bones were broken. There are a great many children, and there isn't enough music. There isn't nearly enough."

"So how do I get out?" She hated admitting that she didn't already know.

The old man smiled and widened up his eyes. "Boo," he said, puffing out his thin beard.

Ana took a step backwards and passed through the stone.

Her face was inches away from her brother's graffiti. It was dark, and she could barely see the colors by moonlight. She looked around. She was alone. Her backpack was gone.

"I told it not to wander off," she said.

There was only one forest path she could find. Ana took a walking stick from a pile of broken branches near the edge of the woods and took a deep breath and set out. She wished she had her flashlight. She wished she had her backpack. In her head she promised to give it a scratch behind the ears if it would come back and to never again hang it up on a dresser drawer knob. It had looked uncomfortable there.

The air smelled like wet leaves, heavy and rich. She followed the path uphill and downhill and around sudden corners cut into the sides of hills. She passed trees that looked like tall, twisted people until she looked at them directly. Ana hoped she was following the right trail. She saw a wispy orange light between the tree trunks and decided to follow that instead.

The orange light brightened as Garth inhaled cigarette smoke. He was leaning on a boulder. He looked up and blew smoke at the moon.

Half of his face was swollen.

"Hey," said Ana. "What are you doing?"

"Nothing," he said. "Waiting for little girls, maybe."

"Your infection's worse."

"True," he said. "But this bit of silver is keeping me from gnawing on your bones."

"Oh," said Ana. "Good. Everybody should stay away from my bones."

He took another drag, brightening up the wispy orange light, and tugged his hat down to cover more of the swollen half of his face. Ana held on to her stick.

"Do you know where Rico is?" she asked.

"Maybe. He plays tonight."

"Can you take me to him?"

"Maybe." Garth dropped the cigarette and stepped on it, crushing the little orange flame. He walked off, away from the path. Ana waited for some signal from him that she should follow. She didn't get one. She followed.

Garth took long strides, and his boots hit the ground like he was trying to punish it for something. Ana tried to keep up, and she tried to keep a little bit behind him at the same time. She didn't want to be too close. He hunched, staring at the ground, and she thought he was moping more than usual until he dove, snarling. He came up holding a lanky thing covered in short, spiky fur.

"Where does the Guard keep watch tonight?" he asked.

The lanky thing shrugged and grinned many teeth.

"Where does the Guard watch the Glen?" He shook the thing in his hand.

It snickered.

"Please?" Ana asked, very sweetly.

The lanky thing blew her a kiss. "Tonight there is no waking Guard," it said. "Tonight he is sleeping and dreaming that he guards, and he crosses no one unless they cross into his dreaming while he sleeps at his post, which is easy to do and see to it that you don't.

Everything within a pebble's toss of him in all directions is only the substance of his dream, and inside it the Guard is a much better guard than he ever was awake. He guards the Western Arch."

"How many arches are there?" Garth asked.

"Tonight there is only the Western Arch. All others are overgrown. It rained today."

"Thank you," Ana said.

The lanky thing bowed, which was difficult to do while Garth held it up by the scruff of its neck. Then it bit him hard on the wrist and dropped to the ground. Garth howled. The lanky thing snickered from somewhere nearby.

"Let me see your wrist," Ana said. She had Band-Aids in her backpack. Then she remembered that she didn't have her backpack.

Garth looked at her. Garth never made eye contact, but he did so now; and he held it, and he also made a little rumbling noise in the back of his throat.

"No," he said.

"Okay," she said.

"You should know that I'm not interested in dying for your brother. He's all right. I like him. But I'm not interested in death on his behalf. I'm not interested in any of the things so close to death that the distinction makes no difference. This is something you should know before we go any further."

"Okay," she said again.

He walked away. She followed. She wondered where her backpack was.

They found an enormous figure in full plate armor asleep. The Guard was dreaming a desert the size of a pebble's throw. All around it was sunlight and sand and nowhere to hide.

"That's the Western Gate," Garth said.

"Where?" Ana whispered.

"Behind the desert. Cut into the wall of thorns there." He pointed. Ana stood at the very edge of the desert and squinted. She could only see sand and sun in front of them.

Garth dropped another finished cigarette, driving it farther into the dirt than he really needed to. "Good luck," he said.

"Wait," Ana told him. "Don't go yet. I'm going to try something."

She picked up a pebble, took aim, and threw it at the precise moment that she stepped forward into desert sand. For just an instant she knew what it was like to be an unimportant part of someone else's dream. Then the pebble struck the Guard's gold helmet, clanging loudly and waking it up.

The desert vanished. Ana ducked behind a tree that hadn't been there before and leaned against the trunk. She could hear the metal movements of plate armor on the other side. She didn't know where Garth was.

"I am a pirate king," Ana whispered to herself. "It's a glorious thing to be a pirate king."

She ran and switched directions twice and tried to circle back towards the Western Gate. She almost stumbled in the dark, but she didn't. The Guard almost caught her anyway. She felt gauntleted fingers snatch at her shoulder. Then she heard it clang and crash against the ground. She stopped, panting, and turned around to look.

Garth stood over the Guard, who was much shorter and less impressive than it had dreamed itself earlier. Garth looked at Ana, snarled, and jerked his chin towards the Gate. Then he spit on the Guard's golden armor.

Ana backed farther away. She watched the Guard pull itself up off the ground. It plucked out Garth's silver piercing with a little spray of blood.

Garth howled, and his face began to change.

Ana turned away and slipped inside.

The Glen was at least as big as a cornfield and covered over with a dome of branches high overhead. Inside the branches were orange wisps of light, glowing and fading again.

It was full of dancers. Ana looked at them and closed her eyes and looked again. She could hear Rico singing over the noise of the crowd.

"I'm still a pirate king," she whispered to herself, weaving her way in between dancers and trying to find the stage. She dodged the dancing things and bumped into some and passed through the shimmering substance of others. She saw colors and antlers and sharp teeth in strange places.

She found the stage. She found her brother. He sang, and the language sounded a little bit like Spanish but not very much. Nick played a red guitar, acoustic and covered in gold ivy. Julia played a yellow-grey flute. Both of them were even taller than they usually were.

Rico saw her, and Ana saw a lot of white around the edges of his eyes when he did. He nudged Julia, and she started a flute solo. Then he got down off the stage and pulled Ana behind it. She opened her mouth. He shushed her.

"Okay, don't eat or drink. Whatever else you do, don't eat anything and don't drink anything. Now tell me what you think you're doing."

"Looking for you," Ana said.

"I'm impressed," he said, biting on his lower lip. "I really am. But this is very, very bad, and I'm not sure how to fix it."

"What's the problem?" Ana asked, folding her arms and looking at him as though she were the older one.

"Okay," Rico said, taking deep breaths. "Do you see those guys over there? The ones with the tattoos?"

"They're the gang?" Ana asked.

"Yeah. Sure. Kind of. And this is supposed to be my last task for them, and then after the concert I'll learn how to sing up every chrome piece of a motorcycle and ride it from town to town, stopping only to hum the fuel tank full again. I'll learn how to sing hurricanes and how to send them away. I'll learn how to sing something people can dance to for a full year and never notice the time passing."

"Sounds like fun," Ana said.

"Sure. The catch is that this crowd has to be happy and dancing until the dawn light comes. If they stop before then, I fail, and I have to serve the guys with the tattoos for at least a hundred years. So you should either go, right now, however you came here, or else hide somewhere and don't eat or drink or talk to anyone until dawn. And don't do anything distracting because the crowd might stop dancing, and that would be very bad. They like children here, but they care about music a lot more than they care about kids."

Ana looked up at Julia and her yellow-grey flute.

"I have go back onstage now," Rico said.

"Okay," Ana said.

"Hide," he said.

"Okay."

He went back onstage. Julia finished her solo, and Rico sang. He was good.

Ana thought she saw her backpack scamper between someone's hooves. She followed. Then she saw Garth, or at least she assumed it was Garth. He had started to eat people near the Western Arch.

"Crap," Ana said. He was distracting the crowd. Some of them weren't dancing anymore.

She ran back to the arch and slipped through. She looked everywhere, kicking up leaves. She found her walking stick and used it to poke through the leaves that were dark and wet and sticky. Then she found one golden gauntlet. Blood pooled underneath it. A small, silver tusk sat in its palm.

She picked up the silver. It was very sharp. She ran back through the arch and followed the screaming.

Garth was gnawing on a severed antler with his long wolf muzzle. Some things in the crowd were shouting; and more were laughing, and most were still dancing but not all of them were.

"Hey, perro muerto," Ana said. She threw her walking stick at him. It got his attention. He dropped the antler, bounded forward, and knocked her to the ground, slavering.

Ana grabbed one of his furry ears with her left hand and shoved the tusk through it with her right. The skin of his ear resisted, stretching a little before the silver broke through.

Garth rolled over and howled. Ana got to her feet and looked around her. The crowd danced. Even those who were bleeding from the fight with Garth were dancing again. She took a deep breath, but she didn't get a chance to let it out all the way before someone's hand took her by the elbow and pulled her towards the stage.

She looked up at the arm attached to the hand. It had green and red letters tattooed all up and down its length.

Rico, Julia, and Nick bowed to the sound of applause and unearthly cries. The sky began to lighten above the branches, grey and rose-colored and pale.

The owner of the green and red arm pushed Ana forward in front of Rico. "What's this?" Rico asked.

"Your last initiation," said a very deep voice behind Ana. She didn't want to turn around. She looked straight ahead at her brother. "Sing her to sleep. Let her sleep for a thousand years, or at least until another glacier passes this way."

"I've already finished my initiation," Rico said. "They all danced until dawn."

"Yes," said the voice. "You held them, most of them, and they were deer in headlights high-beamed by your song. Those you lost, you gained again as they danced, bleeding. It was good. But it was not your last task. The last requires a ten-year-old."

"Crap," said Ana.

Rico took her hand, pulled her closer, and tossed red and green colors into the air between them and the crowd. Colors settled into the shape of his tag. Ana still couldn't read it.

"Home," Rico said. "I'll follow when I can."

"You have to tell me what it says," Ana told him, but he just smiled and pushed her through.

Their parents were as frantic as one might expect. Ana managed to slip into her brother's room. She found green and red spray paint hidden behind the couch before her mother and father and Deputy Chad came in to look for clues to Rico's whereabouts. Ana kept the spray paint hidden under her own bed.

It took a long time for Ana to get back to the high school because her parents kept closer tabs on her after Rico disappeared. Bertha had already sandblasted the graffiti; and Ana couldn't find the forest path, and she didn't know where Garth was. She hoped he wasn't dead or something very close to dead. She walked home and listened to three nervous phone messages from her mother on the answering machine. Ana called her back and told her she was home and that everything was fine even though it wasn't really.

She went up to her room and found her backpack sitting on her bed. She gave it a hug. It purred when she scratched behind its ears. "I'm really, really angry at you for leaving," she said. It kept purring.

Inside she found three pages torn from her notebook. They were folded in half together with "Ana" written on the front.

The first page was in Rico's handwriting. *I'll see you as soon as I find a way out of a hundred years of servitude*, it said. *Don't worry, I'll manage. DO NOT COME LOOKING FOR ME. Keep a pinch of salt in your pocket at all times and stay out of the woods and DO NOT keep following me around. I'm serious.*

Ana snorted and turned the page. It was her seventh drawing with a note written underneath: *This is my name, dumbass.*

She turned to the last page.

This is yours.

Ana looked at it and saw that it was.

She took out her Magic Markers and practiced marking her territory on the back wall of her closet.

Flush

Francesco Verso

● translated by Georgia Emma Gili ●

When I tried it the first time, I didn't know what to expect. Disappearing, maybe dying and then reappearing, but where and, above all, *as what*?

No one knew anything about it. Or rather, no one talked about it without losing track of themselves in grumblings and stumblings. Including those who swore they had survived the most terrifying experience of their life. From the faces they were making, they passed it off as conclusive proof: they were stronger because they were still alive.

So why did I want to do it? Why did I want to subject myself to such torture?

I check the time, then the club sign and say to myself: Simon, are you sure it's worth it?

The trance music making the blood pump in your veins follows its own beat at 150 rpm. It rebounds outside along the chipped walls of the alleyway dripping with humidity and fluorescent paints.

Some shady figures are haggling in the shadows. Everything is competing to distract me.

My clothing is unlikely: beige trousers from when I weighed 90 kilos, a light blue shirt which I didn't know I had, and some old, brown, inveterate tourist sandals.

I switch off my smartphone so as not to be wed to some overly invasive urban application.

The place where I have the appointment, the Lair of the White Noise, is not an establishment that you would want to attract attention in. It's a suburb club haunted by ear-splitting volume fanatics with the type of din that distracts you and can make you change your mind every three minutes. Even less, if you're with someone who'll be your sound box.

Maybe that's why I made up my mind. To drop myself into the "well" and slip into the Lair of Noise. Not very differently from those who had dropped in beforehand and would have done so afterwards. From outside, the Lair looks worse than a hole dug in the ground. The entrance is a leaning metal sheet attached to thick hinges sunk into stone. Beyond that, you plunge into a tunnel lit only by oblique candlelight. The air is moved both by the vibrations of the music and by the large air ducts.

In one wide stretch, a dusty cave serves as a dance floor and around it are set out some nailed boards painted red. Wallowing in a ripped VIRGIN AIRLINES seat is an olive-skinned guy in a paramilitary jumpsuit.

I approach him with a nod, and he offers me a crooked smile and a jeweller's shop set of teeth.

My contact, Charlie Four Fingers, had been a good go-between. Maybe he had asked his girlfriend, a chiquita brazileira, to perform a lap-a-samba for the bloke. Maybe she had been good at making him forget a wretched day. As a matter of fact, Tony has agreed to meet me. He lifts a bony hand and beckons me to follow him.

"In the toilets. In a minute. I go in first."

But he doesn't say anything else. Is there a right way of doing this? Are there any precautions to follow? What should you avoid to keep yourself out of harm's way?

I've eaten a spring roll and drunk two beers. Maybe I should wait. Or maybe I'm hesitating because I'm not convinced.

In spite of things, I've let myself be influenced by the voices going round, those on the air that turns into strings in your head, black holes in your understanding and vortices of alienation.

Absurd voices that talk of decompression voids in your soul and mirror-thoughts from the memories of others. Mental boxes inside other boxes.

Illusions so unpleasant and disturbing as to make you lose your sense of direction and lucidity. Shit, how many versions of the same thing exist?

Okay, it's a subjective fact, something that all of us live *by ourselves* and *for ourselves*, but surely there must be a common denominator, something that can only be associated with the phenomenon of the *Flush*.

The Flush or the Whirlpool is the experience in question's nom de guerre: The Silencer, on the other hand, is the name that half the authorities around the planet have used to ban it.

Nothing remains but for me to discover the reason for this choice of name.

I breathe in and start walking towards the flashing toilet symbol.

To reach it I have to keep an eye out for those getting off to the rhythm of a beat interspliced with cannon booms.

If they call them "schizophonics," there's a reason ...

I've never sniffed happy dust in all my life. Skunk spliffs and hash cakes, some glue fumes and at the very most some subliminal dosers. But I've never touched coke, "H," mescaline, amphetamines, or LSD. I like communing with nature, so to speak. And yet, for the Flush I'm ready to break this rule.

Whatever it was, this experience would circulate inside me, it would flow in my veins or into any other organ it could spread to.

I cross the threshold of the bathroom after having exited the acoustic treatment of the dance floor unscathed.

My ears are whistling and regurgitate excess peaks of melody. Inside, I'm stunned by the thunderous noise from all the taps running, vomiting up a thick, greenish liquid. What they had taught us to use with caution since we were kids: that greenish fluid with a vaguely minty smell (no one is able to tell you the taste without copping a stomach pump) is to be blamed on the chemical agent used to exterminate any noxious substances.

If they call it "preventive hygiene," there's a reason ...

Lying in wait behind the door like a feline, Tony swiftly hangs a sign outside saying OUT OF ORDER and then locks us in. I have almost two minutes before the hunt for a free urinal kicks off.

"Are you Simon?"

"Yes, that's me, Four Fingers' friend."

I go to take out an identity card, but he blocks me.

"I'll take your word for it. In any case, I need to see the money first."

"Wait, I want to try it out. How do I know you're not fobbing me off with some low frequency crap?"

The bloke knits his brows: if I'm coming out with bollocks like that it means it's my *first time*. And so he starts to treat me like a junkie, like any old schizophonic, greedy for novelties to get off on.

"You'll have to trust me, mate. I can't let you sample this stuff."

I shut up. The mystery of the Flush has tricked me at its outset. Nothing remains but to open my hand and offer him the agreed payment.

He reaches out his arm and takes my credits.

Then he smiles sardonically and opens the other cupped hand.

"Have fun and keep shtum. If they catch you, swallow them. They're biodegradable. They won't show up in a feces test. They'd have to open up your stomach within half an hour to nail you."

That said, Tony leaps Siamese cat-style onto the basin and slides through the opening in the top window. He never uses the same door twice.

Before he disappears off into the alleyway, he hisses towards me.

"Mate, take the sign down if you don't want them to smash the door to smithereens for starters and then you."

For a second I'm frozen, doubtful about having lightened myself of a few credits for nothing. Then I lower my gaze to my palm and see what I've bought for the equivalent of two months' rent.

A pair of fucking earphones? Two paltry earplugs?

I can't believe it. They dare to raise these lowly contrivances to the rank of synthetic drug? I flip them over in my hand, intent on digging out a deeper meaning, when threatening blows against the door wake me from the hypnosis of a rip-off. I stick the earphones in my pocket and run out, dodging a couple of wild men whose bursting bladders are the cause of my salvation.

Simple bitchin' in my direction won't hurt me very much. I go back through the tunnel, this time upwards. I pant and gasp for breath.

The smoke blocks my sight and ravages my sense of smell, the incessant noise makes mincemeat of what's left. I shake my head, trying to get a grip. Even just an arm hold to guide me back out. I stagger and reel from one shoulder to the next. Banging into strangers who scoff or round on me angrily.

I count the number of turns and fix my eyes on the walls to make out where I am. The air shakes and rumbles with the echoes of a bass that cuts through your flesh, crackles in your ears, gets absorbed, and is only partly deadened.

I catch sight of the emergency strip lighting in the distance. It has to show the way to the surface.

I have double vision, and blood is trickling from my ears. It feels white hot like the sound frequency. I grab a rail there where every night countless people pass out.

Outside the Lair of the White Noise, I get my breath back.

In the midst of the muffled sounds in the alleyway, with blinded eyes and anaesthetized ears, I am tempted to try the Flush effect right there and then.

I clock two din-armed geezers and three sylphs in a groupette protected by an aura of defensive music. So I give up on the idea. I wouldn't want them to attack me with some unknown sound.

Yet, thinking about it, what could happen to me that could be so horrendous if even plain old earplugs are on the drug blacklist?

I think back to Tony who, at this point, must be knocking back a drink in my name.

With the earplugs in my pocket, I start walking stealthily with bated breath. I turn into Columbus Avenue and while, on the one hand, the Doppler effect emitted by the high-powered muscle cars doesn't bother me very much; on the other, it's a nuisance: I'm carrying illegal stuff and anyone could get out of a car, point a "double-bad sound" at me, and force me to undergo an on-the-spot body search.

The pavement on the stretch of highway where they've unveiled a 24x7 HyperStore is teeming with nocturnals, young and not so young people, with easy banter and One-Man-Sound intent on selling insults and exchangeable pick-up lines.

Right now, my ears hurt all the time if I don't wear my Sennheiser padded headphones to isolate me from sounds, using other sounds. I was fool to leave them at home. Sounds to drive away sounds: if they call it "low-satisfaction therapy," there's a reason ...

I look around for a quiet spot, a park, a garage, or any other disused place where a truce could be offered, even momentarily, from the relentlessness noise, from the spirals that are clogging up my ears.

After all, we all want to escape. Those who escape into the TV or by shopping or at football stadiums or clubs. And no one wants to be anywhere else at *that* moment in time.

Those who shut themselves off inside apparent escape mechanisms are simply acknowledging illusory flights from reality. Prisons inside other prisons. Sounds inside other sounds. With only a worsening effect over time.

Those who really flee don't come back. They don't change channel or go looking for an alternative shop. They don't change political party or join the latest club. Those in flight aren't really looking for something, they've already *found* it.

My soundproof barrier, made out of two lobe-shaped prongs of my ears, has stopped oscillating. It's my dowser's way of finding the X-spot, where sounds can't reach me or entangle me in a web of distractions.

Where I am there's no need to make a commotion to be heard. I glance back in both directions.

The seesawing breeze between the isolated branches continues to require the smallest fraction of my attention.

To compensate, the nearest human being is at least 100 yards away. Such a gap as to reassure me and nudge me into getting the earplugs out of my pocket.

I set myself down on a bench along the tree-lined path. In full control of the neighbourhood sound spectrum, I look at the day's purchases: long, cone-shaped, in a skin-camouflage tone. They're covered in a spongy material that I don't recognise. They're not made of plastic or cork or rubber.

Who knows how the molecules that surround us are shaken in the everyday items that we use?

The more I look at them, the more they seem alien to me, pervaded with a mix of anger about Tony's prohibitively rip-off pricing and curiosity towards an object that, at least in theory, promises to give me a unique experience in return.

I shake them to and fro.

The discussion forums that I took part in before coming to a decision didn't give any advice or tips. Maybe there aren't any. Maybe it's a question of instinct.

Then I run into an obvious fact: such simple objects can't possibly transmit such complex experiences. So I separate the earplugs and hold them up at eye level. I observe the cones pointing at each other, ideally.

In the middle, I'm the one keeping the circuit open. Which is what prompts me. I understand the mystery, but I daren't make the leap.

Slowly as a monk preparing tea, I bring the earplugs up to my ears. I look right, then left. I can't understand if I'm putting myself between them or if they're working through me.

In unison, I bring my hands near one another and let the ambiguous consistency of the wedge-shaped material slip into my ear canal and mould itself to the shape of my eardrum.

It is a rarefied tactile sensation, even perceptible in the obscurity of the skin within my ear.

After having softly pushed in the two ends, I am unaware of *going down*. I'm in the middle of a frown when I instinctively feel the presence of another reality: *total silence*. Almost accommodating this state, I half-close my eyes.

Silence together with pitch black should be taken in very small doses. Infinitesimally small doses.

Shit, if in historical terms, getting off your head has always been connected to some kind of distortion, a pleasing deformation of reality, then I've started on some serious substance abuse.

It's like a pressure drop on a plane, a sense of suction which first lengthens and then compresses you.

It's absurd despite being true, the image of air turning into strings in your head, a rarefied space, vacuous and sidereal where my brain used to be.

The absence of auditory perceptions in contrast with noise permeating everything works subtly from inside: absolute silence is too dizzying and opens up chasms inside itself, ripping apart any false sense of self-control.

At first, alert and aware of where I am, I imagine how increasing doses of the Flush lead to undiscovered places, chasms of self that are normally inaccessible to consciousness, bombarded by sounds.

Then panic.

A *voided mind*, free from even the smallest undulation and distraction, what advanced users prattle and moan about on the sites dedicated to this phenomenon, opens up its path *within* me.

My murkiest fears and most remote hopes are condensed onto a visual, which is as real as it is dreamable.

Cirrus-form visions of my ex-girlfriends form in layers under clouds pregnant with fear and anxiety. In the midst of this, sharp flashes spark off memories.

In the silence of muffled reality, what takes shape can't be controlled or moulded into any gradation.

The office where I work as an IT specialist is no longer the deafening open-plan room where privacy is knowingly violated but seems to be a beehive inhabited by drones who play the part of the victim to business queens bordering on working-time hysteria.

My very own Elisa turns into a vulgar ebony pillar, a Doric column of hard-core scenes, taken and thrown onto flesh as the vessel of my own personal Kama Sutra.

Maybe dreaming is the closest paragon to what I'm living. An hallucinatory thread, lucid and yet blurred, a virulent disorientation whose inconsistency is guided to the smallest degree by the active mind.

The concepts that I measure my identity against and that I recognise myself in are sliding away, scared off by the uncomfortable presence of such a unique and rare event.

In terms of anatomy, history, and culture, as we are human beings, we are all linked to physical communication, what's written and spoken. Even when dumb panic takes hold and silence persists inside us for a longish stretch of time, consciousness is switched on.

Not even the accelerated but constant beat of my heart comforts me. I possess an existence beyond mental fluctuations, but nevertheless, I am in free fall.

Using extraordinary willpower, I open my eyes and surprise! A world as mute as I am reveals its silent face to me.

Leaves rustle between the branches, birds sail through the skies in orderly flocks, and the crickets sing in the grass, driven by a breath of wind.

Everywhere there is irreparable quiet and silence.

A veil has been thrown over the sound side of reality, a slap of reality stings me in the face. How many parts of my brain are taken hostage by sound? How much of us is lost in paying attention to it?

I would never want to be deaf, even if a prosthesis can fully restore the joy of hearing, special effects included. Still I can understand why the Flush is illegal.

The monotony of the absence of sound is a switch that can be flicked to get high on and at the same time is definitive, demonstrative proof of having survived yourself.

Two facts that, if kept apart, can be accused of degenerating the spirit and spreading practices which harm personal safety and well-being but which, if put together in a single, unique moment, reinforce the ability to focus on and free yourself from the shackles of distraction.

The risk is of a PVS (Persistent Vegetative State) and the incommunicability of a silence where each of us is an island in a sea of emotions so fluid, insubstantial, and malleable as to repudiate words. But even these are impediments that can be overcome by diffusing the shared ritual of the Flush: bands of *silenced* youths can already be seen going around absorbed in contemplating a higher existence, immune to the entrapment of shiny shop windows, hymns to consumerism, and a flood of sublime subliminal signals.

They gesture, moving their hands in the complex grammatical manoeuvres of LSD, the Language of Signs for the Devocalised, and wave their arms about in a mime all their own, inaccessible to others.

Stripped of every sound-coating, I get up and wander along the dumb, eloquent paths in *another way*. With a tongue that is free from all discord, communicating more intense forms of truth, senses renewed at the root.

It's a premonition ...

It puts what's below the hearing threshold into focus.

What strikes me is that I'm *out of tune*.

No Kissing the Dolls Unless Jimi Hendrix is Playing

Clifton Gachagua

Posters with the face of a grinning girl with red hair are all over the city's walls. A family of three who have found a home outside an Indian café stitch the posters together into a curtain, her face watching over them. Her name has become infamous. Seventeen murders in the ghettos, no MO, no evidence, and somehow the murders all happen at the same time in the five different ghettos.

The poet has come home to roost. He is in love for the first time after a very long time. He spent the night out with a girl in a leather dress the colours of collage frangipani and a long face under red hair and Bengali bangles and heavy chains stretching from her nose ring to an earring, a girl who would otherwise be living in a hefty loft in the UK with another poet with no medical cover to boast of. A girl who held his hand through the city and showed him her blue blazoned red tongue and the weapons she carried in her nightmares.

He plays something on the record. He's not sure what it is, as long as it is not silence. Love likes noise. He lives alone now. Once in a while he will miss them, the other poets. They fucked indiscriminately and with few inhibitions, smoked, and listened to vintage radio podcasts playing zilizopendwa. There were debates about The Mushrooms. Of course, everyone knew, they were all there when it happened, that The Mushrooms had failed in that event of 67 to keep the noontide in its place. The water had come all the way to their feet, bringing with it the dead bodies of children and Chihuahuas from the Italian villas off the coast of Malindi. No one could write poetry after that. They went back to smoking, fucked less, let silence replace The Mushrooms; their father's favourite musicians had failed them. They listened to their bodies more, the silence of metabolism, spent time fixated on the now obsolete. They all had penises the size of semicolons and made a show for everyone who came to visit. The sky was not enough for them, so there were the Octane tanks hidden in the boiler. How many ways Octane helped them reenact what Marijan Rajab must have felt when he made Zuena, and, more importantly, would Zuena ever come back to him? Their poetry came down to that important question: would the dead lover ever return?

They smoked and smoked and danced to the old tunes better than their fathers ever could, twisting waists and shifting disks in their spines. Koffi Olomide's "Andrada and Effracata," first slow then fast, slow then fast again, a recital about dead children as intermission, then the climax. They imagined dance-fucking their own mothers in those fallen hours of the night when it was possible to see certain constellations when you lived next door to the equator, and in this regard constellations of both the southern and northern hemispheres. They had forgotten lung cancer. They worked in advertising and owned holiday homes in Shela and Pate and failed to train Chihuahuas to sit, roll, stay, jump, do not poop on people's lawns. Some anti-smoking campaign display-glass lungs full of dead babies and filters were enacted next to strip clubs, but the poets knew nothing would ever stop them from smoking.

After a while they all had to leave his loft and find another place for their semicolon parade. That was then.

Dik Dik remains one of them. "One of them" is a phrase he carries with him around his neck, it's something his mother could never and will never offer him, a place where his bow legs meant nothing, when all he ever wanted was for her to stick out her tongue.

He sits alone in the middle of his living room and thinks about the girl with the red hair. He readjusts a register.

Long hallways of palm frond alloys, boulevards of thick baobab, dead children flying dragonflies, cheap foam life-size GSU, and imitation art line Kenyatta Avenue. Beautification programmes. Meja Mwangi, last seen here a long time ago, disappears into Sabina Joy with an amputee prostitute who offers him an hours' worth of conversation in Gikuyu—no longer spoken here—for ten times the normal rate. She holds his hand tight and smiles like two moons, blush on the cheeks. He disappears inside her, never to be seen again. Some people will stalk his grave and spend fifty years waiting, fasting, praying. Cyborgs will find them there and eat their intestines alive. Alive. Pick, roll, unfurl them in their hands like cashew nuts. He will never come back; the sons will never come back to their mothers. The mothers have forgotten they ever had sons. If they meet in the Matrix Way, they will greet each other like strangers, probably sleep next to each other, tired and outworn, and they will kiss with their eyes closed.

The prostitute comes back and the night is on her lips and anyone who asks to kiss her she says yes. What else can she say but yes? Because yes is a sacrifice to all those young twenty-somethings and taxi drivers who have the world in front of them and the government so up their assholes it tastes like the Year of the Colon.

She comes back with those dark lips the colour of night, and she is blowing kisses to the night; and right there at the equator there is a kind of magnetic borealis—a migration of evolving nova from the 456 regions to the Near Death Kentucky Fried Chicken Canto regions, where it says Dante was just looking for the devil to fuck his ass. She is dying and her body is in this experiment of reverse engineering; and she is tearing into ribbons of primary colours—wait wait, are these wings?—no, they are not the wings, they are the roads she must take to get home but as soon as she steps onto the curb they disappear. She goes back to the house, kisses him on the forehead, no eye contact, and he remembers his mother. She just wants someone to accept her love.

She walks out into the street.

A man with an eye patch on his nipple and a single eye on his other nipple pinches himself to look at her. He feels a chill, goose bumps spread across his body—he has not yet learned how not to arouse himself whenever he pinches his nipples. He is a work in progress, he reassures himself.

She sees Dik Dik clear in her closed-eye vision when she finally falls asleep.

He has seen the way many men fall into the night of that smile and never come back, so he simply looks at her from the corner of his eye. For her this is enough. She says her name is Chromosome-1972. He has read on a banned billboard the short history of 70s chromosomes, so he does not ask her anything else. He is playing it cool—some genuses don't take too lightly to old-age categorization. Short history and early death appear together in conversations. He does not offer a smile.

They are at Aga Khan Walk, and the blind man is singing. Dik Dik let's her know he loves the blind man. He doesn't say what he really means is that he loves his father. She knows this. She shows him her tongue, and he sucks some colour from it. His tongue is darker, the contrast of colours not as sharp. No one can save him.

The blind man sings in a baritone. He has long stopped singing in semiquavers. He finds the deepest voices and reenacts dead street children who would have grown up to give Pavarotti a run for his money. He points his walking stick up, demands that God shut up; and the city goes all quiet, and he sings the most beautiful ballads; only he is also deaf, and Dik Dik and Chromosome-1972 stand there marvelling at such talent.

They are deaf.

The city is collecting deaf people in blue rooms; the governor wants to know what the gods are saying.

"What do you think he sees?"

"When he sings or when he dreams?"

"Difference?"

"One is about wavelength, the other is that I'm so damn hungry can we get out of here and get some food?"

Leaving a trail of their favourite love song of distant gunshots, ambulance singsongs, and dead children crying behind them, they walk into Mocha Cola where blown-up balloons smile and stick out their tongues at them. Their tongues are made of old turntables, each taste bud a record with a spindle so that, in addition to the love songs, there's all this beautiful music inside and Dik Dik and Chromosome-1972 just want to stick out their respective tongues and kiss some dolls. They kiss some dolls.

On the wall, on this big red poster is a warning in bold letters: NO KISSING THE DOLLS UNLESS JIMI HENDRIX IS PLAYING. A grinning Chinese man stands below it.

Dik Dik wants to order French fries and some old love songs on the machine. She wants to offer her services to the brotherhood of man and the cleaning of dishes with no pay. Two hours after their meeting they have fallen in love, he knows because she is sticking out her tongue and showing him how many flavours of candy are in the register of her mouth. She's showing him only, not the Chinese man. Soon they fight for a short while about the range of colours on her tongue, and he agrees that she makes better sense. He is Mr. Sinister, hates the primary colours. Truth is he is wasting time for some JIMI HENDRIX. The calendar at the main lobby states the date as 1/2/1972, and the calendar in the kitchen says it's 1/2/1967. He's not sure if this is an elaborate joke. Maybe they have run out of a register. In a Nairobi filled with disreputable fried-chicken-and-cabbage-sandwich Ssebos hiding guns and lipstick under the white meat of genetically modified chicken and drunk clockmakers, who can he believe? He decides to walk into the kitchen and do the dishes if only to prove to her that he can be romantic. To really drive the point home he tells her of this dream he had of transgenders plaiting cornrows on dolls from the one and only most expensive doll shop in Nairobi and possibly all of East, Central, and South Africa—The Most Superficial David Foster Wallace Dolly Dolls Shop.

Nairobi, unlike any other city on earth, is a city of visiting poets, men possessed by the love of other faraway places and Samburu festival dolls—Madilu System, Kanda Bongo Man, Les Wanyika, Fundi Konde, Mbilia Mbel, Dik Dik's long dead absentee father, the man with ears and habits like a September Playboy bunny—all these are poets. Dik Dik is a poet. He has thought of his father as homunculus, as atypical, primitive, strange, as absent and as human, as a man possessed with the ability to discern temperaments in dolls of the same gender and age, as a transgendered doll. But on this night he's thinking of nothing but kissing this girl and possibly hot dogs later in the park. Possibly dog meat.

He still wants to go back to that park despite the frenzied woman who waits there for boys like him, singing siren songs, songs not so unlike those of the blind man.

Dik Dik pauses. Chromo/Domo—what he imagines to be a funky sexyname he has developed in the rush for her acceptance—pauses, too. She does not pause just because he does, no no no. So the lovely couple under a blue umbrella and yellow scissors takes a pause. They are so in love with each other a bridge somewhere falls apart at the beating of a butterfly. He takes out an Octane tank and lets her take three puffs in quick succession. He decides right there this is the only girl he will ever show his Octane tank.

They walk onto Short Lane just when two mellow young boys say goodbye to their ailing mother who has gone out to beg for coins from the big and rich Somali men who now own the city and talk in the language of appreciating dollars. Dik Dik grew up with Somalis, fought with them. He wanted to be them. He loved among them.

Nineteen seventy-seven. He tells her the story he has not told any other girl.

A Gikuyu man spanks a Somali woman. There are unconfirmed rumours that it was a Somali man in a buibui. A Somali man pulls out a sword. Innards the colour of reparations denied and the smell of secessionists spill out into the September sun and into the blocked sewers. Red ceases to be a colour, it becomes everything they know. They are happy to kill and risk being killed in this sweet intermission. War breaks out. No animals spared.

He tells her he was once happy, she smiles and believes the lie, loves him just a bit more for lying. He says he will never forget her name.

She cuts some of the red hair and offers it to him. He puts the hair in his mouth.

The young boys approach them from the darker recesses of the alley; the younger one takes out a tube of hallucinogen and gives it to the other one. Dik Dik gives them a taste of his gin and tonic, a bit of the red hair—if she can belong to him she can belong to them— blesses them in the long way of the cross, a technique he has come to acknowledge as more meaningful than what they taught him to be the truth in catechism classes at an age not so different from the kids he sees in front of him. The initial way of the cross as trailed by the index finger and a reverse of the same, with three insistent kisses on the lips in the fashion of Serie A footballers. It's all he can do in a city like this. The young boys leave without saying a word, not even their eyes are capable of language. They retreat backwards, eyes fixed on the couple.

A giant drive-in cinema shows an Indian film, no cars in the lobby, say, for a woman who sleeps under the tower with her two infants, the older one teaching the other how to cheat at thumb finger sucking. Children in the rows of houses both in the Residentials and ghettos can watch the fuzzy images of Bollywood in the drive-in; this is how from an early age they learn bhangra. The governor discovered this, and, in a new taxation programme, made sure children paid entry fees. The question of where they enter is yet to be resolved. Kenya, 2067. Happiness index better than anywhere else in the world.

Dik Dik remembers coming to the city as a child in search of the orchestra of night and smiling lips: drive-in cinemas; white-chested crows; amputees with placards telling the history of their bad luck; wild pigeons; old women walking so slow they turn into scarecrows, maybe one of them was his grandmother, for he's made sure her grave at Langata Cemetery is empty, so she must be out there, roaming the streets of Nairobi, going around saving the children; the man with long nipples—his father.

The night has a language of empty parking lots, headlights, car horns, incidental white lights on the top of most floors of tall buildings, live bands in famous tourist joints—*Miller's Guide to Nairobi*, 2nd Ed, 2067—rooftop pools illuminated by the light from the eyes of long-dead street children. White skin looks beautiful there, like a Standard Chartered banking hall. Bodies come out of nowhere and occupy the empty spaces.

Dik Dik walks into an alley. Some children are born with congenital heart disorders, holes in the walls of the heart as big as black holes, but he's special enough to be born only with bowlegs. The country missed the World Cup because of these bowlegs. A distant muezzin affirms his belonging to another world but in a language he will never understand. Come here, child. Be good and be gone. Dik Dik tiptoes. Slowly, slowly. Dik Dik tiptoes. Midway through a whistle—John Coltrane, Carnegie Hall, a lost time—he stops, and the language of the arrangement of his bones in the general order of the skeleton appears to say hi to a cobbler in red and green. He smiles, nods back, and reaffirms a long-standing discount, "You will always have a home here." The cobbler's smile is so wide Dik Dik can make out pools of saliva in the gorges of the man's toothless gums. A three-headed mousebird tucks its head from under his apron, he pats its crest and tucks it back, smiles to Dik Dik by way of an apology. Dik Dik needs no shoes owing to the size of his feet. The size of his penis begs to differ.

What is home if you don't have the right size shoes to take you there?

Dik Dik walks into Marienbad, says, "Good morning, M'bad." The people laugh with their mouths closed. In the burrows of their smiles and creases are incomplete guides to difficult museum pieces.

He kisses each man slowly, takes time to get the tilt angle just right, just the right amount of aftershave, just the right amount of tongue. JIMI HENDRIX is playing.

Conversations circle around modern architecture. Ah, Nairobi is a riot in July. The sun is out, Hartlaub's Turacos play in certain gardens. Dead children come out to sing the anthem. So much sun in this city. Wounds fester. Everyone is happy with the government, and the children of diplomats are happier with the dollar rate.

Dik Dik had dated the son of a diplomat not a long time back, he tells them. South Sudan. They toast: here's to wishing for places much farther from the Greenwich Meridian.

There was the her—cinematography and choice of costume notwithstanding—he met along the sands of Casablanca. He forgave her for so many things, pretended not to notice other men (and women), as long as she agreed to sign a memorandum stating their memories would not be erased by the happy men at immigration. Casablanca had old men who reminded him of a rundown smoking zone on Koinange Street, but he stayed there for years, long after his parents had left the place and long after they'd stop sending him postcards. He understood the postcards to be a form of their nostalgia, so he forgave them—it was enough that they suffered. He wanted to be near Europe, in Lampedusa, near the cemetery of sunken boats, in commune with so many West Africans, he could dream dreams where he spoke with an accent and impressed the women almost enough to make them smile but not enough to take them home.

In the end he left, and immigration said the memorandum was a forgery.

Casablanca stayed with him. In a certain dream Dik Dik can smell the loins of a woman who has travelled from Syria through Jordan though Tunisia to Lampedusa only do die at the shallow shores of a European beach. The morning after a child smiles at the shallowness of the shore: she knows it's easy to conquer the ocean for her on this other side; no other truth will be truer than the ocean being conquerable and distance being nothing more than the wet lips of a generous lover between her legs.

Chromosome-1972 calls, says as way of salutation: "What Chromosome sees in the eyes of the goat." He's tired but humours her. She's dialling him in her sleep again. He knows what goat she is speaking of but does not stop her when she goes into the details of its appearance. Finally, she returns to the eyes of the goat. They are far from perfect spheres, she explains. What she means is that she felt something in the way the goat looked at her. It's the same way children born long ago would look at you with tilted heads, thinking: "asshole." It's the same way he looks at her, not entirely trusting her love and all the tongue she offers him, the dead colours, the dead children she brings to life when she licks his anus and tells him it's okay, you don't need to be afraid, there's no shame in enjoying anal. She's saying goat, but he hears ghosts.

A beep goes off, and he notices his register is running low. He dials for the police and gives them her address.

And a Pinch of Salt

Hal Duncan

God works in mysterious ways—down strange back alleys mostly, in enchanting side streets off the boulevard, past the corner boys and through, between the narrow of tenement walls warped to concave overhangs, weird tiered storeys of them rising each side of the cobbled lane to swallow an urban explorer of New Sodom, as a crack in the cityscape, a gorge of interstice all dumpsters and darkness and fire escapes zigzagging up to the jut of rooftops limned with moonlight, and framed between them in the distance up ahead, a queer red iron Tour Eiffel straight from Delaunay's cubist canvas, standing as a foundry-wrought sentinel at avenue's end, down past the rhombuses of red-lit brothel windows where, inside, nine muses are kissing an amorous john called Humphrey to ecstatic death just as is chalked on the pavement underfoot in couplets.

God hawks his services in such mysterious ways, down such entrancing angular wynds, loitering in the doorway of a derelict curio shop, collar upturned to the drizzle, cupping a cigarillo in his hands as he watches out for trade. He doesn't go by God these days, goes by *Che Zeus—Hey, Zeus!* in Español—ever since the old mad blind lame watchmaker, the daddy of Che who ran that hidden emporium of errata, disappeared into the backroom, leaving his orreries and automata to spin and play chess with each other by his equations, the whirs and clicks of rickety clockwork echoing in his empty establishment, sparking the worry of would-be customers dropping in to the ching of the bell above the glass-paneled door, in hope of him tinkering their lives to bliss, the scuttlebutt of his absence slowly spreading until eventually one day Herr Doktor Nietzsche ventured behind the beaded curtain and returned, homburg lowering from his head, hand fiddling at his voluminous handlebar moustache, and indigestion churning in his guts as he declared the old man dead.

It was a sweet relief to Che, truth be told, to be shot of the old loon. Nineteen eons of age and still under the thrall of a tyrant's tantrum surl. He'd tried to steer Sodom's hanging judge to the justice, mercy, and wisdom that the zealous churl laid claim to, standing proud with the whores and faggots of Capernaum and Rome, preaching so-called *sin* to be mere stumble over *skandalon*, a hipster rabbi teaching Hillel's wisdom, but it only ever led to pogroms, inquisitions, and crusades. And a son is always already underling to his dada, damned to at best usurp and become him, as Kronos did Ouranos, as Zeus did Kronos. Scion offshoot and throwback to the aged authoritarian's own infancy in a Cretan cave, struggling not to simply follow a Freudian fate of patricide and powermongering everafter, Che Zeus wept. He wept *a lot*, alone in his cause. There was only ever the two of them, sadly, contrary to popular misconception, just Papa Dada and Junior, the ghost of myth and ritual a mistranslation, Che's *pneuma theos* simply any prophet poet's *holy breath*, their *sacred inspiration*. And Jove Jehovah had no love of the rhapsodes of the figurative, those liemakers to be cast out with the dogs and fornicators and magicians.

So it was a liberation to Che to bury the arcane antiquated Almighty of Himself, to close up the shop peddling its mechanical ceremonies of penitence and perdition, board up the doors and bottleglass windows, take down the marquee lettering that spelled out *LORD*, and let the pillowtalk redeem that epithet to a princely pauper's *adonai*, *Adonis*, sung rather than written as his clients climax under Che's tender ministrations, looking down on the Hand of God cupping their bollocks, the Face of God with lips locked round their cock, gazing up at them with a bottom boi's ardour to know his service is the benediction he aspires to. This is God's deliverance now, the delivery of the perfect blowjob to any and all who happen upon him in an alley of New Sodom—and all will, sooner or later, in some midnight hour of their lives.

He's the best cocksucker you can imagine, you see, the cocksucker you can imagine bested by none—who'd be bested by *every* cocksucker out there if he didn't exist, and so must exist. Who'd be bested by any cocksucker that any son of Sodom ever fucked in the face if every single molly and muscle mary of fair Sodom's citizenry didn't get to jolt their jism down his gulping throat at least once. After all, the ideal is not ideal if it's not actual, as Anselm savvied, scorning the unsustainable paradox of a cocksucker bested by none yet bested by all—albeit Anselm missed that perfection (and more!) in his fancy of the deity. The sainted philosopher of Canterbury missed the knock-ons of his notion, how his human perfections of power, wisdom, love, and truth unfold to perfections of care, of communion. Che, perfect in his cunning and concern, did not, and so, as the exemplary salvator of all hanker, all yen, he stood at his father's grave, placed a stone upon the granite slab, and knew it true: he must perfect his succor with actuality. So saith Anselm. So, lest the ideal is not ideal, Che *will* give you the ultimate blowjob at some point.

Or he'll let you suck his perfect cock, of course, if you'd prefer, if your yen is to swallow the ropy spurted nectar of his cum; or he'll let you fuck his perfect ass, riding you cowboy as a power bottom, pounding you into him, rapturous to be impaled, pierced to the core and filled with your prick, wild as Dionysus ramming a figwood dildo up his arse and crying out to the gentle shepherd Prosymnus; or he'll top you as you've never been topped, splay your legs wide and high with a clamp of hands on ankles, plunging into and pressing over down upon you, hand at your throat, flip you sideways, up to all fours, grip on your hips now, taking you so wholly he takes you *over* in a frenzy of eudaimonia, of *enthousiasmos* in its ancient sense; or he'll be a she, and dive your muff, tongue you to waves of orgasm, an entire Pacific crashing over and through you; she'll fuck or be fucked by you in whatever permutation of whatever options will be, for you, perfection.

All this is proven, ontologically assured by these words themselves conjuring for you the ideal totality of all ideals in the shape of a human, all capacities of power, wisdom, love, and truth fused to a perfect stance, a perfect disposition acting perfectly and so necessarily manifest, that stance substanced in the requisite flesh of requisite fuckability. Even in mysterious ways, Che *works*, and he's working anywhen and everywhen, so sooner or later you're bound to take the right wrong turn hard left and stroll past the hustler in the hoody where he lurks. You'll take a chance on his cruising glance, and you won't regret it.

What you've spent on him, or in him (or her) will be all the payment asked for by this hustler God, Che Zeus. This may be a trade to him, a job to work in his peculiar byways, in the queer passages of New Sodom that slice a non-Euclidean angle between this boulevard of San Francisco and that avenue of Pompeii, but his profession is as much vocation, his craft an art, his knack a nature. And what does a God need coin for anyway, or any such token offerings, when he's drunk the libation from your cock, had your unction splatted over his cheek and chest? Try and pass the bucks to him, with cash or kudos, and he'll wave away a payoff paltry in comparison to the sacred balm. The charity of *caritas* is welcome to the vagabond kid, rough-trading rentboy punk, Che Zeus—*agape* shared simply another aspect of ardour's concord—but soul debt redeemed was Papa Dada's way, the barter of obedience and oblations for grace. Fuck that, says Che.

And you will. You'll fuck that and be fucked. And all you'll offer him in exchange that isn't his already is a hand reached down to where he kneels before you, thumbing a stray gloop at the snick of his smile into a twirl of tongue and smack of lips. In a lock of forearms, you'll haul him to his feet, and kiss him hard, taste yourself on him as he hauls his ratty jeans up, nooks his unskivvied tackle in the pod of denim, and buttons up, and buckles his bullet belt. Maybe you won't still be in the alley, so you'll grab his sleeveless tee for him from the rug at your feet, as you sit on the edge of the hotel bed to prise your heels into his scuffed white vintage baseball boots, and kneel yourself to lace them up for him as his John the Baptist. You'll sniff the armpit of that sleeveless tee, white cotton and lycra blend printed with a pencil sketch of an Antinous statue, snuffling half to test if it's too rank to wear and half to relish the Sweat of God, the gorgeous goaty *kinabra* of God on this skintight second skin of him that you pull on now, to pose, slinked as the hustler Che to have communed in the giving and getting of the perfect lay, so perfect that who can say who's who now in the mingle of flesh scents?

And maybe you'll dig a cigarillo from the pack in the pocket of your jacket, fetched from the hallway where it was dumped, and set it twixt yer lips, and he'll light it for you with his Zippo, or vice versa, and he'll hand you the first, as you light a second one for him. He'll make you coffee in a little scullery off his kitchen living room, in your wee steel moka pot, setting it on one hob of the gas cooker to heat to a rabid gurgle while the butter melts into the olive oil in the frying pan on the hob beside it, and he cracks two eggs into a glass jug, adding dried basil from a flip-top jar, and garlic powder, and a pinch of salt, and a splut of milk, folding and stirring the mix with a fork before pouring it into a sizzle of pan, gently crunkling the edges inward—with a tip of pan after to spread the unsolid egg into the space—until the thin round flattish rumple of omelette is ready to be flip-folded with a spatula and slid onto a plate, and served with the coffee to Che where he sits on your black leather sofa, sunlit, in your candy-striped boxer briefs, checking messages on his Nokia, an unshaven Galilean, swarthy and lithe as a fisher on a Minoan fresco. Fucking A, he'll say. Cheers, man.

No worries, you'll say.

Whether it's you or he who'll scoff the nosh down is … unpredictable, a quirk of the perfection's happenstance actuality which, born of the haccaeity of you, can only be unique in every instance, unique as any instant's thisness. Either way, one of you will blow on your java to cool it, and the other will savour the lush of pursing lips, the *swrrp* of a sip sucking Nicaraguan Arabica, Indonesian Robusta, or Philippine Liberica. Eyes glancing round the room in a comfortably awkward silence, scanning the shelves for totems of identity ... best left for you to fill in as and when the moment's come. Kitsch teraphim? Or trinkets as simply elegant as a nautilus shell? Wait and see.

Take it as it comes.

And then move on with a parting kiss, out the door, down the stairs of the tenement close and out into New Sodom's streets, on a stride of pride, headed wherever home is now, Che, everywhere and anywhere.

Escape to Hell

Iheoma Nwachukwu

Two days in this sewer. Saif and Motassim are where? Saif returns with news from Misrata yesterday as I'm fucking Hana, my smallest bodyguard, a quick one before her shift ends. Saif curses and crawls out—am I crazy because I'm horny in war? Because fuck is neat and sweet in a sewer?

It's hot in here. Midday hot. It's like sensing the world in a black oil drum. I have crushed what must be Afra somewhere, and its smell floats about like a won't-leave ghost. I feel an odd buoyancy like that time I floated in water for the first time here in Sirte. Sound slams into my ears. Ti-ti-dum! Ratatat-titi-dum! Supporters holding the city. I'm a beast on all fours in my yellow jelabia and faded brown trousers, trying to find the least-hurting angle for my back.

I cut my face shaving this morning, and I'm wondering what it would be like to die. They died unable to hurl themselves in my dreams: the stupid students I hanged every April in the gym room beginning in 1977! The Cyprus businessman I told Ramadan to shoot in the mouth, in his office, until he dies! Mahmoud in Tripoli—I packed his body in a short box back to his wife! Political prisoners whose mothers are whores, I fed to crocodiles! Yes! Each one of those scheming rats! How could their deaths affect me? It was my life or theirs! I chose mine!

I feel strange making this tape. Why am I doing this today? Who am I making it for? Am I afraid of something? Will my voice in this rectangle-shaped thing mean what I want it to mean? Mean anything to you? Who are you? I am not a crazy man.

I have been meaning to write another collection of short stories. Like *Escape to Hell*, that first one. Again this one will be called *Escape to Hell, Part Two*.

This whole war, I will talk about it, in an essay in *Escape to Hell*. This life, this funny life, of Muammar Qaddafi. The world is a cuddly chameleon. That's why the hardiest of men are fooled time and again. Anti-American riots in Tripoli in 1962 over the Cuban missile crisis and today the same people, my people, support the same country they rioted against?

I gave them free electricity, go in the cities and look! They pay nothing! I told the banks, "Give loan to man and boy at zero interest."

The banks do it! When any Libyan buys a car, my government takes fifty percent of the cost! Largest oil reserves in Africa! Low cost of oil production! Libya has no external debt! I did it! Libya has foreign reserves of fifty billion dollars! Look in your computers! Look in your computers! Don't be fooled!

Yesterday, Motassim was welcomed by Bill Clinton's wife wearing a red and black dress! Today, she bombs me! Two years ago, Britain, that whore! They sold me military planes, chemical weapons, today they have bombed me seven hundred times! France, two years ago, also, military planes and fuses, today they've bombed me two thousand times! Italy, electronic equipment and military planes, Belgium, small guns! Today, they are all bombing me! Why? Who did I hurt? Who have I hurt? Their people? Because of Lockerbie? That was a long time ago! What else did I do? I did nothing else! Oh, okay, the discotheque I bombed in Berlin? I paid compensation!

I will make a bonfire of the world with the Sarkozy documents waiting for me next week in Algiers when I go to see my wife. You will see! Do you know why NATO is here? This war is for our ...

Sshhhhh ...
—I see many legs approaching in the wrong way, to the sewer, to this sewer. A face.—Peeping.—It's looking at me. Hana?

"Is. Is that you, Motassim?"

"Come out! We have slaughtered your sons like the swines—"

"Who are you—"

"—they are! The whores you surround yourself with, we've raped and killed! Your fighters bleated like sick goats when we cornered and slaughtered them like flies!"

"Liar!"

"This blood-soaked singlet in my hand belongs to that cunt, Motassim. You son of a whore! Come out in peace or die like a dog! Muammar Qaddafi!! The people's revolution is here for justice—"

"*Ah—Alla-hu Ak—bar ...*"

The Lady and the Poet

Walter Tierno

● translated by Christopher Kastensmidt ●

Drizzle

In the old days it drizzled a lot around these parts. Now not so much. Nowadays, the skies punish the people with raging storms, heartless cold, and dog day summers. The drizzles were irritating, it's true, but they had a soft hand. A shameless caress, as the Poet would say. Today, the skies hand us beatings. They take revenge for all the garbage we breathe on them.

I was born in those days, when the drizzle still treated us with affection. It wasn't so long ago. It was a few years after the so-called revolution broke out, won by generals in their bedclothes, without a fight or a shot. Just orders, trickery, and phone calls. A sad revolt carried out by almost normal men full of fear and boasting, their heads burning in rage. Lots of people found it pretty. They still do. They never realized how many soldiers of distorted honor and bandits with recycled files received license to exercise their quirks in a variety of creative and confusing ways.

I was born at a time when disagreement wasn't open to debate, only to a beating. In those times, they silenced voices and songs, dreams and ironies. They hung some from the "parrot perch," so they might sing pleas and the names of their companions. Some spirits ended up broken beyond repair. They rained down blows in the name of so-called liberty, the opposite of communism, a confusing term that even today few people understand. Even Dona Nha, who has an explanation for everything:

"They said 'round here that cumnism was gonna be good. Who knows? I'm too old to understan' these thangs."

Dona Nha's greatest treasure doesn't lie in her political convictions but in her repertoire of stories. She has many to tell. Even from those

times of beatings and kind drizzle. Most, of course, are invented. But good causes are like that. A liar like no other, she says she was born a slave and that she saw and heard more than human eyes and ears should. Among the many lies that inhabit her memory, one beautiful and sad memory speaks of the Lady's love for the Poet.

Of when they met

Dona Nha and the Lady met in a cell. Their bodies naked, intertwined to exchange heat, they also traded names and stories. The Lady told Dona Nha that it drizzled a lot on the day that she met the Poet and drizzled a lot on the first night they had under a black and overcast sky. It was with sweet words that she had never heard that the Poet convinced her to give herself to him up there on the building's flagstones without ceiling, heat, comfort, or shame. Under the drizzle, their heads, backs, and feet got wet, and in those places the water turned icy. The pubes between her legs also got wet, and there the water turned flavorful and hot. He had no qualms and an appetite for everything. He didn't just have her. He devoured her, and for that, he became the Poet. Not this poet or that poet. To the rest of the world, maybe, but not for her. For her, he became the Poet with a capital *P*. He was the Poet less for the force of his art than for the music he played on her body with fingers, tongue, and humidity.

The Lady and the Poet met each other as you might expect for a solitary man with more fire than reason and a whore with less ambition than passion. A night of partying, alcohol, and smoking. An orgy of the alienated and politicized, infidels and believers. Some in search of a release that no one knew how to describe with words, even those they swore to understand. Others in search of something for which to search.

The Lady wasn't working. She had accepted the invite from a friend, a more experienced and disputed professional, those with money to burn and a delicious decadence in their eyes. Those who hadn't visited the beds of both ladies had lived just a bit sadder life.

The ladies' civilian disguises fooled most but not the Poet. He hadn't visited their beds but was infatuated by others of the same nature; he was quite familiar with love professionals and genuinely respected them as only a Poet can.

He was there because he was the friend of someone but didn't quite remember who, and no one seemed to care. It was one more welcome mouth for drinking, smoking, conversing, and—

depending on how the night went—kissing and sucking. When he laid eyes on the Lady and her friend, he smelled their goals and doubts, stories, regrets, and conceits. The goals and doubts of the Lady stirred him the most. He introduced himself. He flowered his brazenness with verse and capped off his conquest with a hot and wet kiss.

And don't think, reader, that the nature of the Lady's profession had dried her heart. The pleasures that she offered "down there" were obtained for short periods of time with large bills. But her spirit, a source of pleasure reserved for few mortals, could only be reached "up there" and never with money. The Lady fell in love, and that's saying a lot. Even Dona Nha's only eye sparkled with sincerity when she spoke of that love because she had seen and confirmed it—later on, I'll tell you how.

Love bloomed, watered by sweat, fertilized by intimacies, rooted in the genitals. The Lady and the Poet connected on beds, sheets, sofas, carpets, tiles, plates, and silverware. They invaded each other under the sun, the rain, and the drizzle. Principally under the drizzle. And they repeated rituals, positions, and scenarios many times.

But never under the full moon.

Never.

The reader might find this strange. But there isn't so much mystery if I say that he was the youngest, the first rod after a progeny of six girls. If you don't understand what kind of life is reserved for that type of unlucky soul, I repeat the words of Dona Nha:

"You don' know? Boy like that 'comes a werewolf."

The Lady knew that recipe.

"You're a wolf?" she whispered in her lover's ear during a random night on the bed. They had just come, their bodies asking for rest and their spirits clamoring for intimacy, and he had just numbered the members of his family.

The Poet neither denied nor confirmed. He just entered into her one more time, a debauched smile on his lips, a loving jolt with his pelvis. Their pubes mixed below, and their mouths pressed up top. Everything trembled when she came again. This time, provocatively, he didn't accompany her. He let her tremble alone: a bit embarrassed, a ton happy.

"You ruin me for clients," she said. And she regretted it. Why talk about clients to a boyfriend?

Boyfriend.

The word sounded sweet in her head, but she didn't repeat it out loud. She was scared of its fragility. Could a whore date? Her older friend said yes, and the Lady pretended that her opinion was worth a lot.

"You're my wolf-boyfriend," she said, but not aloud. She feared the frailty of happiness. She enjoyed her love in silence, and it was for love and silence that she messed up.

The Poet was shameless. He embraced everything that was pleasant and immoral except for the lack of justice. And justice is a slippery thing that everyone tries to grab, feel up, and keep as company.

To make it worse, the Poet wasn't one to simply hate. If he hated, he acted. And he would take up iron and lead to fight in the battles that arose in those times against the old, pajama-wearing generals.

Dona Nha, in her simplicity or wisdom, I don't know which, summed up the gang well:

"A group o' sonbitches, tha's what ..."

His visits to the Lady diminished. He got involved with the comrades. He fought.

The lovers' trysts became every time sadder and more bureaucratic. One day, she gathered her courage and complained. He didn't glance at her eyes when he responded:

"It's not the fight that makes a guy limp. The fight, when there is one, is good. What makes a guy limp is the inglorious thanklessness."

"What happened."

"Our blood for what? For sheep? For people that don't see. Not because it's not in front of their eyes but because they don't want to see it."

"I don't understand."

"I'm tired of this shit. Of living like a warrior, to be remembered as a thief. If that's what's it's for ..."

He didn't say anything else. He just fucked her, quickly and unsatisfactorily. While he put on his underpants, he grumbled:

"Anonymity castrates."

The Lady's pain

A week after that conversation, the Poet landed in the Lady's hovel without warning, breathless. His tongue out, eyes tired. She was on the job, and he was blunt and objective:

"Get out!"

With considerable strength for someone so thin, he booted an old man from the room. The clothes followed right after.

He slammed the door and turned to the Lady.

"You're not going to receive anyone else today!" It had been an order, not a question, and it surprised her so much she didn't know how to respond.

The Poet had brought a full suitcase and pushed it under the bed. As if he hadn't done anything unusual, he hugged and kissed his lover. His lips rubbed her ear while he whispered:

"Don't attend anyone else until I get back."

"What's this? I have to work."

"You're not paying attention," he hollered. "I need you to pay attention. Don't attend anyone. And don't touch the suitcase. Don't open it. Never. And don't talk about it or show it to anyone. Do you understand?"

She hadn't understood.

"When are you coming back?"

"There's going to be a full moon. I'll come back afterwards."

"When?"

"When the moon changes, you know that! Just ... just do what I ask, all right? It will be worth it, I promise."

She looked at him with mistrust, hurt, and excitement.

"What's in the suitcase?"

"Our future."

She tried not to laugh at his strange, solemn silence.

"A big suitcase like that could carry a lot of kinds of future. But it could also be empty."

"It's not. It carries a lot more than it seems. Believe me, that's our future there. A new life, without glory, but with our asses free and happy. And fuck everything."

"You're crazier than usual."

"It's true. But don't open the suitcase. Leave it hidden."

How many other lovers haven't sinned for foolish zeal? For the senseless will to protect the other, keeping them ignorant? If the poet had revealed the suitcase's contents to the Lady, she certainly would have found a better place to hide it. And how many other lovers haven't suffered for blind faith? For the senseless will to obey? Had the Lady searched the suitcase, she would have avoided the men finding it two days later.

They kicked the door in, and the only reason they didn't turn the entire apartment upside down was that the suitcase was in such an easy place to find. They threw it on the bed and opened it with a pocket knife. Inside shone every type of bill from old to fresh. The cops laughed with debauchery and pocketed a lot of it without the least decency.

"Where?" growled the German, a subject with eyes full of disgust and disdain, a soft belly spread over the badly strapped belt. The lackluster hair color had earned him his nickname among his subordinates. German had been a crook. He had a nose for hunting communists. For that, they had forgiven his crimes and given him a troop of scoundrels.

"Where, dammit?" he repeated, confronting the Lady.

"What?"

It wasn't the answer he'd been waiting for. He slapped her with the palm of his calloused hand.

"Where's that cuckold boyfriend of yours? Hurry up, whore, out with it!"

"I don't know," responded the Lady, between tears and pain.

"This one's a whore and stupid? Your boyfriend fucked you over, do you understand? He fucked everybody. You see this money here? Where do you think it came from? From a robbery your boyfriend participated in."

"Lies ..." she sobbed.

"Huh? Speak up, dammit!"

"It's a lie."

"Are you calling me a liar? He smiled. "That's disrespecting authority, isn't it, Sideburns?"

One of his companions, owner of generous sideburns, agreed with a nod.

"He's no bandit," she defended him pathetically. "He's a poet."

"A poet?" German guffawed. "Besides a terrorist, a cuckold, and a son of a bitch, he's a fag! Had to be."

"Don't bother sticking the broom handle into that one, he might like it."

"Shut up, Sideburns!" yelled German, while he turned back to the Lady. "Listen here, you whore. Your little fag poet is a terrorist and communist son of a bitch. He assaulted a bank with a bunch of communist sons of bitches and turned tail on his comrades. They're all singing in jail already. Your fucking boyfriend is the only one left. Where is he?"

The Lady said nothing.

"All you have to do is tell us where the cuckold is, and we'll let you go ..."

The Lady sealed her lips and looked away.

German laughed.

"Is that right? Not going to collaborate? Fuck it! Your problem!" He turned to Sideburns. "That's exactly what I wanted."

"Tasty ..." growled Bubblegum, who stood next to Sideburns and caressed his revolver.

"Frame this bitch," continued German. "We'll talk in the cooler." To the Lady he said, "You don't want to do what's right, go to hell! Shitty bitch."

They dragged the Lady by her hair. They forced her to march with slaps to the neck and thighs, her wrists decorated by handcuffs. They got in a small car, the Lady squeezed between bodies with little care for hygiene. Before the darkness of the hood, a whisper with the smell of sour beer puffed in her right ear:

"This little peacock won't take long to sing like a bird."

They laughed.

The trip lasted longer than the Lady's stomach could manage, and she arrived at the jail with her ears burning for having obliged the cops to stop for her to vomit. They had raised the hood but hadn't uncovered her eyes.

They threw the Lady into a cold, humid, fetid cell. She stayed there for many hours. Between her and the corridor: thick, rusty bars. Over her head, a strong lamp. And growing fear.

When German remembered her, he made a point of getting her personally. Walking down the corridor, they were accompanied by a symphony of shouts and moans. They entered a dark cell. The diligence men were there, sweaty, surrounded by cigarette smoke and the smell of sweat, come, and piss. Their faces were lost in the penumbra. They put her under a lamp brighter than the one in her cell.

"Take off your clothes," said German.

She didn't move.

"Now the whore is embarrassed? I told you to take off your fucking clothes, dammit! Hurry up! If you don't take them off nice, you'll do it under a beating, you bitch."

"What do you ..." she tried to ask.

"Shut up! The one who asks the questions here is me!"

A slap to the face, another to the back of her head, a kick in the thigh, a hand ripping her blouse here, another pulling her skirt there. The tears, inevitable.

"Are you shy? Take off the panties and the bra, too. Move it! A whore with decency, ever seen that before?"

She obeyed.

The Lady felt pain in many forms. Shock, drowning, beaten by a wet rag, and swinging from the parrot perch.

"What are you complaining about? You're a whore, aren't you?" was what each of the five men who raped her said. "And if you get pregnant, you'll remove the little shit because sons of whores turn into communists when they grow up," said the last one who came in her.

They asked about the Poet. Who he was, where he came from, and where he was hiding.

"Open that beak, that's what's best for you. The guy is worthless. He tricked his own associates and filched all the money.

They asked about lots of other things. Many times. She didn't have a response for anything.

"Why are you protecting that fag?" The cop took on a conciliatory tone of voice. He held her head by the back of the neck. The parrot perch stopped swinging. "We know he left the suitcase with you, didn't he?"

They said his name. It sounded strange in her ears and not just because of the buzzing. To her, he was just the Poet. Her wolf-boyfriend. Not that dull, pompous name.

Her love faltered when something in her anus heated up and burned.

Suddenly, the questions stopped. The men, frustrated.

"Wash this whore and take her back. Tomorrow, we'll continue. I have a date with the missus."

Sideburns risked a joke about his boss's tenderness.

"Shut up!" hollered German. "That's why all you fuck is communists and whores on the parrot perch. You have to take care of a decent woman, don't forget it!"

The other didn't let it get to him. He kept laughing.

"Keep on laughing. While you stay here ass-fucking terrorists, I'm going to have a delicious dinner and a clean fuck."

They took down the Lady. The cold floor, wet and filthy against her back. Her body deadened. She lifted her head. Her arms and legs were numb. She gathered some strength from who-knows-where.

"Is tonight a full moon?"

Only German's eyes showed a hint shadow. A point of fear, very discreet and soon stifled. And she—the person with the most cracked, violated spirit in the room—was the only one who noticed.

"And why do you want to know, you whore?" he snarled. "It's none of your business. Move, dammit," he urged the others, "take this sack of shit to her cell. Tomorrow, we'll continue."

They delivered the Lady to her cell. She passed out when her head bounced on the ground but soon awoke, her attention caught by the image of the creature they dragged down the corridor. A woman of dark, dull skin, her hair gray. A mature face marked by experience and sensuality. The left foot missing.

The Lady heard her screams for hours.

In the end, confused or tired, the executioners tossed Nha in the Lady's cell. Some rags covered her parts. Her strong body, full of curves, scars, and stories, had been treated even worse than the Lady's, but the punishment had done less damage to her spirit.

When they were alone, Nha called the torturers names that even the Lady didn't know. Upon finishing her list of swear words, she surprised the Lady with a debauched smile.

"Fuhget it. They dun me bad, but I'll have my revenge."

They had a break from the pain, a crumb of peace. They held each other for heat and comfort. The Lady wanted to back away when she spotted Sideburns in the corridor, watching them. His face twisted in a perverted smile, his right hand on his penis. Nha held her.

"We have ta keep warm," she said. "Fuhget that 'un."

She gently kissed her new companion's face and placed a hand over her left butt cheek.

They heard the heaving respiration and the burping whisper of the man while he masturbated, his moan when he came, half a minute later, and his tottering steps when he left.

"You best believe 'at I keep 'em all up here." Nha pointed to her own head.

They engaged in a murmured conversation like old friends who had just run into each other.

Nha told one of her many tall tales. The Lady paid her back by speaking of her Poet, of how she'd met him and how wonderfully he fucked her. She had barely laid her head on her new friend's firm thighs when she heard the first shots.

Slaughter

And who said there was a weapon that could kill the wretch? He neither sweated nor smiled nor stopped. He advanced through torn-off legs and dilacerated heads. His claws punctured and ripped, his teeth ripped and dismembered, the long, black hairs shone, covered in fresh blood.

Executioners ran and died.

A Poet whose bestiality proclaimed itself in blood and guts, fear and shit. Men who had just tortured and raped without mercy now begged and shat themselves.

Nha and the Lady would have shit themselves too when they saw the beast fill the cell door. But one of them had seen and lived through much worse, and the other recognized him, even covered in fur and fury.

The lock burst under the force of the deformed arms. The Lady helped support Nha, who hobbled without the prosthesis that substituted her lost foot, confiscated upon her arrest.

They passed through bodies and blood, pieces of meat and cloth. Other captives were freed and ran without restraint, guided by a fear much stronger than gratitude.

They reached the liberty of the night. The fresh caress of a fine drizzle. The narrow, deserted street was the end of the world. A miniscule wound in the city, unimportant, without light, without eyes or ears. In a sky without stars through a break in the thick clouds, the moon showed itself. An inebriating, pulsing disk. The Poet, an inexplicable beast, breathed its scanty light and exhaled power and glory. The Lady touched his fur, his snout, his vibrant tongue. He was naked, and his red member, quivering, was an insane invitation. She searched Nha's eyes and found a sly, unabashed smile.

"Don' you know these wolves is like that? You carry they litter, they knows where you be."

The Lady touched her womb. A promise of weeping came from her lips.

"I'm ..."

"Gots ta be. How else you think your wolf done found us?"

"They hit me so much ... Do you think ..." Her voice faltered.

"Sons o' wolves is strong. [Si apuquenti naum]."

The Poet stared at her with welcoming eyes. With his wet snout he smelled the face of his offspring's mother. She felt his shivering and in the heaving groaning could smell the metallic taste of blood. He had killed so many for her. Almost all of her torturers.

Almost.

They heard a crack. A shattered howl of pain. The furry body collapsed. Behind it, the Lady saw German. He held a smoking revolver.

"I knew it!" he said. His eyes bugged out, injected with fear, paranoia, and victory.

The weapon spat two more times. One shot wounded the Lady's leg. The other knocked down Dona Nha.

German's finger didn't stop pulling the trigger, but the gun's hammer struck in vain. Three bullets was all he had in the cylinder. While he put more bullets in the gun, he slobbered and muttered, "Sons of bitches. They're all sons of bitches. I knew that fag was a werewolf. I knew it. I told them so."

The Poet rose up, his body trembling, blood running from his snout, but this time it wasn't from enemies, it was his own. He advanced on the cop. Desperate and afraid beyond reason, German gave up on the gun and fled. Why stay there risking death at the claws of a dying beast? But he wasn't as fast as he should have been. One of the Poet's claws drew a scar on his back that would accompany him for the rest of his life. The tear burned but didn't stop him from fleeing at an insane run, far away from that madness.

Then the Poet died. Without a goodbye, a last stanza, a final kiss. He just died.

The hairs fell out, the face regained its softness, and in death, the human prevailed.

Dona Nha barely escaped death but not without a price. The shot that had brought her down shattered her left eye. With pains that punished them from the surface of their skin to the depths of their souls, she and the Lady braced each other and got out of there.

The newspapers mentioned nothing the following day. No one beyond those present knew, and not many were left.

The bullet that one of Dona Nha's friends pulled from the Lady's leg was a macabre souvenir. A silver bullet. German had known. He had always known that a wolf would come after its lover. He could have put silver bullets in all his colleague's guns but was selfish in his triumph. No one ever knew why or how, but life was generous to German.

There he is now, so many years later.

It's drizzling. The same soft caress that cradled the pleasures of my parents over the flagstones. Dona Nha points him out, but she doesn't need to. He's fat, satisfied. He drops a bag of trash on the sidewalk in front of his house. I've never seen him before, but I know who he is. It impregnates him: all the arrogance, the disorder, the hate.

"The time has come," my mother announces. In her voice, a coldness I don't recognize.

We get out of the car. Dona Nha offers me an accomplice's smile. She's the one who calls the man's attention.

"Gehmun?"

The man freezes. He faces them a bit challenging, a bit frightened.

"Do you know who we are?" my mother asks.

"More or less," he sneers. "I think I've seen your snouts before. Didn't I fuck your assess?"

Dona Nha laughs.

"We ne'er forget you. Our asses don' either. They still hurtin'."

A nervous smile trembles on the man's lips. The realization of the inevitable shines in his old eyes.

"You took a long time."

"No," my mother responds. "We didn't take a long time. We waited. Have you had a good life?"

"I can't complain. Family, cash. Life was good."

"How nice."

"What do you want? An apology."

"We could start there."

He smiles with disdain and sizes me up.

"And that one?"

"My daughter."

"One of mine?"

"No. The Poet's."

"Oh ... A bitch, then? I guess I didn't beat as hard as I should have. I should have made you shit that little turd before she was born. Disgusting, the daughter of a werewolf with a whore."

He growls and tries to pull a gun from his pants. He doesn't have time.

I'm my daddy's girl. And that is his only legacy. I'm not a male son preceded by six sisters. The full moon will never transform me. My incisors will never grow, my hair will not cover me. I'm just a bit stronger. A bit faster. Not much, but enough to take the gun from the hand of my father's assassin. He, a pot-bellied torturer unaccustomed to defending himself, barely sees my strong hand snap over his. The revolver flies. I grab it in the air. I toss it away. We won't need it.

My mother came prepared. She draws her pistol and points it at German. She savors the moment for two seconds. Time enough for German to regret everything he'd never done. Everything he's built and will never enjoy.

She pulls the trigger with neither hurry nor hesitation.

The hole between the eyes is small. The gap that opens on the back of his head lets out blood, brains, and spirit. Dona Nha watches, her glass eye gleaming like a black fire.

We flee without hurry. Practically a stroll. Our chests are light now, uncongested and without sadness. We walk without asking anything of each other. Up in the sky, the moon shines with force, bathing us with promises of anonymous glories and love stories. It congratulates us for the love we've lived and for the revenge that is so cold and sweet.

Like so many other times, they tell me stories. They're all as fake as this one. I promise them that, at home, I'll write about the Lady's love for her Poet Wolf, and like them, I'll insist that it's all true, even the drizzle's caress on our faces.

Salvation

Claudia De Bella

Dislocating. Dismembering. Flaying. It's in your blood, and there's nothing you can do about it.

I've been an executioner since I got to Salvation. Back on Earth, I was hunted, locked away, and drugged to prevent me from relapsing. Here, I get a government salary. And more important, I'm completely happy.

I'm asked to kill them slowly, but sometimes I can't. Some of them whine and beg for mercy, and those are the most annoying. I look at their faces, and I only want to crush them—their eyes popping out of their skulls, their jaws broken in three parts. I can't wait to smash their ribs. I want to see them dead. Then excitement makes me hurry, and they don't get the proper punishment, the suffering quota established by the Law. But the Court Head is satisfied with me. I do my job very well. I'm useful to society, he always tells me.

The crime they've committed doesn't matter. Father Alfonso says that any action against the Doctrine is an equally serious offence and deserves the highest penalty. Here in Salvation there's no difference between insulting a workman and murdering a priest. You are pure, or you're not. You can't damage the Creator's work in any way. Except for me: I'm an executioner, the armed hand of the Divine Justice.

So they come to me. The ritual is very simple. Once they prove to be guilty, which they always do, they're quickly removed from Court and brought here. There are no prisons on this planet, just waiting rooms. I wait for them a little uneasily with that tickle of enthusiasm and anticipation I always feel when work is coming.

The iron door opens, and I see the convict for the first time. I immediately start to consider the method. If they are big and strong, much better. There's a lot to do before they give up. The weak need more subtlety. A powerful, well-applied blow can kill them at once, and that's not the idea. Men, women, young, old … each requires a special, customized treatment adapted to their bone structure, their more or less rebellious personality, their will to fight the punishment or to submit themselves to it.

I've developed my technique to such a point that I can plan the whole procedure in a few seconds. A quick look is enough to diagnose the sequences which guarantee the longest hours of pain with the deepest possible damage, yet keeping them alive. The Law orders they must die at least a week after the verdict. I'm proud to say some of them last as much as three weeks. I've been awarded for making them last that long.

When we're left alone, the first thing I do is remove their cuffs. It's funnier when they're loose, running around the dungeon like frenzied rats, thinking they can escape. Other executioners use tools, but that's not very manly. I think my hands are there for a purpose, and so are my feet, my shoulders, my elbows. No weapon is more sacred than this body the Creator has given me. Knuckles hitting flesh until blood sprays out. From both of us. My colleagues don't know what they're missing.

It's just a matter of hitting and punching and piercing and pulling hair out and dislocating members and tearing skin open and breaking mouths until they can't scream anymore. When they've turned into a bloody mess, you apply different punishments, less frequent but more insidious. And on and on, until one pain or another destroys their last resistance and they let themselves die. That's mercy, Father Alfonso says—giving them enough time to be purified by suffering and to regret their sins.

I've never understood why Salvation is excluded from the usual navigation routes. There's so much holiness here, so much attachment to the true precepts of harmonic cohabitation that everyone should spend some time on this planet and learn and follow its example.

When the Earth jailers dropped me in a field near New Bethlehem, hoping that I, unable to restrain myself, would soon go back to my old tricks and be arrested, judged, and executed by the Salvation Courts, they never imagined I'd become an executioner myself. I'm eternally indebted to them. Thanks to those jailers, I discovered my real vocation, the mission the Creator had set aside for me since I was born. I only had to find the place where my particular skills were needed, not considered a perversion but an exceptional gift. People here appreciate my real value, and I enjoy every single day of my life as I serve the only true religion doing what I like best.

How many sinners have I redeemed? Two hundred and thirty-seven, according to the ecclesiastic records ... two hundred and thirty-seven souls that finally admitted their mistakes thanks to me. I know I've already gained my place in Heaven. But I'm not eager to get there yet. My paradise is here, in Salvation, in this dungeon I'll never leave because Father Alfonso says I must not be blemished by the impurity from outside. That's why he protects me with the padlocks securing my door.

But who cares about freedom? As long as that door keeps opening, as long as there are sinners who challenge the Divine Law, as long as I am the one to lead them along the path of forgiveness, and—above all—as long as I continue hearing their bones shatter when I throw them against the stone walls, I'll always think I'm the most fortunate man in the universe, and I'll thank the Creator for the pleasures He has bestowed on me, which I'm certain I rightfully deserve.

How to Remember to Forget to Remember the Old War

Rose Lemberg

for Bogi Takács

At the budget committee meeting this morning, the pen in my hand turns into the remote control of a subsonic detonator. It is familiar—heavy, smooth, the metal warm to the touch. The pain of recognition cruises through my fingers and up my arm, engorges my veins with unbearable sweetness. The detonator is gunmetal gray. My finger twitches, poised on the button.

I shake my head, and it is gone. Only it is still here, the taste of blood in my mouth, and underneath it, unnamed acidic bitterness. Around the conference table the faces of faculty and staff darken in my vision. I see them—aging hippies polished by their long academic careers into a reluctant kind of respectability; accountants neat in bargain bin clothes for office professionals; the dean, overdressed but defiant in his suit and dark blue tie with a class pin. They've traveled, I am sure, and some had protested in the streets back in the day and thought themselves radicals; but there's none here who would not recoil in horror if I confessed my visions.

I do not twitch. I want to run away from the uncomplicated, slightly puffy expressions of those people who'd never faced the battlefield, never felt the ground shake, never screamed tumbling facedown into the dirt. But I have more self-control than to flee. When it comes my time to report, I am steady. I concentrate on the numbers. The numbers have never betrayed me.

At five p.m. sharp I am out of the office. The airy old space is supposed to delight with its tall, cased windows and the afternoon sun streaming through the redwoods, but there's nothing here I want to see. I walk briskly to the Downtown Berkeley BART station and catch a train to the city. The train rattles underground, all stale air and musty seats. The people studiously look aside, giving each other the safety of not-noticing, bubbles of imaginary emptiness in the crowd. The mild heat of bodies and the artificially illuminated darkness of the tunnel take the edge off.

When I disembark at Montgomery, the sky is already beginning to darken, the edges of pink and orange drawn in by the night. I could have gotten off at Embarcadero, but every time I decide against it—the walk down Market Street towards the ocean gives me a formality of approach which I crave without understanding why. My good gray jacket protects against the chill coming up from the water. The people on the street—the executives and the baristas, the shoppers and the bankers—all stare past me with unseeing eyes.

They shipped us here, I remember. Damaged goods, just like other states shipped their mentally ill to Berkeley on Greyhound buses: a one-way ticket to nowhere, to a place that is said to be restful and warm in the shadow of the buildings, under the bridges, camouflaged from this life by smells of pot and piss. I am luckier than most. Numbers come easy to me, and I look grave and presentable in my heavy jackets that are not armor. Their long sleeves hide the self-inflicted scars.

I remember little. Slivers. But I still bind my chest and use the pronoun they, and I wear a tight metal bracelet on my left arm. It makes me feel secure, if not safe. It's only a ploy, this bracelet I have found, a fool's game at hope. The band is base metal but without any markings, lights, or familiar pinpricks of the signal. Nothing flows. No way for Tedtemár to call, if ever Tedtemár could come here.

Northern California is where they ship the damaged ones, yes, even interstellars.

Nights are hard. I go out to the back yard, barren from my attempts at do-it-yourself landscaping. Only the redwood tree remains and at the very edge, a stray rose bush that blooms each spring in spite of my efforts. I smoke because I need it, to invoke and hold at bay the only full memory left to me: the battlefield, earth ravished by heaving and metal, the screech and whoosh of detonations overhead. In front of me I see the short, broad figure of my commanding officer. Tedtemár turns around. In dreams their visor is lifted, and I see their face laughing with the sounds of explosions around us. Tedtemár's arms are weapons, white and broad and spewing fire. I cannot hear anything for the wailing, but in dreams Tedtemár's lips form my name as the ground heaves.

I have broken every wall in my house, put my fist through the thinness of them as if they're nothing. I could have lived closer to work, but in this El Cerrito neighborhood nobody asks any questions; and the backyard is mine to ravage. I break the walls, then half-heartedly repair them over weekends only to break them again. At work I am composed and civil and do not break anything, though it is a struggle. The beautiful old plaster of the office walls goes gritty gray like barracks, and the overhead lights turn into alarms. Under the table I interlace my fingers into bird's wings, my unit's recognition sign, as my eyes focus resolutely on spreadsheets. At home I repair the useless walls and apply popcorn texture, then paint the whole thing bog gray in a shade I mix myself. It is too ugly even for my mood even though I've been told that gray is all the rage with interior designers these days.

I put my fist through the first wall before the paint dries.

Today, there is music on Embarcadero. People in black and colorful clothing whirl around, some skillfully, some with a good-natured clumsiness. Others are there simply to watch. It's some kind of a celebration, but I have nothing to celebrate and nothing to hope for except for the music to shriek like a siren. I buy a plate of deep-fried cheeseballs and swallow them, taste buds disbelieving the input, eyes disbelieving the revelry even though I know the names of the emotions expressed here. Joy. Pleasure. Anticipation. At the edge of the piers, men cast small nets for crabs to sell to sushi bars, and in the nearby restaurants diners sip wine and shiver surreptitiously with the chill. I went out on dates with women and men and with genderfluid folks, but they have all avoided me after a single meeting. They are afraid to say it to my face, but I can see. Too gloomy. Too intense. Too quiet. Won't smile or laugh.

There is a person I notice among the revelers. I see them from the back—stooped, aloof. Like me. I don't know what makes me single them out of the crowd, the shape of the shoulders perhaps. The stranger does not dance, does not move; just stands there. I begin to approach, then veer abruptly away. No sense in bothering a stranger with—with what exactly? Memories?

I cannot remember anything useful.

I wish they'd done a clean job, taken all my memories away so I could start fresh. I wish they'd taken nothing, left my head to rot. I wish they'd shot me. Wish I'd shoot myself, and have no idea why I don't, what compels me to continue in the conference rooms and in the overly pleasant office and in my now fashionably gray house. Joy or pleasure are words I cannot visualize. But I do want—something. Something.

Wanting itself at least was not taken from me, and numbers still keep me safe. Lucky bastard.

I see the stranger again at night, standing in the corner of my backyard where the redwood used to be. The person has no face, just an empty black oval filled with explosives. Their white, artificial arms form an alphabet of deafening fire around my head.

The next day I see them in the shape of the trees outside my office window, feel their movement in the bubbling of Strawberry Creek when I take an unusual lunch walk. I want, I want, I want, I want. The wanting is a gray bog beast that swallows me awake into the world devoid of noise. The suffocating safe coziness of my present environment rattles me, the planes and angles of the day too soft for comfort. I press the metal of my bracelet, but it is not enough. I cut my arms with a knife and hide the scars old and new under sleeves. I break the walls again and repaint them with leftover bog gray, which I dilute with an even uglier army green.

Over and over again I take the BART to Embarcadero, but the person I seek is not there, not there when it's nearly empty and when it's full of stalls for the arts and crafts fair. The person I seek might never have existed, an interplay of shadows over plastered walls. A coworker calls to introduce me to someone; I cut her off, sick of myself and my well-wishers, always taunting me in my mind. In an hour I repent and reconsider and later spend an evening of coffee and music with someone kind who speaks fast and does not seem to mind my gloom. Under the table my fingers lace into bird's wings.

I remember next to nothing, but I know this: I do not want to go back to the old war. I just want—want—

I see the person again at Montgomery in a long corridor leading from the train to the surface. I recognize the stooped shoulders and run forward, but the cry falls dead on my lips.

It is not Tedtemár. Their face, downturned and worn, betrays no shiver of laughter. They smell unwashed and stale, and their arms do not end in metal. The person does not move or react like the others perhaps-of-ours I've seen here over the years, and their lips move, saying nothing. I remember the date from the other day, cheery in the face of my silence. But I know I have nothing to lose. So I cough, and I ask.

They say nothing.

I turn away to leave when, out of the corner of my eye, I see their fingers interlock to form the wings of a bird.

Imprudent and invasive for this world, I lay my hand on their shoulder and lead them back underground. I buy them a BART ticket, watch over them as even the resolutely anonymous riders edge away from the smell. I take them to my home in El Cerrito, where broken walls need repair and where a chipped cup of tea is made to the soundtrack of sirens heard only in my head. The person holds the cup between clenched fists and sips, eyes closed. I cannot dissuade them when they stand in the corner to sleep, silent and unmoving like an empty battle suit.

At night I dream of Tedtemár crying. Rockets fall out of their eyes to splash against my hands and burst there into seeds. I do not understand. I wake to the stranger huddled to sleep in a corner. Stray moonrays whiten their arms to metal.

In the morning I beg my guest to take sustenance or a bath, but they do not react. I leave them there for work, where the light again makes mockery of everything. Around my wrist the fake bracelet comes to life, blinking, blinking, blinking in a code I cannot decipher, calling to me in a voice that could not quite be Tedtemár's. It is only a trick of the light.

At home I am again improper. The stranger does not protest or recoil when I peel their dirty clothes away, lead them into the bath. They are listless, moving their limbs along with my motions. The sudsy water covers everything—that which I could safely look at and that which I shouldn't have seen. I will not switch the pronouns. When names and memories go, these bits of language, translated inadequately into the local vernacular, remain to us. They are slivers, always jagged slivers of us, where lives we lived used to be.

I remember Tedtemár's hands, dragging me away. The wail of a falling rocket. Their arms around my torso, pressing me back into myself.

I wash my guest's back. They have a mark above their left shoulder as if from a once-embedded device. I do not recognize it as my unit's custom or as anything.

I wanted so much—I wanted—but all that wanting will not bring the memories back, will not return my life. I do not want it to return, that life that always stings and smarts and smolders at the edge of my consciousness, not enough to hold on to, more than enough to hurt—but there's an emptiness in me where people have been once, even the ones I don't remember. Was this stranger a friend? Their arms feel stiff to my touch. For all their fingers interlaced into wings at Montgomery station, since then I had only seen them hold their hands in fists.

Perhaps I'd only imagined the wings.

I wail on my way to work, silent with mouth pressed closed, so nobody will notice. In the office I wail, open-mouthed and silent, against the moving shades of redwoods in the window.

For once I don't want takeaway or minute-meals. I brew strong black tea and cook stewed red lentils over rice in a newly purchased pot. I repair the broken walls and watch Tedtemár-who-is-not-quite-Tedtemár as they lean against the doorway, eyes vacant. I take them to sleep in my bed, then perch on the very edge of it, wary and waiting. At night they cry out once, their voice undulating with the sirens in my mind. Hope awakens in me with that sound, but then my guest falls silent again.

An older neighbor comes by in the morning and chats at my guest, not caring that they do not answer—like the date whose name I have forgotten. I don't know if I'd recognize Tedtemár if I met them here. My guest could be anyone, from my unit or another or a veteran of an entirely different war shipped to Northern California by people I can't know because they always ship us here from everywhere and do not tell us why.

Work's lost all taste and color, what of it there ever was. Even numbers feel numb and bland under my tongue. I make mistakes in my spreadsheets and am reprimanded.

● ● ●

At night I perch again in bed beside my guest. I hope for a scream, for anything; fall asleep in the silent darkness, crouched uncomfortably with one leg dangling off to the floor.

I wake up with their fist against my arm. Rigid fingers press and withdraw to the frequency of an old alarm code that hovers on the edge of my remembrance. In darkness I can feel their eyes on me but am afraid to speak, afraid to move. In less than a minute, when the pressing motion ceases and I no longer feel their gaze, I cannot tell if this has been a dream.

I have taken two vacation days at work. I need the rest but dread returning home, dread it in all the different ways from before. I have not broken a wall since I brought my guest home.

Once back, I do not find them in any of their usual spots. I think to look out of the kitchen window at last. I see my stranger, Tedtemár, or the person who could be Tedtemár—someone unknown to me from a different unit, a different culture, a different war. My commanding officer. They are in the backyard on their knees. There's a basket by their side, brought perhaps by the neighbor.

For many long minutes I watch them plant crocuses into the ravaged earth of my yard. They are digging with their fists. Their arms, tight and rigid as always, seem to caress this ground into which we've been discarded, cast aside when we became too damaged to be needed in the old war. Explosives streak past my eyelids and sink, swallowed by the clumps of the soil around their fists.

I do not know this person. I do not know myself.

This moment is all I can have.

I open the kitchen door, my fingers unwieldy, and step out to join Tedtemár.

Bottled-Up Messages

Basma Abdel Aziz

● translated by Ruth Ahmedzai Kemp ●

What if I were to start my day on a different footing for a change? I could break my habit of a lifetime and leave the house without my usual cup of tea in the kitchen. What if I tried out being lazy? I could shove aside the reams of paper people are always streaming into the office with. I could just ignore it all and let it pile up and clog up the system—accidentally, of course, on purpose.

Or perhaps I could go and sit in the bathroom and idle away a couple of hours in there. I could wander aimlessly from one colleague's office to another, stopping here and there for a chat, maybe a cup of coffee or a bite to eat. I'd sit back with a carefree yawn, my notebooks and files piled up in front of me, gnawing on a pencil that splinters between my teeth. I wouldn't bother with any correspondence or with responding to any queries, no matter how pressing. Instead, I'd gaze on idly as the people wait, crushed by their exasperation. But why should I feel the need to do anything about it?

I could also let myself go, put on a bit of weight. As my clothes got tighter, my bulging ass would shake when I walk. My stomach would rise in shapely contours rather than clinging as it does to my spine. No longer would my bones almost protrude from my flesh, grating on the metal chair when I sit. Instead, they would be generously cushioned by my ample backside. And I could make the most of my new look to try out new outfits like flowing skirts and tight, flowery tops with revealing necklines that give a glimpse of my neck and shoulders. And *silly* leather shoes.

● ● ●

I lie in bed a while after waking up and indulge these vivid daydreams. I stretch out my legs and fidget between the warm and cold patches, ignoring the knock at the door and the fact that the cleaning lady might go if I don't let her in. I get up and stretch lazily as I walk to the bathroom. I turn on the tap and wait for the hot water to trickle out, feeling even more relaxed once the knocking stops and I know that I'm on my own. I massage my face with some moisturizer a colleague gave me a few years ago after a trip to the Gulf and which I've never used. Then I sit down and surrender myself to the sun. I ring round my girlfriends to catch up on the TV news and the latest chart hits. The hum of their voices spills into my ear from the handset, the chatter of girls who have no idea that there is a revolution taking place in the next country, girls who are oblivious to the fact that our neighbours have taken to the streets, that their tyrant has fallen, and that others have followed.

Like them, I change the channel when the news comes on. I stick plugs in my ears and wander off into the kitchen to make myself a snack. I try not to notice the dust kicked up by *everything crashing down* around me. I get out the vacuum cleaner and run it over everything in my path, trying to suck up the words swirling in the air around me, determined not to let them spoil my new mood.

It isn't long before the vacuum cleaner is full and overflowing. Reaching its bursting point, it starts to spew out everything it has sucked up, choking the space I have just cleared around me. I realize that my attempt to slip out of my skin has come crashing down. The moisturizer hasn't made the slightest difference. A frown beckons, tantalizingly—a scowl that has lurked within me for years. If only I'd just let the chubby cleaning lady in and let her do her job, she would have saved me from having to change everything and I could have carried on with life as it was.

I sit at the table, my elbows resting on the vast quantities of notes I've scribbled. I am always writing one thing or another because I am overwhelmed by impossible possibilities because their failure to materialize is wearing me down and because their materialization has become my only dream. And all this time I've been living at the bottom of a huge glass bottle. This bottle is where I wash my clothes, where I eat, where I exercise, where I work, where I write and study and scream out loud. It's where I sleep, where I wake up, where I relieve myself. This bottle is running out of space for me and my *non-proverbial excretions*; but no matter the pressure, the stopper never pops open to let me pour out. The bottle insists on keeping me trapped inside. When it once decided to expand a little, I relaxed, telling myself I could finally breathe. But it wasn't long before it went back to how it was before—hard and inflexible. It pressed against me so tightly and for so long that I was reduced to a mere figment of myself. Nothing remained of me but a hoarse, broken voice.

I resolved years ago that I'd escape, but I never get anywhere, no matter how I twist and contort myself. I've tried every position, every posture—to no avail. But maybe if I get fat and lazy, if I keep quiet and keep my head down and my skin well moisturized—maybe then the bottle will break.

And while I wait for this bottle to shatter around me, I write about an idyllic day when I can finally let my guard down, when I don't need to shout or scream. I walk among the protestors, a little light-headed from the exhaust fumes. I buy myself some sugar cane juice and lean against the metal police barrier, the sun beating down, making me frown. But then I half-smile, my mouth slightly open. The sugar cane juice has doubled in price, but I pay for it without losing that light-headed, happy feeling. I wipe my lips and throw the paper napkin onto the ground, which is covered in little puddles. I watch the edges of the paper soak up the water. I see the sodden tissue expand and stick to the ground. I wipe my shoes with it until they shine, and I walk on in peace.

The sheet of paper I've scrawled on is covered in random, misshapen blobs inching along, trickling from one word to another. Some words have merged, others are illegible. Despite disappearing from the page, these words are still trapped in this bottle. Perhaps *one of them* will find it and crack it open. Perhaps that someone will pour some of the contents down his gullet. And as he belches, the bottle's trapped contents will seep out into the air, filling it with the fresh scent of revolution for everyone to inhale.

Acception

Tessa Kum

I.

Forty-four seconds ago, I heard a knock at the door.
Forty-two seconds ago, I considered ignoring it.
Twenty-seven seconds ago, I answered it.

"Tessa Kum?"
Here we go.
Again.

NOTICE OF RELOCATION

Dear Ms. T. Kum (CID# 19800806-F787-A/C2/M3-2009),

Re: the *Revised and Updated Collective Unconscious Research and Privacy Act* (2009), *Equal Opportunity Act* (1995), *Racial and Religious Tolerance Act* (2001), *Thought Artefact Identification and Spatial Differentiation Act* (2009), and the *Department of Human Services (Housing) and Deep Research and Ethical Oversight Committee Co-operative 2009.*

Thanks to your assistance, the first stage of the Cultural Identification Program has been a resounding success. The joint efforts of DHS and DREOC in recognising and classifying each of Victoria's rich and diverse cultural zones has yielded excellent results. We are now able to begin extrapolating artifacts in the psyche of the collective waking conscious, specifically those stemming from cultural structures. As such, our understanding of the collective unconscious and the human condition is deeper than ever before, and continues to grow.

Your support has been greatly appreciated, and with the insight gained from the initial CID Program, it is now possible for the community to take the next exciting step.

You have been identified as being of Asian Stock (second-tier Chinese/third-tier Malaysian). Our records indicate you have already taken up residence within one of the designated Asian Cultural Zones (Box Hill, SE CHINA, Third Precinct), a neighbourhood reflecting your lush and vibrant heritage.

Psychic Waypoint Tower #ACC217 has returned anomalous readings in the nocturnal waveband in your area. The nocturnal waveband—a state of the art new initiative—monitors the unconscious while asleep, gaining us valuable research data into the true unconscious with no disruption or inconvenience to you. Further investigation has pinpointed you as the aberrant mind within PWT #ACC217's field of surveillance.

Your true unconscious is not compatible with the specifications laid out for an Asian Cultural Zone (Box Hill, SE CHINA, Third Precinct), as stated in the Collective Unconscious Research and Privacy Act (2009).

New accommodation in a more suitable zone has been found for you.

It is our responsibility to lead the world forward in this new and exciting era, and it is with pride, humility, and determination that we accept this responsibility. There has never been a time of greater unity within our nation than now.

Thank you for your cooperation in this matter.

Together, we are building a better future.

DREOC officers are of the same breed as ticket inspectors. Even in plain clothes, they're easy to pick. It's written in their posture, the heavy armour in their voices. They know they're unpopular and they're bracing for pent-up and projectile vitriol. It's building in the four of them now as my gaze is dragged along the sentences. The further down the page I get, the wider they hold their shoulders. They're blocking the light.

Half the breath I have been holding comes out, not a sigh, and I look up at the wall of muscle around me.

"Do you understand?"

The officer asking curls down toward me, a name tag on his coat announcing him as Colin Brown. He looks like a Colin Brown. Clean-cut, neat, and with an odd mix of apprehension and confidence— they outnumber me, but he doesn't want to be here. Ancient acne scars and outgoing ears make him look younger than he is. He taps over his PDA without doing anything.

"Certainly. We're building a better future." I fold the letter and run the seams between my fingers, and that action releases me from their attention. They disperse around the room.

Colin's sarcasm detector isn't switched on. "A better future. Exactly. Let's see here." He scans his PDA again. "Our records indicate you are of Asian stock."

"So you keep telling me. I assume that's why you moved me here to an Asian Cultural Zone, right?"

He won't look at me. "You sound like you disagree."

"It doesn't matter what I think."

In the kitchen his companions coalesce, murmuring and shifting impatiently.

"You know you can contest a cultural classification—"

"I know. I have. Several times."

Colin winces or smiles or attempts to do both and ends up with a face of dishonest wrinkles. He changes the subject. "You seem prepared for this. Were you contacted by DREOC, by any chance?" He gestures at the boxes crowding the room.

"No." I clasp my hands before me and dig my nails and my anger into my palms. "Your agents forcibly removed me from Northcote and placed me here three weeks ago, and I have not unpacked. Doing so would mean accepting a classification you have no right to force on me, accepting the creation of the zones and my nonconsensual relocation, accepting that it is now illegal for me to see my family and friends, accepting that I have let the bad guys destroy my life, and I accept none of these things."

"Oh." Colin taps his PDA once, twice. "Well."

I think Colin would be more comfortable if I were yelling at him.

They have a truck waiting downstairs.

Fifty-eight minutes after I open the door, every trace of me is removed from the apartment I refused to call home.

I have no idea what road we're on. They've taken me through Asian, Mediterranean, British, Sub-Continent, Pacific, and East African Cultural Zones, and now we're out west. I don't know the west. It's almost a foreign country. They do things differently here with big houses on small blocks and not a tree to be seen. The night sky sags over the rooftops, pushing everything down against the dead lawns.

"What was it that singled me out for this special treatment?"

The checkpoint falls away behind us, the glimmer of razor wire in the spotlights slipping back from the road and stretching into the darkness, the border between some African and Middle Eastern Cultural Zone. There are no Indigenous Cultural Zones this close to the city.

Colin winds up the window, the car weaving in the lane. "Ah. I don't know if I should tell you that."

"It's in my head. I already know."

He taps his thumbs thoughtfully on the steering wheel and finally digs his PDA out of his pocket. "It states here you dream of the end of the world—" he quirks an eyebrow, it's oh so amusing—"which is not within the acceptable parameters laid out for Asian stock, Chinese and Malaysian inclusive, according to the *Collective Unconscious Research and Privacy Act* (2009), with particular reference to the Herman-Biscuit Paper, and made legislation last week. Specifically, the inclusion of zombies—" He pauses and reads over that again, his mouth moving silently. It's a good thing it's a straight road. "Zombies? Really?"

Every morning I wake up full of terror and adrenaline after spending my sleep running for my life. Some mornings, I wake before the zombies corner me. Some mornings, I don't.

Mum told me, sitting at the kitchen table with two cups of tea and DREOC bold and unstoppable on the front page of *The Age*, that it was an unsubtle metaphor my unconscious or subconscious or whatever-conscious was employing to act out my waking fears: an unstoppable and uncaring force would invade and destroy my world and stand on my lounge room carpet in dirty shoes and acne scars and smile weakly at me while doing so. At the time I thought she was projecting.

Who knew zombies were against the law?

Some disquiet stirs in the back of my mind, doubt cast on my doubt. They really can read minds. There are no walls left in the world.

"That's an odd thing to dream about."

"Apparently." I stare at him with my dark Asian eyes.

He flicks me a nervous glance without turning his head and licks his lips. He isn't someone who can sit in silence. Unfortunately, he's no good at making conversation.

"Well, I mean, it's odd for a Malaysian to dream about. You know, it's not all that exotic, and Malaysians don't have zombies. Um. Do they?"

"I'm not Malaysian."

"But our records—wait, we've been over this already. You're Chinese. Sorry."

"I'm not Chinese either."

I have this conversation with everyone I meet, eventually.

He looks at me, the road, me, the road, the dash, the road, me, the rearview mirror, me. My face doesn't tell him much.

"Is this how you dispute their findings? Flat out deny everything?"

I turn away and look in the sideview mirror. The truck carrying my boxes is driven by a compulsive tailgater, the headlights bright in my eyes.

It's all in the record he just read, if he paid attention. If any of them paid any attention.

Colin's use of it lodges the word in my head. It's a pretty word with a meaning that is not so pretty.

"A guy at work said my lunch was 'exotic.'"

Dad pulled a face at me, one of his many faces to indicate he had heard but probably wasn't paying attention. He lifted the lid from the wok, dragging up a roil of steam and releasing the smell of pork, char sieu sauce, and cloud mushrooms. The hiss and spit conquered the kitchen, and I waited till he clanged the lid back down.

"It was only two-minute noodles. Not even any meat or veggies. Just the noodles. In the microwave."

Dad pulled another face, disdaining my choice of lunch.

"There are other people in the office who eat the exact same noodles, and they aren't told it's 'exotic.'"

He pointed at the rice cooker, and I obeyed.

"Maybe it's because I was using chopsticks," I said, pushing the steamed bok choi and wom bok aside.

Dad was nodding but not listening. Pork and cloud mushrooms out of the wok into a dish. Oil and garlic into the wok. Soy sauce on the silken tofu. The snapping and cracking garlic and oil on the silken tofu.

This was not exotic either.

Not even those who lived in the western suburbs had much to do with this place. It was intended to be an industrial estate until DREOC claimed it, and overnight it was made over with portable rooms and portable toilets and portable showers, all shuffled in and planted amid scaffolding and abandoned foundations and pipes and silos.

We pull up at the final checkpoint, and as our convoy is confirmed against the registered database, Colin turns to me. "Your new home. What do you think?"

Ropes have been strung between the portables, some laden with laundry. I doubt anything dries quickly in the cold. The area isn't paved; the portables are set on cinder blocks, and all else is pot-holed gravel. Skips sit at the end of a row, lids raised with the bulge of sodden plastic bags, two listing at an angle with the stumps left by missing wheels sunk in the mud. A high fence marks the perimeter. Barbed wire, clean and new and yet unrusted. Puddles glisten sick, little rainbows of oil on leaked grey water, that careless reek wafting in through the car vents.

A couple of women smoking by the toilets watch us, a mixture of apathy and raw seething hatred in the creases around their eyes, the twist of their mouths and the pinch of their noses as smoke leaves and rises around them.

This is so far removed from the eucalypt-lined streets of my home and the tragically-hip and curious alleys of the city. There will be no possums on the roof here, no chai lattes and no urban exploration. No joyous discoveries of great restaurants, surprise street art, secret hot chocolate.

Colin can't keep his hands still on the wheel. Weirdly eager and afraid, as though he'll take any rejection of the place as a personal failure. There was a time I would have been sensitive to his sensitivity. There was a time I'd have even tried to dress the situation in a positive light for my own wellbeing.

I stare at him until he has to look away, and then I stare at him some more. Passive aggressive is all I have in me, and it isn't all that aggressive.

I'm given one half of a portable. A cracked chipboard partition provides a thin veneer of privacy between me and my neighbour but does nothing to drown out the sound of the TV, *60 Minutes* covering something on shopping trolley rage. No curtains, anyone walking by can see my everything. It's not insulated. The air feels heavy, settled, a faint thread of mildew souring the edges. No one has moved through it for some time.

Colin offers to help me put my bed together, but I don't want him to be nice, I won't let him be nice, I'm going to hate him and everything he is.

"I'm just trying to help," he says, too much the kicked puppy.

"You're the bad guy," I say. "You don't get to help."

He ducks his head and leaves me in another place I will not call home.

I pull up Mum's number on my mobile. I pull up close friends, distant friends, coworkers. I cycle through them all over and over and don't call any of them.

There is nothing to say.

Kim lives in the portable across from me, sharing with an elderly Brazilian-Rhodesian man who yells abuse at everyone equally.

She's not a mongrel like me. She grew up in four different countries, her parents doing some sort of diplomatic work, which is enough reason to lock her up in here ("the kennel," she says, without a smile but not without amusement).

"My mind is a spaghetti jambalaya goulash stir fry." There is some pride in this statement, but I've yet to hear her say something unexpected.

She passes me a cigarette. I don't smoke, but I've now confirmed that I cannot leave the camp without "special permission," and even if I could, there are no trains or buses this far out; and thus I cannot get to work and so no longer have a job, not to mention I can't get to any of my stowed books in order to read, so I smoke. Or rather, I suck on the filter, hold the smoke in my mouth, nettled acridity muting fast on my tongue, and dare myself to inhale without choking.

This is how dogs in the kennel pass the time.

"I'm just a banana."

"Like most of the people here. Bananas, coconuts, eggplants—"

"Kiwi fruit."

She laughs.

"I don't get the point of that. Not here." I point at the Psychic Waypoint Tower mounted over an unused silo at the southern end of the camp. "Waste of time. All right for reading all the nicely sorted zones, I mean, there probably are patterns there to recognise, but here?" I watch one of the camp guards jog to the toilet. "They've never explained how the towers work."

She exhales gustily, silent, and smoke spills from her nose.

"It isn't for data, you know. It's so we know we're always being watched. We're the aberrant cultural cells in the larger body of

Australia. Everything else is neat and orderly, and we're the cancer; and they've got their eye on us to make sure we don't get out of hand."

"You sound like Agent Smith."

I return the cigarette. "It isn't neat and orderly. It's never been neat and orderly. This is Australia." The smoke has coated my teeth, and they're tacky against my tongue.

I hate this place; the cold and the mud, the stagnant air infected with stewing sewerage and old steam from the mess hall, the emptiness of trees, the absence of all I've taken for granted—loose leaf tea, magpies stalking me on the nature strip, fog over the railway tracks, hot soft-boiled eggs, overheard laughter, running water, light switches that work, colour, colour, colour—I hate this temporary third world country. I might be in shock.

"Why aren't there any Australian Cultural Zones, anyway?"

I never did fit in the Asian Cultural Zone. To everyone else, I was Asian enough to be labelled "Asian," but to all Asians, I was white. The looks I'd get as I left the railway station at Box Hill varied from surprise to hostility. I didn't belong, and if they must be segregated, then they didn't want me there.

There was never a question of whether I would be placed in a British Cultural Zone.

No one belongs in here either, and there is an equality in that misfitism like a balm on a burn.

Kim squints at me. "You haven't even been here a day."

"Don't tell me I have to earn my bitterness."

She laughs again, and some of the tension slides from my neck.

Colin is in the mess hall. Why is Colin in the mess hall? Too late, I've made eye contact. He parks himself at our table, the plastic chair stammering across the lino, a forced casualness in his white knuckles and clasped hands, that ticket inspector paranoia waiting to be challenged.

"Soooooo." He can't help but fill the silence he's created. "Tess— I can call you Tess, right? You're not Malaysian, and you're not Chinese. What are you then?"

"Fuck off," Kim suggests.

"I'm Australian."

To his credit, he does not say *yeah, but what are you really*? "Your family then."

"It's all in my file."

"I'd rather hear it from you."

The sound Kim makes could be at Colin or at her carbonara.

The look he directs at me, this government-sanctioned bully, this clueless boy, this ordinary guy, unhinges my jaw. He's all expectation, eager and open-minded and trying so hard.

Okay then.

"Mum is white Australian. Her Mum came over from England, and her Dad is seventh generation white settler."

"Then your Dad is Malaysian."

"Yes. No." I poke my carbonara with equal distaste. "He's Chinese-Malaysian, which means the family is Chinese but they live in Malaysia. Not Malaysian, though. Different cultural group. Sorta."

"Doesn't that mean he's just Chinese?"

Dad, tucking into rendang and sneering at the group at the table opposite. "From northern China," he said. "You can tell from the sallow skin and the pudgy faces." Mum met my eyes, and we shared a shrug. "Really?" "Yeah." A disapproving sniff. "You can tell."

"Yes. No. He's never been to China, and the family has been in Malaysia for generations. There's geographical cross-pollination of the culture."

Colin's mouth puckers in thought.

"Like all the Greeks here, who've never been to Greece," I add.

"But there aren't many of them." He dismisses them with an easy wave that floors my appetite faster than the cafeteria food. Kim glances at me, resignation in the slope of her mouth.

"There are enough to make several Mediterranean Cultural Zones."

"Yeah, but not that many—"

"Do you think Australia is white?"

Finding himself suddenly pinned between us, he stalls. He knows the answer he wants to give will be shot down, and we know it, too. He knows we'll sniff out any dishonest reply, and we know he knows that, too.

"The majority is," he offers lamely.

Kim curls her lip. "I'm white. What the fuck am I doing in here?"

He raises his hands helplessly. "It's not my call, you know. I'm just trying to get a fix on Tess here, you see. Your Dad, I mean." He can't change the subject fast enough. "If he were deported—"

"Not 'were.' He has been." *Thirty-nine missed calls. Seventeen messages. Mum standing alone in the kitchen with the dogs sitting in the hallway, waiting for Dad to come home.* "You didn't even give me enough notice to get to the airport and say goodbye."

Colin raises his hands again against the accusation in my voice. "That wasn't me personally, come on now, I'm trying to understand."

Which is more than most DREOC officers do, I'll give him that. I bite down the tired tirade stirring on my tongue.

"So since he was deported from here for not being Australian, will he be deported from Malaysia for not being Malaysian?"

I tell myself I could answer if I chose to.

"Would they send him to China? Would China take your family?"

"It's a detention centre," Dad said, weeks ago, a weak connection forcing his voice under water. "For everyone who gave up their Malaysian citizenship to live overseas. There's not enough space. There isn't any running water. There aren't any beds. They won't let any of your uncles contact me. They don't want us—" He cut himself off but not before I heard the catch in his voice. When he continued, he was steady, collected, even had a weak laugh. "And the squat toilets are just holes in the courtyard. They're not screened off. You should have seen the queue after they served a bad curry for dinner. What a mess. Oh, dear. Oh dear, oh dear."

He was pretending to be okay.

The battery in his phone died, and that was the last I heard of him.

"Sorry. I know you don't know, I shouldn't be asking. Um." Colin's eyes dart to my plate. "Are you going to eat that? No? Thanks." He grabs the plastic fork from my hand and shovels tortellini in his mouth. "It must be hard," he says, cream sauce thickening the saliva strings between his teeth.

"Jesus—" A touch on Kim's arm and she quiets.

I could stop here. I could. I could get up and walk away.

"How do you justify it?" I ask, keeping my voice level.

"Pardon?"

I swallow, control cold and hard in my throat. "You kick people out of the country and divide up families and make people live where you say they can live. DREOC is destroying lives. Destroying *us*. How do you justify it?"

Chewing slower, he shrugs uncomfortably. "*I'm* not destroying anything. I mean, it's only temporary stuff. I don't have any say in it, you know. It's just a job. All the higher-ups make the decisions. We just get told what to do."

I swallow again, control getting harder to hold. "You have to pay the bills?"

"Exactly!"

"Pretty sure that's what a lot of the guards in the World War II Nazi concentration camps said."

"What, hey! That's not fair!" Flecks of pasta spray from between his teeth, and he clasps a hand over his mouth, chewing and swallowing hastily. "We're not going around killing anyone, Jesus! This isn't ethnic cleansing or, or genocide or anything like that, it's not permanent, it's just, just—"

"Bringing some order?" Kim suggests.

"Tidying up?"

"Yeah. Yeah. Tidying up. That's all." He looks down at the plate, oil congealed around the bacon.

I lean forward. "Tidying and cleansing mean the same thing."

"It's not like that, and you know it!"

His shout echoes across the mess hall, a sudden quiet focus unfurling in its wake.

"Do I know it?" I hiss. "Do I fucking know it? Do you? Do you know how it *really* is then? If you do, then please, by all means, educate us!" I can't keep it down. "Have you had men in uniform drag you out your door and throw you in the back of a truck and haul you away without telling you where to? How about being told you are no longer allowed to associate with your friends and family because they're white and you're not? Has your father been kicked out of the country? No? Are you coming to terms with the fact you may never see him again? No? I bet you still live at home and none of this has ever occurred to you, you take it all for granted, you pathetic whitebread fuck!" He looks away, wavering protests silenced. Horrified I said it, horrified I meant it, but not enough to stop, I don't stop, I can't stop, I won't stop. "How about this place then? This prison camp, don't pretend this shithole isn't a fucking prison. Have you just been thrown into a scungy-arse portable with no water and no power and no privacy and nothing, *nothing*, and told you can't leave because you might contaminate the rest of the fucking state?!"

It's a roar an eruption a nova whiting out the mess hall and snarling in my ears. It shakes me and shakes me, my fists on the table, Colin wide-eyed and flinching. There isn't enough air in me, but still it comes out, this final razor opening everyone within earshot.

"Despite being born here and having lived only here, have you been told you are not Australian?"

I can hear nothing. There is nothing to hear. No one says a word. No one can speak over the answering roar in their own hearts. It has shaken me, and I am shaken, frightened by the violence in my blood and bones; but I swallow, taste bile, and swallow it down.

After a long pause spent probing a grey crescent of mushroom with the tip of his fork, Colin shakes his head.

"It's just a job," he repeats, barely a whisper.

"Just a job," I repeat.

"Do you know what you're doing?" Kim murmurs.

"Yes," I lie.

Colin draws in a shuddering breath and looks up, the muscles in his neck taut against his spine, raising his head in rusty wincing judders. There is nothing he rests his gaze on, no safe place to look here among us until he meets my eyes. I don't know what he sees, but in him I see a hunger.

"I'm just ..." His breath is heavy with cream and garlic, which doesn't hide the rank cold sweat. "I want to help."

I loosen my fingers. "We don't want help," I say, and my voice carries, clear and calm in the aftermath, addressing not just him and Kim, but everyone, all the misfits and oddballs and mongrels and mixtures.

"We want change."

This isn't fury. This is an offer.

The realisation widens his eyes and parts his lips. Is the breath he draws laden with hope? With anticipation? I can see right through him and watch that first spark catch and light up. All he needs is one last push.

His eyes are so clear, so bright.

I will change that.

"Tell me how the Psychic Waypoint Towers work."

This enemy, this ordinary person, he doesn't want to be the bad guy.

I won't let him.

II.

There's no escaping the smell.

It saturates the air, lends it a fullness that sits heavy in the lungs, and coats the back of the throat. We cover our faces with rags and masks already carrying the stench. It wends its way into all closed spaces. It seeps into the skin and hair. No one is carefree with the air they breathe. No one gets used to it.

Melbourne's birds, the magpies and seagulls and crows, have grown fat and torpid. They need never hunt, they need never compete. There is more food than they can eat, and they waddle about the streets, complacent and lazy, not even pausing to peck at a thumb rolled into a gutter, the fingernail hanging loose and ready to fall.

Occasionally, when there is a lull in hostilities, new fires are lit.

Whether once revolutionaries or DREOC militia, nearby bodies are collected and heaped. In burnt-out ambulances. In florist kiosks. In derailed trams. Ruins given a new purpose. The dead drape careless arms across each other. They all look the same. Precious fuel and they burn and the smell changes. We don't linger.

We need food, and we do what we must to have it.

And no matter what it is—Spam, tinned asparagus, Vegemite, a jar of anchovies, a can of mock turkey—when opened, when cooked, when that first bite hits the tongue—

It tastes like the dead.

It's come down to this.

"It's not worth it," I say, sitting on the roof of the municipal hall on Ruckers Hill, binoculars pointed towards the city, the sunset in my eyes. Last night, DREOC made an enormous push and took back the Atherton Gardens housing blocks in Fitzroy, despite our best efforts.

Colin rubs his thumb on my hairline, behind my ear, making a clean patch in the grime. "You keep saying that."

"Because it's true."

This was, in another life, my favourite view of Melbourne. It was a grand surprise opening up beyond the petrol station and houses without warning. I'd take long looping walks, always culminating on this hill, with the sun gone and the city rising graceful and clean into the night sky. Full of glass, full of light, full of determinedly individual architecture, each building making a unique statement, each building clashing with its neighbours.

Now the glass is broken and crumbed on the streets, the buildings blasted, and everything is smoke and dust and smoke and dust.

The DREOC militia have wasted no time. A fresh Psychic Waypoint Tower, gleaming clean and orange in the sinking light, is growing on the commission block roof amid the air-conditioning vents and mobile phone towers. If they complete it, they'll have a live feed into Melbourne once again. They'll be able to see us. They'll be able to find us.

They'll know our plan.

"We're not finished. There's still a lot of work to be done. Later, you'll see you're wrong." There is a conviction in his voice that wasn't always there. I haven't seen uncertainty in him for a long time, not since that first day back in the camp, standing in the ruins of the first Psychic Waypoint Tower destroyed, ragtag army of misfits and mongrels around us and the camp's director kneeling at my feet.

I pulled the trigger and watched the spark within him become an inferno.

The wind changes, and smoke obscures my view. Burning tyres, burning houses, burning petrol stations; every sunset is spectacular. "We were a minority." I lower the binoculars. They're dropping smoke flares around the roof to mask the tower's construction, and on the ground mounds of trash are set alight to screen their movements.

I doubt we'll miraculously stumble across any rocket launchers before they bring the tower online. We have to make our move now even if we're not ready.

"Maybe," I say, thinking back to a camp of cheap temporary housing on an industrial site in the far western suburbs, one camp out of an entire state, and I wonder where Mum is, if she got out with the rest of the refugees, or—no, don't think about that. "Maybe we should have been left to suffer, so the majority could live in peace."

He leans in close, close enough I can hear him swallow, throat tight and tense and dry. "It's too late," he says through clenched teeth. "To change your mind."

It's never too late to change, I think, but do not say.

A scuffle on the ladder, and Kim pops up through the trapdoor. "Slop's up. Pickled dace and marmalade, picked it special just for you, Col."

"We should eat before we meet the others." I stand and head back to the trapdoor. He'll follow. He always does.

What signs there are read *Bonds Warehouse* and *WARNING CONDEMNED BUILDING DO NOT ENTER* and *ASBESTOS HAZARD All Personnel Must Wear Protective Clothing.* A derelict storage warehouse in Thomastown, all grime-coated gutters and stone-broken windows, dribbles of rust and pigeon shit caked down the walls. That wet taste of old metal and cold stone in the vast empty spaces surrounding it. A chain-link fence with a crusted gate and padlock sealing off a bare concrete courtyard spackled with weed.

This is not DREOC's primary research facility. That one is sign-posted, advertised, and even ran guided tours on the weekends.

This is DREOC's real research facility.

Before, all transmissions from every Psychic Waypoint Tower in the state came to this site. Everything read in the unconscious, nocturnal, and waking conscious wavebands came silent through the sky to an antenna array concealed within the structure. The neighbourhood died from the psychic pollution although no one knew it at the time. The thoughtfog broke everyone eventually.

The complex extends beneath the surface, surprisingly far down, safe from the poisonous space it created. We have only the original planning blueprints. We could be wrong about a lot of things.

And we certainly are.

When we reach the twelfth sublevel, when we turn the corner and see the featureless corridor terminate at a cell door bearing no name or number, when we finally reach our objective, my hands are still clean, but I am not. I am uninjured, my breathing even, but something inside me cannot stop howling.

With such operations I like to guess how many years of therapy it would take to undo the evening's actions. The answer is always: none. I don't like counsellors. If I can't absolve myself of this, then no one can.

"Stay here." Kim nods, and Colin leaves the team guarding the stairwell and joins me at the door.

"Just a swipe card?" he asks. The reader flicks to green, and the passageway echoes with the thunk of the bolt being flung back. I don't let my relief show. The swipe card cost too much for doubt.

I push the door open.

Small, square, unornamented. Empty walls, no carpet. One hospital bed, devoid of extraneous medical equipment. In it, one girl beneath a doona. A floral doona. With bees. Heavy leather restrains all her limbs with only minimal slack for movement. The smell of piss and shit.

She starts awake—was she asleep?—and I was wrong, she's not a girl, she's a woman. She can't be much older than me. No, that's not true. Maybe her body has only lived for so many years, but her mind is like nothing else on Earth.

A surprised frown dips beneath her matted bed hair, quickly melting away as she rolls her eyes and sighs, this amused exasperation her only greeting. Her head drops back on the pillow, eyes closed. She's seen all she needs to see.

"One at a time." I push Colin back out the door. He resists for a moment, staring at her. She's not unattractive, and a feather of envy brushes up my throat. "Get the helmet." I shut the door behind him.

"I know you probably need some time to figure me out," I say, approaching the bed. My voice rasps too loud in the silent room, tongue and lips dry and coarse from yelling. "I can't give you that time, sorry. We need to be out that door and up that corridor and out of this place, and we needed to have done it ten minutes ago. We've got your helmet, you won't leave this room without it on."

I tug angrily at her straps. She lies here for all hours of all days and can't take herself to the toilet. She reeks. Rage at this small indignity is easier to hold than rage at the greater crime against her.

"You knew." The words form in her mouth slowly as if spooling from a single thread drawn across a great distance. "Right away. Why the straps."

I glance at her face. Proud Greek nose, smooth olive skin gone sallow without the sun, fierce eyebrows. She looks at me looking at her, some tired recognition in the faint tilt to her chin. Already, she *sees* me. Maybe she doesn't need that much time. Maybe I'm not that hard to figure out. I try not to feel insulted by this.

The first strap comes loose. "It's what I'd do in your situation." My knuckles brush against the inside of her wrist and the pearled scars there.

Her hand twists, and her grip is not weak. "How do you know I won't do it again once you've freed me?"

"I don't."

"Will you stop me?"

I don't answer. She can read my mind and see the truth for herself.

She was the first psychic ever created. The lab rat DREOC used to trial and error their research and streamline the process for the mindreaders to come. She woke with all her walls demolished, able to read everyone, unable to hold herself apart from the collective conscious. After weeks alternating between screaming and sedation, they built a shielded room, providing the walls they'd taken from her, and she never left.

Later, she'll try to tell me what it was like. "Like drowning, never dying," she says, or "Noise torture, like they say the CIA use," or "Chemical burn in your brain." Her mind was levered open, and the world swept through and swept her out. She can't explain, and I can't understand.

The records refer to her as Yvonne, but she hasn't been Yvonne for some time. She is everyone and no one.

From her, they were able to design the first Psychic Waypoint Towers and extract some meaning from the data they collected. From her, DREOC built everything.

She is the end of the world, sitting here in green pyjamas.

● ● ●

Kim holds the door open for Colin, huffing beneath the helmet's weight. There's no time, but he launches into his speech before he's crossed the threshold.

"We've been fighting DREOC from the beginning. Anyone could see that tapping into the collective unconscious was the highest breach of privacy, an abuse of power justified as being for 'the good of all mankind.' Exploring the human condition, establishing Australia's psychic signature, enhancing anti-discrimination laws; it never ends, and people were surprised when segregation became legislation." Kim ignores my gesture to leave and darts after Colin, catching the other side of the helmet. He nods briefly, not breaking his monologue. "That's not what Australia is. See Tessa?" He can never quite meet my eye when using me as an example. "Unclassifiable, indefinable, she is her own person. As we all should be. DREOC has forgone the individual. We won't let it happen, not without a fight. Aussie battlers, that's what we are. The underdog. Fighting for a fair go." They heave the helmet onto the bed with a grunt.

I've heard him practicing this in the bathroom. I wonder if he believes it.

"Six minutes," Kim mouths. This is taking too long.

A bemused smile touches Yvonne's face, distant, as everything she says and does comes through so many layers of everyone else she appears to forget her body, and he trails off like a stunned school boy.

"But you know that, of course."

I suck in my cheek and give him a look before turning to the helmet. "Is there a trick to this, or do you just put it on?" It isn't glass but looks it. It's reminiscent of an old diving helmet, and the shoulders are heavily padded to soften its ridiculous weight. Our greasy handprints are all over it. "Kim, get out there and get the others ready to move."

"Wait." Kim hesitates, but Colin isn't talking to her. He nods at Yvonne. "Prove it."

"We don't have time for this." The militia is coming, if not here already. We have to *go*.

"We do," Kim backs him up.

"We can't do this again," Colin says. "If she's the wrong person—"

Yvonne slips from the bed and crosses the floor with small steps and beckons him down to whisper in his ear.

All the blood rushes from his face, etching out his acne scars, the graze on his forehead, and the grime on his chin. He looks down at Kim, and I see something there I don't want to see before he looks at me, then away, resolutely away. The question on Kim's lips stalls with a quiet shake of his head, and some invisible and undeniable chasm opens between us.

What did she tell him? I think I know. I wish I didn't know. I add another year to my hypothetical therapy.

"Satisfied?" I can't keep the edge out of my voice.

He nods, once.

"Kim," I snap, ignoring the half-formed guilt on her face. The lights flicker and die momentarily. There is no time. "I said go tell the others, we're leaving." She can't leave the room fast enough. "Help me with this."

Colin casts quick, furtive looks at my face as we lift the helmet. He never did master forced casualness. The helmet settles, and Yvonne straightens awkwardly beneath it.

"I haven't had any contact with anyone outside for ... I don't know. Time is a different language with too many parallel memories. Not since they made the other mindreaders, at any rate." The helmet fogs with her breath. With halting steps she heads to the door. Too slow, too slow.

She looks at me. "I've read you. I know everything about you." I pause. "Everything."

Old disquiet stirs in the back of my mind. There are no walls left in the world.

"Even the zombies." There's no amusement in that statement.

"I haven't dreamed for a long time."

"Liar." Her smile fades fast. "I know the way they work. I can see why they put you in the reject bin with all the other pieces that didn't fit in their jigsaw. I know what you've done." I expect judgement, but there is none. "I know why you've done it. For Australia."

"No, not for Australia."

I can hear Colin not saying anything. I can read his silences as easily as Yvonne read me.

"You would say this country does not know what it is."

Kids threw rocks at me after school, calling me a dirty chink and telling me to go home. Which is exactly where I was going. At least the irony amused my parents.

"It will know in the end." And it will not like what it sees.

She shakes her head, shuffling ever onward. "You can't lie to me," she says. There is almost a question in her voice, a question she knows there is no point in asking.

I reach out to steady her, swaying beneath the helmet's weight, but don't touch her. "No. I can't. Everything you saw in my head is true."

The corners of her mouth sag.

"I'm sorry," I add as the pitch in the room alters. The air conditioning has stopped.

"I can never go home."

I unholster my gun, signalling for Colin to get the door. "None of us can."

He cracks it, peers through, and confirming the corridor clear, ducks out.

"I'm sorry, too," she murmurs. I can barely hear her. It's not a diving helmet, it's a fish tank.

I stare down the corridor at Colin's back, at the fingertips Kim lays on his wrist. He recoils from her. He knows I'm watching. I keep my finger off the trigger.

"I know you know."

"And you know I chose to say nothing."

Colin flips off signals in a flurry. Fuck. We're not alone.

Yvonne slips a hand into mine. The creases of my palm are black with cordite and sweat, my knuckles bruised, and her skin is paper dry and cold. Back pressed to the wall, I step out, but she doesn't follow and stops me short.

"Choices." The word sounds hollow, drooping from her tongue. "You have given me no choice here. You're no different from DREOC."

There is no time. Kim catches my eye and beckons urgently. Their impatience claws beneath my shoulder blades. Echoing down the stairwell, the sound of boots, the rasp of flak jackets. Deep in the building something rumbles, and the lights go out for good.

There are too many things I can't grant her, but I ask. I have to know. "What do you want?"

She sighs, soft and airless as a failing moth.

"I want to die."

And the shooting starts again.

We speed down the Western Ring Road in an old Jeep. My ribs shriek with every bounce, and on the cracked road there is a lot of bouncing. The freeway is clotted with the husks of burnt-out trucks jack-knifed across the lanes, the remaining wreckage of conquered barricades and cars half-crushed by the passage of tanks. Flitting between the warehouses is the occasional glimpse of what was the city, baleful and weary beyond orange-bellied smoke.

We left at least six behind at the research facility, and beside me

Kim writhes and kicks at the seat in front. She can't breathe, she's choking on her own blood.

Four nooses hang from the sign for Pascoe Vale Road. One of them has snapped. I can't tell if the dead are theirs or ours. Yvonne looks at me, and her look is terrible.

"What have you done?"

She doesn't need to ask. She knew. Now she understands.

Colin is speaking, but no one hears him. They're looking at Yvonne, tired and wilting and ridiculous in her begrimed pyjamas and helmet. They're looking at the unhappy turn of her lips and downcast eyes. They're looking at her hand, clinging fast to mine. They're looking at the bulletproof vest I'm still wearing and the small but significant hole in the outer lining. They're looking at my straight back, set shoulders, and lifted chin. They can't see my pain. Here in the main bunker in our underground base, all they see is the revolution, and our victory.

Colin finishes listing the lost and dead, his voice breaking on Kim's name. Her last packet of cigarettes in his hand, already tapping one out. I never did pick up the habit. "The price was high," he says, meeting my eyes briefly. This time he does not tell me it was worth it.

"There is still a lot of work to be done," I say.

Unlike him, I am very good at pretending nothing is wrong.

Yvonne finally releases my hand after taking it in the corridor all those hours ago. Her flesh is crimped with the impression of my fingers where I'd gripped too hard in pain, the bruising already showing. She shucks off the helmet with a groan of relief.

"It's noisy," she says of the room we prepared, "but keeps enough out."

I sit gingerly on the edge of the bed, too aware of her. As the Psychic Waypoint Tower invaded my sleep, so she is once again invading my thoughts, and I don't like it and don't hide it. Although there's little of interest to see right now. Intense hurt. Colin. Betrayal. Fatigue. Grief. Kim. A sudden savage craving for chicken parmigiana.

She holds up her bruised hand. "If I can touch you, I can read you."

Oh.

There's no small amount of malicious enjoyment in her pronouncement.

I don't deserve to feel betrayed. I assumed her to be passive, just a tool. She's right. I am no different from DREOC.

She shakes her head in agreement. "No, the Face of the Revolution is not."

I could convince her. I could put forth all the reasons she has to work with us. I could.

"But you want to let me choose," she says simply. "You see me as a person first. You would let me choose even though none of your comrades has considered doing so and will oppose you if they find out."

I haven't said a word. There's no need.

Yvonne crouches before me. Her face, protected by the helmet, is starkly clean compared to the rest of her. There's a faint memory of air conditioning in her hair.

"Who am I talking to? The revolutionary leader, the heartbroken daughter, the jilted lover, who?" She touches my face, a touch that is only a touch.

Chicken parmigiana, followed by a lamb souvlaki.

And then hot apple pie and cream.

"Me," I croak. "You're talking to me."

III.

I pull the trigger. Again.

The crack of gunfire joins the echoes already bouncing around Federation Square. None of them truly fade away. I wanted to use a silencer, but Colin said it would ruin the effect.

It's amazing how much blood comes out of a head wound. The body, greasy blonde hair and heavy jowls, is dragged from the stage before it has finished collapsing, but there is still so much blood spilling on top of all the blood spilt before, thick and black.

Colin actually used the phrase "thoughtcrime" that time, and I don't believe he was being ironic. I don't believe he's read *1984* either.

"Bring the next," he says. *Next. Next.* Like the echoing gunshot, the word never fades away.

Pieces of the outside world reach us; a pirate broadcast on shortwave, a briefly stolen satellite hookup, an unreliable spliced phone line. The picture pieced together is contradictory, both hopeful and hopeless. DREOC is proceeding as planned and has started a program for reading the minds of high school students to determine their future occupations. DREOC is tangled in international red tape and is being charged with human rights abuse. Martial law has been declared in all states. More underground rebellions have formed. The cultural zones have become entirely sealed off, and no one can leave them. The rebellions are quite literally underground and go where they please.

Australia is frightened. Australia is joyous. Australia doesn't know what it is or what it is becoming.

The original plan—and it was a fine plan—was to have Yvonne act as our own Psychic Waypoint Tower and gather information regarding DREOC's capabilities and movements, the location of their stations, and their future plans. We had no moles, no inside intelligence to speak of. She was to be the turning point in our campaign.

And she was.

Oh, she was.

Colin pronounces the sentence, and I pull the trigger. Again.

"Bring the next," he says.

We're on the stage backing the Transport Bar. When Prime Minister Rudd made a formal apology to the Indigenous people of Australia, I was here, watching this stage. Colin liked this resonance with the past, thought it fitting. The square is packed, the incline towards the twisted remains of the Atrium rises in the receding distance until all I can see is a wall of faces.

There was cheering when we began, when the first DREOC militia member was executed, and what I saw in those faces sickened me. All these executions later, and there is no cheering, and what I see in those faces now is worse.

We don't have enough ammunition to waste on a firing squad. There are no bullet holes in the wall. We have left no mark to tell those who will come later what has happened here.

There is just me, hand and gun so splattered with blood it drips like an open wound, waiting for the word.

I pull the trigger. Again.

"Bring the next."

This used to be such a *cultured* space; cultural exhibitions, curious art installations, activists and petition signers, street performers and sponsored jazz bands, free tai chi and salsa classes, book fairs and green energy expos; all these things aimed at making the world a better place.

Not all blood smells the same. Not all blood flows the same. It creeps across the stage and oozes around my boot.

I have to be the one to pull the trigger, Colin said. It is symbolic. It is what history wants. I fired the first shot, the shot that started this, and so I must fire the shot that will end it for these criminals.

He said these things, and I knew, blinded by the blaze of his conviction, he couldn't see *me* anymore.

Colin is reading, again, the charges against one of the seventy-nine DREOC militia members remaining in our captivity. Try-hard tribal tattoos, a weak chin and mutton chops. He's just some guy. Some guy who needed a job to get his parents off his back. Some guy who got caught up in the hysteria. Some guy paying rent. Some guy trying to make himself big. Some guy with nothing better to do. Some guy, pulling Samoans and Somalis and Indonesians and Vietnamese and Greeks and Turks and Lebanese and Koreans out of their homes and telling them where to go. I have to keep reminding myself of this. It gets harder each time I pull the trigger.

There is no end to these ordinary people. There never will be.

This guy, this enemy, this guy, he cringes away from Yvonne's hand. Yvonne can't take the helmet off outside or lose her mind in the roar of the world's collective conscious. Her hand has become the hand of judgement, resting on the back of his neck. With a touch she can see, and with a touch she sees him. There are no walls left in the world.

The final charge is read, and Colin pauses to lick his lips, the break in speech tripping my attention. All the charges are the same for all our prisoners. A mass sentencing and execution would be more efficient, I'd joked.

But, no. It is the rights of the individual that DREOC has not respected. Thus, it is the individual we must honour and condemn.

No one talks about Australia anymore. I stopped counting the number of times I've had to reload after the sixth clip.

"We are prepared to waive these charges," Colin says. "If you can put aside your prejudices and judgements and let go of the collective mentality you've so blindly followed, if you can do this, you may join us. You can help us change Australia. You have a choice: to change.

"Together," Colin says. "We are building a better future."

He can't say the DREOC motto without emphasising it. He still thinks it's clever.

Blood seeps over the lip of the stage to the patterned paving below. The slope has funnelled it down through the cracks towards St. Kilda Road, and the crowd has given way before its advance. On the edge by that creeping tide, an Indian woman and red-bearded man stand behind a girl, hands on her shoulders. Her face is dirty, thin, and the features ambiguous in origin. She covers her nose and mouth and hasn't looked up from the blood in a long time.

This enemy, this guy, this frightened man, he is kneeling in the blood of those tried before him. It's soaked his pants, and the stain is climbing the fabric. It isn't much of a choice. He nods. He has no loyalty to DREOC. It was just a job.

Colin looks at Yvonne, and with a small shake of her head, she removes her hand.

She is so quick to judge.

Colin doesn't skip a beat. "You do not possess the qualities necessary to make the world and our future what it must be. You have no place here." I can't tell if Colin enjoys this or not. I don't know if I can even hear him over the memory of all the previous judgements and the growing howl in my heart.

"This is Tessa. You can't classify her just by looking at her face, and her background confuses you because she cannot be so easily defined as 'Asian' or 'Caucasian.' For that, you treated her as less than human."

And you won't let me be only human, merely human, *just* human.

"You locked her up because she was inconvenient."

And you're the one who carried that out.

"She is the face of the future, the Face of the Revolution, and the revolution has won!"

There are no cheers. This is no triumph.

In this breath, in this moment no different from all the others preceding it, I touch my finger to the trigger. The hush in the square is outlined by the complacent murmur of seagulls gathering by the trucks to the side of the stage, the tray beds heaped high with all the people I have executed, no, murdered today. To the other side, the beer garden converted to a cattle pen, are all the prisoners yet to be tried, heads down, some crying.

No please no please no please no his lips move. This frightened man, this enemy, his voice has fled. Yvonne took it from him, negated any choice he might have made with a shake of her head.

My wrist aches, hand gloved in gore, cordite and blood on my tongue, ears ringing, the gun too hot in my hand, but I can't put it down. There are more to come, we have to read them, we have to decide what they are, we have to—

Colin steps back, clear of any spatter, and I say, "No."

The word cuts through all the other words hanging in the air, soft and undeniable and waking the crowd from their acceptance.

"*These blokes, they thought I was some old Chinese fuddy-duddy, they started telling me what I should be saying, and I thought, uh oh, here we go, I'll show them. Nobody tells me what to be."*

"You know I'm just going to throw those words back at you when you tell me what I should be, right, Dad?"

I tilt my chin just enough of a negative to assure the guards below.

"You were this man. Just doing your job. Not malicious. You worked for DREOC and did all that he did. You changed."

"And he won't change," Colin counters. "Yvonne has seen him. She knows. None of us can lie to her."

"No," I repeat. "Seeing is not understanding." A ripple runs through the crowd. These people have lost as much as I have, if not more. They fought beside me. They died doing what I commanded. They did terrible things because I ordered it. They believed.

"His death won't solve anything. None of these deaths will. This isn't what we wanted."

"This is what we *need*." Colin turns to the audience, prisoners and comrades, and points at the enemy, the guy, the victim. "He will not change! He will look at you and see a chink, a wog, a skinny, a boong, a curry, a towelhead. It is ingrained. It cannot be undone."

The audience shivers like wind passing over water. Here and there I see a nod or a frown of doubt. Even the guards, friends who've been with us since that first camp, lean towards each other and whisper uncertainly, eyes darting between us. They all believed because we never gave them a reason not to.

Colin has become a fluent orator in his time, but I am the Face of the Revolution; and there is blood, bone, and brain spattered on my trousers, shirt, face, and hair.

The girl in the crowd isn't listening to Colin. She doesn't need to be told of all the wrongs DREOC perpetuated in the name of a better future. She doesn't need fine speeches to mollify her conscience.

"... It will only happen again unless we erase it. We must remove the minds that pollute the collective with narrow and outdated thoughts ..."

All she can see is the blood at her feet.

"... We can only take what we have learned and start anew. A society that recognises the individual as equally as the group."

Out of my line of sight, Yvonne is silent, still, almost nonexistent. Knowingly or not, she has become the tool DREOC created her to be. I am fortunate for the helmet, and that—here, now—she cannot see what I am thinking.

Colin turns to me, and it's just him, me, and the disappointment in his voice.

"It was you who taught me this simple truth."

"Then why don't you understand?" I whisper.

The crowd stills. I have never grown used to being the focus of so much attention.

This time, I can't give them what they want.

"Don't you see what we're doing? You put me in that camp because someone read my mind and I dreamed of zombies, and that was incompatible with your checklist. Now we're standing here, passing out judgement on these people because we've read their minds and what we find is incompatible with our checklist. This new world order we're building, now we have our own psychic; we're telling people what they are and what they are allowed to be—" I swallow. I can't look at Yvonne. "We've become them."

"This is different, Tessa." He couldn't fake this frightening calm. "You're losing sight of the bigger picture."

"This is not different."

The frown in Colin's brow deepens. He doesn't want to hear this, doesn't want me to be this, doesn't have time for this. "Everything has changed. We're giving this man a chance, which is more than you were given. You know this. You've known this your whole life. This is the change *you* brought about."

The rift is complete. This is what we have become. In the empty space between us is the memory of Kim. This is why he ended up in Kim's bed; he had not put her on a pedestal. She was like him, just some person.

I bow my head and nod.

He says, "Then you know what must be done."

He says, lower, "It is too late to change your mind."

I don't trust myself to speak.

For a moment, I think he's going to reach out a hand to me, or I to him; but the moment passes, and with a final nod, he turns away from me.

"Doubt is in all of us!" He addresses the crowd again as I step up. "Even she, the spark and inspiration that brought us so far, even she doubts! We have endured so much to reach this point, we have suffered and we have lost so much, and there's still a lot of work to be done." The stillness in the audience remains, but the flavour of the air has changed, the welling expectation heavy like a distant storm. "The path forward is still one we must fight for, every step of the way. We all doubt. We will continue to doubt, but we shall never, *never* let doubt win!"

They cheer. They no longer doubt.

Yvonne puts her hand on the back of my neck. I feel a tremble run through her fingers, but she does not pull away.

This enemy, this victim, this guy at my feet, he won't look at me. I don't doubt Yvonne. She sees people clearly, all they have ever been. I judge him, and harshly.

She cannot see what people will become.

In another time, in another place, to another person, my mother said she would be proud of me no matter who I was, and even though he hassled me for not becoming an astronaut, my father agreed.

Finally, I meet Yvonne's eyes.

She's smiling, a broad, relieved smile, and with that smile the world changes, no, the world never changes, and my doubts leave me.

And I put a bullet through her heart.

The Day It All Ended

Charlie Jane Anders

Bruce Grinnord parked aslant in his usual spot and ran inside the DiZi Corp. headquarters. Bruce didn't check in with his team or even pause to glare at the beautiful young people having their toes stretched by robots while they sipped macrobiotic goji-berry shakes and tried to imagine ways to make the next generation of gadgets cooler looking and less useful. Instead, he sprinted for the executive suite. He took the stairs two or three at a time until he was so breathless he feared he'd have a heart attack before he even finished throwing his career away.

DiZi's founder, Jethro Gruber—Barrons' Young Visionary of the Year five years running—had his office atop the central spire of the funhouse castle of DiZi's offices in a round glass turret looking down on the employee oxygen bar and the dozen gourmet cafeterias. If you didn't have the key to the private elevator, the only way up was this spiral staircase, which climbed past a dozen Executive Playspaces, and any one of those people could cockblock you before you got to Jethro's pad. But nobody seemed to notice Bruce charging up the stairs, fury twisting his round face, even when he nearly put his foot between the steps and fell into the Moroccan Spice Cafe.

Bruce wanted to storm into Jethro's office and shout his resignation in Jethro's trendy schoolmaster glasses. He wanted to enter the room already denouncing the waste, the stupidity of it all—but when he reached the top of the staircase, he was so out of breath, he could only wheeze, his guts wrung and cramped. He'd only been in Jethro's office once before: an elegant goldfish bowl with one desk that changed shape (thanks to modular pieces that came out of the floor), a few chairs, and one dot of maroon rug at its center. Bruce stood there, massaging his dumb stomach and taking in the oppressive simplicity.

So Jethro spoke first, the creamy purr Bruce knew from a million company videos. "Hi, Bruce. You're late."

"I'm ... I'm what?"

"You're late," Jethro said. "You were supposed to have your crisis of conscience three months ago." He pulled out his Robo-Bop and displayed a personal calendar, which included one entry: "Bruce Has a Crisis of Conscience." It was dated a few months earlier. "What kept you, man?"

It started when Bruce took a wrong turn on the way to work. Actually, he drove to the wrong office—the driving equivalent of a Freudian slip.

He was on the interstate at 7:30, listening to a banjo solo that he hadn't yet learned to play. Out his right window, every suburban courtyard had its own giant ThunderNet tower just like the silver statue in Bruce's own cul-de-sac—the sleek concave lines and jetstreamed base like a 1950s Googie space fantasy. To his left, almost every passing car had a Car-Dingo bolted to its hood with its trademark sloping fins and whirling lights. And half the drivers were listening to music or making Intimate Confessions on their Robo-Bops. Once on the freeway, Bruce could see much larger versions of the ThunderNet tower dotting the landscape from shopping-mall roofs to empty fields. Plus, everywhere he saw giant billboards for DiZi's newest product, the Crado—empty-faced, multicultural babies splayed out in a milk-white, egg-shaped chair that monitored the baby's air supply and temperature in some way that Bruce still couldn't explain.

Bruce was a VP of marketing at DiZi—shouldn't he be able to find something good to say about even one of the company's products?

So this one morning, Bruce got off the freeway a few exits too soon. Instead of driving to the DiZi offices, he went down a feeder road to a dingy strip mall that had offices instead of dry cleaners. This was the route Bruce had taken for years before he joined DiZi, and he felt as though he'd taken the wrong commute by mistake.

Bruce's old parking spot was open, and he could almost pretend time had rolled back except that he'd lost some hair and gained some weight. He found himself pushing past the white, balsa wood-and-metal door with the cheap sign saying "Eco Gnomic" and into the offices, and then he stopped. A roomful of total strangers perched on beanbags and folding chairs turned and stared, and Bruce had no explanation for who he was or why he was there. "Uh," Bruce said.

The Eco Gnomic offices looked like crap compared with DiZi's majesty but also compared with the last time he'd seen them. Take the giant Intervention Board that covered the main wall: When Bruce had worked there, it'd been covered with millions of multicolored tacks attached to scraps of incidents. This company is planning a major polluting project, so we mobilize culture-jammer flashmobs here and organize protesters at the public hearing there like a giant, multidimensional chess game covering one wall, deploying patience and playfulness against the massive corporate engine. Now though, the Intervention Board contained nothing but bad news without much in the way of strategies. Arctic Shelf disintegrating, floods, superstorms, droughts, the Gulf Stream stuttering, extinctions like dominoes falling. The office furniture teetered on broken legs, and the same computers from five years ago whined and stammered. The young woman nearest Bruce couldn't even afford a proper Mohawk—her hair grew back in patches on the sides of her head, and the stripe on top was wilting. None of these people seemed energized about saving the planet.

Bruce was about to flee when his old boss, Gerry Donkins, showed up, and said, "Bruce! Welcome back to the nonprofit sector, man." Bruce and Gerry wound up spending an hour sitting on crates, drinking expired YooHoo. "Yeah, Eco Gnomic is dying," said Gerry, giant mustache twirling, "but so is the planet."

"I feel like I made a terrible mistake," Bruce said. He looked at the board and couldn't see any pattern to the arrangement of ill omens.

"You did," Gerry replied. "But it doesn't make any difference, and you've been happy. You've been happy, right? We all thought you were happy. How is Marie, by the way?"

"Marie left me two years ago," Bruce said.

"Oh," Gerry said.

"But on the plus side, I've been taking up the banjo."

"Anyway, no offense, but you wouldn't have made a difference if you'd stayed with us. We probably passed the point of no return a while back."

Point of no return. It sounded sexual or like letting go of a trapeze at the apex of its arc.

"You did the smart thing," said Gerry, "going to work for the flashiest consumer products company and enjoying the last little bit of the ride."

Bruce got back in his Prius and drove the rest of the way to work, past the rows of ThunderNet towers and the smoke from far-off forest fires. This felt like the last day of the human race even though it was just another day on the steep slope. As Bruce reached the lavender glass citadel of DiZi's offices, he started to go numb inside, like always. But instead, this time, a fury took him, and that's when he charged inside and up the stairs to Jethro's office, ready to shove his resignation down the CEO's throat.

"What do you mean?" Bruce said to Jethro, as his breath came back. "You were *expecting* me to come in here and resign?"

"Something like that." Jethro gestured for Bruce to sit in one of the plain white, absurdly comfortable teacup chairs. He sat cross-legged in the other one like a yogi in his wide-sleeved linen shirt and camper pants. In person, he looked slightly chubbier and less classically handsome than all his iconic images, but the perfect hipster bowl haircut and sideburns and those famous glasses were instantly recognizable. "But like I said: late. The point is, you got here in the end."

"You didn't *engineer* this. I'm not one of your gadgets. This is real. I really am fed up with making pointless toys when the world is about to choke on our filth. I'm done."

"It wouldn't be worth anything if it wasn't real, bro." Jethro gave Bruce one of his conspiratorial/mischievous smiles that made Bruce want to smile back in spite of his soul-deep anger. "That's why we hired you in the first place. You're the canary in the coal mine. Here, look at the org chart."

Jethro made some hand motions, and one glass surface became a screen, which projected an org chart with a thousand names and job descriptions. And there, halfway down on the left, was Bruce's name with "CANARY IN THE COAL MINE." And a picture of Bruce's head on a cartoon bird's body.

"I thought my job title was junior executive VP for product management," Bruce said, staring at his open-mouthed face and those unfurled wings.

Jethro shrugged. "Well, you just resigned, right? So you don't have a title anymore." He made another gesture, and a bright-eyed young thing wheeled a minibar out of the elevator and offered Bruce beer, whiskey, hot sake, coffee, and Mexican Coke. Bruce felt rebellious, choosing a single-malt whiskey until he realized he was doing what Jethro wanted. He took a swig that burned his throat and eyes.

"So you're quitting; you should go ahead and tell me what you think of my company." Jethro spread his hands and smiled.

"Well." Bruce drank more whiskey and then sputtered. "If you really want to know ... your products are pure evil. You build these sleek little pieces of shit that are designed with all this excess capacity and redundant systems. Have you ever looked at the schematics of the ThunderNet towers? It's like you were *trying* to build something overly complex. And it's the ultimate glorification of form over function—you've been able to convince everybody with disposable income to buy your crap because people love anything that's ostentatiously pointless. I've had a Robo-Bop for years, and I still don't understand what half the widgets and menu options are for. I don't think anybody does. You use glamour and marketing to convince people they need to fill their lives with empty crap instead of paying attention to the world and realizing how fragile and beautiful it really is. You're the devil."

The drinks fairy had started gawking halfway through this rant, then she seemed to decide it was against her pay grade to hear this. She retreated into the elevator and vanished around the time Bruce said he didn't understand half the stuff his Robo-Bop did. Bruce had fantasized about telling Jethro off for years, and he enjoyed it so much he had tears in his eyes by the end. Even knowing that Jethro had put this moment on his Robo-Bop calendar couldn't spoil it.

Jethro was nodding as if Bruce had just about covered the bases. Then he made another esoteric gesture, and the glass wall became a screen again. It displayed a PowerPoint slide:

DIZI CORP. PRODUCT STRATEGY
+ Beautiful Objects That Are Functionally Useless
+ Spare Capacity
+ Redundant Systems
+ Overproliferation of Identical but Superficially Different Products
+ Form Over Function
+ Mystifying Options and Confusing User Interface

"You missed one, I think," Jethro said. "The one about overproliferation. That's where we convince people to buy three different products that are almost exactly the same but not quite."

"Wow." Bruce looked at the slide, which had gold stars on it. "You really are completely evil."

"That's what it looks like, huh?" Jethro actually laughed as he tapped on his Robo-Bop. "Tell you what. We're having a strategy meeting at three, and we need our canary there. Come and tell the whole team what you told me."

"What's the point?" Bruce felt whatever the next level below despair was. Everything was a joke, *and* he'd been deprived of the satisfaction of being the one to unveil the truth.

"Just show up, man. I promise it'll be entertaining if nothing else. What else are you going to do with the rest of your day, drive out to the beach and watch the seagulls dying?"

That was exactly what Bruce had planned to do after leaving DiZi. He shrugged. "Sure. I guess I'll go get my toes stretched for a while."

"You do that, Bruce. See you at three."

The drinks fairy must have gossiped about Bruce because people were looking at him when he walked down to the main promenade. If there'd been a food court in 2001: A Space Odyssey, it would have looked like DiZi's employee promenade. Bruce didn't have his toes stretched. Instead, he ate two organic calzones to settle his stomach after the morning whiskey. The calzones made Bruce more nauseated. The people on Bruce's marketing team waved at him in the cafeteria but didn't approach the radioactive man.

Bruce was five minutes early for the strategy meeting; but he was still the last one to arrive, and everyone was staring at him. Bruce had never visited the Executive Meditation Hole, which also doubled as Jethro's private movie theater. It was a big bunker under the DiZi main building with wall carpets and aromatherapy.

"Hey, Bruce." Jethro was lotus-positioning on the dais at the front, where the movie screen would be. "Everybody, Bruce had a Crisis of Conscience today. Big props for Bruce, everybody."

Everyone clapped. Bruce's stomach started turning again, so he put his face in front of one of the aromatherapy nozzles and huffed calming scents. "So Bruce has convinced me that it's time for us to change our product strategy to focus on saving the planet."

"You what?" Bruce pulled away from the soothing jasmine puff. "Are you completely delusional? Have you been surrounded by yes-men and media sycophants for so long that you've lost all sense of reality? It's way, way too late to save the planet, man." Everybody stared at Bruce until Jethro clapped again. Then everyone else clapped, too.

"Bruce brings up a good point," Jethro said. "The timetable is daunting, and we're late. Partly because your Crisis of Conscience was months behind schedule, I feel constrained to point out. In any case, how would we go about meeting this audacious goal? 'Enterprise audacity' being one of our corporate buzzsaws, of course. And for that, I'm going to turn it over to Zoe. Zoe?"

Jethro went and sat in the front row, and a big screen appeared up front. A skinny woman in a charcoal-gray suit got up and used her Robo-Bop to control a presentation.

"Thanks, Jethro," the stick-figure woman, Zoe, said. She had perfect Amanda Seyfried hair. "It really comes down to what we call product versatility." She clicked on a picture of a nice midrange car with a swooshy device bolted to its roof. "Take the Car-Dingo, for example. What does it do?"

Various people raised their hands and offered slogans like "It makes a Prius feel like a muscle car" or "It awesome-izes your ride."

"Exactly!" Zoe smiled. She clicked the next slide over, and proprietary specs for the Car-Dingo came up. They were so proprietary, Bruce had never seen them. Bruce struggled to make sense of all those extra connections and loops, going right into the engine. She pulled up similar specs for the ThunderNet tower, full of secret logic. Another screen showed all those nonsensical Robo-Bop menus, suddenly unlocking and making sense.

"Wait a minute." Bruce was the only one standing up besides Zoe. "So you're saying all these devices were dual-function all this time? And in all the hundreds of hellish product meetings I've sat through, you never once mentioned this fact?"

"Bruce," Jethro said from the front row, "we've got a little thing at DiZi called the Culture of Listening. That means no interrupting the presentation until it's finished or no artisanal cookies for you."

Bruce sighed and climbed over someone to find a seat and listened to another hour of corporate "buzzsaws." At one point he could have sworn Zoe said something about "end-user velocitization." One thing Bruce did understand in the gathering haze: Even though DiZi officially frowned on the cheap knockoffs of its products littering the Third World, the company had gone to great lengths to make sure those illicit copies used the exact same specs as the real items.

Just as Bruce was passing out from boredom, Jethro thanked Zoe and said, "Now let's give Bruce the floor. Bruce, come on down." Bruce had to thump his own legs to wake them up, and when he reached the front, he'd forgotten all the things he was dying to say an hour earlier. The top echelons of DiZi management stared, waiting for him to say something.

"Uh." Bruce's head hurt. "What do you want me to say?"

Jethro stood up next to Bruce and put an arm around him. "This is where your Crisis of Conscience comes in, Bruce dude. Let's just say, as a thought embellishment, that we could fix it." ("Thought embellishment" was one of Jethro's buzzsaws.)

"Fix ... it?"

Jethro handed Bruce a Robo-Bop with a pulsing Yes/No screen. "It's all on you, buddy. You push Yes, we can make a difference here. There'll be some disruptions, people might be a mite inconvenienced, but we can ameliorate some of the problems. Push No and things go on as they are. But bear in mind—if you push Yes, you're the one who has to explain to the people."

Bruce still didn't understand what he was saying yes to, but he hardly cared. He jabbed the Yes button with his right thumb. Jethro whooped and led him to the executive elevator, so they could watch the fun from the roof.

"It should be almost instantaneous," Jethro said over his shoulder as he hustled into the lift. "Thanks to our patented 'snaggletooth' technology that makes all our products talk to each other. It'll travel around the world like a wave. It's part of our enterprise philosophy of Why-Not-Now."

The elevator lurched upward, and in moments they had reached the roof. "It's starting," Jethro said. He pointed to the nearest ThunderNet tower. The sleek lid was opening up like petals until the top resembled a solar dish. And a strange haze was gathering over the top of it.

"This technology has been around for years, but everybody said it was too expensive to deploy on a widespread basis," Jethro said with a wink. "In a nutshell, the tops of the towers contain a photocatalyst material, which turns the CO_2 and water in the atmosphere into methane and oxygen. The methane gets stored and used as an extra power source. The tower is also spraying an amine solution into the air that captures more CO_2 via a proprietary chemical reaction. That's why the ThunderNets had to be so pricey."

Just then, Bruce felt a vibration from his own Robo-Bop. He looked down and was startled to see a detailed audit of Bruce's personal carbon footprint—including everything he'd done to waste energy in the past five years.

"And hey, look at the parking lot," Jethro said. All the Car-Dingos were reconfiguring themselves, snaking new connections into the car engines. "We're getting most of those vehicles as close to zero emissions as possible, using amines that capture the cars' CO_2. You can use the waste heat from the engine to regenerate the amines." But the real gain would come from the cars' GPSs, which would start nudging people to carpool whenever another Car-Dingo user was going to the same destination, using a "packet-switching" model to optimize everyone's commute for greenness. Refuse to carpool and your car might start developing engine trouble—and the Car-Dingos, Bruce knew, were almost impossible to remove.

As for the Crados? Jethro explained how they were already hacking into every appliance in people's homes to make them energy efficient whether people wanted them to be or not.

Zoe was standing at Bruce's elbow. "It's too late to stop the trend or even reverse all the effects," she said over the din of the ThunderNet towers. "But we can slow it drastically, and our most optimistic projections show major improvements in the medium term."

"So all this time—all this hellish time—you had the means to make a difference, and you just ... sat on it?" Bruce said. "What the fuck were you thinking?"

"We wanted to wait until we had full product penetration." Jethro had to raise his voice now; the ThunderNet towers were actually thundering for the first time ever. "And we needed people to be ready. If we had just come out and told the truth about what our products actually did, people would rather die than buy them. Even after Manhattan and Florida. We couldn't give them away. But if we claimed to be making overpriced, wasteful pieces of crap that destroy the environment? Then everybody would need to own two of them."

"So my Crisis of Conscience—" Bruce could only finish that sentence by wheeling his arms.

"We figured the day when you no longer gave a shit about your own future would be the day when people might accept this," Jethro said, patting Bruce on the back like a father even though he was younger.

"Well, thanks for the mind games." Bruce had to shout now. "I'm going to go explore something I call my culture of drunkenness."

"You can't leave, Bruce," Jethro yelled in his ear. "This is going to be a major disruption, everyone's gadgets going nuts at once. There will be violence and wholesale destruction of public property. There will be chainsaw rampages. There may even be Twitter snark. We need you to be out in front on this, explaining it to the people."

Bruce looked out at the dusk, red-and-black clouds churning as millions of ThunderNet towers blasted them with scrubber beams. Even over that racket, the chorus of car horns and shouts as people's Car-Dingos suddenly had minds of their own started to ring from the highway. Bruce turned and looked into the gleam of his boss's schoolmaster specs. "Fuck you, man," he said. Followed a moment later by "I'll do it."

"We knew we could count on you." Jethro turned to the half dozen or so executives cluttering the roof deck behind him. "Big hand for Bruce, everybody." Bruce waited until they were done clapping, then leaned over the railing and puked his guts out.

Acknowledgment is Made for Permission to Reprint the Following Materials:

"Walking Awake" by N.K. Jemisin. Copyright © 2014 by N.K. Jemisin. First published in *Lightspeed*, June 2014. Reprinted by permission of the author.

"The Black Box" by Malka Older. Copyright © 2016 by Malka Older. First published in *WIRED*, January 2017. Reprinted by permission of the author.

"A Song Transmuted" by Sarah Pinsker. Copyright © 2016 by Sarah Pinsker. First published in *Cyber World: Tales of Humanity's Tomorrow* (Hex Publishers, 2016). Reprinted by permission of the author.

"Water" by Ramez Naam. Copyright © 2013 2013 by Ramez Naam. First published in *Networked Matter,* edited by The Institute for the Future. Reprinted by permission of the author.

"Underworld 101" by Mame Bougouma Diene. Copyright © 2017 by Mame Bougouma Diene. First published electronically online in *Omenana #9*. Reprinted by permission of the author.

"The Faithful Soldier, Prompted" by Saladin Ahmed. Copyright © 2010 by Saladin Ahmed. First published in *Apex Magazine, Issue 18*. Reprinted by permission of the author.

"Beautiful Curse" by Kristine Ong Muslim. Copyright © 2013 by Kristine Ong Muslim. An early version of "Beautiful Curse" first appeared in the anthology Smoking Mirrors (Connotation Press, 2013). The story was later collected in Age of Blight (Unnamed Press, 2016) and then reprinted in Weird Fiction Review, September 2016. Reprinted by permission of the author.

"Real Boys" by Clara Kumagai. Copyright © 2016 by Clara Kumagai. First published in *The Stinging Fly* (November, 2016). Reprinted by permission of the author.

"Born Out of Frost" by Mélanie Fazi. Translated from the French by Lynn E. Palermo. Copyright © by Mélanie Fazi. First published in *Anomaly 25,* September 2017. Reprinted by permission of the author and translator.

About the Editor

Bill Campbell is the author of *Sunshine Patriots, My Booty Novel, Pop Culture: Politics, Puns, "Poohbutt" from a Liberal Stay-at-Home Dad, Koontown Killing Kaper,* and the spaceploitation comic, *Baaaad Muthaz,* with David Brame and Damian Duffy. Along with Edward Austin Hall, he co-edited the groundbreaking anthology, *Mothership: Tales from Afrofuturism and Beyond.* He also co-edited the Glyph Award-winning comics anthology, *APB: Artists against Police Brutality,* with Jason Rodriguez and John Jennings, the Locus Award-nominated anthology, *Stories for Chip: A Tribute to Samuel R. Delany,* with Nisi Shawl, and *Future Fiction: New Dimensions in International Science Fiction and Fantasy* with Italian publisher, Francesco Verso. Campbell founded Rosarium Publishing in 2013.

About the Authors

Basma Abdel Aziz is an award-winning writer, sculptor, and psychiatrist. A long-standing vocal critic of government oppression in Egypt, she is the author of several works of non-fiction books and a columnist for *Al-Shorouk*. In 2016 she was named one of Foreign Policy's Global Thinkers for her debut novel *The Queue*, which was also nominated in 2017 in the long list of BTBA. She lives in Cairo.

Saladin Ahmed was born in Detroit. His 2012 fantasy novel, *Throne of the Crescent Moon*, received starred reviews from *Publishers Weekly*, *Kirkus Reviews*, and *Library Journal*, was nominated for the Hugo Award and the Nebula Award, and won the Locus Award for Best First Novel. His essays have appeared in the *New York Times*, the *Boston Globe*, *BuzzFeed*, and *Salon*. He is currently writing *Black Bolt* for Marvel Comics and *Abbott* for Boom! Studios.

William Alexander is a National Book Award-winning, *New York Times* best-selling author of fantasy and science fiction for kids. He is also a second generation Cuban-American immigrant to the United States. He studied theater and folklore at Oberlin College, English at the University of Vermont, and creative writing at Clarion. He now teaches at the Vermont College of Fine Arts program in Writing for Children and Young Adults. Find him online at goblinsecrets.com.

Charlie Jane Anders is the author of *All the Birds in the Sky*, which won the Nebula, Locus, and Crawford Awards. Her short fiction has appeared in *Wired Magazine*, Tor. com, *Asimov's Science Fiction, Fantasy & Science Fiction, Tin House, ZYZZYVA, The McSweeney's Joke Book of Book Jokes*, and elsewhere, and her story, "Six Months Three Days," won a Hugo Award. She runs the long-running *Writers With Drinks* reading series in San Francisco and used to spout off on io9.com. She won the Emperor Norton Award for "extraordinary invention and creativity unhindered by the constraints of paltry reason."

K. Tempest Bradford is a speculative fiction writer by night, a media critic and writing instructor by day, and a podcaster in the interstices. Her short fiction has appeared in multiple anthologies and magazines including *Strange Horizons, Electric Velocipede, Diverse Energies, In the Shadow of the Towers*, and many more. She's the host of *ORIGINality*, a podcast about the roots of creative genius, and contributes to several more. Her media criticism and reviews can be found on NPR, io9, and in books about Time Lords. When not writing, she teaches classes on writing inclusive fiction through LitReactor and WritingtheOther.com. Visit her blog at KtempestBradford.com and her Patreon at patreon.com/ktempestbradford.

Jennifer Marie Brissett is the author of the novel *Elysium* (Aqueduct Press), winner of the Philip K. Dick Award Special Citation. Her short fiction has appeared in *Fantastic Stories, Morpheus Tales, The Future Fire, FIYAH Magazine, Terraform, Thaumatrope, Uncanny Magazine*, and *Halfway Down the Stairs*, and she has contributed to the anthology, *Warrior Wisewoman 2* (Norilana Books). She holds a BS from Boston University and an MFA in Creative Writing from the University of Southern Maine.

A community organizer and teacher, **Maurice Broaddus**'s work has appeared in magazines like *Lightspeed Magazine, Weird Tales, Beneath Ceaseless Skies, Asimov's, Cemetery Dance, Uncanny Magazine*, with some of his stories having been collected in *The Voices of Martyrs* (Rosarium Publishing). His books include the urban fantasy trilogy, *The Knights of Breton Court*, and the (upcoming) middle grade detective novel, *The Usual Suspects*. His latest novella is *Buffalo Soldier* (Tor.com). As an editor, he's worked on *Dark Faith, Dark Faith: Invocations, Streets of Shadows, People of Colo(u)r Destroy Horror*, and *Apex Magazine*. Learn more at MauriceBroaddus.com.

Christopher Brown is the author of *Tropic of Kansas*, a novel published in 2017 by Harper Voyager. He was a World Fantasy Award nominee for *Three Messages and a Warning: Contemporary Mexican Short Stories of the Fantastic*, an anthology he co-edited. His short fiction and criticism has appeared in a variety of magazines and anthologies, including *MIT Technology Review's Twelve Tomorrows, The Baffler*, and *Reckoning*.

Nadia Bulkin writes scary stories about the scary world we live in, three of which have been nominated for a Shirley Jackson Award. Her stories have been included in volumes of *The*

Year's Best Horror (Datlow), *The Year's Best Dark Fantasy and Horror* (Guran) and *The Year's Best Weird Fiction*; in venues such as *Nightmare, Fantasy, The Dark,* and *ChiZine*; and in anthologies such as *She Walks in Shadows* (winner of the World Fantasy Award) and *Aickman's Heirs* (winner of the Shirley Jackson Award). She spent her childhood in Indonesia with a Javanese father and an American mother, then relocated to Nebraska. She now has a B.A. in political science, an M.A. in international affairs, and lives in Washington, D.C.

Chesya Burke is a doctoral candidate in the Department of English at the University of Florida. She has written and published nearly a hundred fiction and articles within the genres of science fiction, fantasy, noir, and horror. Her story collection, *Let's Play White*, is being taught in universities around the country and her novel, *The Strange Crimes of Little Africa*, debuted in December 2015. Poet Nikki Giovanni compared her writing to that of Octavia Butler and Toni Morrison, and Samuel Delany called her "a formidable new master of the macabre." Chesya received her Master's degree in African American Studies from Georgia State University.

Joyce Chng lives in Singapore. Their fiction has appeared in *The Apex Book of World SF II, We See A Different Frontier, Cranky Ladies of History,* and *Accessing the Future.* Joyce also co-edited *The SEA Is Ours: Tales of Steampunk Southeast Asia* (Rosarium Publishing) with Jaymee Goh. Their recent space opera novels deal with wolf clans and vineyards. Occasionally, they wrangle article editing at *Strange Horizons* and *Umbel & Panicle.* Their alter ego, J. Damask, writes about werewolves in Singapore. You can find them at http://awolfstale.wordpress.comand @jolantru.

John Chu is a microprocessor architect by day, a writer, translator, and podcast narrator by night. His fiction has appeared or is forthcoming at *Boston Review, Uncanny, Asimov's Science Fiction, Clarkesworld,* and Tor.com among other venues. His translations have been published or is forthcoming at *Clarkesworld, The Big Book of SF,* and other venues. His story "The Water That Falls on You from Nowhere" won the 2014 Hugo Award for Best Short Story.

Argentinian **Claudia De Bella** was an author, English teacher, rock singer, and award-winning translator. Her short stories have appeared in Argentina, Brazil, and Italy. She passed away in April 2018.

Mame Bougouma Diene is a Franco–Senegalese American humanitarian living in Brooklyn, New York, and the US/Francophone spokesperson for the African Speculative Fiction Society (http://www.africansfs.com/), with a fondness for progressive metal, tattoos, and policy analysis. You can find his work in *Brittle Paper, Omenana, Galaxies Magazine* (French), *Edilivres* (French), *Fiyah! Magazine, Truancy Magazine,* and *Strange Horizons,* and in anthologies such as *AfroSFv2* (Storytime), *Myriad Lands* (Guardbridge Books), *You Left Your Biscuit Behind* (Fox Spirit Books), and *This Book Ain't Nuttin to Fuck Wit* (New English Press). Follow him @mame_bougouma on Twitter.

Hal Duncan is the author of *Vellum* and *Ink,* more recently *Testament,* and numerous short stories, poems, essays, even some musicals. Homophobic hatemail once dubbed him "THE.... Sodomite Hal Duncan!!" (sic), and you can find him online at http://www.halduncan.com or at his Patreon for readings, revelling in that role.

Corinne Duyvis is the award-winning author of critically acclaimed young adult novels, *Otherbound* (2014) and *On the Edge of Gone* (2016), as well as the superhero prose novel, *Guardians of the Galaxy: Collect Them All* (2017). Corinne was born in Amsterdam, The Netherlands, where she still resides.

Amal El-Mohtar is an award-winning writer of fiction, poetry, and criticism. Her stories and poems have appeared in magazines including Tor.com, *Fireside Fiction, Lightspeed, Uncanny, Strange Horizons, Apex, Stone Telling,* and *Mythic Delirium;* anthologies including *The Djinn Falls in Love and Other Stories* (2017), *The Starlit Wood: New Fairy Tales* (2016), *Kaleidoscope: Diverse YA Science Fiction and Fantasy Stories* (2014), and *The Thackery T. Lambshead Cabinet of Curiosities* (2011); and in her own collection, *The Honey Month* (2010). Her articles and reviews have appeared in the *New York Times, NPR Books* and on Tor.com. She became the Otherworldly columnist at the *New York Times* in February 2018.

Born in 1976 in Dunkerque, **Mélanie Fazi** splits her time between writing and translating authors such as Graham Joyce, Lisa Tuttle, or Brandon Sanderson into French. She has published two novels (*Trois pépins du fruit des morts* and *Arlis des forains*) and three collections of stories (*Serpentine, Notre-Dame-aux-Ecailles, Le Jardin des silences*) and was published in *Kadath*, an homage to the village created by HP Lovecraft.

Tang Fei is a speculative fiction writer whose fiction has been featured (under various pen names) in magazines in China such as *Science Fiction World, Jiuzhou Fantasy*, and *Fantasy Old and New*. She has written fantasy, science fiction, fairy tales, and wuxia (martial arts fantasy), but prefers to write in a way that straddles or stretches genre boundaries. She is also a genre critic, and her critical essays have been published in *The Economic Observer*. She lives in Beijing and considers herself a foodie with a particular appreciation for dark chocolate, cleverer, and single malt Scotch Whisky.

Jeffrey Ford is the author of the novels T*he Physiognomy, Memoranda, The Beyond, The Portrait of Mrs. Charbuque, The Girl in the Glass, The Cosmology of the Wider World, The Shadow Year,* and *The Twilight Pariah*. 2018 will see the publication of a new novel, *Ahab's Return or The Last Voyage,* from Morrow/Harper Collins. His short story collections are *The Fantasy Writer's Assistant, The Empire of Ice Cream, The Drowned Life, Crackpot Palace,* and *A Natural History of Hell*. Ford's short fiction has appeared in a wide variety of magazines and anthologies. Ford is the recipient of the World Fantasy Award, Nebula, Edgar Allan Poe Award, the Shirley Jackson Award, the Hayakawa Award, and Gran Prix de l'Imaginaire. He lives in Ohio in a 100 plus-year-old farm house surrounded by corn and soybean fields and teaches part time at Ohio Wesleyan University.

Clifton Gachagua is the winner of the Sillerman Prize for African Poetry, 2013. He has recently published a volume of poetry, *Madman at Kilifi* (University of Nebraska Press), and appears in a chapbook box set, *Seven New Generation African Poets* (University of Nebraska Press). He was recently selected for Africa39, Clifton works at Kwani? as an assistant editor.

Sergio Gaut vel Hartman is an Argentine writer and editor. Among others, he published the following books: *Cuerpos descartables* (1985), *Las Cruzadas* (2006), *El universo de la ciencia ficción* (2006), *Espejos en fuga* (2009), *Sociedades secretas de la historia argentina* (2010), *Historia de la Segunda Guerra Mundial* (2011), *Vuelos* (2011)

Avatares de un escarabajo pelotero (2017), *Otro camino* (2017), *La quinta fase de la Luna* (2018) and *El juego del tiempo* (2018). He has compiled more than twenty anthologies and was a finalist in the Minotauro and U.P.C. awards.

Hiromi Goto is an emigrant from Japan who gratefully resides on the Unceded Musqueam, Skwxwú7mesh, and Tsleil Waututh Territories. Her first novel, *Chorus of Mushrooms*, was awarded the Commonwealth Writers' Prize Best First Book, Canada and Caribbean Region, and co-winner of the Canada-Japan Book Award. Her second novel, *The Kappa Child*, was awarded the 2001 James Tiptree Jr. Memorial Award. Her first YA novel, *Half World*, won The Sunburst Award and the Carl Brandon Parallax Award. Hiromi is a mentor in The Writer's Studio Program at Simon Fraser University, and a mentor for The Pierre Elliott Trudeau Foundation. www.hiromigoto.com

Margrét Helgadóttir was born in Ethiopia to Norwegian and Icelandic parents. She currently lives in Oslo, Norway. Her stories have appeared in a number of both magazines and print anthologies such as *Gone Lawn, Luna Station Quarterly*, and *Girl at the End of the World*. Her debut book, *The Stars Seem So Far Away*, was shortlisted to British Fantasy Awards 2016. Margrét is editor of the anthology *Winter Tales* (2016) and the book series, *Fox Spirit Books of Monsters*. *African Monsters* and *Asian Monsters* were both shortlisted to British Fantasy Awards as Best Anthology (2016 and 2017). Margrét is also a charter member of the African Speculative Fiction Society.

Sabrina Li-Chun Huang is a Chinese writer born in Taipei in 1979. She studied philosophy at the National Chengchi University and after graduation, went on to work in media. She has published three collections of short stories: *Fallen Xiao Luren* (2001) and *Eight Flowers Blossom, Nine Seams Split* (2005), which were published under the pseudonym Jiu Jiu, and *Welcome to the Dollhouse* (2012). Huang's short fiction has won every major short story prize in Taiwan, including the China Times Literary Award and the United Daily Literary Award. In 2012, she was named by *Unitas Magazine* as one of the 20 best Sinophone writers under 40.

N.K. Jemisin is a Hugo- and Locus-Award-winning Brooklyn author. Her short fiction and novels have also been multiply nominated for the Nebula and the World Fantasy Award and shortlisted for the Crawford and the Tiptree. Her speculative works range from fantasy to science fiction to the undefinable; her themes include resistance to oppression, the inseverability of the liminal, and the coolness of Stuff Blowing Up. She is a member of the Altered Fluid writing group, and she has been an instructor for the Clarion and Clarion West workshops. In her spare time she is a biker, an adventurer, and a gamer; by profession she is a counselor; and she is also single-handedly responsible for saving the world from KING OZZYMANDIAS, her ginger cat. Her essays and fiction excerpts are available at nkjemisin.com.

Csilla Kleinheincz is a Hungarian-Vietnamese writer. She has three fantasy novels published in Hungarian as well as a short story collection. Her stories in English have been published by *Interfictions, Expanded Horizons*, and the *Apex Book of World SF 2*. Currently, she works as an editor for the Hungarian publishing house, Gabo, and translates fiction by Peter S. Beagle, Ann Leckie, Ursula K. Le Guin, Catherynne M. Valente, and others.

Tessa Kum once started a social justice movement by accident, and if she learned anything from the experience, it is that she does not wish to lead the revolution. Ever. She lives in Melbourne with one old dog and one angry bird, and she studies plants. Other publications of her work can be found at the *Review of Australian Fiction* and the forthcoming anthology, *Mechanical Animals*.

Clara Kumagai writes fiction, non-fiction, and plays for young people and for grown-ups. She has been published in *The Stinging Fly, Banshee, Cicada*, and *The Irish Times*. She is currently based in Tokyo, where she is writing a young adult novel. Clara is from Canada, Japan, and Ireland.

Victor LaValle is the author of a story collection, four novels, and two novellas. His 2016 novella, *The Ballad of Black Tom*, won a Shirley Jackson Award and British Fantasy Award and was a finalist for the Hugo, World Fantasy, and Nebula Awards. His most recent novel is *The Changeling*, which has won a Dragon Award. He is also the writer and creator of a comic book, *Victor LaValle's Destroyer*. He has been the recipient of a Guggenheim Fellowship, an American Book Award, and a Whiting Award, among other honors. He teaches at Columbia University and lives in New York City with his wife and two kids.

Rose Lemberg is a queer, bigender immigrant from Eastern Europe and Israel. Their fiction and poetry have appeared in Lightspeed's *Queers Destroy Science Fiction, Uncanny, Beneath Ceaseless Skies*, and many other venues. Rose's work has been a finalist for the Nebula, Rhysling, Crawford, and other awards. Their poetry collection, *Marginalia to Stone Bird*, is available from Aqueduct Press (2016). For a full bibliography, please visit http://roselemberg.net.

Karin Lowachee was born in South America, grew up in Canada, and worked in the Arctic. Her first novel, *Warchild*, won the 2001 Warner Aspect First Novel Contest. Both *Warchild* and her third novel, *Cagebird*, were finalists for the Philip K. Dick Award. *Cagebird* won the Prix Aurora Award in 2006 for Best Long-Form Work in English and the Spectrum Award also in 2006. Her books have been translated into French, Hebrew, and Japanese, and her short stories have appeared in anthologies edited by Nalo Hopkinson, John Joseph Adams, Jonathan Strahan, and Ann VanderMeer. Her fantasy novel, *The Gaslight Dogs*, was published through Orbit Books USA. She can be found on twitter @karinlow.

Kuzhali Manickavel is an Indian writer who writes in English. She was born in Winnipeg, Canada, and moved to India when she was thirteen. She currently lives in Chidambaram, Tamil Nadu. Her first book, *Insects Are Just Like You And Me Except Some Of Them Have Wings*, was published by Blaft Publications in 2008. *The Guardian* named the book as one of the best independently published ebooks in the weird fiction genre, calling it "just very, very beautiful." Manickavel's short stories have also appeared in print magazines like *Shimmer Magazine, Versal, AGNI, PANK, FRiGG*, and *Tehelka*, and in anthologies such as *Best American Fantasy 3* and *Breaking the Bow: Speculative Fiction Inspired by the Ramayana*. A second book, *Things We Found During the Autopsy*, was released in 2014.

Juan Martinez is the author of *Best Worst American*. He lives in Chicago, where he's an assistant professor at Northwestern University. His work has appeared in many literary journals and anthologies, including *Glimmer Train, McSweeney's, Ecotone*, National Public Radio's *Selected Shorts*, and elsewhere. Visit and say hi at http://fulmerford.com.

Brandon Mc Ivor is a Trinidadian author living in Ehime, Japan. With his sister, he is the co-founder of People's Republic of Writing, and has had his fiction published in *The Caribbean Writer, Existere, The Corner Club Press, Buffalo Almanack,* and elsewhere. In 2016, he was shortlisted for the Small Axe Short Fiction Literary Prize.

Silvia Moreno-Garcia is the critically-acclaimed author of *Signal to Noise*—winner of a Copper Cylinder Award, finalist of the British Fantasy, Locus, Sunburst and Aurora awards—and *Certain Dark Things,* selected as one of NPR's best books of 2016. Her latest novel is *The Beautiful Ones,* a fantasy of manners. She won a World Fantasy Award for her work as an editor.

Kristine Ong Muslim is the author of eight books of fiction and poetry, including the short story collections, *Age of Blight* (Unnamed Press, 2016) and *Butterfly Dream* (Snuggly Books, 2016), as well as the poetry collections, *Lifeboat* (University of Santo Tomas Publishing House, 2015), *Meditations of a Beast* (Cornerstone Press, 2016), and *Black Arcadia* (University of the Philippines Press, 2017). She is poetry editor of *LONTAR: The Journal of Southeast Asian Speculative Fiction,* a literary journal published by Epigram Books in Singapore, and was co-editor with Nalo Hopkinson of the original fiction section of the *Lightspeed Magazine* special issue, *People of Colo(u)r Destroy Science Fiction.* Her stories recently appeared in *Sunvault: Stories of Solarpunk & Eco-Speculation* (Upper Rubber Boot Books, 2017) and *Weird Fiction Review.* She grew up and continues to live in southern Philippines.

Ramez Naam was born in Cairo, Egypt, and came to the US at the age of 3. He's a computer scientist who spent 13 years at Microsoft, leading teams working on email, web browsing, search, and artificial intelligence. He holds almost 20 patents in those areas. Ramez is the winner of the 2005 H.G. Wells Award for his non-fiction book, *More Than Human: Embracing the Promise of Biological Enhancement.* He is also the author of *The Nexus Trilogy,* the first book of which, *Nexus,* was nominated for the Campbell Award and won the Prometheus Award. The third novel, *Apex,* won the Philip K. Dick Award.

Shweta Narayan was born in India, has lived in Malaysia, Saudi

Arabia, the Netherlands, Scotland, and California, and feels kinship with shapeshifters and other liminal beings. Their short fiction and poetry have appeared in places like *Lightspeed, Strange Horizons, Tor.com*, and the 2012 *Nebula Showcase* anthology. Shweta was a recipient of the Octavia E. Butler Memorial Scholarship. They've been mostly dead since 2010 but have a few stories in the works again and are trying not to do an Orpheus and look back.

Iheoma Nwachukwu has won fellowships from the Michener Center for Writers and the Chinua Achebe Center for Writers, Bard College, New York. His fiction has appeared in *The Iowa Review, The Southern Review, Black Renaissance Noire*, and elsewhere. His poetry has been published in *PRISM International, Rusty Toque, Forklift Ohio*, and elsewhere. He has non-fiction in *Electric Literature*.

Irenosen Okojie is a writer and Arts Project Manager. Her debut novel, *Butterfly Fish*, won a Betty Trask Award and was short-listed for an Edinburgh International First Book Award. Her work has been featured in *The Observer,The Guardian*, the BBC, and the *Huffington Post,* amongst other publications. Her short stories have been published internationally, including Salt's *Best British Short Stories 2017, Kwani?*, and *The Year's Best Weird Fiction*. She was presented at the London Short Story Festival by Ben Okri as a dynamic writing talent to watch and was featured in the *Evening Standard Magazine* as one of London's exciting new authors. Her short story collection, *Speak Gigantular* (Jacaranda Books), was short-listed for the Edgehill Short Story Prize, the Jhalak Prize, the Saboteur Awards, and nominated for a Shirley Jackson Award.

Malka Older is a writer, aid worker, and PhD candidate. Her science fiction political thriller, *Infomocracy*, was named one of the best books of 2016 by *Kirkus, Book Riot*, and the *Washington Post*, and the sequel, *Null States*, came out in September 2017. She was nominated for the 2016 John W. Campbell Award for Best New Writer. Named Senior Fellow for Technology and Risk at the Carnegie Council for Ethics in International Affairs for 2015, she has more than a decade of experience in humanitarian aid and development. Her doctoral work on the sociology of organizations at the Institut d'Études Politques de Paris (Sciences Po) explores the dynamics of multi-level governance and disaster response using the cases of Hurricane Katrina and the Japan tsunami of 2011.

Johary Ravaloson is an author and visual artist, in addition to his day job as a lawyer. Born in Antananarivo, Madagascar, in 1965, he lived and studied in Paris and Réunion before returning to his hometown in 2007. He has won numerous prizes for his novels and short stories, including the Grand Prix de l'Océan Indien and the Prix roman de la Réunion des livres. With his wife, the contemporary artist Sophie Bazin, he founded a new publishing house in the 2000s, starting a new trend of in-country publishing in Madagascar and Réunion. His most recent novel, *Vol à vif*, was published simultaneously in France and Madagascar in February 2016.

Sarah Pinsker is the author of the Nebula winning novelette, *Our Lady of the Open Road*, and the Theodore Sturgeon Award-winning novelette, *In Joy, Knowing the Abyss Behind*. Her stories have appeared in *Asimov's, Strange Horizons, Fantasy & Science Fiction, Lightspeed*, and *Uncanny*, among others, and in anthologies, including *Long Hidden* and *The New Voices of Fantasy*. She is also a singer/songwriter and toured nationally behind three albums on various independent labels. A fourth is forthcoming. She lives with her wife and dog in Baltimore, Maryland. Find her online at sarahpinsker.com and on Twitter @sarahpinsker.

SF writer **Geoff Ryman** was born in Canada in 1951, went to high school and college in the United States, and has lived most of his adult life in Britain. His longer works include *The Unconquered Country*, the novella version of which won the World Fantasy Award in 1985; *The Child Garden*, which won the Arthur C. Clarke Award and the John W. Campbell Memorial Award in 1990; the hypertext novel, *253*, the "print remix" of which won the Philip K. Dick Award in 1999; and *Air*, which won the Arthur C. Clarke and James Tiptree, Jr. Awards in 2006. An early Web design professional, Ryman led the teams that designed the first web sites for the British monarchy and the Prime Minister's office. He also has a lifelong interest in drama and film; his 1992 novel, *Was*, looks at America through the lens of *The Wizard of Oz* and has been adapted for the stage, and Ryman himself wrote and directed a stage adaptation of Philip K. Dick's *The Transmigration of Timothy Archer*.

Eve Shi is Indonesian, a lifelong fangirl, and writer. She has published six novels in Indonesian with more coming in 2018 and written several short stories in English. Since 2011 she has been the Indonesian municipal liaison for NaNoWriMo. You can reach her on

Twitter at @Eve_Shi or via email at stormofblossoms@gmail.com.

Angela Slatter's debut novel, *Vigil*, was published by Jo Fletcher Books in 2016, with *Corpselight* following in 2017; *Restoration* is slated for release in 2018. She is the author of eight short story collections (two co-authored). Angela has won a World Fantasy Award, a British Fantasy Award, one Ditmar Award, and six Aurealis Awards. She has been a Queensland Writers Fellow, the Established Writer-in-Residence at the Katharine Susannah Prichard Writers Centre, and has an MA and a PhD in Creative Writing. Her work has been translated into Bulgarian, Chinese, Russian, Spanish, Japanese, Polish, Romanian, and French.

Gabriel Teodros is a musician and writer from South Seattle who first made a mark with the group Abyssinian Creole, and reached an international audience with his critically-acclaimed solo debut, *Lovework*. In 2015, Teodros made his speculative fiction debut with a story published in *Octavia's Brood: Science Fiction Stories from Social Justice Movements*, and in 2016 he graduated from the Clarion West Writers Workshop for Speculative Fiction. For more information log on to www.gabrielteodros.com

Walter Tierno studied graphic arts and journalism and worked as an adman for almost twenty years. He has also taken his chances on comic books and theater projects. His first novel, *Cira*, was published in 2010, followed by *Anardeus: In the Heat of Destruction* in 2013. In 2016, he published the novel, *Like a Tattoo*. He is also the co-author of two coloring books, *Love in Every Color* and *From Father to Son*. Walter is an illustrator, an editor, a writer, and a very honest liar. He lives in São Paulo.

Francesco Verso has published several novels, *Antidoti Umani* (finalist at 2004 Urania Mondadori Award), *e-Doll* (2008 Urania Mondadori Award), and *Livido* (aka *Nexhuman* in English; 2013 Odissea Award, 2014 Italia Award for Best SF Novel). In 2015 he won the Urania Award for the second time with *BloodBusters*. His stories have appeared in various Italian magazines (*Robot, iComics, Fantasy Magazine, Futuri*) and has been produced for the stage (The Milky Way); they have also been sold abroad (*International Speculative Fiction #5, Chicago Quarterly Review #20*). In 2014 Verso founded Future Fiction (a book series by Mincione Edizioni), publishing the best speculative fiction from around the world.

Bryan Thao Worra is author of *Demonstra* (2013); *Barrow* (2009); *Winter Ink* (2008); *On the Other Side of the Eye* (2007); and *The Tuk-Tuk Diaries: Our Dinner with Cluster Bombs* (2003). His work appears in over 100 international publications, including *Astropoetica, Cha, Asian Pacific American Journal, Hyphen, Lantern Review, Kartika Review, Journal of the Asian American Renaissance, Expanded Horizons, Quarterly Literary Review Singapore, Strange Horizons, Tales of the Unanticipated*, and Innsmouth Free Press. He was selected as a Cultural Olympian during the 2012 London Summer Olympics' Poetry Parnassus convened by the Southbank Centre. He works on Lao and Southeast Asian American refugee resettlement issues across the United States.

Printed in the USA
CPSIA information can be obtained
at www.ICGtesting.com
JSHW022202140824
68134JS00018B/815

9 780998 705972